The Best
AMERICAN
SHORT
STORIES
2004

The *Best* AMERICAN SHORT STORIES® 2004

Selected from
U.S. and Canadian Magazines
by LORRIE MOORE
with KATRINA KENISON

With an Introduction by Lorrie Moore

HOUGHTON MIFFLIN COMPANY
BOSTON • NEW YORK   2004

Visit our Web site: www.houghtonmifflinbooks.com.

ISSN 0067-6233
ISBN 0-618-19734-6
ISBN 0-618-19735-4 (pbk.)

Printed in the United States of America

MP 10 9 8 7 6 5 4 3 2 1

Contents

Foreword

FIFTEEN YEARS AGO, when I became the annual editor of the *Best American Short Stories,* my first job was to ensure that the three hundred or so magazines publishing short fiction in America and Canada all sent their issues to me. Within a few months' time, as I negotiated the narrowing path through my office, I realized that I also had to figure out what to do with all those magazines once I'd looked through them.

After offering free magazines to local hospitals, schools, and prisons, and being turned down everywhere, I met a used bookseller named Vincent McCaffrey, who said he'd be glad to take the intact issues and offer them for sale in his Newbury Street store, Avenue Victor Hugo. It was the beginning of a long love affair with the shop a local magazine dubbed "the black hole of Newbury Street, because once you walk in, it's almost impossible to extract yourself."

Several times a year, I would deliver boxes of literary journals to Vincent's doorstep, and then proceed into the bowels of the store, past Blue Bart, the cat, in his sunny window, and on to the ceiling-high shelves of volumes both old and new, rare and run-of-the-mill. Relieved of my several hundred magazines (which found their way onto display shelves near the door or deep into the basement to join the more than quarter million catalogued copies of vintage and used magazines), I would always find a few books to carry home. There were modest little treasures, of the sort that appeal to a casual reader as opposed to a real collector — a first edition of Thornton Wilder's *Bridge of San Luis Rey,* inscribed by the author's brother Amos to one Edna Richner; pristine volumes of C. S. Lewis and Roald Dahl for my sons; a well-worn hardcover of *The Seed and the Sower* by Laurens van der Post. Best of all, though, were the unexpected finds, the books I had no idea I wanted — no idea, for that matter, that they existed — until my roving eye fell upon them on the crowded shelves: *Speak to the Earth: Pages from a Farmwife's Journal* by Rachel Peden, who proved to be a naturalist of the first order, though her name now is utterly forgotten; or, one of my all-time favorites, *How to Be Happy on Nothing a Year* by Charles A. David, published in 1933 by the long-defunct Bobbs Merrill Company at a hardcover price of $1.50.

It always felt like a good trade, knowing that the exquisitely produced magazines I mine for stories each year would go on to another life, in another's hands, rather than ending up directly in the recycling pile, the poems and essays and literary criticism mostly unread. And the books I carried home live on on my own shelves, years after they've gone out of print, still alive, somehow, by virtue of the fact that they were chosen by me, paid for, read once again.

In a world in which we value little and consider almost everything disposable — from used razors to outdated computers to inconvenient relationships — Avenue Victor Hugo was one small voice for preservation and reuse, a place where old things were valued, catalogued, offered anew to a clientele that ranged from penny-pinching students to passionate bibliophiles. One morning my husband and I bore witness as a tidy, elderly couple in threadbare overcoats lugged two paper grocery sacks up to Vincent's front desk and offered him a pile of lightly read Louis Auchincloss novels. Vincent received their wares graciously, offered them a modest credit for trade, and the pair happily stepped into the dusty stacks, on the prowl for a fresh batch of fiction. Watching this bit of small business made us, two lifelong publishing types, immeasurably happy.

There are not many places left in this land where, in one stop, you can find old issues of *The New Yorker* from 1940 to the present; or nearly any volume of *Fantasy & Science Fiction Magazine* from 1953 on; as well as the latest fiction offering from Small Beer Press; the complete works of Andre Brink and Lawrence Durrell; a pristine illustrated edition of *Heidi*, circa 1952; a leatherbound volume of *A Tale of Two Cities;* a first edition of Theodore White's *Making of a President* . . . Avenue Victor Hugo was such a place, an irresistible repository for the written word in all its forms, a place where, it seemed, very little was ever thrown away, where the word *disposable* was perhaps not uttered.

I use the past tense because, in May, after nearly thirty years of business, the store closed its doors, having fallen victim to a variety of financial pressures resulting from changing reading patterns among consumers (the increasing tendency of book buyers, for example, to all seek out the same few titles that have received mass publicity through venues like TV book clubs); widespread Internet access for buyers and sellers, enabling consumers to buy exclusively online and anyone with a few old books to become a book dealer; rising rents and lighter foot traffic along Newbury Street.

As I write, the old magazines at the store are being bundled and sold off in groups; in a few weeks, whatever is left will be thrown away or donated. Meanwhile, the piles in my own basement are growing ever higher. The magazines are, once again, disposable. The short stories contained in those many pages, having been selected by an editor, published, and read by me, may or may not live again elsewhere. It seems a shame to throw them all away, but as yet there are no new takers for my back issues of *The Georgia Review*, as pleasing as those lovingly printed pages are to the book lover's eye.

A novel, bound between hard covers and complete unto itself, is considered a respectable object, something worthy of permanent shelf space in a home, while last month's *Harper's* or *Atlantic Monthly* may well go to the trash bin largely unread, to make way for the current issues as they arrive in the mailbox. In this culture of abundance, cleaning up usually means throwing away.

Last year, in an essay in *Descant* entitled "The State of the Short Story," Aleksandar Hemon suggested that the very disposability of the short story can work to its advantage. Knowing that a story published in a magazine might or might not be read, that the magazine will most likely be thrown away, renders the work, in the author's mind at least, somehow less lasting, less "important" than a novel — thereby allowing the story to be a more courageous form. "It is easier," writes Hemon, "to risk with a short story, it is easier to try and it is easier to fail."

The twenty stories chosen for this volume each represent risks that succeeded. Here are twenty stories that, for whatever reason,

were simply not disposable, the ones that demanded second readings, thirds, or fourths. As Lorrie Moore observes in her introduction, only the strict space limitations imposed on her prevented the
current volume from being much larger than it is. The field of fine
stories was vast; the initial harvest, abundant. But in the end, we are
held to twenty. These twenty stories, by writers both widely acclaimed and as yet unknown, all had their first appearances in the
ephemeral world of magazines and are reborn here in book form,
to endure a while longer and reach a wider circle of readers. It's my
hope that many if not all of the year's other notable short stories
will live on elsewhere as well, in other anthologies and collections
and public readings. For good stories, as we all know, are not really
disposable, no matter where they first appear; good stories are read
and passed on, published and republished, studied and remembered, long after today's trash has been carried to the bin, long after one year's "best of" collection has been supplanted by the next.

This week, I'll make one last visit to Avenue Victor Hugo, where
the remaining stock is being sold at 50 percent off, and I'll come
home with a pile of books I didn't know I wanted till I saw them.
And I'll be reminded once again that when it comes to words and
those who write them, we can all help to save what is worth saving,
we can all make sure that what is good endures, simply by reading,
and reading again.

Has ever a guest editor, asked to read some 120-odd short stories
on a deadline and select from those his or her favorites, been perfectly delighted by the task at hand? Not, to my knowledge, until
this year. Is Lorrie Moore just, by nature, a cheerful worker? Does
she rake leaves and iron shirts with as much pleasure as she reads
mountains of short stories? I have no idea. But her continued enthusiasm over the course of the last year, even as she delayed work
on her novel to read stories, made my own job of reading and selecting considerably more pleasant as well. In choosing this year's
collection of *Best American Short Stories,* Lorrie Moore has done writers and readers a great service, for her own love for the form and
keen sensibility have resulted in a volume that fairly hums with life.
We are grateful for her efforts, despite the fact that she claims to
have thoroughly enjoyed herself.

The stories chosen for this anthology were originally published
between January 2003 and January 2004. The qualifications for se-

lection are (1) original publication in nationally distributed American or Canadian periodicals; (2) publication in English by writers who are American or Canadian, or who have made the United States or Canada their home; (3) original publication as short stories (excerpts of novels are not knowingly considered). A list of magazines consulted for this volume appears at the back of the book. Editors who wish their short fiction to be considered for next year's edition should send their publications to Katrina Kenison, c/o The Best American Short Stories, Houghton Mifflin Company, 222 Berkeley Street, Boston, MA 02116.

K.K.

Introduction

OVER THE YEARS I have listened to fellow teachers and writers pronounce on literary fiction — its predators, prey, habits, and habitats — and as I've gotten older I have stopped taking notes and attempted instead not to fidget rudely in my seat. For some reason it seems that everything I hear now sounds increasingly untrue. Or at least no more true than its exact opposite. It seems that no matter what one says about reading and writing, or about short stories and novels, a hundred exceptions support the opposite case. Short stories are for busy people or short attention spans: Well, then why can a reader duck in and out of a novel for ten-minute intervals but not do so successfully with a short story? People don't read anymore: Then why are books being published — and sold — at a record number? There is no literary community: What are all these writing programs and reading series and book-groups-in-the-middle-of-nowhere? Perhaps all these assertions occur because, too often, and more and more, writers are asked to speak publicly of their art (oh, dear) or their approach to their craft (that alarmingly nautical phrase), and what has resulted may be simply the desperate, improvised creative-writing yack of good people uncomfortably far from their desks.

Nonetheless, opportunities such as this introduction encourage implausible pronouncements and sweeping generalizations, and though I am not easily encouraged, I am surely immune from nothing — a lesson learned from literature.

There is no thoroughly convincing theory of the short story — it is technically a genre, not a form, but resists the definitions that usually cluster around both. There is the defining length (an unedifying fifty-page range), there is the short story's lonely voice from a submerged population (Frank O'Connor's famous hypothesis), and there are various "slice of life" ideas and notions of literary apprenticeship (stories are what writers do on their way to a novel). All of these convey what happens sometimes — what happens a lot — but in lieu of a truly winning overriding theory, we should rely perhaps on simple descriptions, in which case the more the merrier. Let me throw some into the pot. Many that I've heard — and used myself — are fashioned as metaphors comparing shorter and longer narratives, attempting to define the one through its relationship to the other. *A short story is a love affair; a novel is a marriage. A short story is a photograph; a novel is a film. A short story is a weekend guest; a novel is a long-term boarder. A story is a brick; a novel is a brick wall.* And my favorite, the asymmetrical *a short story is a flower; a novel is a job.*

From its own tradition, the novel arrives to reader and writer alike, baggy, *ad hoc,* bitter with ambition, already half ruined. The short story arrives, modest, prim, and purposeful, aiming for perfection, though the lengthier it is, the more novel-like, the more it puts all that at risk, acquiring instead, in a compelling trade, the greater, sustained attention of the reader, upon whom a more lasting impression will be made, if all goes well. (This year's anthology, I think, tends to favor the longer short story.)

Yet a story's very shortness ensures its largeness of accomplishment, its selfhood and purity. Having long lost its ability to pay an author's rent (in that golden blip between Henry James and television, F. Scott Fitzgerald, for one, wrote stories to fund his novels), the short story has been freed of its commercial life to become serious art, by its virtually every practitioner. As a result, short or long, a story lies less. It sings and informs and blurts. It has nothing to lose.

In adding my own heedless descriptions to the stew, I have often liked to think that short stories have something in common with songs — not just the digested-in-a-single-sitting aspect of them, but their distillation of emotion and circumstance, their interest in beautiful pain. Like songs, there is often more urgency to them, less forewarning and professional calculation in their creation. Similarly, like songs, they are often about some kind of love gone

bad — love for an overcoat, a tenor, a babysitter, to name three famous ones (by Gogol, Joyce, and Cheever) — or, at random from
this book, love for a ranch, a waitress, a goat, a daughter (Proulx,
Boyle, Munro, Lewis). These love objects represent lives and possibilities, spiritual entrances and exits, which are at one time within
reach of a person but, as the story tells us, due to interesting, musical, and sorrowful particularities, soon pass by and away and without — like a long, empty train at a crossing.

Oh, darlin'.

For now, for my purposes here, this may have to do for a coarse,
working hypothesis of the short story.

If literature exists, as one wag has it, so that readers can spend
time with people they would never want to in real life, then a short
story might be considered doubly, deeply literary in that even its
author — not just its reader — has decided to spend an abbreviated amount of time with its inhabitants (the characters a writer
commits a lot of time to end up in novels).

Perhaps this limitation accounts for the prevailing sadness of
short stories. Authors of short stories are interested in the difficult
emotions of their protagonists only up to a point. They are more
interested in constructing a quick palimpsest of wounds and tones
and triggering events. After that, the authors depart, exactly where
the reader must depart: pre-noose. That is part of a story's melancholy and civility. Leave the bustling communities, cathartic weddings, and firing squads for novels.

As for their oft stated affinity with poetry, short stories do have in
common with poems an interest in how language completes one's
understanding of the world, although the way language is used by
ordinary people (registered within a story as the voices of its characters) can also disguise and obscure that understanding, a psychological and dramatic element a story usually takes more interest in
than a poem. I would say that all the stories included herein are
interested in how people talk. They are interested in the value,
beauty, and malarkey of words that people utter to themselves
or others. That is how human life is best captured on the page:
through its sound. The stories here are interested, too, in the set-
tings that shape this sound — landscapes are given vivid paint and
life. Finally, stories generally, and certainly the ones here, are interested in some cultural truth delivered and given amnesty through

the paradoxical project of narrative invention and the mechanisms of imagination. Unlike novels or poems, but more akin to a play, the short story is also an end-oriented form, and in the best ones the endings shine a light back upon the story illumining its meaning with both surprise and inevitability. If a story is not always, therapeutically, an axe for the frozen sea within us, then it is at least a pair of brutally sharpened ice skates.

As for this year's story selection itself, correctly or not, I didn't view the process as a contest — why pit an apple against an orange — but as the assembling of a book, and the great variety of first-rate reading that is in it, I think, speaks to the health of the North American short story. (Eat your fruit!) Much has been made in this series about the editorial custom of "reading blind" — an honorable phrase suggestive of a fluency in Braille — and I did, late in the process, gruesomely burst a blood vessel in my eye, which made it difficult sometimes to see. But I must confess: I had read some of these stories before they came to me with their authors' names blackened out. I did so simply because I was not going to forego my usual habit of reading short stories as they appeared throughout the year in various magazines. This did not affect my opinions one way or the other, however, nor — I swear — did holding those babies up to the window light to see if I could make out any of those blacked-out names. Friends? Relatives? Could I pretend that brazen copyediting had caused me to fail to recognize one of my own stories and accidentally-on-purpose choose it? With all too many stories to pick from, in the end, as editorial criteria, I was left with only my own visceral responses to the stories themselves: Was I riveted? Did a story haunt me for days? Or did one nail drive out the other, as I ultimately read them in that most ungenerous but revealing of ways: from piles. Before reading all of them, as I received them in large packets in the mail (from Katrina Kenison, whose lovely name, in a spell of midwinter doldrums, I began to covet), I imagined my "editorial criteria" might be a simple matter of suicide prevention — which stories, for instance, did not send my own hands flying to my throat — though somewhat unexpectedly the reading became a joyous activity I felt disappointed to conclude (in the end, coveting Katrina Kenison's job, as well).

The stories collected here impressed me with their depth of knowledge and feeling of character, setting, and situation — or at least with their convincingly fabricated semblance thereof. They spoke with amused intelligence, compassion, and dispassion, and I trusted their imaginative sources, which seemed not casual but from the deep center of a witnessing life and a thoughtful mind. True eloquence, said Daniel Webster, a little theatrically, cannot be brought from afar but must exist in the person, the subject, the occasion. "If it comes at all it comes like the outbreaking of a fountain from the earth or the bursting of volcanic fires with spontaneous, original, native force, the clear conception outrunning the deductions of logic." Outrunning the deductions of logic is what literature does and why we read it. And a story — with its narrative version of a short man's complex — aims for quick eloquence and authority in voice and theme. But emotional heart and dramatic unpredictability are part of why it is the preferred form of fiction writers learning their art and why it has taken over much of our literary education — the Napoleon of the narrative world. A story's economy, its being one writer's intimate response to a world (as opposed to a novelist's long creation of a world), a response that must immerse a reader vividly and immediately, allows a gathering of twenty such responses in an anthology such as this and offers a kind of group portrait of how humanity is currently faring. Is that not, too, why we read short stories? To see in ways that television and newspapers cannot show us what others are up to — those who are ostensibly like us, as well as those ostensibly not? The stories here, I felt, did that.

In the end, I noticed an assortment of perhaps not accidental things, such as the number of stories set in the distant past which failed to win me over entirely (is the short story sometimes too abbreviated a space to close that distance authentically and make the long ago seem real?). On the other hand, I noticed that a number of stories I'd chosen were written from the point of view of the opposite sex of the author (those by Fox, Smith, Proulx, Eisenberg, Waters). (Is the short story especially hospitable to this kind of transgendered sympathy and ventriloquism?)

Mostly, however, I was intrigued by the very different stories I'd chosen that had certain random themes in common — or I assume random. One would be reluctant, even foolish, to offer these things up as indicative of something that in a widespread way is on the American mind. Nonetheless, two stories — Nell Freudenberger's "The Tutor" and Sarah Shun-lien Bynum's "Accomplice" — focus on a girl's academic ambitions and the awkward relationship those ambitions have to each girl's devoted father. "'A toast,' said Julia's father," writes Freudenberger in a moment charged with love and irony. "'To my daughter the genius.'" And in Bynum's "Accomplice": "There she saw her father, leaning forward very slightly, and holding onto the pew in front of him. He was smiling at her. Hugely. She lost her bearings entirely."

Two urban romances — "Grace" by Paula Fox and "Tooth and Claw," T. C. Boyle's loose update of "The Lady or the Tiger?" — use animals as MacGuffins, emblems, touchstones, and substitutes for human emotion, character, and appetite, as does Alice Munro's "Runaway." Here is Munro's quite useful description of a goat: "At first she had been Clark's pet entirely, following him everywhere, dancing for his attention. She was as quick and graceful and provocative as a kitten, and her resemblance to a guileless girl in love had made them both laugh. But as she grew older she seemed to attach herself to Carla, and in this attachment she was suddenly much wiser, less skittish — she seemed capable, instead, of a subdued and ironic sort of humor." And here is Boyle's wild African serval locked in a bedroom: "The carpeting — every last strip of it — had been torn out of the floor, leaving an expanse of dirty plywood studded with nails, and there seemed to be a hole in the plasterboard just to the left of the window. A substantial hole. Even through the closed door I could smell the reek of cat piss or spray or whatever it was. 'There goes my deposit,' I said."

Two stories — by the poet R. T. Smith and by Mary Yukari Waters — compassionately satirize the custodial culture that can spring up decades later in a war-vanquished land. Waters's "Mirror Studies" begins: "The Kashigawa district, two hours from the Endos' home in Tokyo, was an isolated farming community with two claims to distinction: indigenous harrier monkeys up in the hills, and a new restaurant — Fireside Rations — that served 'rice' made from locally grown yams. This restaurant had been featured in an *Asahi Shimbun* article about the trendy resurgence of wartime food, also known as nostalgia cuisine . . . City dwellers, jaded by French and Madeiran cuisine, were flocking out on weekends to try it." In Smith's dramatic monologue, "Docent," a romantically jilted tour guide, done up with Confederate absurdity in a hoop skirt and hairnet, warns, "If you have a morbid curiosity about the Fall of the South — which is not the same as a healthy historical interest — please save your comments for your own diaries and private conversations."

Edward Jones's "A Rich Man" and Thomas McGuane's "Gallatin Canyon" pull no punches in their sharply written tales of masculine vanity's bravado and backfirings. In "A Rich Man," Horace, set up for a fall, sees himself as "the cock of the walk." When, in "Gallatin Canyon," the protagonist, proud of his recent material success, asks his girlfriend what she thinks of the new prosperity around them, she says, presciently, "I'm not sure it's such a good thing, living in a boomtown. It's basically a high-end carny atmosphere." Which is what, in a way, ensues in both stories.

Jill McCorkle's "Intervention" and Deborah Eisenberg's "Some Other, Better Otto" look with resignation and poignant humor at the judgment of family members upon one another's life choices. Writes Eisenberg: "'So,' Corinne had said in a loud and artificially genial tone as if she were speaking to an armed high school student, 'where did you and William meet, Otto?' . . . The table fell silent; Otto looked out at the wolfish ring of faces. 'On Third Avenue,' he said distinctly, and returned to his meal." Otto later says of his family, "The truth is, they've *never* sanctioned my way of life. Or, alternately, they've always *sanctioned* it. Oh, what on earth good is it to have a word that means only itself and its opposite!"

"I have to say I'm glad to see them leave," says the father in "Intervention" of his own grown children. "I say adios, motherfuckers," says his wife.

Love imprecisely understood by onlookers is also a theme in Catherine Brady's mournfully restrained "Written in Stone" and Angela Pneuman's wonderfully funny "All Saints Day" — as is fundamentalist religion and its dissenters. The tragic fate of a child, and its eternal shadow for the adults living beyond it, is the subject of Trudy Lewis's emotionally intricate "Limestone Diner" and John Edgar Wideman's "What We Cannot Speak About We Must Pass Over in Silence." "She blamed her remaining children for their good health and sound instincts," thinks the matriarch and heroine of "Limestone Diner." "I have a friend with a son in prison," begins Wideman's obliquely heartbreaking, almost Kafkaesque meditation. "About once a year he visits his son . . . He's told me the planning, the expense, the long day spent flying there and longer day flying back are the least of it."

The criminal life is looked at from deep within, in Stuart Dybek's "Breasts," the better part of whose braided narrative is a vivid reexamination of that American mythic figure, the Chicago gangster. It is a story that stands a bit alone here in terms of its garish material (grafted to a subtle technique). With its trio of points of view, its Puzo plot, and Tarantino turns, it is a *tour de force*, complex in construction and saturated in social and sensual information not to be forgotten by the squeamish.

If within these pages there seems to be a preponderance of selections from *The New Yorker*, it is more proof that there is no such thing as a *New Yorker* story anymore — as Robert Stone already said in these pages over ten years ago. The Beckettian drift of Sherman Alexie's "What You Pawn I Will Redeem," the gothic menace of Alice Munro's "Runaway," the village elegy of John Updike's "The Walk with Elizanne," would seem to have little in common with one another. Nor would Annie Proulx's richly drawn portrait of a western rancher resisting loss and the twenty-first century, nor Charles D'Ambrosio's haunting rendition of two broken souls in a Manhattan mental hospital. *The New Yorker* probably publishes fiction more frequently than any well-paying magazine and is bound to have more stories in the running for this anthology than other publications: the high quality of these stories is hard to ignore. "Do you know how many good men live in this world?" exclaims Alexie's own *New Yorker* story. "Too many to count!"

Stories that I received (from the lyrically named Katrina Kenison) but reluctantly set aside, I discovered, included those by Arthur Miller, Joyce Carol Oates, E. L. Doctorow, Stephen King, Louise Erdrich, Tobias Wolff (who does, however, make an appearance in the pages of Bynum's story "Accomplice"), Jayne Anne Phillips, Wendell Berry, Annie Dillard, James Salter, Ann Beattie, Dave Eggers, Thom Jones, Frederick Busch, Tony Earley, Antonya Nelson, David Gates, Stephen Barthelme, Amy Hempel, Robert Olen Butler, Margot Livesey, Ward Just, Leonard Michaels, George Saunders, Jim Shepard, Mary Morris, Max Apple, Donald Antrim, Joanna Scott, Peter Ho Davies, Joy Williams, Jonathan Lethem — to name, say, some. Shocking omissions! But they testify less to the idiosyncrasies of one person's reading than to the constraints of bookbinding glue. I had virtually no "No" pile. I had "Yes" and an unhelpfully towering "Probably." Twenty stories — all that was allowed — is a severe limitation (and, given that, the writers left out will necessarily exceed in aggregate stature those left in, which may be why this series annually delegates the selection task to a new, here-today-gone-tomorrow guest editor, so as to avoid an accumulation of ill will and derision and possible petty violence upon the offices of the publisher).

But look what gloriously remains.

LORRIE MOORE

The Best
AMERICAN
SHORT
STORIES
2004

SHERMAN ALEXIE

What You Pawn I Will Redeem

FROM THE NEW YORKER

Noon

ONE DAY YOU HAVE A HOME and the next you don't, but I'm not going to tell you my particular reasons for being homeless, because it's my secret story, and Indians have to work hard to keep secrets from hungry white folks.

I'm a Spokane Indian boy, an Interior Salish, and my people have lived within a hundred-mile radius of Spokane, Washington, for at least ten thousand years. I grew up in Spokane, moved to Seattle twenty-three years ago for college, flunked out after two semesters, worked various blue- and bluer-collar jobs, married two or three times, fathered two or three kids, and then went crazy. Of course, crazy is not the official definition of my mental problem, but I don't think asocial disorder fits it, either, because that makes me sound like I'm a serial killer or something. I've never hurt another human being, or, at least, not physically. I've broken a few hearts in my time, but we've all done that, so I'm nothing special in that regard. I'm a boring heartbreaker, too. I never dated or married more than one woman at a time. I didn't break hearts into pieces overnight. I broke them slowly and carefully. And I didn't set any land-speed records running out the door. Piece by piece, I disappeared. I've been disappearing ever since.

I've been homeless for six years now. If there's such a thing as an effective homeless man, then I suppose I'm effective. Being homeless is probably the only thing I've ever been good at. I know where to get the best free food. I've made friends with restaurant and convenience store managers who let me use their bathrooms. And I don't mean the public bathrooms, either. I mean the employees' bathrooms, the clean ones hidden behind the kitchen or the pantry or the cooler. I know it sounds strange to be proud of this, but it means a lot to me, being trustworthy enough to piss in somebody else's clean bathroom. Maybe you don't understand the value of a clean bathroom, but I do.

Probably none of this interests you. Homeless Indians are everywhere in Seattle. We're common and boring, and you walk right on by us, with maybe a look of anger or disgust or even sadness at the terrible fate of the noble savage. But we have dreams and families. I'm friends with a homeless Plains Indian man whose son is the editor of a bigtime newspaper back east. Of course, that's his story, but we Indians are great storytellers and liars and mythmakers, so maybe that Plains Indian hobo is just a plain old everyday Indian. I'm kind of suspicious of him, because he identifies himself only as Plains Indian, a generic term, and not by a specific tribe. When I asked him why he wouldn't tell me exactly what he is, he said, "Do any of us know exactly what we are?" Yeah, great, a philosophizing Indian. "Hey," I said, "you got to have a home to be that homely." He just laughed and flipped me the eagle and walked away.

I wander the streets with a regular crew — my teammates, my defenders, my posse. It's Rose of Sharon, Junior, and me. We matter to one another if we don't matter to anybody else. Rose of Sharon is a big woman, about seven feet tall if you're measuring overall effect and about five feet tall if you're only talking about the physical. She's a Yakama Indian of the Wishram variety. Junior is a Colville, but there are about 199 tribes that make up the Colville, so he could be anything. He's good-looking, though, like he just stepped out of some "Don't Litter the Earth" public service advertisement. He's got those great big cheekbones that are like planets, you know, with little moons orbiting them. He gets me jealous, jealous, and jealous. If you put Junior and me next to each other, he's the Before Columbus Arrived Indian and I'm the After Columbus Arrived Indian. I am living proof of the horrible damage that colonialism has done to us Skins. But I'm not going to let you know how scared I sometimes get of history and its ways. I'm a strong man, and I know that silence is the best method of dealing with white folks.

This whole story really started at lunchtime, when Rose of Sharon, Junior, and I were panning the handle down at Pike Place Market. After about two hours of negotiating, we earned five dollars — good enough for a bottle of fortified courage from the most beautiful 7-Eleven in the world. So we headed over that way, feeling like warrior drunks, and we walked past this pawnshop I'd never noticed before. And that was strange, because we Indians have built-in pawnshop radar. But the strangest thing of all was the old powwow-dance regalia I saw hanging in the window.

"That's my grandmother's regalia," I said to Rose of Sharon and Junior.

"How you know for sure?" Junior asked.

I didn't know for sure, because I hadn't seen that regalia in person ever. I'd only seen photographs of my grandmother dancing in it. And those were taken before somebody stole it from her, fifty years ago. But it sure looked like my memory of it, and it had all the same color feathers and beads that my family sewed into our powwow regalia.

"There's only one way to know for sure," I said.

So Rose of Sharon, Junior, and I walked into the pawnshop and greeted the old white man working behind the counter.

"How can I help you?" he asked.

"That's my grandmother's powwow regalia in your window," I said. "Somebody stole it from her fifty years ago, and my family has been searching for it ever since."

The pawnbroker looked at me like I was a liar. I understood. Pawnshops are filled with liars.

"I'm not lying," I said. "Ask my friends here. They'll tell you."

"He's the most honest Indian I know," Rose of Sharon said.

"All right, honest Indian," the pawnbroker said. "I'll give you the benefit of the doubt. Can you prove it's your grandmother's regalia?"

Because they don't want to be perfect, because only God is perfect, Indian people sew flaws into their powwow regalia. My family always sewed one yellow bead somewhere on our regalia. But we always hid it so that you had to search really hard to find it.

"If it really is my grandmother's," I said, "there will be one yellow bead hidden somewhere on it."

"All right, then," the pawnbroker said. "Let's take a look."

He pulled the regalia out of the window, laid it down on the glass counter, and we searched for that yellow bead and found it hidden beneath the armpit.

"There it is," the pawnbroker said. He didn't sound surprised. "You were right. This is your grandmother's regalia."

"It's been missing for fifty years," Junior said.

"Hey, Junior," I said. "It's my family's story. Let me tell it."

"All right," he said. "I apologize. You go ahead."

"It's been missing for fifty years," I said.

"That's his family's sad story," Rose of Sharon said. "Are you going to give it back to him?"

"That would be the right thing to do," the pawnbroker said. "But I can't afford to do the right thing. I paid a thousand dollars for this. I can't just give away a thousand dollars."

"We could go to the cops and tell them it was stolen," Rose of Sharon said.

"Hey," I said to her. "Don't go threatening people."

The pawnbroker sighed. He was thinking about the possibilities.

"Well, I suppose you could go to the cops," he said. "But I don't think they'd believe a word you said."

He sounded sad about that. As if he was sorry for taking advantage of our disadvantages.

"What's your name?" the pawnbroker asked me.

"Jackson," I said.

"Is that first or last?"

"Both," I said.

"Are you serious?"

"Yes, it's true. My mother and father named me Jackson Jackson. My family nickname is Jackson Squared. My family is funny."

"All right, Jackson Jackson," the pawnbroker said. "You wouldn't happen to have a thousand dollars, would you?"

"We've got five dollars total," I said.

"That's too bad," he said, and thought hard about the possibilities. "I'd sell it to you for a thousand dollars if you had it. Heck, to make it fair, I'd sell it to you for nine hundred and ninety-nine dollars. I'd lose a dollar. That would be the moral thing to do in this case. To lose a dollar would be the right thing."

"We've got five dollars total," I said again.

"That's too bad," he said once more, and thought harder about the possibilities. "How about this? I'll give you twenty-four hours to come up with nine hundred and ninety-nine dollars. You come back here at lunchtime tomorrow with the money and I'll sell it back to you. How does that sound?"

"It sounds all right," I said.

"All right, then," he said. "We have a deal. And I'll get you started. Here's twenty bucks."

He opened up his wallet and pulled out a crisp twenty-dollar bill and gave it to me. And Rose of Sharon, Junior, and I walked out into the daylight to search for nine hundred and seventy-four more dollars.

1 P.M.

Rose of Sharon, Junior, and I carried our twenty-dollar bill and our five dollars in loose change over to the 7-Eleven and bought three bottles of imagination. We needed to figure out how to raise all that money in only one day. Thinking hard, we huddled in an alley beneath the Alaska Way Viaduct and finished off those bottles — one, two, and three.

2 P.M.

Rose of Sharon was gone when I woke up. I heard later that she had hitchhiked back to Toppenish and was living with her sister on the reservation.

Junior had passed out beside me and was covered in his own vomit, or maybe somebody else's vomit, and my head hurt from thinking, so I left him alone and walked down to the water. I love the smell of ocean water. Salt always smells like memory.

When I got to the wharf, I ran into three Aleut cousins, who sat on a wooden bench and stared out at the bay and cried. Most of the homeless Indians in Seattle come from Alaska. One by one, each of them hopped a big working boat in Anchorage or Barrow or Juneau, fished his way south to Seattle, jumped off the boat with a pocketful of cash to party hard at one of the highly sacred and traditional Indian bars, went broke and broker, and has been trying to find his way back to the boat and the frozen north ever since.

These Aleuts smelled like salmon, I thought, and they told me they were going to sit on that wooden bench until their boat came back.

"How long has your boat been gone?" I asked.

"Eleven years," the elder Aleut said.

I cried with them for a while.

"Hey," I said. "Do you guys have any money I can borrow?"

They didn't.

3 P.M.

I walked back to Junior. He was still out cold. I put my face down near his mouth to make sure he was breathing. He was alive, so I dug around in his blue jeans pockets and found half a cigarette. I smoked it all the way down and thought about my grandmother.

Her name was Agnes, and she died of breast cancer when I was fourteen. My father always thought Agnes caught her tumors from the uranium mine on the reservation. But my mother said the disease started when Agnes was walking back from a powwow one night and got run over by a motorcycle. She broke three ribs, and my mother always said those ribs never healed right, and tumors take over when you don't heal right.

Sitting beside Junior, smelling the smoke and the salt and the vomit, I wondered if my grandmother's cancer started when somebody stole her powwow regalia. Maybe the cancer started in her broken heart and then leaked out into her breasts. I know it's crazy, but I wondered whether I could bring my grandmother back to life if I bought back her regalia.

I needed money, big money, so I left Junior and walked over to the Real Change office.

4 P.M.

Real Change is a multifaceted organization that publishes a newspaper, supports cultural projects that empower the poor and the homeless, and mobilizes the public around poverty issues. Real Change's mission is to organize, educate, and build alliances to create solutions to homelessness and poverty. It exists to provide a voice for poor people in our community.

I memorized Real Change's mission statement because I sometimes sell the newspaper on the streets. But you have to stay sober to sell it, and I'm not always good at staying sober. Anybody can sell the paper. You buy each copy for thirty cents and sell it for a dollar, and you keep the profit.

"I need one thousand four hundred and thirty papers," I said to the Big Boss.

"That's a strange number," he said. "And that's a lot of papers."

"I need them."

The Big Boss pulled out his calculator and did the math.

"It will cost you four hundred and twenty-nine dollars for that many," he said.

"If I had that kind of money, I wouldn't need to sell the papers."

"What's going on, Jackson-to-the-Second-Power?" he asked. He is the only person who calls me that. He's a funny and kind man.

I told him about my grandmother's powwow regalia and how much money I needed in order to buy it back.

"We should call the police," he said.

"I don't want to do that," I said. "It's a quest now. I need to win it back by myself."

"I understand," he said. "And, to be honest, I'd give you the papers to sell if I thought it would work. But the record for the most papers sold in one day by one vender is only three hundred and two."

"That would net me about two hundred bucks," I said.

The Big Boss used his calculator. "Two hundred and eleven dollars and forty cents," he said.

"That's not enough," I said.

"And the most money anybody has made in one day is five hundred and twenty-five. And that's because somebody gave Old Blue five hundred-dollar bills for some dang reason. The average daily net is about thirty dollars."

"This isn't going to work."

"No."

"Can you lend me some money?"

"I can't do that," he said. "If I lend you money, I have to lend money to everybody."

"What can you do?"

"I'll give you fifty papers for free. But don't tell anybody I did it."

"O.K.," I said.

He gathered up the newspapers and handed them to me. I held them to my chest. He hugged me. I carried the newspapers back toward the water.

5 P.M.

Back on the wharf, I stood near the Bainbridge Island Terminal and tried to sell papers to business commuters boarding the ferry.

I sold five in one hour, dumped the other forty-five in a garbage can, and walked into McDonald's, ordered four cheeseburgers for a dollar each, and slowly ate them.

After eating, I walked outside and vomited on the sidewalk. I hated to lose my food so soon after eating it. As an alcoholic Indian with a busted stomach, I always hope I can keep enough food in me to stay alive.

6 P.M.

With one dollar in my pocket, I walked back to Junior. He was still passed out, and I put my ear to his chest and listened for his heartbeat. He was alive, so I took off his shoes and socks and found one dollar in his left sock and fifty cents in his right sock.

With two dollars and fifty cents in my hand, I sat beside Junior and thought about my grandmother and her stories.

When I was thirteen, my grandmother told me a story about the Second World War. She was a nurse at a military hospital in Sydney, Australia. For two years, she healed and comforted American and Australian soldiers.

One day, she tended to a wounded Maori soldier, who had lost his legs to an artillery attack. He was very dark-skinned. His hair was black and curly and his eyes were black and warm. His face was covered with bright tattoos.

"Are you Maori?" he asked my grandmother.

"No," she said. "I'm Spokane Indian. From the United States."

"Ah, yes," he said. "I have heard of your tribes. But you are the first American Indian I have ever met."

"There's a lot of Indian soldiers fighting for the United States," she said. "I have a brother fighting in Germany, and I lost another brother on Okinawa."

"I am sorry," he said. "I was on Okinawa as well. It was terrible."

"I am sorry about your legs," my grandmother said.

"It's funny, isn't it?" he said.

"What's funny?"

"How we brown people are killing other brown people so white people will remain free."

"I hadn't thought of it that way."

"Well, sometimes I think of it that way. And other times I think of it the way they want me to think of it. I get confused."

She fed him morphine.

"Do you believe in heaven?" he asked.

"Which heaven?" she asked.

"I'm talking about the heaven where my legs are waiting for me."

They laughed.

"Of course," he said, "my legs will probably run away from me when I get to heaven. And how will I ever catch them?"

"You have to get your arms strong," my grandmother said. "So you can run on your hands."

They laughed again.

Sitting beside Junior, I laughed at the memory of my grandmother's story. I put my hand close to Junior's mouth to make sure he was still breathing. Yes, Junior was alive, so I took my two dollars and fifty cents and walked to the Korean grocery store in Pioneer Square.

7 P.M.

At the Korean grocery store, I bought a fifty-cent cigar and two scratch lottery tickets for a dollar each. The maximum cash prize was five hundred dollars a ticket. If I won both, I would have enough money to buy back the regalia.

I loved Mary, the young Korean woman who worked the register. She was the daughter of the owners, and she sang all day.

"I love you," I said when I handed her the money.

"You always say you love me," she said.

"That's because I will always love you."

"You are a sentimental fool."

"I'm a romantic old man."

"Too old for me."

"I know I'm too old for you, but I can dream."

"O.K.," she said. "I agree to be a part of your dreams, but I will only hold your hand in your dreams. No kissing and no sex. Not even in your dreams."

"O.K.," I said. "No sex. Just romance."

"Goodbye, Jackson Jackson, my love. I will see you soon."

I left the store, walked over to Occidental Park, sat on a bench, and smoked my cigar all the way down.

Ten minutes after I finished the cigar, I scratched my first lottery ticket and won nothing. I could win only five hundred dollars now, and that would be only half of what I needed.

Ten minutes after I lost, I scratched the other ticket and won a free ticket — a small consolation and one more chance to win some money.

I walked back to Mary.

"Jackson Jackson," she said. "Have you come back to claim my heart?"

"I won a free ticket," I said.

"Just like a man," she said. "You love money and power more than you love me."

"It's true," I said. "And I'm sorry it's true."

She gave me another scratch ticket, and I took it outside. I like to scratch my tickets in private. Hopeful and sad, I scratched that third ticket and won real money. I carried it back inside to Mary.

"I won a hundred dollars," I said.

She examined the ticket and laughed.

"That's a fortune," she said, and counted out five twenties. Our fingertips touched as she handed me the money. I felt electric and constant.

"Thank you," I said, and gave her one of the bills.

"I can't take that," she said. "It's your money."

"No, it's tribal. It's an Indian thing. When you win, you're supposed to share with your family."

"I'm not your family."

"Yes, you are."

She smiled. She kept the money. With eighty dollars in my pocket, I said goodbye to my dear Mary and walked out into the cold night air.

8 P.M.

I wanted to share the good news with Junior. I walked back to him, but he was gone. I heard later that he had hitchhiked down to Portland, Oregon, and died of exposure in an alley behind the Hilton Hotel.

9 P.M.

Lonesome for Indians, I carried my eighty dollars over to Big Heart's in South Downtown. Big Heart's is an all-Indian bar. Nobody knows how or why Indians migrate to one bar and turn it into an official Indian bar. But Big Heart's has been an Indian bar for twenty-three years. It used to be way up on Aurora Avenue, but a crazy Lummi Indian burned that one down, and the owners moved to the new location, a few blocks south of Safeco Field.

I walked into Big Heart's and counted fifteen Indians — eight men and seven women. I didn't know any of them, but Indians like to belong, so we all pretended to be cousins.

"How much for whiskey shots?" I asked the bartender, a fat white guy.

"You want the bad stuff or the badder stuff?"

"As bad as you got."

"One dollar a shot."

I laid my eighty dollars on the bar top.

"All right," I said. "Me and all my cousins here are going to be drinking eighty shots. How many is that apiece?"

"Counting you," a woman shouted from behind me, "that's five shots for everybody."

I turned to look at her. She was a chubby and pale Indian woman, sitting with a tall and skinny Indian man.

"All right, math genius," I said to her, and then shouted for the whole bar to hear. "Five drinks for everybody!"

All the other Indians rushed the bar, but I sat with the mathematician and her skinny friend. We took our time with our whiskey shots.

"What's your tribe?" I asked.

"I'm Duwamish," she said. "And he's Crow."

"You're a long way from Montana," I said to him.

"I'm Crow," he said. "I flew here."

"What's your name?" I asked them.

"I'm Irene Muse," she said. "And this is Honey Boy."

She shook my hand hard, but he offered his hand as if I was supposed to kiss it. So I did. He giggled and blushed, as much as a dark-skinned Crow can blush.

"You're one of them two-spirits, aren't you?" I asked him.

"I love women," he said. "And I love men."

"Sometimes both at the same time," Irene said.

We laughed.

"Man," I said to Honey Boy. "So you must have about eight or nine spirits going on inside you, enit?"

"Sweetie," he said. "I'll be whatever you want me to be."

"Oh, no," Irene said. "Honey Boy is falling in love."

"It has nothing to do with love," he said.

We laughed.

"Wow," I said. "I'm flattered, Honey Boy, but I don't play on your team."

"Never say never," he said.

"You better be careful," Irene said. "Honey Boy knows all sorts of magic."

"Honey Boy," I said, "you can try to seduce me, but my heart belongs to a woman named Mary."

"Is your Mary a virgin?" Honey Boy asked.

We laughed.

And we drank our whiskey shots until they were gone. But the other Indians bought me more whiskey shots, because I'd been so generous with my money. And Honey Boy pulled out his credit card, and I drank and sailed on that plastic boat.

After a dozen shots, I asked Irene to dance. She refused. But

Honey Boy shuffled over to the jukebox, dropped in a quarter, and selected Willie Nelson's "Help Me Make It Through the Night." As Irene and I sat at the table and laughed and drank more whiskey, Honey Boy danced a slow circle around us and sang along with Willie.

"Are you serenading me?" I asked him.

He kept singing and dancing.

"Are you serenading me?" I asked him again.

"He's going to put a spell on you," Irene said.

I leaned over the table, spilling a few drinks, and kissed Irene hard. She kissed me back.

10 P.M.

Irene pushed me into the women's bathroom, into a stall, shut the door behind us, and shoved her hand down my pants. She was short, so I had to lean over to kiss her. I grabbed and squeezed her everywhere I could reach, and she was wonderfully fat, and every part of her body felt like a large, warm, soft breast.

Midnight

Nearly blind with alcohol, I stood alone at the bar and swore I had been standing in the bathroom with Irene only a minute ago.

"One more shot!" I yelled at the bartender.

"You've got no more money!" he yelled back.

"Somebody buy me a drink!" I shouted.

"They've got no more money!"

"Where are Irene and Honey Boy?"

"Long gone!"

2 A.M.

"Closing time!" the bartender shouted at the three or four Indians who were still drinking hard after a long, hard day of drinking. Indian alcoholics are either sprinters or marathoners.

"Where are Irene and Honey Boy?" I asked.

"They've been gone for hours," the bartender said.

"Where'd they go?"

"I told you a hundred times, I don't know."

"What am I supposed to do?"

"It's closing time. I don't care where you go, but you're not staying here."

"You are an ungrateful bastard. I've been good to you."

"You don't leave right now, I'm going to kick your ass."

"Come on, I know how to fight."

He came at me. I don't remember what happened after that.

4 A.M.

I emerged from the blackness and discovered myself walking behind a big warehouse. I didn't know where I was. My face hurt. I felt my nose and decided that it might be broken. Exhausted and cold, I pulled a plastic tarp from a truck bed, wrapped it around me like a faithful lover, and fell asleep in the dirt.

6 A.M.

Somebody kicked me in the ribs. I opened my eyes and looked up at a white cop.

"Jackson," the cop said. "Is that you?"

"Officer Williams," I said. He was a good cop with a sweet tooth. He'd given me hundreds of candy bars over the years. I wonder if he knew I was diabetic.

"What the hell are you doing here?" he asked.

"I was cold and sleepy," I said. "So I lay down."

"You dumb-ass, you passed out on the railroad tracks."

I sat up and looked around. I was lying on the railroad tracks. Dockworkers stared at me. I should have been a railroad-track pizza, a double Indian pepperoni with extra cheese. Sick and scared, I leaned over and puked whiskey.

"What the hell's wrong with you?" Officer Williams asked. "You've never been this stupid."

"It's my grandmother," I said. "She died."

"I'm sorry, man. When did she die?"

"Nineteen seventy-two."

"And you're killing yourself now?"

"I've been killing myself ever since she died."

He shook his head. He was sad for me. Like I said, he was a good cop.

"And somebody beat the hell out of you," he said. "You remember who?"

"Mr. Grief and I went a few rounds."

"It looks like Mr. Grief knocked you out."

"Mr. Grief always wins."

"Come on," he said. "Let's get you out of here."

He helped me up and led me over to his squad car. He put me in the back. "You throw up in there and you're cleaning it up," he said.

"That's fair."

He walked around the car and sat in the driver's seat. "I'm taking you over to detox," he said.

"No, man, that place is awful," I said. "It's full of drunk Indians."

We laughed. He drove away from the docks.

"I don't know how you guys do it," he said.

"What guys?" I asked.

"You Indians. How the hell do you laugh so much? I just picked your ass off the railroad tracks, and you're making jokes. Why the hell do you do that?"

"The two funniest tribes I've ever been around are Indians and Jews, so I guess that says something about the inherent humor of genocide."

We laughed.

"Listen to you, Jackson. You're so smart. Why the hell are you on the street?"

"Give me a thousand dollars and I'll tell you."

"You bet I'd give you a thousand dollars if I knew you'd straighten up your life."

He meant it. He was the second-best cop I'd ever known.

"You're a good cop," I said.

"Come on, Jackson," he said. "Don't blow smoke up my ass."

"No, really, you remind me of my grandfather."

"Yeah, that's what you Indians always tell me."

"No, man, my grandfather was a tribal cop. He was a good cop. He never arrested people. He took care of them. Just like you."

"I've arrested hundreds of scumbags, Jackson. And I've shot a couple in the ass."

"It don't matter. You're not a killer."

"I didn't kill them. I killed their asses. I'm an ass-killer."

We drove through downtown. The missions and shelters had already released their overnighters. Sleepy homeless men and women stood on street corners and stared up at a gray sky. It was the morning after the night of the living dead.

"Do you ever get scared?" I asked Officer Williams.

"What do you mean?"

"I mean, being a cop, is it scary?"

He thought about that for a while. He contemplated it. I liked that about him.

"I guess I try not to think too much about being afraid," he said. "If you think about fear, then you'll be afraid. The job is boring most of the time. Just driving and looking into dark corners, you know, and seeing nothing. But then things get heavy. You're chasing somebody, or fighting them or walking around a dark house, and you just know some crazy guy is hiding around a corner, and hell, yes, it's scary."

"My grandfather was killed in the line of duty," I said.

"I'm sorry. How'd it happen?"

I knew he'd listen closely to my story.

"He worked on the reservation. Everybody knew everybody. It was safe. We aren't like those crazy Sioux or Apache or any of those other warrior tribes. There've only been three murders on my reservation in the last hundred years."

"That is safe."

"Yeah, we Spokane, we're passive, you know. We're mean with words. And we'll cuss out anybody. But we don't shoot people. Or stab them. Not much, anyway."

"So what happened to your grandfather?"

"This man and his girlfriend were fighting down by Little Falls."

"Domestic dispute. Those are the worst."

"Yeah, but this guy was my grandfather's brother. My great-uncle."

"Oh, no."

"Yeah, it was awful. My grandfather just strolled into the house.

He'd been there a thousand times. And his brother and his girlfriend were drunk and beating on each other. And my grandfather stepped between them, just as he'd done a hundred times before. And the girlfriend tripped or something. She fell down and hit her head and started crying. And my grandfather kneeled down beside her to make sure she was all right. And for some reason my great-uncle reached down, pulled my grandfather's pistol out of the holster, and shot him in the head."

"That's terrible. I'm sorry."

"Yeah, my great-uncle could never figure out why he did it. He went to prison forever, you know, and he always wrote these long letters. Like fifty pages of tiny little handwriting. And he was always trying to figure out why he did it. He'd write and write and write and try to figure it out. He never did. It's a great big mystery."

"Do you remember your grandfather?"

"A little bit. I remember the funeral. My grandmother wouldn't let them bury him. My father had to drag her away from the grave."

"I don't know what to say."

"I don't, either."

We stopped in front of the detox center.

"We're here," Officer Williams said.

"I can't go in there," I said.

"You have to."

"Please, no. They'll keep me for twenty-four hours. And then it will be too late."

"Too late for what?"

I told him about my grandmother's regalia and the deadline for buying it back.

"If it was stolen, you need to file a report," he said. "I'll investigate it myself. If that thing is really your grandmother's, I'll get it back for you. Legally."

"No," I said. "That's not fair. The pawnbroker didn't know it was stolen. And, besides, I'm on a mission here. I want to be a hero, you know? I want to win it back, like a knight."

"That's romantic crap."

"That may be. But I care about it. It's been a long time since I really cared about something."

Officer Williams turned around in his seat and stared at me. He studied me.

"I'll give you some money," he said. "I don't have much. Only

thirty bucks. I'm short until payday. And it's not enough to get back
the regalia. But it's something."

"I'll take it," I said.

"I'm giving it to you because I believe in what you believe. I'm
hoping, and I don't know why I'm hoping it, but I hope you can
turn thirty bucks into a thousand somehow."

"I believe in magic."

"I believe you'll take my money and get drunk on it."

"Then why are you giving it to me?"

"There ain't no such thing as an atheist cop."

"Sure, there is."

"Yeah, well, I'm not an atheist cop."

He let me out of the car, handed me two fivers and a twenty, and
shook my hand.

"Take care of yourself, Jackson," he said. "Stay off the railroad
tracks."

"I'll try," I said.

He drove away. Carrying my money, I headed back toward the
water.

8 A.M.

On the wharf, those three Aleuts still waited on the wooden bench.

"Have you seen your ship?" I asked.

"Seen a lot of ships," the elder Aleut said. "But not our ship."

I sat on the bench with them. We sat in silence for a long time. I
wondered if we would fossilize if we sat there long enough.

I thought about my grandmother. I'd never seen her dance in
her regalia. And, more than anything, I wished I'd seen her dance
at a powwow.

"Do you guys know any songs?" I asked the Aleuts.

"I know all of Hank Williams," the elder Aleut said.

"How about Indian songs?"

"Hank Williams is Indian."

"How about sacred songs?"

"Hank Williams is sacred."

"I'm talking about ceremonial songs. You know, religious ones.
The songs you sing back home when you're wishing and hoping."

"What are you wishing and hoping for?"

"I'm wishing my grandmother was still alive."

"Every song I know is about that."

"Well, sing me as many as you can."

The Aleuts sang their strange and beautiful songs. I listened. They sang about my grandmother and about their grandmothers. They were lonesome for the cold and the snow. I was lonesome for everything.

10 A.M.

After the Aleuts finished their last song, we sat in silence for a while. Indians are good at silence.

"Was that the last song?" I asked.

"We sang all the ones we could," the elder Aleut said. "The others are just for our people."

I understood. We Indians have to keep our secrets. And these Aleuts were so secretive they didn't refer to themselves as Indians.

"Are you guys hungry?" I asked.

They looked at one another and communicated without talking.

"We could eat," the elder Aleut said.

11 A.M.

The Aleuts and I walked over to the Big Kitchen, a greasy diner in the International District. I knew they served homeless Indians who'd lucked into money.

"Four for breakfast?" the waitress asked when we stepped inside.

"Yes, we're very hungry," the elder Aleut said.

She took us to a booth near the kitchen. I could smell the food cooking. My stomach growled.

"You guys want separate checks?" the waitress asked.

"No, I'm paying," I said.

"Aren't you the generous one," she said.

"Don't do that," I said.

"Do what?" she asked.

"Don't ask me rhetorical questions. They scare me."

She looked puzzled, and then she laughed.

"O.K., professor," she said. "I'll only ask you real questions from now on."

"Thank you."

"What do you guys want to eat?"

"That's the best question anybody can ask anybody," I said. "What have you got?"

"How much money you got?" she asked.

"Another good question," I said. "I've got twenty-five dollars I can spend. Bring us all the breakfast you can, plus your tip."

She knew the math.

"All right, that's four specials and four coffees and fifteen percent for me."

The Aleuts and I waited in silence. Soon enough, the waitress returned and poured us four coffees, and we sipped at them until she returned again, with four plates of food. Eggs, bacon, toast, hash brown potatoes. It's amazing how much food you can buy for so little money.

Grateful, we feasted.

Noon

I said farewell to the Aleuts and walked toward the pawnshop. I heard later that the Aleuts had waded into the saltwater near Dock 47 and disappeared. Some Indians swore they had walked on the water and headed north. Other Indians saw the Aleuts drown. I don't know what happened to them.

I looked for the pawnshop and couldn't find it. I swear it wasn't in the place where it had been before. I walked twenty or thirty blocks looking for the pawnshop, turned corners and bisected intersections, and looked up its name in the phone books and asked people walking past me if they'd ever heard of it. But that pawnshop seemed to have sailed away like a ghost ship. I wanted to cry. And just when I'd given up, when I turned one last corner and thought I might die if I didn't find that pawnshop, there it was, in a space I swear it hadn't occupied a few minutes ago.

I walked inside and greeted the pawnbroker, who looked a little younger than he had before.

"It's you," he said.

"Yes, it's me," I said.

"Jackson Jackson."

"That is my name."

"Where are your friends?"

"They went traveling. But it's O.K. Indians are everywhere."

"Do you have the money?"

"How much do you need again?" I asked, and hoped the price had changed.

"Nine hundred and ninety-nine dollars."

It was still the same price. Of course, it was the same price. Why would it change?

"I don't have that," I said.

"What do you have?"

"Five dollars."

I set the crumpled Lincoln on the countertop. The pawnbroker studied it.

"Is that the same five dollars from yesterday?"

"No, it's different."

He thought about the possibilities.

"Did you work hard for this money?" he asked.

"Yes," I said.

He closed his eyes and thought harder about the possibilities. Then he stepped into the back room and returned with my grandmother's regalia.

"Take it," he said, and held it out to me.

"I don't have the money."

"I don't want your money."

"But I wanted to win it."

"You did win it. Now take it before I change my mind."

Do you know how many good men live in this world? Too many to count!

I took my grandmother's regalia and walked outside. I knew that solitary yellow bead was part of me. I knew I was that yellow bead in part. Outside, I wrapped myself in my grandmother's regalia and breathed her in. I stepped off the sidewalk and into the intersection. Pedestrians stopped. Cars stopped. The city stopped. They all watched me dance with my grandmother. I was my grandmother, dancing.

T. CORAGHESSAN BOYLE

Tooth and Claw

FROM THE NEW YORKER

THE WEATHER had absolutely nothing to do with it — though the rain had been falling off and on throughout the day and the way the gutters were dripping made me feel as if despair were the mildest term in the dictionary — because I would have gone down to Daggett's that afternoon even if the sun were shining and all the fronds of the palm trees were gilded with light. The problem was work. Or, more specifically, the lack of it. The boss had called at 6:30 A.M. to tell me not to come in, because the guy I'd been replacing had recovered sufficiently from his wrenched back to feel up to working, and, no, he wasn't firing me, because they'd be on to a new job next week and he could use all the hands he could get. "So take a couple days off and enjoy yourself," he'd rumbled into the phone in his low, hoarse, uneven voice, which always seemed on the verge of morphing into something else altogether — squawks and bleats or maybe just static. "You're young, right? Go out and get yourself some tail. Get drunk. Go to the library. Help old ladies across the street. You know what I mean?"

It had been a long day: breakfast out of a cardboard box while cartoon images flickered and faded and reconstituted themselves on the TV screen, and then some desultory reading, starting with the newspaper and a couple of *National Geographic*s I'd picked up at a yard sale; lunch at the deli, where I had ham and cheese in a tortilla wrap and exchanged exactly eleven words with the girl behind the counter ("Number seven, please, no mayo." "Have a nice day." "You, too"), and a walk to the beach that left my sneakers sodden. And, after all that, it was still only 3:00 in the afternoon and I had to force myself to stay away from the bar till 5:00, 5:00 at least.

I wasn't stupid. And I had no intention of becoming a drunk like all the hard-assed old men in the shopping-mall-blighted town I grew up in, silent men with hate in their eyes and complaint eating away at their insides — like my own dead father, for that matter — but I was new here, or relatively new (nine weeks now and counting), and Daggett's was the only place I felt comfortable. And why? Precisely because it was filled with old men drinking themselves into oblivion. It made me think of home. Or feel at home, anyway.

The irony wasn't lost on me. The whole reason I'd moved out to the Coast to live, first with my aunt Kim and her husband, Waverley, and then in my own one-bedroom apartment with kitchenette and a three-by-six-foot balcony with a partially obscured view of the Pacific, half a mile off, was so that I could inject a little excitement into my life and mingle with all the college students in the bars that lined State Street cheek to jowl, but here I was hanging out in an old man's bar that smelled of death and vomit and felt as closed in as a submarine, when just outside the door were all the exotic, sunstruck glories of California. Where it never rained. Except in winter. And it was winter now.

I nodded self-consciously at the six or seven regulars lined up at the bar, then ordered a Jack-and-Coke, the only drink besides beer that I liked the taste of, and I didn't really like the taste of beer. There were sports on the three TVs hanging from the ceiling — this was a sports bar — but the volume was down and the speakers were blaring the same tired hits of the sixties that I could have heard back home. *Ad nauseam.* When the bartender — *he* was young, at least, as were the waitresses — set down my drink, I made a comment about the weather, "Nice day for sunbathing, isn't it?," and the two regulars nearest me glanced up with something like interest in their eyes. "Or maybe bird watching," I added, feeling encouraged, and they swung their heads back to the familiar triangulation of their splayed elbows and cocktail glasses, and that was the end of that.

It must have been seven or so, the rain still coming down and people briefly enlivened by the novelty of it as they came and went in spasms of umbrella furling and unfurling, when a guy about my age — or, no, he must have been thirty, or close to it — came in and took the seat beside me. He was wearing a baseball cap, a jean jacket, and a T-shirt that said OBLIGATORY DEATH, which I took to be the name of a band, though I'd never heard of it. His hair was blond, cut short around the ears, and he had a soul beard that was like a pale stripe painted under his lip by an unsteady hand. We exchanged the standard greeting — *What's up?* — and then he flagged down the bartender and ordered a draft beer, a shot of tomato juice, and two raw eggs.

"Raw eggs?" the bartender echoed, as if he hadn't heard right.

"Yeah. Two raw eggs, in the shell."

The bartender — his name was Chris, or maybe it was Matt — gave a smile and scratched the back of his head. "We can do them over easy or sunny-side up or poached even, but *raw*, I don't know. I mean, nobody's ever requested raw before —"

"Ask the chef, why don't you?"

The bartender shrugged. "Sure," he said, "no problem." He started off in the direction of the kitchen, then pulled up short. "You want toast with that, home fries, or what?"

"Just the eggs."

Everybody was watching now, any little drama worth the price of admission, especially on a night like this, but the bartender — Chris, his name was definitely Chris — just went down to the other end of the bar and communicated the order to the waitress, who made a notation in her pad and disappeared into the kitchen. A moment went by, and then the man turned to me and said in a voice loud enough for everybody to hear, "Jesus, this music sucks. Are we caught in a time warp here, or what?"

The old men — the regulars — glanced up from their drinks and gave him a look, but they were gray-haired and slack in the belly and they knew their limits.

"Yeah," I heard myself say, "it really sucks," and before I knew it I was talking passionately about the bands that meant the most to me even as the new guy poured tomato juice in his beer and sipped the foam off the top, while the music rumbled defiantly on and people with wet shoes and dripping umbrellas crowded in behind us. The eggs, brown-shelled and naked in the middle of a standard dinner plate, were delivered by Daria, a waitress I'd had my eye on, though I hadn't yet worked up the nerve to say more than hello and good-bye to her. "Your order, sir," she said, easing the plate down on the bar. "You need anything with that? Ketchup? Tabasco?"

"No," he said, "that's fine," and everyone was waiting for him to crack the eggs over his beer, but he didn't even look at them. He was looking at Daria, holding her with his eyes. "So, what's your name?" he asked, grinning.

She told him, and she was grinning, too.

"Nice to meet you," he said, taking her hand. "I'm Ludwig."

"Ludwig," she repeated, pronouncing it with a *v*, as he had, though as far as I could tell — from his clothes and accent, which was pure southern California — he wasn't German. Or if he was, he sure had his English down.

"Are you German?" Daria was flirting with him, and the realization of it began to harden me against him in the most rudimentary way.

"No," he said. "I'm from Hermosa Beach, born and raised. It's the name, right?"

"I had this German teacher last year? His name was Ludwig, that's all."

"You're in college?"

She told him she was, which was news to me. Working her way through. Majoring in business. She wanted to own her own restaurant someday.

"It was my mother's idea," he said, as if he'd been mulling it over. "She was listening to the *Eroica* Symphony the night I was born." He shrugged. "It's been my curse ever since."

"I don't know," she said. "I think it's kind of cute. You don't get many Ludwigs, you know?"

"Yeah, tell me about it," he said, sipping his beer.

She lingered, though there were other things she could have been doing. "So, what about the eggs?" she said. "You going to need utensils, or —"

"Or what? Am I going to suck them out of the shell?"

"Yeah," she said, "something like that."

He reached out a hand cluttered with silver to embrace the eggs and gently roll them back and forth across the gleaming expanse of the plate. "No, I'm just going to fondle them," he said, and got the expected response: she laughed. "But does anybody still play dice around here?" he called down the bar as the eyes of the regulars slid in our direction and then away again.

In those days — and this was ten years ago or more — the game of Horse was popular in certain California bars, as were smoking, unprotected sex, and various other adult pleasures that may or may not have been hazardous to your health. There were five dice, shaken in a cup, and you slammed that cup down on the bar, trying for the highest cumulative score, which was thirty. Anything could be bet on, from the next round of drinks to ponying up for the jukebox.

The rain hissed at the door, and it opened briefly to admit a stamping, umbrella-less couple. Ludwig's question hung unanswered on the air. "No? How about you, Daria?"

"I can't — I'm working."

He turned to me. I had no work in the morning or the next morning, either — maybe no work at all. My apartment wasn't what I'd thought it would be, not without somebody to share it with, and I'd already vowed to myself that I'd rather sleep on the streets than go back to my aunt's, because going back there would represent the worst kind of defeat. *Take good care of my baby, Kim,* my mother had said when she dropped me off. *He's the only one I've got.*

"Sure," I said. "I guess. What're we playing for — for drinks, right?" I began fumbling in my pockets, awkward — I was drunk, I could feel it. "Because I don't have, well, maybe ten bucks —"

"No," he said, "no," already rising from his seat, "you just wait here, just one minute, you'll see," and then he was out the door and into the grip of the rain.

Daria hadn't moved. She was dressed in the standard outfit for Daggett's employees — shorts, white ankle socks, and a T-shirt with the name of the establishment blazoned across the chest, her legs pale and silken in the flickering light of the fake fireplace in the corner. She gave me a sympathetic look, and I shrugged to show her that I was ready for anything, a real man of the world.

There was a noise at the door — a scraping and shifting — and we all looked up to see Ludwig struggling with something there against the backdrop of the rain. His hat had been knocked askew and water dripped from his nose and chin. It took a moment, one shoulder pinning the door open, and then he lifted a cage — a substantial cage, two and a half feet high and maybe four feet long — through the doorway and set it down against the wall. No one moved. No one said a word. There was something in the cage, the apprehension of it as sharp and sudden as the smell it brought with it, something wild and alien and very definitely out of the ordinary on what to this point had been a painfully ordinary night.

Ludwig wiped the moisture from his face with a swipe of his sleeve, straightened out his hat, and came back to the bar, looking jaunty and refreshed. "All right," he said, "don't be shy — go have a look. It won't bite. Or it will, it definitely will, just don't get your fingers near it, that's all."

I saw coiled limbs, claws, yellow eyes. Whatever it was, the thing hadn't moved, not even to blink. I was going to ask what it was when Daria, still at my side, said, "It's a cat, some kind of wildcat, right? A what — a lynx or something?"

"You can't have that thing in here," one of the regulars said, but already he was getting up out of his seat to have a look at it — everyone was getting up now, shoving back chairs and rising from the tables, crowding around.

"It's a serval," Ludwig was saying. "From Africa. Thirty-five pounds of muscle and quicker than a snake."

And where had he got it? He'd won it, in a bar in Arizona, on a roll of the dice.

How long had he had it? Two years.

What was its name? Cat. Just Cat. And, yes, it was a male, and, no, he didn't want to get rid of it but he was moving overseas on a new job and there was just no way he could take it with him, so he felt that it was apropos — that was the word he used, "apropos" — to give it up in the way he'd got it.

He turned to me. "What was your name again?"

"Junior," I said. "James, Jr., Turner, I mean. James Turner, Jr. But everybody calls me Junior." I wanted to add, "Because of my father, so people wouldn't confuse us," but I left it at that, because it got even more complicated considering that my father was six months dead and I could be anybody I wanted.

"O.K., Junior, here's the deal," Ludwig said. "Your ten bucks against the cat, one roll. What do you say?"

I wanted to say that I had no place for the thing, that I didn't want a cat of any kind or even a guinea pig or a fish in a bowl and that the ten dollars was meaningless, but everyone was watching me and I couldn't back out without feeling the shame rise to my face — and there was Daria to consider, because she was watching me, too. "Yeah," I said. "Yeah, O.K., sure."

Sixty seconds later, I was still solvent and richer by one cat and one cage. I'd got lucky — or unlucky, depending on how you want to look at it — and rolled three fives and two fours; Ludwig rolled a combined eleven. He finished his beer in a gulp, took my hand to seal the deal, and then started toward the door. "But what do I feed it?" I called. "I mean, what does it eat?"

"Eggs," he said. "It loves eggs. And meat. Raw. No kibble, forget kibble. This is the real deal, this animal, and you need to treat it right." He was at the door, looking down at the thing with what might have been wistfulness or satisfaction, I couldn't tell which, then he reached down behind the cage to unfasten something there — a gleam of black leather — and toss it to me: it was a glove, or a gauntlet, actually, as long as my arm. "You'll want to wear this when you feed him," he said, and then he was gone.

For a long moment, I stared at the door, trying to work out what had happened, and then I looked at the regulars — at the expressions on their faces — and at the other customers, locals or maybe even tourists, who'd come in for a beer or a burger or the catch of the day and had all this strangeness thrust on them, and finally at the cage. Daria was bent beside it, cooing to the animal inside, Ludwig's eggs cradled in one hand. She was short and compact, conventionally pretty, with the round eyes and symmetrical features of an anime heroine, her running shoes no bigger than a child's, her blond hair pulled back in a ponytail, and I'd noticed all that before, over the course of weeks of study, but now it came to me with the force of revelation. She was beautiful, a beautiful girl propped on one knee, while her shorts rode up in back and her T-shirt bunched beneath her breasts, offering this cat — my cat — the smallest comfort, as if it were a kitten she'd found abandoned on the street.

"Jesus, what are you going to do with the thing?" Chris had come out from behind the bar and he was standing beside me now, looking awed.

I told him that I didn't know. That I hadn't planned on owning a wildcat, hadn't even known they existed — servals, that is — until five minutes ago.

"You live around here?"

"Bayview Apartments."

"They accept pets?"

I'd never really given it much thought, but they did, they must have — the guy next door to me had a pair of yapping little dogs with bows in their hair, and the woman down the hall had a Doberman that was forever scrabbling its nails on the linoleum when she came in and out with it, which she seemed to do about a hundred times a day. But this was something different. This was something that might push at the parameters of the standard lease. "Yeah," I said, "I think so."

There was a single slot where the door of the cage fastened that was big enough to receive an egg without crushing its shell, and Daria, still cooing, rolled first one egg, then the other, through the aperture. For a moment, nothing happened. Then the cat, hunched against the mesh, shifted position ever so slightly and took the first egg in its mouth — two teeth like hypodermics, a crunch, and then the soft frictive scrape of its tongue.

Daria rose and came to me with a look of wonder. "Don't do a thing till I get off, O.K.?" she said, and in her fervor she took hold of my arm. "I get off at nine, so you wait, O.K.?"

"Yeah," I said. "Sure."

"We can put him in the back of the storage room for now, and then, well, I guess we can use my pickup."

I didn't have the leisure to reflect on how complex things had become all of a sudden, and even if I had I don't think I would have behaved any differently. I just nodded at her, stared into her plenary eyes, and nodded.

"He's going to be all right," she said, and added, "He will," as if I'd been disagreeing with her. "I've got to get back to work, but you wait, O.K.? You wait right here." Chris was watching. The manager was watching. The regulars had all craned their necks and half the dinner customers, too. Daria patted down her apron, smoothed back her hair. "What did you say your name was again?"

So I had a cat. And a girl. We put the thing in the back of her red Toyota pickup, threw a tarp over it to keep the rain off, and drove to Vons, where I watched Daria march up and down the aisles seeking out kitty litter and the biggest cat pan they had (we settled for a dishpan, hard blue plastic that looked all but indestructible), and then it was on to the meat counter. "I've only got ten bucks," I said.

She gave me a withering look. "This animal's got to eat," she informed me, and she reached back to slip the band from her ponytail so that her hair fell glistening across her shoulders, a storm of hair, fluid and loose, the ends trailing down her back like liquid in motion. She tossed her head impatiently. "You do have a credit card, don't you?"

Ten minutes later, I was directing her back to my building, where she parked next to the Mustang I'd inherited when my father died, and then we went up the outside stairs and along the walkway to my apartment, on the second floor. "I'm sorry," I said, swinging open the door and hitting the light switch, "but I'm afraid I'm not much of a housekeeper." I was going to add that I hadn't expected company, either, or I would have straightened up, but Daria just strode right in, cleared a spot on the counter, and set down the groceries. I watched her shoulders as she reached into the depths of one bag after another and extracted the forty-odd dollars' worth of chicken parts and rib-eye steak (marked down for quick sale) that we'd selected in the meat department.

"O.K.," she said, turning to me as soon as she'd made space in the refrigerator for it all, "now where are we going to put the cat, because I don't think we should leave it out there in the truck any longer than we have to, do you? Cats don't like the rain, I know that — I have two of them. Or one's a kitten, really." She was on the other side of the kitchen counter, a clutter of crusted dishes and glasses sprouting colonies of mold between us. "You have a bedroom, right?"

I did. But if I was embarrassed by the state of the kitchen and living room — this was my first venture at living alone, and the need for order hadn't really seemed paramount to me — then the thought of the bedroom, with its funk of dirty clothes and unwashed sheets, the reeking work boots and the duffel bag out of which I'd been living, gave me pause. Here was this beautiful apparition in my kitchen, the only person besides my aunt who'd ever stepped through the door of my apartment, and now she was about to discover the sad, lonely disorder at the heart of my life. "Yeah," I said. "That door there, to the left of the bathroom." But she was already in the room, pushing things aside, a frown of concentration pressed between her eyes.

"You're going to have to clear this out," she said. "The bed, everything. All your clothes."

I was standing in the doorway, watching her. "What do you mean, 'clear it out'?"

She lifted her face. "You don't think that animal can stay caged up like that, do you? There's hardly room for it to turn around. And that's just cruel." She drilled me with that look again, then put her hands on her hips. "I'll help you," she said. "It shouldn't take ten minutes."

Then it was up the stairs with the cat, the two of us fighting the awkwardness of the cage. We kept the tarp knotted tightly in place, both to keep the rain off the cat and to disguise it from any of my neighbors who might happen by, and, though we shifted the angle of the thing coming up the stairs, the animal didn't make a sound. We had a little trouble getting the cage through the doorway — the cat seemed to concentrate its weight as if in silent protest — but we managed, and then we maneuvered it into the bedroom and set it down in the middle of the rug. Daria had already arranged the litter box in the corner, atop several sheets of newspaper, and she'd taken my biggest stew pot, filled it with water, and placed it just inside the door, where I could get to it easily. "O.K.," she said, glancing up at me with a satisfied look, "it's time for the unveiling," and she bent to unfasten the tarp.

The overhead light glared, the tarp slid from the cage and puddled on the floor, and there was the cat, pressed to the mesh in a compression of limbs, its yellow eyes seizing on us. "Nice kitty," Daria cooed. "Does he want out of that awful cage? Hmm? Does he? And meat — does he want meat?"

So far, I'd gone along with everything in a kind of daze, but this was problematic. Who knew what the thing would do, what its habits were, its needs? "How are we going to —" I began, and left the rest unspoken. The light stung my eyes, and the alcohol whispered in my blood. "You remember what that guy said about feeding him, right?" In the back of my head, there was the smallest glimmer of a further complication: once he was out of the cage, how would we — how would I — ever get him back into it?

For the first time, Daria looked doubtful. "We'll have to be quick," she said.

And so we were. Daria stood at the bedroom door, ready to slam it shut, while I leaned forward, my heart pounding, and slipped the bolt on the cage. I was nimble in those days — twenty-three years old and with excellent reflexes despite the four or five Jack-and-Cokes I'd downed in the course of the evening — and I sprang for the door the instant the bolt was released. Exhilaration burned in

me. It burned in the cat, too, because at the first click of the bolt it
came to life as if it had been hot-wired. A screech tore through the
room, the cage flew open, and the thing was an airborne blur slamming against the cheap plywood panel of the bedroom door, even
as Daria and I fought to force it shut.

In the morning (she'd slept on the couch, curled up in the fetal position, faintly snoring; I was stretched out on the mattress we'd removed from the bedroom and tucked against the wall under the
TV), I was faced with a number of problems. I'd awakened before
her, jolted out of a dreamless sleep by a flash of awareness, and for
a long while I just lay there watching her. I could have gone on
watching her all morning, thrilled by her presence, her hair, the repose of her face, if it weren't for the cat. It hadn't made a sound,
and it didn't stink, not yet, but its existence was communicated to
me nonetheless — it was there, and I could feel it. I would have to
feed it, and after the previous night's episode, that was going to require some thought and preparation, and I would have to offer
Daria something, too, if only to hold her here a little longer. Eggs, I
could scramble some eggs, but there was no bread for toast, no
milk, no sugar for the coffee. And she would want to freshen up in
the bathroom — women always freshened up in the morning, I was
pretty sure of that. I thought of the neatly folded little matching
towels in the guest bathroom at my aunt's and contrasted that image with the corrugated rag wadded up on the floor somewhere in
my own bathroom. Maybe I should go out for bagels or muffins or
something, I thought — and a new towel. But did they sell towels at
7-Eleven? I didn't have a clue.

We'd stayed up late, sharing the last of the hot cocoa out of the
foil packet and talking in a specific way about the cat that had
brought us to that moment on the greasy couch in my semi-
darkened living room and then more generally about our own
lives and thoughts and hopes and ambitions. I'd heard about her
mother, her two sisters, the courses she was taking at the university.
Heard about Daggett's, the regulars, the tips — or lack of them.
And her restaurant fantasy. It was amazingly detailed, right down to
the number of tables she was planning on, the dinnerware, the cut-
lery, and the paintings on the walls, as well as the décor and the clientele — "Late twenties, early thirties, career people, no kids" —

and a dozen or more of the dishes she would specialize in. My ambitions were more modest. I'd told her how I'd finished community college without any particular aim or interest, and how I was
working setting tile for a friend of my aunt and uncle; beyond that,
I was hoping to maybe travel up the coast and see Oregon. I'd
heard a lot about Oregon, I told her. Very clean. Very natural up
there. Had she ever been to Oregon? No, but she'd like to go. I remembered telling her that she ought to open her restaurant up
there, someplace by the water, where people could look out and
take in the view. "Yeah," she'd said, "that'd be cool," and then she'd
yawned and dropped her head to the pillow.

I was just getting up to see what I could do about the towel in the
bathroom, thinking vaguely of splashing some after-shave on it to
fight down any offensive odors it might have picked up, when her
eyes flashed open. She didn't say my name or wonder where she
was or ask for breakfast or where the bathroom was. She just said,
"We have to feed that cat."

"Don't you want coffee or anything — breakfast? I can make
breakfast."

She threw back the blanket and I saw that her legs were bare. She
was wearing the Daggett's T-shirt over a pair of shiny black panties;
her running shoes, socks, and shorts were balled up on the rug beneath her. "Sure," she said. "Coffee sounds nice." And she pushed
her fingers through her hair on both sides of her head and then let
it all fall forward to obscure her face. She sat there a moment before leaning forward to dig a hair clip out of her purse, arch her
back, and pull the hair tight in a ponytail. "But I am worried about
the cat, in new surroundings and all. The poor thing — we should
have fed him last night."

Perhaps so. And I certainly didn't want to contradict her — I
wanted to be amicable and charming, wanted to ingratiate myself
in any way I could — but we'd both been so terrified of the animal's power in that moment when we'd released it from the cage
that neither of us had felt up to the challenge of attempting to feed
it. Attempting to feed it would have meant opening that door
again, and that was going to take some thought and commitment.
"Yeah," I said. "We should have. And we will, we will, but coffee, coffee first — you want a cup? I can make you a cup?"

So we drank coffee and ate the strawberry Pop-Tarts I found in the cupboard above the sink and made small talk as if we'd awakened together a hundred mornings running, and it was so tranquil and so domestic and so right I never wanted it to end. We were talking about work and about what time she had to be in that afternoon, when her brow furrowed and her eyes sharpened and she said, "I wish I could see it. When we feed it, I mean. Couldn't you, like, cut a peephole in the door or something?"

I was glad for the distraction, damage deposit notwithstanding. And the idea appealed to me: now we could see what the thing — my pet — was up to, and if we could see it, then it wouldn't seem so unapproachable and mysterious. I'd have to get to know it eventually, have to name it and tame it, maybe even walk it on a leash. I had a brief vision of myself sauntering down the sidewalk, this id with claws at my side, turning heads and cowing the weightlifters with their Dobermans and Rottweilers, and then I fished my power drill out from under the sink and cut a neat hole, half an inch in diameter, in the bedroom door. As soon as it was finished, Daria put her eye to it.

"Well?"

"The poor thing. He's pacing back and forth like an animal in a zoo."

She moved to the side and took my arm as I pressed my eye to the hole. The cat flowed like molten ore from one corner of the room to the other, its yellow eyes fixed on the door, the dun, faintly spotted skin stretched like spandex over its seething muscles. I saw that the kitty litter had been upended and the hard blue plastic pan reduced to chewed-over pellets, and wondered about that, about where the thing would do its business if not in the pan. "It turned over the kitty pan," I said.

She was still holding my arm. "I know."

"It chewed it to shreds."

"Metal. We'll have to get a metal one, like a trough or something."

I took my eye from the peephole and turned to her. "But how am I going to change it — don't you have to change it?"

Her eyes were shining. "Oh, it'll settle down. It's just a big kitty, that's all" — and then for the cat, in a syrupy coo — "Isn't that right, kittums?" Next, she went to the refrigerator and extracted one of the steaks, a good pound and a half of meat. "Put on the glove," she said, "and I'll hold onto the doorknob while you feed him."

"What about the blood — won't the blood get on the carpet?" The gauntlet smelled of saddle soap and it was gouged and pitted down the length of it; it fit me as if it had been custom-made.

"I'll press the blood out with a paper towel — here, look," she said, dabbing at the meat in the bottom of the sink and then lifting it on the end of a fork. I took the fork from her and together we went to the bedroom door.

I don't know if the cat smelled the blood or if it heard us at the door, but the instant I turned the knob it was there. I counted three, then jerked the door back just enough to get my arm and the dangle of meat into the room even as the cat exploded against the doorframe and the meat vanished. We pushed the door to — Daria's face was flushed and she seemed to be giggling or gasping for air — and then we took turns watching the thing drag the steak back and forth across the rug as if it still needed killing. By the time the cat was done, there was blood everywhere, even on the ceiling.

After Daria left for work, I didn't know what to do with myself. The cat was ominously silent and when I pressed my eye to the peephole I saw that it had dragged its cage into the far corner and was slumped behind it, apparently asleep. I flicked on the TV and sat through the usual idiocy, which was briefly enlivened by a nature show on the Serengeti that gave a cursory glimpse of a cat like mine — "The serval lives in rocky kopjes, where it keeps a wary eye on its enemies, the lion and the hyena, feeding principally on small prey, rabbits, birds, even snakes and lizards," the narrator informed me in a hushed voice — and then I went to the sandwich shop and ordered the No. 7 special, no mayo, and took it down to the beach. It was a clear day, all the haze and particulate matter washed out of the air by the previous day's deluge, and I sat there with the sun on my face and watched the waves ride in on top of one another while I ate and considered the altered condition of my life. Daria's face had got serious as she stood at the door, her T-shirt rumpled, her hair pulled back so tightly from her scalp I could make out each individual strand. "Take care of our cat now, O.K.?" she said. "I'll be back as soon as I get off." I shrugged in a helpless, submissive way, the pain of her leaving as acute as anything I'd ever felt. "Sure," I said, and then she reached for my shoulders and pulled me to her for a kiss — on the lips. "You're sweet," she said.

So I was sweet. No one had ever called me sweet before, not since childhood, anyway, and I have to admit the designation thrilled me, bloomed inside me like the promise of things to come. I began to see her as a prime mover in my life, her naked legs stretched out on the couch, the hair falling across her shoulders at the kitchen table, her lips locked on mine. But as I sat there eating my ham-and-cheese wrap a conflicting thought came to me: there had to be someone in her life already, a girl that beautiful, working in a bar, and I was deluding myself to think I had a chance with her. She had to have a boyfriend — she could even be engaged, for all I knew. I tried to focus on the previous night, on her hands and fingers — had she been wearing a ring? And, if she had, then where was the fiancé, the boyfriend, whoever he was? I hated him already, and I didn't even know if he existed.

The upshot of all this was that I found myself in the cool subterranean glow of Daggett's at 3:30 in the afternoon, nursing a Jack-and-Coke like one of the regulars while Daria, the ring finger of her left hand as unencumbered as mine, cleared up after the lunch crowd and set the tables for the dinner rush. Chris came on at 5:00, and he called me by my name and refreshed my drink before he even glanced at the regulars, and for the next hour or so, during the lulls, we conversed about any number of things, beginning with the most obvious — the cat — but veering into sports, music, books, and films, and I found myself expanding into a new place altogether. At one point, Daria stopped by to ask if the cat was settling in — was he still pacing around neurotically or what? — and I could tell her with some assurance that he was asleep. "He's probably nocturnal," I said, "or something like that." And then, with Chris looking on, I couldn't help adding, "You're still coming over, right? After work? To help me feed him, I mean."

She looked to Chris, then let her gaze wander out over the room. "Oh, yeah," she said, "yeah," and there was a catch of hesitation in her voice. "I'll be there."

I let that hang a moment, but I was insecure and the alcohol was having its effect and I couldn't leave it alone. "We can drive over together," I said, "because I didn't bring my car."

*

She was looking tired by the end of her shift, the bounce gone out of her step, her hair a shade duller under the drab lights, and even as I switched to coffee I noticed Chris slipping her a shot of something down at the end of the bar. I'd had a sandwich around 6:00, and then, so as not to seem overanxious, I'd taken a walk, which brought me into another bar down the street, where I had a Jack-and-Coke and didn't say a word to anyone, and then I'd returned at 8:00 to drink coffee and hold her to her promise.

We didn't say much on the way over to my place. It was only a five-minute drive, and there was a song on that we both liked. Plus, it seemed to me that when you were comfortable with someone you could respect the silences. I'd gone to the cash machine earlier and in a hopeful mood stocked up on breakfast things — eggs, English muffins, a quart each of no-fat and two-percent milk, an expensive Chinese tea that came in individual foil packets — and I'd picked up two bottles of a local Chardonnay that was supposed to be really superior, or at least that was what the guy in the liquor department had told me, as well as a bag of corn chips and a jar of salsa. There were two new bathroom towels hanging on the rack beside the medicine cabinet, and I'd given the whole place a good vacuuming and left the dishes to soak in a sink of scalding water and the last few molecules of dish soap left in the plastic container I'd brought with me from my aunt's. The final touch was a pair of clean sheets and a light blanket folded suggestively over the arm of the couch.

Daria didn't seem to notice — she went straight to the bedroom door and affixed her eye to the peephole. "I can't see anything," she said, leaning into the door, the muscles of her calves flexing as she went up on her toes. "It's too bad we didn't think of a night-light or something."

I was watching her out of the corner of my eye — admiring her, amazed all over again at her presence — while working the corkscrew in the bottle. I asked her if she'd like a glass of wine. "Chardonnay," I said. "It's a local one, really superior."

"I'd love a glass," she said, turning away from the door and crossing the room to me. I didn't have wineglasses, so we made do with the milky-looking water glasses my aunt had dug out of a box in her basement. "I wonder if you could maybe slip your arm in the door and turn on the light in there," she said. "I'm worried about him. And, plus, we've got to feed him again, right?"

"Sure," I said, "yeah, no problem," but I was in no hurry. I re-filled our glasses and broke out the chips and salsa, which she seemed happy enough to see. For a long while, we stood at the kitchen counter, dipping chips and savoring the wine, and then she went to the refrigerator, extracted a slab of meat, and began pat-ting it down with paper towels. I took her cue, donned the gaunt-let, braced myself, and jerked the bedroom door open just enough to get my hand in and flick on the light. The cat, which of course had sterling night vision, nearly tore the glove from my arm, and yet the suddenness of the light seemed to confuse it just long enough for me to salvage the situation. The door slammed on a puzzled yowl.

Daria immediately put her eye to the peephole. "Oh my God," she murmured.

"What's he doing?"

"Pacing. But here, you have a look."

The carpeting — every last strip of it — had been torn out of the floor, leaving an expanse of dirty plywood studded with nails, and there seemed to be a hole in the plasterboard just to the left of the window. A substantial hole. Even through the closed door I could smell the reek of cat piss or spray or whatever it was. "There goes my deposit," I said.

She was right there beside me, her hand on my shoulder. "He'll settle down," she assured me, "once he gets used to the place. All cats are like that — they have to establish their territory is all."

"You don't think he can get inside the walls, do you?"

"No," she said, "no way. He's too big."

The only thing I could think to do, especially after an entire day of drinking, was to pour more wine, which I did. Then we repeated the ritual of the morning's feeding — the steak on the fork, the blur of the cat, the savage thump at the door — and took turns watching it eat. After a while, bored with the spectacle — or per-haps *sated* is a better word — we found ourselves on the couch and there was a movie on TV and we finished the wine and the chips and we never stopped talking, a comment on this movie leading to a discussion of movies in general, a reflection on the wine dredging up our mutual experiences of wine tastings and the horrors of Cribari red and Boone's Farm and all the rest. It was midnight be-fore we knew it and she was yawning and stretching.

"I've really got to get home," she said, but she didn't move. "I'm wiped. Just wiped."

"You're welcome to stay over," I said, "I mean, if you don't want to drive, after the wine and all —"

A moment drifted by, neither of us speaking, and then she made a sort of humming noise — "Mmm" — and held out her arms to me even as she sank down into the couch.

I was up before her in the morning, careful not to wake her as I eased myself from the mattress where we'd wound up sleeping because the couch was too narrow for the two of us. My head ached — I wasn't used to so much alcohol — and the effigy of the cat lurked somewhere behind that ache, but I felt buoyant and optimistic. Daria was asleep on the mattress, the cat was hunkered down in his room, and all was right with the world. I brewed coffee, toasted muffins, and fried eggs, and when she woke I was there to feed her. "What do you say to breakfast in bed?" I murmured, easing down beside her with a plate of eggs over easy and a mug of coffee.

I was so intent on watching her eat that I barely touched my own food. After a while, I got up and turned on the radio and there was that song again, the one we'd heard coming home the night before, and we both listened to it all the way through without saying a word. When the DJ came on with his gasping juvenile voice and lame jokes, she got up and went to the bathroom, passing right by the bedroom door without a thought for the cat. She was in the bathroom a long while, running water, flushing, showering, and I felt lost without her. I wanted to tell her that I loved her, wanted to extend a whole list of invitations to her: she could move in with me, stay here indefinitely, bring her cats with her, no problem, and we could both look after the big cat together, see to its needs, tame it, and make it happy in its new home — no more cages, and meat, plenty of meat. I was scrubbing the frying pan when she emerged, her hair wrapped in one of the new towels. She was wearing makeup and she was dressed in her Daggett's outfit. "Hey," I said.

She didn't answer. She was bent over the couch now, stuffing things into her purse.

"You look terrific," I said.

There was a sound from the bedroom then, a low moan that

might have been the expiring gasp of the cat's prey, and I wondered if it had found something in there, a rat, a stray bird attracted to the window, an escaped hamster or lizard. "Listen, Junior," she said, ignoring the moaning, which grew higher and more attenuated now, "you're a nice guy, you really are."

I was behind the Formica counter. My hands were in the dishwater. Something pounded in my head, and I knew what was coming, heard it in her voice, saw it in the way she ducked her head and averted her eyes.

"I can't — I have to tell you something, O.K.? Because you're sweet, you are, and I want to be honest with you."

She raised her face to me all of a sudden, let her eyes stab at mine and then dodge away again. "I have a boyfriend. He's away at school. And I don't know why . . . I mean, I just don't want to give you the wrong impression. It was nice. It was."

The moaning cut off abruptly on a rising note. I didn't know what to say — I was new at this, new and useless. Suddenly I was desperate, looking for anything, any stratagem, the magic words that would make it all right again. "The cat," I said. "What about the cat?"

Her voice was soft. "He'll be all right. Just feed him. Be nice to him." She was at the door, the purse slung over one shoulder. "Patience," she said, "that's all it takes. A little patience."

"Wait," I said. "Wait."

"I've got to go."

"Will I see you later?"

"No," she said. "No, I don't think so."

As soon as her pickup pulled out of the lot, I called my boss. He answered on the first ring, raising his voice to be heard over the ambient noise. I could hear the tile saw going in the background, the irregular banging of a hammer, the radio tuned to some jittery right-wing propagandist. "I want to come in," I said.

"Who is this?"

"Junior."

"Monday, Monday at the earliest."

I told him I was going crazy cooped up in my apartment, but he didn't seem to hear me. "What is it?" he said. "Money? Because I'll advance you on next week if you really need it, though it'll mean a trip to the bank I wasn't planning on. Which is a pain in the ass. But I'll do it. Just say the word."

"No, it's not the money, it's just —"

He cut me off. "Don't you ever listen to anything I say? Didn't I tell you to go out and get yourself laid? That's what you're supposed to be doing at your age. It's what I'd be doing."

"Can't I just, I don't know, help out?"

"Monday," he said.

I was angry suddenly and I slammed the phone down. My eyes went to the hole cut in the bedroom door and then to the breakfast plates, egg yolk congealing there in bright yellow stripes, the muffin, Daria's muffin, untouched but for a single neat bite cut out of the round. It was Friday. I hated my life. How could I have been so stupid?

There was no sound from the bedroom, and as I laced my sneakers I fought down the urge to go to the peephole and see what the cat had accomplished in the night — I just didn't want to think about it. Whether it had vanished like a bad dream or chewed through the wall and devoured the neighbor's yapping little dogs or broken loose and smuggled itself onto a boat back to Africa, it was all the same to me. The only thing I did know was that there was no way I was going to attempt to feed that thing on my own, not without Daria there. It could starve, for all I cared, starve and rot.

Eventually, I fished a jean jacket out of a pile of clothes on the floor and went down to the beach. The day was overcast and a cold wind out of the east scoured the sand. I must have walked for hours and then, for lack of anything better to do, I went to a movie, after which I had a sandwich at a new place downtown where college students were rumored to hang out. There were no students there as far as I could see, just old men who looked exactly like the regulars at Daggett's, except that they had their square-shouldered old wives with them and their squalling unhappy children. By 4:00 I'd hit my first bar, and by 6:00 I was drunk.

I tried to stay away from Daggett's — *Give her a day or two,* I told myself. *Don't nag, don't be a burden* — but at quarter of 9:00 I found myself at the bar, ordering a Jack-and-Coke from Chris. Chris gave me a look, and everything had changed since yesterday. "You sure?" he said.

I asked him what he meant.

"You look like you've had enough, buddy."

I craned my neck to look for Daria, but all I saw were the regulars, hunched over their drinks. "Just pour," I said.

The music was there like a persistent annoyance, dead music, ancient, appreciated by no one, not even the regulars. It droned on. Chris set down my drink and I lifted it to my lips. "Where's Daria?" I asked.

"She got off early. Said she was tired. Slow night, you know?"

I felt a stab of disappointment, jealousy, hate. "You have a number for her?"

Chris gave me a wary look, as if he knew something I didn't. "You mean she didn't give you her number?"

"No," I said. "We never — well, she was at my house . . ."

"We can't give out personal information."

"To me? I said she was at my house. Last night. I need to talk to her, and it's urgent — about the cat. She's really into the cat, you know?"

"Sorry."

I threw it back at him. "You're sorry? Well, fuck you — I'm sorry, too."

"You know what, buddy —"

"Junior, the name's Junior."

He leaned into the bar, both arms propped before him, and in a very soft voice he said, "I think you'd better leave now."

It had begun to rain again, a soft patter in the leaves that grew steadier and harder as I walked home. Cars went by on the boulevard with the sound of paper tearing, and they dragged whole worlds behind them. The streetlights were dim. There was nobody out. When I came up the hill to my apartment, I saw the Mustang standing there under the carport, and though I'd always been averse to drinking and driving — a lesson I'd learned from my father's hapless example — I got behind the wheel and drove up to the job site with a crystalline clarity that would have scared me in any other state of mind. There was an aluminum ladder there, and I focused on that — the picture of it lying against the building — until I arrived and hauled it out of the mud and tied it to the roof of the car, without a thought for the paint job or anything else.

When I got back, I fumbled in the rain with my overzealous knots until I got the ladder free and then I hauled it around back of the apartment building. I was drunk, yes, but cautious, too — if anyone had seen me, in the dark, propping a ladder against the wall of an apartment building, even my own apartment building, things could have got difficult in a hurry. I couldn't very well claim to be painting, could I? Not at night. Not in the rain. Luckily, though, no one was around. I made my way up the ladder, and when I got to the level of the bedroom the odor hit me, a rank fecal wind sifting out of the dark slit of the window. The cat. The cat was in there, watching me. I was sure of it. I must have waited in the rain for fifteen minutes or more before I got up the nerve to fling the window open, and then I ducked my head and crouched reflexively against the wall. Nothing happened. After a moment, I made my way down the ladder.

I didn't want to go into the apartment, didn't want to think about it, didn't know if a cat that size could climb down the rungs of a ladder or leap twenty feet into the air or unfurl its hidden wings and fly. I stood and watched the dense black hole of the window for a long while and then I went back to the car and sat listening to the radio in the dark until I fell asleep.

In the morning — there were no heraldic rays of sunshine, nothing like that, just more rain — I let myself into the apartment and crept across the room as stealthily as if I'd come to burgle it. When I reached the bedroom door, I put my eye to the peephole and saw a mound of carpet propped up against an empty cage — a den, a makeshift den — and only then did I begin to feel something for the cat, for its bewilderment, its fear and distrust of an alien environment: this was no rocky kopje, this was my bedroom on the second floor of a run-down apartment building in a seaside town a whole continent and a fathomless ocean away from its home. Nothing moved inside. Surely it must have gone by now, one great leap and then the bounding limbs, grass beneath its feet, solid earth. It was gone. Sure it was. I steeled myself, pulled open the door, and slipped inside. And then — and I don't know why — I pulled the door shut behind me.

CATHERINE BRADY

Written in Stone

FROM ZYZZYVA

HASSAN COMES TO ME on Tuesday nights. He is having more difficulty than I am with our separation. I don't know how other people manage to cancel each other out of their lives. I can't. He can't.
Hassan can't do anything by half measures; he won't be reassured
that we remain friends unless I see him every week.

He lets himself in — he still has a key — while I am at the gym,
and by the time I get home, I can smell lamb in the oven, and the
sauce, *khoresht*, bubbling away on the stove, seeping the scent of cinnamon and garlic and stewed cherries. The Persian rice steams
over a low flame, a dishcloth laid under the lid of the pot, part of
the process of fussing over it that doesn't seem to account for the
spectacular results, flaky rice that forms a crunchy golden crust on
the bottom.

We kiss. I take off my jacket and go to the sink to wash lettuce for
salad. He says I don't have to help, I look tired, but I insist that I'm
fine. Hassan watches me anxiously. He expects to read in my body
some distressing proof of injury — circles under the eyes, stooped
shoulders, the abrupt collapse of muscles that will make me literally an old woman, a thrown-away woman. I'm forty-six, and I go to
the gym five days a week, and I've told him he can forget it, I'm not
going to make it that easy for him.

I tell him about the new orthopedic surgeon at the hospital; the
guy seems O.K., only he plays country-and-western music during
surgery. Hassan is quick to see this as domineering. Surgeons are as
cocky as fighter pilots, but they bear the entire burden of risk; no

one has yet sued me for handing a surgeon the wrong piece of gauze. I shrug. "Maybe he just has bad taste in music."

When we talk about Hassan's job, we're talking about the problems of the entire world. Somehow, with a degree in structural engineering, Hassan ended up working for a nonprofit here in San Francisco that arranges conferences between government officials and scientists and businesspeople from all over the globe. He pursues the world's grievances without any of the pessimism his country's history should have instilled in him. And he happens to be awfully good at parties and getting people interested in one another. He has three hundred names in his e-mail address book. He loves every person on that list, from his colleagues to the security guy in his building to the earnest minor bureaucrats from Uruguay and Indonesia.

Hassan complains to me about his job, which he never used to do. Sometimes I wonder if he means to console me — he may have left me for another, but he is not perfectly happy — but then he'd started complaining before he left.

"Now that we're respectable, everyone becomes cautious," Hassan says. "I am not supposed to enjoy myself so much at the cocktail parties and banquets. What does this mean? What's too much enjoyment?"

He met this woman when she performed at some benefit. I don't know if he decided to love her in particular or if, out of innocence and boldness, she forced his hand by taking literally his long-standing and general offer to the world.

My husband — my soon-to-be ex-husband? — is a warm and affectionate man, a nostalgic creature. When we went back to Iran, we lived under one roof with his entire family. The man badgered his mother to teach him to make all the foods he'd missed when he was at college in the United States. He and I were happy — very happy — for twenty years. He brought me tulips on every anniversary. I always knew where he had left his reading glasses. He used to save the notes I left under his coffee cup every morning when I left for work, stuff the scraps of paper in the top drawer of his dresser, where they accumulated until he moved out. Hassan is in a predicament, all right.

Hassan turns the rice out of the pot, shapes it into a perfect cone, and makes an impression into which he ladles the lamb and the *khoresht*. We eat by candlelight — something we had forgotten to do anymore when we lived together — and Hassan works steadily at a bottle of red wine.

He slips toward her; he can't help it. He's tired, he says, because she didn't sleep last night. She works late, is used to staying up late. When he first told me about her, so proud to announce she was a singer, I almost burst out laughing. The wife — suited up every day in surgical scrubs, paper cap hiding my frosted hair, plastic booties over my orthopedic shoes, so desexed you can tell my gender only by the size of my bones. The lover — a sultry chanteuse.

Hassan tells me he has discovered that Monica is an insomniac. "She stays up, then she feels blue, and then she can't stand it, so she brings a bottle of brandy back to bed and wakes me up to talk."

It could be too that this is her way of testing him. She must have plenty of younger men available to her. "Maybe she has to find out if you can keep up."

"Do you know," Hassan says, "how old and slow she makes me feel? If it's any comfort."

This is his way of testing *me*, the limits of my tolerance. "I don't feel that way," I say. "It's not like that for me at all."

"I won't talk about her if it bothers you."

Why does everyone expect me to be bitter? I've been avoiding my girlfriends, who want to take me out on Saturdays, who seem to think it's going to save my life to sit in a bar with them and consider the forms of torture appropriate to husbands who take up with younger women.

"No," I say. "I'm interested."

He wonders how she manages for so long on so little sleep. She has to get up and go to work in the mornings, too, boring temp jobs to pay the rent, at least until she can earn steady money as a singer, graduate from wedding gigs to a local opera company. Then he tells me what else he's just discovered about her.

"She has some kind of dyslexia when it comes to directions," he says. "The other night I let her drive home from a party, and I fell asleep in the car. She had to wake me up in order to find the way to her own house. She can't tell left from right. She finds her way by memorizing landmarks, only she has a harder time at night, and if she strays from her route, she has no idea where she is."

Hassan embroiders the moment until the dyslexia becomes some touching spiritual dislocation, a signifying vulnerability.

He didn't fall asleep. He passed out. I worry about him without me. I never drink as much as he does and can always get him home.

Hassan's stories of his courtship — the trouble he takes to elaborate — remind me of the traditional Persian dances he and his friends used to perform when we were in college. All of the Persians were studying engineering or computer science or medicine, things that would be useful to the shah's technological society. They shared apartments, they kissed one another, they cooked together. They paired off to dance to tapes they'd brought with them from Iran. One of them would take the role of the woman and make everyone laugh at the exaggerated sinuousness of his rolling hips and unfurling arms, his pursed lips. Their tradition codified this lasciviousness, cleared a space for it, a secret out in the open.

Hassan and I went back to Iran in 1977, after we graduated from college. Hassan's mother had been widowed the year before, and he felt a duty to return to his family, to repay his country for his education. We'd just gotten married. There's the story of what happened to us in those years in Iran — Hassan tells it better than I could — and then there are those vivid memories that continue to live in me like sensation, not recollected but reborn whenever they are aroused. I can still return to the garden of his mother's house, an inner courtyard walled in by overgrown pink climbing roses, their branches so thick and luxuriant that anyone who dared their thorns could be hidden entirely beneath their leaves. A path of stones wound through salvia and fanning clusters of white lilies. In a shady corner a flowering vine shaped itself in fluid arabesques in its drive for light. The English word *paradise* comes from the Persian word for an enclosed garden, *pairi-da–za*.

On Ashura, the tenth day of Muharram, I watched from the window as men marched past the house, their wailing echoing off the walls of the buildings that faced the narrow street. They lashed themselves with chains and belts, scoring the skin of their bare backs. Some of them flinched when they drew blood; others did not waver in their intoxicated chanting. Their faces were not hungry but hard with satisfaction. Hassan was in such a hurry to explain. These men were commemorating the death of Hossein, their long-ago martyr, and this was their atonement, their allotment of his sacrifice. Hassan shrugged. They had so little else. This was just the sort of thing that the West sensationalized; I mustn't make that mistake. I did see what was before my eyes: how real God is to the poor.

The shah's regime was already crumbling, with all the randomly intensified dangers of collapse. The mullahs had grown intransigent; Hassan's sister had taken to wearing a head scarf so she wouldn't be harassed in the street; her brothers debated how this concession might be understood politically; and their mother remembered how the shah's father had forced women to give up the chador. The world might begin to move at a raging pace, with the moan and roar of those men in the street, and still one lives a slower life in private, stubborn and tentative and intricate in its flourishing. I'd sneak out to that garden to enjoy the relief of being alone, to savor all that I was learning about my husband's family — Hassan and his two brothers, cracking pistachio nuts between their fingers, arguing with the same vivid energy of the boys I'd known in the United States; his mother snipping roses and dropping them in a bucket, smiling and nodding to supplement the Farsi words I did not understand.

I cook this time, so it's simple: steak, baked potatoes, peas. I stand all day at work. I sterilize slender implements and lay them out in exacting order on a paper-sheeted tray. In an orthopedic surgical unit, every gesture, like the implements, is scaled to the miniature — the surgeon slices a precisely calibrated seam through tissue, scrapes away at bone in increments that will minimize nerve damage, or studies a video screen that projects images captured by a camera lens so small it can be threaded into the body. I don't want to come home to core or peel or dice or fillet.

Hassan is in trouble from another quarter. He has wooed a little too zealously the representative of a foundation that might fund his organization.

He takes both my hands in his to plead his case. "We went out for drinks. We're relaxing, I think. And the next day she calls my boss and says she's uncomfortable dealing with me. I've sexualized the interaction."

Another time, his need to befriend a fundraiser might yield a grant, or he might take a guest from India to a drag show and delight him instead of shock him. More than once he's gotten conference delegates drunk in order to soften their attitudes toward one another. If it doesn't work out, he is undaunted. He'd roll the dice again if he had to, and let someone else hold his breath. No one wrote to tell him when his mother got sick, for fear he'd rush back to Iran. His brother waited to tell Hassan until it was too late for him to come to the funeral. Maybe it was safe for Hassan to return, maybe he could have visited years ago, and only superstition made us believe that history was written in stone.

Hassan frowns. "I think I touched her elbow. A couple of times."

And probably he pressed too close, the way he must lean across the table now in order to talk, really talk, to me. Persians routinely invade what an American would consider inviolate personal space. Hassan is so Americanized now, and yet these essential habits persist.

"Would it do any good to call her and apologize?" I say.

"I am forbidden to contact her. Forbidden."

"Do they understand at work that she just misread you?"

"They say, 'Don't drink. Don't drink on the job.'"

He did stop drinking for a few months last year, after he learned that his mother had died. He didn't decide to quit; he just lost interest for a while, the way he lost interest in everything else. Maybe they should have written him that his mother was ill. Hassan hadn't seen her for nearly twenty years, not since we left Iran.

Hassan strokes my hands. "With this woman — I thought we were sympathetic, that's all. Remember the good old days, when we were so delighted by the freedom to be sexual? Now we must hide it. We must behave like automatons in our professional lives."

I smile. "Nobody has any fun anymore."

"Exactly," Hassan says. He smiles back at me. "Are you? Having any fun?"

"What?"

"Dating someone."

"Don't feel up to it yet."

"What about that new doctor? You have such expressive eyes. Why don't you give him a come-hither look the next time you're handing him a scalpel or changing a CD for him? What if he wants you already? 'Nurse, oh, nurse, I have an itch. Can you scratch it for me?'"

"What happened? Did you and your girl have a fight?"

"She's not a girl. We're going to drive up to Tahoe this weekend and go skiing. She's going to teach me."

"I'll be seeing you in the ortho unit on Monday."

"Don't be silly. I'm staying on the bunny hill. I'm planning to fall down a lot. It must be very safe to fall down in the snow. She will have to come and help me up every time. She'll fall in love with me a thousand times more."

A thousand times he'd flirted, a thousand times been taken too seriously, and then he brought these interesting people home to introduce them to me. He didn't bring her home, though he kept talking about her. I made him leave. I didn't want to beg. I still remember the hurt, stunned look on his face when I told him to go.

"It's true that we fight," Hassan says. "But the fights — they're very good, actually. Big scenes."

Ever since we lived in Iran, I've been afraid for Hassan, the way you are afraid ever after for a child who's long since recovered from some serious illness. I never want to be as afraid again as I was during those two years. He'd found work right away, consulting with construction crews who were building the roads and bridges and office towers of the shah's future, and he was popular with the crews. He told jokes; he brought pastries to the site; he had some story about a goat crossing a bridge that was meant to illustrate the principles of weight distribution. He shrugged when bribes had to be paid. And then he was taken in for questioning. He'd told a joke that everyone was telling: the shah makes a phone call to hell, and when he asks the operator for the charges, he is told there aren't any, it's a local call. Hassan was picked up by the secret police at a jobsite, and one of the foremen risked his own neck by sending a worker to the house to tell us.

We were not sure where Hassan had been taken. His oldest brother made a few hopeless phone calls, and then we waited. We sat in the living room on chairs covered with crocheted doilies. Later that afternoon, Hassan walked in the door with his jacket over his arm, his shirt soaked through with sweat. He had to work a little this time at being himself. "Nothing to worry about," he said. He had only been questioned for a few hours; the SAVAK men had let him off easy. His mother cried, and he promised her he would be careful. He'd tell a different joke the next time.

I was afraid whenever he left the house after that. I never ran into trouble on the street; I dyed my hair brown and wore a scarf like Hassan's sister, gave shots at the clinic where I'd found useful work, and stopped trying to make conversation with the patients. But Hassan could not choose to be careful. Some urge in him that he couldn't repress would prompt him to make up a story about materials disappearing daily from the jobsite, or burst out singing some American rock song, or flare up when his instructions for placing rebar hadn't been followed to the letter.

Any of these things could have sealed his fate, and that didn't change when the revolution came, relatively bloodless but not peaceful. Hassan greeted the revolution with anticipation — from such ardor anything might flow. He could no longer find work as an engineer, but he could teach math to high school students. Only he could not help sympathizing with faculty who were denounced by their students. He would not relinquish the necktie he so hated, because someone wished to make him. He would not give up visiting friends in the evening, even though the guards at the checkpoints on the road beat anyone they suspected of drinking. He chewed parsley to disguise the smell of liquor on his breath.

The frenzy would die down soon, Hassan said. Ayatollah Khomeini loved the Sufi poet Rumi, had written poems himself as a younger man. When the *komitehs* began to appear and issue their own laws over their neighborhood fiefdoms, because the revolution had succeeded so far in advance of its ability to govern, Hassan was the one who stood in line to get permission to buy food, fluid at the task of bartering, teasing, and cajoling the armed young men who wanted not bribes but a tithe for the mullahs. He'd joke, to them, that the cost of living hadn't changed a bit.

Hassan's sister left the country, smuggling out jewelry as insurance not just for herself but for the rest of the family. His family wanted Hassan to go next. But Persians prefer not to confront one another. They chose intermediaries — an aunt, an uncle — to hint at this. Without result. I felt as if my nerves had been soaked in some flammable solution, priming me forever for dread. I burst into tears one day when Hassan came home from the market on time, as promised. Hassan applied for an exit visa a week later, but he was refused. Finally, we left illegally, crossing the border into Turkey on foot, like refugees. From there we returned to America, a place where his impulsiveness would not cost him his life.

Hassan cancels on the next Tuesday, but comes the following week. I arrive after he does. I don't want to sit and wait for him. He serves me *dolmeh,* rice flecked with the golden bits of crust and sprinkled with saffron threads, and duck baked with pomegranates and basted with their juice. He has brought a bottle of vodka this time, instead of a bottle of wine, and he fills two tumblers full. If I didn't know better, I'd accuse Hassan of courting me.

"Why are we getting drunk?" I ask.

"You know I like vodka," he says. "And I have to celebrate. I believe I've been demoted again."

"Why?"

"They're claiming we've raised enough money to hire someone whose job it is to raise money, so I can concentrate on event planning. They put it very nicely." He sighs. "I must have said something to that woman that I can't remember."

"I had no idea they were so puritan."

"It's inevitable," Hassan says. "It's been coming for a long time."

"Don't be too unhappy."

He smiles at me. "They're taking away from me the part of my job that I hate the most. Really, I should celebrate. Life is good. We have a plan afoot to hold regional conferences, and this would be a great thing. Give little countries a chance to solve their problems for themselves. Oh! And I didn't break any bones when we went skiing."

"Why do you have to tempt fate?"

"It was an adventure. And did I tell you I am going to be on the stage? Monica and I are going to be extras in the opera. She gets to sing a few lines. I get to stand at the back and hold a spear."

He's still slender, and he has the kind of dark, striking looks that come across well on stage. There's a reason so many women have misread his intentions.

"Will you come to see me?" Hassan asks.

"No. I'd like to see you, but I'll pass on seeing her."

He looks stricken.

"I just don't want to have to set eyes on her and discover she's a luscious young thing. I'd rather think of her as nothing special. Kind of dumpy."

"Will you feel better if I tell you things are not perfect with us?"

"She's not dumpy, is she?"

"Because she's mad at me. I'm in the doghouse. I banged up the car on the way home from a planning meeting last week. I hit a pole when I was backing out of a parking spot, and that doesn't even really count. But now she's thinking I'm drinking too much, that's the reason. I ask her if she wants to sign on as a consultant to my boss, she throws things. My God, she throws my shoes out the window, so I'll have to go downstairs to get them and she can lock me out. It's terrible."

"That's why you brought the vodka."

"If it's good vodka," he says, "no one can smell it on your breath."

"Isn't this a case of the pot calling the kettle black? Didn't you tell me she drags a bottle of brandy to bed and wakes you up in the middle of the night?"

"But you see, this is the rub. She threw out the last of her very good brandy. She wants to prove to me that this is important to her. She will do anything for me. She will quit drinking with me."

"Now that I didn't expect," I say. "I thought she was supposed to be so arty."

"I know. But no. She is strict. So, all right, I say to myself, this would be a sacrifice. But then I want to know, what could be on the other side of that? What would it be like? Do you think I should quit? Maybe I should try it."

Hassan pours himself another tumbler of vodka. "So. We toast. Here's to our friends and well-wishers. Here's to my last glass of vodka."

We clink glasses.

"Also," he says, "she turns out to be jealous. She wants to know why I have to come and have dinner with you."

What story of me does he tell her, of all that binds us, without intending this consequence?

"Tell her I'm being a harridan about money," I say. "That way she won't worry."

If I didn't see him every week, I wouldn't know if he had dinged a post or found a new crusade at work or fallen asleep at the wheel and awakened just in time.

Our first years back in the United States, we worried all the time about Hassan's family in Iran. His middle brother got out, but Hassan's mother refused to leave, and so his oldest brother stayed with her. There was the hostage crisis, the gas shortage, the embargo. We had to contrive ways to get money to Hassan's family, all illegal. Hassan's sister came out to us from New York, where she'd first gone; she'd married and had a little boy and gotten divorced in short order, another worry. Hassan had difficulty finding work as an engineer — we persuaded ourselves it was the recession — and he didn't like the work when he got it. Someone threw a cup of coffee at him one morning when he was in a long line at the gas station. He wouldn't have told me except that he ruined his sport coat trying to wash out the stain himself. "Well," he said, "he called me a dirty Arab, and I decided it wasn't a good time to inform him that I was Iranian, and Iranians are not Arabs."

None of this could keep us from being happy. We lived carefully, so Hassan could send money home, but we always had enough for little trips. We went away at least once a month, even if it was only to a friend's cabin in Inverness. We enjoyed having our nephew in the house, making forts out of sofa cushions and filling the house with balloons for his birthday, and it was only a favor, not a duty, to give up a concert or a party when his mother needed us to watch him. I never agonized about the value of my work the way Hassan did; I was already doing enough living after hours. We had huge, raucous parties. We invited Hassan's fellow exiles, people he'd met at some futile political committee or on a construction site, a couple of nurses, teachers, his sister's friends from graduate school. If people weren't dancing, they were arguing fiercely, and Hassan would be in the middle of them, usually standing, wavering on his feet. He would tease and cajole and browbeat his friends in his desire for agreement. They must not complain so bitterly about Reagan; his election was necessary to the survival of the left in America, just as the frenzy in Iran was every day making possible the triumph of democracy and reason. I never argued; I plied people with food and drink and smiled a lot. I was a bleached blonde then, with a collection of beaded and silky dresses I wore for these parties, and I enjoyed the dismay and suspicion of some of Hassan's friends, their assumption that the marriage must be about sex. I wanted them to think that.

Once, for a Fourth of July party, Hassan smuggled in some fireworks from Oregon, and he set them off in the backyard of our rented house, surrounded by an audience, of course. One of the Roman candles misfired and shot into the pine tree that shaded the yard. The tree ignited like a torch, its trunk becoming a slender column of flame. Someone called the fire department; I hid what was left of the fireworks; and Hassan got the hose and doused the fire. We should have been arrested, but Hassan convinced the firefighters that a spark from the barbecue had ignited the tree. Hours later, after everyone had gone home, I was still nervous that a spark might reignite in that dry Monterey pine. So Hassan and I kept vigil in the yard, wrapped in blankets, looking up through the blackened branches at the stars. In his arms, I fell asleep to the sound of the pinecones in the tree snapping and crackling, releasing the residual heat and energy of the fire.

Hassan cancels on me two Tuesdays in a row. When he calls the next Tuesday afternoon, to cancel again, I tell him I don't want to hear another made-up excuse. He doesn't have to torture me; he can just say that he won't be coming anymore.

"No, no, no," he says, "that's not it." He is silent for a moment. "I stopped drinking. Pretty much. I am supposed to go to the meeting on Tuesday night."

"That's where you've been?"

"No, no. Tonight is the first time. This is a condition — a big condition — she sets for me. I don't know about this. I'm not very good at organized activities."

"Where is this meeting? I could meet you when it's over, and we could go for pizza."

"Would you?" he says. "Would you come in with me, just this first time?"

"Isn't that against the rules?"

"If we have to, we will come up with a story for you to confess too."

I consider staying home alone. I've been trying to break that habit. I've been dating a guy I met at work, a medical-instrument salesman who sat in on surgery to demonstrate a new arthroscope. We've gone out for two Saturdays in a row. We kissed on the second date, a chaste, closed-mouth kiss.

"Give me the address."

Hassan is waiting for me outside the church social room. When we go inside, the meeting is already under way, so we find seats in the back. People take turns going to the front of the room to announce that they are alcoholics. Some of them describe their most recent temptation; others tell stories of the way that alcohol has rotted their lives. A man does not know how to begin to beg his children for forgiveness. A woman describes how she followed the AA formula for resisting temptation: she stopped to register her emotion, unburdened herself of her anger, got a good night's sleep, made sure she ate a hearty breakfast. Hassan whispers in my ear, "She looks like she eats a hearty breakfast." After a few more minutes, he nudges me again. "Why does everybody discover that they drink for the exact same reasons? Why do you have to go to bed at exactly ten P.M. to stay sober?"

I giggle. He snickers. The urge to laugh becomes so strong that it's like a spasm. Soon both of us are shaking with the effort to stifle our laughter.

We beat a hasty retreat, shutting the door quietly behind us, and once we are outside, we yield to the irresistible impulse to hoot and howl.

We sit on the back bumper of my car while we decide where to go. Hassan says he would really like a drink. He holds out his hand, level and steady. "I am not shaking or anything. So I cannot be addicted. Which means I can have a drink."

He sits so that his shoulder touches mine. "This AA," he says. "This indoctrination. I can't stomach it."

I wonder if he is even conscious of his mania for contact. When I closed my eyes to kiss that salesman, I felt careful, vigilant, the way I am in surgery, where it's my job, not the surgeon's, to preserve the sterile field. "You don't have to come to these meetings," I say. "You don't even have to quit drinking."

"I just jumped off that cliff — sure, sure, I would promise this woman the moon, and they'll stop nagging me at work into the bargain. What did I do this for? I must be a crazy alcoholic. I act like one."

He takes my hand, and my fingers grip his instinctively.

I am so intently focused on his hand in mine that it hurts. As if I'm a new wife, not one accustomed to this habit.

Hassan kicks at the bumper of the car. "You know, she doesn't eat, all day. So many opera singers are fat; maybe it's an edge for her if she can starve herself. And I hate this in her."

My patience, my forbearance, has finally been rewarded. I am a new wife. I am again stealing off to the garden to indulge my delirium. Here are the roses, the salvia, the vine that cunningly, effort-lessly, routes its growth toward the light.

"I can't stop myself from trying to tempt her," Hassan says. "Eat, eat, eat! It's myself I'm trying to encourage. I'm not so greedy as I thought."

I did not worry when Hassan curled up into a silent mourning after his mother died. It was in his nature. No half measures. He reread all her letters, thin onionskin pages saved for years in a fat manila envelope. One night, I sat with him while he read. He said, "We should have had children." He never said it to me again. He didn't really mean it. He was grieving.

Hassan makes a sound that is not quite a laugh, not quite a moan. "Why have I done this to you? Behaving like an idiot! And what for?"

He lifts an arm, but something catches at the gesture, and he lets his hand drop heavily in his lap.

When I want him to flow like water over stone.

I watch his face for a moment. I begin the story for him. I tell him, "You fell in love."

He seems to gather himself. And then he's off. "It's terrible, this kind of love. Always butting heads. Always struggling."

I let him lean against me. Soon all those AA people will come out of their meeting and give us dirty looks. I've been afraid too long to register so small a threat. Only I didn't know enough to be frightened all those years ago, when those men were marching in the street, flogging their bodies, driving themselves forward.

SARAH SHUN-LIEN BYNUM

Accomplice

FROM THE GEORGIA REVIEW

IT WASN'T EVEN HALLOWEEN YET, but Ms. Hempel was already
thinking about her anecdotals. The word, with all its expectations
of intimacy and specificity, bothered her: a noun in the guise of an
adjective, an obfuscation of the fact that twice a year she had to produce eighty-two of these ineluctable *things*. Not reports, like those
written by other teachers at other schools, but anecdotals: loving
and detailed accounts of a student's progress, enlivened by descriptions of the child offering a piercing insight or aiding a struggling
classmate or challenging authority. It was a terrible responsibility:
to render, in a recognizable way, something as ineffable as another
human being, particularly a young one. On average she would
spend an hour writing about each child, and then waste up to another hour rereading what she had just written, in the hopes that
her words might suddenly reveal themselves as judicious. But too
often Ms. Hempel's anecdotals reminded her of those blurry portraits from photography's early days: Is that a hand I see? A bird?
The sitter has squirmed, readjusted her skirts, swatted at a fly: she is
no longer a child, but a smudge of light. This is how Ms. Hempel's
students appeared, captured in her anecdotals: bright and beautiful and indistinct.

The cubicle where she now sat, peeling an orange, would, in less
than two months, become a Faculty Work Station. Other faculty
members would sit in the work stations next to hers; they would
peer over and say, "Don't kill yourself. You're not writing a novel."
But now there was only Mr. Polidori, humming faintly and balancing equations.

The science and math teachers had it easy. During anecdotal season, Ms. Hempel would berate her younger, student self: she never should have turned away from the dark and gleaming surfaces of the lab. She had chosen instead the squishy embrace of the humanities, where nothing was quantifiable and absolute, and now she was paying for all those lovely, lazy years of sitting in circles and talking about novels. Mrs. Beasley, the head of the math department, had perfected an anecdotal formula: she entered the student's test scores, indicated whether his ability to divide fractions was "strong," "improving," or "a matter of concern," and then ended with either congratulations or exhortations, whichever seemed more appropriate. The formulaic would not do, however, for an English teacher. Ms. Hempel could not complain of a child's limited vocabulary or plodding sentences without putting on a literary fireworks display of her own. Because there was always that skepticism: students who didn't quite believe that she could do all the things that she required of them ("vary your sentence structure," "incorporate metaphors," "analyze, not summarize!"), as if she were a fleshy coach who relaxes on the bleachers while the team goes panting around the gym.

So the anecdotals must be beautiful. But she didn't want them to sound florid or excessive. She didn't want to sound insincere. (Oh, superlatives! Ms. Hempel's undoing.) She wanted to offer up tiny, exact, tender portraits of the children she taught, like those miniature paintings that Victorians would keep inside their lockets, along with a wisp of hair. And though she would fail to do so every time, she had not resigned herself to failure, could not experience that relief; every December and every May she would sit down to write, dogged by the fear that she would misrepresent a child, or that through some grievous grammatical error, some malapropism, some slip, she would expose herself and by her own hand reveal the hoax.

"If I started my anecdotals this afternoon, I would have to write only one and a half a day. That sounds manageable."

"Recycle," Mr. Polidori said, from the depths of his cubicle.

"I do recycle," Ms. Hempel said. "I make my kids recycle, too."

Mr. Polidori's face appeared above her. "Use your anecdotals from last year. Just insert new names — if you go under Edit, then slide your arrow down to Replace, it's quite straightforward."

"Oh," she said. "I can't do it. Because the material is all new this year. They're not reading *A Light in the Forest* anymore. Or *April Morning*. But it's a wonderful idea." This possibility had never occurred to her.

For the new seventh-grade curriculum, Ms. Hempel picked a book that had many swear words in it. She felt an attraction to swear words, just as she did to cable television, for both had been forbidden in her youth. Her father had considered swear words objectionable on the grounds of their very ordinariness. "Everyone uses the same old expletives over and over again," he said. "And *you* are not everyone." He grasped her cranium gently in one hand and squeezed, as if testing a cantaloupe at the farmers' market. "Utterly unordinary," he declared.

But to Ms. Hempel, swear words were beautiful precisely because they were ordinary, just as gum snapping and hair flipping were beautiful. She once longed to become a gum-snapping, foulmouthed person, a person who could describe every single thing as *fucking* and not even realize she was doing it.

In this, she never succeeded. When she read *This Boy's Life*, when she saw *shit* and even *fuck* on the page, she quietly thrilled. Then she ordered copies for the seventh grade.

"First impressions?" she asked, perched atop her desk, her legs swinging. "What do you think?"

The seventh-graders looked at one another uneasily. They had read the opening chapter for homework. A few stroked the books' covers, of which they had already declared their approval; it was sleek and muted. Grown-up. A cover that promised they were venturing into new territory: no more shiny titles, endorsements from the American Library Association, oil paintings of teenagers squinting uncertainly into the distance.

"Do you like it?" Ms. Hempel tried again. She smiled entreatingly; her shoes banged against her desk. Teaching, she now understood, was a form of extortion; you were forever trying to extract from your students something they didn't want to part with: their attention, their labor, their trust.

David D'Souza, ladies' man, came to her assistance. Even though he was a little chubby and overcurious about sex, he was a very popular boy in the seventh grade. He had gone out with a lot of girls.

He walked down the hallways with the rolling, lopsided gait of the rappers that he so fervently admired. In the classroom, his poise deserted him; he sputtered a lot, rarely delivering coherent sentences. He batted away his ideas just as they were escaping from his mouth.

But David was a gentleman, and ready to sacrifice his own dignity in order to rescue Ms. Hempel's. *Cooperative* and *responsive,* she thought. *Willing to take risks.*

"It's like . . . ," he began, and stopped. Ms. Hempel smiled at him, nodding furiously, as if pumping the gas pedal on a car that wouldn't start. "It's . . ." He grabbed his upper lip with his bottom teeth. He ground his palm into the desk. The other kids delicately averted their eyes; they concentrated on caressing the covers of their books. "It's . . . *different* from the other stuff I've read in school."

The class exhaled: yes, it was different. They spoke about it as if they didn't quite trust it, particularly the boys, as if there was something inherently suspicious about a book whose characters seemed real. Toby, for example. He wanted to be a good kid, but couldn't stop getting into trouble; he loved his mother a lot, but wasn't above manipulating her into buying things that he wanted — it was all uncannily familiar. They were also puzzled by the everyday nature of his struggles: there was no sign that soon Toby would be surviving on his own in the wilderness, or traveling into the future to save the planet from nuclear disaster.

"It doesn't really sound like a book," said Emily Borowitz, capricious child, aspiring trapeze artist, lover of Marc Chagall. Ms. Hempel would write, *gifted.*

"I normally don't like books," said Henry Woo, sad sack, hanger-on, misplacer of entire backpacks. Ms. Hempel would write, *has difficulty concentrating.*

"It's O.K. for us to be reading this?" said Simon Grosse, who needed to ask permission for everything. Ms. Hempel would write, *conscientious.*

On Parents Night, Ms. Hempel felt fluttery and damp. She knew, from past experience, that she would make a burlesque of herself, that her every sentence would end with an exclamation point, and her hands would fly about wildly and despairingly, like two bats trapped inside a bedroom. The previous year, a boy named Zachary Bouchet had reported, "My mother says that you smile too much."

In the faculty room, Mr. Polidori threw an arm around her and whispered, "Just pretend they're naked."

That was the last thing Ms. Hempel wanted to imagine.

Instead, she decided to picture her own parents sitting in front of her. She pictured her mother, who would make them late because she misplaced the car keys; and her father, who would station himself in the front row and ask embarrassing questions. Embarrassing not in their nature, but embarrassing simply because he had asked them. Her father liked to attract attention. "Ni hao ma!" he would greet the waiters at the Chinese restaurant. "Yee-haw!" he would whoop at the fourth-grade square dance recital. "Where's the defense?" he would wail from the sidelines of soccer games. "Brava! Brava!" he would sing out, the first to rise to his feet. Ms. Hempel, as a child, had received several standing ovations, all induced by her beaming, cheering, inexorable father.

Each of these parents, Ms. Hempel told herself, is as mortifying as mine were. A mother began: "This book they're reading — I was just wondering if anyone else was troubled by the language."

Ms. Hempel smiled bravely at the instigator. "I'm glad you brought that up," she said, and reminded herself: This woman can never find her car keys. This woman is always running late.

A classroom of parents, squeezed into the same chairs that their children occupied during the day, looked at Ms. Hempel.

She couldn't say, Your kids are O.K. with me. I promise.

Instead she said, "When I chose this book, I was thinking of *The Catcher in the Rye.* Because every time I teach *Catcher* to the eighth grade, I feel like I'm witnessing the most astonishing thing. It's like they've stuck their finger in a socket and all their hair is standing on end. They're completely *electrified.* What they're responding to, I think, is the immediacy and authenticity of the narrator's voice. And part of what makes Holden sound authentic to them is the language he uses. This book's impact on them is just — *immeasurable.* Even on the ones who don't like to read, who don't like English. It suddenly opens up to them all of literature's possibilities. Its power to speak to their experiences."

Ms. Hempel paused, surprised. She had recovered.

"I thought to myself, shouldn't the seventh grade get the chance to feel that? That shock of recognition?"

And she meant it, in a way, now that she had to say it.

What happened then? Ms. Hempel doubted it had anything to do with her speech. Perhaps an insurgency had been building quietly against the concerned mother, who probably hijacked PTA meetings, or else was always suggesting another bake sale. Maybe they heard in her complaint an echo of their own parents, or they believed on principle that words could never be dirty. Maybe sitting in the plastic desk chairs reminded them of what school felt like.

One after another, the parents began describing their children: She talks about it at dinner. He takes it with him into the bathroom. You don't understand — the last thing that she enjoyed reading was the PlayStation manual.

They spoke in wonder.

At night, I hear him chuckling in his bedroom. He says that he wants me to read it, that he'll loan me his copy when he's done. When I offered to rent the movie for her, she said that she didn't want to ruin the book.

"I knew it!" a father announced. "It was just a question of finding the right book."

And the parents nodded again, as if they had always known it, too.

"Well done!" Another father, sitting in the back row, began to clap. He smiled at Ms. Hempel. Three more giddy parents joined in the applause.

Ms. Hempel, standing at the front of the classroom, wanted to bow. She wanted to throw a kiss. She wanted to say thank you. Thank you.

And then it occurred to her: perhaps what had so humiliated her about her father had made someone else — a square dancer, a waiter, the director of the seventh-grade production of *The Pirates of Penzance* — feel wonderful.

The next morning, in homeroom, Ms. Hempel helped Cilia Matsui free herself from her crippling backpack. "Your dad," she noted, "has this very benevolent presence."

"Benevolent?" Cilia Matsui asked.

Ms. Hempel always used big words when she spoke; they also appeared frequently in her anecdotals, words like *acuity* and *perspicacious*. It was all part of her ambitious schemes for vocabulary expansion. Most kids took interest in new words only if they felt they had something personal at stake. "You're utterly depraved, Patrick," she would say. "No, I won't. Look it up. There are about six dictionaries sitting in the library."

So Adelaide's comments were astute. Gloria had an agile mind. Rasheed's spelling was irreproachable. Even those who weren't academically inclined deserved a dazzling adjective. David D'Souza, for instance, was chivalrous. These words, Ms. Hempel knew, were now permanently embedded. Even after the last layer of verbal detritus had settled, they would still be visible, winking brightly: yes, I *was* an iconoclastic thinker.

Because one never forgets a compliment. "You looked positively beatific during the exam," Miss Finnegan, her tenth-grade English teacher, had told her. "Staring out the window, a secret little smile on your face. I was worried, to tell the truth. But then you turned in the best of the bunch."

Thus, *beatific* — blissful, saintly, serenely happy — was forever and irrevocably hers. She shared the new word with her father; she showed him the grade she had received. Aha, he said, with great vindication. Aha!

Uncomplimentary words, however, seemed to overshadow the complimentary ones. That wasn't it, exactly. But whereas an ancient compliment would suddenly, unexpectedly, descend upon her, spinning down from the sky like a solitary cherry blossom, words of criticism were familiar and unmovable fixtures in the landscape: fire hydrants, chained trash cans, bulky public sculptures. They were useful, though, as landmarks. Remember? she used to say to her father: Mr. Ziegler. White hair. He made us memorize Milton. And when that failed, she would say: Don't you remember him? He was the one who called me lackadaisical.

Her mother's memory was terrible, but her father could always be counted on. In his neat, reliable way, he sorted and shelved all the slights she had endured. Oh yes, he'd say. *Mr. Ziegler.* Looking back on those conversations, she wondered if perhaps it was unfair to make him revisit the unhappy scene of her high school career. Remembering old criticisms is fun only once they have been proven laughably incorrect. Fractions! the famous mathematician hoots: Mrs. Beasley said I was hopeless at fractions!

When her father died, a year ago that spring, Ms. Hempel had spoken at his memorial service, along with her brother and sister. Calvin talked about a day they went hiking together in Maine, and Maggie, before she started crying, remembered how he used to read aloud to her, every night before she went to bed. Ms. Hempel's story sounded unsentimental by comparison. She described her father picking her up from play practice, when she was maybe fourteen or fifteen. It was winter, and too cold to wait for the bus. Before parking the car in the garage, he would deposit her at the back door, so that she wouldn't have to walk through the slush. As she balanced her way up the path, he would flick his headlights on and off. The beams cast shadows across the lawn, making everything seem bigger than it really was: the randy cat, her mother's beloved gazebo, the fur sprouting from the hood of her parka. Right before she reached the door, she would turn around and wave at him. She couldn't see him, because the headlights were too bright, but she could hear him. Click, click. Click, click. Only after she stepped inside would he steer the car back out of the driveway.

When Ms. Hempel finished speaking, she looked out at her family. They looked back at her expectantly, waiting to hear the end of the story. The last time she stood on this pulpit, many years before, she had received the same anxious look. She was the narrator for the Christmas pageant, and though she had spoken her part clearly and with dramatic flourish, she forgot to say her final line: "So the three wise men followed the star of Bethlehem." A long pause followed, and then the three wise men stumbled out of the sacristy, as if a great force had propelled them.

For the rest of the pageant, she had to stay inside the pulpit, from where she was supposed to look down on the manger with a mild and interested expression; instead, she watched the other children wolfishly, willing someone else to make a mistake more terrible than her own. No one did. It could have happened to anyone, her mother would tell her, but she knew differently: it could have happened only to her. During her narration, she had fastened her eyes on the choir loft, but as she neared the end, in anticipation of the delicious relief that she would soon feel, she allowed her gaze to slip down onto the congregation below. There she saw her father, leaning forward very slightly, and holding onto the pew in front of him. He was smiling at her. Hugely. She lost her bearings entirely.

Now, standing in the same pulpit, she looked out at her family as they waited hopefully for a final paragraph. She looked at them in defiance: That's all! He clicked the headlights on and off. The End. And she wished something that she used to never wish: that her father was there, on the edge of his pew. He would have liked the story; it would have made sense to him.

"Is being benevolent a good thing or a bad thing?" Cilia Matsui asked.

"A good thing!" said Ms. Hempel. "Benevolent means generous and kind."

"Oh yes," Cilia said. "That sounds like my dad."

Dwight, Toby's stepfather, was the character in the book who her kids despised most. They shuddered at the humiliations that he made Toby endure: shucking whole boxes full of foul-smelling horse chestnuts, attending Boy Scouts in a secondhand uniform, playing basketball in street shoes because he wouldn't fork out the money for sneakers. They hated him for coming between Toby and his mother. They hated him for being petty and insecure and cruel. "Dwight . . . ," they would mutter helplessly. "I want to kill the guy."

As Toby's situation worsened, they would turn over their books and study the author's photograph: his handsome, bushy mustache, his gentle eyes. "He teaches at Syracuse," they would point out. "He lives with his family in upstate New York."

They loved these facts, because reading about the abusive stepdad, the failures at school, the yearnings to escape, to be someone else — it made them feel terrible. "He had such a tough life," they repeated, shaking their heads. "A really tough life."

But, according to the back of the book, Toby prevailed. The kids saw, in the felicitous pairing of picture and blurb, a happy ending to his story: he became a writer! He didn't turn into a drunk or a bum. The back cover promised that it was possible to weather unhappy childhoods, that it was possible to do lots of bad things and have lots of bad things done to you — and the damage would not be irreparable. Often, a particularly somber discussion of Toby's struggles would conclude with this comforting thought: And now he's a famous and successful writer. *Tobias Wolff.*

Fame and success: did that count as revenge? The seventh grade had a lively sense of justice. They wanted to see Dwight pay for all that he had done to Toby and his mother, for all the pain he had inflicted. They longed for a climactic, preferably violent, showdown between the boy and the stepfather. Barring that, they wanted Dwight to suffer, in some specific and prolonged way. The fact that he had to live with the meagerness of his own soul — this was not considered punishment enough.

"He's probably read the book, right?" Will Bean asked.

"And he knows that Toby's a famous writer?"

They relished this idea: Dwight as an unrepentant old man, hobbling down to the liquor mart, pausing by the brilliant window of a bookstore. And there's Toby. Mustached, mischievous Toby, the same photograph from the back cover, only much larger. A careful pyramid of his books is pointing toward the sky. NUMBER ONE BESTSELLER, the sign reads. Through the plate glass, the old man can hear the faint slamming of the cash register. He can see the customers taking their place in line. And he can make out, even though his eyes are old and rheumy, the title of the book that they hold in their hands.

"If he's read it, he knows that millions of people now hate him, right?"

Which would mean, of course, banishment from the Elks Club. Divorce papers from his latest wife. Bushels of hate mail thumping against his screen door. Furtive trips to the convenience store, his mechanic's jacket pulled up over his head.

"Well," said Ms. Hempel. "I think he's dead already."

A howl filled the classroom.

"Usually writers don't publish this kind of book until the main characters have all passed away. So people's feelings don't get hurt."

Dwight, cold in the ground before the book even reached the stores. It was the greatest unfairness of all.

"And Rosemary? She's dead? She didn't get to see how good a writer her son is? She didn't get to see how well he turned out?" This, too, struck them as terribly unjust.

"No, no," Ms. Hempel said. "Rosemary is still alive. I think. Look in the front pages of your book — he thanks her, he says that she corrected him on certain facts, on the chronology of the events."

"Good." The class looked relieved. "O.K."

An opportunity for moral inquiry presented itself. "If you were writing a book about your life," Ms. Hempel asked, "and you cast a person in an unflattering light, would you wait until that person died? Before you published your book?"

The kids didn't see her point. "I couldn't write a book. I don't have enough to write about," Simon Grosse said.

"That's not true!" said Ms. Hempel. "Each of you could write a book. Several books, in fact." She tried to remember what Flannery O'Connor had said on the subject. "Anyone who's made it through childhood has enough material to last them until the day they die."

"We haven't made it through yet," Henry Woo said.

"But you will," said Ms. Hempel. "And when you do, you'll have lots to write about. Everyone does interesting things when they're kids."

"And bad things, like Toby?"

"And bad things. Everyone has, even if everyone won't admit it."

The kids waited for a moment, as if they needed, for the sake of politeness, to make a show of digesting this information.

"Did you do bad things, Ms. Hempel?"

She should have expected it.

"Well. Be logical. Everyone includes me, doesn't it?"

Greedily, the kids leaned forward. "What kinds of bad things?" The back legs of desk chairs rose into the air.

Ms. Hempel heaved an enormous sigh of resignation. She let her arms drop heavily to her sides. "You really want to know?" she groaned, as if she were finally, under great duress, capitulating to their demands. "You're really going to make me do this?" In truth, she loved talking about herself. Especially to her students.

All heads nodded vigorously.

"I watched TV when I wasn't supposed to. And sometimes I stayed out past my curfew."

The back legs returned to the floor. "That's it?"

"I wasn't always considerate of my parents."

David D'Souza offered her a wan smile.

"And I pierced my nose with a sewing needle," Ms. Hempel said. "My mother turned her face away every time I walked into the room, like she does when she's watching a violent movie. She was furious at me."

"Caroline Pratt pierced her bellybutton," Adelaide observed. Caroline was an eighth-grader. "She didn't even use ice."

Ms. Hempel shuffled through her collected misdeeds, trying to find ones that she could, in good conscience, share with seventh-graders. "I used to like skateboarders. I would help them dye their hair — it made my hands all blotchy. And I was always getting in trouble for breaking the dress code at my school. Once I wore —"

"Ms. Hempel, did you always want to be a teacher?"

It startled her, the conversation veering off in this direction. But then it made sense to her: they believed they already knew the answer. Of course she always wanted to be a teacher. They were giving her a way out. A way of explaining her unremarkable youth.

"No!" she said. "I certainly didn't."

"Why not?" And the question sounded reproachful. "You like teaching, don't you?" Because suddenly there was the possibility that she didn't. "You like being a teacher. And you were good at school."

They said it with confidence. They treated it as a commonplace, an assumption that needn't be challenged. But the fact that they had said it, the fact that the issue had arisen, in the midst of this tour through Ms. Hempel's offenses, suggested that somewhere, in some part of themselves, they knew differently. It was astonishing, the efficiency with which they arrived at the truth. This was probably why children were so useful in stories and films about social injustice, like *To Kill a Mockingbird*. But Ms. Hempel didn't think that this ability was particularly ennobling. It was just something they could do, the way dogs can hear certain high-pitched sounds, or the way x-rays can see past skin and tissue, down to the ghostly blueprint of the bones.

Ms. Hempel sighed. A real one, this time.

"My school — it was demanding, academically. They had very high expectations of us."

"So you were a really good student?"

"No," Ms. Hempel said. "I wasn't."

And this, finally, impressed them.

"I did well on all the standardized tests — like the ERBs? — I scored very high on those. Anything with bubbles I was excellent at, or multiple choice. Even short answer. But it was hard for me to develop my ideas at length. You know, stick with an argument, weave different threads together.

"And my school placed a lot of emphasis on that. On essays, term papers, the final question on exams. It's not because I didn't have anything to say, or because I didn't have any ideas. I had lots of them, too many of them. My papers were hard to make sense of.

"Has anyone ever told you that you have lots of potential? But that you aren't fulfilling it? That's what I heard all throughout high school.

"So I would get terribly nervous before a paper was due. I would tell myself, I'm really going to fulfill my potential on this one. I'm going to make an outline, do a rough draft, write a paragraph a night. I'm going to plan my time effectively. And I would spend two weeks telling myself this, and there I'd be, three o'clock in the morning, the paper's due in five hours, and I can't get my ideas to sit still long enough for me to write any of them down.

"That's why," Ms. Hempel concluded, "I make you turn in your outlines. And your rough drafts. Even though you hate me for it."

But the attempt at levity went unremarked. Her class gazed at her, soberly.

"So how'd you become a good student?" Cilia Matsui asked. "How did you get into a good college and become a teacher?"

"I don't know," Ms. Hempel said. "Worked harder, I guess. What do they say? — I buckled down."

It wasn't until high school that all of this unfulfilled potential was discovered; up until then, she had been simply great: great kid, great student. *A pleasure to have in class.* But beginning in the ninth grade, she felt her greatness gently ebbing away, retreating to a cool, deep cistern hidden somewhere inside her. I think it's there! her teachers hollered down into the darkness. It *is* there! her father insisted. But where? she felt like asking. Because there was something faintly suspicious, faintly cajoling, about the way they spoke to her, as if she alone knew the location, and was refusing to tell them for the sake of being contrary.

Dear Parents,
   You recently have received an "anecdotal" about your child. Although it might not have been immediately apparent, this anecdotal was written BY your child, from the perspective of one of his or her teachers. In response to the students' entreaties, I did not include a note of explanation. They wanted to explain the exercise to you themselves, and I hope you have had a chance to talk with your children about the letters they wrote. At this point, though, I would like to offer my own thoughts about the assignment and provide a context in which to understand these anecdotals.
   The assignment was inspired by a passage from the memoir we currently are reading, *This Boy's Life* by Tobias Wolff. When this passage oc-

curs, Toby is longing to escape his abusive stepfather and the dead-end town he lives in. When his older brother suggests that Toby apply to boarding school, he becomes excited about the idea, but then discouraged when he realizes that with his poor grades, he will never be accepted. Help arrives in the form of his best friend, who volunteers in the school office and supplies Toby with all the official stationery he needs to create his own letters of recommendation.

> I felt full of things that had to be said, full of stifled truth. That was what I thought I was writing — the truth. It was truth known only to me, but I believed in it more than I believed in the facts arrayed against it. I believed that in some sense not factually verifiable I was a straight-A student. In the same way, I believed that I was an Eagle Scout, and a powerful swimmer, and a boy of integrity. These were ideas about myself that I had held onto for dear life. Now I gave them voice.
>   . . . I wrote without heat or hyperbole, in the words my teachers would have used if they had known me as I knew myself. These were their letters. And in the boy who lived in their letters, the splendid phantom who carried all my hopes, it seemed to me I saw, at last, my own face.

I had hoped that through this exercise students could give voice to their own visions of themselves, visions that might differ from those held by teachers, parents, or friends. I wanted to give them a chance to identify and celebrate what they see as their greatest strengths. During this crucial stage of their development, kids need, I think, to articulate what they believe themselves capable of.

The students approached the assignment with an enthusiasm that overwhelmed me. In their efforts to sound like their teachers, they wrote at greater length, in sharper detail, with more sophisticated phrasing and vocabulary, than they ever have before. Spelling and grammatical errors instantly disappeared; drafts were exhaustively revised. They felt it important that their anecdotals appear convincing.

The decision to mail these anecdotals home was fueled by my desire to share with you these very personal and often revealing self-portraits. When I read them, I found them by turns funny, poignant, and, as Tobias Wolff writes, full of truth. I thought that you, as parents, would value this opportunity to see your children as they see themselves. The intention was not, as I think a few students have mistaken, to play a joke.

I hope that this assignment has offered some meaningful insights into your child, and I deeply regret if it has been the cause of any misunderstanding or distress. Please feel free to contact me if you have further questions or concerns.

*

Ms. Hempel distributed the letters, each of which she had signed by hand. "Please," she said. "It's imperative that you deliver these to your parents. First thing tonight, before you do anything else. Its contents are extremely important." She had omitted certain details: the glee with which she had brandished the school stationery, pulling it out from beneath her cardigan; the instructions she had provided as to perfecting her signature on the anecdotals, the way she had leaned over her students' shoulders and adjusted the loops in their *l*'s. How they had jigged up and down, and laughed wickedly, and rubbed their palms together in a villainous way. How she hadn't the heart to tell them that their anecdotals, so carefully fashioned, would be, upon first glance, apprehended as false.

They didn't sound quite right. And the signatures were awful.

Ms. Hempel had contemplated forgery, once, when she was still a student. Her school instituted a new policy: throughout the semester, parents had to sign all tests and papers, so that when final grades were sent home, there wouldn't be any unwelcome surprises. In accordance with the policy, she left her essay on her father's desk, with a little note requesting his signature. The essay had earned a C+.

Later that evening, she was lying face-down on her bed, air-drying. Her skin was still ruddy from the bath, and as she peeked over her shoulder, surveying the damp expanse of her own body, it reminded her, in a satisfying way, of a walrus. But the comparison wasn't very complimentary. She amended it to a seal, a sleek and shining seal. She imagined a great, gruff hunter coveting her pelt.

But then she was interrupted: the sound of something sliding beneath her door. Disappointingly, only her essay. She padded over from the bed and bent down to retrieve it.

It was horrible to behold. Her father had written not only at the top of the essay, per her instructions, but in the margins as well. His firm handwriting had completely colonized the page. The phrases were mysterious — "No, no, she's being ironic" — agitated and without context, like the cries of people talking in their sleep. Upon closer inspection, she realized that his comments were in response to what her teacher, Mr. Amis, had already written. To his accusations of "Obscure," her father rejoined: "Nicely nuanced." When he wondered how one paragraph connected to the next, her father explained: "It seems a natural transition to move from a general definition to a particular instance." The dialogue continued until the final page, where her father arrived at his jubilant conclusion: that this was an essay unequaled in its originality, its unpredictable leaps of imagination, its surprising twists and turns. On the bottom of the page, he had printed, neatly: A−. It was protected inside a circle.

"Your name!" she bellowed down the staircase. "Why is it so hard for you to just sign your name?"

Back inside her bedroom, she heard the methodical stamp of her father's feet, climbing the stairs. "I don't want any part in this!" she yelled, tucking the essay inside her binder, though she would apologize to Mr. Amis; she would say, My father lost it.

She stood up and spoke through the crack in the door. "Don't ever do that again."

"I'm sorry, sweetheart," her father said, his voice muffled. He was right on the other side. "But I can't promise you I won't."

It was at that moment forgery first presented itself as an option. But instead she decided to ask, from then on, for her mother's signature. It seemed much easier than fraud. And she knew, anyhow, that even if she did try, she would inevitably get caught. Teachers were alert to that sort of crime.

Ms. Hempel thought that parents would be, too. They were supposed to be vigilant. They were supposed to reprogram the cable box, listen to lyrics, sniff sweaters, check under the mattress. Or, at the least, distinguish between Ms. Hempel's prose and that of a seventh grader. She had read every one of the anecdotals herself, yet she could not account for the lapse.

Some were panegyrics, plain and simple: *Adelaide is without a doubt the most outstanding French student I have ever encountered in my twenty-six years of teaching.* Some were recantations: *Please ignore my phone call of last week. Matthew is no longer disrupting my class.* Some suggested publication: *Elliott's five-paragraph essay was so superb, I think he should send it to* Newsweek. Some recommended immediate acceleration: *Judging by her excellence in all areas, I think that Emily is ready to take the SATs, and maybe start college early.* Some anecdotals did everything at once.

Dear Melanie Bean,

   I am writing to you about your son. He has been doing exceedingly well in English class. He has gotten a perfect score on every test or quiz we have had in English. He is completely outscoring, outtalking, outparticipating everyone in the class. I look forward to spending my time elaborating his mind in his field of expertise. I would like to consider moving him up to the eighth grade level, which I think would be more suited to his ability. Even though he would miss Spanish every day, I think that Spanish is an inferior class for any person of his mental state, and is simply ruining his skills. I have framed many of his works and find them all inspirational, especially his poetry. William is an inspirational character and I will never forget him. I suggest that you encourage him to use his skills constantly.

Sincerely,
Beatrice Hempel

Will Bean looked nothing like his mother. He was small and impish and pale, and had assumed the role of a friendly, benign irritant, someone who pops up from behind desks and briskly waves. His greatest joy was a series of books about a religious community made up of mice, voles, and hedgehogs. They had taken the Benedictine vows, and created a devout but merry life for themselves. Will frequently alluded to them. He produced a radio play in which he performed all the parts: the sonorous voice of the badger abbot, the tittering of the field mice, who were still novices and had to work in the monastery's kitchens. He pestered Ms. Hempel into borrowing a tape deck and making the whole class listen to his production. In anecdotal terms, he could be described as *whimsical,* or *inventive,* or *delightfully imaginative.*

Ms. Bean, however, was tall and gaunt and harried. When Ms. Hempel saw her, standing outside the school's gates, she was swaddled in bags: one for her computer, another for her dry cleaning, for her groceries, for Will's soccer uniform. It was strange, how clearly Ms. Hempel could picture her students' lives — Will had tae kwon do on Tuesday afternoons, and every Wednesday night he spent with his dad — and how murky their parents' lives seemed by comparison. All she could see in Ms. Bean was evidence of a job, an exhausting one.

"Do you have a moment?" she said.

Ms. Hempel said of course.

"I wanted to speak with you about the assignment."

Would she find it deceitful, and dishonest, as Mrs. Woo did? Or maybe, like Mrs. Galvin, she had telephoned all the relatives, even the ones in California, to tell them the wonderful news. It was unlikely, though, that she loved the assignment, thought it original and brilliant and bold. Only Mr. Borowitz seemed to feel that way.

What Ms. Bean wanted her to know was that she felt the assignment to be unkind. Or maybe not unkind. Maybe just unfair. Because she had been waiting a long time for someone else to finally notice what she had always known about Will. And then to discover that it was an assignment, merely.

The disappointment was terrible — could Ms. Hempel understand that?

Mr. Dunne, her college counselor, was the one who first noticed the discrepancy. Impressive scores, mediocre grades. A specialist was consulted, a series of tests administered, and a medication prescribed. The bitter pills, her father used to call them. The prescription made her hands shake a little, but that wore off after a while. And then: a shy, newfound composure. Her mother entrusted her with the holiday newsletter. She wrote film reviews for the university paper. She had a nice way with words, a neat way of telling a story.

To her ears, though, her stories sounded smushed, as if they had been sat upon by accident. None of the interesting parts survived. Yes, her father flashed the headlights, and yes, she waved at him before she stepped inside. Those details were resilient. Not these: how she waved glamorously, and smiled radiantly, how the headlights heralded the arrival of a star. How her shadow, projected onto the snow, looked huge.

"That was beautiful," her grandmother said to her, when she returned to her pew. "I can see Oscar doing just that — making sure you got in safely."

Beautiful was not what she intended. Her story was not about safety and concern and anxious attentions. It was a tale of danger, intrigue. A story from the days before her medicine, the days of their collusion, when they communicated in code — click, click — as true accomplices do. When they were still plotting to prove everyone woefully mistaken. This was the story she wanted to tell. Then how did something altogether different emerge? Something she didn't even recognize as her own. Even her father — her co-conspirator, her fan — had been changed into someone she didn't quite know. A kind and shadowy figure, sitting in the car. *Benevolent. Thoughtful. Considerate of others.*

CHARLES D'AMBROSIO

Screenwriter

FROM THE NEW YORKER

HOW WAS I SUPPOSED TO know that any mention of suicide to the phalanx of doctors making Friday rounds would warrant the loss of not only weekend-pass privileges but also the liberty to take a leak in private? My first suicidal ideations occurred to me when I was ten, eleven, twelve, something like that, and by now I was habituated to them and dreams of hurting myself (in the parlance of those places) formed a kind of lullaby I often used to rock myself to bed at night. I got into trouble when I told my p-doc I couldn't fall asleep until I'd made myself comfortable by drawing the blankets over my head and imagining I was closing the lid of my coffin. In confessing to him, I was trying only to be honest and accurate, a good patient, deserving. But no dice: the head p-doc put me on Maximum Observation and immediately I was being trailed around by a sober ex-athlete who, introducing himself, put a fatherly hand on my shoulder and squeezed and told me not to worry, he was a screenwriter, too — not as successful or rich as me, sure, but a screenwriter nonetheless. He said that his name was Bob and he let it be known that he'd taken this position on the mental ward only to gather material for his next script. Half the reason I was in the ward was to get away from the movies, but my whole time with Bob I kept wondering, Is this, or that, or this or that, or this, or this, or this going to be in a *movie?* Everywhere I went, he went, creeping along a few sedate paces back in soft-soled shoes, a shadow that gave off a disturbing susurrus like the maddening sibilance settling dust must make to the ears of ants.

One morning I was lying on my mattress, flipping through women's magazines, but after a while Bob started scratching his ankle, so I got up and went to the bathroom. Bob stood right behind me and in my state of excited self-consciousness the splashing of piss against the urinal cake was deafening, a cataract so loud it was like I'd managed, somehow, to urinate directly into my own ear. After that I watched a television show about a guy with massive arms but no legs climbing a mountain; with a system of pulleys and ropes he managed to belay himself up the slope like a load of bananas. He planted an American flag on the summit. This ruined man's struggle and eventual triumph moved me; in fact I began to cry. To calm myself I listened to the languorous *pick-pock* of two heavily medicated patients thwacking a Ping-Pong ball in the rec room, but there was a final *phut* and then that unnerving nothing, nothing at all, and finally an attack of the fantods drove me out to the patio. Where I sat, Bob sat, and pretty soon the patio started making me crazy, too. Sitting still — just sitting! — was like an equestrian feat. But if I stood up, if I walked in circles, then Bob would have to stand up and walk in circles with me.

The patio was perched high above the FDR and the East River and caged in with chainlink fencing. Concrete benches were scattered around like cuttlebone, and there were potted shrubs in each corner. Scavenging pigeons and seagulls flocked overhead, vaguely white and whirling in the wind. I crushed saltines in their cellophane packets and poured the crumbs in the lap of my paper gown and fed the pieces to the birds.

Bob said, "Are you gonna get better?"

I looked up from my lap and said, "This isn't very interesting, is it?"

"I didn't say that."

"I know you want to write a movie. You're looking for material. But this — it's not a thriller, that's for sure."

"And it's not a whodunit because, like, you're not doing anything."

A young woman known on the ward as the ballerina was dancing across the patio. By the way she kept her hair twisted into a prim, tight bun, and by her body, which seemed to have a memory separate from her mind, a strict memory of its own, you immediately guessed she was a dancer. Her grandparents were with her, two

hunched-up people in colossal overcoats and tiny black shoes, people I assumed were immigrants or refugees, because their clothes
were so out-of-date, like from the nineteenth century, and because,
all bent over, they looked wary and vigilant, as though they were
ducking. Lumpen, I kept thinking, or lumpenproletariat — when I
probably meant just plain lumpy. Every evening they came to visit
their granddaughter, and now they sat on a bench and watched
as she swooped like a bird through the lengthening shadows. The
old man smoked an unfiltered cigarette, working his tongue in a
lizardy fashion to free the flecks of tobacco lodged in his teeth. The
old lady sat with her knucklelike face rapt, a Kleenex balled in her
fist. She was crying for the beauty of her granddaughter, and in motion the girl *was* beautiful, she was ecstatic. She wore a sacklike stan-
dard-issue paper gown the same as me and she was barefoot. Her
arms floated away from her body as though she were trying to balance a feather on the tip of each finger. Then she jumped around,
modern and spasmodic, as if the whole point of dance were to leap
free of your skin. She raced from one end of the patio to the other,
flew up, twirling and soaring, clawing the fence with her fingers
and setting the links to shiver. But as soon as her grandparents left,
blam, the dance in her died. She went cataleptic.

I clapped, and said, "That was nice. *Brava, brava. Bravissima!*"

"Got a smoke?" she said.

I rose to hand her a cigarette and my lighter and to look into her
strange blue eyes. "You're really a good dancer," I said.

"No I'm not," she said.

Her voice had no affect and its deadness sat me right back
down on the bench. She turned away and flicked the wheel of the
lighter, cupping the cigarette out of the wind. A paper plate rolled
as if chased, around and around the patio, like a child's game without the child. A white moth fell like a flower petal from the sky,
dropped through a link in the fence, and came to light on my
hand. The cooling night wind raised goose flesh on my arms, and a
cloud of smoke ripped into the air. The girl's gown was smoldering.
A leading edge of orange flame was chewing up the hem. I rose
from my seat to tell the ballerina she was on fire. The moth flew
from my hand, a gust fanned the flames, there was a flash, and the
girl ignited, lighting up like a paper lantern. She was cloaked in
fire. The heat moved in waves across my face and I had to squint

against the brightness. The ballerina spread her arms and levitated, *sur les pointes,* leaving the patio as her legs, ass, and back emerged phoenixlike out of this paper chrysalis, rising up until finally the gown sloughed from her shoulders and sailed away, a tattered black ghost ascending in a column of smoke and ash, and she lowered back down, naked and white, standing there, pretty much unfazed, in first position.

After a month on the p-ward you don't get telegrams or get-well cards or stuffed animals anymore, and the petals fall off your flowers and curl like dead skin on the dresser top while the stems go soft and rot in their vases. That's a bad stretch, that Sargasso in the psych ward when the last winds of your old life die out. In the real world I was still legally married — my wife was a film producer, but she'd left me for a more glamorous opportunity, the star of our most recent movie. The script I'd written was somewhat autobiographical and the character he played was modeled after my dead father. So now my wife was banging Dad's doppelgänger and I hadn't talked to her in I don't know how long. In between therapy sessions and the administration of the usual battery of tests (Thematic Apperception, Rorschach, MMPI), as well as blood draws and vitals, I sat on the sofa in the lounge, hoping for a certain zazen zeroness — serene and stupid — but mostly getting hung up on cravings for tobacco. One night after dinner I sat on the sofa and moved my finger to different locations around my head — below the ear, right in the ear, above the eyeball, against the roof of my mouth — experimenting with places to put the gun. I tried filling the dreary hours with poetry — my first love — but I'd been a script doctor too long. I hadn't futzed with an iamb in ages, and the words just dog-paddled around the page senselessly. I was desperate enough for a nicotine high to harvest some of the more smokable butts out of the Folgers coffee cans the staff filled with kitty litter and set out on the patio. The pickings were slim, though; in the p-ward people tend to smoke their cigarettes ravenously. You look around, and everybody's got burnt, scabby fingers just like the Devil.

Finally I worked up the nerve to bum a smoke from Carmen, an operatic Italian woman who was my next-door neighbor on the ward. She tapped one free of her pack. It looked like a sterile, all-white, hospital-issue ciggie that would never do anything bad, such as give you cancer. I drew it under my nose, giving it a sniff in the manner of a man with a fine cigar.

"You saved my life," I said. "Could I bother you for a match?"

"You know," she said, "I grew up an only child and was chased by every kid in my school! Teased all my life, my mom's dressin' me didn't help! I was the school clown, I can never remember being happy as a child, sexually abused from eleven to fourteen, then I started to run away at sixteen, raped several times, tried suicide several times . . . then I met a thirty-five-year-old man, got pregnant, married him, suffered beatings for seven years, left him, alone, had nowhere to go, three kids, I collapsed, went for the sixth time into the hospital . . . came out, nowhere to go, so I stayed with this guy, a friend, we started to mess around, I had my fourth child, now when I look back at it all, phew, I never had love, I hate my life, I wish I was never born, I get days when I feel so stupid that taking a bath takes two hours 'cause I can't think!"

Man, on the p-ward you asked for a match and people told you stuff. After a week you knew everybody's etiology. Illness was our lingua franca. Patients announced their worst infirmities right off, but no one dared talk about normal life. Oh, no — that was shameful and embarrassing, a botch you didn't bring up in polite conversation. Fearing I might blow my chance for a pass if I hung around Carmen, I grabbed a book of matches from a table in the Ping-Pong room and stepped out onto the patio. But the ballerina was out there, dancing.

"Got an extra smoke?" she asked.

"I don't want any encore of the last time," I said. "Besides, I only got this one. I'll share it with you if you want."

She sat beside me on the bench. Her skin smelled of ointments and steroid creams.

I said, "Are you a professional?"

"Professional nut case," she said.

"No, really."

"I've been in here and uptown at Columbia for like a donkey's year."

"I meant are you a dancer."

"Not with this body."

"Why do you say that?"

"Do you have a knife?"

"I haven't worn pants in five weeks."

"What's that supposed to mean?"

"Nothing. I just don't have any pockets. No wallet, no keys, no spare change, no lint, no rabbit's foot, and no knife. It's emasculating. Why do you want a knife, anyway?"

"Never mind."

Her nose was fat and fruitlike, a nose for pratfalls and slapstick, not jetés and pirouettes and pliés and whatnot. But her lips were lovely, the color of cold meat, and her eyes, sunk deep in their sockets, were clear blue. When you looked into them, you half expected to see fish swimming around at the back of her head, shy ones.

"All I ever wanted to do was dance, all I've ever done is dance, and I grew up into a linebacker."

"Yeah, well, I wanted to be a screenwriter, and guess what. I am one. That's the other tragedy in life." I eased back against the fence. "Anyway, you got nice legs. I don't know what you're talking about."

"My thighs, stupid!"

From the patio you could see the red gondolas rising over the East River, pendent and swaying as they made their way to Roosevelt Island. The sun was setting and I thought it would be so calm and beautiful to be hanging in a bucket way above everything, especially if they could just ride you out over the river and suspend you there, bobbing around, twilight for all time, the sun never going down, the glass forever warm, just hanging out in a lovely red bucket with that senile light dusting your cheeks.

"Calm down." I lit the cigarette and passed it to her. "Your legs are fine."

She smiled. "Well, thank you," she said. Then she puckered her lips, made a loud wet smack, sucked down a single deep drag, exhaled, and drove the cigarette into her thigh. She twisted and snubbed and jammed the coal against her skin, staring at the burn, red and flecked with ash, until the last live cinder died out.

"You ought to quit smoking," I said.

Bob followed us back to her room, where she applied some kind of topical anodyne, smoothing the white cream into her wound, as dreamy as a lover, and crawled into bed.

"Why'd you do that?"

"If I knew, I wouldn't be here, now would I?"

"Sure you might. You might know exactly why you did it but you might not be able to stop yourself anyway."

I leaned over her bed and tried to kiss her, but she put a hand to my lips.

After that, I came to see her every night. I totally dug her broken bohemian thing, it was so the opposite of my trajectory, my silly success. I'd made a million dollars each of the last four years running and never felt worse in my life. I'm not whining — I'm not one of those whiners. One of those affluent crybabies. But I'd lost the plot and was afraid that if my life improved anymore I'd vanish. By contrast a woman setting herself on fire seemed very real; on doctor's orders, she was strapped in at 9:00 sharp, pinned to the flat board of her bed like a specimen. At first it was unnerving to talk to a woman who was lashed to her bed with a contraption of leather belts and heavy brass buckles, so I angled my seat away from her face and spoke to her knees, which looked, in the faint blue light, as though they'd been carved by water from a bar of soap.

"How are you?" I said.

She seesawed her wrist, *comme ci, comme ça*, beneath a band of heavy saddle leather. The leather was burnished to a rich gloss by the straining of a thousand sweaty wrists on a thousand other agonized nights.

"Would you grab me an orange?"

I fetched an orange from a basket and peeled it; it was especially fragrant in the semidark. Bob was sitting in a chair in the hallway and I could hear the dry scratch of his pencil as he took notes. I didn't care. The ballerina's window was open and in the breeze the heavy curtains swept aside and the hospital courtyard, with its scalloped pattern of cobblestones, its wet bare trees and February emptiness, seemed like a scene recollected from an expatriate life in Paris that I'd never lived, a moment out of some tawdry romance I'd never had in my youth.

"Make sure you peel as much of the yuck off as possible," she said. "I hate the yuck."

"I hate the yuck, too," I said, and held a jeweled segment over her mouth. Her lips spread and her tongue slid forward. It had been ages since I'd fed anyone. It was excellent the way, when

I held the crescent of orange there, poised above her blue lips, her mouth just opened. I dangled another piece and watched her mouth open like a little starveling bird's and then I pulled the piece away and watched her mouth close. Then I gave it to her.

"You don't have a match, do you?" I put a cigarette in my mouth. "A pyro like yourself."

"I'd love a smoke."

"I bet you would. Why do you burn yourself?"

"My doctor's theory is it puts the pain in a place I can find it. On the outside."

"I know exactly what he means. I thought making movies was going to be that way. Now I'd just rather be crucified."

"I don't like your mind."

"Yeah, well, I'm not here for a pedicure."

"Untie me," she whispered.

"No can do," I said.

"Please."

"Can't."

"We'll just smoke that cig and then you can buckle me right back up."

"I don't have any matches."

She smiled. "I do."

She told me to lift the table lamp, and underneath it I found a cache of contraband matches. Each individual match had been ripped from the book and mustered in a neat, soldierly line, and the strip of striking was there, too, the whole kit flat enough to hide beneath the green felt base.

"Great, but I'll just hold the cig to your lips. I'm going to leave you strapped in for now."

We worked the cig down to a nub, fanning the smoke out the window, and then she yanked at the sides of her gown. A couple of the snaps popped open, and she pulled aside the paper. It made a rustling like the thin parchment pages of a Bible.

"This was the first time, after an audition for the Albany Ballet," she said, using her finger to trace a faint cicatrix the size of postage stamp. "I wanted a sharp blade, I just had the idea. I had a disposable razor for shaving my legs, so I put that in my mouth. I bit down on it real hard, trying to crack the plastic so I could get the blade free. But I couldn't get it. It wouldn't come out. I was so frustrated.

I started crying. I lit a cigarette. I had no idea what that hand with the cigarette would do — it was like it was somebody else's.

"Sometimes, like this, I'm just tense," she said, pointing out an ellipsis of brown dots down the length of her belly, marks the size of moles she'd made by extinguishing stick matches against her skin. All along her body, a palimpsest of older lesions darkened beneath the rawer, more recent burns. Her arms were crosshatched with brands she'd seared into her skin with a coat hanger heated over a gas stove.

"Can I touch?" I asked.

She nodded.

I put my finger against a dark, hard burl on her outer thigh, an elevated lump as smooth as a chestnut. I ran the flat of my hand over her hip and down her leg. Whatever I touched prompted a story, some account: auditions, classes, Tuesday nights, phone calls, weddings. I'd been horny, but now I felt detached. This display of her body wasn't sexy, the way a tour of a battlefield isn't bloody.

In the p-hosp, of course, it was seriously against the rules to touch another patient, and being under Bob's constant surveillance didn't make it easy for us. In line at the cafeteria I'd palm my food tray with one hand and feel her solid balletic rump with the other. Or I'd play footsie with her under the table at Friday-night bingo. Or I'd grope her up in the little gymnasium where, for R.T., we played some of the sorriest games of volleyball you can imagine. In the typical draft that goes on against the fence at school, you know who the athletes are, who the sissies are, who to crib from in a history exam and avoid on the kickball team, but up on psych choosing a squad of decent players was primarily a pharmacological matter, something where, really, you wanted to consult the *DSM-IV* before you made your first selection. Choosing an appropriate sexual partner in a mental hospital was probably supposed to work along similar lines. You needed records!

With her malady, the ballerina wasn't really into fooling around, but I hoped her new medication, Manerix, which was supposed to dampen some of her desire to burn herself, might also lead by inverse ratio to an upsurge in her passion for old-fashioned sex. After a week, two weeks, I was getting frustrated. Most of the contact we made, skin to skin, was glancing and accidental, hardly more than what passes acceptably between strangers on the street. She had this terrific body, so looking and fantasizing was fine — for a while. But of course about this time I discovered that I couldn't whack off. My medication was giving me erectile hassles, plus Bob outside my open door didn't help. In anticipation of the day when the ballerina's Manerix would kick in I started pitching my cocktail of bupropion and lithium and clonazepam out the window.

But the ballerina made such great progress on her new meds that by the end of February her p-doc wanted her to practice sleeping through the night without restraints. After dinner we'd sit outside, on the patio, and watch the sun go down, knowing she was about to be released. And one morning, sure enough, I saw her dragging a wicker basket and a pillowcase full of clothes to the nurses' station. Departures on the psych ward were a big deal. People always swore they'd come back and visit, but they never did. By the time you were a ward veteran like myself, a little bit of your hope left with them and never fully returned. I expected I'd never see her again. She was cured, and that was tantamount to being gone, gone off to reside in some unfamiliar land. Her grandparents met her in the lounge with their hopeless, past-tense faces and their old leafy clothes; standing beside them in a gauzy spring dress, the ballerina seemed a mere puff of self, passing like a spirit out of their heavy Old World sadness, whatever it was about. She told me that as soon as I managed to wrangle my first pass she wanted to see me. She used a red felt pen to write her name and number across the hem of my gown, and we shook hands, but after she was gone and I took up my station on the sofa, I felt certain I wouldn't rise again until some angel came by and blew a trumpet.

It was maybe a couple weeks later, and I was no longer on Maximum Observation. Bob was gone and I was on my own. My window was open and little things stirred as they had in my childhood, so that the clothes scattered on the floor were once again the bodies of dead men. When I was a boy, my father and his six brothers seined for salmon out of Ilwaco, Washington, and every couple years one or another of them would wash up in the frog water around Chehalis Slough, drowned. The funerals seemed to last days, weeks, even months, as the remaining brothers gathered nightly in the Riptide bar and stared drunkenly into one another's eyes like dazed, speechless toads. Left at home, sleepless and alone — I have a mother somewhere, but I never knew her — I imagined that each shirt on the floor was a dead uncle and I could not leave the tipsy life raft of my bed, waiting out those long nights when the ocean fog was cool and full of premonitions and the beacon at the end of the breakwater threw green shadows against the walls of my room. Now I drew the blanket over my head. "Our Father who art in heaven . . . etc. . . . etc. . . . now and at the hour of our death amen!" When the coffin thing didn't put me to sleep I peeked over the satiny selvage of my blanket and stared at the ceiling and listened to the tedious complaints of patients as they wept into the pay phone across the hall: (8:02) . . . My parents had a bad marriage, then divorced and married worse people . . . (8:07) . . . I'll show you what's the matter with me. Then I get my razor. I cut down sharp and quick. I scream and go out onto the court and bleed all over . . . (8:47) . . . It's hard to kill yourself by taking Tylenol. You die from liver failure, which takes a long time . . .

This kind of serial conversation went on night after night, a litany of complaint and outrage, right outside my door. People were hospitalized when their feelings reached an acute phase, but if you eavesdropped on all the jabbering, all the lonely, late-night calls, the whole long history of pain and madness fused into a single humdrum story, without much drama. It went flat. I'd been revolving in and out of various mental wards my whole life and previously had always considered myself touched and unique. I was kind of snobby about it — like a war vet, bitter and proud — but now I flipped the covers to the floor and queued up with all the other lunatics, waiting my turn.

"Look," I said, "can I come see you?"

"You can get out?" the ballerina asked.

"What're you saying?"

"Are you better?"

"No," I said. "Not really. But I'm off M.O."

She didn't say anything. On the p-ward you often found the pay phone swaying from the end of its metal cord like the pendulum of a clock, no one in sight. People just drifted away from conversations, too frazzled and forgetful to end the call or maybe too medicated and lethargic to hang up. That's what I was imagining when the ballerina went silent, the dangling phone.

"O.K.?" I said, finally.

"O.K.," she said.

I hung up and crawled back into bed and stared at the ceiling and listened: (9:31) . . . I swear I spent 60 percent of my life puking . . . (9:33) . . . Then can you explain to me why every time I got in my car to go somewhere "Mr. Bojangles" was playing . . . (9:45) . . . I started keeping a journal almost two years ago. I used to write only when I was happy. Then I realized that I'd look back and think that my whole life was happy, so I started only writing when I was depressed. And I realized that I wasn't always depressed, so I started to write every day. Now I calculate I'm 50 percent happy and 50 percent depressed so I don't see the point of writing at all anymore . . . (10:07) . . . It hurts.

I used my very first pass to visit the ballerina. With three hours before lockdown, I caught a cab, stopped for a bottle of wine, then hustled over to her place, a small apartment just off Varick. She showed me around with exactly three gestures. "Kitchen," she said. "Bedroom. Bathroom." We uncorked the wine and toasted my new freedom.

After being abstemious for so long, I was drunk in no time. I bent and gave the ballerina a kiss on the tip of her big old nose and crossed the room in that deliberate way of drunks. Her bathroom was a frilly gift that one girl might give to another, an assortment of powders, soaps, oils, lotions, perfumes, sea sponges, lava stones, and so on. There were yellow candles set at the corners of the tub. Bath beads in translucent caps sat in jars like sapphires. A fragrant potpourri filled a blue glass bottle, and there was a bar of brown soap with chunks of something abrasive, like sawdust, embedded in it. The whole place was stockpiled with not just your boring brandname products but all these totally recherché and esoteric potions searched out in faraway quarters of the city. I opened the medicine cabinet and fingered through the shelves, reading. A jar of astringent lotion said that it would rid your skin of the toxins that are an inescapable part of modern life. I didn't believe it, of course, and yet who doesn't want to "revive" and "replenish," who doesn't love the words "pure" and "essential"? My p-doc hadn't been using any of this uplifting language, and after a couple months on the ward the exotica listed on the backs of these bottles — olive, kukui, St.

John's wort, wild yam — sounded good to me, sounded like the fruits of some heavenly place, an island off somewhere in the blue future. Hadn't Columbus set sail in search of these very ingredients?

Mixed in with all that humbug were the serious amber bottles of medication: Effexor, Paxil, Wellbutrin, Prozac, Zoloft, the whole starting roster of antidepressants. The ballerina couldn't have been taking them in combination, so what was the history here? I lined the bottles up according to the date the script had been filled at the pharmacy, but the timeline gave out about a month before she entered the psych ward. No refill for Manerix in sight. What was the deal? In a back row of the medicine chest she kept the scrubs and utility players, and I popped a few Tuinals, washing them down with water from the faucet, and then tapped a couple Xanax and Valium into my palm, to save for a rainy day. I took a leak and flushed the toilet and stared at myself in the mirror. My eyes were dark pits and my gums had turned a pulpy red. I seemed to be looking at the portrait of a man who hadn't eaten a piece of fruit in years.

When I came out she said, "Lots of medications, huh?"

"You got the whole library in there," I said.

"You were snooping around, trying to get a read on me. I know, so don't even bother saying you weren't."

"I said I was looking."

"I don't care. I always look, too. It's O.K."

I shrugged. "What's up with the Manerix?"

"That new antidepressant that's supposed to depress my depression better than the old antidepressants did?"

"Yeah, that one."

"I ditched it."

"Is that a good idea? How's it going, without meds?"

"I feel like burning myself, if that's what you mean."

For ten years I'd been dutiful and hardworking, cranking out those bigtime Hollywood screenplays in order to bankroll a lifestyle that broke the silly-meter. Now it was like, Bring on the degradation! Let's break through the bullshit and get real! I wished I'd brought another bottle of wine, to help lower me back into the bohemian hopes I'd had at twenty-five — literature and pussy. Baudelaire and women that stank like Gruyère! I'd never really wanted to write screenplays. I'd wanted to be a poet. And here I was, in poetry central. There were candles on the shelves, on the floor, fat and thin candles, tall and short, red and green and all the gradients of soft pastel, scented with the sweet and cloying flavors of guava, pomegranate, mango. Everything here was *luxe, calme,* and *volupté,* all right. In his Tahitian diary Gauguin wrote, "Life being what it is, we dream of revenge," a phrase whose ruthlessness used to be right up my alley. But what kind of revenge did I need when last year I'd managed to enjoy three summers, two springs, and four falls — one in Moscow, another in Florence, two more in Cairo and Burma? I was a touch manic, and after I walked off the set of my last movie, winter just didn't make it onto the itinerary. I was like a god, laughing at the weather. Who needed Gauguin and his gaudy painted paradise? For me, now, the most extreme, remote, Polynesian corner of the globe was inside the ballerina's skull.

She crawled across the floor on her hands and knees and the front of her dress gaped open and showed her breasts just hanging in that lovely, lovely way, guavaish and weighty, ready for plucking. I reached in and pinched a nipple. She shrank back and told me she didn't feel like being touched tonight.

"You don't?"

"Not really," she said. "You look scared. Are you scared?"

"Scared?" I looked up at her. "I don't know. I don't even know who I am right now. I'm all bottomed out. I'm down here with the basal ganglia and the halibuts."

"Did you take any of my pills?"

"You bet."

"You liar! You did, too."

"I said I did, you goofy bitch!"

That started the ballerina pacing, head erect, back swayed, tense. Her heels pounded the floor like a ball-peen hammer. She marched over to her dresser and rearranged some objects. I heard glass clinking and jars slamming down. She jerked a chair away from the window and set it by the door. She slapped shut a book that had been lying open beside a cereal bowl on the table. She disappeared into the kitchen alcove. She stomped back in with a cup of ice in her hand. She chewed the ice, and the broken shards fell out of her mouth to the floor. She grabbed the chair at the door and returned it to its original place by the window. Her whole, total animal thing took over, while for me, thanks to the downers, all memory of the upright life was gone. I would never again walk into a room and shake someone's hand. I could barely turn my head to keep track of the ballerina. Some words came out of her mouth, but I don't know where in the room they went. I never heard them.

Her dress dropped to the floor and she sat on the bed. Her panties were black, webby things; it looked as if a huge hairy spider had clamped itself onto her. Beside her she had a pack of cigarettes and a candle and a green knitting needle I wasn't too crazy about. She lifted the candle and lit the cigarette and drained some of the hot wax on her thigh. All the while she watched me, and after a few minutes she had me hooked, I was mesmerized, charmed, I was down way deep into that blue pool where the fish shyly waited. She took a drag of the cigarette, exhaled, then turned the hot coal around and twirled the ash off against her nipple. Another drag, and she turned her attention to the other nipple. Pretty soon both aureoles were ashy smudges. Her eyes remained wide open and, I guess, fixed on me, but they were blue and unfocused, and the pain was miles away.

I watched her, but something had gone wrong. Her torment wasn't turning me on. I didn't feel a thing. Obviously the drugs I'd snatched from her medicine cabinet weren't elevating my mood, and the thought of all those sundries in her bathroom was bringing me down, hard. Every last, sad soap in that utopian toilet was bumming me out. They were all part of a repertoire of hope I'd already lived through. I'd already washed myself with that crap. I'd taken those pills. I'd tried to feel loose and relaxed in a tub of hot water, beneath that shadowy candlelight. It all seemed so familiar. Her paisley sheets and the fan of peacock feathers above the futon and the tasseled lampshade screamed *boudoir*. The little shells and rocks and twigs italicized *a special moment long ago*. In the little syncretic boutiquey spiritual figurines lined up on the windowsill and the crystal prisms strung from the ceiling on threads of monofilament, I saw the very same occult trinkets that had decorated every bedroom I'd ever been in. My anticipation was gone, I couldn't lust or desire. All this intense specialness, along with the way she was effortfully trying to turn her pain to pleasure, was ending up as a very dull result in my brain.

I heard the tindery snap, the kindling crackle, of burning hair. She was burning herself, *là-bas*. The whole room stank. As she closed in on a climax, soot washed down her thigh like the aftermath of a calamity when the uncaring rain begins to carry it all out to sea . . .

"Here," she said, passing me the cigarette.

"No, thanks," I said.

"Burn me."

I'm a screenwriter and my movies gross millions and when I write "THE CAR BLOWS UP" there's a pretty good chance a real car will indeed blow up, but I am not particularly keen on the idea of roasting this woman's cunt over a hot coal. I can't even say the word *cunt* convincingly. The Frenchy sangfroid I'd felt leaving the psych ward was completely gone now. I wasn't Henry Miller, I wasn't Eugène-Henri-Paul Gauguin, I wasn't any of those expat guys. My career as a sexual adventurer was about half an hour old, and it was over already. I've read Baudelaire, but I wouldn't want to have his big ugly forehead. I was known among my friends as a major cork dork, and the wine I'd bought I wouldn't even have cooked with at home, fricasseeing stew meat for the dog. When I left the ballerina, if I chose, I could check myself out of the hospital and into the Plaza, stay a month, order room service, conduct business through my agent, while I watched other people out the window, real lunatics, splashing in the fountain, singing holy songs, dancing and shouting hosannas into the sky until the police came and Tasered them back into submission. When I squared up my tab at the p-hosp it would run me about thirty-five grand and at that rate the Plaza would be a bargain.

I needed air. I managed to stand and make it to the window and was swinging a foot onto the fire escape when a wet gob of something hit with a splat on the back of my neck. I thought for sure it was bird shit. I looked up. A blue rain was falling through the streetlamps, and at the Korean deli on the corner a crippled man leaned on a wooden cane, picking through a pyramid of oranges. An old Korean woman sat on a white bucket, cutting the stems on peonies, huge lion-headed flowers with pink petals that shook loose in the wind and were pasted to the wet sidewalk like découpage. Everything seemed to have been given a new coat of varnish sometime in the night. Every wire and railing glistened, and the air was clean and cool. Above the intersection a traffic signal turned green. Several cars went by, their sleepy wipers blinking away the drizzle. Down at the deli the cripple reached into his pocket and paid for the orange, and the old woman went back to cutting her peonies. How could so much peace and calm reign between two people? I balanced on the windowsill and looked back at the ballerina.

She was a mess, ghoulish with a plastering of soot and ash. Her body, crisscrossed with brandings and burned by match heads, looked fully clothed. She'd never be naked again, not with the textile weave of her scars, the plaids and polka dots she'd made of her skin.

She said, "What?"

I hadn't said anything. "Isn't there anything else you like to do?"

"I don't know."

"It's raining out."

"Why?"

"Why?" I said. "Why is it raining?"

The air in the room was stale and as hot as a kiln, the motion baked out of it. I opened another window in the kitchen alcove. Instantly a sort of pulmonary breeze blew a green curtain into the room, expanding the space. I saw a forgotten slice of bread in the chrome slot of her toaster and a used tea bag set to rest on the edge of her sink, the stub of a cigarette going soggy inside it. When I returned to the bedroom the ballerina hadn't moved. She'd sleep in these ashes, like some black-feathered bird. Her back was to me, and I went to her, but the burns covering her body — how would you even hold such a woman? Where exactly do you put your hands on somebody who hurts everywhere? I stopped short. I'd never seen her back before, and it was pristine. The skin was flawless, a cold hibernal blue where her blood flowed beneath. I blew on my fingers, warming them, and then laid my hand between her shoulder blades, lightly, as though to press too hard would leave a print.

"How about cleaning up?" I said.

"Oh," she sniffled. "I don't know."

In the bathroom I plugged the drain with a dry cracked stopper and dialed the spigots until the water running over my wrist was hot and tropical. I looked around at all the ingredients. The stuff in jars looked like penny candy, and I spilled some of that in. The beaded things were especially pretty, and I tossed a combination of yellow and green gel caps in the tub, followed by a pill that effervesced and changed the color of the water to a pale Caribbean blue. I gave up on any idea of alchemy and just went wild. Pine Forest, Prairie Grass, Mountain Snow, Ocean Breeze. Once I got into it, I saw no reason to stop — juniper, vanilla, cranberry. A capful of almond oil, a splash of *bain moussant,* some pink and blue flakes from a box that turned out to be ordinary bubble bath.

"O.K.," I said, closing the bathroom door to trap the steam.

She hadn't budged from her place on the bed. I hooked her arm over my shoulder. For a ballerina she had pretty much zero *ballon* at this point. Her feet dragged across the floor like the last two dodoes. I was afraid that when I lowered her into the tub she'd sink to the bottom. I made her sit upright. With steam curling down from above and a heady lather of bubble bath rising over the edge of the tub, the bathroom was now one massive cumulus cloud.

"A candle," she said.

I snapped the chain on a bare bulb above the sink. "No more candles tonight." I grabbed a soft white cloth from the shelf and sat beside the tub, in a pillow of suds.

"My life is so simple a one-year-old could live it."

"You're just having one of those days," I said. I wrung the washcloth and let the warm water dribble down her chest. "What's up with those old people? Your grandparents?"

"They emigrated here after my mom died."

"Where'd they come from?"

"Yugoslavia," she said. "Bosnia, Herzegovina, Croatia, Serbia, Slovenia, Macedonia, that whole thing."

"You speak their language?"

"Mala kolicina."

I soaped her shoulders and neck, rinsed the cloth and ran it slowly along the length of her arm, studying the scars. I was stupidly surprised when the wounds didn't wash away. A siren passed in the street. Her startled fingers took off in flight, fluttering up from the sea of foam and sailing through the fragrant steam, darting here and there.

"What's wrong with you?" she asked.

"I don't know," I said.

"You must have a diagnosis. Everyone has a diagnosis."

"Well, just before I came to the hospital I spent three hundred dollars on AstroTurf and PVC pipe, trying to build a driving range in my dining room."

"It's your dining room," she said. "You can do what you want."

"I've never owned a golf club in my life."

"Oh."

"Travel brochures are a bad sign, too, but you know what's the worst? Messing with the medications. Like lithium — it makes my hands shake and I can't walk steadily. So I decide to back the lithium off a little and titrate up on something like BuSpar or Lamictal. My hands stop shaking but I can't remember anything or I start eating like a pig. I keep trying, you know, making all these little adjustments, but it's like — I don't know. I don't know what it's like."

"There's no like about it," she said.

"Eventually I can't move. I'll have the thought, Oh, I want to go out, so I put on my hat and stare at the door. Right about then I check into the hospital, they fix me up, send me back out. I kick ass for a while and then collapse."

"You know your diagnosis," she said.

"Whatever — bipolar II, Fruit of the Loom IV, it doesn't make a difference."

"We'll never get out," she said.

"*Au contraire* — I'm getting myself discharged A.M.A., first thing tomorrow."

"But at least we have our own language."

"Yeah, Greek."

"In grade school," she said, "I wrote a report about how a myth was a female moth. We were studying the Greeks."

"You have a beautiful mouth," I said. "I'd like to crawl in it and die."

"I'm twenty-nine years old," she said. "My mouth is full of dead boys." She blew me a kiss. "Sometimes your mind gives me a feeling of great tiredness. Aren't you exhausted?"

"My curfew," I said feebly.

"The fires are going out, it's true." She sank down in the tub and submerged so that only her knees, her small dancer's breasts, her big nose, her lovely mouth and blue eyes, these isolated islands of herself, rose above the darkening water. Flecks of ash floated over the surface. "Here's my idea for your next screenplay," she said. "Sirens are going everywhere. People are weeping. It doesn't really matter where you are, it's all black. You can't open your eyes anyway."

"What are you saying?"

"And there's a donkey marooned on an island in the middle of the ocean. A volcano is erupting on the island and rivers of hot lava are flowing toward the donkey. In addition, all around the small island is a ring of fire. What would you do?"

I considered the possibilities. "I don't know."

Smiling, she said, "The donkey doesn't know, either."

"That's a good one."

She poked at the remaining bubbles with her finger, popping them. I checked my watch. It was midnight on the nose and all that awaited me back at the p-ward was another morning and a long walk down a putty-colored corridor and, at the end of it, a paper cup full of pills. And in a month or a year the ballerina would touch a scar on her breast and tell a rather pointless story about a screenwriter she'd met in the psych ward. Waves of dirty water lapped against the sides of the tub, and her skin, moist and gleaming, was fragrant with wild yam and almond. Then everything went briefly quiet in one of those strange becalmed moments where it's hard to believe you're still in Manhattan.

STUART DYBEK

Breasts

FROM TIN HOUSE

SUNDAYS HAVE ALWAYS been depressing enough without having to do a job. Besides, he's hung-over, so fuck Sunday. Taking somebody out on Sunday is probably bad luck.

And Monday: no wheels. He's got an appointment at the Marvel station on Western with the Indian. That man's a pro — can listen to an engine idle and tell you the wear on the belts, can hear stuff that won't break for months already going bad. The Indian is the only one he lets touch the Bluebird, his powder blue, 312 Y-block, twin Holley, four-barrel T-bird.

Tuesday, it's between Sovereign or hauling more than a month's laundry to the Chink's. Not to mention another hangover. He strips the sheets, balls them into the pillowcases, stuffs in the towels. He's tired of their stink, of his stink, of the dirty clothes all over the floor, all over the apartment. He's been wearing the same underwear how long? He strips naked, pulls off his underwear and socks, stares at himself in the bedroom mirror. His reflection looks smudged and he wipes the mirror with a sock, then he drops to the carpet to do a hundred pushups — that always sharpens the focus.

He does only seventy, and, chest pounding hard enough to remind him that his father's heart gave out at age forty-five, lights a cigarette. He slaps on some Old Spice, slips back into his trousers and shirt without bothering to check the mirror, stuffs another pillowcase with dirty clothes, and, since he's cleaning, starts on the heaps of dishes unwashed for weeks. Then, wham, it hits him: who needs all this shit? Into trash bags go not only pizza cardboards and Chinese food cartons, but bottles, cans, cereal boxes, plates, bowls, glasses, dirty pots. The silverware can stay. Next it's the refrigerator's turn: sour milk, moldy cheese, rancid butter, all the scummy, half-empty bottles of mustard, mayo, pickles, jam, until the fridge is completely empty except for its cruddy shelves.

He removes the shelves.

Now he's got room for the giant mortadella that Sal brought from Italy. Sal came back from his trip bearing gifts and saying, *"Allora!,"* whatever that means. The mortadella is scarred with wounds from another souvenir Sallie brought him, a stiletto. He'd wanted an authentic stiletto for his knife collection, and this one is a piece of work, a slender pearl handle contoured to slide the thumb directly to the switch, and the most powerful spring he's ever seen on a knife. When the six-inch blade darted out, the knife actually recoiled in his hand. It felt as if the blade could shoot through Sheetrock, let alone flesh. He tested it on the mortadella, a thick sausage more muscular than Charles f-ing Atlas. He wondered if the knife could penetrate the rind, and was amazed when the thrust of the spring buried the blade to the hilt. It was a test he found himself repeating, and the mortadella, now propped in the empty refrigerator, looks like it's seen gladiatorial combat, like Julius f-ing Caesar after Brutus got done with him.

Whitey calls. "Joey, you take care of business?"

"Still in the planning stage."

"Well, the decision's been made, you know? Let's not be indecisive on this."

"No problem, Whitey."

Taking care of business. Last Saturday night at Fabio's what Whitey said was "Blow the little skimming fuck's balls off and leave him for the birds."

"Not like there's vultures circling the neighborhood," he told Whitey, and Whitey said, "Joey, it was a manner of fuckin' speaking."

O.K., *allora!* motherfucker, no more procrastination. He can haul out the garbage, drop his laundry at the Chink's, *and* take care of Johnny Sovereign. Let's get this fucking thing over with, even though he hasn't made a plan yet and that's not like him. Things are chancy enough without leaving them to chance. The man who's prepared, who knows exactly what he's going to do, always has the advantage. What seems as inevitable as fate to such a man seems to others like a surprise. Problems invariably arise and he wants to be able to anticipate them, like the Indian who can listen to an engine and hear what will go bad. He wants to see the scars that appear before the wounds that caused them.

With a cotton swab he oils the .22, then sets the Hoppes oil on a glass ashtray on his dresser next to the Old Spice so it doesn't leave a ring, and tests the firing mechanism. He fills the clip with hollow-point shells and slides it into the Astra Cub, a Spanish-made Saturday night special that fits into the pocket of his sport coat. The sport coat is a two-button, powder blue splash — same shade as the Bluebird. He'd conceal the stiletto in his sock, but he's stuffed all his socks into the dirty laundry, which forces him to dig through the pillowcases until he comes up with a black and pink argyle with a good elastic grip to it. He can't find the match, so he puts the argyle on his right foot and a green Gold Toe on the left — nobody's going to be checking his fucking socks — then slides the stiletto along his ankle.

From his bedroom closet he drags out the locked accordion case that belonged to his grandfather. There's a lacquered red accordion inside that came from Lucca, where Puccini lived. In a cache Joe made by carefully detaching the bellows from the keyboard is an emergency roll of bills — seven Gs — and uppers, downers, Demerol, codeine, a pharmacopeia he calls his painkillers. In a way, they're for emergencies, too. Inside the accordion case there's also a sawed-off shotgun, and a Walther PPK like James Bond uses except this one is stolen and the serial number filed off, and a Luger stamped with a swastika, supposedly taken off a dead German officer, which his father kept unloaded and locked away. After his father's death, Joe found ammo for it at a gun show. There's a rubber-banded cigarillo box with photos of girlfriends baring their breasts, breasts of all sizes, shapes, and shades of skin, a collection which currently features Whitey's girlfriend, Gloria Candido, and her silver-dollar nipples. She told Joe that the size of her nipples prevented her from wearing a bikini. It's the kind of photo that could get Joe clipped, but he's gambling that Gloria Candido is clever enough to play Whitey. Whitey's getting old, otherwise a punk-ass like Johnny Sovereign wouldn't be robbing him blind.

Capri St. Clare is in the cigarillo box, too, not that she belongs with the others. Her letters he keeps in his bureau drawer. She was shy about her breasts because the left was wine-stained. No matter that they were beautiful. For her, it was the single flaw that gives a person something to hide. Joe understood that, though he didn't understand her. There's always some vulnerability that a personality is reorganized to protect, a secret that can make a person unpredictable, devious, mysterious. Capri was all those, and still he misses her, misses her in a way that threatens to become his own secret weakness. Her very unpredictability is what he misses. Often enough it seemed like spontaneity. He doesn't have a photo of her breasts, but one surprising afternoon he shot a roll of her blond muff. He'd been kidding her about being a bottle blonde and with uncharacteristic swagger she hiked her skirt, thumbed down her panties, and said, "Next time you want to know is it real or is it Clairol ask them to show you this." She'd been sitting on his windowsill, drinking a Heineken, and when she stood the sun streamed across her body, light adhering not just to her bush but to the golden down on her stomach and thighs, each hair a prism, and a crazy notion possessed him with the force of desire, so strong he almost told her. He wanted to wake to that sight, to start his day to it, to restart his life to it, and maybe end his life to it, too. The breasts could stay stashed in the cigarillo box, but he wanted a blowup on his bedroom wall of her hands, that's what fascinated him, her hands, the right lifting her bunched skirt and the left thumbing down her turquoise panties. He took the roll of film to Walgreens to be developed and when he picked it up, photos were missing. He could tell from the weight of the envelope, but went down the Tooth Care aisle to open it and be sure. He returned to the photo counter and asked the pimply kid with STEVORINO on his nametag who'd waited on him, "You opened these, didn't you? You got something that belongs to me."

"No way," the kid said, his acne blazing up.

"Zit-head, I should smash your face in now, but I don't want pus on my shirt. It's a nice shirt, right? So, see this?" He opened his hand and a black switchblade the width of a garter snake flicked out a silver fang. "I'm going to count to five and, if I don't have the pictures by then, I'm going to cut off Stevo's dickorino right here to break him of the habit of yanking it over another man's intimate moments."

"O.K.," the kid said. "I'm sorry." He reached into the pocket of his Walgreens smock and slid the pictures over, face-down.

"How many of my boob shots have you been snitching, Stevorino? What is it? You think of me as the Abominable Titman, the fucking Hugh Hefner of St. Michael's parish? See me coming in with a roll of Kodak and you get an instant woodie?"

"No, sir," the kid said.

Joe went outside and sat in his idling car, studying the photos, thinking of Capri, of the intensity of being alone with her, of her endless inventions and surprises, but then he thought of her deceptions, their arguments, and her talk of leaving for L.A. It was there, in the car with her photos on the dashboard, that he let her go, accepted, as he hadn't until that moment, that she had to want to stay or it wasn't worth it. He didn't let that distract him from his plan of action, which required watching the Walgreens exit. A plan was the distinction between a man with a purpose and some joker sitting in a car, working himself into a helpless rage. Two hours passed before the kid came out. He was unlocking his bicycle when he saw Joe Ditto.

"Mister, I said I was sorry," the kid pleaded.

"Stevo, when they ask how it happened, say you fell off your bike," Joe said, and, with an economically short blur of a kick, a move practiced in steel-toed factory shoes on a heavy bag, on buckets and wooden planks, hundreds, maybe thousands of times until it was automatic, cracked the kid's kneecap.

He never did get around to making that blowup of Capri. Joe hasn't heard from her in months, which is unlike her, but he knows she'll get in touch, there's too much left unfinished between them for her not to, and until she's back, he doesn't need her muff on the wall.

Tuesday afternoon at the Zip Inn is a blue clothespin day. That's the color that Roman Ziprinski, owner and one-armed bartender, selects from the plastic clothespins clamped to the wire of Christmas lights that hang year-round above the cash register. With the blue clothespin Zip fastens the empty right sleeve of his white shirt that he's folded as neatly as one folds a flag.

It's an afternoon when the place is empty. Just Zip and, on the TV above the bar, Jack Brickhouse, the play-by-play announcer for the Cubs. The Cubbies are losing again, this time to the Pirates. It's between innings, and Brickhouse says it's a good time for a Hamm's, the official beer of the Chicago Cubs.

"Official," Zip says to Brickhouse, "that's pretty impressive, Jack."

To the tom-tom of a tribal drum the Hamm's theme song plays: *From the land of sky blue waters,* and Zip hums along, *from the land of pine and lofty balsam comes the beer refreshing, Hamm's the beer refreshing . . .*

Hamm's is brewed in Wisconsin. Zip has a place there, way up on Lac Court Oreilles in the Chain of Lakes region famous for muskies. It's a little fisherman's cottage no one knows he has, where he goes to get away from the city. A land of sky blue waters is what Zip dreamed about during the war. Daydreamed, this is. If he could have controlled his night dreams, those would have been of sky blue water, too, instead of the nightmares and insomnia that began after he was wounded and continued for years. Sometimes, like last night, Zip still wakes in a sweat as sticky as blood, with the stench of burning flesh lingering in his nostrils, to the tremors of a fist hammering a chest — a medic's desperate attempt to jump-start a dead body. No matter how often that dream recurs, Zip continues to feel shocked when in the dark he realizes the chest is his, and the fist pounding it is attached to his missing right arm.

When he joined the Marines out of high school, his grandmother gave him a rosary blessed in Rome to wear like a charm around his neck and made him promise to pray. But Zip's true prayer was one that led him into the refuge of a deep northern forest, a place he'd actually been only once, as a child, on a fishing trip with his father. He summoned that place from his heart before landings and on each new day of battle and on patrol as, sick with dysentery, he slogged through what felt like poisonous heat with seventy pounds of flamethrower on his back. He'd escape the stench of shit and the hundreds of rotting corpses that the rocky coral terrain of Peleliu made impossible to bury, into a vision of cool, fresh water and blue-green shade scented with pine. When I make it through this, that's where I'm going, he vowed to himself. Sky blue water was the dream he fought for — his private American Dream. And so is the Zip Inn, his own tavern in the old neighborhood. He's his own boss here. Zip uncaps a Hamm's. It's on the house. The icy bottle sweats in his left hand. He raises it to his lips and lets it suds down his throat: he came back missing an arm, but hell, a lot of guys didn't come back at all.

He can't control his night dreams, but, during the day, Zip

makes it a practice not to think about the war. Today he wishes for a customer to come in and give him something else to think about. The pounding in his temples has Zip worrying about his blood pressure. He has the urge to take a dump, but knows his bowels are faking it. The symptoms of stress bring back Peleliu — the way his bowels cramped as the amtrac slammed toward the beach. They lost a third of the platoon on a beachhead called Rocky Point to a butchering mortar barrage that splintered the coral rock into razors of shrapnel. Zip stands wondering how does a man in a place so far from home summon up whatever one wants to call it — courage, duty, insanity — in the face of that kind of carnage, and then say nothing when two goombahs from across Western Avenue come into *his* place, the Zip Inn, and tell him it would be good business to rent a new jukebox from them. Instead of throwing those parasites out, he said nothing. Nothing.

Only a two-hundred-dollar initial installation fee, they told him.

Two of them smelling of after-shave: a fat guy, Sal, the talker, and Joe — he'd heard of Joe — a psycho with a Tony Curtis haircut and three-day growth of beard, wearing a sharkskin suit and factory steel-toes. The two hoods together like a pilot fish and a shark.

"Then every month only fifty for service," fat Sal said, "and that includes keeping up with all the new hits. And we service the locked coin box so you won't have to bother. Oh yeah, and to make sure nobody tries to mess with the machine we guarantee its protection — only twenty-five a month for that — and believe me, when we say protection we mean protection. Nobody will fuck with your jukebox. Or your bar."

"So you're saying I pay you seventy-five a month for something I pay fifteen for now. I mean the jukebox don't net me more than a few bucks," Zip told them. "It's for the enjoyment of my customers. You're asking me to lose money on this."

"You ain't getting protection for no fifteen bucks," Sal said.

"Protection from what?" Zip asked.

The hoods looked at each other and smiled. *"Allora!"* Sal shrugged to Joe, then told Zip, "A nice little setup like you got should be protected."

"I got Allstate," Zip said.

"See, that kind of insurance pays *after* something happens — a break-in, vandalism, fire. The kind we're talking here guarantees nothing like that is going to happen in the first place. All the other taverns in the neighborhood are getting it too. You don't want to be odd man out."

"A two-hundred-dollar installation fee?" Zip asked.

"That covers it."

"Some weeks I don't clear more than that."

"Come on, man, you should make that in a night. Start charging for the eggs," Sal said, helping himself to one. "And what's with only six bits for a shot and a beer? What kinda businessman are you? Maybe you'd like us to set up a card game in your back room on Fridays. And put in a pinball machine. We're getting those in the bars around here, too."

"Installation was fifty for the box I got. Service is fifteen a month."

Joe, the guy in the sharkskin suit, rose from his bar stool and walked over to the jukebox. He read the selections aloud: "Harbor Lights," "Blue Moon," "The She's Too Fat Polka," "CuCuRoo CuCu Paloma," "Sing, Sing, Sing" . . .

"These songs are moldy, man," Joe said. "Where's Sinatra, where's Elvis the Pelvis? Your jukebox dealer's a loser. They're gonna be out of business in a year. Their machines ain't dependable. Sallie, got a coin?"

"Here, on me," Zip said, reaching into the till.

"No, no, Sallie's got it."

"Yeah, I got it," Sal said, flipping the coin to Joe.

"Requests, Mr. Zip?" Joe asked.

"I hear it anytime I want."

"So what's your favorite song?"

"Play 'Sing, Sing, Sing,'" Sal said, yolk spitting from his mouth. "Did you know Benny Goodman's a yid from Lawndale? Lived on Francisco before the *tutsones* moved in."

Joe dropped in the coin and punched some buttons. Zip could hear from the dull clunk that the coin was a slug.

"Goddamn thing ate my quarter!" Joe exclaimed. "I fuckin' hate when machines snitch from me. Those new newspaper boxes are the worst. Selling papers used to be a job for blind guys and crips. No offense, Mr. Zip, I'm just saying a paper stand was decent work for these people, and then they put in newspaper boxes and not only does it turn crips into beggars, but the fucking boxes rob you.

I'm trying to buy a *Trib* the other day and the box eats my quarter. No change, no nothing. You think maybe a fucking Republican paper like the *Trib* rigs its box to screw you? Know what I did to that newspaper box?"

"Here," Zip said. "Here's a refund."

"But, see, Mr. Zip, it's bad business you having to cover for these lousy fucking jukes. You know if you whack them just right it's like hitting the jackpot." Joe kicked the jukebox knee-high and its lights blinked out. From the crunch, Zip knew he'd kicked in the speaker. "No jackpot? Well, guess it ain't my lucky day." Joe laughed. "So listen, Mr. Zip, we got a deal to shake on?" Joe extended his hand. Then, eyeing Zip's clothespinned sleeve, Joe withdrew his right hand and extended his left.

"Let me think it over," Zip said. He didn't offer his hand. He wasn't trying to make a statement. It was the only hand he had.

"No problem," Joe said. "No pressure. Give it some careful thought. I'll come by next week, maybe Friday, and you can give me your answer." He pulled out a roll of bills, peeled off a twenty, and set it on the mess of eggshells Sal had left on the bar. "For the egg."

Big shots leaving a tip stolen from the pocket of some workingman. After they walked out of his bar, Zip snapped open his lighter and watched the burning twenty turn the eggshells sooty. In the war, he'd operated an M2 flamethrower. They must have figured a kid his size could heft it, not just lug the napalm-filled tanks, but brace against the backward thrust of the jetting flame. The flame had a range of only thirty yards, so Zip had to crawl close to the mouths of caves and apertures of pillboxes, close enough to smell the bodies burning. It made him an easy target. Each pillbox was its own beachhead. For the Japs it was death rather than dishonor, a warrior code called *bushido*. It made them seem crazy, alien, inhuman: gooks. But now, when Zip sees neighborhood kids killing and dying over who's wearing what gang colors, or mob goons like Joe Ditto, he wonders if whatever code they live by is any less fucked than *bushido*?

He thought he'd paid the price to live in peace, yet here in the old neighborhood, U.S.A., Zip stands behind the bar powerless while the days tick down to when Joe Ditto comes back. Zip could call the cops, but he can't prove anything, and besides, hoods wouldn't be canvassing taverns if the cops weren't on the take. Calling the cops would be stupid. What if he merely closed down the bar, packed his Chevy, and drove for sky blue waters, disappeared into green shadow and mist? But Zip knows from experience, that's a daydream.

Whitey calls in the middle of a dream.

Little Julio is supposed to be in his room practicing, but he's playing his flute in the bedroom doorway. Julio's mother, Gloria Candido, is wearing a pink see-through nightie, and Joe can't believe she lets Little Julio see her like that because Little Julio is not *that* little and he's just caught Joe circumnavigating Gloria's nipples with his tongue and Little Julio wants some, too. "He's playing his nursing song," Gloria says. The flute amplifies the kid's breath until it's as piercing as an alarm. To shut him up, Joe gropes for the phone.

"Joe," Whitey says, "what's going on?"

Drugged on dream, Joe wakes to his racing heart. "What?" he says, even though he hates guys who say *what* or *huh*. It's a response that reveals weakness.

"Whatayou mean *what*? What the fuck? You know *what*. What's with you?"

What day is this? Joe wants to ask, but he knows that's the wrong thing to say, so instead he says, "I had a weird night."

"Joe, are you fuckin' on drugs?"

"No," Joe says. He's coming out of his fog and it occurs to him that Whitey can't possibly be calling about Gloria Candido. A confrontation on the phone is not how Whitey would handle something like that. Whitey wouldn't let on he knew. "Well, what's the problem, then?" Whitey demands.

It's Johnny Sovereign that Whitey is calling about, and as soon as Joe realizes that, his heart stops racing. "Ran into a minor complication. I went to see him yesterday and . . ."

"Maronn!" Whitey yells. "Joe, we're on the fucking phone here. I don't care what the dipshit excuses are, just fucking get it done."

"Hey, Whitey, suck this," Joe says, and puts the receiver to his crotch. "Who the fuck do you think you're yelling at, you vain old sack of shit with your wrinkled *minchia*. Your girlfriend's slutting around behind your back making a fucking *cornuto* of you. You don't like it, I'll cut you, I'll bleed you like a stuck pig."

Joe says all that to the dial tone. Telling off the dial tone doesn't leave him feeling better, just the opposite, and he makes a rule on the spot: never again talk to dial tones after someone's hung up on you. It's like talking to mirrors. Mirrors have been making him nervous lately. There's a dress draped over his bedroom mirror and Joe gets out of bed and looks through the apartment for the woman to go with it. That would be April. She's nowhere to be found and for a moment Joe wonders if she's taken his clothes and left him her dress. But his clothes are piled on the chair beside the bed where he stripped them off — shoes, trousers with keys and wallet, sport coat with the .22 weighting one pocket. He's naked but for his mismatched socks. The stiletto is still sheathed in the black and pink argyle.

Yesterday was supposed to have been a cleanup day. His plan was to pitch the trash, drop his laundry at the Chink's, and then to stop by Johnny Sovereign's house on Twenty-fifth Street. The plan depended on Sovereign not being home, so Joe called from a pay phone and Sovereign's good-looking young wife answered and said Johnny would be back around 4:00. O.K., things were falling into place. Joe would wait in the gangway behind Sovereign's house for him to come home, and suggest they go for a drink in order to discuss Johnny setting up gambling nights in the back rooms of some of the local taverns. Once Joe got Sovereign alone in the car, well, he'd have to improvise from there.

So around 3:00 in the afternoon, Joe parked beside the rundown one-car garage behind Sovereign's house. The busted garage door gaped open and he saw that Sovereign's Pontiac Bonneville was gone. Bonnevilles with their 347-cubic-inch engines that could do zero to sixty in eight-point-one were the current badass car — in Little Village, they call them Panchos. Sovereign's splurging on that car was what made Whitey suspect he was skimming on the numbers. New wheels and already leaking oil, Joe thought, as he looked at the warped, bird shit–crusted floorboards of the garage. If Sovereign wasn't careless and all for show, he'd have taken that Pancho to the Indian.

Johnny Sovereign's back fence was warped, too, and overgrown with morning glories. His wife must have planted them. She'd made an impression on Joe the one time he'd been inside their house. Johnny had invited him in and they'd gone the back way, the entrance Joe figures it's Johnny's habit to use. Johnny didn't bother to announce their arrival and they caught his wife — Vi, that was her name — vacuuming in her slip. When she saw Joe standing there a blush heated her bare shoulders before she ran into the bedroom. She was wearing a pale yellow slip. Joe would have liked to slide its thin straps down her skinny arms to see if her blush mottled her breasts the way some women flush when they come. Sovereign's Pontiac was yellow, too, but canary yellow, and Joe wondered if there was some connection between Vi's slip and the car.

He sat in the Bluebird and lit a cigarette, then unscrewed the top from a pinch bottle of Scotch and washed down a couple painkillers. He could hear sparrows twittering on the wires and pigeons doing owl imitations inside Sovereign's shitty garage. The alley was empty except for the humped, hooded figure of a woman slowly approaching in the rearview mirror — a bag lady in a black winter coat and babushka, stopping to inspect each trash can. Except for the stink of trash, Joe didn't mind the waiting. He needed time to think through his next moves. From where he parked, he could watch the gangway and intercept Sovereign before he entered the house. He'd ask Sovereign to have a drink and Sovereign would want to know where. "Somewhere private," Joe would tell him. And then — wham — it came to Joe, as it always did, how he'd work it. He'd tell Sovereign, "Let's take *your* wheels. I want to ride in a new yellow Bonneville." He'd bring the bottle of Scotch, a friendly touch, and suggest they kill it on the deserted side street where the dragsters raced. Sovereign could show him what the Pancho could do there. He couldn't think of a way to get the shotgun into Sovereign's car, so he'd have to forget about that. Joe was scolding himself for not thinking it all through earlier when a woman's voice startled him.

"Hi, Joe, got an extra smoke?"

"What are you doing here?" Joe asked.

"Trying to bum a Pall Mall off an old lover," April said. "You still smoke Pall Malls, don'tcha?"

Her hair was bleached corn silk blond and she wore a dress the shade of morning glories. Joe wondered how she'd come down the alley without him seeing her. The neckline exposed enough cleavage so that he could see a wingtip from the tiny blue seagull tattooed on her left breast. She looked more beautiful than he'd re-membered.

"I thought you went to Vegas," he said. "I heard you got married to some dealer at Caesars." He didn't add that he'd also heard she'd OD'd.

"Married? *Me?*" She showed him her right hand: nails silvery pink, a cat's-eye on her index finger going from gray to green the way her eyes did. Joe lifted her palm and leaned to kiss the pale band of flesh where a wedding ring would have been, but he paused when sunlight hit her hand in a way that made it appear freckled and old with dirty, broken fingernails. She brought her hand the rest of the way and sighed when it met his lips.

"You used to do that thing with my hand that would drive me crazy," April said.

"Hey, we were kids," Joe said.

He'd worked back then for a towing service Whitey ran and he met April when he went to tow her Chevy from a private lot off Rush Street. He'd traded not towing her car for a date. She was a senior at Our Lady of Lourdes High, still a virgin, and on the first date she informed him that she was sorry, but she didn't put out. That was the phrase she'd used. Joe had laughed and told her, "Sweetheart, it's not like I even asked you. And anyway, there's other things than *putting out*." "Such as?" April asked, and from that single question, Joe knew he had her. It was nothing about him in particular, she was just ready. "Imagine the knuckles on your fingers are knees and the knuckles on your hands are breasts," Joe had told her, extending her index and middle fingers into a V and outlining an imaginary torso with his finger. "O.K., I see. So?" she asked. "So this," he whispered, and kissed the insides of her fingers, then licked their webbing. She watched him as if amused, then closed her eyes. Even after she was putting out three times a day, nothing got her more excited than when he kissed her hand. "Lover," she'd once told him, "that goes right to my pussy."

"Aren't you going to ask me if I'm still using?" April asked. "I'm clean. And I been thinking about you ever since I've been back in the neighborhood. I'm staying with my sister, Renee. Remember her? She had a crush on you, too. I dreamed last night I'd find you here and when I woke I thought, Forget it, you can't trust dreams, but then I thought, What the hell, all that will happen is I'll feel foolish."

"You dreamed of meeting me here?" Joe asked.

"Amazing, huh? Like the commercial, you know? 'I dreamed I met my old boyfriend in an alley, wearing my Maidenform bra.' Nice ride," she said, gliding her fingertips along the Bluebird like stroking a cat. She came around the passenger side, climbed in, leaned back into the leather seat, and sighed. "Just you, me, and a thousand morning glories."

Joe flicked away his cigarette and kissed her.

"You taste good, like Scotch," she said.

He reached for the pinch bottle and she took a sip and kissed him, letting the warm liquor trickle from her mouth into his.

"What are *you* doing here?" she asked.

"That information wasn't in your dream?"

"In my dream you were a lonely void waiting for your soul mate." April took another sip of Scotch and swallowed it this time. "Maybe we should have a private homecoming party," she said.

Joe remembers driving with April down the alleys back to his place, stopping on the way for a fifth of Bacardi and a cold six-pack of tonic water, and later, covering his kitchen table with Reynolds Wrap and laying out the lines of coke. He remembers the *plink* of blood on foil when her nose began to bleed, and April calling from the bathroom, "Joe, where's all the towels?"

"Forgot to pick them up from the Chink's."

"No towels, no sheets. You sure you live here? Good thing I'm not hungry. What's in the fridge? Anything at all? I dread to look."

They lay soul-kissing on the bare mattress while darkness edged up his bedroom walls. How still the city suddenly sounded. Between shrieks of nighthawks, an accordion faintly wheezed from some open window. Joe's bedroom window was open, too, and a breeze that tingled the blinds they hadn't bothered to draw seemed tinted with the glow of the new arc lights the city had erected. Before the mirror, April, streaked in bluish glow, undid her ponytail. Mimicked by a reflection, deep in the dark glass, she slipped her dress over her head. No Maidenform bra. He came up behind her and bit her shoulders. He could see what appeared to be disembodied blue hands — his hands — cupping her luminous breasts. Otherwise he was a shadow. His thumb traced the tiny seagull flying across her breast. In the mirror it looked graceless, like an insignia a gang punk might have India-inked on his forearm. Her reflection appeared suddenly to surge to the surface of the glass, and he could see that the mirror was blemished with hairline fractures superimposed on her face like wrinkles. She flipped the dress she was still holding over the mirror as if to snuff a chemical reaction. It snuffed the residual light, and in the darkness he could feel something flying wildly around the room, and they lost their balance, banged off a wall, and fell to the bare mattress. She took his cock, fit it in, crammed his fingers in her mouth, then brought her free hand, smelling of herself, to his lips.

Joe remembers all that, but none of it — the booze, the coke, the Demerol, the waking up repeatedly in the dark already fucking — explains how it could be nearly 3:00 P.M., or what her dress is doing left behind. He yanks the dress off the mirror and is surprised to find a crack zigzagging down the center. Maybe it was the mirror they'd staggered into. He staggers into the kitchen, washes down a couple painkillers with what's left in a bottle of flat tonic water, then palms Old Spice on his face and under his arms, tugs on his clothes, and dials Sovereign's number. He knows it's not a good idea to be calling from his place, but that can't be helped. When Vi answers on the second ring, he asks, "Johnny there?"

"He'll be home around four," she says. "Can I tell him who's calling?"

Joe hangs up.

From the closet, he digs out a gym bag stuffed with dirty gym gear and canvas gloves for hitting the heavy bag. He lifts the mirror from the bedroom wall, bundles it in the dress, totes it into the alley, and sets it beside the garbage cans, then throws the gym bag into the Bluebird. Joe drives down the alleys, formulating an idea of how to get the shotgun into Sovereign's car. Off Twenty-fifth he scatters a cloud of pigeons and nearly sideswipes a blind old bag lady in a babushka and dark glasses, who's feeding them. A little after 3:00 P.M., he pulls behind Sovereign's house. Joe can smell the baking motor oil spotting the warped floorboards of the empty, run-down garage. Demerol tends to heighten his sense of smell. Wind rustling down the alley leaves an aftertaste of rotten food and all the mildewed junk people pitch. He makes sure the alley is empty, then slips the sawed-off shotgun from under the seat and buries it in the gym bag, beneath his workout gear. The bottle of Scotch rests on top, and as he zips the bag, the whiff of old gym sweat vanishes in a gust of a sweet, familiar perfume.

When Joe looks up, Marisol stands as if she's emerged from the morning glories. She has a white flower in her auburn hair. Her flower scent obliterates the mix of pigeons, garbage, and motor oil he's come to associate with Johnny Sovereign. She's dressed in white cotton x-rayed by sunlight: shirt opened a button beyond modest, tied in a knot above her exposed navel, and tight white toreador pants. The laces of the wedged shoes he used to call her goddess sandals snake around her ankles. Her oversized shades seem necessary to shield her from her own brightness.

"See you're still driving the B-bird," she says, sauntering toward the car. "That's cute how you name your cars. Kind of surprisingly boyish of you, Joe, though when you first told me your car had a name, know what I thought? I thought, Oh no, don't let this be one of those pathetic jerks who names his penis, too. And, hey, I like the color-coordinated touch with the sport coat. That splash pattern is perfect for eating spaghetti with tomato sauce. Recognize the shirt? It's yours. Want it back?"

Wounded wing, how strange to fall from blue. Like a fish that suddenly forgets the way to swim. When men fly, they know, by instinct, they defy. But to a bird, as to a god, nothing's more natural than sky . . .

Needing somewhere to think about the lyrics to the song he's composing to a nonstop percussion in his mind, not to mention needing a cold brew, Teo gimps out of daylight into the Zip Inn. A slab of sunshine extends from the doorway. Beyond it, the dimness of the narrow shotgun barroom makes the flowing blue water of the illuminated Hamm's beer sign on the back wall look like a mirage. The TV screen flickers with white static that reflects off the photos of the local softball teams decorating the walls. Teo doesn't remove his dark glasses. Zip, the folded right sleeve of his white shirt fastened with a yellow clothespin, stands behind the bar before a bottle of whiskey and raises a shot glass.

"*Qué pasa, amigo!*" Zip says, a little loudly given there's just the two of them.

"*Nada, hombre.*" Teo is surprised to see him drinking alone in the afternoon. Alcoholism is an occupational hazard for bartenders, but Zip has always seemed immune.

"Knee acting up? Have one with me," Zip says, filling a second shot glass.

"What's the occasion?" Teo hooks his cane on the lip of the bar, carefully sets down the bowling bag he's carrying, and eases onto the stool beside it.

"Today is Thursday," Zip says, "and if you ask me, and I know nobody did, Thursday's a reason for celebrating."

"To Thursday," Teo says. *"Salud!"*

"Na zdrowie," Zip answers. He draws a couple beer chasers.

"Let me get the beers," Teo says, laying some bills on the bar. Zip ignores his money.

After a meditative swallow, Teo asks, "TV broke?"

"No game today," Zip says. "Giants are in tomorrow. You work Goldblatt's?"

"No, Leader Store," Teo says. He pushes a dollar at Zip. "At least let me buy a bag of pretzels."

"I heard Leader's is going under. Any shoplifters even there to pinch?" Zip asks, ringing up the pretzels.

"A kid in Pets trying to steal one of those hand-painted turtles. A pink polka-dotted turtle."

"Give him the full nelson?" Zip asks.

"Only the half nelson. He was just a grade-schooler."

"I think the dress disguise actually reduces your effectiveness, my friend. I mean if there was a problem in my tavern, you know, say theoretically speaking, somebody pocketing eggs —"

"The eggs are free," Teo says.

"Then pretzels, say I got a problem with some pretzel sneak thief, so I hire you and you're sitting here, supposedly undercover, in a polka-dotted dress wearing a wig and dark glasses and a cane and maybe smoking a cigar. I mean, you wouldn't be fooling nobody. It might be a deterrent, but not a disguise. You might as well be sitting there in your secret wrestler's getup. Whatever the hell it is."

"Amigo, you really want to see the wrestler's outfit?"

"Why not?" Zip says. "Liven things up. This place could use a little muscle."

"You'd be disappointed. And, by the way, it was the turtle with the polka dots, not the dress."

Lately, Teo has been stopping at the Zip Inn on weekday afternoons when the bar is mostly empty. Zip seems to know when Teo is in a mood to sit reading or simply to sink into his own thoughts and leaves him alone then, but other times they swap stories. Zip has told Teo hilarious tales of the world-record muskies he's lost, and Teo, trying to make his story funny, too, told Zip how his knee was injured when he was thrown from the ring onto the pavement during an outdoor wrestling match.

"You mean like those masked wrestlers when they set up a ring on Nineteenth Street for Cinco de Mayo?" Zip had asked. "What are they called?"

"*Luchadores*," Teo told him.

"So, you're a . . . *luchador* . . . with a secret masked identity?" Zip had sounded genuinely curious.

"Not anymore," Teo had answered.

Now, from the bowling bag, Teo pulls the hem of the dress he dons occasionally as part of his store security job. It's the dress they gave him when he began working for Goldblatt's — blue paisley, not polka dots — and, contrary to Zip's wisecracks, Teo has caught so many shoplifters that he's begun moonlighting at Leader Store on his days off.

"Yeah, this one is more you," Zip says, fingering the fabric, then asks, "What the hell else you got in there?"

Teo lifts out the pigeon.

This morning, he tells Zip, on his way to work he found the pigeon — a blue checker cock, *Columba affinis* — dragging its wounded wing down an alley, and took it with him to Leader's, kept it in an empty parrot cage in Pets, fed it water and the hemp seed he carries with him as a treat for his own birds. Teo thinks of it as the Spanish pigeon. He doesn't mention the message, in Spanish, that he found tied to its unhanded leg.

"So it ain't one of your birds?" Zip asks.

"No." Teo shakes his head. He's told Zip how he keeps a *palomar* — a pigeon loft — on the roof of the three-story building on Blue Island Avenue where he rents a room, but he hasn't told Zip about the messages arriving there either. Teo hasn't told anyone but the sax player, and he's gone missing. Over the last month, Teo's pigeons have been coming home with scraps of paper fastened with red twine to their banded legs. The first message arrived on a misty day, attached to the leg of one of his bronzed archangels. It wasn't Teo who noticed it but the sax player, Lefty Antic, who practiced his saxophone on the roof. Teo untied the message and he and Lefty

read the smeared ink: *marlin*. "Mean anything to you?" Lefty Antic
had asked.

"Just a big fish, man," Teo told him.

"Maybe it's his name, Marlin the Pigeon," Lefty Antic said.

"No," Teo said, "they don't tell us their names."

The next morning, slipped under his door, Teo found 250 dollars in crisp bills rubber-banded in a folded page from a Sportsman
Park harness racing form with *Merlin* circled in the fourth race,
and a note that read, *Thanks for the tip. Lefty.*

Teo saved the winnings and the message in a White Owl Cigar
box. A few days later, out of a drizzle, a second, barely legible message arrived fastened to one of his racing homers. So far as Teo
could tell, it read: *tibet.* He took the message and half his winnings
and knocked on Lefty Antic's door. There was no answer and Teo
had turned to go when the door opened, emitting the smell of marijuana. The sax player looked hung-over, unshaven, eyes bloodshot, and Teo was sorry he'd disturbed him, but Lefty Antic insisted
he come in. Together they studied the harness races in the newspaper and found a seven-to-one shot named Tidbit in the fifth race.
There was also a buggy driver, J. Tippets, racing in the third and
eighth races. Lefty decided they'd better bet both the horse and
the driver and went to book it with Johnny Sovereign. That night,
Teo had a dream in which his cousin Alaina was riding him. She
hadn't aged — the same bronze-skinned, virgin body he'd spy on
through the bird shit–splattered skylight on the roof in El Paso
where his uncle, Jupo, kept a *palomar.* Uncle Jupo had taken him in
when Teo was fourteen after his mother had run off with a cowboy.
It became Teo's job to care for his uncle's pigeons. He was seventeen when Uncle Jupo caught him on the roof with his trousers
open, spying on Alaina in her bath. His uncle knocked him down
and smashed Teo's face into the pebbled roof as if trying to grind
out his eyes, then sent him packing with eight dollars in his pocket.
Alaina still looked so young that Teo was ashamed even to have
dreamed it. The pain of her love bites woke him at dawn, and even
after waking, his nipples ached from the fierce way her small teeth
had pulled at his body, as if his flesh was taffy. Waiting under his
door was an envelope with eight hundred dollars and a note: *It was
the driver. Thanks, Lefty.*

The third message arrived in a rainstorm. *Lonestar.* Teo woke

Lefty Antic out of a drunken stupor. They pored over the harness races, but the only possibility was a driver named T. North whose first name, Lefty thought, was Tex, and whose last name suggested the North Star. Then they checked the thoroughbreds at Arlington, and found a long shot named Bright Venus. "The Evening Star!" Lefty said, smiling. Track conditions would be sloppy, and Bright Venus was a mudder. Lefty had the shakes so bad he could barely get dressed, but, convinced it was the score they'd been building to, he went off to lay their bets with Sovereign. Teo bet a thousand to win. That night he had a nightmare that he was in El Paso, where he'd began his career as a *luchador* wrestling on the Lucha Libre circuit at fiestas and rodeos. In the dream he was wrestling the famous Ernesto "La Culebra" Aguirre, the Snake, named for the plumed serpent, Quetzalcoatl, the Aztec god of human sacrifice. Lucha Libre wrestlers often took the names of superheroes and Aztec warriors, and Teo once really had wrestled the Snake, though not in El Paso. That match was in Amarillo, back in the days when Teo was making a name for himself as a masked *luchador* called the Hummingbird. He'd come upon his identity in an illustrated encyclopedia of the gods of Mexico. The Hummingbird was Huitzilopochtli, the Mayan sun god; the illustration showed a hawklike warrior bird rising from a thorny maguey plant. Huitzilopochtli's sacred colors were sun white and sky blue, so those were the colors of the costume — mask, tank top, and tights — that Teo wore. When Teo put on the mask he'd feel transformed by a surge of energy and strength. As the Hummingbird, he defied the limitations of his body and performed feats that marveled the crowds. He flew from the ropes, survived punishing falls, and lifted potbellied fighters twice his size high off their feet and slammed them into submission. To keep his identity secret, he would put his mask on miles from the ring, and afterward he wore it home. The night before bouts he took to sleeping in his mask. It was at a carnival in El Paso that he saw Alaina again, standing ringside with a group of high school friends, mostly boys. It had been three years since his uncle had thrown him out without giving him a chance to say goodbye to her. The boys must have come to see the *rudo* billed as El Huracan — the Hurricane — but known to fans as El Flatoso for his flatulence in the ring. El Flatoso, with his patented move of applying a head scissors, then gassing his opponent into unconsciousness, was beloved by high school boys and drunks. Teo had been prepared to be part of the farce of fighting him until he saw Alaina in the crowd. He could feel her secretly watching him through her half-lowered eyelashes with the same intensity he knew she'd watched him when he'd spied on her through the skylight. Suddenly, the vulgar spectacle he was about to enact was intolerable. The match was supposed to last for a half-hour, but when El Flatoso came clownishly farting across the ring, the Hummingbird whirled up and delivered a spinning kick that knocked the *rudo* senseless. He didn't further humiliate El Flatoso by stripping off his mask, and the boys at ringside cursed, demanding their money back, before dejectedly dragging Alaina off with them. But he saw her look back and wave, and he bowed to her. Later that night, there was a light rap on the door of the trailer that served as his dressing room. Alaina stood holding a bottle of mescal. "Don't take it off," she whispered as he began to remove his mask. Though they'd yet to touch, she stood unbuttoning her blouse. "I don't believe this is happening," he said, and she answered, "Unbelievable things happen to people on the edge." She spoke like a woman, not a girl, and, when she unhooked her bra, her breasts were a woman's, full, tipped with nipples the shade of roses going brown, not the buds of the girl he'd spied on. He knelt before her and kissed her dusty feet. She raised her skirt and he buried his face in her woman smell. He wanted the mask off so he could smear his cheeks with her. "Leave it on," she commanded, "or I'll have to go." He rose kissing up her body, until his lips suckled her breasts and their warm, sweet-sour sweat coated his tongue, and suddenly her sighs turned to a cry. "No, too sensitive," she whispered, pushing him gently away, then she opened his shirt and kissed him back hard, fiercely biting and sucking his nipples as if he were a woman. "My *guainambi*," she said, using the Indian word for hummingbird. It was months before he saw her again, this time at a rodeo in Amarillo — a long way from El Paso — where he stood in the outdoor ring waiting for his bout with the Snake. The loose white shirt she wore didn't conceal her pregnancy and for a moment he wondered if the child could be his, then realized she'd already been with child when she'd knocked on his trailer door. La Culebra, in his plumed sombrero, rainbow-sequined cape, and feathered boa, was the star of the Lucha Libre circuit, and it had been agreed that the

Hummingbird was to go down to his first defeat in a close match that would leave his honor intact so that a rivalry could be built. But when Teo saw Alaina there ringside, he couldn't accept defeat. He and the Snake slammed each other about the ring, grappling for the better part of an hour under a scorching sun with Teo refusing to be pinned, and finally in a clinch the Snake told him, "It's time, *pendejo,* stop fucking around," and locked him in his signature move, the boa constrictor. But the Hummingbird slipped it and when the Snake slingshotted at him off the ropes, the Hummingbird spun up into a helicopter kick. The collision dropped them both on their backs in the center of the ring. "Cocksucker, this isn't El Flatoso you're fucking with," the Snake told him as he rose spitting blood. The legend surrounding La Culebra was that he had once been a heavyweight boxer. He'd become a *luchador* only after he'd killed another boxer in the ring, and when he realized they weren't following the script, he used his fists. The first punch broke Teo's nose and blood discolored his white and blue mask, swelling like a blood blister beneath the fabric. The usual theatrics disappeared, and it became a street fight that had the fans on their feet cheering, a battle that ended with the Snake flinging the Hummingbird from the ring. The fall fractured Teo's kneecap, his head bounced off the pavement, and as he lay stunned, unable to move for dizziness and pain, the Snake leaped down onto his chest from the height of the ring, stomping the breath from his body, and tore off the bloodied mask of the Hummingbird as if skinning him, then spat in his flattened face. Teo, his face a mask of blood, looked up into the jeering crowd, but he never saw Alaina again.

In Teo's nightmare, not only did the Snake humiliate him by tearing off his Hummingbird mask and exposing his identity to the crowd, but, derisively shouting *"Las tetas!,"* he also tore off Teo's tank top, exposing a woman's breasts weeping milky tears. At dawn, when Teo groaned out of his dream, with his stomped, body-slammed chest aching and his heart a throbbing bruise, there was no envelope of winnings waiting. That morning, Teo knocked repeatedly on Lefty Antic's door without an answer. The thought occurred to him that the saxophone player had taken off with their money, not out of crookedness, but on a drunken binge. It was only in the afternoon, when Teo bought a newspaper and checked the racing scores at Arlington, that he learned Bright Venus had finished dead last. He checked the harness results at Sportsman's and there was a story about a buggy overturning in the third race and its driver, Toby North, being critically injured when a trotting horse crushed his chest.

It seemed as if a vicious practical joke had been played on them all, but when the next message came, Teo knocked again on Lefty Antic's door. He hadn't seen the saxophone player since Lefty had staggered out to place their bets on Bright Venus. There still was no answer, and Teo, filled with a terrible sense of abandonment and foreboding, and sure that Lefty Antic was dead inside, got the landlord to open the door, only to find the room empty and orderly. Alone, feeling too apprehensive to simply ignore the message, Teo studied the racing pages looking for clues as he'd seen Lefty Antic do. It seemed likely to him that the new rain-smudged message, *delay plaza*, referred to the mayor, Richard Daley, and when he could find no connection whatsoever at any of the racetracks, he took the el train downtown. There wasn't a Daley Plaza in Chicago, but there was an open square near City Hall and Teo walked there, not sure what he was looking for, yet hoping to recognize it when he saw it. But no sign presented itself, nothing was going on in the square but a rally for a young senator from Massachusetts, an Irish-Catholic like the mayor, who was running for president in a country that Teo figured would never elect a Catholic.

The messages have continued to arrive, and Teo continues to save them, and the cigar box fills with scraps of paper his pigeons have brought home from God knows where. Teo can't shake the foreboding or the loneliness. His sleep is haunted by the recurrent dream of a funeral that extends the length of a country of ruined castles and burning ghettos from which he wakes and, unable to return to sleep, sometimes he spreads the messages on the table and tries to piece them together, to see if the torn edges fit like the pieces of a jigsaw puzzle, if the words can be arranged into a coherent sentence. He senses some story, some meaning, connecting them, but the words themselves baffle him: *knoll, motorcade, six seconds, bloodstone* . . .

And it's not dreams alone that disrupt his sleep. There's an increasing tenderness in his chest that waking doesn't dispel. In the darkness, his nipples ache as if they've been pinched with tongs; the palpitations of his heart resonate like spasms through soft tissue. His flesh feels foreign to his breastbone. He can feel his in-flamed chest swelling beneath his undershirt, and he brushes his fingertips across his chest afraid of what he'll find. He's put on weight and his once sculpted chest has grown flabby, his weight-lifter's pectorals drooping to fat. Come morning, he reassures him-self that's all it is — fat, he's simply getting fat, and the strange pain will also pass. Better to ignore it. He avoids studying the bathroom mirror when he shaves.

Sometimes, after midnight, he thinks he hears Lefty Antic play-ing his saxophone softly on the roof, but it's only wind vibrating the rusted chimney hood, streaming clouds rasping against a rusty moon, the hoot of pigeons. He hasn't seen the sax player since they lost their stake on *lone star.*

Teo has written his own notes — *Who are you? What do you want?* — and attached them to those pigeons of his who have brought him the strange messages. Like Noah, he's sent them flying out over the wet rooftops to deliver his questions, but those pigeons haven't returned home, and it takes a lot to lose a homing pigeon. They fly in a dimension perilous with hawks and the *ack-ack* fire of boys armed with rocks, slingshots, and pellet guns. Fog and bliz-zards disorient them, storms blow them down, and yet instinct brings them home on a single wing, with flight feathers broken, missing a leg or the jewel of an eye.

Teo has decided that since his communiques go unanswered and his birds don't return, then he will refuse to accept further mes-sages. All week he has kept his pigeons cooped. And now this morning, attached to a strange pigeon, another message, the first in Spanish: *asesino.* Murder or assassin, Teo doesn't know which.

He'd like to ease the loneliness, if not the foreboding, and tell Zip about the messages. But, until this afternoon, when he found Zip drinking alone and obviously needing someone to talk to, Teo has been reluctant to talk about anything more personal than Zip's favorite subject: fishing. True, Zip was obviously curious about Teo's wrestling career, but it didn't seem right to tell the insig-nificant story of the Hummingbird to a man who is so careful to never speak of war wounds.

"This feels like we're in some kind of joke," Zip says, opening his palm and allowing the pigeon to step from Teo's hand to his.

"What do you mean?" Teo asks.

"You know," Zip says, "there's all these jokes that start: a man walks into a bar with a parrot, or a man walks into a bar with a dog, or a gorilla, or a cockroach. You know, all these guys walking into all these bars with every animal on the ark. So in this one, a man — no, a wrestler, a masked wrestler — walks into a bar with a pigeon."

"So what's the punch line," Teo asks.

"You're asking me?" Zip says. "It's *your* pigeon."

"No, not one of mine."

"Yeah, but you brought it in here."

"But the joke is your idea."

"Jesus, we got no punch line," Zip says. "You know what that means?"

"What?"

"We'll never get out of the joke."

Whitey calls.

Joe, lying on the bare mattress, naked but for mismatched socks, doesn't answer.

He's staring at the ceiling as if watching a movie. Scene: The alley behind Johnny Sovereign's house. All in white, Marisol steps from a fragrance of morning glories. He'd heard she broke her Audrey Hepburn neck in Europe when she blew off the back of some Romeo's BSA on the Autobahn. Who starts these rumors about dead babes? Maybe Sal, a reputed bullshitter. Well, fucking *allora*, Sallie, if a very much alive Marisol, trailing perfume, doesn't get into the Bluebird, help herself to a smoke from the pack on the dash, and ask, "Know where a girl can get a drink around here?"

Joe unzips the gym bag, hands her the bottle of Scotch, and she asks as if she already knows, "What else you got in that bag, Joe?"

"Whataya mean, what else? Gym stuff."

"Whew! Smells like your athletic supporter's got balls of sca-morze," Marisol says, "but what do I know about the secret lives of jockstraps?"

Joe looks at her and laughs. She always could break him up, and not many beautiful women dare to be clowns. Capri was funny like that, too, and no matter who he's with he misses her. Where's Capri now, with who, and are they laughing? Marisol laughs, too, then quenches her laughter with a belt of Scotch, and turns to be kissed, and Joe kisses her, expecting the fire of alcohol to flow from her mouth into his.

"What?" Marisol says.

"I thought you were going to share."

"Dahlink," she says in her Zsa Zsa accent, "you don't remember I'm a swallower?"

Joe remembers. Remembers a blowjob doing eighty down the Outer Drive after the first night he met her at the Surf, a bar on Rush where she worked as a cocktail waitress; remembers the improv theater he'd go see her in at a crummy little beatnik space in Old Town where you'd just say something obscene about Ike or Nixon or McCarthy and you'd get a laugh — shit, he laughed, too. He remembers the weekend they dropped the top on the Bluebird right after he got it and drove the dune highway along the coast of Indiana to a so-called chalet Whitey owns overlooking the lake, water indigo to the horizon, and at night lit by the foundries in Gary.

Joe's gazing at the ceiling wondering, What time is it, what fucking day is it? He can have that conversation with Whitey without bothering to lift the receiver.

Joe, what the fuck's going on with you?

Hey, Whitey, you ball-buster, Vaffancul'!

Today must be Thursday because yesterday it was Wednesday — a day's reprieve Johnny Sovereign never knew he had — it was Wednesday, late afternoon, when Joe stopped for a fifth of Rémy, Marisol's drink of choice, then brought Marisol back to his place. "Where's all the sheets and towels?" she asked. "Joe, how the hell can you live like this?"

"They're at the Chink's. I been meaning to get them, but I been busy."

"You better watch it before you turn into an eccentric old bachelor, hon. I think maybe you're missing a woman's touch."

That's all she had to say, *touch,* and they were on the bare mattress. Her blouse, an old white shirt of his, came undone and he pressed his face to her breasts, then straddled her rib cage, thrusting slicked with a bouquet of sweat, spit, and sperm between perfumed breasts she mounded together with her hands. A *woman's touch.* When he woke with Marisol beside him it was night and his room musky with the incense of her body — low tide beneath the roses. An accordion was playing, the tune familiar, from long ago. It sounded close, as if someone in the alley was squeezing out a tango. "Hear that?" he asked, not sure she was awake.

"They're loud enough to wake the dead. That's one eerie aria they sing," Marisol said.

"I didn't mean the nighthawks," Joe said. "It's those new mercury vapor lights — they're bug magnets and bring the birds."

Marisol rose from the dark bed and crossed through streaky bluish beams, then raised the blinds on an illuminated window. The glare bestowed on her bare body the luster of a statue. She saw him staring and asked, "Ever think of a window as an erogenous zone?"

"Always the exhibitionist," Joe said, "and hey, why not? You're beautiful, like a statue."

"Statues are by nature exhibitionists, shameless, even if they've lost their arms or boobs or penises. Where's your mirror? I want to see us."

"No mirror.

"You don't have a mirror? Don't tell me — it's at the Chink's."

"It's in the alley."

"That's a novel place to keep it. I may be an exhibitionist, but I'm not going to fuck in the alley."

"It's broken."

"Seven years' bad luck, Joe. Poor unlucky you doesn't get to watch the statues with their shameless minds."

"*Allora!*" Joe said. "It's not that broke."

He went down the back stairs into the alley. The mirror was still where he'd set it against a fence beside the trash. April's violet dress was gone; some size-six bag lady must have had a lucky day. The mirror no longer appeared to be cracked, as if it had healed itself. It reflected the arc light: a stabbing flare. Nighthawks screeched. No one was playing an accordion in the alley, not that Joe thought there would be, but he could still hear it — a melody almost recognizable, one he'd heard as a child, maybe one his grandpa played when he'd accompany scratchy old 78s on his red accordion. Joe listened, trying to identity the open window from which the song wafted. Every window was dark. The music was coming from *his* window. He saw the spark and flame of a lighter, and a silhouette with its head at an awkward angle, gazing silently down at him.

Marisol was still at the window, smoking a reefer, her back to him, when he returned to the room. He propped the mirror against the wall.

"I'll share," she said, inhaling, and then exhaled smoke into his mouth, and he felt her breath smoldering along the corridors of his mind. She handed him the reefer and the crackle of the paper as he sucked in smoke seemed to echo off the ceiling. "That paper's soaked in hash oil," she said. The accordion pumped louder, as if it played in the next room. She was in his arms and he smoothed his hands over her shoulders, down her spine, over her hips, lingering on and parting the cheeks of her perfectly sculpted ass.

"Have any oil?" she whispered.

"What kind of oil?"

"Like you don't want me that way. Almond oil, apricot oil, baby oil, Oil of Olay . . ."

"Hoppe's Number Nine," he said.

"That's a new one on me."

He gestured with the glowing reefer to the bottle in the ashtray next to the Old Spice on the bureau top. She picked it up, sniffed, and by the lighter's flame, she read the label aloud: "DO NOT SWALLOW. SOLVENT FREES GUN BORES OF CORROSIVE PRIMER FOULING AND RESIDUE. PRESERVES ACCURACY! Jesus, Joe, don't you have some good, old-fashioned olive oil? What-a kind-a Day-glo are-a you?"

"Maybe in the kitchen," Joe said.

Brandishing the lighter like a torch, she went to the kitchen. Joe waited on the bed, listening to the accordion playing with the mesmerizing intensity that marijuana imparts to music, when Marisol screamed. "God, what am stepping in? What's leaking out of your fridge, Joe? You have a body in there?"

It's Whitey on the phone. Joe can almost smell the smoke of his cigar.

Maybe these ball-breaking phone calls are some kind of psychological warfare. It occurs to Joe that maybe Whitey knows about Gloria Candido and this whole thing with Johnny Sovereign is a setup. Maybe it's Whitey arranging for these women to distract Joe from doing his job, giving Whitey an excuse other than being a fucking *cornuto* to have Joe clipped. Could Whitey be that smart, that devious? Maybe Whitey has tipped off Sovereign to watch his back around Joe, and Sovereign is waiting for Joe to make his move. Or maybe the women are good-luck angels protecting him from some scheme of Whitey's?

Joe quietly lifts the receiver from the cradle. He listens for

Whitey to begin blaring, *Yo, Joe, whatthefuck?* but whoever is on the line is listening, too. Joe can hear the pursy breathing. It could be Whitey's cigar-sucking, emphysemic huff. Joe slides the stiletto from his right sock, holds it to the mouthpiece, thumbs off the safety, touches the trigger button, and the blade hisses open. *Ssswap!* Then Joe gently sets down the receiver.

He dresses quickly. The shirt he's been wearing since Tuesday reeks, so he switches to the white shirt Marisol left behind even though it smells of perfume. She's left a trail of rusty footprints down the hall from the kitchen as if she stepped on broken glass, and Joe splashes them with Rémy and mops them with the dirty shirt he won't be wearing, then swallows down a mix of painkillers. He sits on the edge of the bathtub, listening to a wheeze from his closet, as if an accordion is shuddering in its sleep, then he dials Johnny Sovereign's number. Vi answers on the third ring.

"Johnny home?"

"He'll be back around six or so," Vi says. "Can I take a message?"

"So, where is he?"

"Can I take your number and have him call you back?"

"Do you even know?"

"Know what?" Vi asks. "Who's calling?"

"An acquaintance."

"You called yesterday and the day before."

Joe hangs up.

The Bluebird is doing sixty down the cracked alleys, and when a bag lady steps from between two garbage cans, she has to drop her bag to get out of the way. He rolls over her shopping bag, bulging from a day's foraging, and in the rearview mirror sees her throwing hex signs in his wake. He pulls up behind Sovereign's abandoned garage and there's that smell of trash, oil, and pigeons, compounded by a summer breeze. Joe can sense someone eyeing him from inside the garage and he eases his right hand into the pocket of his sport coat and flicks off the safety of the .22, uncomfortably aware of how useless the small-caliber pistol is at anything but point-blank range. A gray cat emerges from Sovereign's garage carrying in its mouth a pigeon that looks too big for it, still waving a wing. The cat looks furtively at Joe, then slinks into the morning glories, and from the spot where the cat disappeared, Grace steps out. Morning glories are clipped to her tangled black curls. She's wearing a morning-glory-vine necklace, vine bracelets, and what looks like a bedraggled bridesmaid's gown, if bridesmaids wore black. Her bare feet are bloody probably from walking on glass. "Long time, no see, Joey," she says. "I been with the Carmelites."

Joe remembers Sal asking if he was going to her closed-casket wake. "You had a thing with her, didn't you?" Sal had asked.

"No way!" Joe told him, "A little kissy-face after a party once. I don't know why she made up all those stories."

"That whole Fandetti family is bonkers," Sal said.

Bruno, her father, a Sicilian from Taylor Street, operates an escort service, massage parlors, and a strip bar on South Wabash, but he brought his four daughters up in convent school. The official story was that Grace wasted away with leukemia, but rumor had it that it was a botched abortion. Now, Joe realizes old man Fandetti is even crazier than he thought, faking his daughter's death in order to avoid the humiliation of an illegitimate pregnancy. No surprise she's a nut case. He wonders if they collected insurance on her while they were at it.

"If you stick your finger inside you can feel the electric," Grace tells him, and demonstrates by poking her finger inside a flower. "That hum isn't bees. Electric's what gives them their blue. You should feel it. Come here and put your finger in."

"Where's your shoes, Grace?"

"Under the bed, so they think I'm still there."

"Still where? What are you doing here?"

"Come here, Joey, and put your finger in. You'll feel what the bee's born for. They're so drunk on flower juice!" She walks to the car and leans in through the window on the passenger side, and the straps of the black gown slip off her shoulders and from its décolletage breasts dangle fuller than he remembers them from that one night after a birthday party at Fabio's when he danced with her and they snuck out to the parking lot and necked in his car. She'd looked pretty that night, made up like a doll, pearls in her hair, and wearing a silky dress with spaghetti straps. He'd slipped them down, kissed her breasts, and she wanted to go further, pleaded with him to take her virginity, but he didn't have a rubber and it wasn't worth messing with her connected old man.

"Know what was on the radio?"

"When?" Joe asks. He's aware that he's staring, but, apparently still stoned on that hash oil, he can't take his eyes off her breasts. His reactions feel sluggish; he has to will them. He realizes he's been in a fog since . . . he's not sure how long, but it's getting worse.

She opens the door and sinks into the leather seat and, humming tunelessly, flicks on the car radio. "I Only Have Eyes for You" is playing. "Our song, Joey!"

"Grace, we don't have a song."

"The night we became lovers."

"Why'd you tell people that?"

"You got me in trouble, Joey, and in the Carmelites I had to confess it to the bishop. We weren't supposed to talk, but he made me show and tell."

Joe flicks off the radio; it's like turning on the afternoon: birdsong, cooing pigeons, the bass of bees from a thousand blue gramophones.

"All the sisters were jealous. They called me Walkie-Talkie behind my back. They thought I didn't understand the sacredness of silence, but that's not true. They think silence is golden, but real silence is terrifying. We're not made for it. I could tell you things, Joey, but they're secrets."

"Like what, Grace? Things somebody told you not to tell me?"

"Things God whispers to me. Joey, you smell like a girl."

"I think you can't tell 'cause you don't know. Tell me one secret God said just so I see if either of you knows anything."

"I know words on an accordion. If you turn on your radio you'll hear stars sing the song of a thousand crackles. I know about you and girls. I know what's in your gym bag."

"Yeah, what?"

"They're your way of being totally alone."

"What's in the gym bag, Grace?"

"I know you can't stop staring at my tits. I don't mind; you can see. Oh, God! Windshields glorify the sun! Feel."

"Not here, Grace."

"O.K., at your place."

"That's not such a good idea," Joe says, but he can't stay here with her either, so he eases the car into gear and drives slowly up the alley. The top of her dress is down, and against his better judgment — almost against his will — he turns left onto Twenty-fifth, crosses Rockwell, the boundary between two-flats and truck docks. He drives carefully, his eyes on a street potholed by semis, but aware of her beside him with her dirty feet bloody and her bare breasts in plain view, but Rockwell is empty, not unusual for this time of day. They're approaching a railroad viaduct that floods during rainstorms. A block beyond the viaduct is Western Avenue, a busy street that in grade school he learned is the longest street in the world, just like the Amazon is the longest river. Western won't be deserted, and across Western, on its east bank, is the little Franciscan church of St. Michael's and the old Italian parish where he lives.

"I'm a Sister of Silence, so you need to be nice to me like I always was to you."

"I've always been nice to you, too, Grace."

"I could have had men hurt you, Joey, but I didn't."

They're halfway through the shadowy tunnel of the railroad viaduct and he hits the brakes and juts his arm out to brace her from smacking the windshield. "I don't like when people threaten me, Grace. It really makes me crazy."

"Let's go to your place, Joey. Please drive. I hate viaducts when the trains go over. All those tons of steel on top of you, and the echoes don't stop in your head even after the train is gone."

"There's no train."

"It's coming. I can feel it in my heart. My heart is crying." She squeezes a nipple and catches a milky tear on a fingertip and offers it to him, reaching up to brush it across his lips, but Joe turns his face away. When he does, she slaps him. He catches her arm before she can slap him again and under the viaduct, minus the glare of sun in his eyes, her morning-glory-vine bracelets are scars welted across her wrists. Whistle wailing, a freight hurtles over, vibrating the car. He releases her arm, and she clamps her hands over her ears. Her bare feet stamp a tantrum of bloody imprints on the floor mat.

"Get out!" Joe yells over the thunder of boxcars, and reaches across her body to open the door. She looks at him in amazement, then mournfully steps out into the gutter, her breasts still exposed. Without looking back, he guns into the daylight on the other side, catches the green going yellow on Western, veers into traffic, rattles across the gull-and-pigeon-wheeled bridge spanning the Sanitary

Canal. He isn't going back to his place; he's not heading to pick up his laundry; and until he finishes the job he's not going to Fabio's or any of the hangouts where he might run into Whitey. It's Thursday and Joe's been seeing Gloria Candido on the sly on Thursdays, when Julio goes to his grandmother's after school, but Joe isn't going to Gloria's, either. He's driving south on Western, popping painkillers, Grace's handprint still burning on his face. He drives in silence, no radio. All he wants to feel is the flow of traffic as he heads south to the end of the longest street in the world.

He drives into the dark until he has to pull over, and when he wakes he's parked on a dirt road bordered by rusty barbed wire, across from a collapsed barn and a corroded windmill. He thinks, I could just keep going.

A tank of gas and three jumbo coffees later, he stops at a Texaco on the Illinois side of the Mississippi. On an impulse, he tries calling from a pay phone, but doesn't have enough change. "Make it collect, for Vi Sovereign," he tells the operator.

"Who should I say is calling?" the operator asks.

"Tell her a friend who's been calling, she'll know." And when the operator does, Vi accepts the call. "Where you calling from?" Vi asks. "I hear cars."

"A phone booth off Western Avenue. Johnny home?"

"You're calling early." she says. "He'll be home around noon or so for lunch."

"You don't know where he is or what he's doing? I can hear it in your voice. Did he even come home last night?"

"What do you keep calling for? If you're trying to tell me something about Johnny, just say it. You somebody's husband? What's your name?"

"Maybe we'll meet sometime. I'd pay you back for the phone call, but then you'd know it was me."

"I'll recognize your voice."

"Better you don't," Joe says, and hangs up.

Before noon, he pulls up behind Johnny Sovereign's. From the longest street in the world, he's back to idling in a block-length alley, and yet it's oddly peaceful there, private, a place that's come to feel familiar, and he's so tired and wired at the same time that he'd be content just to drowse awhile with the sun soothing his eyelids. He lights a smoke, chucks the crushed, empty pack out the window, checks the empty alley in the rearview mirror and notices the handprint still looking hot on his face, then catches his own eyes glancing uncomfortably back at him, embarrassed by the intimacy of the moment, as if neither he nor his reflection want anything to do with each other. He puts on the pair of sunglasses he keeps in the visor and when he looks up through their green lenses, a tanned blonde with slender legs in short turquoise shorts and a navy blue halter punctuated by her nipples stands beside the morning glories. There's a rose silk scarf knotted at her throat and she's wearing sunglasses, too.

"Hi, Joe, they told me I'd find you here. I been waiting all morning, thinking how it would be when I saw you. I missed you so much, baby. I thought I could live without you, but I can't."

"Capri," he says.

She smiles at the sound of her name. "My guy, my baby."

"Oh, fuck, fuck! Not you, baby. I didn't care about the others, but not you, too." He's shocked to see her, but not surprised. He hasn't realized until now that he's been waiting for this moment ever since, without warning, her letters stopped, and were replaced by a silence that has become increasingly ominous. Her last letter ended: *Sometimes I read the weather in your city, and imagine you waking up to it, living your life without me.* After a month with no word, he'd asked Sal if he'd heard anything about her, but he hadn't. In all likelihood she'd met someone, and Joe thought he'd be making a fool of himself getting in touch. Even so, he tried calling, but her number was disconnected.

"Baby, I'm back. Aren't you glad to see me?" She steps toward the car and removes her sunglasses. He can't meet her eyes. If he could speak, the words he'd say — *I'm crying in my heart* — wouldn't be his, and when she reaches her arms out, Joe slams the car into reverse, floors it, and halfway down the alley, skidding along garbage cans, hits a bag lady. He can hear her groan as the air goes out of her. Her sausage legs spasmodically kick from where he's knocked her, pinned and thrashing between two garbage cans. Joe keeps going.

"You need a fuckin' ark to get through that shit," Johnny Sovereign says.

The flooded side street is a dare: sewers plugged, hydrants uncapped, scrap wood wedged against each gushing hydrant mouth to fashion makeshift fountains.

"Think of it as a free car wash," Joe says.

"I don't see you driving your T-bird through."

"I might if it was whitewashed with baked pigeon shit. Go, man!"

They crank up the windows and Sovereign guns the engine and drops the canary yellow Pancho into first. By second gear, water sheets from the tires like transparent wings, then the blast of the first hydrant cascades over the windshield, and Sovereign, driving blind, flicks the wipers on and leans on the horn. By the end of the block, they're both laughing.

"You can turn your wipers off now," Joe says. He can hear the tires leaving a trail of wet treads as they turn down Cermak. "Where you going, man?" Joe asks.

"Expressway," Sovereign says. "I thought you wanted to see what this muther can do opened up. You sure you don't want to drive?"

"I'll ride shotgun. But I want to see what it does from jump. I heard zero to sixty in eight-point-one. Go where the dragsters go."

"By Three V's?"

"Yeah, Three V's is good." Joe says. "Private. We can talk a little business there, too."

The 3 V's Birdseed Company, a five-story, dark brick factory with grated windows, stands at the end of an otherwise deserted block. The east side of the street is a stretch of abandoned factories; the west side is rubble — mounds of bricks like collapsed pyramids where factories stood before they were condemned. Both sides of the curb are lined with dumped cars too junky to be repoed or sold, some stripped, some burned. Summer nights kids drag-race there.

"Park here a sec. We'll oil up," Joe says. They've driven blocks, but he can still hear the wet treads of the tires as Sovereign pulls into a space among the junkers. Joe unzips the gym bag he's lugged with him into Sovereign's Bonneville and hoists out the Scotch bottle. There's not more than a couple swallows left. "Haig pinch. Better than Chivas."

Sovereign takes a swig, "Chivas is smoother," he says. He offers Joe a Marlboro. Joe nips off the filter; Sovereign lights them up and flicks on the radio to the Cubs' station. "I just want to make sure it's Drabowsky pitching. I took bets."

"Who'd bet on the fuckin' Cubs?"

"Die-hard fans, some loser who woke up from a dream with a

hunch, the DPs around here bet on Drabowsky. Who else but the Cubs would have a pitcher from Poland? Suckers always find a way to figure the odds are in their favor."

It's Moe Drabowsky against the Giants' Johnny Antonelli. Sovereign flashes an in-the-know smile, flicks the radio off, then takes a victorious belt of Scotch and passes it to Joe. "Kill it," Joe says, and when Sovereign does, Joe lobs the empty pinch bottle out the window and it cracks on a sidewalk already glittering with shards of muscatel pints and shattered fifths of rotgut whiskey. Sun cascades over the yellow Bonneville. Out the back window Joe can see the tread of Sovereign's tires like skid marks trailing them. "Man, those mynahs scream," Sovereign says. "Sounds like goddamn Brookfield Zoo. Hear that one saying a name?"

In summer, the windows behind the grates on the fifth floor of 3 V's are opened. The lower floors of the factory are offices and stockrooms. The top floor houses live exotic birds — parakeets, java birds, finches, canaries, mynahs.

"It's the sparrows," Joe says. "They torment the fancy-ass birds. *'Cheep-cheep,* asshole, you're jackin' off on the mirror in a fuckin' cage while I'm out here singing and flying around.' Drives the 3 V's birds crazy and they start screeching and plucking out their feathers. You ever felt that way?"

"What? In a cage?" Sovereign asks. "No fuckin' way, and I don't intend to. So, what's the deal?" he asks Joe, and actually checks his jeweled Bulova as if suddenly realizing it's time in his big-shot day for him to stop gabbing about birds and get down to business. "Whitey say something about me getting a little more of the local action? Setting craps up on weekends?"

"Yeah, local action," Joe says, "that's what I want to talk to you about."

"I'm in," Johnny says. "I'm up for whatever moves you guys have in mind, Joe."

"There's just one minor problem to work out," Joe says. "Whitey thinks you're skimming."

"Huh?" Sovereign says.

"You heard me," Joe says. "Look, I know your mind is suddenly going from fuckin' zero to sixty, but the best thing is to forget trying to come up with bullshit no one's going to believe anyway and to work this situation out."

"Joe, what you talking about? I keep books. I always give an honest count. No way I would pull that."

"See, that's pussy-ass bullshit. A waste of our precious time. Whitey checked your books. They double-checked. You fucked up, Johnny, so don't bullshit me."

"I never took a nickel beyond my percentage. There gotta be a mistake."

"You saying you may have made a miscalculation? That your arithmetic is bad?"

"Not that I know of."

"Where'd you get the scratch for this car?"

"Hey, I'm doing all right. I mean, I owe on it. The bank fucking owns it."

"More bullshit, you paid cash. Whitey checked. You been making book here and gambling in Uptown and losing, drinking hard, cheating on Vi . . ."

"Vi? What you talking about? She's got nothing to do with nothing."

"Why wouldn't you stay home with a primo lady like that? You're out of control, man. Your fuckin' Pancho's leaking oil. Next you'll be talking to the wrong people. You're a punk-ass bullshitter and a bad risk."

"Joe, I swear to you —"

"You swear?"

"On my mother's grave. Swear it on my children."

"You cross your heart and hope to die, too?"

"Huh?"

"Like little kids say."

"I know how kids talk, Joe. I got a baby girl and a little boy, Johnny Junior."

"So swear it like you mean it," Joe says, exhaling smoke and flicking his cigarette out the window. "I cross my heart . . ." Sovereign looks at Joe as if he can't be serious and Joe stares him down.

"Cross my heart . . ." Sovereign says.

"No, you got to actually cross your heart," Joe says, crossing his own heart, and when, to illustrate further, Joe reaches with his left hand to open Sovereign's sport coat, Sovereign flinches, then smiles, chagrined for being so jumpy. Instead of making a move to resist Joe touching him, Sovereign drags on his cigarette.

"Sure there's a heart in there to cross?" Joe asks, holding Sovereign by the lapel, reaching up with his right hand to check for a heartbeat. "Relax, Johnny, I'm just fucking with you." Joe smiles, then touches the trigger and the stiletto he's palmed from his argyle sock darts out as he thrusts, slamming Sovereign back against the car door, the cigarette shooting from Sovereign's mouth as he groans *uuuhhh!*

Sovereign's hands are pressed to where the blade is buried. He looks down at the bloodied pearl handle of the stiletto sticking from his chest, his eyes bulging, teeth gritted so that the muscles knot out from his jaw.

"Don't move, it's in clean," Joe says, "just let it go."

"Oh, my God, oh, oh," Sovereign exhales, and an atomized spray of blood hangs in the sunlit air between them. The 3 V's birds raise a jungly chatter against the everyday chirp of sparrows. The hot car fills with Sovereign's gasping for breath, and the smell of garlic, of the mortadella sausage on the blade, and then an acrid smell, calling to Joe's mind a line of kindergartners. Sovereign has peed his pants. Sovereign groans from the soul, then closes his eyes. Tears well out from under his red lashes. His skin has gone translucent white, making his liverish freckles stand out like beads of blood forced through his pores.

"Not Vi," Sovereign says. "Oh please, not Vi. I got little kids." Blood gurgles in his throat, and he's breathing hard, but otherwise not struggling as if the pain of the knife has pinned him to the door.

"I told you not to talk. Just let it go. I tried to do you a favor, man. Whitey wants you turned into hamburger. I let you off easy," Joe says.

Sovereign shakes his head no-no, trying to form words with his open mouth. A bubble of bloody spit breaks on his lips. Their faces are close, Sovereign's body slouched so that Joe looks into Sovereign's dilated nostrils, which are throwing cavernous shadows, and Joe leans closer, their faces almost touching, to hear what Sovereign is trying to whisper.

"Bullshit," Johnny Sovereign manages. The word sends up a tiny hanging reddish spray. "You just wanted to see if it worked."

"Fuck you," Joe says. "You got a reprieve you didn't even know you had. What did you do with the time?" But even as he says it, Joe realizes Sovereign is right. He wanted to see what the knife could do, and how stupid was that, because now he's stuck talking with a dying mook. He should have just put a couple caps into Sovereign's brain and walked the fuck away instead of getting cute, sitting here listening to birds chatter, beside a guy with his jaw grinding and red eyelashes pasted to his skin by tears leaking down his cheeks as his life hemorrhages away, the muscle that pumped five quarts a minute, a hundred thousand heartbeats a day — how many in a life? — no longer keeping time. Joe's not sure how long they've been here. He wants the knife back but worries that if he pulls it out Sovereign will start to thrash and yell, that the wound will gush. Sovereign makes a sound as if he's gargling, syrupy blood dribbles from the corner of his mouth as his head rolls to the side, and then he's quiet. Tears dry on his cheeks.

"Sovereign," Joe says, "Johnny. You still here?" Joe can hardly speak for the dryness of his own mouth. He's aware of how terribly thirsty he is, and of how suddenly alone. White heat rays in as if the windshield of the Bonneville is God's magnifying glass. Now, Joe can hear the name Sovereign was talking about — some 3 V's bird repeating *betty betty betty*. He can't sit any longer listening to the nonstop jabber of the last sounds Sovereign heard.

Joe digs the shotgun out of the gym bag. He uses his jockstrap to wipe down the sawed-off shotgun he'll leave behind jammed in Sovereign's piss-soaked crotch. He tries to ease out the stiletto. Blood wells up without gushing. Joe tugs harder but can't dislodge the knife, maybe because his hands have started to shake. He's drenched in sweat, and takes his jacket off. How did his white shirt get spattered with blood? He removes his shirt. The lapels of his powder blue sport coat are speckled, too, but the splash pattern that's good for eating spaghetti makes it look as if the blood might be part of the coat. He wipes the car and the knife handle down with the shirt. In the gym bag, there's a wrinkled gray tank top with the faded maroon lettering CHAMPS over an insignia of crossed boxing gloves, and Joe pulls that on and slips his jacket over it, and then, for no reason, fits the jockstrap over Sovereign's face as if he's wearing a mask or a blindfold so he doesn't have to look. At the shotgun blast, pigeon flocks rise, detonated from the factory roofs, and Joe imagines how on the top floor of 3 V's the spooked birds batter their cages.

Friday afternoon, a red clothespin day at the Zip Inn. Ball game on the TV, Drabowsky against the Giants' Johnny Antonelli — top of the fifth and the Cubs down 2–0 on a Willie Mays homer. The juke-box, Zip apologizes, is on the fritz. No "Ebb Tide," no "Sing, Sing, Sing," no "Cucurucucu Paloma."

Teo sits on a stool, balancing the quarters that he was going to feed to the jukebox, on the wooden bar.

"One more, on the house," Zip says. His white shirt looks slept in, his bow tie askew, his furrowed face stubbled, eyes bloodshot. It's clear he's continued the pace from yesterday. Teo turns his shot glass upside down. Zip turns it back up. "To Friday," Zip says.

"We already drank to Friday." Teo says. "We drank to Friday yesterday, and to Saturday, Sunday, Monday, Tuesday, and Wednesday."

"We missed Thursday."

"Yesterday was Thursday, we started out drinking to Thursday."

"Yeah, but today's fucking special."

"Every day's special, isn't that the point of drinking to them?" Teo asks.

"There is no point," Zip says. "That's the point."

Teo shrugs. "So, why's today special? An anniversary?"

"Special's the wrong word," Zip says. He looks as if the right word might be *doomed*.

Something is eating at Zip, but Teo doesn't know how to ask what. Yesterday, Teo stayed drinking with him until the after-work crowd started filtering in. By then, Teo was half-loaded. He put the wounded Spanish pigeon back in his gym bag and went home, tended to the coop, then fell into bed and, for the first night in weeks, slept undisturbed by dreams. "Look, compadre, if there's something I can do . . ."

"Have a brew," Zip says. He sets a Hamm's before Teo, and a bag of pretzels, and rings up one of the quarters that Teo has balanced on the bar. "You bring your feathered friend with the bum wing?"

"No," Teo says, "but I got something you been asking about." From the bowling bag on the barstool beside him, Teo lifts out a blue head mask, and sets it face-up, flat on the bar. The face has the design of a golden beak and iridescent white feathers. The luminous colors are veined with brownish bloodstains. "You wanted to see, so I brought it."

"Goddamn." Zip smiles, looking, for the moment, like his old self. "This is what you wrestled in? Pretty wild. So, what was your ring name?"

"La Colibri."

"Like the vegetable?"

"It's a kind of bird," Teo says.

"You got the rest of the outfit in there?"

Teo unfolds the matching blue tights and Zip holds them up, smiling skeptically at Teo.

"They stretch," Teo says.

"Not that much, they don't."

"Yeah, they do. I'm wearing the top. Same material." Teo unbuttons his short-sleeved shirt. Underneath, he's wearing an iridescent blue tank top. Its bulgy front is spotted with faded blood like the canvas of a ring.

"I wish I could of seen you in the ring, *amigo*. Must have been something." Zip picks up the mask. He looks as if he'd like to try it on if he had two hands to pull it over his head. "Can you actually see to fight out of this?"

"Sure," Teo says, "it's got holes for the eyes."

"Let's see." Zip hands the mask to Teo to try on, and, when Teo hesitates, Zip says, "Come on. What the hell?"

"What the hell," Teo agrees, and pulls it over his head. It's the first time in years that he's worn it, and he's amazed to feel a reminiscent surge of energy, but maybe that's merely the whiskey kicking in on an empty stomach.

"You are one fierce-looking warrior," Zip says. "You should come in here wearing the whole outfit, just amble in and sit down, open up your book, and if somebody asks, 'Who's that?' I'll tell them: 'Him? The new security. Guards the hard-boiled eggs.'"

On the TV, the Hamm's commercial, *From the land of sky blue waters,* plays between innings.

"Can you drink beer through that?" Zip asks.

When Teo laughs, it's the mask itself that seems to be laughing, the mask that chugs down a bottle of Hamm's.

"Why's Goldblatt's got you disguised in a dress when they could have a goddamn superhero patrolling the aisles? You're wasting your talent. You could be a rent-a-wrestler, make up business cards: HEADLOCKS FOR HIRE . . . HALF NELSONS FIFTY PERCENT OFF. I need an autographed picture for my wall. Hey, I could sponsor you, advertise on your jersey."

"HAVE A NIP AT THE INN OF ZIP," Teo says.

"Very catchy!" Zip sets them up with two more cold ones and rings up another of the quarters Teo has balanced on the bar. "Can the Kohlrabi still kick ass?" Zip asks.

"Fight again?" Teo asks. Even wearing the blue tank top and the mask, even after the first good night's sleep in a long time, even with the sunlight streaming through the door and whiskey through his veins, on a Friday afternoon, and nowhere to be but here, drinking cold beer and joking with his new friend, Teo knows that's impossible.

"What if there was no choice?" Zip asks. "If it was him or you? Say you catch somebody stealing and he pulls a knife? Could you do whatever it took? Is it worth it? You asked, is there something you could do? Purely theoretical, what if somebody hired you to watch their back in a situation like that?"

There's an undisguised undercurrent of desperation in Zip's questions that makes Teo recall the message from the Spanish pigeon: *Asesino*. Murder. The slip of paper is still in Teo's pocket. More than ever, there's an eerie feeling of premonition about it. He'd been thinking maybe of showing it to Zip to see what he made of it, but not now. "Purely theoretical, you keep protection back there?" Teo asks.

"Funny you should ask, I was just looking through my purely theoretical ordnance last night," Zip says. "Swiss Army knife, USMC .45 missing the clip, ever seen one of these?" Zip reaches beneath the bar and sets a short, gleaming sword before Teo.

Teo runs his finger along the oriental lettering engraved on the blade.

"Careful, it's razor-sharp," Zip says. "Never found out what the letters mean. Guys said the Japs used to sharpen these with silk. I don't know if that's true, but all the dead Jap soldiers had silk flags on them that their families gave them when they went to war. Made good souvenirs. G.I.s took everything you could imagine for souvenirs. Bloody flags, weapons, gold teeth, polished Jap skulls until there was an order against those. Wonder what happened to all that shit? Probably stuffed away forgotten in boxes in basements and attics all over the country. Only thing I took was this. It's a samurai knife they'd used for hari-kari. They'd sneak in at night and cut your throat while you slept, so we slept two in a foxhole, one dozing, the other doing sentry. You'd close your eyes dead tired knowing your life depended on your buddy staying awake." Zip puts the sword back under the bar and lifts a length of sawed-off hickory bat handle that dangles by a loop of rawhide from a hook beside the cash register. "This used to be enough," Zip says, "but the way things are these days you gotta get serious if you want to defend yourself. Whoa!" Zip exclaims, gesturing with the bat at the TV screen. "Banks got all of that one."

On the TV, Jack Brickhouse is into his home run call: "Back she goes . . . way back . . . back! . . . back! Hey! Hey!"

"Hey! Hey!" Joe Ditto says. He stands in the emblazoned doorway in his sunglasses and factory steel-toes, his powder blue sport coat looking lopsided and pouchy where the gun weighs down his right pocket. He's wearing the sport coat over a wrinkled gym top, and in his left hand he holds a gym bag. He's sweating as if he's just come from a workout. "Didn't mean to startle you, Mr. Zip. I thought you were going to brain your customer here. This masked marauder didn't pay his bar tab? You want I should speak to him?"

Zip hangs the bat back on its hook, and Joe sets the gym bag down and straddles a stool beside Teo. No introductions are made. On the right side of Joe's face, beneath a four-day growth of beard, there's a hot-looking handprint. "What's so interesting?" Joe asks, when he catches Zip staring. "You don't like the new look from the other side of Western?" He tucks in his Champs tank top as if it's his gym shirt–sport coat combination that Zip was staring at. "Fuckin' hot out there," Joe says. "I need a cold one. You need an air conditioner in here, Mr. Zip."

"They're too noisy," Zip says. "You can't hear the ball game."

"Hey, I'm not trying to sell you one," Joe says. "I don't care for them either." He drains his beer in three gulps, slams down the bottle. Teo's remaining two quarters teeter onto their sides. "Hit me again, Mr. Zip. And a shot of whatever you're drinking. What's the score?"

"Cubs down two to one. Banks just hit one."

"Drabowsky still pitching? You know where he's from?"

"Ozanna, Poland," Zip says like it's a stupid question. "He's throwing good."

"You bet on him?" Joe asks. When he raises the shot glass, his hand is so shaky that he has to bring his mouth to the glass.

"I don't bet on baseball," Zip says.

"Hit me again, Mr. Zip. And one for yourself." From a roll of bills,

Joe peels a twenty onto the bar. "What are you drinking, Masked Marvel? Zip, give Zorro here a Hamm's-the-beer-refreshing."

Zip sets them up and the three men sit in silence, looking from their drinks to the ball game as if waiting for some signal to down their whiskeys. Their dark reflections in the long mirror behind the liquor bottles opposite the bar wait, too. Teo glances at the mirror where a man in a blue Hummingbird mask glances back. He knows the guy in sunglasses beside him is mob, and can't help but notice that Zip has gone tensely quiet, unfriendlier than Teo's ever seen him. Teo thinks of the samurai sword within reach under the bar, and of the message from the Spanish pigeon.

On the TV, Jack Brickhouse says, "Oh brother, looks like a fan fell out of the bleachers," and his fellow sportscaster Vince Lloyd adds, "Or jumped down, Jack." Brickhouse, as if doing play by play, announces, "Now, folks, he's running around the outfield!" and Vince Lloyd adds, "Jack, I think he's trying to hand Willie Mays a beer!"

"That's Lefty!" Teo exclaims.

"Lefty? Lefty Antic?" Zip asks. "You sure?"

"The sax player. He's my neighbor."

"Here come the Andy Frain ushers out on the field," Brickhouse announces. "They'll get things back under control."

"Look at him run!" Teo says.

"Go, Lefty!" Zip yells. "He ain't going down easy."

Without warning, the TV blinks into a commercial: *From the land of sky blue waters* . . .

"Shit!" Joe says. "That was better than the fucking game. Guy had some moves."

"You know Lefty, the sax player?" Teo asks Zip.

"Hell, I got him on the wall," Zip says, and from among the photo gallery of softball teams with ZIP INN lettered on their jerseys he lifts down a picture of a young boxer with eight-ounce gloves cocked. The boxer doesn't have a mustache, but it's easy to recognize the sax player. "He made it to the Golden Glove Nationals," Zip says. "Got robbed on a decision."

"That southpaw welterweight from Gonzo's gym. I remember him from when I was growing up," Joe Ditto says. "Kid had fast hands." He raises his shot glass and they all drink as if to something.

"Well, back to baseball, thank goodness," Jack Brickhouse says.

"Vince, it's unfortunate but a few bad apples just don't belong with the wonderful fans in the beautiful confines of Wrigley Field."

"Best fans in the game, Jack," Vince says.

"They didn't want to show him beating the piss out of the Andy Frains," Joe says.

"Lefty's good people. Hasn't put Korea behind him yet, that's all," Zip says.

Until yesterday, Teo couldn't gimp on his bum knee into the Zip Inn without wondering how Zip could put the war that took his arm behind him. Now, he knows the answer: Zip hasn't.

"Hit me again, Mr. Zip," Joe says. "A double. And get yourself and the Masked Man, here." Joe turns Teo's shot glass up.

Teo turns it back down.

Joe turns it back up. "Hey, mystery challenger, we're having a toast." Joe props Lefty's photo up against a bottle of Hamm's. "To a man who knows how to really enjoy a Cubs game."

This time, his hands steadier, Joe clinks each of their glasses.

"Gimme a pack of Pall Malls, Mr. Zip. So, what's with the mask?" Joe asks Teo. "Off to rob a savings and loan? A nylon's not good enough? Goddamn, you got the whole outfit here," he says, examining the tights that Teo hasn't stuffed back into his bowling bag. "You one of those Mexican wrestlers on Cinco de Mayo or something?"

"Used to be," Teo says.

With his long-neck beer bottle, Joe parts Teo's open shirt to get a look at his tank top. "Who'd you fight as, the Blue Titman? Jesus, Mr. Zip, check the boobs out on this guy. That's some beery-looking bosom you're sporting, hombre. They squirt Hamm's? This might be the best tit in Little Village." Joe lights a smoke, offers one to Teo, who refuses. "Mr. Zip, hit me again, and Knockers here, too," Joe says. He's holding Teo's glass so that Teo can't turn it over. Zip pours and Joe takes a sip of beer, then his hand snakes along the bar and into Teo's bag of pretzels. Joe munches down a pretzel, and his hand snakes back for another, except this time it snakes inside Teo's shirt for a quick feel before Teo pulls away.

"Ever go home at night after a hard day's wrestling and just spend a quiet evening getting some off yourself, or do you need more commitment for that?" Joe asks. "I'm just fucking with you, friend. I used to love to watch wrestling when I was kid. I didn't know it was fake. You know, I didn't mind finding out Santa Claus was bullshit, but Gorgeous George and Zuma the Man from Mars — he wrestled in a mask, too — that hurt."

"It's not always fake," Teo says.

"What fuckin' planet are you from? How do you think Gorgeous George could have done against Marciano? Would you consider a little private contest that wasn't fixed?"

"I don't wrestle anymore," Teo says.

"See, but this may be my only chance to say I wrestle a pro. I'm just talking arm wrestling here," Joe says, and assumes the position, with his elbow on the bar. "We'll wrestle for a drink, or a twenty, or the world championship of the Zip Inn, whatever you want."

"I'm retired," Teo says.

"Come on," Joe says, "besides experience you got fifty pounds on me. If your friend, Lefty, can jump out of the bleachers and take on the Andy Frain ushers, you and me can have a friendly little match. Mr. Zip has a winner. Left-handed, of course. You can referee, Mr. Zip, and hey, that little matter of business for today, let's forget about it. Another time, maybe. Who you betting on, or do you not bet on arm wrestling either?"

"Twenty on El Kohlrabi," Zip says.

Teo looks at Zip surprised.

"Purely theoretical," Zip says, "but you can take him."

"Purely," Teo says, and smiles, then leans his arm on the bar and he and Joe Ditto clench hands.

"*Una momento,*" Joe says. He removes his sport coat and folds it over his gym bag, takes a puff of Pall Mall, then drops to the floor and does ten quick pushups with a hand clap in between each. "Needed to warm up."

Teo removes his shirt to free up his shoulder. Both men, now in tank tops, clench hands again. Joe is still wearing his sunglasses and his half-smoked cigarette dangles from his lip. Zip counts one . . . two . . . wrestle! and they strain against each other, muscle and tendons surfacing, knotting along their forearms. Joe gives slightly, then struggles back to even, seems to gain leverage, and gradually forces Teo's arm downward.

The crowd at Wrigley is cheering and Jack Brickhouse breaks into his home run call: "Back she goes, back, back, way back . . ."

"Goddamn, come on, *luchador,*" Zip urges. His left hand slaps the bar with a force that sends the red clothespin flying off the sleeve folded over the stump of his right arm.

Gripping the edge of the bar with his left hand and grunting, Teo heaves his right arm up until it's back even, but his surge of momentum stalls. He and Joe Ditto lean into each other. They've both begun to sweat, their locked hands are turning white, arms straining, faces close together, separated by the smoke of Joe's dangling Pall Mall. "My friend," Joe says from the side of his mouth, "you smell like pigeons."

Out on the street, sirens wail as if every cop, ambulance, and fire truck in the neighborhood is rushing past. The lengthening ash of Joe's cigarette tumbles to the bar. Joe spits out the butt and it rolls across the bar top onto the floor where Zip grinds it out. Their arms have begun trembling as if in time to each other, but neither budges. Teo turns his face away from Joe and finds himself looking into the mirror. A man in a blue mask looks back. I won't be the one to give up, the man in the mirror is thinking, I won't let them see me defeated again. Teo closes his eyes and concentrates on breathing. He's resolved to ignore the pain, to welcome it, to endure until Joe's arm tires to the point when he'll make one last desperate move. Teo knows if he can hold off that last assault, he'll win.

From the land of sky blue waters tom-toms from the TV, while Joe's left hand slowly snakes to Teo's tank top. At its touch, Teo pushes back harder, but Joe won't give. He holds Teo's concentrated force upright with his right arm while his left hand gently brushes Teo's tank top, then fondles his chest.

"Got you where I want you now," Joe says. "Cootchie-cootchie-coo, motherfucker."

DEBORAH EISENBERG

Some Other, Better Otto

FROM THE YALE REVIEW

"I DON'T KNOW WHY I committed us to any of those things," Otto said. "I'd much prefer to be working or reading, and you'll want all the time you can get this week to practice."

"It's fine with me," William said. "I always like to see Sharon. And we'll survive the evening with your —"

Otto winced.

"Well, we will," William said. "And don't you want to see Naomi and Margaret and the baby as soon as they get back?"

"Everyone always says, 'Don't you want to see the baby, don't you want to see the baby,' but if I did want to see a fat, bald, confused person, obviously I'd have only to look in the mirror."

"I was reading a remarkable article in the paper this morning about holiday depression," William said. "Should I clip it for you? The statistics were amazing."

"The statistics cannot have been amazing, the article cannot have been remarkable, and I am not 'depressed.' I just happen to be bored sick by these inane — waving our little antennae, joining our little paws to indicate — Oh, what is the point? Why did I agree to any of this?"

"Well," William said. "I mean, this is what we do." Hmm. Well, true. And the further truth was, Otto saw, that he himself wanted, in some way, to see Sharon; he himself wanted, in some way, to see Naomi and Margaret and the baby as soon as possible. And it was even he himself who had agreed to join his family for Thanksgiving. It would be straining some concept — possibly the concept of "wanted," possibly the concept of "self" — to say that he himself had wanted to join them, and yet there clearly must have been an implicit alternative to joining them that was even less desirable, or he would not, after all, have agreed to it.

It had taken him — how long? — years and years to establish a viable, if not pristine, degree of estrangement from his family. Which was no doubt why, he once explained to William, he had tended, over the decades, to be so irascible and easily exhausted. The sustained effort, the subliminal concentration that was required to detach the stubborn prehensile hold was enough to wear a person right out and keep him from ever getting down to anything of real substance.

Weddings had lapsed entirely, birthdays were a phone call at the most, and at Christmas, Otto and William sent lavish gifts of out-of-season fruits, in the wake of which would arrive recriminatory little thank-you notes. From mid-December to mid-January they would absent themselves, not merely from the perilous vicinity of Otto's family, but from the entire country, to frolic in blue water under sunny skies.

When his mother died, Otto experienced an exhilarating melancholy; most of the painful encounters and obligations would now be a thing of the past. Life, with its humorous theatricality, had bestowed and revoked with one gesture, and there he abruptly was, in the position he felt he'd been born for: he was alone in the world.

Or alone in the world, anyway, with William. Marching ahead of his sisters and brother, Corinne, Martin, and Sharon, Otto was in the front ranks now, death's cannon fodder and so on; he had become old overnight, and free.

Old and free! Old and free. . . .

Still, he made himself available to provide legal advice or to arrange a summer internship for some child or nephew. He saw Sharon from time to time. From time to time there were calls: "Of course you're too busy, but . . ." "Of course you're not interested, but . . ." was how they began. This was the one thing Corinne and her husband and Martin and whichever wife were always all in accord about — that Otto seemed to feel he was too good for the rest of them, despite the obvious indications to the contrary.

Who was too good for whom? It often came down to a show of force. When Corinne had called a week or so earlier about Thanksgiving, Otto, addled by alarm, said, "We're having people ourselves, I'm afraid."

Corinne's silence was like a mirror, flashing his tiny, harmless lie back to him in huge magnification, all covered with sticky hairs and microbes.

"Well, I'll see what I can do," he said.

"Please try," Corinne said. The phrase had the unassailable authority of a road sign appearing suddenly around the bend: FALL-ING ROCK. "Otto, the children are growing up."

"Children! What children? Your children grew up years ago, Corinne. Your children are old now, like us."

"I meant, of course, Martin's. The new ones. Martin and Laurie's. And there's Portia."

Portia? Oh, yes. The little girl. The sole, thank heavens, issue of Martin's marriage to that crazy Viola.

"I'll see what I can do," Otto said again, this time less cravenly. It was Corinne's own fault. A person of finer sensibilities would have written a note or used e-mail — or would face-savingly have left a message at his office, giving him time to prepare some well-crafted deterrent rather than whatever makeshift explosive he would obviously be forced to lob back at her under direct attack.

"Wesley and I are having it in the city this year," Corinne was saying. "No need to come all the way out to the nasty country. A few hours and it will all be over with. Seriously, Otto, you're an integral element. We're keeping it simple this year."

"'This year'? Corinne, there have been no other years. You do not observe Thanksgiving."

"In fact, Otto, we do. And we all used to."

"Who?"

"All of us."

"Never. When? Can you imagine Mother being thankful for anything?"

"We always celebrated Thanksgiving when Father was alive."

"I remember no such thing."

"I do. I remember, and so does Martin."

"Martin was four when Father died!"

"Well, you were little, too."

"I was twice Martin's age."

"Oh, Otto — I just feel sad, sometimes, to tell you the truth, don't you? It's all going so fast! I'd like to see everyone in the same room once a century or so. I want to see everybody well and happy. I mean you and Martin and Sharon were my brothers and sister.

What was *that* all about? Don't you remember? Playing together all the time?"

"I just remember Martin throwing up all the time."

"You'll be nice to him, won't you, Otto? He's still very sensitive. He won't want to talk about the lawsuit."

"Have you spoken to Sharon?"

"Well, that's something I wanted to talk to you about, actually. I'm afraid I might have offended her. I stressed the fact that it was only to be us this year. No aunts or uncles, no cousins, no friends. Just us. And husbands or wives. Husband. And wife. Or whatever. And children, naturally, but she became very hostile."

"Assuming William to be 'whatever,'" Otto said, "why shouldn't Sharon bring a friend if she wants to?"

"William is *family*. And surely you remember when she brought that person to Christmas! The person with the feet? I wish you'd go by and talk to her in the next few days. She seems to listen to you."

Otto fished up a magazine from the floor — one of the popular science magazines William always left lying around — and idly opened it.

"Wesley and I reach out to her," Corinne was saying. "And so does Martin, but she doesn't respond. I know it can be hard for her to be with people, but we're not people — we're family."

"I'm sure she understands that, Corinne."

"I hope you do, too, Otto."

How clearly he could see, through the phone line, this little sister of his — in her fifties now — the six-year-old's expression of aggrieved anxiety long etched decisively on her face.

"In any case," she said, "I've called."

And yet there was something to what Corinne had said; they had been one another's environs as children. The distance among them had been as great, in any important way, as it was now, but there had been no other beings close by, no other beings through whom they could probe or illumine the mystifying chasms and absences and yearnings within themselves. They had been born into the arid clutter of one another's behavior, good and bad, their measles, skinned knees, report cards . . .

A barren landscape dotted with clutter. Perhaps the life of the last dinosaurs, as they ranged, puzzled and sorrowful, across the comet-singed planet, was similar to childhood. It hadn't been a pleasant time, surely, and yet one did have an impulse to acknowledge one's antecedents, now and again. Hello, that was us, it still is, goodbye.

"I don't know," William said. "It doesn't seem fair to put any pressure on Sharon."

"Heaven forfend. But I did promise Corinne I'd speak with Sharon. And, after all, I haven't actually seen her for some time."

"We could just go have a plain old visit, though. I don't know. Urging her to go to Corinne's — I'm not really comfortable with that."

"Oof, William, phrase, please, jargon."

"Why is that jargon?"

"Why? How should I know why? Because it is. You can say, 'I'm uncomfortable *about* that,' or 'That makes me uncomfortable.' But 'I'm uncomfortable *with* that' is simply jargon." He picked up a book sitting next to him on the table and opened it. *Relativity for Dummies.* "Good heavens," he said, snapping the book shut, "*obviously* Martin doesn't want to talk about the lawsuit. Why bother to mention that to me? Does she think I'm going to ask Martin whether it's true that he's been misrepresenting the value of his client's stock? Am I likely to talk about it? I'm perfectly happy to read about it in the *Times* every day, like everyone else."

"You know," William said, "we could go away early this year. We could just pick up and leave on Wednesday, if you'd like."

"I would not like. I would like you to play in your concert, as always."

William took the book from Otto and held Otto's hand between his own. "They're not really so bad, you know, your family," he said. Sometimes William's consolations were oddly like provocations.

"Easy for you to say," Otto said.

"Not that easy."

"I'm sorry," Otto said. "I know."

Just like William to suggest going away early for Otto's sake, when he looked forward so much to his concert! The little orchestra played publicly only once a year, the Sunday after Thanksgiving. Otto endured the grating preparatory practicing, not exactly with equanimity, it had to be admitted, but with relative forbearance, just for the pleasure of seeing William's radiant face on the occasion. William in his suit, William fussing over the programs, William busily arranging tickets for friends. Otto's sunny, his patient, his deeply good William. Toward the end of every year, when the city lights glimmered through the fuzzy winter dark, on the Sunday after Thanksgiving, William with his glowing violin, urging the good-natured, timid audience into passionate explorations of the unseen world. And every year now, from the audience, Otto felt William's impression stamped on the planet, more legible and valuable by one year — all the more legible and valuable for the one year's diminution in William's beauty.

How spectacular he had been the first time Otto brought him to a family event, that gladiatorial Christmas thirty-odd years earlier. How had Otto ever marshaled the nerve to do it?

Oh, one could say till one was blue in the face that Christmas was a day like any other, what difference would it make if he and William were to spend that particular day apart, and so on. And yet.

Yes, the occasion forced the issue, didn't it. Either he and William would both attend, or Otto would attend alone, or they would not attend together. But whatever it was that one decided to do, it would be a declaration — to the family, and to the other. And, the fact was, to oneself.

Steeled by new love, in giddy defiance, Otto had arrived at the house with William, to all intents and purposes, on his arm.

A tidal wave of nervous prurience had practically blown the door out from inside the instant he and William ascended the front step. And all evening aunts, uncles, cousins, mother, and siblings had stared at William beadily, as if a little bunny had loped out into a clearing in front of them.

William's beauty, and the fact that he was scarcely twenty, had embarrassed Otto on other occasions, but never so searingly. "How *intelligent* he is!" Otto's relatives kept whispering to one another loudly, meaning, apparently, that it was a marvel he could speak. Unlike, the further implication was, the men they'd evidently been imagining all these years.

Otto had brought someone to a family event only once before — also on a Christmas, with everyone in attendance: Diandra Fetlin, a feverishly brilliant colleague, far less beautiful than William. During the turkey, she thumped Otto on the arm whenever he made a good point in the argument he was having with Wesley, and continued to eat with solemn assiduity. Then, while the others applied themselves to dessert, a stuccolike fantasy requiring vigilance, Diandra had delivered an explication of one of the firm's recent cases that was worth three semesters of law school. No one commented on *her* intelligence. And no one had been in the least deceived by Otto's tepid display of interest in her.

"So," Corinne had said in a loud and artificially genial tone as if she were speaking to an armed high school student, "where did you and William meet, Otto?"

The table fell silent; Otto looked out at the wolfish ring of faces.

"On Third Avenue," he said distinctly, and returned to his meal.

"Sorry," he said, as he and William climbed into the car afterward. "Sorry to have embarrassed you. Sorry to have shocked them. Sorry, sorry, sorry. But what was I supposed to say? All that *interest.* The *solicitude.* The truth is, they've *never* sanctioned my way of life. Or, alternately, they've always *sanctioned* it. Oh, what on earth good is it to have a word that means only itself and its opposite!"

Driving back to the city, through the assaultively scenic and demographically uniform little towns, they were silent. William had witnessed; his power over Otto had been substantially increased by the preceding several hours, and yet he was exhibiting no signs of triumph. On the contrary, his habitual chipper mood was — where? Simply eclipsed. Otto glanced at him; no glance was returned.

Back in the apartment, they sat for a while in the dark. Tears stung Otto's eyes and nose. He would miss William terribly. "It was a mistake," he said.

William gestured absently. "Well, we had to do it sooner or later."

We? We did? It was as if snow had begun to fall in the apartment — a gentle, chiming, twinkling snow. And sitting there, looking at each other silently, it became apparent that what each was facing was his future.

Marvelous to watch William out in the garden, now with the late chrysanthemums. It was a flower Otto had never liked until William instructed him to look again. Well, all right, so it wasn't a merry flower. But flowers could comfortably embrace a range of qualities, it seemed. And now, how Otto loved the imperial colors, the tensely arched blossoms, the cleansing scent that seemed dipped up from the pure well of winter, nature's ceremony of end and beginning.

The flat little disk of autumn sun was retreating, high up over the neighbors' buildings. As Otto gazed out the window, William straightened, shaded his eyes, waved, and bent back to work. Late in the year, William in the garden . . .

Otto bought the brownstone when he and William had decided to truly move in together. Over twenty-five years ago, that was. The place was in disrepair and cost comparatively little at the time. While Otto hacked his way through the barbed thickets of intellectual property rights issues that had begun to spring up everywhere, struggling to disentangle tiny shoots of weak, drab good from vibrant, hardy evil, William worked in the garden. He worked on the house as well, and to earn, as he insisted on doing, a modest living of his own, he proofread for a small company that published books about music. Eventually they rented out the top story of the brownstone, for a purely nominal sum, to Naomi, whom they'd met around the neighborhood and liked. It was nice to come home late and see her light on, to run into her on the stairs.

She'd been just a girl when she'd moved in, really, nodding and smiling and ducking her head when she encountered them at the door or on the way up with intractable brown paper bags, bulging as if they were full of cats but tufted with peculiar groceries — vegetables sprouting globular appendages and sloshing cartons of liquids made from grain. Then, further along in the distant past, Margaret had appeared.

Where there had been one in the market, at the corner bar, on the stairs, now there were two. Naomi, short and lively, given to boots and charming cowgirl skirts; tall, arrestingly bony Margaret with arched eyebrows and bright red hair. Now there were lines around Naomi's eyes; she had widened and settled downward. One rarely recalled Margaret's early, sylvan loveliness.

So long ago! Though it felt that way only at moments, when Otto passed by a mirror unprepared, or when he bothered to register the probable ages (in comparison with his own) of people whom — so recently! — he would have taken for contemporaries, or when he caught a glimpse of a middle-aged person coming toward him on the street who turned into William. Or sometimes when he thought of Sharon.

And right this moment, Naomi and Margaret were on their way

back from China with their baby. The adoption went through! Naomi's recent, ecstatic e-mail had announced. Adoption. Had the girls upstairs failed to notice that they had slid into their late forties?

Sharon's apartment looked, as always, as if it had been sealed up in some innocent period of the past against approaching catastrophes. There were several blond wood chairs and a sofa, all slipcovered in a nubby, unexceptionable fabric that suggested nuns' sleepwear, and a plastic hassock. The simple, undemanding shapes of the furnishings portrayed the humility of daily life — or at least, Otto thought, of Sharon's daily life. The Formica counter was blankly unstained, and in the cupboards there was a set of heavy, functional white dishes.

It was just possible, if you craned, and scrunched yourself properly, to glimpse through the window a corner of Sharon's beloved planetarium, where she spent many of her waking hours; the light that made its way to the window around the encircling buildings was pale and tender, an elegy from a distant sun. Sharon herself sometimes seemed to Otto like an apparition from the past. As the rest of them aged, her small frame still looked like a young girl's; her hair remained an infantine flaxen. To hold it back she wore bright plastic barrettes.

A large computer, a gift from Otto, sat in the living room, its screen permanently alive. Charts of the constellations were pinned to one of the bedroom walls, and on the facing wall were topographical maps. Peeking into the room, one felt as if one were traveling with Sharon in some zone between earth and sky; yes, down there, so far away — that was our planet.

Why did he need so many things in his life, Otto wondered; and why did all these things have to be so special? Special, beautiful plates; special, beautiful furniture; special, beautiful everything. And all that specialness, it occurred to him, only to ensure that no one — especially himself — could possibly underestimate his worth. Yet it actually served only to illustrate how corroded he was, how threadbare his native resources, how impoverished his discourse with everything that lived and was human.

Sharon filled a teakettle with water and lit one of the stove burners. The kettle was dented but oddly bright, as if she'd just scrubbed it. "I'm thinking of buying a sculpture," she said. "Nothing big. Sit down, Otto, if you'd like. With some pleasant vertical bits."

"Good plan," Otto said. "Where did you find it?"

"Find it?" she said. "Oh. It's a theoretical sculpture. Abstract in that sense, at least. Because I realized you were right."

About what? Well, it was certainly plausible that he had once idly said something about a sculpture, possibly when he'd helped her find the place and move in, decades earlier. She remembered encyclopedically her years of education, pages of print, apparently arbitrary details of their histories. And some trivial incident or phrase from their childhood might at any time fetch up from her mind and flop down in front of her, alive and thrashing.

No, but it couldn't be called "remembering" at all, really, could it? That simply wasn't what people meant by "remembering." No act of mind or the psyche was needed for Sharon to reclaim anything, because nothing in her brain ever sifted down out of precedence. The passage of time failed to distance, blur, or diminish her experiences. The nacreous layers that formed around the events in one's history to smooth, distinguish, and beautify them never materialized around Sharon's; her history skittered here and there in its original sharp grains on a depthless plane that resembled neither calendar nor clock.

"I just had the most intense episode of déjà vu," William said, as if Otto's thoughts had sideswiped him. "We were all sitting here —"

"We *are* all sitting here," Otto said.

"But that's what I mean," William said. "It's supposed to be some kind of synaptic glitch, isn't it?"

"In the view of many neurologists," Sharon said. "But our understanding of time is dim. It's patchy. We really don't know to what degree time is linear, and under what circumstances. Is it manifold? Or pleated? Is it frilly? And our relationship to it is extremely problematical."

"I think it's a fine idea for you to have a sculpture," Otto said. "But I don't consider it a necessity."

Her face was as transparent as a child's. Or at least as hers had been as a child, reflecting every passing cloud, rippling at the tiniest disturbance. And her smile! The sheer wattage — no one over eleven smiled like that. "We're using the tea bag in the cup method," she said. "Greater scope for the exercise of free will, streamlined technology . . ."

"Oh, goody," William said. "Darjeeling."

Otto stared morosely at his immersed bag and the dark halo spreading from it. How long would Sharon need them to stay? When would she want them to go? It was tricky, weaving a course between what might cause her to feel rejected and what might cause her to feel embattled . . . Actually, though, how did these things work? Did bits of water escort bits of tea from the bag, or what? "How is flavor disseminated?" he said.

"It has to do with oils," Sharon said.

Strange, you really couldn't tell, half the time, whether someone was knowledgeable or insane. At school Sharon had shown an astounding talent for the sciences — for everything. For mathematics, especially. Her mind was so rarefied, so crystalline, so adventurous, that none of the rest of them could begin to follow. She soared into graduate school, practically still a child; she was one of the few blessed people, it seemed, whose destiny was clear.

Her professors were astonished by her leaps of thought, by the finesse and elegance of her insights. She arrived at hypotheses by sheer intuition and with what eventually one of her mentors described as an almost alarming speed; she was like a dancer, he said, out in the cosmos springing weightlessly from star to star. Drones, merely brilliant, crawled along behind with laborious proofs that supported her assertions.

A tremendous capacity for metaphor, Otto assumed it was, a tremendous sensitivity to the deep structures of the universe. Uncanny. It seemed no more likely that there would be human beings thus equipped than human beings born with satellite dishes growing out of their heads.

He himself was so literal-minded he couldn't understand the simplest scientific or mathematical formulation. Plain old electricity, for example, with its amps and volts and charges and conductivity! Metaphors, presumably — metaphors to describe some ectoplasmic tiger in the walls just spoiling to shoot through the wires the instant the cage door was opened and out into the bulb. And molecules! What on earth were people talking about? If the table was actually just a bunch of swarming motes, bound to one another by nothing more than some amicable commonality of form, then why didn't your teacup crash through it?

But from the time she was tiny, Sharon seemed to be in kindly, lighthearted communion with the occult substances that lay far within and far beyond the human body. It was all as easy for her as reading was for him. She was a creature of the universe. As were they all, come to think of it, though so few were privileged to feel it. And how hospitable and correct she'd made the universe seem when she spoke of even its most rococo and far-fetched attributes!

The only truly pleasurable moments at the family dinner table were those rare occasions when Sharon would talk. He remembered one evening — she would have been in grade school. She was wearing a red sweater; pink barrettes held back her hair. She was speaking of holes in space — holes in nothing! No, not in nothing, Sharon explained patiently — in space. And the others, older and larger, laid down their speared meat and listened, uncomprehending and entranced, as though to distant, wordless singing.

Perhaps, Otto sometimes consoled himself, they could be forgiven for failing to identify the beginnings. How could the rest of them, with their ordinary intellects, have followed Sharon's rapid and arcane speculations, her penetrating apperceptions, closely enough to identify with any certainty the odd associations and disjunctures that seemed to be showing up in her conversation? In any case, at a certain point as she wandered out among the galaxies, among the whirling particles and ineffable numbers, something leaked in her mind, smudging the text of the cosmos, and she was lost.

Or perhaps, like a light bulb, she was helplessly receptive to an overwhelming influx. She was so physically delicate, and yet the person to whom she was talking might take a step back. And she, in turn, could be crushed by the slightest shift in someone's expression or tone. It was as if the chemistry of her personality burned off the cushion of air between herself and others. Then one night she called, very late, to alert Otto to a newspaper article about the sorting of lettuces; if he were to give each letter its numerological value ... The phone cord thrummed with her panic.

When their taxi approached the hospital on that first occasion, Sharon was dank and electric with terror; her skin looked like wet plaster. Otto felt like an assassin as he led her in, and then she was ushered away somewhere. The others joined him in the waiting room, and after several hours had the opportunity to browbeat various doctors into hangdog temporizing. Many people got better, didn't they, had only one episode, didn't they, led fully functioning lives? Why wouldn't Sharon be part of that statistic — she, who was so able, so lively, so sweet — so, in a word, healthy? When would she be all right?

That depended on what they meant by "all right," one of the doctors replied. "We mean by 'all right' what you mean by 'all right,' you squirrelly bastard," Wesley had shouted, empurpling. Martin paced, sizzling and clicking through his teeth, while Otto sat with his head in his hands, but the fateful, brutal, meaningless diagnosis had already been handed down.

"I got a cake," Sharon said. She glanced at Otto. "Oh. Was that appropriate?"

"Utterly," William said.

"Appropriate?" What if the cake turned out to be decorated with invisible portents and symbols? What if it revealed itself to be invested with power? To be part of the arsenal of small objects — nail scissors, postage stamps, wrapped candies — that lay about in camouflage to fool the credulous doofus like himself just as they were winking their malevolent signals to Sharon?

Or what if the cake was, after all, only an inert teatime treat? A cake required thought, effort, expenditure — all that on a negligible scale for most people, but in Sharon's stripped and cautious life, nothing was negligible. A cake. Wasn't that enough to bring one to one's knees? "Very appropriate," Otto concurred.

"Do you miss the fish?" Sharon said, lifting the cake from its box.

Fish? Otto's heart flipped up, pounding. Oh, the box, fish, nothing.

"We brought them home from the dime store in little cardboard boxes," she explained to William, passing the cake on its plate and a large knife over to him.

"I had a hamster," William said. The cake bulged resiliently around the knife.

"Did it have to rush around on one of those things?" Sharon asked.

"I think it liked to," William said, surprised.

"Let us hope so," Otto said. "Of course it did."

"I loved the castles and the colored sand," Sharon said. "But it was no life for a fish. We had to flush them down the toilet."

William, normally so fastidious about food, appeared to be happily eating his cake, which tasted, to Otto, like landfill. And William had brought Sharon flowers, which it never would have occurred to Otto to do.

Why had lovely William stayed with disagreeable old him for all this time? What could possibly explain his appeal for William, Otto wondered? Certainly not his appearance, nor his musical sensitivity — middling at best — nor, clearly, his temperament. Others might have been swayed by the money that he made so easily, but not William. William cared as little about that as did Otto himself. And yet, through all these years, William had cleaved to him. Or at least, usually. Most of the uncleavings, in fact, had been Otto's — brief, preposterous seizures having to do with God knows what. Well, actually he himself would be the one to know what, wouldn't he, Otto thought. Having to do with — who *did* know what? Oh, with fear, with flight, the usual. A bit of glitter, a mirage, a chimera . . . A lot of commotion just for a glimpse into his own life, the real one — a life more vivid, more truly his, than the one that was daily at hand.

"Was there something you wanted to see me about?" Sharon asked.

"Well, I just . . ." Powerful beams of misery intersected in Otto's heart. Was it true? Did he always have a reason when he called Sharon? Did he never drop in just to say hello? Not that anyone ought to "drop in" on Sharon. Or on anyone, actually. How barbarous.

"Your brother's here in an ambassadorial capacity," William said. "I'm just here for the cake."

"Ambassadorial?" Sharon looked alarmed.

"Oh, it's only Thanksgiving," Otto said. "Corinne was hoping — I was hoping —"

"Otto, I can't. I just can't. I don't want to sit there being an exhibit of robust good health, or non-contaminatingness, or the triumph of the human spirit, or whatever it is that Corinne needs me to illustrate. Just tell them everything is O.K."

He looked at his cake. William was right. This was terribly unfair. "Well, I don't blame you," he said. "I wouldn't go myself, if I could get out of it."

"If you had a good-enough excuse."

"I only —" But of course it was exactly what he had meant; he had meant that Sharon had a good-enough excuse. "I'm —"

"Tell Corinne I'm all right."

Otto started to speak again, but stopped.

"Otto, please." Sharon looked at her hands, folded in her lap. "It's all right."

"I've sometimes wondered if it might not be possible, in theory, to remember something that you — I mean the aspect of yourself that you're aware of — haven't experienced yet," William said later. "I mean, you really *don't* know whether time is linear, so —"

"Would you stop that?" Otto said. "*You're* not insane."

"I'm merely speaking theoretically."

"Well, don't! And your memory has nothing to do with whether time is 'really,' whatever you mean by that, linear. It's plenty linear for us! Cradle to grave? Over the hill? It's a one-way street, my dear. My hair is not sometimes there and sometimes not there. We're *not* getting any younger."

At moments it occurred to Otto that what explained his appeal for William was the fact that they lived in the same apartment. That William was idiotically accepting, idiotically pliant. Perhaps William was so deficient in subtlety, so insensitive to nuance, that he simply couldn't tell the difference between Otto and anyone else. "And, William — I wish you'd get back to your tennis."

"It's a bore. Besides, you didn't want me playing with Jason, as I remember."

"Well, I was out of my mind. And at this point it's your arteries I worry about."

"You know," William said — he put his graceful hand on Otto's arm — "I don't think she's any more unhappy than the rest of us, really, most of the time. That smile! I mean, that smile can't come out of nowhere."

There actually were no children to speak of. Corinne and Wesley's "boys" put in a brief, unnerving appearance. When last seen, they had been surly, furtive, persecuted-looking, snickering, hulking, hairy adolescents, and now here they were, having undergone the miraculous transformation. How gratified Wesley must be! They had shed their egalitarian denim chrysalis and had risen up in the crisp, mean mantle of their class.

The older one even had a wife, whom Corinne treated with a stricken, fluttery deference as if she were a suitcase full of weapons-grade plutonium. The younger one was restlessly on his own.

When, early in the evening the three stood, and announced to Corinne with thuggish placidity that they were about to leave ("I'm afraid we've got to shove off now, Ma"), Otto jumped to his feet. As he allowed his hand to be crushed, he felt the relief of a mayor watching an occupying power depart his city.

Martin's first squadron of children (Maureen's) weren't even mentioned. Who knew what army of relatives, step-relatives, half relatives they were reinforcing by now. But there were — Otto shuddered faintly — Martin's two newest (Laurie's). Yes, just as Corinne had said, they, too, were growing up. Previously indistinguishable wads of self-interest, they had developed perceptible features — maybe even characteristics; it appeared reasonable, after all, that they had been given names.

What on earth was it that William did to get children to converse? Whenever Otto tried to have a civilized encounter with a child, the child just stood there with its finger in its nose. But Martin's two boys were chattering away, showing off to William their whole heap of tiresome electronics.

William was frowning with interest. He poked at a keyboard, which sent up a shower of festive little beeps, and the boys flung themselves at him, cheering, while Laurie smiled meltingly. How times had changed. Not so many years earlier, such a tableau would have had handcuffs rattling in the wings.

The only other representative of "the children" to whom Corinne had referred with such pathos was Martin's daughter, Portia (Viola's). She'd been hardly more than a toddler at last sight, though she now appeared to be about — what? Well, anyhow, a little girl. "What are the domestic arrangements?" Otto asked. "Is she living with Martin and Laurie these days, or is she with her mother?"

"That crazy Viola has gone back to England, thank God; Martin has de facto custody."

"Speaking of Martin, where is he?"

"I don't ask," Corinne said.

Otto waited.

"I don't ask," Corinne said again. "And if Laurie wants to share, she'll tell you herself."

"Is Martin in the pokey already?" Otto asked.

"This is not a joke, Otto. I'm sorry to tell you that Martin has been having an affair with some girl."

"Again?"

Corinne stalled, elaborately adjusting her bracelet. "I'm sorry to tell you she's his trainer."

"His *trainer*? How can Martin have a trainer? If Martin has a trainer, what can explain Martin's body?"

"Otto, it's not funny," Corinne said with ominous primness. "The fact is, Martin has been looking very good lately. But of course you wouldn't have seen him."

All those wives — and a trainer! How? Why would any woman put up with Martin? Martin, who always used to eat his dessert so slowly that the rest of them had been made to wait, squirming at the table, watching as he took his voluptuous, showy bites of chocolate cake or floating island long after they'd finished their own.

"I'm afraid it's having consequences for Portia. Do you see what she's doing?"

"She's —" Otto squinted over at Portia. "What is she doing?"

"Portia, come here, darling," Corinne called.

Portia looked at them for a moment, then wandered sedately over. "And now we'll have a word with Aunt Corinne," she said to her fist as she approached. "Hello, Aunt Corinne."

"Portia," Corinne said, "do you remember Uncle Otto?"

"And Uncle Otto," Portia added to her fist. She regarded him with a clear, even gaze. In its glade of light and silence they encountered each other serenely. She held out her fist to him. "Would you tell our listeners what you do when you go to work, Uncle Otto?"

"Well," Otto said, to Portia's fist, "first I take the elevator up to the twentieth floor, and then I sit down at my desk, and then I send Bryan out for coffee and a bagel —"

"Otto," Corinne said, "Portia is trying to learn what it is you *do*. Something I'm sure we'd all like to know."

"Oh," Otto said. "Well, I'm a lawyer, dear. Do you know what that is?"

"Otto," Corinne said wearily, "Portia's father is a lawyer."

"Portia's father is a global-money mouthpiece!" Otto said.

"Aunt Corinne is annoyed," Portia commented to her fist. "Now Uncle Otto and Aunt Corinne are looking at your correspondent. Now they're not."

"Tell me, Portia," Otto said. The question had sprung insistently into his mind: "What are you going to be when you grow up?"

Her gaze was strangely relaxing. "You know, Uncle Otto," she said pensively to her fist, "people used to ask me that a lot."

Huh! Yes, that was probably something people asked only very small children, when speculation would be exclusively a matter of amusing fantasy. "Well, I was only just mulling it over," Otto said.

"Portia, darling," Corinne said, "why don't you run into the kitchen and do a cooking segment with Bea and Cleveland?"

"It's incredible," Otto said when Portia disappeared, "she looks exactly like Sharon did at that age."

"Ridiculous," Corinne said. "She takes after her father."

Martin? Stuffy, venal Martin, with his nervous eyes and scoopy nose and squashy head balanced on his shirt collar? Portia's large, gray eyes, the flaxen hair, the slightly oversized ears and fragile neck, recapitulated absolutely Sharon's appearance in this child who probably wouldn't remember ever having seen Sharon. "Her father?"

"Her father," Corinne said. "Martin. Portia's father."

"I know Martin is her father. I just can't divine the resemblance."

"Well, there's certainly no resemblance to — Wesley —" Corinne called over to him. "Must you read the newspaper? This is a social occasion. Otto, will you listen, please? I'm trying to tell you something. The truth is, we're all quite worried about Portia."

Amazing how fast one's body reacted. Fear had vacuumed the blood right through his extremities. One's body, the primeval parts of one's brain — how fast they were! Much faster than that recent part with the words and thoughts and so on, what was it? The cortex, was that it? He'd have to ask William, he thought, his blood settling back down. That sort of wrinkly stuff on top that looked like crumpled wrapping paper.

"Laurie is worried sick. The truth is, that's one reason I was so anxious for you to join us today. I wanted your opinion on the matter."

"On what matter?" Otto said. "I have no idea what this is about. She's fine. She seems fine. She's just playing."

"I know she's just playing, Otto. It's *what* she's playing that concerns me."

"What she's playing? What is she playing? She's playing radio, or something! Is that so sinister? The little boys seem to be playing something called Hammer Her Flat."

"I'm sure not. Oh, gracious. You and Sharon were both so right not to have children."

"Excuse me?" Otto said incredulously.

"It's not the radio aspect per se that I'm talking about, it's what that represents. The child is an observer. She sees herself as an outsider. As alienated."

"There's nothing wrong with being observant. Other members of this family could benefit from a little of that quality."

"She can't relate directly to people."

"Who can?" Otto said.

"Half the time Viola doesn't even remember the child is alive! You watch. She won't send Portia a Christmas present. She probably won't even call. Otto, listen. We've always said that Viola is 'unstable,' but, frankly, Viola is *psychotic*. Do you understand what I'm saying to you? Portia's *mother*, Otto. It's just as you were saying, *there's a geneti* ——"

"I was saying *what?* I was saying nothing! I was only saying —"

"Oh, dear!" Laurie exclaimed. She had an arm around Portia, who was crying.

"What in hell is going on now?" Wesley demanded, slamming down his newspaper.

"I'm afraid Bea and Cleveland may have said something to her," Laurie said, apologetically.

"Oh, terrific," Wesley said. "Now I know what I'm paying them for."

"It's all right, sweetie," Laurie said. "It all happened a long time ago."

"But why are we celebrating that we killed them?" Portia asked, and started crying afresh.

"We're not celebrating because we killed the Indians, darling," Laurie said. "We're celebrating because we ate dinner with them."

"Portia still believes in Indians!" one of the little boys exclaimed.

"So do we all, Josh," Wesley said. "They live at the North Pole and make toys for good little —"

"Wesley, please!" Corinne said.

"Listener poll," Portia said to her fist. "Did we eat dinner with the Indians, or did we kill them?" She strode over to Otto and held out her fist.

"We ate dinner with them and *then* we killed them," Otto realized, out loud to his surprise.

"Who are you to slag off Thanksgiving, old boy?" Wesley said. "You're wearing a fucking bow tie."

"So are you, for that matter," Otto said, awkwardly embracing Portia, who was crying again.

"And *I* stand behind my tie," Wesley said, rippling upward from his chair.

"It was Portia's birthday last week!" Laurie interrupted loudly, and Wesley sank back down. "Wasn't it!"

Portia nodded, gulping, and wiped at her tears.

"How old are you now, Portia?" William asked.

"Nine," Portia said.

"That's great," William said. "Get any good stuff?"

Portia nodded again.

"And Portia's mommy sent a terrific present, didn't she," Laurie said.

"Oh, what was it, sweetie?" Corinne said.

Laurie turned pink and her head seemed to flare out slightly in various directions. "You don't have to say, darling, if you don't like."

Portia held on to the arm of Otto's chair and swung her leg aimlessly back and forth. "My mother gave me two tickets to go to Glyndebourne on my eighteenth birthday," she said in a tiny voice.

Wesley snorted. "Got your outfit all picked out, Portia?"

"I won't be going to Glyndebourne, Uncle Wesley," Portia said with dignity.

There was a sudden silence in the room.

"Why not, dear?" Otto asked. He was trembling, he noticed.

Portia looked out at all of them. Tears still clung to her face. "Because." She raised her fist to her mouth again. "Factoid: According to the Mayan calendar, the world is going to end in the year 2012, the year before this reporter's eighteenth birthday."

"All right," Corinne whispered to Otto. "Now do you see?"

"You're right, as always," Otto said, in the taxi later, "they're no worse than anyone else's. They're all awful. I really don't see the point in it. Just think! Garden garden garden garden garden, two happy people, and it could have gone on forever! They knew, they'd been told, but they ate it anyway, and from there on out, *family*! Shame, fear, jobs, mortality, envy, murder . . ."

"Well," William said brightly, "and sex."

"There's that," Otto conceded.

"In fact, you could look at both family and mortality simply as by-products of sexual reproduction."

"I don't really see the point of sexual reproduction, either," Otto said. "*I* wouldn't stoop to it."

"Actually, that's very interesting, you know; they think that the purpose of sexual reproduction is to purge the genome of harmful mutations. Of course, they also seem to think it isn't working."

"Then why not scrap it?" Otto said. "Why not let us divide again, like our dignified and immortal forebear, the amoeba."

William frowned. "I'm not really sure that —"

"Joke," Otto said.

"Oh, yes. Well, but I suppose sexual reproduction is fairly entrenched by now — people aren't going to give it up without a struggle. And besides, family confers certain advantages as a social unit, doesn't it."

"No. What advantages?"

"Oh, rudimentary education. Protection."

"'Education'! Ha! 'Protection'! Ha!"

"Besides," William pointed out. "It's broadening. You meet people in your family you'd never happen to run into otherwise. And anyhow, obviously the desire for children is hard-wired."

"'Hard-wired.' You know, that's a term I've really come to loathe! It explains nothing, it justifies anything; you might as well say, 'Humans want children because the Great Moth in the Sky requires them to.' Or 'Humans want children because humans want children.' 'Hard-wired,' please! It's lazy, it's specious, it's perfunctory, and it's utterly without depth."

"Why does it have to have depth?" William said. "It *refers* to depth. It's good, clean science."

"It's not science at all, it's a cliché. It's a redundancy."

"Otto, why do you always scoff at me when I raise a scientific point?"

"I don't! I don't scoff at you. I certainly don't mean to. It's just that this particular phrase, used in this particular way, isn't very interesting. I mean, you're telling me that something is biologically *inherent* in human experience, but you're not telling me anything *about* human experience."

"I wasn't intending to," William said. "I wasn't trying to. If you want to talk about human experience, then let's talk about it."

"All right," Otto said. It was painful, of course, to see William irritated, but almost a relief to know that it could actually happen.

"Let's, then. By all means."

"So?"

"Well?"

"Any particular issues?" William said. "Any questions?"

Any! *Billions.* But that was always just the problem: how to disentangle one; how to pluck it up and clothe it in presentable words? Otto stared, concentrating. Questions were roiling in the pit of his mind like serpents, now a head rising up from the seething mass, now a rattling tail . . . He closed his eyes. If only he could get his brain to relax . . . Relax, relax . . . Relax, relax, relax . . . "Oh, you know, William — is there anything at home to eat? Believe it or not, I'm starving again."

There was absolutely no reason to fear that Portia would have anything other than an adequately happy, adequately fruitful life. No reason at all. Oh, how prudent of Sharon not to have come yesterday. Though in any case, she had been as present to the rest of them as if she had been sitting on the sofa. And the rest of them had probably been as present to her as she had been to them.

When one contemplated Portia, when one contemplated Sharon, when one contemplated one's own apparently pointless, utterly trivial being, the questions hung all around one, as urgent as knives at the throat. But the instant one tried to grasp one of them and turn it to one's own purpose and pierce through the murk, it became as blunt and useless as a piece of cardboard.

All one could dredge up were platitudes: one comes into the world alone, snore snore; one, snore snore, departs the world alone . . .

What would William have to say? Well, it was a wonderful thing to live with an inquiring and mentally active person; no one could quarrel with that. William was immaculate in his intentions, unflagging in his efforts. But what drove one simply insane was the vagueness. Or, really, the banality. Not that it was William's job to explicate the foggy assumptions of one's culture, but one's own ineptitude was galling enough; one hardly needed to consult a vacuity expert!

And how could one think at all, or even just casually ruminate, with William practicing, as he had been doing since they'd awakened. Otto had forgotten what a strain it all was — even without any exasperating social nonsense — those few days preceding the concert; you couldn't think, you couldn't concentrate on the newspaper. You couldn't even really hear the phone, which seemed to be ringing now —

Nor could you make any sense of what the person on the other end of it might be saying. "What?" Otto shouted into it. "You what?"

Could he — the phone cackled into the lush sheaves of William's arpeggios — *bribery, sordid out* —

"William!" Otto yelled. "Excuse me? Could I what?"

The phone cackled some more. "Excuse me," Otto said. *"William —"*

The violin went quiet. "Excuse me?" Otto said again into the phone, which was continuing to emit gibberish. "Sort *what* out? Took her *where* from the library?"

"I'm trying to explain, sir," the phone said. "I'm calling from the hospital."

"She was *taken* from the library *by force?*"

"Unfortunately, sir, as I've tried to explain, she was understood to be homeless."

"And so she was taken away? By force? That could be construed as kidnapping, you know."

"I'm only reporting what the records indicate, sir. The records do not indicate that your sister was kidnapped."

"I don't understand. Is it a crime to be homeless?"

"Apparently your sister did not claim to be homeless. Apparently your sister claimed to rent an apartment. Is this not the case? Is your sister in fact homeless?"

"My sister is not homeless! My sister rents an apartment! Is that a crime? What does this have to do with why my sister was taken away, by force, from the library?"

"Sir, I'm calling from the hospital."

"I'm a taxpayer!" Otto shouted. William was standing in the doorway, violin in one hand, bow in the other, watching gravely. "I'm a lawyer! Why is information being withheld from me?"

"Information is not being withheld from you, sir, please! I understand that you are experiencing concern, and I'm trying to explain this situation in a way that you will understand what has occurred.

It is a policy that homeless people tend to congregate in the library, using the restrooms, and some of these people may be removed, if, for example, these people exhibit behaviors that are perceived to present a potential danger."

"Are you reading this from something? Is it a crime to use a public bathroom?"

"When people who do not appear to have homes to go to, appear to be confused and disoriented —"

"Is it a *crime* to be *confused*?"

"Please calm *down,* sir. The evaluation was not ours. What I'm trying to tell you is that according to the report, your sister became obstreperous when she was brought to the homeless shelter. She appeared to be disoriented. She did not appear to understand why she was being taken to the homeless shelter."

"Shall I go with you?" William said, when Otto put down the phone.

"No," Otto said. "Stay, please. Practice."

So, once again. Waiting in the dingy whiteness, the fearsome whiteness no doubt of heaven, heaven's sensible shoes, overtaxed heaven's obtuse smiles and ruthless tranquillity, heaven's asphyxiating clouds dropped over the screams bleeding faintly from behind closed doors. He waited in a room with others too dazed even to note the television that hissed and bristled in front of them or to turn the pages of the sticky, dog-eared magazines they held, from which they could have learned how to be happy, wealthy, and sexually appealing; they waited, like Otto, to learn instead what it was that destiny had already handed down: bad, not that bad, very, very bad.

The doctor, to whom Otto was eventually conducted through the elderly bowels of the hospital, looked like an epic hero — shining, arrogant, supple. "She'll be fine, now," he said. "You'll be fine now, won't you?"

Sharon's smile, the sudden birth of a little sun, and the doctor's own brilliant smile met, and ignited for an instant. Otto felt as though a missile had exploded in his chest.

"Don't try biting any of those guys from the city again," the doctor said, giving Sharon's childishly rounded, childishly humble shoulder a companionable pat. "They're poisonous."

"Bite them!" Otto exclaimed, admiration leaping up in him like a dog at a chainlink fence, on the other side of which a team of uniformed men rushed at his defenseless sister with clubs.

"I did?" Sharon cast a repentant, sidelong glance at the doctor.

The doctor shrugged and flipped back his blue-black hair, dislodging sparkles of handsomeness. "The file certainly painted an unflattering portrait of your behavior. 'Menaced dentally,' it says, or something of the sort. Now, listen. Take care of yourself. Follow Dr. Shiga's instructions. Because I don't want to be seeing you around here, O.K.?"

He and Sharon looked at each other for a moment, then traded a little, level, intimate smile. "It's O.K. with me," she said.

Otto took Sharon to a coffee shop near her apartment and bought her two portions of macaroni and cheese.

"How was it?" she said. "How was everyone?"

"Thanksgiving? Oh. You didn't miss much."

She put down her fork. "Aren't you going to have anything, Otto?"

"I'll have something later with William," he said.

"Oh," she said. She sat very still. "Of course."

He was a monster. Well, no one was perfect. But in any case, her attention returned to her macaroni. Not surprising that she was ravenous. How long had her adventures lasted? Her clothing was rumpled and filthy.

"I didn't know you liked the library," he said.

"Don't think I'm not grateful for the computer," she said. "It was down."

He nodded, and didn't press her.

There was a bottle of wine breathing on the table, and William had managed to maneuver dinner out of the mysterious little containers and the limp bits of organic matter from the fridge, which Otto had inspected earlier in a doleful search for lunch. "Bad?" William asked.

"Fairly," Otto said.

"Want to tell me?" William said.

Otto gestured impatiently. "Oh, what's the point."

"O.K.," William said. "Mustard with that? It's good."

"I can't stand it that she has to live like this!" Otto said.

William shook his head. "Everyone is so alone," he said.

Otto yelped.

"What?" William said. "What did I do?"

"Nothing," Otto said. He stood, trying to control his trembling. "I'm going to my study. You go on upstairs when you get tired."

"Otto?"

"Just — please."

He sat downstairs in his study with a book in his hand, listening while William rinsed the dishes and put them in the dishwasher, and went, finally, upstairs. For some time, footsteps persisted oppressively in the bedroom overhead. When they ceased, Otto exhaled with relief.

A pale tincture spread into the study window; the pinched little winter sun was rising over the earth, above the neighbors' buildings. Otto listened while William came down and made himself breakfast, then returned upstairs to practice once again.

The day sat heavily in front of Otto, like an opponent judging the moment to strike. How awful everything was. How awful he was. How bestial he had been to William; William, who deserved only kindness, only gratitude.

And yet the very thought of glimpsing that innocent face was intolerable. It had been a vastly unpleasant night in the chair, and it would be hours, he knew, before he'd be able to manage an apology without more denunciations leaping from his treacherous mouth.

Hours seemed to be passing, in fact. Or maybe it was minutes. The clock said 7:00, said 10:00, said 12:00, said 12:00, said 12:00, seemed to be delirious. Fortunately there were leftovers in the fridge.

Well, if time was the multiplicity Sharon and William seemed to believe it was, maybe it contained multiple Sharons, perhaps some existing in happier conditions, before the tracks diverged, one set leading up into the stars, the other down to the hospital. Otto's mind wandered here and there amid the dimensions, catching glimpses of her skirt, her hair, her hand, as she slipped through the mirrors. Did things have to proceed for each of the Sharons in just exactly the same way?

Did each one grieve for the Olympian destiny that ought to have been hers? Did each grieve for an ordinary life — a life full of ordinary pleasures and troubles — children, jobs, lovers?

Everyone is so alone. For this, all the precious Sharons had to flounder through their loops and tucks of eternity; for this, the shutters were drawn on their aerial and light-filled minds. Each and every Sharon, thrashing through the razor-edged days only in order to be absorbed by this spongy platitude: *Everyone is so alone!* Great God, how could it be endured? All the Sharons, forever and ever, discarded in a phrase.

And those Ottos, sprinkled through the zones of actuality — what were the others doing now? The goldfish gliding, gliding, within the severe perimeter of water, William pausing to introduce himself . . .

Yes, so of course one felt incomplete; of course one felt obstructed and blind. And perhaps every creature on earth, on all the earths, was straining at the obdurate membranes to reunite as its own original entity, the spark of unique consciousness allocated to each being, only then to be irreconcilably refracted through world after world by the prism of time. No wonder one tended to feel so fragile — it was exasperating enough just trying to have contact with a few other people, let alone with all of one's selves!

To think there could be an infinitude of selves, and not an iota of latitude for any of them! An infinitude of Ottos, lugging around that personality, those circumstances, that appearance. Not only once dreary and pointless, but infinitely so.

Oh, was there no escape? Perhaps if one could only concentrate hard enough they could be collected, all those errant, enslaved selves. And in the triumphant instant of their reunification, distilled to an unmarked essence, the suffocating Otto-costumes dissolving, a true freedom at last. Oh, how tired he was! But why not make the monumental effort?

Because Naomi and Margaret were arriving at 9:00 to show off this baby of theirs, that was why not.

And anyhow, what on earth was he thinking?

Still, at least he could apologize to William. He was himself, but at least he could go fling that inadequate self at William's feet!

No. At the *very* least he could let poor, deserving William practice undisturbed. He'd wait — patiently, patiently — and when William was finished, William would come downstairs. Then Otto could apologize abjectly, spread every bit of his worthless being at William's feet, comfort him and be comforted, reassure him and be reassured . . .

At a few minutes before 9:00, William appeared, whistling.

Whistling! "Good practice session?" Otto said. His voice came out cracked, as if it had been hurled against the high prison walls of himself.

"Terrific," William said, and kissed him lightly on the forehead.

Otto opened his mouth. "You know —" he said.

"Oh, listen —" William said. "There really is a baby!" And faintly interspersed among Naomi and Margaret's familiar creakings and bumpings in the hall Otto heard little chirps and gurgles.

"Hello, hello!" William cried, flinging open the door. "Look, isn't she fabulous?"

"We think so," Naomi said, her smile renewing and renewing itself. "Well, she is."

"I can't see if you do that," Margaret said, disengaging the earpiece of her glasses and a clump of her red, crimpy hair from the baby's fist as she attempted to transfer the baby over to William.

"Here." Naomi held out a bottle of champagne. "Take this, too. Well, but you can't keep the baby. Wow, look, she's fascinated by Margaret's hair. I mean, who isn't?"

Otto wasn't, despite his strong feelings about hair in general. "Should we open this up and drink it?" he said, his voice a mechanical voice, his hand a mechanical hand accepting the bottle.

"That was the idea," Naomi said. She blinked up at Otto, smiling hopefully, and rocking slightly from heel to toe.

"Sit. Sit everyone," William said. "Oh, she's sensational!"

Otto turned away to open the champagne and pour it into the lovely glasses somebody or another had given to them sometime or another.

"Well, cheers," William said. "Congratulations. And here's to —"

"Molly," Margaret said. "We decided to keep it simple."

"We figured she's got so much working against her already," Naomi said, "including a couple of geriatric moms with a different ethnicity, and God only knows what infant memories, or whatever you call that stuff you don't remember. We figured we'd name her something nice, that didn't set up all kinds of expectations. Just a nice, friendly, pretty name. And she can take it from there."

"She'll be taking it from there in any case," Otto said, grimly.

The others looked at him.

"I love Maggie," Naomi said. "I always wanted a Maggie, but Margaret said —"

"Well." Margaret shrugged. "I mean —"

"No, I know," Naomi said. "But."

Margaret rolled a little white quilt out on the rug. Plunked down on it, the baby sat, wobbling, with an expression of surprise.

"Look at her!" William said.

"Here's hoping," Margaret said, raising her glass.

So, marvelous. Humans were born, they lived. They glued themselves together in little clumps, and then they died. It was no more, as William had once cheerfully explained, than a way for genes to perpetuate themselves. "The selfish gene," he'd said, quoting, probably detrimentally, someone; you were put on earth to fight for your DNA.

Let the organisms chat. Let them talk. Their voices were as empty as the tinklings of a player piano. Let the organisms talk about this and that; it was what (as William had so trenchantly pointed out) this particular carbon-based life form did, just as its cousin (according to William) the roundworm romped ecstatically beneath the surface of the planet.

He tried to intercept the baby's glossy, blurry stare. The baby was actually attractive, for a baby, and not bald at all, as it happened. Hello, Otto thought to it, let's you and I communicate in some manner far superior to the verbal one.

The baby ignored him. Whatever she was making of the blanket, the table legs, the shod sets of feet, she wasn't about to let on to Otto. Well, see if he cared.

William was looking at him. So, what was he supposed to do? Oh, all right, he'd contribute. Despite his current clarity of mind.

"And how was China?" he asked. "Was the food as bad as they say?"

Naomi looked at him blankly. "Well, I don't know, actually," she said. "Honey, how was the food?"

"The food," Margaret said. "Not memorable, apparently."

"The things people have to do in order to have children," Otto said.

"We toyed with the idea of giving birth," Margaret said. "That is, Naomi toyed with it."

"At first," Naomi said, "I thought, what a shame to miss an experience that nature intended for us. And, I mean, there was this guy at work, or of course there's always — But then I thought, What, am I an idiot? I mean, just because you've got arms and legs, it doesn't mean you have to —"

"No," William said. "But still. I can understand how you felt."

"Have to what?" Margaret said.

"I can't," Otto said.

"Have to what?" Margaret said.

"I *can't* understand it," Otto said. "I've just never envied the capacity. Others are awestruck. Not I. I've never even remotely wished I were able to give birth, and in fact, I've never wanted a baby. Of course it's inhuman not to want one, but I'm just not human. I'm not a human being. William is a human being. Maybe William wanted a baby. I never thought to ask. Was that what you were trying to tell me the other day, William? Were you trying to tell me that I've ruined your life? *Did* you want a baby? *Have* I ruined your life? Well, it's too bad. I'm sorry. I was too selfish ever to ask if you wanted one, and I'm too selfish to want one myself. I'm more selfish than my own genes. I'm not fighting for my DNA, I'm fighting against it!"

"I'm happy as I am," William said. He sat, his arms wrapped tightly around himself, looking at the floor. The baby coughed. "Who needs more champagne?"

"You see?" Otto said into the tundra of silence William left behind him as he retreated into the kitchen. "I really am a monster."

Miles away, Naomi sat blushing, her hands clasped in her lap. Then she scooped up the baby. "There, there," she said.

But Margaret sat back, eyebrows raised in semicircles, contemplating something that seemed to be hanging a few feet under the ceiling. "Oh, I don't know," she said, and the room shuttled back into proportion. "I suppose you could say it's human to want a child, in the sense that it's biologically mandated. But I mean, you could say that, or you could say it's simply unimaginative. Or you could say it's unselfish or you could say it's selfish, or you could say pretty much anything about it at all. Or you could just say, Well, I want one. But when you get right down to it, really, one what? Because, actually — I mean, well, look at Molly. I mean, actually, they're awfully specific."

"I suppose I meant, like, crawl around on all fours, or something," Naomi said. "I mean, just because you've got — look, there they already are, all these babies, so many of them, just waiting, waiting, waiting on the shelves for someone to take care of them. We could have gone to Romania, we could have gone to Guatemala, we could have gone almost anywhere — just, for various reasons, we decided to go to China."

"And we both really liked the idea," Margaret said, "that you could go as far away as you could possibly get, and there would be your child."

"Uh-huh." Naomi nodded soberly. "How crazy is that?"

"I abase myself," Otto told William as they washed and dried the champagne glasses. "I don't need to tell you how deeply I'll regret having embarrassed you in front of Naomi and Margaret." He clasped the limp dishtowel to his heart. "How deeply I'll regret having been insufficiently mawkish about the miracle of life. I don't need to tell you how ashamed I'll feel the minute I calm down. How deeply I'll regret having trampled your life, and how deeply I'll regret being what I am. Well, that last part I regret already. I profoundly regret every tiny crumb of myself. I don't need to go into it all once again, I'm sure. Just send back the form, pertinent boxes checked: 'I intend to accept your forthcoming apology for —'"

"Please stop," William said.

"Oh, how awful to have ruined the life of such a marvelous man! Have I ruined your life? You can tell me; we're friends."

"Otto, I'm going upstairs now. I didn't sleep well last night, and I'm tired."

"Yes, go upstairs."

"Good night," William said.

"Yes, go to sleep, why not?" Oh, it was like trying to pick a fight with a dog toy! "Just you go on off to sleep."

"Otto, listen to me. My concert is tomorrow. I want to be able to play adequately. I don't know why you're unhappy. You do interesting work, you're admired, we live in a wonderful place, we have wonderful friends. We have everything we need and most of the things we want. We have excellent lives by anyone's standard. I'm happy, and I wish you were. I know that you've been upset these last few days, I asked if you wanted to talk, and you said you didn't. Now you do, but this happens to be the one night of the year when I most need my sleep. Can it wait till tomorrow? I'm very tired, and you're obviously very tired, as well. Try and get some sleep, please."

"'Try *and* get some sleep'? 'Try *and* get some sleep'? This is unbearable! I've spent the best years of my life with a man who doesn't know how to use the word 'and'! 'And' is not part of the infinitive! 'And' means *'in addition to.'* It's not 'Try *and* get some sleep,' it's 'Try *to* get some sleep' — *to! to! to! to! to! to! to! Please try to get some sleep!"*

Otto sat down heavily at the kitchen table and began to sob.

How arbitrary it all was, and cruel. This identity, that identity: Otto, William, Portia, Molly, the doctor . . .

She'd be up now, sitting at her own kitchen table, the white enamel table with a cup of tea, thinking about something, about numbers streaming past in stately sequences, about remote astral pageants . . . The doctor had rested his hand kindly on her shoulder. And what she must have felt then! Oh, to convert that weight of the world's compassion into something worthwhile — the taste, if only she could have lifted his hand and kissed it, the living satin feel of his skin . . . Everyone had to put things aside, to put things aside for good.

The way they had smiled at each other, she and that doctor! What can you do, their smiles had said. The handsome doctor in his handsome-doctor suit and Sharon in her disheveled-lunatic suit: what a charade. In this life, Sharon's little spark of consciousness would be costumed inescapably as a waif at the margins of mental organization and the doctor's would be costumed inescapably as a flashing exemplar of supreme competence; in this life (and, frankly, there would be no other) the hospital was where they would meet.

"Otto —"

A hand was resting on Otto's shoulder.

"William," Otto said. It was William. They were in the clean, dim kitchen. The full moon had risen high over the neighbors' buildings, where the lights were almost all out. Had he been asleep? He blinked up at William, whose face, shadowed against the light of the night sky, was as inflected, as ample in mystery as the face in the moon. "It's late, my darling," Otto said. "I'm tired. What are we doing down here?"

PAULA FOX

Grace

FROM HARPER'S MAGAZINE

ONCE THEY WERE OUT ON THE STREET, Grace, his dog, paid no attention to John Hillman, unless she wanted to range farther than her leash permitted. She would pause and look back at him, holding up one paw instead of lunging ahead and straining against her collar as John had observed other dogs do.

On her suddenly furrowed brow, in the faint tremor of her extended paw, he thought he read an entreaty. It both touched and irritated him. He would like to have owned a dog with more spirit. Even after he had put her dish of food on the kitchen floor, she would hesitate, stare fixedly at his face until he said, heartily, "Go ahead, Grace," or, "There you are! Dinner!"

He entered Central Park in the early evening to take their usual path, and the farther he walked from the apartment house where he lived, the more benign he felt. A few of the people he encountered, those without dogs of their own, paused to speculate about Grace's age or her breed.

"The classical antique dog," pronounced an elderly man in a long raincoat, the hem of which Grace sniffed at delicately.

John had decided she was about three years old, as had been estimated by the people at the animal shelter where he had found her. But most of the people who spoke to him in the park thought she looked older.

"Look at her tits. She's certainly had one litter. And some of her whiskers are white," observed a youngish woman wearing a black sweatshirt and baggy gray cotton trousers. As she looked at John her expression was solemn, her tone of voice impersonal. But he thought he detected in her words the character of a proclamation: *Tits* was a matter-of-fact word a woman could say to a man unless he was constrained by outmoded views.

What if, he speculated, inflamed by her use of the word, he had leaped upon her and grabbed her breasts, which, as she spoke, rose and fell behind her sweatshirt like actors moving behind a curtain?

"You're probably right," he said as he glanced up at a park lamp that lit as he spoke, casting its glow on discarded newspapers, fruit juice cartons, crushed cigarette packs, and empty plastic bottles that had contained water. He had seen people, as they walked or ran for exercise, pausing to nurse at such bottles, holding them up at an angle so that the water would flow more quickly into their mouths. Perhaps they were merely overheated.

"I don't know much about dogs," he added.

She was pleasant-looking in a fresh, camp-counselor style, about his age, he surmised, and her stolid-footed stance was comradely. He would have liked to accompany her for a few minutes, a woman who spoke with such authority despite the ugliness of her running shoes. He knew people wore such cartoon footwear even to weddings and funerals these days. Meanwhile, he hoped she wouldn't suddenly start running in place or stretch her arms or do neck exercises to ease whatever stress she might be experiencing, emitting intimate groans as she did so.

When he was speaking with people, he found himself in a state of apprehension, of nervous excitement, lest he be profoundly offended by what they said or did. For nearly a year, he had dated a girl who did such neck cycles at moments he deemed inappropriate. After completing one she had done in a bar they frequented, she had asked him, "Didn't I look like a kitty cat?" "No!" he replied, his voice acid with distaste. At once he regretted it. They spent the night lying in her bed like wooden planks. The next morning she dressed in silence, her face grim. He had tried to assuage her with boyish gaiety. She had broken her silence with one sentence: "I don't want to see you anymore."

"Have a good day," said the woman in the baggy trousers, crimping her fingers at him as she sloped down the path. He bent quickly to Grace and stroked her head. "But it's night," he muttered.

Was the interest expressed by people in the park only for his dog? Was he included in their kindly looks? When the walk was over,

John felt that he was leaving a country of goodwill, that the broad avenue he would cross when he emerged from the park to reach his apartment house was the border of another country, New York City, a place he had ceased to love this last year.

Grace made for frequent difficulty at the curb. If the traffic light was green and northbound cars raced by, she sat peacefully on her haunches. But when the light changed to red and the traffic signal spelled WALK, Grace balked, suddenly scratching furiously at the hardened earth at the base of a spindly tree or else turning her back to the avenue. John would jerk on the leash. Grace would yelp. It was such a high, thin, frightened yelp. John would clench his jaw and yank her across the avenue, half wishing a car would clip her.

In the elevator, a few seconds later, he would regret his loss of control. If only Grace would look up at him. But she stared straight ahead at the elevator door.

The trouble with owning a dog is that it leaves you alone with a private judgment about yourself, John thought. If a person had accused him of meanness, he could have defended himself. But with a dog — you did something cheap to it when you were sure no one was looking, and it was as though you had done it in front of a mirror.

John hoped that Grace would forget those moments at the curbside. But her long silky ears often flattened when he walked by her, and he took that as a sign. The idea that she was afraid of him was mortifying. When she cringed, or crept beneath a table, he murmured endearments to her, keeping his hands motionless. He would remind himself that he knew nothing about her past; undoubtedly, she'd been abused. But he always returned, in his thoughts, to his own culpability.

To show his good intentions, John brought her treats, stopping on his way home from work at a butcher shop to buy knucklebones. When Grace leaped up and whimpered and danced as John was opening the door, he would drop his briefcase and reach into a plastic bag to retrieve and show Grace what he had brought her. She would begin at once to gnaw the bone with the only ferocity she ever showed. John would sit down in a chair in the unlit living room, feeling at peace with himself.

After he gave her supper he would take her to the park. If all went well, the peaceful feeling lasted throughout the evening. But if Grace was pigheaded when the traffic light ordered them to walk — or worse, if the light changed when they were in the middle of the avenue and they were caught in the rush of traffic and Grace refused to move, her tail down, her rump turned under — then John, despite his resolution, would jerk on the leash, and Grace would yelp. When this happened, he had to admit to himself that he hated her.

This murderous rage led him to suspect himself the way he suspected the men who walked alone in the park, shabbily dressed and dirty, men he often glimpsed on a path or standing beneath the branch of a tree halfway up a rise. In his neighborhood there were as many muggings during the day as there were at night. Only a week earlier a man had been strangled less than one hundred yards from the park entrance. Now that it was early summer, the foliage was out, and it was harder to see the direction from which danger might come.

A day after the murder, he wondered if his cry would be loud enough to bring help. He had never had to cry out. He stood before his bathroom mirror, opened his mouth, and shut it at once, imagining he had seen a shriek about to burst forth, its imminence signaled by a faint quivering of his uvula.

Grace didn't bark — at least he'd never heard her bark — and this fact increased his worry. Would she silently observe his murder, then slink away, dragging her leash behind her?

Sometimes he wished she would run away. But how could she? He didn't let her off the leash as some owners did their dogs. Were he to do so, she was likely to feel abandoned once again.

He had got Grace because he had begun to feel lonely in the evenings and on weekends since the end of his affair with the kitty-cat girl, as he named her in memory. In his loneliness, he had begun to brood over his past. He had been slothful all his life, too impatient to think through the consequences of his actions. He had permitted his thoughts to collapse into an indeterminate tangle when he should have grappled with them.

When regret threatened to sink him, he made efforts to count his blessings. He had a passable job with an accounting firm, an affectionate older sister living in Boston with whom he spoke once a month, and a rent-controlled apartment. He still took pleasure in books. He had been a comparative literature major in college before taking a business degree, judging that comp lit would get him nowhere. His health was good. He was only thirty-six.

Only! Would he tell himself on his next birthday that he was *only* thirty-seven, and try to comfort himself with a word that mediated between hope and dread?

He had little time to brood over the past during work, yet in the office he felt himself slipping into a numbness of spirit and body broken only by fits of the looniness he had also observed in colleagues and acquaintances. He called the phenomenon "little breakdowns in big cities."

His own little breakdowns took the form of an irritability that seemed to increase by the hour. He became aware of a thick, smothering, oily smell of hair in the packed subway trains he rode to and from work. There was so much hair, lank or curly, frizzed or straight, bushy or carved in wedges, adorned with wide-toothed combs, metal objects, bits of leather, rubber bands. There were moments when John covered his mouth and nose with one hand.

Then there was the bearded man he shared an office with. Throughout the day, with his thumb and index finger, he would coil a hair in his beard as though it were a spring he was trying to force back into his skin. When John happened to look up and catch his officemate at it, he couldn't look away or take in a single word the man was saying.

He was in a fire of rage. Why couldn't the man keep his picking and coiling for private times?

That was the heart of it, of course: privacy. No one knew what it meant anymore. People scratched and groomed themselves, coiled their hair, shouted, played their radios at full volume, ate, even made love in public. Not that anyone called it lovemaking.

On a scrap of paper that he found on his desk, John wrote:

Name's Joe Sex
You can call me Tex
You kin have me, have me
At 34th and Lex.

He rolled it up into a ball and aimed at but missed the wastebasket. Later that day, a secretary retrieved it and read it aloud to the staff.

People grew merry and flirtatious. He was thanked by everyone for cheering them up, for lightening the day.

On the weekend before he found Grace at the animal shelter, he wrote three letters to the *New York Times*. The first was to a noted psychiatrist who had reviewed a study of child development, calling it an "instant classic." John wrote: "An instant classic is an oxymoron. A classic is established over time, not in an instant."

The second was sent to a book reviewer who had described a detective story as "lovingly written." "Lovingly," John wrote, "is not an adverb that applies to literature, especially thrillers when they concern criminal activity."

His third letter was about a term, "street-smart," used by a writer to describe a novel's heroine. "This is a superficially snappy but meaningless cliché that trivializes reality," he wrote. "On the street, the truth is that people stumble about in confusion and dismay even when they are making fortunes selling illegal drugs. People are smart for only a few minutes at a time."

While he was writing the letters he felt exalted. He was battling the degradation of language and ideas. But the intoxication soon wore off. He stared down at the letters on his desk. They looked less than trivial. He crumpled them and threw them into a wastebasket.

He came to a decision then. What he needed was a living creature to take care of; an animal would be a responsibility that would anchor him in daily life.

On weekends, Grace was a boon. John played with her, wearing an old pair of leather gloves so her teeth wouldn't mark his hands. He bought rubber toys in a variety store, and she learned to chase and fetch them back to him. Once, while he lay half-asleep in his bathtub, she brought him a rubber duck. "Why, Grace," he said, patting her with a wet hand, "how appropriate!"

Perhaps dogs had thoughts. How else to explain the way Grace would suddenly rise from where she was lying and go to another room? Something must have occurred to her.

She followed him about as he shaved, made breakfast, washed his socks, dusted the furniture with an old shirt. When he sat down with his newspaper, she would curl up nearby on the floor. In the three months he had owned her, she had grown glossy and sleek. He liked looking at her. Where had she come from?

As if feeling his gaze, she stared up at him. At such moments of mutual scrutiny, John felt that time had ceased. He sank into the natural world reflected in her eyes, moving toward an awareness to which he was unable to give a name.

But if he bent to pet her, she would flatten her ears. Or if he touched her when she was up, her legs would tremble with the effort to remain upright yet humble. Or so he imagined.

One day he came home from work at noon. He had felt faint while drinking coffee at his desk in the office. Grace was not at the door to welcome him. He called her. There was no response.

After a thorough search, surprised by the violent thumping of his heart, he discovered her beneath the box spring of his bed. "Oh, Grace!" he exclaimed reproachfully. As soon as he had extricated her, he held her closely, her small hard skull pressed against his throat. After a moment he put her down. "You gave me a scare," he said. Grace licked her flank. Had his emotion embarrassed her?

John's throat was feeling raw and sore, but he took Grace for a walk right away. She might have been confused by the change in her routine. At the park entrance, she sat down abruptly. He tugged at the leash. She sat on — glumly, he thought. He picked her up and walked to a patch of coarse grass and placed her on it. Dutifully, she squatted and urinated. A dozen yards or so away, John saw a black dog racing around a tree while its owner watched it, swinging a leash and smiling.

Grace seemed especially spiritless today. Later, propped up by pillows in bed and drinking tea from a mug printed with his initials — a gift from the kitty-cat girl — he wondered if Grace, too, was sick.

She was lying beneath the bedroom window, her paws twitching, her eyes rolled back leaving white crescents below her half-closed lids. He tried to forget how he had dragged her back home after their brief outing.

Of course, animals didn't hold grudges. They forgave, or forgot, your displays of bad temper. Yet they must have some form of recollection, a residue of alarm that shaped their sense of the world around them. Grace would have been as exuberant as the black dog circling the tree if her puppyhood had been different. She pranced and cried when John came home from work, but wasn't that simply relief? My God! What did she do in the apartment all day long, her bladder tightening as the hours accumulated, hearing, without understanding, the din of the city beyond the windows?

John felt better toward dusk, after waking from a nap. He determined to take Grace to a veterinarian. He ought to have done so long ago. In the telephone directory, he found a vet listed in the West Eighties, a few blocks from his apartment house.

The next morning he called his office to say that he wouldn't be in until after lunch; he had to go to the doctor. Did the secretary sense an ambiguity in his voice when he mentioned a doctor? She didn't know that he had a dog. No one in the office knew.

Yet was it possible that his evasions, his lies, were transparent to others? And they chose not to see through them because the truth might be so much more burdensome?

He recognized that people thought him an oddball at best. His friends warned him that, at worst, he would dry up, he was so wanting in emotion. But he considered most of them to be sentimentalists, worshiping sensations that they called feelings.

"You have a transient sensation. At once you convert it into a conviction," he said to a woman sitting beside him at a dinner party. The hostess heard him, sprang to her feet, grabbed the salad bowl, with its remaining contents, and emptied it onto his head. He was dismayed, but he managed to laugh along with the other guests, who helped to pick leaves of lettuce and strips of carrot and radish from his collar and neck.

For the rest of the evening, desolation wrapped itself around him like a mantle. Everyone, including himself, was wrong. Somehow he knew he was alive. Life was an impenetrable mystery cloaked in babble. He couldn't get the olive oil stains out of his shirt and had to throw it out.

In the vet's waiting room, Grace sat close to John's feet, her ears rising and falling at the cries of a cat in a carrier. The cat's owner tapped the carrier with an index finger and smiled at John. "Sorry about the noise," she said. "We all get scared in the doctor's office."

She may have been right, but he shied away from her all-encompassing "we." He smiled minimally and picked up a copy of *Time* magazine from a table.

When the receptionist told him to go to Room 1, Grace balked. He picked her up and carried her, turning away from the cat owner's sympathetic gaze. He placed Grace on a metal examination table in the middle of a bare cubicle. A cat howled in another room.

As the doctor entered, his lab coat emanating the grim, arid smell of disinfectant, he nodded to John and looked at Grace. She had flattened herself against the table; her head was between her paws. The doctor's pink hands moved Grace's envelope of fur and skin back and forth over her bones as he murmured, "Good girl, good dog."

He took her temperature, examined her teeth, and poked at her belly. With each procedure, Grace grew more inert. "Distemper shots?" the doctor asked. John shook his head mutely. The doctor asked him more questions, but John couldn't answer most of them. Finally John explained that he'd found her in an animal shelter. The doctor frowned. "Those places weren't great even before the city cut funding for them," he said. John nodded as though in agreement, but it was all news to him. What he'd known about dogs was that they could get rabies and had to be walked at least twice a day.

The doctor said that Grace had a bit of fever. It would be best to leave her overnight for observation. John could pick her up in the morning on Saturday.

John went to his office. People remarked on his paleness and asked him what the doctor had said. "I had a fever yesterday. Probably a touch of flu," he replied. After his words they kept their distance. A secretary placed a bottle of vitamin C tablets on his desk, averting her face as she told him they were ammunition in the war against colds.

"I have leprosy," John said.

She giggled and backed away from his desk. She doesn't know what leprosy is, he guessed, or senses that it's vaguely un-American.

He kept to his section of the office the rest of the day. He was gratified that his colleagues had him pegged as a bit crazy. He had no desire to dislodge the peg. It made it easier. Thinking about that now, as he drank his third carton of tea, he didn't know what "it" was that was made easier.

After work, with no special reason to go home, he stopped at a bar on Columbus Avenue. He ordered a double whiskey. As he drank it, his brain seemed to rise in his skull, leaving a space that filled up with serene emptiness. He ordered a repeat, wanting to sustain the feeling, which recalled to him the moments that followed lovemaking, almost a pause of being. But as he lifted his glass, he became cautious at the thought of four whiskeys on an empty stomach, and asked a passing waiter for a steak, medium. He took his drink to a booth.

The steak, when it came, was leathery, and it reminded him of the gloves he wore when he played with Grace. At this very moment she was in a cage in the dark, bewildered but stoical. Long-suffering was more like it, poor thing, carried along on the current of existence. No wonder she suddenly got up and went to another room to lie down. It wasn't thought that roused her, only a need for a small movement of freedom inside of fate. Why, after all, had he stopped in this awful, shadowy bar?

He had a few friends, most of them cocooned in partial domesticity, living with someone or seeing someone steadily. His oldest friend was married, the father of a child. Occasionally someone would introduce him to a woman in an attempt at matchmaking, feebly disguised as a dinner party.

One showed no interest in him, but another had taken him aside and asked him why he had lent himself to what was, basically, a slave auction. His impulse was to remark that no one had bid for her. Instead he asked why she had agreed to meet him. She replied that she had a sociological interest in the lifestyles of male loners in New York. He observed that life, like death, was not a style. She called him a dinosaur.

The only woman over the years for whom he had felt even a shred of interest was the mother of his friend's child. When he recognized the interest, stirred once more to life after he stopped seeing the kitty-cat girl, a sequence of scenes ran through his mind like a movie: betrayal, discovery, family disruption, himself a stepfather, late child-support checks. She was steadfast and not especially drawn to him.

There had been a time when he took the kitty-cat girl out for social evenings with his friends. Their enthusiasm for her was tinged by hysteria, he noted, as though he'd been transformed from a lone wolf to a compliant sheep. Walking away from a friend's apartment where they had spent an evening, he felt like a figure in a heroic illustration: a woman-saved prodigal son.

Now he was down to a sick dog. An apartment filled with unattractive furniture awaited him. But Grace would not be there.

He was dizzy after downing such a quantity of whiskey. His fork slid from his hand to fall beneath the table. He didn't bother to search for it but continued to sit motionless in the booth, most of the steak uneaten on the plate.

It might be only the strange weakness that had come over him like a swoon, but he imagined he could feel his bodily canals drying up, his eyes dimming, the roots of his hair drying with tiny explosions like milkweed pods pressed between two fingers.

His resounding no to the kitty-cat girl, from months ago, echoed in his ears. What had prevented him from saying yes? She might have laughed and embraced him. By that magic of affection that can convert embarrassment into merriment, they might have averted all that followed. Instead she had turned away and, he thought, gone to sleep, leaving him in an agitated wakefulness in which his resentment at her fatuity kept at bay, he knew now, a harsh judgment on his own nature.

She was, after all, a very nice woman: kind, generous, fullhearted. What did it matter that in bending to someone's pet or a friend's small child she assumed a high, squeaky voice, that she held her hand over her heart when she was moved, that she struck actressy poses when she showed him a new outfit or hairstyle? What had it mattered? Body to body — what did it all really matter?

He sighed and bent to retrieve the fork. In the darkness beneath the table he found a whole cigarette lying among the damp pickleends and crumpled napkins. *Smoke it,* he told himself as he felt the strength returning to his arms and hands. Smoking was the one thing that aroused the kitty-cat girl to anger. He'd been startled by it, so much so that he'd given up the pleasure of an infrequent cigarette after dinner in the evening. "Don't make it a religion," he'd chided her. "It's only one of a thousand things that kill people."

He summoned a waiter and asked him for a match. While he was speaking, he heard a voice boom out, ". . . and this will impact the economy." Someone at the bar had turned up the volume on a suspended television set. John glimpsed the speaker on the screen, an elderly man wearing steel-rimmed eyeglasses. "Impact is a noun, you stupid son of a bitch," he muttered, puffing on the cigarette.

"Always correcting my English," she had protested to him more than once. It suddenly came to him that he'd been lying to himself about how the affair had ended. He'd convinced himself that she had left his apartment, angrily, the morning after their quarrel about "kitty cat." In fact it had taken a week, during which they met at the end of the day in his or her apartment, ate together, went to a movie, slept in bed side by side. They had not made love. When they spoke, it was of mundane matters, and when they parted in the morning, he to his office and she to the private school where she taught first grade, she had briefly pressed her cheek against his. Life has its rhythms, he told himself.

But at the end of the week, after staring down at the light supper he'd prepared, she burst out at him in words that suggested a continuation of an angry interior monologue, "— and it's not only the way I talk. You're trying to change the way I am!" She paused, then shouted, "Why don't you say anything you really mean? My God! You wouldn't acknowledge the Eiffel Tower if it fell right on you!"

He had laughed, startled at such an extravagant image. "I'd be speechless then, all right," he'd said. But he admitted he'd been clumsy.

She asked then, as she wept, how he could have said no to her so savagely. Afterward, when she was dying inside, he'd walked around the apartment with a foolish smile — as though nothing had happened between them.

She picked up her purse from the chair where she'd been sitting, not eating while he ate, and kept on talking cheerfully.

"You're one big NO!" she burst out. "And you're smiling this instant . . ."

He recalled touching his face. What she'd said was true. "I don't mean to smile," he'd said. She got up and dropped her key on a kitchen counter and left the apartment.

He'd eaten her untouched supper, his mind like an empty pail. Then he'd waited for her to telephone him. He'd waited for himself to telephone her. But something had gone out of him. He had slumped into a mulish opposition to her: she skirted life's real troubles, chirping platitudes.

He dropped the cigarette the waiter had lit for him, got to his feet, and hurried from the bar. Behind him came the waiter. John paid his bill on the sidewalk, all too aware of the stares of the public.

I will not think about her, he ordered himself as he walked home. I have cleared the decks. I'm better off.

As he unlocked the door, he called, "Grace!" Then he remembered. "Oh, Christ . . . ," he said aloud.

He took a long hot shower, emerging slack-limbed and unpleasantly warm. Naked, he walked through the rooms, letting the air dry him, waving his arms, a heavy object trying to fly.

He paused before the bedroom window that looked out on Central Park. Perhaps the comradely woman out for a run, who had remarked on Grace's tits, would look up and observe to a friend, "See the cock hanging up there in that window?" But he was on the seventh floor, invisible to everything but passing birds.

He put on a ragged T-shirt and turned on the television set. As a rule he watched opera, a Friday-evening news program, and now and then an old movie. Tonight he would settle for diversion. He was finding it hard to keep his mind off the way he'd left the bar without paying his check.

A news anchor was saying, "The crisis centers around . . ." He switched channels and turned up a psychologist with devilish red hair and a sharp jaw who was discussing role models and sharing. "We must share," she asserted in a tone John found menacing. "Share what?" he asked the screen. "Give me a noun or give me death. And isn't 'role model' a tautology?"

On another channel a middle-aged actress declared that after years of substance abuse — "yeah, cocaine, the whole megillah" — and loveless promiscuity, she had become a sexually mature woman, in charge of her body and her life. The male interviewer smiled and nodded without pause.

On a call-in interview, a very large Arab emir was addressed as Abdul by a caller who then asked him, "How ya doin'?" The emir's expression of stolid indifference didn't change, but he appeared to send out a glow like a hot coal.

John switched channels more quickly. In every mouth that spoke from the screen, that word, *hopefully,* ownerless, modifying nothing, inserted itself amid sentences like the white synthetic packing material that protected china or glasses.

The telephone rang. Startled — no one called at this time of evening — he picked it up, and a buoyant male voice asked, "John?" The voice was not familiar. Perhaps he'd forgotten its owner; he wasn't good with voices. "Yes," he answered. He discovered at once that it was a selling call. "Do you know me?" John asked. The voice chuckled. "Well, no, John. I don't," it replied. John hung up.

It was nearly midnight when he turned off the set and went to bed. On a nearby table lay a volume of short stories by a British writer. In one of them, the writer had stated: "You can't help having the diseases of your time."

He thought of the letters to the newspaper he'd thrown away. Why had he bothered? The apocalypse would not be brought about by debased language, would it? "I've been cracked in the head, Grace," he said to the absent dog.

His body, his brain, began a slow descent into the formless stuff of sleep. His hands fluttered at the light switch until, with what felt like his last particle of energy, he pressed it off.

At once his heart began to pound. His eyelids flew open, and he was fully awake, recalling the kitty cat's account of her only brother's death. It had happened several months before he met her. Her brother was visiting her from the Midwest. While shaving one morning in her bathroom, he toppled over, dead from a heart attack. He had been twenty-eight.

She'd telephoned the news to their mother in Norman, Oklahoma. Their father had died of the same ailment several years earlier.

"Oh, Lord — where will we get the money to fly him home and bury him?" were her mother's first words, she'd told John.

He had expressed indignation at such petty concerns in a woman whose son had died.

"You don't understand," she had cried. "She was putting something in front of her grief — like you bar a door against a burglar. And money isn't petty when there's so little of it!"

She had been right and wrong, as he had been. But he could hardly have pursued the subject while her cheeks were covered with tears.

He turned the light back on and picked up the book of short stories, opening it at random. He read several sentences. Unable to make sense of them, he dropped the book on the table. The phone rang. He grabbed it, aware that he was breathless with hope it would be the girl. "Hello, hello?" he pleaded. A muffled voice at the other end asked, "Manuel?"

The next morning he returned to the vet's office. The waiting room was crowded with animals and their owners. Dogs panted or moved restlessly or whimpered. A brilliant-eyed cat sat on a man's lap, one of its ears nearly severed from its bloodied head.

To John's relief, the receptionist sent him at once to an examining room. The doctor was waiting for him with a grave expression on his face.

"I'm sorry to inform you that" — he turned to glance at a card lying on the table — "Grace has passed away."

John was astonished to hear himself groan aloud. The doctor gripped his arm. "Steady! Relationships with pets are deeply meaningful," he said softly. "You shouldn't blame yourself. Grace was a casebook of diseases. But it was the heartworm that finished her off."

"Heartworm!" cried John.

"It's carried by mosquitoes," the doctor replied. He relinquished John's arm.

"She didn't seem that sick," John said dully, leaning against the examining table.

"She was," the doctor stated brusquely. "And please don't lean against the table or it'll give way. Let me advise a grieving period, after which, hopefully, you'll move on. Get a new pet. Plenty of them need homes." He nodded at the door.

John held up a hand. "Wait! Had she littered?"

The doctor frowned momentarily. "Yes. I believe she had."

"What do you do with the bodies?" John asked at the door.

"We have a disposal method in place. You'll be notified," the doctor answered, taking a bottle of pink liquid from a shelf and shaking it.

On the sidewalk, John stood still, trying to compose himself. He felt a jab of pain over his navel. He loosened his belt, and the pain ceased. He had been eating stupidly of late and had certainly gained weight. He set off for his apartment.

The ceiling paint in the living room was flaking. Really he ought to do something about it. He took a dust mop from a closet and passed it over the floor. The dust collected in feathery little piles, which he gathered up on a piece of cardboard.

Had any of Grace's puppies survived? For a few minutes, he rearranged furniture. He discovered a knucklebone beneath an upholstered chair, where Grace must have stored it. A question formed in his mind as he stooped to pick it up. Was it only her past that had made her afraid? Her puppies lost, cars bearing down on her, endless searching for food, the worm in her heart doing its deadly work. He stared at the bone, scored with her teeth marks.

As if suddenly impelled by a violent push, he went to the telephone. In a notebook written down amid book titles, opera notices, and train schedules to Boston was a list of phone numbers. He had crossed out kitty cat's name but not her phone number. Still clutching Grace's bone, he dialed it.

On the fifth ring, she answered.

"Hello, Jean," he said.

He heard her gasp. "So. It's you," she said.

"It's me," he agreed.

"And what do you want?" She was breathing rapidly.

"I'd like to see you."

"What for?"

"Jean. I know how bad it was, the way I spoke to you."

"You were so — contemptuous!"

"I know. I had no right —"

She broke in. "No one has."

They fell silent at the same moment. Her breathing had slowed down.

"I haven't just been hanging around, you know," she said defiantly.

"I only want to speak to you."

"You want! You have to think about what other people want once a year!"

"Jean, please . . ." He dropped the bone on the table.

In a suddenly impetuous rush, she said, "It was so silly what I asked you! I'll never forget it. I can't even bear describing it to myself — what happened. All I feel is my own humiliation."

"We are born into the world and anything can happen," he said.

"What?"

"Listen. I had a dog. Grace. She got sick. Last night she died at the animal hospital. I guess I wanted to tell someone."

"I don't know what I'm supposed to do with that news," she said. "But I'm really sorry." She paused, then went on. "Poor thing," she said gently, as if speaking to someone standing beside her.

Something painful and thrilling tore at his throat. He held his breath, but still a sob burst from him. Despite its volume, he heard her say, "John? Are you all right?"

"Yes, yes . . . I don't know."

"Oh, John, I can come over this minute. I've been running, but I can change clothes in a jiffy. I don't feel you're all right."

The few tears had already dried on his cheeks. They stood in their apartments, hanging onto their telephones, trying to make up their minds if they really wanted to see each other again.

The Tutor

FROM GRANTA

SHE WAS AN AMERICAN GIRL, but one who apparently kept Bombay time, because it was 3:30 when she arrived for their 1:00 appointment. It was a luxury to be able to blame someone else for his wasted afternoon, and Zubin was prepared to take full advantage of it. Then the girl knocked on his bedroom door.

He had been in the preparation business for four years, but Julia was his first foreign student. She was dressed more like a Spanish or an Italian girl than an American, in a sheer white blouse and tight jeans that sat very low on her hips, perhaps to show off the tiny diamond in her bellybutton. Her hair was shiny, reddish brown — chestnut you would call it — and she'd ruined her hazel eyes with a heavy application of thick, black eyeliner.

"I have to get into Berkeley," she told him.

It was typical for kids to fixate on one school. "Why Berkeley?"

"Because it's in San Francisco."

"Technically Berkeley's a separate city."

"I know that," Julia said. "I was born in San Francisco."

She glanced at the bookshelves that covered three walls of his room. He liked the kids he tutored to see them, although he knew his pride was irrelevant: most didn't know the difference between Spender and Spenser, or care.

"Have you *read* all of these?"

"Actually that's the best way to improve your verbal. It's much better to see the words in context." He hated the idea of learning words from a list; it was like taking vitamin supplements in place of eating. But Julia looked discouraged, and so he added: "Your dad says you're a math whiz, so we don't need to do that."

"He said that?"

"You aren't?"

Julia shrugged. "I just can't believe he said 'whiz.'"

"I'm paraphrasing," Zubin said. "What were your scores?"

"Five hundred and sixty verbal, seven hundred sixty math."

Zubin whistled. "You scored higher than I did on the math."

Julia smiled, as if she hadn't meant to, and looked down. "My college counselor says I need a really good essay. Then my verbal won't matter so much." She dumped out the contents of an expensive-looking black leather knapsack and handed him the application, which was loose and folded into squares. Her nails were bitten, and decorated with half-moons of pale pink polish.

"I'm such a bad writer, though." She was standing expectantly in front of him. Each time she took a breath, the diamond in her stomach flashed.

"I usually do lessons in the dining room," Zubin said.

The only furniture in his parents' dining room was a polished mahogany table, covered with newspapers and magazines, and a matching sideboard — storage space for jars of pickles, bottles of Wild Turkey from his father's American friends, his mother's bridge trophies, and an enormous, very valuable Chinese porcelain vase, which the servants had filled with artificial flowers: red, yellow, and salmon-colored cloth roses beaded with artificial dew. On nights when he didn't go out, he preferred having his dinner served to him in his room; his parents did the same.

He sat down at the table, but Julia didn't join him. He read aloud from the form. "Which book that you've read in the last two years has influenced you most, and why?"

Julia wandered over to the window.

"That sounds O.K.," he encouraged her.

"I hate reading."

"Talk about the place where you live, and what it means to you." Zubin looked up from the application. "There you go. That one's made for you."

She'd been listening with her back to him, staring down Ridge Road toward the Hanging Garden. Now she turned around — did a little spin on the smooth tiles.

"Can we get coffee?"

"Do you want milk and sugar?"

Julia looked up, as if shyly. "I want to go to Barista."

"It's loud there."

"I'll pay," Julia said.

"Thanks. I can pay for my own coffee."

Julia shrugged. "Whatever — as long as I get my fix."

Zubin couldn't help smiling.

"I need it five times a day. And if I don't get espresso and a ciga-rette first thing in the morning, I have to go back to bed."

"Your parents know you smoke?"

"God, no. Our driver knows — he uses it as blackmail." She smiled. "No smoking is my dad's big rule."

"What about your mom?"

"She went back to the States to find herself. I decided to stay with my dad," Julia added, although he hadn't asked. "He lets me go out."

Zubin couldn't believe that any American father would let his teenage daughter go out at night in Bombay. "Go out where?"

"My friends have parties. Or sometimes clubs — there's that new place, Fire and Ice."

"You should be careful," Zubin told her.

Julia smiled. "That's so Indian."

"Anyone would tell you to be careful — it's not like the States."

"No," Julia said.

He was surprised by the bitterness in her voice. "You miss it."

"I am missing it."

"You mean now in particular?"

Julia was putting her things back into the knapsack haphazardly — phone, cigarettes, datebook, Chap Stick. She squinted at the window, as if the light were too bright. "I mean, I don't even know what I'm missing."

Homesickness was like any other illness: you couldn't remember it properly. You knew you'd had the flu, and that you'd suffered, but you didn't have access to the symptoms themselves: the chills, the swollen throat, the heavy ache in your arms and legs as if they'd been split open and something — sacks of rock — had been sewn up inside. He had been eighteen, and in America for only the second time. It was cold. The sweaters he'd bought in Bombay looked wrong — he saw that the first week — and they weren't warm enough anyway. He saw the same sweaters, of cheap, shiny wool, in too bright colors, at the international table in the Freshman Union. He would not sit there.

His roommate saw him go out in his T-shirt and windbreaker, and offered to lend him one of what seemed like dozens of sweaters: brown or black or wheat-colored, the thickest, softest wool Zubin had ever seen. He went to the Harvard Coop, where they had a clothing section, and looked at the sweaters. He did the calculation several times: the sweaters were "on sale" for eighty dollars, which worked out to roughly 3,300 rupees. If it had been a question of just one he might have managed, but you needed a minimum of three. When the salesperson came over, Zubin said that he was just looking around.

It snowed early that year.

"It gets like, how cold in the winter in India?" his roommate Bennet asked.

Zubin didn't feel like explaining the varied geography of India, the mountains and the coasts. "About sixty degrees Fahrenheit," he said.

"*Man,*" said Bennet. Jason Bennet was a nice guy, an athlete from Natick, Massachusetts. He took Zubin to eat at the lacrosse table, where Zubin looked not just foreign, but as if he were another species — he weighed at least ten kilos less than the smallest guy, and felt hundreds of years older. He felt as if he were surrounded by enormous and powerful children. They were hungry, and then they were restless; they ran around and around in circles, and then they were tired. Five nights a week they'd pledged to keep sober; on the other two they drank systematically until they passed out.

He remembered the day in October that he'd accepted the sweater (it was raining) and how he'd waited until Jason left for practice before putting it on. He pulled the sweater over his head and saw, in the second of woolly darkness, his father. Or rather, he saw his father's face, floating in his mind's eye like the Cheshire Cat. The face was making an expression that Zubin remembered from the time he was ten, and had proudly revealed the thousand rupees he'd made by organizing a betting pool on the horseraces among the boys in the fifth standard.

He'd resolved immediately to return the sweater, and then he had looked in the mirror. What he saw surprised him: someone small but good-looking, with fine features and dark, intense eyes, the kind of guy a girl, not just a girl from home but any girl — an American girl — might find attractive.

And he wanted one of those: there was no use pretending he didn't. He watched them from his first-floor window, as close as fish in an aquarium tank. They hurried past him, laughing and calling out to one another, in their boys' clothes: boots, T-shirts with cryptic messages, jeans worn low and tight across the hips. You thought of the panties underneath those jeans, and in the laundry room you often saw those panties: impossibly sheer, in incredible colors, occasionally, delightfully torn. The girls folding their laundry next to him were entirely different from the ones at home. They were clearly free to do whatever they wanted — a possibility that often hit him, in class or the library or on the historic brick walkways of the Radcliffe Quad, so intensely that he had to stop and take a deep breath, as if he were on the point of blacking out.

He wore Jason's sweater every day, and was often too warm; the classrooms were overheated and as dry as furnaces. He almost never ran into Jason, who had an active and effortless social schedule to complement his rigorous athletic one. And so it was a surprise, one day in late October, to come back to the room and find his roommate hunched miserably over a textbook at his desk.

"Midterms," Jason said, by way of an explanation. Zubin went over and looked at the problem set, from an introductory physics class. He'd taken a similar class at Cathedral; now he laid out the equations and watched as Jason completed them, correcting his roommate's mistakes as they went along. After the third problem Jason looked up.

"Man, thanks." And then, as if it had just occurred to him. "Hey, if you want to keep that —"

He had managed so completely to forget about the sweater that he almost didn't know what Jason meant.

"It's too small for me anyway."

"No," Zubin said.

"Seriously. I may have a couple of others too. Coach has been making us eat like hogs."

"Thanks," Zubin said. "But I want something less preppy."

Jason looked at him.

"No offense," Zubin said. "I've just been too fucking lazy. I'll go tomorrow."

The next day he went back to the Coop with his almost new textbooks in a bag. These were for his required classes (what they called the Core, or general knowledge), as well as organic chemistry. If you got to the reserve reading room at 9:00, the textbooks were almost always there. He told himself that the paperbacks for his nineteenth-century novel class weren't worth selling — he'd bought them used anyway — and when he took the rest of the books out and put them on the counter, he realized he had forgotten the *Norton Anthology of American Literature* in his dorm room. But the books came to $477.80 without it. He took the T downtown to a mall, where he bought a down jacket for $300, as warm as a sleeping bag, the same thing the black kids wore. He got a wool watchman's cap with a Nike swoosh.

When he got home, Jason laughed. "Dude, what happened? You're totally ghetto." But there was approval in it. Folding the brown sweater on Jason's bed, Zubin felt strong and relieved, as if he had narrowly avoided a terrible mistake.

Julia had been having a dream about losing it. There was no sex in the dream; she couldn't remember whom she'd slept with, or when. All she experienced was the frustrating impossibility of getting it back, like watching an earring drop and scatter in the bathroom sink, roll and clink down the drain before she could put her hand on it. The relief she felt on waking up every time was like a warning.

She had almost lost it in Paris, before they moved. He was German, not French, gangly but still handsome, with brown eyes and blondish hair. His name was Markus. He was a year ahead of her at the American School and he already knew that he wanted to go back to Berlin for university, and then join the Peace Corps. On the phone at night, he tried to get her to come with him.

At dinner Julia mentioned this idea to her family.

"*You* in the Peace Corps?" said her sister Claudia, who was visiting from New York. "I wonder if Agnès B. makes a safari line?"

When Claudia came home, she stayed with Julia on the fourth floor, in the *chambre de bonne* where she had twin beds and her Radiohead poster, all her CDs organized by record label, and a very old stuffed monkey named Frank. The apartment was half a block from the Seine, in an old hotel on the rue des Saints-Pères; in the living room were two antique chairs, upholstered in red-and-gold-striped brocade, and a porcelain clock with shepherdesses on it. The chairs and the clock were Louis XVI, the rugs were from Tehran, and everything else was beige linen.

Claudia, who now lived with her boyfriend in a railroad apartment on the Lower East Side, liked to pretend she was poor. She talked about erratic hot water and rent control and cockroaches, and when she came to visit them in Paris she acted surprised, as if the houses she'd grown up in — first San Francisco, then Delhi, then Dallas, Moscow, and Paris — hadn't been in the same kind of neighborhood, with the same pair of Louis XVI chairs.

"I can't believe you have a Prada backpack," she said to Julia. Claudia had been sitting at the table in the kitchen, drinking espresso, and eating an orange indifferently, section by section. "Mom's going crazy in her old age."

"I bought it," Julia said.

"Yeah, but with what?"

"I've been selling my body on the side — after school."

Claudia rolled her eyes and took a sip of her espresso; she looked out the window into the little back garden. "It's so *peaceful* here," she said, proving something Julia already suspected: that her sister had no idea what was going on in their house.

It started when her father's best friend, Bernie, left Paris to take a job with a French wireless company in Bombay. He'd wanted Julia's father to leave with him, but even though her father complained all the time about the oil business, he wouldn't go. Julia heard him telling her mother that he was in the middle of an important deal.

"This is the biggest thing we've done. I love Bernie — but he's afraid of being successful. He's afraid of a couple of fat Russians."

Somehow Bernie had managed to convince her mother that Bombay was a good idea. She would read the share price of the wireless company out loud from the newspaper in the mornings, while her father was making eggs. It was a strange reversal; in the past, all her mother had wanted was for her father to stay at home. The places he traveled had been a family joke, as if he were trying to outdo himself with the strangeness of the cities — Istanbul and Muscat eventually became Tbilisi, Ashkhabad, Tashkent. Now, when Julia had heard the strained way that her mother talked about Bernie and wireless communication, she had known she was hearing part of a larger argument — known enough to determine its size, if not its subject. It was like watching the exposed bit of a dangerous piece of driftwood, floating just above the surface of a river.

Soon after Claudia's visit, in the spring of Julia's freshman year, her parents gave her a choice. Her mother took her to Galeries Lafayette, and then to lunch at her favorite crêperie on the Ile Saint-Louis where, in between *galettes tomate-fromage* and *crêpe pomme-chantilly,* she told Julia about the divorce. She said she had found a two-bedroom apartment in the West Village: a "feat," she called it.

"New York will be a fresh start — psychologically," her mother said. "There's a bedroom that's just yours, and we'll be a five-minute train ride from Claudie. There are wonderful girls' schools — I know you were really happy at Hockaday —"

"No I wasn't."

"Or we can look at some coed schools. And I'm finally going to get to go back for my master's —" She leaned forward confidentially. "We could both be graduating at the same time."

"I want to go back to San Francisco."

"We haven't lived in San Francisco since you were three."

"So?"

The sympathetic look her mother gave her made Julia want to yank the tablecloth out from underneath their dishes, just to hear the glass breaking on the rustic stone floor.

"For right now that isn't possible," her mother said. "But there's no reason we can't talk again in a year."

Julia had stopped being hungry, but she finished her mother's crêpe anyway. Recently her mother had stopped eating anything sweet; she said it "irritated her stomach," but Julia knew the real reason was Dr. Fabrol, who had an office on the Ile Saint-Louis very near the crêperie. Julia had been seeing Dr. Fabrol once a week during the two years they'd been in Paris; his office was dark and tiny, with a rough brown rug and tropical plants, which he misted from his chair with a plastic spritzer while Julia was talking. When he got excited he swallowed, making a clicking sound in the back of his throat.

In front of his desk Dr. Fabrol kept a sandbox full of little plastic figures: trolls with brightly colored hair, toy soldiers, and little dollhouse people dressed in American clothes from the fifties. He said that adults could learn a lot about themselves by playing "*les jeux des enfants.*" In one session, when Julia couldn't think of anything to say, she'd made a ring of soldiers in the sand, and then without looking at him, put the mother doll in the center. She thought this might be over the top even for Dr. Fabrol, but he started arranging things on his desk, pretending he was less interested than he was so that she would continue. She could hear him clicking.

The mother doll had yellow floss hair and a full figure and a red-and-white-polka-dotted dress with a belt, like something Lucille Ball would wear. She looked nothing like Julia's mother — a fact that Dr. Fabrol obviously knew, since Julia's mother came so often to pick her up. Sometimes she would be carrying bags from the nearby shops; once she told them she'd just come from an exhibit at the new Islamic cultural center. She brought Dr. Fabrol a postcard of a Phoenician sarcophagus.

"I think this was the piece you mentioned?" Her mother's voice was louder than necessary. "I think you must have told me about it — the last time I was here to pick Julia up?"

"Could be, could be," Dr. Fabrol said, in his stupid accent. They both watched Julia as if she were a TV and they were waiting to find out about the weather. She couldn't believe how dumb they must have thought she was.

Her father asked her if she wanted to go for an early-morning walk with their black Labrador, Baxter, in the Tuileries. She would've said no — she wasn't a morning person — if she hadn't known what was going on from the lunch with her mother. They put their coats on in the dark hall with Baxter running around their legs, but by the time they left the apartment, the sun was coming up. The river threw off bright sparks. They crossed the bridge, and went through the archway into the courtyard of the Louvre. There were no tourists that early, but a lot of people were walking or jogging on the paths above the fountain.

"Look at all these people," her father said. "A few years ago, they wouldn't have been awake. If they were awake they would've been having coffee and a cigarette. Which reminds me."

Julia held the leash while her father took out his cigarettes. He wasn't fat, but he was tall and pleasantly big. His eyes squeezed shut when he smiled, and he had a beard, mostly gray now, which he trimmed every evening before dinner with special scissors. When she was younger, she had looked at other fathers and felt sorry for their children; no one else's father looked like a father to her.

In the shade by the stone wall of the Tuileries, with his back to the flashing fountain, her father tapped the pack, lifted it to his mouth, and pulled a cigarette out between his lips. He rummaged in the pocket of his brown corduroys for a box of the tiny wax matches he always brought back from India, a white swan on a red box. He cupped his hand, lit the cigarette, and exhaled away from Julia. Then he took back Baxter's leash and said: "Why San Francisco?"

She wasn't prepared. "I don't know." She could picture the broad stillness of the bay, like being inside a postcard. Was she remembering a postcard?

"It's quiet," she said.

"I didn't know quiet was high on your list."

She tried to think of something else.

"You know what I'd like?" her father asked suddenly. "I'd like to watch the sunrise from the Golden Gate — do you remember doing that?"

"Yes," Julia lied.

"I think you were in your stroller." Her father grinned. "That was when you were an early riser."

"I could set my alarm."

"You could set it," her father teased her.

"I'm awake now," she said.

Her father stopped to let Baxter nose around underneath one of the gray stone planters. He looked at the cigarette in his hand as if he didn't know what to do with it, dropped and stamped it out, half-smoked.

"Can I have one?"

"Over my dead body."

"I'm not sure I want to go to New York."

"You want to stay here?" He said it lightly, as if it were a possibility.

"I want to go with you," she said. As she said it, she knew how much she wanted it.

She could see him trying to say no. Their shadows were very sharp on the clean paving stones; above the bridge, the gold Mercury was almost too bright to look at.

"Just for the year and a half."

"Bombay," her father said.

"I liked India last time."

Her father looked at her. "You were six."

"Why are you going?"

"Because I hate oil and I hate oilmen. And I hate these goddamn *kommersants*. If I'd done it when Bernie first offered —" Her father stopped. "You do not need to hear about this."

Julia didn't need to hear about it; she already knew. Her father was taking the job in Bombay — doing exactly what her mother had wanted him to do — just as her parents were getting a divorce. The only explanation was that he'd found out about Dr. Fabrol. Even though her mother was going to New York (where she would have to find another psychologist to help her get over Julia's), Julia could see how her father wouldn't want to stay in Paris. He would want to get as far away as possible.

Julia steered the conversation safely toward business: "It's like, mobile phones, right?"

"It is mobile phones." Her father smiled at her. "Something you know about."

"I'm not *that* bad."

"No, you're not."

They'd walked a circle in the shade, on the promenade above the park. Her father stopped, as if he wasn't sure whether he wanted to go around again.

"It's not even two years," Julia said. There was relief just in saying it, the same kind she'd felt certain mornings before grade school, when her mother had touched her head and said *fever.*

Her father looked at the Pont Neuf; he seemed to be fighting with himself.

"I'd rather start over in college — with everybody else," she added.

Her father was nodding slowly. "That's something we could explain to your mother."

As you got older, Zubin noticed, very occasionally a fantasy that you'd been having forever came true. It was disorienting, like waking up in a new and better apartment, remembering that you'd moved, but not quite believing that you would never go back to the old place.

That was the way it was with Tessa. Their first conversation was about William Gaddis; they had both read *Carpenter's Gothic,* and Zubin was halfway through *JR.* In fact he had never finished *JR,* but after the party he'd gone home and lay on his back in bed, semierect but postponing jerking off with the relaxed and pleasant anticipation of a sure thing, and turned fifty pages. He didn't retain much of the content of those pages the next morning, but he remembered having felt that Gaddis was an important part of what he'd called his "literary pedigree," as he and Tessa gulped cold red wine in the historic, unheated offices of the campus literary magazine. He even told her that he'd started writing poems himself.

"Can I read them?" she asked. As if he could show those poems to anyone!

Tessa moved closer to him; their shoulders and their hips and their knees were pressed together.

"Sure," he said. "If you want."

They had finished the wine. Zubin told her that books were a kind of religion for him, that when things seemed unbearable the only comfort he knew was to read. He did not tell her that he was more likely to read science fiction at those times than William Gaddis; he hardly remembered that himself.

"What do you want to do now?" he'd asked, as they stepped out onto the narrow street, where the wind was colder than anything he could have imagined at home. He thought she would say she had class in the morning, or that it was late, or that she was meeting her roommate at 11:00, and so it was a surprise to him when she turned and put her tongue in his mouth. The wind disappeared then, and everything was perfectly quiet. When she pulled away, her cheeks and the triangle of exposed skin between her scarf and her jacket were pink. Tessa hung her head, and in a whisper that was more exciting to him than any picture he had ever seen, print or film, said: "Let's go back to your room for a bit."

He was still writing to Asha then. She was a year below him in school, and her parents had been lenient because they socialized with his parents (and because Zubin was going to Harvard). They had allowed him to come over and have a cup of tea, and then to take Asha for a walk along Marine Drive, as long as he brought her back well before dark. Once they had walked up the stairs from Hughes Road to Hanging Garden and sat on one of the benches, where the clerks and shopgirls whispered to one another in the foliage. He had ignored her flicker of hesitation and pointed down at the sun setting over the city: the Spenta building with a pink foam of cloud behind it, like a second horizon above the bay. He said that he wouldn't change the worst of the concrete-block apartments, with their exposed pipes and hanging laundry and water-stained, crumbling facades, because of the way they set off plain Babulnath Temple, made its tinseled orange flag and bulbous dome rise spectacularly from the dense vegetation, like a spaceship landed on Malabar Hill.

He was talking like that because he wanted to kiss her, but he sometimes got carried away. And when he noticed her again he saw that she was almost crying with the strain of how to tell him that she had to get home *right now*. He pointed to the still blue sky over the bay (although the light was fading and the people coming up the path were already dark shapes) and took her hand and together they climbed up to the streetlight, and turned left toward her parents' apartment. They dropped each other's hand automatically when they got to the driveway, but Asha was so relieved that, in the mirrored elevator on the way up, she closed her eyes and let him kiss her.

That kiss was the sum of Zubin's experience, when he lost it with Tessa on Jason Bennet's green futon. He would remember forever the way she pushed him away, knelt in front of him, and, with her jeans unbuttoned, arched her back to unhook her bra and free what were still the breasts that Zubin held in his mind's eye: buoyant and pale with surprising long, dark nipples.

Clothed, Tessa's primary feature was her amazing acceptability; there was absolutely nothing wrong with the way she looked or dressed or the things she said at the meetings of the literary magazine. But when he tried to remember her face now, he came up with a white oval into which eyes, a nose, and a pair of lips would surface only separately, like leftover Cheerios in a bowl of milk.

When he returned from the States the second time, Asha was married to a lawyer and living in Cusrow Baug. She had twin five-year-old boys and a three-year-old girl. She had edited a book of essays by famous writers about Bombay. The first time he'd run into her, at a wine tasting at the Taj President, he'd asked her what she was doing and she did not say, like so many Bombay women he knew, that she was married and had three children. She said: "Prostitution." And when he looked blank, she laughed and said, "I'm doing a book on prostitution now. Interviews and case histories of prostitutes in Mumbai."

When their city and all of its streets had been renamed overnight, in 1994, Zubin had had long discussions with Indian friends in New York about the political implications of the change. Now that he was back those debates seemed silly. The street signs were just something to notice once and shake your head at, like the sidewalks below them — constantly torn up and then abandoned for months.

His mother was delighted to have him back. "We won't bother you," she said. "It will be like you have your own artist's loft."

"Maybe I should start a salon," Zubin joked. He was standing in the living room, a few weeks after he'd gotten back, helping himself from a bottle of Rémy Martin.

"Or a saloon," his father remarked, passing through.

He didn't tell his parents that he was writing a book, mostly because only three of the thirty poems he'd begun were actually finished; that regrettable fact was not his fault, but the fault of the crow that lived on the sheet of tin that was patching the roof over his bedroom window. He'd learned to ignore the chain saw from the new apartment block that was going up under spindly bamboo scaffolding, the hammering across the road, the twenty-four-hour traffic and the fishwallah who came through their apartment block between 10:00 and 10:30 every morning, carrying a steel case on his head and calling *"hell-o, hell-o, hell-o."* These were routine sounds, but the crow was clever. It called at uneven intervals so that just as Zubin was convinced it had gone away, it began again. The sound was mournful and rough, as depressing as a baby wailing; it sounded to Zubin like despair.

When he'd first got back to Bombay, he'd been embarrassed about the way his students' parents introduced him: "BA from Harvard; Henry fellow at Oxford; Ph.D. from Columbia." He would correct them and say that he hadn't finished the Ph.D. (in fact, he'd barely started his dissertation) when he quit. That honesty had made everyone unhappy, and had been bad for business. Now he said his dissertation was in progress. He told his students' parents that he wanted to spend a little time here, since he would probably end up in the States.

The parents assumed that he'd come back to get married. They pushed their children toward him, yelling at them: "Listen to Zubin; he's done three degrees — two on scholarship — not lazy and spoiled like you. Aren't I paying enough for this tutoring?" They said it in Hindi, as if he couldn't understand.

The kids were rapt and attentive. They did the practice tests he assigned them; they wrote the essays and read the books. They didn't care about Harvard, Oxford, and Columbia. They were thinking of Boston, London, and New York. He could read their minds. The girls asked about particular shops; the boys wanted to know how many girlfriends he had had, and how far they'd been willing to go.

None of his students could believe he'd come back voluntarily. They asked him about it again and again. How could he tell them that he'd missed his bedroom? He had felt that if he could just get back *there* — the dark wood floor, the brick walls of books, the ancient roll-top desk from Chor Bazaar — something would fall back into place, not inside him but in front of him, like the lengths of replacement track you sometimes saw them fitting at night on dark sections of the Western Railway commuter line.

He had come home to write his book, but it wasn't going to be a book about Bombay. There were no mangoes in his poems, and no beggars, no cows or Hindu gods. What he wanted to write about was a moment of quiet. Sometimes sitting alone in his room there would be a few seconds, a silent pocket without the crow or the hammering or wheels on the macadam outside. Those were the moments he felt most himself; at the same time, he felt that he was paying for that peace very dearly — that life, his life, was rolling away outside.

"But why did you wait three years?" his mother asked. "Why didn't you come home right away?"

When he thought about it now, he was surprised that it had taken only three years to extract himself from graduate school. He counted it among the more efficient periods of his life so far.

He saw Julia twice a week, on Tuesdays and Thursdays. One afternoon when his mother was hosting a bridge tournament, he went to her house for the first time. A servant showed him into her room and purposefully shut the door, as if he'd had instructions not to disturb them. It was only 4:00, but the blinds were drawn. The lights were on and the door to her bathroom was closed; he could hear the tap running. Zubin sat at a small, varnished desk. He might have been in any girl's room in America: stacks of magazines on the bookshelf, tacked-up posters of bands he didn't know, shoes scattered across a pink rag rug, and pieces of pastel clothing crumpled in with the sheets of the bed. A pair of jeans was on the floor where she'd stepped out of them, and the denim held her shape: open, round, and paler on the inside of the fabric.

Both doors opened at once. Zubin didn't know whether to look at the barefoot girl coming out of the bathroom, or the massive, bearded white man who had appeared from the hall.

"Hi, Daddy," Julia said. "This is Zubin, my tutor."

"We spoke on the phone, sir," said Zubin, getting up.

Julia's father shook hands as if it were a quaint custom Zubin had insisted on. He sat down on his daughter's bed, and the springs protested. He looked at Zubin.

"What are you working on today?"

"*Dad.*"

"Yes."

"He just got here."

Julia's father held up one hand in defense. "I'd be perfectly happy if you didn't get into college. Then you could just stay here."

Julia rolled her eyes, a habit that struck Zubin as particularly American.

"We'll start working on her essay today." Zubin turned to Julia: "Did you do a draft?" He'd asked her the same thing twice a week for the past three, and he knew what the answer would be. He wouldn't have put her on the spot if he hadn't been so nervous himself. But Julia surprised him: "I just finished."

"What did you write about?" her father asked eagerly.

"The difficulties of being from a broken home."

"Very interesting," he said, without missing a beat.

"I couldn't have done it without you."

"I try," he said casually, as if this were the kind of conversation they had all the time. "So maybe we don't even need Zubin — if you've already written your essay?"

Julia shook her head: "It isn't good."

Zubin felt he should say something. "The new format of the SAT places much greater emphasis on writing skills." He felt like an idiot.

Julia's father considered Zubin. "You do this full-time?"

"Yes."

"Did you always want to be a teacher?"

"I wanted to be a poet," Zubin said. He could feel himself blushing but mostly he was surprised, that he had told these two strangers something he hadn't even told his parents.

"Do you write poems now?"

"Sometimes," Zubin said.

"There are some good Marathi poets, aren't there?"

"That's not what I'm interested in." Zubin thought he'd spoken too forcefully, but it didn't seem to bother Julia's father.

"I'll leave you two to work now. If you want, come to dinner some time — our cook makes terrible Continental food, because my daughter won't eat Indian."

Zubin smiled. "That sounds good — thank you, sir."

"Mark," Julia's father said, closing the door gently behind him.

"Your dad seems cool."

Julia was gathering up all of her clothes furiously from the bed and the floor. She opened her closet door — a light went on automatically — and threw them inside. Then she slammed it. He didn't know what he'd done wrong.

"Do you want me to take a look at what you have?"

"What?"

"Of the essay."

"I didn't write an essay."

"You said —"

Julia laughed. "Yeah."

"How do you expect to get into Berkeley?"

"You're going to write it."

"I don't do that." He sounded prim.

"I'll pay you."

Zubin got up. "I think we're finished."

She took her hair out of the band and redid it, her arms above her head. He couldn't see any difference when she finished. "A hundred dollars."

"Why do you want me to write your essay?"

Suddenly Julia sank down on to the floor, hugging her knees. "I have to get out of here."

"You said that before." He wasn't falling for the melodrama. "I'll help you do it yourself."

"A thousand. On top of the regular fee."

Zubin stared. "Where are you going to get that much money?"

"Half a *lakh*."

"That calculation even I could have managed," Zubin said, but she wasn't paying attention. She picked up a magazine off her night table and flopped down on the bed. He had the feeling that she was giving him time to consider her offer and he found himself — in that sealed-off corner of his brain where these things happened — considering it.

With two hundred dollars a week, plus the thousand-dollar bonus, he easily could stop all the tutoring except Julia's. And with all of that time, there would be no excuse not to finish his manuscript. There were some prizes for first collections in England and America; they didn't pay a lot, but they published your book. Artists, he thought, did all kinds of things for their work. They made every kind of sacrifice — financial, personal, moral — so as not to compromise the only thing that was truly important.

"I'll make a deal with you," Zubin said.

Julia looked bored.

"You try it first. If you get really stuck — then maybe. And I'll help you think of the idea."

"They *give* you the idea," she said. "Remember?"

"I'll take you to a couple of places. We'll see which one strikes you." This, he told himself, was hands-on education. Thanks to him, Julia would finally see the city where she had been living for nearly a year.

"Great," said Julia sarcastically. "Can we go to Elephanta?"

"Better than Elephanta."

"To the Gateway of India? Will you buy me one of those big spotted balloons?"

"Just wait," said Zubin. "There's some stuff you don't know about yet."

They walked from his house, past the Hanging Garden, to the small vegetable market in the lane above the Walkeshwar Temple.

They went down a flight of uneven steps, past small, open electronic shops where men clustered around televisions waiting for the cricket scores. The path wound between low houses, painted pink or green, a primary school, and a tiny, white temple with a marble courtyard and a black *nandi* draped in marigolds. Two vegetable vendors moved to the side to let them pass, swiveling their heads to look, each with one hand lightly poised on the flat basket balanced on her head. Inside the baskets, arranged in an elegant multicolored whorl, were eggplants, mint, tomatoes, Chinese lettuces, okra, and the smooth white pumpkins called *dudhi*. Farther on a poster man had laid out his wares on a frayed blue tarpaulin: the usual movie stars and glossy deities, plus kittens, puppies, and an enormous white baby in a diaper and pink headband. Across the bottom of a composite photo — an English cottage superimposed on a Thai beach, in the shadow of Swiss mountains dusted with yellow and purple wildflowers and bisected by a torrential Amazonian waterfall — were the words *Home is where. When you go there, they have to let you in.* Punctuation aside, it was difficult for Zubin to imagine a more depressing sentiment.

"You know what I hate?"

Zubin had a strange urge to touch her. It wasn't a sexual thing, he didn't think. He just wanted to take her hand. "What?"

"Crows."

Zubin smiled.

"You probably think they're poetic or something."

"No."

"Like Edgar Allan Poe."

"That was a raven."

"Edgar Allan Po*etic*." She giggled.

"This kind of verbal play is encouraging," Zubin said. "If only you would apply it to your practice tests."

"I can't concentrate at home," Julia said. "There are too many distractions."

"Like what?" Julia's room was the quietest place he'd been in Bombay.

"My father."

The steps opened suddenly onto the temple tank: a dark green square of water cut out of the stone. Below them, a schoolgirl in a purple jumper and a white blouse, her hair plaited with two red ribbons, was filling a brass jug. At the other end a laborer cleared muck from the bottom with an iron spade. His grandmother had brought him here when he was a kid. She had described the city as it had been: just the sea and the fishing villages clinging to the rocks, the lush, green hills, and in the hills these hive-shaped temples, surrounded by the tiny colored houses of the priests. The concrete block apartments were still visible on the Malabar side of the tank, but if you faced the sea you could ignore them.

"My father keeps me locked up in a cage," Julia said mournfully.

"Although he lets you out for Fire and Ice," Zubin observed.

"He doesn't. He ignores it when I go to Fire and Ice. All he'd have to do is look in at night. I don't put pillows in the bed or anything."

"He's probably trying to respect your privacy."

"I'm his *kid*. I'm not supposed to have privacy." She sat down suddenly on the steps, but she didn't seem upset. She shaded her eyes with her hand. He liked the way she looked, looking — more serious than he'd seen her before.

"Do you think it's beautiful here?" he asked.

The sun had gone behind the buildings and was setting over the sea and the slum on the rocks above the water. There was an orange glaze over half the tank; the other, shadowed half was green and cold. Shocked-looking white ducks with orange feet stood in the shade, each facing a different direction, and on the opposite side two boys played an impossibly old-fashioned game, whooping as they rolled a worn-out bicycle tire along the steps with a stick. All around them bells were ringing.

"I think lots of things are beautiful," Julia said slowly. "If you see them at the right time. But you come back and the light is different, or someone's left some trash, or you're in a bad mood — or whatever. Everything gets ugly."

"This is what your essay is about." He didn't think before he said it; it just came to him.

"The Banganga Tank?"

"Beauty," he said.

She frowned.

"It's your idea."

She was trying not to show she was pleased. Her mouth turned up at the corners, and she scowled to hide it. "I guess that's O.K. I guess it doesn't really matter what you choose."

*

Julia was a virgin, but Anouk wasn't. Anouk was Bernie's daughter; she lived in a fancy house behind a carved wooden gate, on one of the winding lanes at Cumbala Hill. Julia liked the ornamental garden, with brushed-steel plaques that identified the plants in English and Latin, and the blue ceramic pool full of lumpy-headed white and orange goldfish. Behind the goldfish pond was a cedar sauna, and it was in the sauna that it had happened. The boy wasn't especially cute, but he was distantly related to the royal house of Jodhpur. They'd only done it once; according to Anouk that was all it took, before you could consider yourself ready for a real boyfriend at university.

"It's something to get over with," Anouk said. "You simply hold your breath." They were listening to the Shakira album in Anouk's room, which was covered with pictures of models from magazines. There were even a few pictures of Anouk, who was tall enough for print ads but not to go to Europe and be on runways. She was also in a Colgate commercial that you saw on the Hindi stations. Being Anouk's best friend was the thing that saved Julia at the American School, where the kids talked about their fathers' jobs and their vacation houses even more than they had in Paris. At least at the school in Paris they'd gotten to take a lot of trips — to museums, the Bibliothèque Nationale, and Monet's house at Giverny.

There was no question of losing her virginity to any of the boys at school. Everyone would know about it the next day.

"You should have done it with Markus," Anouk said, for the hundredth time, one afternoon when they were lying on the floor of her bedroom, flipping through magazines.

Julia sometimes thought the same thing; it was hard to describe why they hadn't done it. They'd talked about it, like they'd talked about everything, endlessly, late at night on the phone, as if they were the only people awake in the city. Markus was her best friend — still, when she was sad, he was the one she wanted to talk to — but when they kissed he put his tongue too far into her mouth and moved it around in a way that made her want to gag. He was grateful when she took off her top and let him put his hand underneath her bra, and sometimes she thought he was relieved too, when she said no to other things.

"You could write him," Anouk suggested.

"I'd love him to come visit," Julia allowed.

"Visit and come."

"Gross."

Anouk looked at her sternly. She had fair skin and short hair that flipped up underneath her ears. She had cat-shaped green eyes exactly like the ones in the picture of her French grandmother, which stared out of an ivory frame on a table in the hall.

"What about your tutor?"

Julia pretended to be horrified. "Zubin?"

"He's cute, right?"

"He's about a million years older than us."

"How old?"

"Twenty-nine, I think."

Anouk went into her dresser and rummaged around. "Just in case," she said innocently, tossing Julia a little foil-wrapped packet.

This wasn't the way it was supposed to go — you weren't supposed to be the one who got the condom — but you weren't supposed to go to high school in Bombay, to live alone with your father, or to lose your virginity to your SAT tutor. She wondered if she and Zubin would do it on the mattress in his room, or if he would press her up against the wall, like in *9½ Weeks*.

"You better call me, like, the second after," Anouk instructed her.

She almost told Anouk about the virginity dream, and then didn't. She didn't really want to hear her friend's interpretation.

It was unclear where she and Markus would've done it, since at that time boys weren't allowed in her room. There were a lot of rules, particularly after her mother left. When she was out, around 11:00, her father would message her mobile, something like: WHAT TIME, MISSY? or simply, ETA? If she didn't send one right back, he would call. She would roll her eyes, at the cafe or the party or the club, and say to Markus, "My dad."

'Well," Markus would say. "You're his daughter."

When she came home, her father would be waiting on the couch with a book. He read the same books over and over, especially the ones by Russians. She would have to come in and give him a kiss, and if he smelled cigarettes he would ask to see her bag.

"You can't look in my bag," she would say, and her father would hold out his hand. "Everybody else smokes," she told him. "I can't help smelling like it." She was always careful to give Markus her Dunhills before she went home.

"Don't you trust me?" she said sometimes (especially when she was drunk).

Her father smiled. "No. I love you too much for that."

It was pouring and the rain almost shrieked on Zubin's tin roof, which still hadn't been repaired. They were working on reading comprehension; a test two years ago had used Marvell's "To His Coy Mistress." Zubin preferred "The Garden," but he'd had more success teaching "To His Coy Mistress" to his students; they told him it seemed "modern." Many of his students seemed to think that sex was a relatively new invention.

"It's a persuasive poem," Zubin said. "In a way, it has something in common with an essay."

Julia narrowed her eyes. "What do you mean, persuasive?"

"He wants to sleep with her."

"And she doesn't want to."

"Right," Zubin said.

"Is she a virgin?"

"You tell me." Zubin remembered legions of teachers singsonging exactly those words. "Look at line twenty-eight."

"That's disgusting."

"Good," he said. "You understand it. That's what the poet wanted — to shock her a little."

"That's so manipulative!"

It was amazing, he thought, the way Americans all embraced that kind of psychobabble. *Language* is manipulative, he wanted to tell her.

"I think it might have been very convincing," he said instead.

"*Vegetable* love?"

"It's strange, and that's what makes it vivid. The so-called metaphysical poets are known for this kind of conceit."

"That they were conceited?"

"Conceit," Zubin said. "Write this down." He gave her the definition; he sounded conceited.

"*The sun is like a flower that blooms for just one hour,*" Julia said suddenly.

"That's the opposite," Zubin said. "A comparison so common that it doesn't mean anything — you see the difference?"

Julia nodded wearily. It was too hot in the room. Zubin got

up and propped the window open with the wooden stop. Water sluiced off the dark, shiny leaves of the magnolia.

"What is that?"

"What?"

"That thing, about the sun."

She kicked her foot petulantly against his desk. The hammering outside was like an echo, miraculously persisting in spite of the rain. "Ray Bradbury," she said finally. "We read it in school."

"I know that story," Zubin said. "With the kids on Venus. It rains for seven years, and then the sun comes out and they lock the girl in the closet. Why do they lock her up?"

"Because she's from Earth. She's the only one who's seen it."

"The sun."

Julia nodded. "They're all jealous."

People thought she could go out all the time because she was American. She let them think it. One night she decided to stop bothering with the outside stairs; she was wearing new jeans that her mother had sent her; purple cowboy boots and a sparkly silver halter top that showed off her stomach. She had a shawl for outside, but she didn't put it on right away. Her father was working in his study with the door cracked open.

The clock in the hall said 10:20. Her boots made a loud noise on the tiles.

"Hi," her father called.

"Hi."

"Where are you going?"

"A party."

"Where?"

"Juhu." She stepped into his study. "On the beach."

He put the book down and took off his glasses. "Do you find that many people are doing Ecstasy — when you go to these parties?"

"Dad."

"I'm not being critical — I read an article about it in *Time*. My interest is purely anthropological."

"Yes," Julia said. "All the time. We're all on Ecstasy from the moment we wake up in the morning."

"That's what I thought."

"I have to go."

"I don't want to keep you." He smiled. "Well I do, but . . ." Her father was charming; it was like a reflex.

"See you in the morning," she said.

The worst thing was that her father *knew* she knew. He might have thought Julia knew even before she actually did; that was when he started letting her do things like go out at 10:30 and smoke on the staircase outside her bedroom. It was as if she'd entered into a kind of pact without knowing it; and by the time she found out why they were in Bombay for real, it was too late to change her mind.

It was Anouk who told her, one humid night when they were having their tennis lesson at Willingdon. The air was so hazy that Julia kept losing the ball in the sodium lights. They didn't notice who'd come in and taken the last court next to the parking lot until the lesson was over. Then Anouk said: "Wow, look — *Papa!*" Bernie lobbed the ball and waved; as they walked toward the other court, Julia's father set up for an overhead and smashed the ball into the net. He raised his fist in mock anger and grinned at them.

"Good lesson?"

"Julia did well."

"I did not."

"Wait for Bernie to finish me off," Julia's father said. "Then we'll take you home."

"How much longer?"

"When we're finished," said Bernie sharply.

"On sort ce soir."

"On va voir," her father said. Anouk started to say something and stopped. She caught one ankle behind her back calmly, stretched, and shifted her attention to Julia's father. "How long?"

He smiled. "Not more than twenty."

They waited in the enclosure, behind a thin white net that was meant to keep out the balls, but didn't, and ordered fresh lime sodas.

"We need an hour to get ready, at least."

"I'm not going."

"Yes you are."

Anouk put her legs up on the table and Julia did the same and they compared: Anouk's were longer and thinner, but Julia's had a better shape. Julia's phone beeped.

"It's from Zubin."

Anouk took the phone.

"It's just about my lesson."

Anouk read Zubin's message in an English accent: CAN WE SHIFT FROM FIVE TO SIX ON THURSDAY?

"He doesn't talk like that," Julia said, but she knew what Anouk meant. Zubin was the only person she knew who wrote SMS in full sentences, without any abbreviations.

Anouk tipped her head back and shut her eyes. Her throat was smooth and brown and underneath her sleeveless white top, her breasts were outlined, the nipples pointing up. "Tell him I'm hot for him."

"You're a flirt."

Anouk sat up and looked at the court. Now Bernie was serving. Both men had long, dark stains down the fronts of their shirts. A little bit of a breeze was coming from the trees behind the courts; Julia felt the sweat between her shoulders. She thought she'd gone too far, and she was glad when Anouk said, "When are they going to be finished?"

"They'll be done in a second. I think they both just play 'cause the other one wants to."

"What do you mean?"

"I mean, my dad never played in Paris."

"Mine did," Anouk said.

"So maybe he just likes playing with your dad."

Anouk tilted her head to the side for a minute, as if she were thinking. "He would have to, though."

The adrenaline from the fight they'd almost had, defused a minute before, came flooding back. She could feel her pulse in her wrists. "What do you mean?"

Her friend opened her eyes wide. "I mean, your dad's probably grateful."

"Grateful for *what*?"

"The job."

"He had a good job before."

Anouk blinked incredulously. "Are you serious?"

"He was the operations manager in Central Asia."

"Was," Anouk said.

"Yeah, well," Julia said. "He didn't want to go back to the States after my mom did."

"My God," Anouk said. "That's what they told you?"

Julia looked at her. *Whatever you're going to say, don't say it.* But she didn't say anything.

"You have it backwards," Anouk said. "Your mother left because of what happened. She went to America, because she knew your father couldn't. There was an article about it in *Nefte Compass* — I couldn't read it, because it was in Russian, but my dad read it." She lifted her beautiful eyes to Julia's. "My dad said it wasn't fair. He said they shouldn't've called your dad a crook."

"Four-five," her father called. "Your service."

"But I guess your mom didn't understand that."

Cars were inching out of the club. Julia could see the red brake lights between the purple blossoms of the hedge that separated the court from the drive.

"It doesn't matter," Anouk said. "You said he wouldn't have gone back anyway, so it doesn't matter whether he *could* have."

A car backed up, beeping. Someone yelled directions in Hindi.

"And it didn't get reported in America or anything. My father says he's lucky he could still work in Europe — probably not in oil but anything else. He doesn't want to go back to the States anyway — *alors, c'est pas grand chose.*"

The game had finished. Their fathers were collecting the balls from the corners of the court.

"Ready?" her father called, but Julia was already hurrying across the court. By the time she got out to the drive she was jogging, zig-zagging through the cars clogging the lot, out into the hot night-time haze of the road. She was lucky to find an empty taxi. They pulled out into the mass of traffic in front of the Hagi Ali and stopped. The driver looked at her in the mirror for instructions.

"Malabar Hill," she said. "Hanging Garden."

Zubin was actually working on the essay, sitting at his desk by the open window, when he heard his name. Or maybe hallucinated his name: a bad sign. But it wasn't his fault. His mother had given him a bottle of sambuca, which someone had brought her from the duty-free shop in the Frankfurt airport.

"I was thinking of giving it to the Mehtas, but he's stopped drinking entirely. I could only think of you."

"You're the person she thought would get the most use out of it," his father contributed.

Now Zubin was having little drinks (really half drinks) as he tried to apply to college. He had decided that there would be nothing wrong with writing a first draft for Julia, as long as she put it in her own words later. The only problem was getting started. He remembered his own essay perfectly, unfortunately on an unrelated subject. He had written, much to his English teacher's dismay, about comic books.

"Why don't you write about growing up in Bombay? That will distinguish you from the other applicants," she had suggested.

He hadn't wanted to distinguish himself from the other applicants, or rather, he'd wanted to distinguish himself in a much more distinctive way. He had an alumni interview with an expatriate American consultant working for Arthur Andersen in Bombay; the interviewer, who was young, Jewish, and from New York, said it was the best college essay he'd ever read.

"Zu-bin."

It was at least a relief that he wasn't hallucinating. She was standing below his window, holding a tennis racket. "Hey, Zubin, can I come up?"

"You have to come around the front," he said.

"Will you come down and get me?"

He put a shirt over his T-shirt, and then took it off. He took the glass of sambuca to the bathroom sink to dump it, but he got distracted looking in the mirror (he should've shaved) and drained it instead.

He found Julia leaning against a tree, smoking. She held out the pack.

"I don't smoke."

She sighed. "Hardly anyone does anymore." She was wearing an extremely short white skirt. "Is this a bad time?"

"Well —"

"I can go."

"You can come up," he said, a little too quickly. "I'm not sure I can do antonyms now, though."

In his room Julia gravitated to the stereo. A Brahms piano quartet had come on.

"You probably aren't a Brahms person."

She looked annoyed. "How do *you* know?"

"I don't," he said. "Sorry — are you?"

Julia pretended to examine his books. "I'm not very familiar with his work," she said finally. "So I couldn't really say."

He felt like hugging her. He poured himself another sambuca instead. "I'm sorry there's nowhere to sit."

"I'm sorry I'm all gross from tennis." She sat down on his mattress, which was at least covered with a blanket.

"Do you always smoke after tennis?" he couldn't help asking.

"It calms me down."

"Still, you shouldn't —"

"I've been having this dream," she said. She stretched her legs out in front of her and crossed her ankles. "Actually it's kind of a nightmare."

"Oh," said Zubin. Students' nightmares were certainly among the things that should be discussed in the living room.

"Have you ever been to New Hampshire?"

"What?"

"I've been having this dream that I'm in New Hampshire. There's a frozen pond where you can skate outside."

"That must be nice."

"I saw it in a movie," she admitted. "But I think they have them — anyway. In the dream I'm not wearing skates. I'm walking out onto the pond, near the woods, and it's snowing. I'm walking on the ice, but I'm not afraid — everything's really beautiful. And then I look down and there's this thing — this dark spot on the ice. There are some mushrooms growing on the dark spot. I'm worried that someone skating will trip on them, so I bend down to pick them."

Her head was bent now; she was peeling a bit of rubber from the sole of her sneaker.

"That's when I see the guy."

"The guy."

"The guy in the ice. He's alive, and even though he can't move, he sees me. He's looking up and reaching out his arms and just his fingers are coming up — just the tips of them through the ice. Like white mushrooms."

"Jesus," Zubin said.

She misunderstood. "No — just a regular guy."

"That's a bad dream."

"Yeah, well," she said proudly. "I thought maybe you could use it."

"Sorry?"

"In the essay."

Zubin poured himself another sambuca. "I don't know if I can write the essay."

"You have to." Her expression changed instantly. "I have the money — I could give you a check now, even."

"It's not the money."

"Because it's dishonest?" she said in a small voice.

"I —" But he couldn't explain why he couldn't manage to write even a college essay, even to himself. "I'm sorry."

She looked as if she'd been about to say something else, and then changed her mind. "O.K.," she said dejectedly. "I'll think of something."

She looked around for her racket, which she'd propped up against the bookshelf. He didn't want her to go yet.

"What kind of a guy is he?"

"Who?"

"The guy in the ice — is he your age?"

Julia shook her head. "He's old."

Zubin sat down on the bed, at what he judged was a companionable distance. "Like a senior citizen?"

"No, but older than you."

"Somewhere in that narrow window between me and senior citizenship."

"You're not old," she said seriously.

"Thank you." The sambuca was making him feel great. They could just sit here and get drunk and do nothing, and it would be fun, and there would be no consequences; he could stop worrying for tonight, and give himself a little break.

He was having that comforting thought when her head dropped lightly to his shoulder.

"Oh."

"Is this O.K.?"

"It's O.K., but —"

"I get so tired."

"Because of the nightmares."

She paused for a second, as if she was surprised he'd been paying attention. "Yes," she said. "Exactly."

"You want to lie down a minute?"

She jerked her head up — nervous all of a sudden. He liked it better than the flirty stuff she'd been doing before.

"Or I could get someone to take you home."

She lay down and shut her eyes. He put his glass down carefully on the floor next to the bed. Then he put his hand out; her hair was very soft. He stroked her head and moved her hair away from her face. He adjusted the glass beads she always wore, and ran his hand lightly down her arm. He felt that he was in a position where there was no choice but to lift her up and kiss her very gently on the mouth.

"Julia."

She opened her eyes.

"I'm going to get someone to drive you home."

She got up very quickly and smoothed her hair with her hand.

"Not that I wouldn't like you to stay, but I think —"

"O.K.," she said.

"I'll just get someone." He yelled for the servant.

"I can get a taxi," Julia said.

"I know you *can*," he told her. For some reason, that made her smile.

In September she took the test. He woke up early that morning as if he were taking it, couldn't concentrate, and went to Barista, where he sat trying to read the same *India Today* article about regional literature for two hours. She wasn't the only one of his students taking the SAT today, but she was the one he thought of, at the 8:40 subject change, the 10:00 break, and at 11:25, when they would be warning them about the penalties for continuing to write after time was called. That afternoon he thought she would ring him to say how it had gone, but she didn't, and it wasn't until late that night that his phone beeped and her name came up: JULIA : VERBAL IS LIKE S-SPEARE : PLAY. It wasn't a perfect analogy, but he knew what she meant.

He didn't see Julia while the scores were being processed. Without the bonus he hadn't been able to give up his other clients, and the business was in one of its busy cycles; it seemed as if everyone in Bombay was dying to send their sixteen-year-old child halfway around the world to be educated. Each evening he thought he might hear her calling up from the street, but she never did, and he didn't feel he could phone without some pretense.

One rainy Thursday he gave a group lesson in a small room on the first floor of the David Sassoon library. The library always reminded him of Oxford, with its cracked chalkboards and termite-riddled seminar tables, and today in particular the soft, steady rain made him feel as if he were somewhere else. They were doing triangles (isosceles, equilateral, scalene) when all of a sudden one of the students interrupted and said: "It stopped."

Watery sun was gleaming through the lead glass windows. When he had dismissed the class, Zubin went upstairs to the reading room. He found Bradbury in a tattered ledger book and filled out a form. He waited while the librarian frowned at the call number, selected a key from a crowded ring, and, looking put-upon, sent an assistant into the reading room to find "All Summer in a Day" in the locked glass case.

> It had been raining for seven years; thousands upon thousands of days compounded and filled from one end to the other with rain, with the drum and gush of water, with the sweet crystal fall of showers and the concussion of storms so heavy they were tidal waves come over the islands.

He'd forgotten that the girl in the story was a poet. She was different from the other children, and because it was a science fiction story (this was what he loved about science fiction) it wasn't an abstract difference. Her special sensitivity was explained by the fact that she had come to Venus from Earth only recently, on a rocket ship, and remembered the sun — it was like a penny — while her classmates did not.

Zubin sat by the window in the old seminar room, emptied of students, and luxuriated in a feeling of potential he hadn't had in a long time. He remembered when a moment of heightened contrast in his physical surroundings could produce this kind of elation; he could feel the essay wound up in him like thread. He would combine the Bradbury story with the idea Julia had had, that day at the tank. Beauty was something that was new to you. That was why tourists and children could see it better than other people, and it was the poet's job to keep seeing it the way the children and the tourists did.

He was glad he'd told her he couldn't do it because it would be that much more of a surprise when he handed her the pages. He felt noble. He was going to defraud the University of California for her gratis, as a gift.

*

He intended to be finished the day the scores came out and, for perhaps the first time in his life, he finished on the day he'd intended. He waited all day, but Julia didn't call. He thought she would've gone out that night to celebrate, but she didn't call the next day, or the next, and he started to worry that she'd been wrong about her verbal. Or she'd lied. He started to get scared that she'd choked — something that could happen to the best students, you could never tell which. After ten days without hearing from her, he rang her mobile.

"Oh yeah," she said. "I was going to call."

"I have something for you," he said. He didn't want to ask about the scores right away.

She sighed. "My dad wants you to come to dinner anyway."

"O.K.," Zubin said. "I could bring it then."

There was a long pause, in which he could hear traffic. "Are you in the car?"

"Uh-huh," she said. "Hold on a second?" Her father said something and she groaned into the phone. "My dad wants me to tell you my SAT scores."

"Only if you want to."

"Eight hundred math."

"Wow."

"And six-ninety verbal."

"You're kidding."

"Nope."

"Is this the Julia who was too distracted to do her practice tests?"

"Maybe it was easy this year," Julia said, but he could tell she was smiling.

"I don't believe you."

"Zu*bin*!" (He loved the way she added the extra stress.) "I *swear.*"

They ate *coquilles St. Jacques* by candlelight. Julia's father lit the candles himself, with a box of old-fashioned White Swan matches. Then he opened Zubin's wine and poured all three of them a full glass. Zubin took a sip; it seemed too sweet, especially with the seafood. "A toast," said Julia's father. "To my daughter the genius."

Zubin raised his glass. All week he'd felt an urgent need to see her; now that he was here he had a contented, peaceful feeling, only partly related to the two salty dogs he'd mixed for himself just before going out.

"Scallops are weird," said Julia. "Do they even have heads?"

"Did any of your students do better?" her father asked.

"Only one, I think."

"Boy or girl?"

"Why does *that* matter?" Julia asked. She stood up suddenly: she was wearing a sundress made of blue and white printed Indian cotton, and she was barefoot. "I'll be in my room if anyone needs me."

Zubin started to get up.

"Sit," Julia's father said. "Finish your meal. Then you can do whatever you have to do."

"I brought your essay — the revision of your essay," Zubin corrected himself, but she didn't turn around. He watched her disappear down the hall to her bedroom: a pair of tan shoulders under thin, cotton straps.

"I first came to India in 1976," her father was saying. "I flew from Moscow to Paris to meet Julia's mom, and then we went to Italy and Greece. We were deciding between India and North Africa — finally we just tossed a coin."

"Wow," said Zubin. He was afraid Julia would go out before he could give her the essay.

"It was February, and I'd been in Moscow for a year," Julia's father said. "So you can imagine what India was like for me. We were staying in this pension in Benares — Varanasi — and every night there were these incredible parties on the roof.

"One night we could see the burning ghats from where we were — hardly any electricity in the city, and then this big fire on the ghat, with the drums and the wailing. I'd never seen anything like that — the pieces of the body that they sent down the river, still burning." He stopped and refilled their glasses. He didn't seem to mind the wine. "Maybe they don't still do that?"

"I've never been to Benares."

Julia's father laughed. "Right," he said. "That's an old man's India now. And you're not writing about India, are you?"

Writing the essay, alone at night in his room, knowing she was out somewhere with her school friends, he'd had the feeling, the delusion, really, that he could hear her. That while she was standing on the beach or dancing in a club, she was also telling him her life story: not the places she'd lived, which didn't matter, but the time in third grade when she was humiliated in front of the class;

the boy who wrote his number on the inside of her wrist; the weather on the day her mother left for New York. He felt that her voice was coming in the open window with the noise of the motor-bikes and the televisions and the crows, and all he was doing was hitting the keys.

Julia's father had asked a question about India.

"Sorry?" Zubin said.

He waved a hand dismissively in front of his face. "You don't have to tell me — writers are private about these things. It's just that business guys like me — we're curious how you do it."

"When I'm here, I want to write about America, and when I'm in America, I always want to write about being here." He wasn't slur-ring words, but he could hear himself emphasizing them: "It would have made *sense* to stay there."

"But you didn't."

"I was homesick, I guess."

"And now?"

Zubin didn't know what to say.

"Far be it from me, but I think it doesn't matter so much, whether you're here or there. You can bring your home with you." Julia's father smiled. "To some extent. And India's wonderful — even if it's not your first choice."

It was easy if you were Julia's father. He had chosen India be-cause he remembered seeing some dead bodies in a river. He had found it "wonderful." And that was what it was to be an American. Americans could go all over the world and still be Americans; they could live just the way they did at home and nobody wondered who they were, or why they were doing things the way they did.

"I'm sure you're right," Zubin said politely.

Finally Julia's father pressed a buzzer and a servant appeared to clear the dishes. Julia's father pushed back his chair and stood up. Before disappearing into his study, he nodded formally and said something — whether "Good night," or "Good luck," Zubin couldn't tell.

Zubin was left with a servant, about his age, with big, south-ern features and stooped shoulders. The servant was wearing the brown uniform from another job: short pants and a shirt that was tight across his chest. He moved as if he'd been compensating for his height his whole life, as if he'd never had clothes that fit him.

"Do you work here every day?" Zubin asked in his schoolbook Marathi.

The young man looked up as if talking to Zubin was the last in a series of obstacles that lay between him and the end of his day.

"Nahin," he said. *"Mangalwar ani guruwar."*

Zubin smiled — they both worked on Tuesdays and Thursdays. "Me too," he said.

The servant didn't understand. He stood holding the plates, waiting to see if Zubin was finished and scratching his left ankle with his right foot. His toes were round and splayed, with cracked nails and a glaucous coating of dry, white skin.

"O.K.," Zubin said. *"Bas."*

Julia's room was, as he'd expected, empty. The lights were burning and the stereo was on (the disk had finished), but she'd left the window open; the bamboo shade sucked in and out. The mirror in the bathroom was steamed around the edges — she must've taken a shower before going out; there was the smell of some kind of fragrant soap and cigarettes.

He put the essay on the desk, where she would see it. There were two Radiohead CDs, still in their plastic wrappers, and a detritus of pens and pencils, hair bands, fashion magazines — French *Vogue, Femina,* and *YM* — gum wrappers, an OB tampon, and a miniature brass abacus with tiny ivory beads. There was also a diary with a pale blue paper cover.

The door to the hall was slightly open, but the house was absolutely quiet. It was not good to look at someone's journal, especially a teenage girl's. But there were things that would be worse — jerking off in her room, for example. It was a beautiful notebook with a heavy cardboard cover that made a satisfying sound when he opened it on the desk.

"It's empty."

He flipped the diary closed, but it was too late. She was climbing in through the window, lifting the shade with her hand.

"That's where I smoke," she said. "You should've checked."

"I was just looking at the notebook," Zubin said. "I wouldn't have read what you'd written."

"My hopes, dreams, fantasies. It would've been good for the essay."

"I finished the essay."

She stopped and stared at him. "You wrote it?"

He pointed to the neatly stacked pages, a paper island in the clutter of the desk. Julia examined them, as if she didn't believe it.

"I thought you weren't going to?"

"If you already wrote one —"

"No," she said. "I tried, but —" She gave him a beautiful smile. "Do you want to stay while I read it?"

Zubin glanced at the door.

"My dad's in his study."

He pretended to look through her CDs, which were organized in a zippered binder, and snuck glances at her while she read. She sat down on her bed with her back against the wall, one foot underneath her. As she read she lifted her necklace and put it in her mouth, he thought unconsciously. She frowned at the page.

It was better if she didn't like it, Zubin thought. He knew it was good, but having written it was wrong. There were all these other kids who'd done the applications themselves.

Julia laughed.

"What?" he said, but she just shook her head and kept going.

"I'm just going to use your loo," Zubin said.

He used it almost blindly, without looking in the mirror. Her towel was hanging over the edge of the counter, but he dried his hands on his shirt. He was drunker than he'd thought. When he came out, she had folded the three pages into a small square, as if she were getting ready to throw them away.

Julia shook her head. "You did it."

"It's O.K.?"

Julia shook her head. "It's perfect — it's spooky. How do you even know about this stuff?"

"I was a teenager — not a girl teenager, but you know."

She shook her head. "About being an American, I mean? How do you know about that?"

She asked the same way she might ask who wrote *The Fairie Queene* or the meaning of the word *synecdoche*.

Because I am not any different, he wanted to tell her. He wanted to grab her shoulders: *If we are what we want, I am the same as you.*

But she wasn't looking at him. Her eyes were like marbles he'd had as a child, striated brown and gold. They moved over the pages he'd written as if they were hers, as if she were about to tear one up and put it in her mouth.

"This part," Julia said. "About forgetting where you are? D'you know, that *happens* to me? Sometimes coming home I almost say the wrong street — the one in Paris, or in Moscow when we used to have to say 'Pushkinskaya.'"

Her skirt was all twisted around her legs.

"Keep it," he said.

"I'll write you a check."

"It's a present," Zubin told her.

"Really?"

He nodded. When she smiled, she looked like a kid. "I wish I could do something for *you*."

Zubin decided that it was time to leave.

Julia put on a CD — a female vocalist with a heavy bass line. "This is too sappy for daytime," she said. Then she started to dance. She was not a good dancer. He watched her fluttering her hands in front of her face, stamping her feet, and knew, the same way he always knew these things, that he wasn't going anywhere at all.

"You know what I hate?"

"What?"

"Boys who can't kiss."

"All right," Zubin said. "You come here."

Her bed smelled like the soap — lilac. It was amazing, the way girls smelled, and it was amazing to put his arm under her and take off each thin strap and push the dress down around her waist. She made him turn off the lamp, but there was a streetlamp outside; he touched her in the artificial light. She looked as if she were trying to remember something.

"Is everything O.K.?"

She nodded.

"Because we can stop."

"Do you have something?"

It took him a second to figure out what she meant. "Oh," he said. "No — that's good I guess."

"I have one."

"You do?"

She nodded.

"Still. That doesn't mean we have to."

"I want to."

"Are you sure?"

"If you do."

"If I do — yes." He took a breath. "I want to."

She was looking at him very seriously.

"This isn't —" he said.

"Of course not."

"Because you seem a little nervous."

"I'm just thinking," she said. Her underwear was light blue, and it didn't quite cover her tan line.

"About what?"

"America."

"What about it?"

She had amazing gorgeous perfect new breasts. There was nothing else to say about them.

"I can't wait," she said, and he decided to pretend she was talking about this.

Julia was relieved when he left and she could lie in bed alone and think about it. Especially the beginning part of it: she didn't know kissing could be like that — sexy and calm at the same time, the way it was in movies that were not *9½ Weeks*. She was surprised she didn't feel worse; she didn't feel regretful at all, except that she wished she'd thought of something to say afterward. *I wish I didn't have to go* was what he had said, but he put on his shoes very quickly. She hadn't been sure whether she should get up or not, and in the end she waited until she heard the front door shut behind him. Then she got up and put on a T-shirt and pajama bottoms and went into the bathroom to wash her face. If she'd told him it was her first time, he would've stayed longer, probably, but she'd read enough magazines to know that you couldn't tell them that. Still, she wished he'd touched her hair the way he had the other night, when she'd gone over to his house and invented a nightmare.

Zubin had left the Ray Bradbury book on her desk. She'd thanked him, but she wasn't planning to read it again. Sometimes when you went back you were disappointed, and she liked the rocket ship the way she remembered it, with silver tail fins and a red lacquer shell. She could picture herself taking off in that ship — at first like an airplane, above the hill and the tank and the bay with its necklace of lights — and then straight up, beyond the sound barrier. People would stand on the beach to watch the launch: her father, Anouk, and Bernie, everyone from school, and even Claudie and her mother and Dr. Fabrol. They would yell up to her, but the yells would be like the tails of comets, crusty blocks of ice and dust that rose and split in silent, white explosions.

She liked Zubin's essay too, although she wasn't sure about the way he'd combined the two topics; she hoped they weren't going to take points off. Or the part where he talked about all the different perspectives she'd gotten from living in different cities, and how she just needed one place where she could think about those things and articulate what they meant to her. She wasn't interested in "articulating." She just wanted to get moving.

Zubin walked all the way up Nepean Sea Road, but when he got to the top of the hill he wasn't tired. He turned right and passed his building, not quite ready to go in, and continued in the Walkeshwar direction. The market was empty. The electronics shops were shuttered and the Just Orange advertisements twisted like kites in the dark. There was the rich, rotted smell of vegetable waste, but almost no other trash. Foreigners marveled at the way Indians didn't waste anything, but of course that wasn't by choice. Only a few useless things flapped and flattened themselves against the broad, stone steps: squares of folded newsprint from the vendors' baskets, and smashed matchbooks — extinct brands whose labels still appeared underfoot: "Export quality premium safety matches" in fancy script.

At first he thought the tank was deserted, but a man in shorts was standing on the other side, next to a small white dog with standup, triangular ears. Zubin picked a vantage point on the steps out of the moonlight, sat down, and looked out at the water. There was something different about the tank at night. It was partly the quiet; in between the traffic sounds a breeze crackled the leaves of a few desiccated trees, growing between the paving stones. The night intensified the contrast, so that the stones took on a kind of sepia, sharpened the shadows, and gave the carved and whitewashed temple pillars an appropriate patina of magic. You could cheat for a moment in this light and see the old city, like taking a photograph with black-and-white film.

The dog barked, ran up two steps, and turned expectantly toward the tank. Zubin didn't see the man until his slick, seal head surfaced in the black water. Each stroke broke the black glass; his hands made eddies of light in the disturbed surface. For just a moment, even the apartment blocks were beautiful.

EDWARD P. JONES

A Rich Man

FROM THE NEW YORKER

HORACE AND LONEESE PERKINS — one child, one grandchild
— lived most unhappily together for more than twelve years in
Apartment 230 at Sunset House, a building for senior citizens at
1202 Thirteenth Street Northwest. They moved there in 1977, the
year they celebrated forty years of marriage, the year they made
love for the last time — Loneese kept a diary of sorts, and that fact
was noted on one day of a week when she noted nothing else. "He
touched me," she wrote, which had always been her diary euphe-
mism for sex. That was also the year they retired, she as a pool secretary at the Commerce Department, where she had known one
lover, and he as a civilian employee at the Pentagon, as the head of
veteran records. He had been an army sergeant for ten years before becoming head of records; the secretary of defense gave him a
plaque as big as his chest on the day he retired, and he and the secretary of defense and Loneese had their picture taken, a picture
that hung for all those twelve years in the living room of Apartment
230, on the wall just to the right of the heating and air-conditioning unit.

A month before they moved in, they drove in their burgundy
and gold Cadillac from their small house on Chesapeake Street in
Southeast to a Union Station restaurant and promised each other
that Sunset House would be a new beginning for them. Over blackened catfish and a peach cobbler that they both agreed could have
been better, they vowed to devote themselves to each other and become even better grandparents. Horace had long known about the
Commerce Department lover. Loneese had told him about the

man two months after she had ended the relationship, in 1969.
"He worked in the mailroom," she told her husband over a spaghetti supper she had cooked in the Chesapeake Street home. "He
touched me in the motel room," she wrote in her diary, "and after
it was over he begged me to go away to Florida with him. All I could
think about was that Florida was for old people."

At that spaghetti supper, Horace did not mention the dozens of
lovers he had had in his time as her husband. She knew there had
been many, knew it because they were written on his face in the
early years of their marriage, and because he had never bothered
to hide what he was doing in the later years. "I be back in a while. I
got some business to do," he would say. He did not even mention
the lover he had slept with just the day before the spaghetti supper,
the one he bid goodbye to with a "Be good and be sweet" after telling her he planned to become a new man and respect his marriage
vows. The woman, a thin schoolbus driver with clanking bracelets
up to her elbows on both arms, snorted a laugh, which made Horace want to slap her, because he was used to people taking him seriously. "Forget you, then," Horace said on the way out the door. "I
was just tryin to let you down easy."

Over another spaghetti supper two weeks before moving, they re-
iterated what had been said at the blackened-catfish supper and
did the dishes together and went to bed as man and wife, and over
the next days sold almost all the Chesapeake Street furniture. What
they kept belonged primarily to Horace, starting with a collection
of 639 record albums, many of them his "sweet babies," the 78s. If a
band worth anything had recorded between 1915 and 1950, he
bragged, he had the record; after 1950, he said, the bands got
sloppy and he had to back away. Horace also kept the Cadillac he
had painted to honor a football team, paid to park the car in the
underground garage. Sunset had once been intended as a luxury
place, but the builders, two friends of the city commissioners, ran
out of money in the middle and the commissioners had the city-
government people buy it off them. The city-government people
completed Sunset, with its tiny rooms, and then, after one commis-
sioner gave a speech in Southwest about looking out for old people, some city-government people in Northeast came up with the
idea that old people might like to live in Sunset, in Northwest.

Three weeks after Horace and Loneese moved in, Horace went

down to the lobby one Saturday afternoon to get their mail and happened to see Clara Knightley getting her mail. She lived in Apartment 512. "You got this fixed up real nice," Horace said of Apartment 512 a little less than an hour after meeting her. "But I could see just in the way that you carry yourself that you got good taste. I could tell that about you right off." "You swellin my head with all that talk, Mr. Perkins," Clara said, offering him coffee, which he rejected, because such moments always called for something stronger. "Whas a woman's head for if a man can't swell it up from time to time. Huh? Answer me that, Clara. You just answer me that." Clara was fifty-five, a bit younger than most of the residents of Sunset House, though she was much older than all Horace's other lovers. She did not fit the city people's definition of a senior citizen, but she had a host of ailments, from high blood pressure to diabetes, and so the city people had let her in.

Despite the promises, the marriage, what little there had been of it, came to an end. "I will make myself happy," Loneese told the diary a month after he last touched her. Loneese and Horace had fixed up their apartment nicely, and neither of them wanted to give the place up to the other. She wanted to make a final stand with the man who had given her so much heartache, the man who had told her, six months after her confession, what a whore she had been to sleep with the Commerce Department mailroom man. Horace, at sixty, had never thought much of women over fifty, but Clara — and, after her, Willa, of Apartment 1001, and Miriam, of Apartment 109 — had awakened something in him, and he began to think that women over fifty weren't such a bad deal after all. Sunset House had dozens of such women, many of them attractive widows, many of them eager for a kind word from a retired army sergeant who had so many medals and ribbons that his uniform could not carry them. As far as he could see, he was cock of the walk: many of the men in Sunset suffered from diseases that Horace had so far escaped, or they were not as good-looking or as thin, or they were encumbered by wives they loved. In Sunset House he was a rich man. So why move and give that whore the satisfaction?

They lived separate lives in a space that was only a fourth as large as the Chesapeake Street house. The building came to know them as the man and wife in 230 who couldn't stand each other. People talked about the Perkinses more than they did about anyone else, which was particularly upsetting to Loneese, who had been raised to believe family business should stay in the family. "Oh, Lord, what them two been up to now?" "Fight like cats and dogs, they do." "Who he seein now?" They bought separate food from the Richfood on Eleventh Street or from the little store on Thirteenth Street, and they could be vile to each other if what one bought was disturbed or eaten by the other. Loneese stopped speaking to Horace for nine months in 1984 and 1985, when she saw that her pumpkin pie was a bit smaller than when she last cut a slice from it. "I ain't touch your damn pie, you crazy woman," he said when she accused him. "How long you been married to me? You know I've never been partial to pumpkin pie." "That's fine for you to say, Horace, but why is some missing? You might not be partial to it, but I know you. I know you'll eat anything in a pinch. That's just your dirty nature." "My nature ain't no more dirty than yours."

After that, she bought a small icebox for the bedroom where she slept, though she continued to keep the larger items in the kitchen refrigerator. He bought a separate telephone, because he complained that she wasn't giving him his messages from his "associates." "I have never been a secretary for whores," she said, watching him set up an answering machine next to the hide-a-bed couch where he slept. "Oh, don't get me started bout whores. I'd say you wrote the damn book." "It was dictated by you."

Their one child, Alonzo, lived with his wife and son in Baltimore. He had not been close to his parents for a long time, and he could not put the why of it into words for his wife. Their boy, Alonzo Jr., who was twelve when his grandparents moved into Sunset, loved to visit them. Horace would unplug and put away his telephone when the boy visited. And Loneese and Horace would sleep together in the bedroom. She'd put a pillow between them in the double bed to remind herself not to roll toward him.

Their grandson visited less and less as he moved into his teenage years, and then, after he went away to college, in Ohio, he just called them every few weeks, on the phone they had had installed in the name of Horace and Loneese Perkins.

In 1987, Loneese's heart began the countdown to its last beat and she started spending more time at George Washington University Hospital than she did in the apartment. Horace never visited her.

She died two years later. She woke up that last night in the hospital and went out into the hall and then to the nurses' station but could not find a nurse anywhere to tell her where she was or why she was there. "Why do the patients have to run this place alone?" she said to the walls. She returned to her room and it came to her why she was there. It was nearing 3:00 in the morning, but she called her own telephone first, then she dialed Horace's. He answered, but she never said a word. "Who's this playin on my phone?" Horace kept asking. "Who's this? I don't allow no playin on my phone." She hung up and lay down and said her prayers. After moving into Sunset, she had taken one more lover, a man at Vermont Avenue Baptist Church, where she went from time to time. He was retired, too. She wrote in her diary that he was not a big eater and that "down there, his vitals were missing."

Loneese Perkins was buried in a plot at Harmony Cemetery that she and Horace had bought when they were younger. There was a spot for Horace, and there was one for their son, but Alonzo had long since made plans to be buried in a cemetery just outside Baltimore.

Horace kept the apartment more or less the way it was on the last day she was there. His son and daughter-in-law and grandson took some of her clothes to the Goodwill and the rest they gave to other women in the building. There were souvenirs from countries that Loneese and Horace had visited as man and wife — a Ghanaian carving of men surrounding a leopard they had killed, a brass menorah from Israel, a snow globe of Mount Fuji with some of the snow stuck forever to the top of the globe. They were things that did not mean very much to Alonzo, but he knew his child, and he knew that one day Alonzo Jr. would cherish them.

Horace tried sleeping in the bed, but he had been not unhappy in his twelve years on the hide-a-bed. He got rid of the bed and moved the couch into the bedroom and kept it open all the time.

He realized two things after Loneese's death: his own "vitals" had rejuvenated. He had never had the problems other men had, though he had failed a few times along the way, but that was to be expected. Now, as he moved closer to his seventy-third birthday, he felt himself becoming ever stronger, ever more potent. God is a strange one, he thought, sipping Chivas Regal one night before he went out: He takes a man's wife and gives him a new penis in her place.

The other thing he realized was that he was more and more at- tracted to younger women. When Loneese died, he had been keep- ing company with a woman of sixty-one, Sandy Carlin, in Apart- ment 907. One day in February, nine months after Loneese's death, one of Sandy's daughters, Jill, came to visit, along with one of Jill's friends, Elaine Cunningham. They were both twenty-five years old. From the moment they walked through Sandy's door, Horace began to compliment them — on their hair, the color of their fingernail polish, the sharp crease in Jill's pants ("You iron that yourself?"), even "that sophisticated way" Elaine crossed her legs. The young women giggled, which made him happy, pleased with himself, and Sandy sat in her place on the couch. As the ice in the Pepsi-Cola in her left hand melted, she realized all over again that God had never promised her a man until her dying day.

When the girls left, about 3:00 in the afternoon, Horace offered to accompany them downstairs, "to keep all them bad men away." In the lobby, as the security guard at her desk strained to hear, he made it known that he wouldn't mind if they came by to see him sometime. The women looked at each other and giggled some more. They had been planning to go to a club in Southwest that evening, but they were amused by the old man, by the way he had his rap together and put them on some sort of big pedestal and shit, as Jill would tell another friend weeks later. And when he saw how receptive they were he said why not come on up tonight, shucks, ain't no time like the present. Jill said he musta got that from a song, but he said no, he'd been sayin that since before they were born, and Elaine said thas the truth, and the women giggled again. He said I ain't gonna lie bout bein a seasoned man, and then he joined in the giggling. Jill looked at Elaine and said want to? And Elaine said what about your mom? And Jill shrugged her shoulders and Elaine said O.K. She had just broken up with a man she had met at another club and needed something to make the pain go away until there was another man, maybe from a better club.

At about 11:30, Jill wandered off into the night, her head liq- uored up, and Elaine stayed and got weepy — about the man from the not-so-good club, about the two abortions, about running away from home at seventeen after a fight with her father. "I just left him nappin on the couch," she said, stretched out on Horace's new liv- ing room couch, her shoes off and one of Loneese's throws over her feet. Horace was in the chair across from her. "For all I know, he's still on that couch." Even before she got to her father, even before the abortions, he knew that he would sleep with her that night. He did not even need to fill her glass a third time. "He was a fat man," she said of her father. "And there ain't a whole lot more I remember."

"Listen," he said as she talked about her father, "everything's gonna work out right for you." He knew that, at such times in a seduction, the more positive a man was the better things went. It would not have done to tell her to forget her daddy, that she had done the right thing by running out on that fat so-and-so; it was best to focus on tomorrow and tell her that the world would be brighter in the morning. He came over to the couch, and before he sat down on the edge of the coffee table he hiked up his pants just a bit with his fingertips, and seeing him do that reminded her vaguely of something wonderful. The boys in the club sure didn't do it that way. He took her hand and kissed her palm. "Everything's gonna work out to the good," he said.

Elaine Cunningham woke in the morning with Horace sleeping quietly beside her. She did not rebuke herself and did not look over at him with horror at what she had done. She sighed and laid her head back on the pillow and thought how much she still loved the man from the club, but there was nothing more she could do: not even the five-hundred-dollar leather jacket she had purchased for the man had brought him around. Two years after running away, she had gone back to where she had lived with her parents, but they had moved and no one in the building knew where they had gone. But everyone remembered her. "You sure done growed up, Elaine," one old woman said. "I wouldna knowed if you hadn't told me who you was." "Fuck em," Elaine said to the friends who had given her a ride there. "Fuck em all to hell." Then, in the car, heading out to Capitol Heights, where she was staying, "Well, maybe not fuck my mother. She was good." "Just fuck your daddy then?" the girl in the back seat said. Elaine thought about it as they went down Rhode Island Avenue, and just before they turned onto New Jersey Avenue she said, "Yes, just fuck my daddy. The fat fuck."

She got out of Horace's bed and tried to wet the desert in her mouth as she looked in his closet for a bathrobe. She rejected the blue and the paisley ones for a dark green one that reminded her of something wonderful, just as Horace's hiking up his pants had. She smelled the sleeves once she had it on, but there was only the strong scent of detergent.

In the half room that passed for a kitchen, she stood and drank most of the orange juice in the gallon carton. "Now, that was stupid, girl," she said. "You know you shoulda drunk water. Better for the thirst." She returned the carton to the refrigerator and marveled at all the food. "Damn!" she said. With the refrigerator door still open, she stepped out into the living room and took note of all that Horace had, thinking, *A girl could live large here if she did things right.* She had been crashing at a friend's place in Northeast, and the friend's mother had begun to hint that it was time for her to move on. Even when she had a job, she rarely had a place of her own. "Hmm," she said, looking through the refrigerator for what she wanted to eat. "Boody for home and food. Food, home. Boody. You shoulda stayed in school, girl. They give courses on this. Food and Home the first semester. Boody Givin the second semester."

But, as she ate her eggs and bacon and Hungry Man biscuits, she knew that she did not want to sleep with Horace too many more times, even if he did have his little castle. He was too tall, and she had never been attracted to tall men, old or otherwise. "Damn! Why couldn't he be what I wanted and have a nice place, too?" Then, as she sopped up the last of the yolk with the last half of the last biscuit, she thought of her best friend, Catrina, the woman she was crashing with. Catrina Stockton was twenty-eight, and though she had once been a heroin addict, she was one year clean and had a face and a body that testified not to a woman who had lived a bad life on the streets but to a nice-looking Virginia woman who had married at seventeen, had had three children by a truck-driving husband, and had met a man in a Fredericksburg McDonald's who had said that women like her could be queens in D.C.

Yes, Elaine thought as she leaned over the couch and stared at the photograph of Horace and Loneese and the secretary of defense, Catrina was always saying how much she wanted love, how it didn't matter what a man looked like, as long as he was good to her and loved her morning, noon, and night. The secretary of defense was in the middle of the couple. She did not know who he was, just that she had seen him somewhere, maybe on the television. Horace was holding the plaque just to the left, away from the secretary. Elaine reached over and removed a spot of dust from the picture with her fingertip, and before she could flick it away a woman said her name and she looked around, chilled.

She went into the bedroom to make sure that the voice had not been death telling her to check on Horace. She found him sitting up in the bed, yawning and stretching. "You sleep good, honey bunch?" he said. "I sure did, sweetie pie," she said and bounded across the room to hug him. A breakfast like the one she'd had would cost at least four dollars anywhere in D.C. or Maryland. "Oh, but Papa likes that," Horace said. And even the cheapest motels out on New York Avenue, the ones catering to the junkies and prostitutes, charged at least twenty-five dollars a night. What's a hug compared with that? And, besides, she liked him more than she had thought, and the issue of Catrina and her moving in had to be done delicately. "Well, just let me give you a little bit mo, then."

Young stuff is young stuff, Horace thought the first time Elaine brought Catrina by and Catrina gave him a peck on the cheek and said, "I feel like I know you from all that Elaine told me." That was in early March.

In early April, Elaine met another man at a new club on F Street Northwest and fell in love, and so did Horace with Catrina, though Catrina, after several years on the street, knew what she was feeling might be in the neighborhood of love, but it was nowhere near the right house. She and Elaine told Horace the saddest of stories about the man Elaine had met in the club, and before the end of April he was sleeping on Horace's living room floor. It helped that the man, Darnell Mudd, knew the way to anyone's heart, man or woman, and that he claimed to have a father who had been a hero in the Korean War. He even knew the name of the secretary of defense in the photograph and how long he had served in the cabinet.

By the middle of May, there were as many as five other people, friends of the three young people, hanging out at any one time in Horace's place. He was giddy with Catrina, with the blunts, with the other women who snuck out with him to a room at the motel across Thirteenth Street. By early June, more than a hundred of his old records had been stolen and pawned. "Leave his stuff alone," Elaine said to Darnell and his friends as they were going out the door with ten records apiece. "Don't take his stuff. He loves that stuff." It was 11:00 in the morning and everyone else in the apartment, including Horace, was asleep. "Sh-h-h," Darnell said. "He got so many he won't notice." And that was true. Horace hadn't played records in many months. He had two swords that were originally on the wall opposite the heating and air-conditioning unit. Both had belonged to German officers killed in the Second World War. Horace, high on the blunts, liked to see the young men sword-fight with them. But the next day, sober, he would hide them in the bottom of the closet, only to pull them out again when the partying started, at about 4:00 in the afternoon.

His neighbors, especially the neighbors who considered that Loneese had been the long-suffering one in the marriage, complained to the management about the noise, but the city-government people read in his rental record that he had lost his wife not long ago and told the neighbors that he was probably doing some kind of grieving. The city-government people never went above the first floor in Sunset. "He's a veteran who just lost his wife," they would say to those who came to the glass office on the first floor. "Why don't you cut him some slack?" But Horace tried to get a grip on things after a maintenance man told him to be careful. That was about the time one of the swords was broken and he could not for the life of him remember how it had happened. He just found it one afternoon in two pieces in the refrigerator's vegetable bin.

Things toned down a little, but the young women continued to come by and Horace went on being happy with them and with Catrina, who called him Papa and pretended to be upset when she saw him kissing another girl. "Papa, what am I gonna do with you and all your hussies?" "Papa, promise you'll only love me." "Papa, I need a new outfit. Help me out, willya please?"

Elaine had become pregnant not long after meeting Darnell, who told her to have the baby, that he had always wanted a son to carry on his name. "We can call him Junior," he said. "Or Little Darnell," she said. As she began showing, Horace and Catrina became increasingly concerned about her. Horace remembered how solicitous he had been when Loneese had been pregnant. He had not taken the first lover yet, had not even thought about anyone else as she grew and grew. He told Elaine no drugs or alcohol until the baby was born, and he tried to get her to go to bed at a decent hour, but that was often difficult with a small crowd in the living room.

Horace's grandson called in December, wanting to come by to see him, but Horace told him it would be best to meet someplace downtown, because his place was a mess. He didn't do much cleaning since Loneese died. "I don't care about that," Alonzo Jr. said. "Well, I do," Horace said. "You know how I can be bout these things."

In late December, Elaine gave birth to a boy, several weeks early. They gave him the middle name Horace. "See," Darnell said one day, holding the baby on the couch. "Thas your grandpa. You don't mind me callin you his granddad, Mr. Perkins? You don't mind, do you?" The city-government people in the rental office, led by someone new, someone who took the rules seriously, took note that the old man in Apartment 230 had a baby and his mama and daddy in the place and not a single one of them was even related to him, though if one had been it still would have been against the rules as laid down in the rule book of apartment living.

By late February, an undercover policeman had bought two packets of crack from someone in the apartment. It was a woman, he told his superiors at first, and that's what he wrote in his report, but in a subsequent report he wrote that he had bought the rocks from a man. "Start over," said one of his superiors, who supped monthly with the new mayor, who lived for numbers, and in March the undercover man went back to buy more.

It was late on a warm Saturday night in April when Elaine woke to the crackle of walkie-talkies outside the door. She had not seen Darnell in more than a month, and something told her that she should get out of there because there might not be any more good times. She thought of Horace and Catrina asleep in the bedroom. Two men and two women she did not know very well were asleep in various places around the living room, but she had dated the brother of one of the women some three years ago. One of the men claimed to be Darnell's cousin, and, to prove it to her, when he knocked at the door that night he showed her a Polaroid of him and Darnell at a club, their arms around each other and their eyes red, because the camera had been cheap and the picture cost only two dollars.

She got up from the couch and looked into the crib. In the darkness she could make out that her son was awake, his little legs kicking and no sound from him but a happy gurgle. The sound of the walkie-talkie outside the door came and went. She could see it all on the television news — "Drug Dealing Mama in Jail. Baby Put in Foster Care." She stepped over the man who said he was Darnell's cousin and pushed the door to the bedroom all the way open. Catrina was getting out of bed. Horace was snoring. He had never snored before in his life, but the drugs and alcohol together had done bad things to his airway.

"You hear anything?" Elaine whispered as Catrina tiptoed to her.

"I sure did," Catrina said. Sleeping on the streets required keeping one eye and both ears open. "I don't wanna go back to jail."

"Shit. Me, neither," Elaine said. "What about the window?"

"Go out and down two floors? With a baby? Damn!"

"We can do it," Elaine said, looking over Catrina's shoulder to the dark lump that was Horace mumbling in his sleep. "What about him?"

Catrina turned her head. "He old. They ain't gonna do anything to him. I'm just worried bout makin it with that baby."

"Well, I sure as hell ain't gonna go without my child."

"I ain't said we was," Catrina hissed. "Down two floors just ain't gonna be easy, is all."

"We can do it," Elaine said.

"We can do it," Catrina said. She tiptoed to the chair at the foot of the bed and went through Horace's pants pockets. "Maybe fifty dollars here," she whispered after returning. "I already got about three hundred."

"You been stealin from him?" Elaine said. The lump in the bed turned over and moaned, then settled back to snoring.

"God helps them that helps themselves, Elaine. Les go." Catrina had her clothes in her hands and went on by Elaine, who watched as the lump in the bed turned again, snoring all the while. Bye, Horace. Bye. I be seein you.

The policeman in the unmarked car parked across Thirteenth Street watched as Elaine stood on the edge of the balcony and jumped. She passed for a second in front of the feeble light over the entrance and landed on the sloping entrance of the underground parking garage. The policeman was five years from retirement and he did not move, because he could see quite well from where he sat. His partner, only three years on the job, was asleep in the passenger seat. The veteran thought the woman jumping might have hurt herself, because he did not see her rise from the ground for several minutes. I wouldn't do it, the man thought, not for all a rich man's money. The woman did rise, but before she did he saw another woman lean over the balcony dangling a bundle. Drugs? he thought. Nah. Clothes? Yeah, clothes more like it. The bundle was on a long rope or string — it was too far for the man to make out. The woman on the balcony leaned over very far and the woman on the ground reached up as far as she could, but still the bundle was a good two feet from her hands.

Just let them clothes drop, the policeman thought. Then Catrina released the bundle and Elaine caught it. Good catch. I wonder what she looks like in the light. Catrina jumped, and the policeman watched her pass momentarily in front of the light, and then he looked over at his partner. He himself didn't mind filling out the forms so much, but his partner did, so he let him sleep on. I'll be on a lake fishin my behind off and you'll still be doin this. When he looked back, the first woman was coming up the slope of the entrance with the bundle in her arms and the second one was limping after her. I wonder what that one looks like in a good light. Once on the sidewalk, both women looked left, then right, and headed down Thirteenth Street. The policeman yawned and watched through his sideview mirror as the women crossed M Street. He yawned again. Even at 3:00 in the morning people still jaywalked.

The man who was a cousin of Darnell's was on his way back from the bathroom when the police broke through the door. He frightened easily, and though he had just emptied his bladder, he peed again as the door came open and the light of the hallway and the loud men came spilling in on him and his sleeping companions.

Horace began asking about Catrina and Elaine and the baby as soon as they put him in a cell. It took him that long to clear his head and understand what was happening to him. He pressed his face against the bars, trying to get his bearings and ignoring everything behind him in the cell. He stuck his mouth as far out of the bars as he could and shouted for someone to tell him whether they knew if the young women and the baby were all right. "They just women, y'all," he kept saying for some five minutes. "They wouldn't hurt a flea. Officers, please. Please, officers. What's done happened to them? And that baby . . . That baby is so innocent." It was a little after 6:00 in the morning, and men up and down the line started hollering for him to shut up or they would stick the biggest dick he ever saw in his mouth. Stunned, he did quiet down, because, while he was used to street language coming from the young men who came and went in his apartment, no bad words had ever been directed at him. They talked trash with the filthiest language he had ever heard, but they always invited him to join in and "talk about how it really is," talk about his knowing the secretary of defense and the mayor. Usually, after the second blunt, he was floating along with them. Now someone had threatened to do to him what he and the young men said they would do to any woman that crossed them.

Then he turned from the bars and considered the three men he was sharing the two-man cell with. The city-jail people liked to make as little work for themselves as possible, and filling cells beyond their capacity meant having to deal with fewer locks. One man was cocooned in blankets on the floor beside the tiered metal beds. The man sleeping on the top bunk had a leg over the side, and because he was a tall man the leg came down to within six inches of the face of the man lying on the bottom bunk. That man was awake and on his back and picking his nose and staring at Horace. His other hand was under his blanket, in the crotch of his pants. What the man got out of his nose he would flick up at the bottom of the bunk above him. Watching him, Horace remembered that a very long time ago, even before the Chesapeake Street house, Loneese would iron his handkerchiefs and fold them into four perfect squares.

"Daddy," the man said, "you got my smokes?"

"What?" Horace said. He recalled doing it to Catrina about 2:00 or 3:00 in the morning and then rolling over and going to sleep. He also remembered slapping flies away in his dreams, flies that were as big as the hands of policemen.

The man seemed to have an infinite supply of boogers, and the more he picked the more Horace's stomach churned. He used to think it was such a shame to unfold the handkerchiefs, so wondrous were the squares. The man sighed at Horace's question and put something from his nose on the big toe of the sleeping man above him. "I said do you got my smokes?"

"I don't have my cigarettes with me," Horace said. He tried the best white man's English he knew, having been told by a friend who was serving with him in the army in Germany that it impressed not only white people but black people who weren't going anywhere in life. "I left my cigarettes at home." His legs were aching and he wanted to sit on the floor, but the only available space was in the general area of where he was standing and something adhered to his shoes every time he lifted his feet. "I wish I did have my cigarettes to give you."

"I didn't ask you bout *your* cigarettes. I don't wanna smoke them. I ask you bout *my* cigarettes. I wanna know if you brought *my* cigarettes."

Someone four cells down screamed and called out in his sleep: "Irene, why did you do this to me? Irene, ain't love worth a damn anymore?" Someone else told him to shut up or he would get a king-sized dick in his mouth.

"I told you I do not have any cigarettes," Horace said.

"You know, you ain't worth shit," the man said. "You take the cake and mess it all up. You really do. Now, you know you was comin to jail, so why didn't you bring my goddamn smokes? What kinda fuckin consideration is that?"

Horace decided to say nothing. He raised first one leg and then the other and shook them, hoping that would relieve the aches. Slowly, he turned around to face the bars. No one had told him what was going to happen to him. He knew a lawyer, but he did not know if he was still practicing. He had friends, but he did not want any of them to see him in jail. He hoped the man would go to sleep.

"Don't turn your fuckin back on me after all we meant to each other," the man said. "We have this long relationship and you do this to me. Whas wrong with you, Daddy?"

"Look," Horace said, turning back to the man. "I done told you I ain't got no smokes. I ain't got your smokes. I ain't got my smokes. I ain't got nobody's smokes. Why can't you understand that?" He was aware that he was veering away from the white man's English, but he knew that his friend from Germany was probably home asleep safely in his bed. "I can't give you what I don't have." Men were murdered in the D.C. jail, or so the *Washington Post* told him. "Can't you understand what I'm sayin?" His back stayed as close to the bars as he could manage. Who was this Irene, he thought, and what had she done to steal into a man's dreams that way?

"So, Daddy, it's gonna be like that, huh?" the man said, raising his head and pushing the foot of the upper-bunk man out of the way so he could see Horace better. He took his hand out of his crotch and pointed at Horace. "You gon pull a Peter-and-Jesus thing on me and deny you ever knew me, huh? Thas your plan, Daddy?" He lowered his head back to the black-and-white-striped pillow. "I've seen some low-down dirty shit in my day, but you the lowest. After our long relationship and everything."

"I never met you in my life," Horace said, grabbing the bars behind him with both hands, hoping, again, for relief.

"I won't forget this, and you know how long my memory is. First, you don't bring me my smokes, like you know you should. Then you deny all that we had. Don't go to sleep in here, Daddy, thas all I gotta say."

He thought of Reilly Johnson, a man he had worked with in the Pentagon. Reilly considered himself something of a photographer. He had taken the picture of Horace with the secretary of defense. What would the bail be? Would Reilly be at home to receive his call on a Sunday morning? Would they give him bail? The policemen who pulled him from his bed had tsk-tsked in his face. "Sellin drugs and corruptin young people like that?" "I didn't know nothin about that, officer. Please." "Tsk tsk. An old man like you."

"The world ain't big enough for you to hide from my righteous wrath, Daddy. And you know how righteous I can be when I get started. The world ain't big enough, so you know this jail ain't big enough."

Horace turned back to the bars. Was something in the back as painful as something in the stomach? He touched his face. Rarely, even in the lost months with Catrina, had he failed to shave each morning. A man's capable demeanor started with a shave each morning, his sergeant in boot camp had told him a thousand years ago.

The man down the way began calling for Irene again. Irene, Horace called in his mind. Irene, are you out there? No one told the man to be quiet. It was about 7:00 and the whole building was waking up and the man calling Irene was not the loudest sound in the world anymore.

"Daddy, you got my smokes? Could use my smokes right about now."

Horace, unable to stand anymore, slowly sank to the floor. There he found some relief. The more he sat, the more he began to play over the arrest. He had had money in his pocket when he took off his pants the night before, but there was no money when they booked him. And where had Catrina and Elaine been when the police marched him out of the apartment and down to the paddy wagon, with the Sunset's female security guard standing behind her desk with an "Oh, yes, I told you so" look? Where had they been? He had not seen them. He stretched out his legs and they touched the feet of the sleeping man on the floor. The man roused. "Love don't mean shit anymore," the man on the lower bunk said. It was loud enough to wake the man on the floor all the way, and that man sat up and covered his chest with his blanket and looked at Horace, blinking and blinking and getting a clearer picture of Horace the more he blinked.

Reilly did not come for him until the middle of Monday afternoon. Somebody opened the cell door and at first Horace thought the policeman was coming to get one of his cellmates.

"Homer Parkins," the man with the keys said. The doors were supposed to open electronically, but that system had not worked in a long time.

"Thas me," Horace said and got to his feet. As he and the man with the keys walked past the other cells, someone said to Horace, "Hey, pops, you ain't too old to learn to suck dick." "Keep moving," the man with the keys said. "Pops, I'll give you a lesson when you come back."

As they poured his things out of a large manila envelope, the two guards behind the desk whispered and laughed. "Everything there?" one of them asked Horace. "Yes." "Well, good," the guard said. "I guess we'll be seein you on your next trip here." "Oh, leave that old man alone. He's somebody's grandfather." "When they start that old," the first man said, "it gets in their system and they can't stop. Ain't that right, pops?"

He and Reilly did not say very much after Reilly said he had been surprised to hear from Horace and that he had wondered what had happened to him since Loneese died. Horace said he was eternally grateful to Reilly for bailing him out and that it was all a mistake as well as a long story that he would soon share with him. At Sunset, Reilly offered to take him out for a meal, but Horace said he would have to take a rain check. "Rain check?" Reilly said, smiling. "I didn't think they said that anymore."

The key to the apartment worked the way it always had, but something was blocking the door, and he had to force it open. Inside, he found destruction everywhere. On top of the clothes and the mementos of his life, strewn across the table and the couch and the floor were hundreds and hundreds of broken records. He took three steps into the room and began to cry. He turned around and around, hoping for something that would tell him it was not as bad as his eyes first reported. But there was little hope — the salt and pepper shakers had not been touched, the curtains covering the glass door were intact. There was not much beyond that for him to cling to.

He thought immediately of Catrina and Elaine. What had he done to deserve this? Had he not always shown them a good and kind heart? He covered his eyes, but that seemed only to produce more tears, and when he lowered his hands the room danced before him through the tears. To steady himself, he put both hands on the table, which was covered in instant coffee and sugar. He brushed broken glass off the chair nearest him and sat down. He had not got it all off, and he felt what was left through his pants and underwear.

He tried to look around but got no farther than the picture with the secretary of defense. It had two cracks in it, one running north to south and the other going northwest to southeast. The photograph was tilting, too, and something told him that if he could straighten the picture it all might not be so bad. He reached out a hand, still crying, but he could not move from the chair.

He stayed as he was through the afternoon and late into the evening, not once moving from the chair, though the tears did stop at around 5:00. Night came and he still did not move. My name is Horace Perkins, he thought just as the sun set. My name is Horace Perkins and I worked many a year at the Pentagon. The apartment became dark, but he did not have it in him to turn on the lights.

The knocking had been going on for more than ten minutes when he finally heard it. He got up, stumbling over debris, and opened the door. Elaine stood there with Darnell Jr. in her arms.

"Horace, you O.K.? I been comin by. I been worried about you, Horace."

He said nothing but opened the door enough for her and the baby to enter.

"It's dark, Horace. What about some light?"

He righted the lamp on the table and turned it on.

"Jesus in heaven, Horace! What happened! My Lord Jesus! I can't believe this." The baby, startled by his mother's words, began to cry. "It's O.K.," she said to him, "it's O.K.," and gradually the baby calmed down. "Oh, Horace, I'm so sorry. I really am. This is the worst thing I've ever seen in my life." She touched his shoulder with her free hand, but he shrugged it off. "Oh, my dear God! Who could do this?"

She went to the couch and moved enough trash aside for the baby. She pulled a pacifier from her sweater pocket, put it momentarily in her mouth to remove the lint, then put it in the baby's mouth. He appeared satisfied and leaned back on the couch.

She went to Horace, and right away he grabbed her throat. "I'm gonna kill you tonight!" he shouted. "I just wish that bitch Catrina was here so I could kill her, too." Elaine struggled and sputtered out one "please" before he gripped her tighter. She beat his arms, but that seemed to give him more strength. She began to cry. "I'm gonna kill you tonight, girl, if it's the last thing I do."

The baby began to cry, and she turned her head as much as she could to look at him. This made him slap her twice, and she started to fall, and he pulled her up and, as he did, went for a better grip, which was time enough for her to say, "Don't kill me in front of my son, Horace." He loosened his hands. "Don't kill me in front of my boy, Horace." Her tears ran down her face and over and into his hands. "He don't deserve to see me die. You know that, Horace."

"Where, then!"

"Anywhere but in front of him. He's innocent of everything."

He let her go and backed away.

"I did nothin, Horace," she whispered. "I give you my word, I did nothin." The baby screamed, and she went to him and took him in her arms.

Horace sat down in the same chair he had been in.

"I would not do this to you, Horace."

He looked at her and at the baby, who could not take his eyes off Horace, even through his tears.

One of the baby's cries seemed to get stuck in his throat, and to release it the baby raised a fist and punched the air, and finally the cry came free. How does a man start over with nothing? Horace thought. Elaine came near him, and the baby still watched him as his crying lessened. How does a man start from scratch?

He leaned down and picked up a few of the broken albums from the floor and read the labels. "I would not hurt you for anything in the world, Horace," Elaine said. Okeh Phonograph Corporation. Domino Record Co. RCA Victor. Darnell Jr.'s crying stopped, but he continued to look down at the top of Horace's head. Cameo Record Corporation, N.Y. "You been too good to me for me to hurt you like this, Horace." He dropped the records one at a time: "It Takes an Irishman to Make Love." "I'm Gonna Pin a Medal on the Girl I Left Behind." "Ragtime Soldier Man." "Whose Little Heart Are You Breaking Now." "The Syncopated Walk."

TRUDY LEWIS

Limestone Diner

FROM MERIDIAN

THE MORNING AFTER her granddaughter's frantic phone call,
Lorraine skipped her usual coffee session at the Limestone Diner
and drove out to the accident scene instead. Of course, no one had
bothered to clean up yet; there were mysterious pieces from deep
in the engine scattered all over the road and the green field nearby
was covered with smashed yellow cupcakes. Lorraine, still agile at
sixty-eight, set her travel mug on a fence post, lifted the barbed
wire, and climbed on through. The field belonged to the Graysons,
she supposed. They still grazed a few cattle, despite the fact that
their income came almost exclusively from the axle factory two
towns over. Here and there, a cupcake had survived whole, its yellow face still decorated with two black eyes and a thin slice of smile.
How did it happen? She remembered the wildflowers that seemed
to blossom in her mama's lawn all in the same day, remembered
Sharee tumbling out of the car in that checked blue playsuit, the
one Lorraine had cut and wrangled out of a scrap of white-sale
bedsheet. Sharee must've been seven at the time, her cheeks spotted with excitement, one of her long red-brown curls caught in
a button and stretched out nearly straight, as she declared that
Easter had come early this year, there was candy poking out all over
the yard. How did some fail and some survive and how did He pick
and choose between them?

Lorraine located a likely stick and scraped off a stray streak of
frosting that had stuck to her shoe. It was suspiciously spreadable
— probably the cheap kind made with shortening instead of real
butter, if she knew Kris's mom. She pictured the wiry bleached-

blond pot smoker working late in the cramped kitchen of her trailer frosting cupcakes for the Lady Rangers' bake sale, then sending poor Kris out at the last minute like that to drop them off at the high school while the gym door was still unlocked for the track team.

And just as others had blamed her, she blamed the mother — who else was there to blame? In the twenty-nine years since Sharee's accident, Lorraine had tried every other possible angle. She blamed her husband for teaching the girl to drive before she was fifteen. She blamed her remaining children — Sally and Trev — for their good health and sound instincts. She blamed her sister's girl for naming her baby daughter after Sharee before a proper generation had passed, thereby stirring up bad luck for Lorraine's youngest. She blamed the WPA workers who had built the road, the French trappers and traders who had settled the county, the glaciers that had formed the ridge. She got as far back as God, and then she blamed the Rock of Ages too — a dirty old man with clay-stained fingers and halitosis, who didn't let anyone know the breath of life stank like rotted egg salad at the end of a late summer family reunion in the sun.

Still, in the end, it was always the mother who paid. Lorraine squatted down for a closer look and felt the arthritis pinch her knee, as if death was feeling her up in preparation for his next big move. Ha, she told him, you'll have to do better than that. The earth was still damp from this weekend's rain. She dug idly with her stick until she came to the place where the clay gave back its resistance and the smell of iron clogged her nose, then thought of Kris pawing the ground, Kris winding up for a fast ball, Kris raising the dust. The girl was only the relief pitcher, but that was due to inconsistency and a moody temperament. As far as talent went, she could outpitch Daisy Wycliff on three days out of four. On the fourth, however, Kris would shout obscenities at the ref, jam her finger, walk two batters in a row, then sit down on the bench and argue with her spinster coach while inking up the bottom of her shoe, as the other girls, Lorraine's granddaughter Reenie among them, floundered out on the field without her. It was Kris who had gotten them to the Kansas City tournament in the first place, and now she wouldn't be there to pitch them through. Lorraine picked up a cupcake and brought it up to her face, tasted the icing to confirm her suspicions, then buried it in the hole she'd made, sugar still burning on her gums.

Over the rise of the hill, through the white-hot glare of the early morning sun, she saw a woman coming toward her. Old woman, she thought, by the drab loose clothes and the sorrowful walk, or rather a woman just coming into the suspicion of her old age. Lorraine stood up and shaded her eyes, the glare parted, and she saw her daughter Sally, a wry silver blonde sliding toward fifty, in the gray-green work shirt and cargo pants she wore for her job at the State Park Service. Her face still pretty but dry and rough; the wrinkles clawed in next to the eyes and over the forehead like she'd gotten careless with a feral cat. Every time Lorraine saw those marks, she wanted to lift her hand and wipe them away, as she had wiped away the pudding and jam, the dirt and the gravy, for the first ten years of Sally's life.

Sally glanced down at the cupcakes on the ground, then looked at Lorraine with a tentative squint. "Trev called me this morning. He said it was probably over as soon as she hit the ground. They excused the teammates from school, you know, so poor little Reenie's home just sitting in her room and playing that awful music over and over."

"That girl was something else. She had the whole crew blasting them Donnas, when all they ever wanted before was their Shania Twains and their Britney Spears."

"Well, all I'm saying is, they could probably use you over there."

"Let an old woman have her meditation, sister."

Sally's lip pinched inward; Lorraine could always tell when the girl's patience was coming to an end by the way she bit at one corner of her lip until she'd practically sucked the whole side of her face in. Giving rise to even more wrinkles, no doubt. "Really, Ma, why'd I know that you'd be out here? Can't you ever let anything alone? You're like some horrible old turkey hawk. People see you coming, they know some kind of destruction's up and roaming the land."

"Now, don't go having a hot flash on me. I told you, I'm contemplating. I'll get moving here in a St. Louis minute."

How would Sally know? She'd never had kids of her own, and now it was too late. She'd taken up with one fellow after another, finally settled in with a widower who ran the concession up at the

Park. The two of them seemed to get along, grew a garden that kept the whole family in squash and tomatoes, ran their matching chocolate Labs through the woods, threw big bonfire parties whenever there was a controlled burn in the forest. To tell the truth, Trev, with his three kids, his furniture dealership, and his twenty-five-year marriage, didn't seem half as happy. But Lorraine could never get used to the fact that Sally had just meandered along from bud to seed without ever coming into a satisfying bloom.

She had to admit that it was a comfort to have someone look up on her, though, to call every evening in the quiet spell between the jays and the whippoorwills, to help with the lawn work now that Earl had lost interest, to go out to the movies and the mall. Would Sharee have done the same if she'd lived? Sharee with that fine brown woman-down on her calves since before she even started school, the long bony nose with the diamond-cut nostrils that made her seem constantly mad about something, the strawberry-rhubarb smell of sharp sweat on a sweet temperament, the thrill the girl took in packing a suitcase or a picnic, the embroidered denim jacket with its clumsy knots of red and blue and yellow silk hanging out the other side.

Not knowing, Lorraine gave up, speared another cupcake, and let Sally lead her back to the car.

Sharee lives in Kansas City now, far enough from home that her relatives don't include her in their Sunday plans, close enough that she can drive back for the holidays on a single tank of gas and a large thermos of overly sweetened coffee. She is connected to the sticky web of her extended family only by her inherited name and her mother's viscous commentary over the phone line: Cousin Amy got divorced from that drunken auto repairman, Aunt Erma finally quit her job at the Limestone Diner at seventy-three, Cel got him another HUD house and toted it back to the farm on a trailer, Paul Dee knocked up his junior high girlfriend and had to drop out of school to get married and start in full-time at Nolan's Filling and Towing, Aunt Lorraine has pretty much taken over as den mother and mascot of her granddaughter's softball team. As much as she loves her mom, a modernized woman who wears sweater sets half buttoned over her plump plummy breasts, gets Dad to cook burgers or pork chops on his own one night a week, reads mysteries with snappy female detectives and has a euphemistic word for everyone, Sharee wants nothing to do with that backward lot of hillbillies. When she graduated high school, she insisted on going out of state to KU for college, even though it meant taking out extra loans for tuition and working twenty hours a week in a local T-shirt shop. Lawrence, with its import stores and microbreweries, its hordes of unattached singles, amazed her; here, she could finally become herself, separate from the rest of the family and their soap opera plots.

Something about crossing that state line changed Sharee. In Missouri, she couldn't see anything for the caves and creeks and sinkholes, the limestone cliffs, the broken-backed Ozarks, the vine-covered trees, and the clapboard billboards by the highway advertising fetal life and walnut bowls. In Kansas, the horizon is straight like the edge of a place mat; the sky comes at you honestly, every streak of pink visible as the lines in your palm. This plainness Sharee finds appealing because it mirrors Sharee herself: the straight wholewheat hair, the long nose, the pale unmarked body with its modest round breasts and solid hips. She bought a dress at a thrift store during that first year of college and not another soul in her family would have worn it; it had no shape, no color, it did not do a thing to accentuate her form. It had a huge white Puritan collar; boxy straight seams down the sides, a tiny blue pinstripe on white cotton, a pencil-sized kick pleat at the calf. Only in this dress did Sharee begin to become who she was; in this dress she ate her first tamale baked in a genuine cornhusk, instead of just a paper wrapper from Burrito Bell. In this dress she attended her first live theater — even if it was just a few of her classmates wearing bustles and top hats and stumbling over their *fin-de-siècle* lines. In this dress she felt the pangs that would lead her to surrender her long-contested virginity to a boy all the way from Chicago, who stroked her pale flawless cheek, her long smooth buttocks, and told her she was the "pride of the prairie" even though she feared in her heart she was really only a broke-back belle.

By the time Sally got Lorraine over to Trev's house, the whole team was there, eating doughnuts and drinking milk, their legs and elbows taking over the dining table, the breakfast nook, and the bar. Something about the sight of these big girls comforted Lorraine; they were so healthy and strong, inches taller than she and her five

sisters — even some of her brothers — had been at that age, and
more thickly muscled, despite the lack of discipline and farm work.
All that milk, she thought, all that meat. Nothing like the steady
diet of grease-soaked beans and greens and fried eggs she remembered from her own childhood and which still made her give in
and splurge on packaged snacks and out-of-season fruit at the grocery store. Close up, the girls smelled mostly of the junk food they
downed in great boy-sized portions, of coconut suntan lotion and
citrus perfumes that went acid in the sunshine, mango lip-gloss,
and cinnamon chewing gum.

Lorraine knew, she had been attending nearly every practice,
even touring with them when they went to tournaments, or rather
following along behind the schoolbus in the tin-can mobile home
she and Earl had bought to celebrate her retirement from her sec-
retarial job at Boonslick High. At every stop, Lorraine held a concession in the parking lot, serving up sweet fizzy sodas in tall lem-
onade glasses printed with flamingos and sunflowers, filling milky
marbled candy bowls with the salty snacks she remembered from
her own kids' adolescence. She listened to the shortstop's complaints about her mother's boyfriends, the third baseman's love
troubles, and Kris the relief pitcher's blow-by-blow accounts of her
arguments with Hettie Barnes, the spinster coach who made them
keep their nails short and their grades high. Meanwhile, Lorraine
let the girls play their music — Britney Spears, Christina Aguilera,
Shania Twain — on the new CD player she bought with her Green
Stamps, even through she still preferred the country tunes she
grew up with: Louvin Brothers, Hank Williams, Woody Guthrie,
Patsy Cline. But the music Kris liked was even worse. She had a
boyfriend at the state university who sent her tapes of howls and
yelps and curses trussed up as regular tunes. Kris's favorite was the
Donnas, an all-girl group who sang about nothing but drinking and
boy-hopping. On the CD cover, four pretty brunettes in evening
clothes sat drinking at a table covered with empty shot glasses. All
of them were named Donna, supposedly, and you couldn't really
tell them apart, except for the fact that each had her hair parted
and her body pierced in a slightly different location.

In Trev's kitchen, the girls rippled in the speckled sunlight, constantly shifting their long limbs and playing with their hair, while
Trev sat as still as a scarecrow among them, his overstuffed shirt ex-

ploding with graying chest hair above and expanding love handles below as he tried to maintain control of his *USA Today*. Without ever hearing her daughter go, Lorraine was aware that Sally had disappeared behind her, off for another day of poking and puttering in the park.

"Still, I can't believe it," Irene Mason was saying. "I mean, she was with me yesterday afternoon at the car wash at Burrito Bell, spraying guys' shorts when they walked by. 'How else are you going to know?' she said. I was kind of mortified. But the guys seemed to be into it."

"Like that time she made us all strip in Kirksville and do that Spanish dance."

"Donna A, Donna C, Donna F. She never called anybody by their name anymore. She just yelled for more Donnas to get up and get down."

"'Forty Boys in Forty Nights,' that was her favorite tune," Lorraine said. "She was always telling folks we were on tour with the band."

Some of the girls nodded, as seriously as if they were listening to a teacher talk on about Shakespeare, and Trev dropped the money section of his paper, surprised by his mother's voice and annoyed, no doubt, by her familiarity with the flimflam that seemed to him beneath the attention of a grown-up person, although she could assure him he'd had plenty to say about the Stones and Eagles and Led Zeppelin when he was sixteen. Reenie, the sweet girl with the chin dimple and a single cherry-wood braid, got up to greet her old gran and hand off a cup of coffee. She gave Lorraine a wordless hug, then absent-mindedly rubbed Trev's bald head on the way back to her seat.

"Hmm, needs more polish," she said. "Someone pass the Lemon Pledge."

A second girl — Daisy Wycliff — mimicked passing a bottle, and Reenie proceeded to bring the blood back to her father's scalp. As she did, her boat-necked T-shirt took a dip, and Lorraine spotted the butterfly tattoo that sat folded, as still as a resting swallowtail, on the leeward side of Reenie's left breast.

Due to National Softball Association regulations, the girls couldn't wear jewelry in the game, so they settled for ornamental tattoos instead: bracelets of doodles around their upper arms, tiny hearts and daisies inside the inner slopes of the cleavage where the charm of a necklace might hang, diamonds dotting the vertebrae of their lower backs, so that a row of jeweled peaks emerged from the bottom of the gray Lady Rangers uniform shirt whenever a player swooped down to retrieve a ball. The girls all seemed to have the same color hair too, as if this were part of the team uniform — streaks of blond and brown like caramel and chocolate in a candy bar, the healthy good looks that would bleach out into ordinary un-varnished pine after they'd sat too long in the sun. Reenie was the best of them, a girl with her mother's height and her father's flat-faced determination. She'd slimmed down considerably since she started playing the game; she'd made a whole new level of friends with these teammates who'd known one another all their lives, but who somehow never connected until they picked up a bat and ball.

"Did you know that she actually made out with that security guard in Sedalia?" a girl offered. "He must've been twenty-five at least, and he got bothered enough to pull out a lubricated bad boy before she told him she was engaged."

"Engaged? I didn't know she was engaged."

"Engaged to get pre-engaged, is more like. Besides, the guy's practically her cousin."

"Wait," said Trev, "Just let a dad finish his breakfast here. And Mama Lorraine, could you possibly please get a hold of yourself, show some respect for the — for the family and all?"

Trev's wife came in, red eyes and raw lips, her hands rummaging up the sleeves of her robe as if she were cold on this warm May morning, and the room went still. Lorraine couldn't face her, not without an extra spot of coffee, at least. She got up and poured an-other half cup, touched the poor woman on the small of her back, corralled her into an embrace, and let her go again without ever looking her in the face. But, even so, Lorraine still smelled the dread that she couldn't afford to remember, the turpentine bile of empty insides after hours of vomiting or fasting, the fish-entrails scent of insomnia. It was as if Trev's Catherine were the grieving mother, not Lorraine.

Something about the woman's defenselessness made Lorraine angry, despite her best intentions. The trouble with this middle generation was that they operated without a foundation: they didn't believe in God, they didn't believe in the devil, they didn't believe in the almanac or the Democratic party or the rod. You could hardly get them excited over anything. No use waiting for Trev and Catherine to serve as examples for these young people. It was obviously up to Lorraine to set the tone. "The main thing is, girls, we can't let Kris down now. She'd expect us to go ahead and play this KC tournament best as we can."

"You really think we should try and play?" Daisy said. "Wouldn't that be disrespecting her?" A tear stood in the corner of her chicory blue eye, enhanced, Lorraine knew, by a costly contact lens that had had to be replaced more than once in the course of her brief pitching career.

"Not if you do it in the right spirit. That's just the way things are in this evil world. You never know who's at the wheel of some black chariot waiting to mow your sister down. But you gotta get up and get right back on the business seat anyway. Otherwise, it's just the same as inviting the devil to your shivaree. The sin against the Holy Spirit, girls."

"Sin against the Holy Spirit — what's that?"

"Doing it with a Catholic, according to my mom," Elaine Michaels smirked.

"No — it's overrunning third with one out to go and the bases loaded."

"Peeing on your granny's grave," Reenie said. "Then wiping yourself with the pinky finger of her Sunday gloves."

Today, Sharee is making chicken and dumplings for her husband, the same Chicago native who scored her virginity with a sly Midwestern compliment and a few well-executed sexual maneuvers eleven years back. Usually, it's Matt who makes dinner for her — pierogi, kielbasa, cheesy potatoes, and grilled steak — but Sharee's on an extended leave from her administrative job at Ozark Airlines and she feels she ought to do something, at least, to justify her existence.

Something besides peeing in a cup, that is, giving herself a shot in the hip, taking a blood test to determine the level of her hormones, reading through moms-in-waiting magazines as she sips herbal tea to relieve the symptoms of her long-awaited pregnancy. Four weeks ago, in her second attempt at in vitro, Sharee had five of her own fertilized eggs transferred into her uterus; this afternoon, her pregnancy has been confirmed by ultrasound. Where for years her uterine walls had remained bare and unadorned, there were now four viable embryos clinging to the lush endometrial lining, perhaps too many for her body to accommodate. Maybe she concentrated too hard, she thinks, when she was lying there on the examining table with her legs in the air, the nurse coordinator leading her through a guided meditation and Matt stroking her belly for good luck.

She rolls out the dough for the dumplings and smells the yeasty scent, good as a microbrewery any day. She marvels at her own fertility, her body's ability to double and triple itself. For years, she has been angry at her body's failures, the good round breasts without a reason, the intricate internal pockets and tubes like a malfunctioning pinball game, the childbearing hips with nothing to hold. It poisoned sex for her, that anger, made her just want to roll over and grow old when Matt pressed against her hip or teased her nipple at a futile point in the cycle. She cuts the dough into strips, remembering her own violence, the punishments she wanted to inflict upon herself. "Visualize a beautiful nursery," the nurse had told her at the moment of the transfer. "Pink, blue, farm animals, jungle theme, anything you like. Now look at the wallpaper. Feel the flocking. It's got to be thick, it's got to be sticky, all plumped out with blood and nutrients. These little eggs are counting on it. They're getting ready to climb your wall." But the idea of fertilized eggs didn't necessarily appeal to Sharee, who's just rural enough to remember encountering a fertilized chicken egg with an offending spot of blood on the Melmac platter at her grandma's breakfast table. The fertilized eggs were the ones you wanted to avoid, the old ones, the ruined ones, with possible chicken parts gelling in their soggy centers. So Sharee had envisioned regular hard-boiled eggs instead: Easter eggs with a little purple dye clinging to the meat, deviled eggs topped with fluffy yolk filling and chives, over-boiled eggs with green rings emanating from the yolks. They all climbed the walls with their little suction feet, but then began dripping, wet and formless again, down the fresh zoo-scape wallpaper.

Sharee drops the dumplings, one by one, into the boiling pot and thinks about how she'll pose the problem to her husband, who has possibly reached the end of what he's able to process, in terms of complications. The dumplings puff out quickly, rising to the surface of the boiling water and chicken fat, and as they do Sharee feels the nausea curdle in her abdomen like the fibroid tumors that brought her to this juncture in the first place.

At 5:20, she's lying on the couch in her sea-horse pajamas when she hears Matt's car in the driveway. She notices how he switches off the engine and leaves the radio playing the end of a rock anthem. Smashing Pumpkins, it sounds like. Matt doesn't even like the Pumpkins, despite their Chicago origins. He's just delaying having to hear the good or bad news, which he pointedly resisted having delivered over the phone. The car door opens, closes, opens again. He forgot his sunglasses, he's checking the mileage, he's getting something out of the glove compartment. Once he finally enters the house, she sees that he's brought her flowers — a neutral bouquet of purple blazing stars and yellow daisies, congratulations if it's a go and consolation if it's just another wash. Which, she wonders, is finally more appropriate?

Three days after Kris's death, Lorraine was at her usual table in the Limestone Diner, working out a batting order for the Kansas City tournament. This was Hettie Barnes's job, she knew, but Hettie hadn't been herself, had been out of school with a migraine, and who knew when she'd get around to it. Lorraine, on the contrary, felt energized by the state of emergency. What was this strange excitement, like a fresh redeye gravy lubricating her old bones? She'd been up since 4:30 dusting her living room and waiting for the diner to open. At 5:45, when Earl shuffled into the room in his railroad-striped overalls to turn on the TV, she slipped on her loafers and reached for her pocketbook, which her husband then grabbed out of her grasp with surprising speed, given his age and the hour of day.

"What's your hurry, woman? You think the gossip will be all dried up before you get there?"

Earl didn't appear to be affected by the accident, seemed, in fact, oblivious to the parallels between this death and their own daughter's. Lorraine often doubted that he remembered Sharee at all, despite the photos in the albums and on the walls, the little altar covered with scraps of dresses and award ribbons in the back bedroom where he never went. When the children were coming up, each night after they went to sleep and the parents finally had a minute to themselves, Lorraine and Earl would tally up the day's gains and losses, his run-ins at the garage, her adventures at the high school. Then the conversation would turn, like a dusty road winding into a hidden spring, onto the subject of their children. What about Sally tying a leash on that box turtle? What about the mouth on that Trev? One night a few weeks after the accident, Lorraine tried to slip Sharee's name back into their nightly talk and Earl's face went blank, as if someone had smoothed it over with a trowel. He grasped the coffee table in front of him, then stood up very straight, walked out of the room, out of the house, started the engine of the new pickup the insurance had paid for, and didn't return for over an hour. After that Sharee was a closed subject. Lorraine guessed she understood, although she could never truly forgive him. Only a male god could turn his back on his dying child; only a man would cut off a daughter just because she defied him by going and getting herself killed.

At the diner, Lorraine accepted another half cup and ripped open a sugar packet with her teeth, trying to determine whether to put Elaine Michaels, with her large biceps and uneven motor development, before or after the delicate but precise Daisy Wycliff. She watched as the old-timers filed in to sit at the counter in their caps and overalls, making competitive claims about the heat, and the granny women gathered at a table under a local artist's rendering of a stand of dogwood in the shadow of a rugged cross, a magnified thorn in the right-hand corner beading up with a single drop of dew. A bit later, you'd see the people in the prime of life dragging in, flaunting their soft underbellies and undeveloped wrinkles, full of trouble about their baby's colic or their teenager's boyfriend or their boss's new policy. Relax, she wanted to tell them, you better pace yourself, because you haven't seen the hind end of trouble yet. She stirred in a creamer and began to focus in on the granny women, skin cracked like gray mud dried in the sunshine, bright eyes and crooked fingers, false white teeth that they constantly clicked and readjusted in their mouths. Those three were always looking for something evil to relish, they could never get enough brine to suit their pickled old taste buds. Today they were gumming and jawing on about one of the granddaughters who'd gone and gotten herself tattooed.

"Not a pretty little doodad, mind you, but this big bloody heart with a dead girl's name trailed across it. Right on the thigh, to where you could see it in a pair of decent-length shorts. All the girls on the team are getting them. Boy, is my daughter-in-law up in arms. Some of the moms are gonna pay a visit to the coach and give her a good talking-to."

Lorraine stiffened like a beaten egg white. Why hadn't they told her, at least consulted with her first? The green marbled tabletop swirled beneath her; the deer horns by the door shifted and repositioned themselves as if they were getting ready to spar with Satan; the jam in the jelly jar crystallized before her eyes. She could have talked them out of it, or at least gone with them to supervise the ink. She imagined a tattoo on her own thigh, where the green and blue veins converged to form a map of her complaints; she imagined Earl whooping and taunting her, she imagined Trev's rude grunt of dismay.

She got up, walked over to the granny women, and spit a half-chewed wad of jelly toast on their table.

"That's for backbiting, you old horny toads," she said. Then she spat again, her own clear juices this time, smelling of coffee and cough drops. "And that's for poisoning the chew."

Clearing her head out by the accident scene, she thought of what she could do to raise morale and protect poor Hettie Barnes, whose only crime was to fall in love with a Gulf War hero who then picked up and headed off to Pensacola on his own, leaving his jilted sweetheart to squander all her affection on a shifting squad of ungrateful high school softball players. Hettie had huge squash-shaped bosoms and straight boyish hips, so many reddish freckles she resembled a hunting hound, and a supple apple butter voice that turned just a bit too sugary when she felt a migraine coming on. Her exaggerated arm motions and brisk manner undercut the effect of those monumental breasts, as if she'd had to keep her body in check all her life. That's what made her such an excellent tonic for the girls. But something in her was sad, incomplete, making Lorraine want to lighten old Hettie's sorrow sack whenever she could.

Lorraine walked over the field again, tracing out a circle in the grass. The day was so blue it shaded into purple, and the morning primroses were starting to come into bloom. But no one had bothered to pick up the cupcakes, which were now soggy with dew and spotted with gnats and flies. Kris's funeral was this afternoon, and the tournament was two days after. Lorraine couldn't let anything get in the way of the trip, which more and more seemed like the last dab of pleasure on her horizon. She'd buy Reenie a new outfit, she'd go to the yarn store and pick up a supply for Christmas sweaters, she'd get in a visit with her great-niece, who must be over thirty by now, just to see if the old girl was living up to her name. In the meantime, someone had to give the girls a pep talk and warn Hettie about the town gossip. As Lorraine was heading back to her vehicle, she saw the truck with the state park emblem: a coneflower, a deer, a flying trout on a disk of green.

"Patrolling the area, ma'am?" It was Sally, her hair pulled back into a ponytail and a fast-food biscuit crumbled in a paper wrapper on her lap.

"I suppose you think you're the police now, just because you got a uniform on your back."

"I suppose you think you're family, just because you tipped a couple of colas with the girl. Now how about you go home and see if Daddy's taken his pill?"

Sharee's mother is on the phone again, relaying the latest in the long saga of death, inbreeding, and destruction in Boonslick, Missouri. This week, a young girl, barely sixteen, had been passing a slow-moving vehicle on Highway 63 when she got into a head-on collision with an oncoming SUV and was killed on the spot. "Those things are a menace. Out-of-state tourists speeding along with their cell phones in their armored cars. And the girl's poor family lives in a trailer, doesn't have any kind of insurance to speak of. Your aunt Lorraine is real upset because Kris was on Cousin Reenie's softball team. And you know, it's got to bring up bad memories for her."

Sharee, high on hormones like a chemically treated turkey, is already weeping before her mother even reaches the punch line; after all, she knows some disaster or another is on its way. In these stories it always is, looming over the next hill of purple coneflowers, lurking in a hidden sinkhole, keeping fresh and cool in a devil's icebox of a cave. She tries to focus on the flowers Matt bought for her, still blooming tall and handsome on their slender stalks, the golden apple wallpaper of the kitchen, her own short fingernails in their barely there beige polish. Her nose tickles as if she is about to sneeze, and she feels the physical pleasure of giving in to her grief. All day, on and off, she has been crying over Matt's reaction, which was basically no reaction, to her news. "It's your body after all, the decision's up to you." The truth is, he's too terrified of her emotional state to offer an opinion. He keeps coming up the periphery of her personal space and then standing there with a plate of crackers or a newspaper or a glass of milk, hoping she'll rise to take the bait. A single brutal pimple has appeared on the side of her face, hard to the touch, as painful as a bruise, and she feels like a teenager again, countering her body's rebellions on her own.

"That's terrible, Ma, if there's anything I can do, you just let me know."

"Come to think of it, the girls are going up there for a tournament next week; your aunt's been saying how she'd love to see you." Ma's tried this kind of setup before, with the cousin taking a graduation trip to the big city, the local band teacher in town for a music convention, the divorced trucker uncle with heavy conscience and a cross-country load. Sharee has seen them all, tried to make conversation in parks and diners and hamburger joints, even over her own blue-tiled table, where more than one hillbilly has tasted pierogi or chutney for the first time, and where she has done her best to find some common point of genetic connection. But she's never understood the compulsion to intersect with one's own kin.

Of course, if she told her mother about her current situation, she'd have an excuse not to see her aunt. But she and Matt have agreed to keep the pregnancy a secret until she reaches the end of the dangerous first trimester, which is also the deadline for selectively terminating one or more of the fetuses. Meaning, of course, she thinks bitterly, that she'll never have the opportunity to discuss her decision with anyone until it's already been made.

Sharee has another reason for wanting to avoid Aunt Lorraine: that creepy story that comes attached to her like a bloody shroud or placenta. Twenty-nine years ago, Sharee's mom named her first daughter after a teenage cousin with red hair and iron calves, the star kick-the-can player in the family and the favorite among the scrappy brood Ma had babysat as a teenager herself. That Sharee, Sharee the first, was killed in a car accident a few weeks after Sharee the second was born. The girl was driving her father's truck to the next town, not even sixteen yet and flooring the gas pedal into the next world when she lost control and crashed into the limestone bluff at the side of the road. And then, three days after she buried her daughter, Aunt Lorraine was over to her niece's house with a lawyer, trying to get Ma to legally change Sharee's name. "For the good of both of them," she said. "It's just unlucky, having two girls with the same name in a single generation, it's like having a double or a twin. This little angel's what, all of a month old? She'll never remember that she was once lifted by some other handle. Anyway, we got loads of freed-up names in the family from those who have passed before: Caroline, Mariah, Josephine."

The lawyer, of course, wasn't a legitimate professional contact, but just another relative, an in-law who'd gotten his degree that spring and wasn't yet gainfully employed. He sat on the porch drinking beer with Sharee's dad while the women wrangled inside. Daddy still claims he could see the house moving, the porch swing rocking, the glass shaking in the window frames "Looked like the earthquake of New Madrid all over again. Thought we was going to have to call an exorcist in on the thing."

Sharee, for one, wishes that her mother had given in to Lorraine's demands and named her something with fewer strings attached. The choices were all old-fashioned, it was true, but they could have been easily transformed into something modern like Cara or Jo. She's been told that her name means "beloved friend" in French, and maybe that was good enough for Sharee the first. But Sharee the second, who's actually been to college and studied a language or two, knows that Cherie also means "too expensive," and that's just what these connections always turn out to be.

At the funeral, Lorraine convinced the usher, a former class president at Boonslick High, to squeeze her in next to her granddaughter, even though the pew was practically full. Earl was left to sit in the row behind, staring at the nearly identical heads of a dozen teenage girls with beer-colored braids and buns and ponytails trussed up in what looked to be black glitter shoestrings.

"Is it true?" Lorraine whispered, "When did you have it done?" Reenie just pulled up her skirt and revealed the silver-dollar-sized tattoo, fuzzy under the nylons, which were, after the local fashion, at least three shades darker than her skin. Lorraine shook her head at the sight and all down the row, girls shifted their thighs to lift the right side of their skirts and display their newly illustrated skin. One of them, Doris McClain, was fresh enough to go without nylons, even in church, and the reds and greens and blues of her tattoo stood out as clear as Sunday morning on her muscled thigh. A pumping anatomical heart. A short brutal dagger. A menstrual drip of blood. But the ribbon across the palpitating organ didn't say "Kris" — there were too many letters for that. Lorraine took her reading glasses out of her pocketbook and read: "Donnas 4-ever, '01."

"That's what Kris would've wanted," Reenie whispered, and Lorraine couldn't tell if there was any sass in it or not.

At the front of the church, Kris sat propped up in a white and silver coffin, purchased, in part, by the Baptist church and Boonslick High. Even the Lady Rangers, urged by Hettie Barnes, had contributed a healthy percentage of their tournament fund. Despite all the comments to the contrary, Kris looked entirely unlike herself, wearing a white dress with tiny black polka dots whose folds nearly drowned out the insistent softball breasts that had always posed a substantial challenge to a sports bra. The dress's puffed sleeves weren't quite long enough to cover the barbed-wire tattoo around her muscular upper arm, and the silver crosses in her ears seemed sadly blasphemous under the holes that ran up the entire length of each lobe like empty pouches in an ammunition belt. Kris's short spiky haircut had obviously frustrated the beautician, who'd tried to soften it into a matronly cowl, but missed one lone cowlick, which now flicked up out of the part in a Pentecostal tongue of flame.

Lorraine stood to lead her team past the coffin and felt her feet moving over the familiar path, each corn and bunion singing its separate strand of harmony. How many times would she tread this road before she got to sit inside the chariot for herself? She stood close and peeked into the driver's seat anyway. Underneath the makeup, Kris looked determined to get off the bench for good. Her right dimple vibrated like the mark of a pebble in a still pond; her pale brown eyebrows were raised as if in anticipation of a good piece of gossip or a dirty joke. In her pitching hand, she gripped a bouquet of prairie dock, coneflowers, and blazing stars like she'd pulled them up by the roots herself. Lorraine reached in to press the girl's hand and felt the sweat in her palm, her own pulse bearing in the wrist.

At least Kris's mother, wearing a black leotard with a flowered skirt and twisting her Kleenex in the front row, had the satisfaction of seeing her daughter look as respectable as anybody else's dead. They'd had to bury Sharee in a closed casket, depriving her mother of the pleasure of dressing her for public one last time. Lorraine had done her best anyway with the bruised and mangled body. She brought out the pink-trimmed bra and underpants Sharee had gotten as a gift for her fifteenth birthday, she washed the soft purple dress with its lotus flowers and pagodas, she restrung the favorite necklace of purple and green glass beads which had been cut from around Sharee's neck in the hospital. But oh the bitterness when the dress had to be ripped to accommodate the swollen waist, the misaligned arm, when the ragged red hair had to be shorn. The sorrow in the barely recognizable purple face. Lorraine remembered the rich ripe skin of babies and very young children, how a cut or bruise would disappear on them overnight, and she couldn't believe that Sharee's wounds would never heal, and that they'd sit there on the beautiful body forever, scarring the best thing she'd ever made.

Lorraine pressed Kris's hand until she felt the blood drain from her own fingertips. Would she bring the girl back if she could? When there had been nothing anyone could do for Sharee? The longer she held onto that hand with its smooth palm and strong bones, the more it seemed like a living thing, a fish or a tree limb, that, caught, killed, or broken, would lead her back to the secret location of her own mistake. She lifted the arm in its barbed-wire bracelet. She kissed the knuckle in its blue birthstone ring. Then she felt an arm on her back, soothing the spot where her bra strap had dug into her for all these years.

Sally took her hand and somehow found the way to unlock it from Kris's fingers, placing the arm back in the casket as the congregation gasped. For a minute, Lorraine believed that she had actually done it. Then she looked back and saw what was really going on.

Behind her, the girls had dropped to their knees in front of the coffin and, one by one, they were lifting their skirts, displaying their tattoos, twisting off their black garters, and dropping them into the coffin. As they enacted this sad backward cancan, they sang a song by the Donnas, one of the rare numbers without underwear or drug references. But between their hoarse voices and swollen sobs, it came out sounding more like a Catholic chant: gloomy, mumbled, and off-key. "Stop Driving Thru My Heart," they pleaded, and Lorraine cringed, remembering the drift of the lyrics. Halfway through, the ramshackle tune broke down entirely, and the girls gathered round the coffin, surrounding it as if it were a cradle. Then they held hands and began to sway, saying Kris's name over and over.

The congregation breathed normally again, and some wise woman toward the back dipped into the first bar of "Shall We Gather at the River?" gliding on alone in her shaky soprano until the rest of the group followed her down to the shore. Then, as Lorraine broke the girls' circle to get a good strong grip on her granddaughter's hand, she could swear she saw the corpse take its pinky finger and flick a black garter away from its wildflower bouquet.

Outside, the mica in the concrete steps gave off a glare that caught Lorraine by surprise, and she saw Earl actually applying a handkerchief to the region of his eyelids. Hettie Barnes, in her white blouse and black culottes, stood draped in girls, blotting mascara and handing out Kleenexes. Over by the marquee, the granny women loomed; a navy print dress, a gray fedora, a brown sweater set, blocking out the Scripture, darkening the sun. Lorraine stepped in between them and the team.

"Now you have your satisfaction, gals, you might as well go back to the diner and chew on the cud."

"I hope you been practicing your fastball, hon, because you ain't going to get many permission slips for your tournament after a display such as that."

"Lucky it's a sacred occasion," Lorraine said. "Otherwise, I might be tempted to give you a jagged piece of my mind. But as it is, I just recommend you to the blue-plate special. Go and get it while it's hot." Then she handed them a few extra memorial programs and escorted them out to their cars.

Sharee is throwing up for the seventh time today, and Matt is standing outside the bathroom door, holding the phone. Every time he tries to hand it over, she feels another surge and has to backtrack to the toilet to disgorge one more mouthful of the water, which is the only nourishment she's been able to take in since last night.

Each of the four fetuses seems to be emitting its own high-pitched scream inside her hollow head. How will she stay alive to keep her wallpaper up and blooming? How will she ever regain enough consciousness to make a choice? She looks at the yellow tiles on the floor and finds a single chip to hold her focus as she gathers her energy for the next upheaval.

On top of all this, her aunt Lorraine has been calling every few hours with news of the softball tournament. The Lady Rangers, despite the loss of their pitcher, have been knocking them out of the ballpark today, defeating teams from all over the state. Lorraine was supposed to drop by at 11:00, after the morning game, then called to delay until 1:00, then 3:30, and now 7:00 as her team keeps advancing through the finals. Sharee's changed shirts three times, wondering what her aunt will see in her, whether she will live up to the image of the cousin she has never known. Now she just wonders if she'll manage to stay awake. For the millionth time, Matt tells her she should go ahead and cancel, tell her aunt she has the flu, this is getting ridiculous, and given the softball schedule, he doubts the old lady will ever make it over anyway. But Sharee doesn't want to give up yet; she feels a physical craving for her relatives — the jagged jarring accent, the deep-fried fat and suffering, the long brittle family nose — just when it seems as if she has to fight against every cell in her body to make a connection.

She tells Matt to arrange the details with her aunt, then stumbles back to her bed with its scattered body pillows and sticky blankets. Her legs ache as if she has walked every mile from Boonslick, Missouri, to this haven on the open plains. When she rolls over onto her side, she falls into a deep sinkhole of sleep, where she is thirteen again and attending a slumber party. One of the girls has an idea: they should hold a dumb supper, like their mothers used to do, where you all make dinner in complete silence, moving backward, and set a plate by each girl. When the wind blows and the house quakes, then you'll see your future husband sitting there next to you at the table in all his glory, but in complete silence, eating a dumb supper from the provided plate. Sharee is willing to give it a try. But when her turn comes, she sees a woman instead, or a girl, really, sitting turned away from the dinner of sliced tomatoes and macaroni and cheese, and crying into a cell phone. The girl's auburn hair covers her face, her arm is beaded with long jeweled scabs, her knee pumps up and down with the rhythm of her sobs, and one flowered sandal moves back and forth on her heel, the other dangling empty from the table leg at her feet. Sharee is terrified of what she'll see if the girl shows her face, so she tries to concentrate on her own meal instead: the dark yellow cheese paste sticking to the noodles like pollen, the sugar-sprinkled homegrown tomatoes as veined and luminous as panes of stained glass. Her stomach buckles inside her, she's too sick to eat, and in the end she has to face her vision just because there's nowhere else to turn. The girl takes a deep breath, digs her fingernails into her widow's peak, and drags the hair out of her eyes, to reveal a flawless face Sharee has seen only in photographs. Sharee remembers all the individual traits — the high freckled forehead, the heart-shaped jaw that looks romantic or stubborn depending on the angle, the steep, nearly perpendicular nose — but she never realized how they fit together before. Now she can't believe she hasn't always known.

In the end, it was no problem to get the girls' parents to agree to Kansas City. Most of them felt the commotion at the funeral had been innocent, and that the girls could definitely use a change of scene. And for the hard cases, Lorraine just gave in and did her grieving-mother routine. She had lived so long, her story had been dragged through the county so many years it had become a dirty joke, and still she wasn't through with it. She took it out and polished it up again like an old toenail: the blue and gold day, the winding road, the redheaded girl with a scab on her elbow and a green bikini top knotted at her neck. Sharee hadn't spoken to her mother for two days; she'd gotten the idea she wanted to go out to see a boy, an older boy, a German boy, who worked at the quarry in Augustin. He'd invited her for a swim, she said, he was packing the picnic, and all she needed was a ride. Lorraine had flat-out refused, and Earl, Earl couldn't deny her anything, not until he saw the boy for himself and drove the fifteen miles back to Boonslick with Sharee screaming obscenities at him from the passenger seat. Even now, Lorraine couldn't help but feel the satisfaction of that moment, Sharee safe in her bedroom, angry at her father for once, Earl making a ruckus in the garage rather than coming in and admitting that Lorraine had been right. When she went to survey the damage, she found Sharee tearing apart her pillow with a pair of

nail scissors, the real goose feathers floating around her and clinging to her swimsuit and her hair. "I just wanted to have a day," she
said. "Just one day when I could feel like my life was going somewhere. I could sit in this town until my teeth fall out. You'd like
that, wouldn't you? I could sit here and get as old as you and never
do anything but marry some cross-eyed loser, then have a bunch of
ugly kids I could blame."

Lorraine went from warm to overheated in a single surge of energy; twisting the scissors out of Sharee's sweaty hand, she grasped
the girl's head down as if to baptize her, then cut off a swatch of
hair from the back of her penny-colored head. "You can say all you
want against me, sister," she said. "But don't you ever mock my
work."

And all the while, Sally was lying there doing her senior history
homework on her bed. Her long ash blond hair covered her face;
only once, when she heard the squawk of the scissor, did she shift
on her elbow and turn a page, then lift her hand to push her hair
behind her pink and blushing ear. Half an hour later, when Lorraine was in the basement doing laundry and Earl had settled into
his Sunday nap, Sharee took the spare car keys out of the Green
Stamp drawer, got in her father's pickup, and drove off on her own.

"And that's why I go with them now," Lorraine would always say.
"Instead of letting them go on alone. Take up your cross and follow
me, the Lord tells us. I have my cross by the highway. I have my fork
in the road. But I got to keep moving to preserve the faith." She
wasn't even certain she believed it anymore, as she stood at the ballpark concession stand with its smells of cotton candy, hot dogs, and
warm pee, picked up the receiver of the pay phone, and dialed her
great-niece's number, which she had memorized through the long
day of victories and reversals. The Lord was one hard character; he
didn't have the time to read a softball schedule or watch a baby die.
Behind her, she heard a bat crack; she turned and strained to make
out the play, another score for the Lady Rangers. Each time the ball
connected with the bat, she felt the impact in her own body: the
road, the bluff, the ground, the rock, the dirt, the clay. Looking at
the girls lined up by the dugout, every one of them a piece of work,
she wondered who would be the next to go under. Daisy turning
up the cuff of her shorts to check on her tan. Elaine positioning
her foot in its tattooed ankle bracelet and striking at a phantom

ball. Knock on wood, not Reenie, leaning back on the bench with her pretty braided head resting on Hettie Barnes's bare freckled shoulder.

On the other end of the phone line, Sharee's husband said he'd see if his wife could take the call. But before Lorraine could get an answer out of him, she saw Sally, who'd taken the day off work to help her mother with the drive, striding up from the field on her long legs, a few electric white hairs bristling over the limp blond pageboy, her breasts swinging as if they were tied around her neck on a string, and her neck itself wreathed in a row of dusty wrinkles, making Lorraine relive the frustration of trying to keep the dirt out of all those rolls of baby fat under her children's chins.

"I've got to talk with you, Ma . . . Reenie wanted me to ask . . . well some of the girls think it's a little disturbing, the story you've been telling around, and they wondered how long you plan on repeating it."

"Just a minute. Just keep your uniform pants on," Lorraine warned, lifting the stiff metal phone cord and turning her face away from the worn face in front of her so she could say her daughter's name.

Intervention

FROM PLOUGHSHARES

THE INTERVENTION is not Marilyn's idea, but it might as well be. She is the one who has talked too much. And she has agreed to go along with it, nodding and murmuring an all-right into the receiver while Sid dozes in front of the evening news. They love watching the news. Things are so horrible all over the world that it makes them feel lucky just to be alive. Sid is sixty-five. He is retired. He is disappearing before her very eyes.

"O.K., Mom?" She jumps with her daughter's voice, once again filled with the noise at the other end of the phone — a house full of children, a television blasting, whines about homework — all those noises you complain about for years only to wake one day and realize you would sell your soul to go back for another chance to do it right.

"Yes, yes," she says.

"Is he drinking right now?"

Marilyn has never heard the term *intervention* before her daughter, Sally, introduces it and showers her with a pile of literature. Sally's husband has a master's in social work and considers himself an expert on this topic, as well as many others. Most of Sally's sentences begin with "Rusty says," to the point that Sid long ago made up a little spoof about "Rusty says," turning it into a game like Simon Says. "Rusty says put your hands on your head," Sid said the first time, once the newly married couple was out of earshot. "Rusty says put your head up your ass." Marilyn howled with laughter, just as she always did and always has. Sid can always make her laugh. Usually she laughs longer and harder. A stranger would have assumed that she was the one slinging back the vodka. Twenty years earlier, and the stranger would have been right.

Sally and Rusty have now been married for a dozen years — three kids and two Volvos and several major vacations (that were so educational they couldn't have been any fun) behind them — and still, Marilyn and Sid cannot look each other in the eye while Rusty is talking without breaking into giggles like a couple of junior high school students. And Marilyn knows junior high behavior; she taught language arts for many years. She is not shocked when a boy wears the crotch of his pants down around his knees, and she knows that Sean Combs has gone from that perfectly normal name to Sean Puffy Combs to Puff Daddy to P. Diddy. She knows that the kids make a big circle at dances so that the ones in the center can do their grinding without getting in trouble, and she has learned that there are many perfectly good words that you cannot use in front of humans who are being powered by hormonal surges. She once asked her class: How will you ever get ahead? only to have them all — even the most pristine honor roll girls — collapse in hysterics. Just last year — her final one — she had learned never to ask if they had hooked up with so-and-so, learning quickly that this no longer meant locating a person but having sex. She could not hear the term now without laughing. She told Sid it reminded her of the time two dogs got stuck in the act just outside her classroom window. The children were out of control, especially when the assistant principal stepped out there armed with a garden hose, which didn't faze the lust-crazed dogs in the slightest. When the female — a scrawny shepherd mix — finally took off running, the male — who was quite a bit smaller — was stuck and forced to hop along behind her like a jackrabbit. "His thang is stuck," one of the girls yelled and broke out in a dance, prompting others to do the same.

"Sounds like me," Sid said that night when they were lying there in the dark. "I'll follow you anywhere."

Now, as Sid dozes, she goes and pulls out the envelope of information about "family intervention." She never should have told Sally that she had concerns, never should have mentioned that there were times when she watched Sid pull out of the driveway only to catch herself imagining that this could be the last time she ever saw him.

"Why do you think that?" Sally asked, suddenly attentive and leaning forward in her chair. Up until that minute, Marilyn had felt invisible while Sally rattled on and on about drapes and chairs and her book group and Rusty's accolades. "Was he visibly drunk? Why do you let him drive when he's that way?"

"He's never visibly drunk," Marilyn said then, knowing that she had made a terrible mistake. They were at the mall, one of those forced outings that Sally had read was important. Probably an article Rusty read first called something like: "Spend Time with Your Parents So You Won't Feel Guilty When You Slap Them in a Urine-Smelling Old-Folks' Home." Rusty's parents are already in such a place; they share a room and eat three meals on room trays while they watch television all day. Rusty says they're ecstatic. They have so much to tell that they are living for the next time Rusty and Sally and the kids come to visit.

"I pray to God I never have to rely on such," Sid said when she relayed this bit of conversation. She didn't tell him the other parts of the conversation at the mall, how even when she tried to turn the topic to shoes and how it seemed to her that either shoes had gotten smaller or girls had gotten bigger (nine was the average size for most of her willowy eighth-grade girls), Sally bit into the subject like a pit bull.

"How much does he drink in a day?" Sally asked. "You must know. I mean, *you* are the one who takes out the garbage and does the shopping."

"He helps me."

"A fifth?"

"Sid loves to go to the Super Stop and Shop. They have a book section and everything."

"Rusty has seen this coming for years." Sally leaned forward and gripped Marilyn's arm. Sally's hands were perfectly manicured with pale pink nails and a great big diamond. "He asked me if Dad had a problem before we ever got married." She gripped tighter. "Do you know that? That's a dozen years."

"I wonder if the Oriental folks have caused this change in the shoe sizes?" Marilyn pulled away and glanced over at Lady's Foot Locker as if to make a point. She knows that "Oriental" is not the thing to say. She knows to say "Asian," and though Sally thinks that she and Rusty are the ones who teach her all of these things, the truth is that she learned it all from her students. She knew to say

Hispanic and then Latino, probably before Rusty did, because she sometimes watches the MTV channel so that she's up on what is happening in the world and thus in the lives of children at the junior high. Shocking things, yes, but also important. Sid has always believed that it is better to be educated even if what is true makes you uncomfortable or depressed. Truth is, she can understand why some of these youngsters want to say motherfucker this and that all the time. Where *are* their mommas, after all; and where are their daddies? Rusty needs to watch MTV. He needs to watch that and *Survivor* and all the other reality shows. He's got children, and unless he completely rubs off on them they will be normal enough to want to know what's happening out there in the world.

"Asian," Sally whispered. "You really need to just throw out that word *Oriental* unless you're talking about lamps and carpets. I know what you're doing, too."

"What about *queer*? I hear that word is O.K. again."

"You have to deal with Dad's problem," Sally said.

"I hear that even the Homo sapiens use that word, but it might be the kind of thing that only one who is a member can use, kind of like —"

"Will you stop it?" Sally interrupted and banged her hand on the table.

"Like the *n* word," Marilyn said. "The black children in my class used it, but it would have been terrible for somebody else to."

Sally didn't even enunciate *African American* the way she usually does. "This doesn't work anymore!" Sally's face reddened, her voice a harsh whisper. "So cut the Gracie Allen routine."

"I loved Gracie. So did Sid. What a woman." Marilyn rummaged her purse for a tissue or a stick of gum, anything so as not to have to look at Sally. Sally looks so much like Sid they could be in a genetics textbook: those pouty lips and hard blue eyes, prominent cheekbones and dark curly hair. Sid always told people his mother was a Cherokee and his father a Jew, that if he was a dog, like a cockapoo, he'd be a Cherojew, which Marilyn said sounded like TheraFlu, which they both like even when they don't have colds, so he went with Jewokee instead. Marilyn's ancestors were all Irish, so she and Sid called their children the Jewokirish. Sid said that the only thing that could save the world would be when everybody was so mixed up with this blood and that that nobody could pronounce the resulting tribe name. It would have to be a symbol — like the name of the artist formerly known as Prince, which was something she had just learned and had to explain to Sid. She doubts that Sally and Rusty even know who Prince is, or Nelly, for that matter. Nelly is the reason all the kids are wearing Band-Aids on their faces, which is great for those just learning to shave.

"Remember that whole routine Dad and I made up about ancestry?" Marilyn asked. She was able to look up now, Sally's hands squeezing her own, Rusty's hands on her shoulders. If she had had an ounce of energy left in her body, she would have run into Lord and Taylor's and gotten lost in the mirrored cosmetics section.

"The fact that you brought all this up is a cry for help whether you admit it or not," Sally said. "And we are here, Mother. We are here for you."

She wanted to ask why Mother — what happened to Mom and Mama and Mommy? — but she couldn't say a word.

There are some nights when Sid is dozing there that she feels frightened. She puts her hand on his chest to feel his heart. She puts her cheek close to his mouth to feel the breath. She did the same to Sally and Tom when they were children, especially with Tom, who came first. She was up and down all night long in those first weeks, making sure that he was breathing, still amazed that this perfect little creature belonged to them. Sometimes Sid would wake and do it for her, even though his work as a grocery distributor in those days caused him to get up at 5:00 A.M. The times he went to check, he would return to their tiny bedroom and lunge toward her with a perfect Dr. Frankenstein imitation: "He's alive!" followed by maniacal laughter. In those days she joined him for a drink just as the sun was setting. It was their favorite time of day, and they both always resisted the need to flip on a light and return to life. The ritual continued for years and does to this day. When the children were older they would make jokes about their parents, who were always "in the dark," and yet those pauses, the punctuation marks of a marriage, could tell their whole history spoken and unspoken.

The literature says that an intervention is the most loving and powerful thing a loved one can do. That some members might be apprehensive. Tom was apprehensive at first, but he always has been; Tom is the noncombative child. He's an orthopedist living in Den-

ver. Skiing is great for his health and his business. And his love life.
He met the new wife when she fractured her ankle. Her marriage
was already fractured, his broken, much to the disappointment of
Marilyn and Sid, who found the first wife to be the most loving and
open-minded of the whole bunch. The new wife, Sid says, is too
young to have any opinions you give a damn about. In private they
call her Snow Bunny.

Tom was apprehensive until the night he called after the hour
she had told everyone was acceptable. "Don't call after nine unless it's an emergency," she had told them. "We like to watch our
shows without interruption." But that night, while Sid dozed and
the made-for-TV movie she had looked forward to ended up (as
her students would say) sucking, she went to run a deep hot bath,
and that's where she was, incapable of getting to the phone fast
enough.

"Let the machine get it, honey," she called as she dashed with
just a towel wrapped around her dripping body, but she wasn't fast
enough. She could hear the slur in Sid's speech. He could not say
slalom to save his soul, and instead of letting the moment pass, he
kept trying and trying — What the shit is wrong with my tongue,
Tom? Did I have a goddamn stroke? Sllllmmmm — sla, sla.

Marilyn ran and picked up the extension. "Honey, Daddy has
taken some decongestants, bless his heart, full of a terrible cold.
Go on back to sleep now, Sid, I've got it."

"I haven't got a goddamned cold. Your mother's a kook!" He
laughed and waved to where she stood in the kitchen, a puddle of
suds and water at her feet. "She's a good-looking naked kook. I see
her bony ass right now."

"Hang up, Tommy," she said. "I'll call you right back from the
other phone. Daddy is right in the middle of his program."

"Yeah, right," Tom said.

By the time she got Sid settled down, dried herself off, and put
on her robe, Tom's line was busy, and she knew before even dialing
Sally that hers would be busy, too. It was a full hour later, Sid fast
asleep in the bed they had owned for thirty-five years, when she
finally got through, and then it was to a more serious Tom than she
had heard in years. Not since he left the first wife and signed off on
the lives of her grandchildren in a way that prevented Marilyn from
seeing them more than once a year if she was lucky. She could get
mad at him for *that*. So could Sid.

"We're not talking about my life right now," he said. "I've given Dad the benefit of the doubt for years, but Sally and Rusty are right."

"Rusty! You're the one who said he was full of it," she screamed. "And now you're on his side?"

"I'm on your side, Mom, your side."

She let her end fall silent and concentrated on Sid's breath. He's alive, only to be interrupted by a squeaky girly voice on Tom's end — Snow Bunny.

Sid likes to drive, and Marilyn has always felt secure with him there behind the wheel. Every family vacation, every weekend gathering. He was always voted the best driver of the bunch, even when a whole group had gathered down at the beach for a summer cook-out where both men and women drank too much. Sid mostly drank beer in those days; he kept an old Pepsi-Cola cooler he once won throwing baseballs at tin cans at the county fair, iced down with Falstaff and Schlitz. They still have that cooler. It's out in the garage on the top shelf, long ago replaced with little red and white Playmates. Tom gave Sid his first Playmate, which has remained a family joke until this day. And Marilyn drank then. She liked the taste of beer but not the bloat. She loved to water-ski, and they took turns behind a friend's powerboat. The men made jokes when the women dove in to cool off. They claimed that warm spots emerged wherever the women had been and that if they couldn't hold their beer any better than that, they should switch to girl drinks. And so they did. A little wine or a mai tai, vodka martinis. Sid had a book that told him how to make everything, and Marilyn enjoyed buying little colored toothpicks and umbrellas to dress things up when it was their turn to host. She loved rubbing her body with baby oil and iodine and letting the warmth of the sun and salty air soak in while the radio played and the other women talked. They all smoked cigarettes then. They all had little leather cases with fancy lighters tucked inside.

Whenever Marilyn sees the Pepsi cooler she is reminded of those days. Just married. No worries about skin cancer or lung cancer. No one had varicose veins. No one talked about cholesterol. None of their friends were addicted to anything other than the sun and the desire to get up on one ski — to slalom. The summer she was pregnant with Tom (compliments of a few too many mai tais, Sid told the group), she sat on the dock and sipped her ginger ale. The motion of the boat made her queasy, as did anything that had to do with poultry. It ain't the size of the ship but the motion of the ocean, Sid was fond of saying in those days, and she laughed every time. Every time he said it, she complimented his liner and the power of his steam. They batted words like throttle and wake back and forth like a birdie until finally, at the end of the afternoon, she'd go over and whisper, "Ready to dock?"

Her love for Sid then was overwhelming. His hair was thick, and he tanned a deep smooth olive without any coaxing. He was everything she had ever wanted, and she told him this those summer days as they sat through the twilight time. She didn't tell him how sometimes she craved the vodka tonics she had missed. Even though many of her friends continued drinking and smoking through their pregnancies, she would allow herself only one glass of wine with dinner. When she bragged about this during Sally's first pregnancy, instead of being congratulated on her modest intake, Sally was horrified. "My God, Mother," she said. "Tom is lucky there's not something wrong with him!"

Tom set the date for the intervention. As hard as it was for Rusty to relinquish his power even for a minute, it made perfect sense, given that Tom had to take time off from his practice and fly all the way from Denver. The Snow Bunny was coming, too, even though she really didn't know Sid at all. Sometimes over the past five years, Marilyn had called up the first wife just to hear her voice or, even better, the voice of one or more of her grandchildren on the answering machine. Now there was a man's name included in the list of who wasn't home. She and Sid would hold the receiver between them, both with watering eyes, when they heard the voices they barely recognized. They didn't know about *69 until a few months ago when Margot, the oldest child, named for Sid's mother, called back. "Who is this?" she asked. She was growing up in Minnesota and now was further alienated by an accent Marilyn knew only from Betty White's character on *The Golden Girls*.

"Your grandmother, honey. Grandma Marilyn in South Carolina."

There was a long silence, and then the child began to speak rapidly, filling them in on all that was going on in her life. "Mom says you used to teach junior high," Margot said, and she and Sid both grinned, somehow having always trusted that their daughter-in-law would not have turned on them as Tom had led them to believe.

Then Susan got on the phone, and as soon as she did, Marilyn burst into tears. "Oh, Susie, forgive me," she said. "You know how much we love you and the kids."

"I know," she said. "And if Tom doesn't bring the kids to you, I will. I promise." Marilyn and Sid still believe her. They fantasize during the twilight hour that she will drive up one day and there they'll all be. Then, lo and behold, here will come Tom. "He'll see what a goddamned fool he's been," Sid says. "They'll hug and kiss and send Snow Bunny packing."

"And we'll all live happily ever after," Marilyn says.

"You can take that to the bank, baby," he says, and she hugs him close, whispers that he has to eat dinner before they can go any-where.

"You know I'm a very good driver," she says, and he just shakes his head back and forth; he can list every ticket and fender-bender she has had in her life.

The intervention day is next week. Tom and Bunny plan to stay with Sally and Rusty an hour away so that Sid won't get suspicious. Already it is unbearable to her — this secret. There has been only one time in their whole marriage when she had a secret, and it was a disaster.

"What's wrong with you?" Sid keeps asking. "So quiet." His eyes have that somber look she catches once in a while; it's a look of hurt, a look of disillusionment. It is the look that nearly killed them thirty-odd years ago.

There have been many phone calls late at night. Rusty knows how to set up conference calls, and there they all are, Tom and Sally and Rusty, talking nonstop. If he resists, we do this. If he gets angry, we do that. All the while, Sid dozes. Sometimes the car is parked crooked in the drive, a way that he never would have parked even two years ago, and she goes out in her housecoat and bedroom slip-pers to straighten it up so the neighbors won't think anything is wrong. She has repositioned the mailbox many times, touched up paint on the car and the garage that Sid didn't even notice. Sometimes he is too tired to move or undress, and she spreads a blanket over him in the chair. Recently she found a stash of empty bottles in the bottom of his golf bag. Empty bottles in the Pepsi cooler, the trunk of his car.

"I suspect he lies to you about how much he has," Rusty says. "We are taught not to ask an alcoholic how much he drinks, but to phrase it in a way that accepts a lot of intake, such as 'How many fifths do you go through in a weekend?'"

"Sid doesn't lie to me."

"This is as much for you," Rusty says, and she can hear the impatience in his voice. "You are what we call an enabler."

She doesn't respond. She reaches and takes Sid's warm limp hand in her own.

"If you really love him," he pauses, gathering volume and force in his words, "you have to go through with this."

"It was really your idea, Mom," Sally says. "We all suspected as much, but you're the one who really blew the whistle." Marilyn remains quiet, a picture of herself like some kind of Nazi woman blowing a shrill whistle, dogs barking, flesh tearing. She can't answer; her head is swimming. "Admit it. He almost killed you when he went off the road. It's your side that would have smashed into the pole. You were lucky."

"I was driving," she says now, whispering so as not to wake him. "I almost killed him!"

"Nobody believed you, Marilyn," Rusty says, and she is reminded of the one and only student she has hated in her career, a smart-assed boy who spoke to her as if he were the adult and she were the child. Even though she knew better, knew that he was a little jerk, it had still bothered her.

"You're lucky Mr. Randolph was the officer on duty, Mom," Tom says. "He's not going to look the other way next time. He told me as much."

"And what about how you told me you have to hide his keys sometimes?" Sally asks. "What about that?"

"Where are the children?" Marilyn asks. "Are they hearing all of this?"

"No," Rusty says. "We won't tell this sort of thing until they're older and can learn from it."

"We didn't," she whispers and then ignores their questions. Didn't what? Didn't what?

"The literature says that there should be a professional involved," she says and, for a brief anxious moment, relishes their silence.

"Rusty is a professional," Sally says. "This is what he does for a living."

Sid lives for a living, she wants to say, but she lets it all go. They are coming, come hell or high water. She can't stop what she has put into motion, a rush of betrayal and shame pushing her back to a dark place she has not seen in years. Sid stirs and brings her hand up to his cheek.

Sid never told the children anything. He never brought up anything once it had passed, unlike Marilyn, who sometimes gets stuck in a groove, spinning and spinning, deeper and deeper. Whenever anything in life — the approach of spring, the smell of gin, pine sap thawing and coming back to life — prompts her memory, she cringes and feels the urge to crawl into a dark hole. She doesn't recognize that woman. That woman was sick. A sick, foolish woman, a woman who had no idea that the best of life was in her hand. It was late spring, and they went with a group to the lake. They hired babysitters around the clock so the men could fish and the women could sun and shop and nobody had to be concerned for all the needs of the youngsters. The days began with coffee and bloody marys and ended with sloppy kisses on the sleeping brows of their babies. Sid was worried then. He was bucking for promotions right and left, taking extra shifts. He wanted to run the whole delivery service in their part of the state and knew that he could do it if he ever got the chance to prove himself. Then he would have normal hours, good benefits.

Marilyn had never even noticed Paula Edwards's husband before that week. She spoke to him, yes; she thought it was Paula's good fortune to have married someone who had been so successful so young. ("Easy when it's a family business and handed to you," Sid said, the only negative thing she ever heard him say about the man.) But there he was, not terribly attractive but very attentive. Paula was pregnant with twins and forced to a lot of bed rest. Even now, the words of the situation, playing through Marilyn's mind, shock her.

"You needed attention," Sid said when it all exploded in her face. "I'm sorry I wasn't there."

"Who are you — Jesus Christ?" she screamed. "Don't you hate me? Paula hates me!"

"I'm not Paula. And I'm not Jesus." He went to the cabinet and mixed a big bourbon and water. He had never had a drink that early in the day. "I'm a man who is very upset."

"At me!"

"At both of us."

She wanted him to hate her right then. She wanted him to make her suffer, make her pay. She had wanted him even at the time it was Paula's husband meeting her in the weeks following in dark, out-of-the-way parking lots — rest areas out on the interstate, run-down motels no one with any self-esteem would venture into. And yet there she had been. She bought the new underwear the way women so often do, as if that thin bit of silk could prolong the masquerade. Then later, she had burned all the new garments in a huge puddle of gasoline, a flame so high the fire department came, only to find her stretched out on the grass of her front yard, sobbing. Her children, ages four and two, were there beside her, wide-eyed and frightened. "Mommy? Are you sick?" She felt those tiny hands pulling and pulling. "Mommy? Are you sad?" Paula's husband wanted sex. She could have been anyone those times he twisted his hands in her thick long hair, grown the way Sid liked it, and pulled her head down. He wanted her to scream out and tear at him. He liked it that way. Paula wasn't that kind of girl, but he knew that she was.

"But you're not," Sid told her in the many years to follow, the times when self-loathing overtook her body and reduced her to an anguished heap on the floor. "You're not that kind."

People knew. They had to know, but out of respect for Sid, they never said a word. Paula had twin girls, and they moved to California, and to this day, they send a Christmas card with a brag letter much like the one that Sally and Rusty have begun sending. Something like: We are brilliant, and we are rich. Our lives are perfect, don't you wish yours was as good? If Sid gets the mail, he tears it up and never says a word. He did the same with the letter that Paula wrote to him when she figured out what was going on. Marilyn never saw what the letter said. She only heard Sid sobbing from the other side of a closed door, the children vigilant as they waited for him to come out. When his days of silence ended and she tried to talk, he simply put a finger up to her lips, his eyes dark and shadowed in a way that frightened her. He mixed himself a drink and offered her one as they sat and listened with relief to the giggles of the children playing outside. Sid had bought a sandbox and put it over the burned spot right there in the front yard. He said that in the fall when it was cooler, he'd cover it with sod. He gave up on advancing to the top, and settled in instead with a budget and all the investments he could make to ensure college educations and decent retirement.

Her feelings each and every year when spring came had nothing to do with any lingering feelings she might have had about the affair — she had none. Rather, her feelings were about the disgust she felt for herself, and the more disgusted she felt, the more she needed some form of self-medication. For her, alcohol was the symptom of the greater problem, and she shudders with recall of all the nights Sid had to scoop her up from the floor and carry her to bed. The times she left pots burning on the stove, the time Tom as a five-year-old sopped towels where she lay sick on the bathroom floor. "Mommy is sick," he told Sid, who stripped and bathed her, placed cool sheets around her body, a cool cloth to her head. It was the vision of her children standing there and staring at her, their eyes as somber and vacuous as Sid's had been the day he got Paula's letter, that woke her up.

"I'm through," she said. "I need help."

Sid backed her just as he always had. Rusty would have called him her enabler. He nursed her and loved her. He forgave her and forgave her. I'm a bad chemistry experiment, she told Sid. Without him she would not have survived.

On the day of intervention, the kids come in meaning business, but then can't help but lapse into discussion about their own families and how great they all are. Snow Bunny wants a baby, which makes Sid laugh, even though Marilyn can tell he suspects something is amiss. Rusty has been promoted. He is thinking about going back to school to get his degree in psychology. They gather in the living room, Sid in his chair, a coffee cup on the table beside him. She knows there is bourbon in his cup but would never say a word. She doesn't have to. Sally sweeps by, grabs the cup, and then is in the kitchen sniffing its contents. Rusty gives the nod of a man in charge. Sid is staring at her, all the questions easily read: Why are they here? Did you know they were coming? Why did you keep this from me? And she has to look away. She never should have let this happen. She should have found a way to bring Sid around to his own decision, the way he had led her.

Now she wants to scream at the children that she did this to Sid. She wants to pull out the picture box and say: This is me back when I was fucking my friend's husband while you were asleep in your beds. And this is me when I drank myself sick so that I could forget what a horrible woman and wife and mother I was. Here is where I passed out on the floor with a pan of hot grease on the stove, and here is where I became so hysterical in the front yard that I almost burned the house down. I ruined the lawn your father worked so hard to grow. I ruined your father. I did this, and he never told you about how horrible I was. He protected me. He saved me.

"Well, Sid," Rusty begins, "we have come together to be with you because we're concerned about you."

"We love you, Daddy, and we're worried."

"Mom is worried," Tom says, and as Sid turns to her, Marilyn has to look down. "Your drinking has become a problem, and we've come to get help for you."

I'm the drunk, she wants to say. I was here first.

"You're worried, honey?" Sid asks. "Why haven't you told me?"

She looks up now, first at Sid and then at Sally and Tom. If you live long enough, your children learn to love you from afar, their lives are front and center and elsewhere. Your life is only what they can conjure from bits and pieces. They don't know how it all fits together. They don't know all the sacrifices that have been made.

"We're here as what is called an intervention," Rusty says.

"Marilyn?" He is gripping the arms of his chair. "You knew this?"

"No," she says. "No, I didn't. I have nothing to do with this."

"Marilyn." Rusty rises from his chair, Sally right beside him. It's like the room has split in two and she is given a clear choice — the choice she wishes she had made years ago, and then maybe none of this would have ever happened.

"We can take care of this on our own," she says. "We've taken care of far worse."

"Such as?" Tom asks. She has always wanted to ask him what he remembers from those horrible days. Does he remember finding her there on the floor? Does he remember her wishing to be dead?

"Water under the bridge," Sid says. "Water under the bridge." Sid stands, shoulders thrown back. He is still the tallest man in the room. He is the most powerful man. "You kids are great," he says. "You're great, and you're right." He goes into the kitchen and ceremoniously pours what's left of a fifth of bourbon down the sink. He breaks out another fifth still wrapped with a Christmas ribbon and pours it down the sink. "Your mother tends to overreact and exaggerate from time to time, but I do love her." He doesn't look at her, just keeps pouring. "She doesn't drink, so I won't drink."

"She has never had a problem," Sally says, and for a brief second Marilyn feels Tom's eyes on her.

"I used to," Marilyn says.

"Yeah, she'd sip a little wine on holidays. Made her feel sick, didn't it, honey?" Sid is opening and closing cabinets. He puts on the teakettle. "Mother likes tea in the late afternoon like the British. As a matter of fact," he continues, still not looking at her, "sometimes we pretend we are British."

She nods and watches him pour out some cheap Scotch he always offers to cheap friends. He keeps the good stuff way up high behind her mother's silver service. "And we've been writing our own little holiday letter, Mother and I, and we're going to tell every single thing that has gone on this past year like Sally and Rusty do. Like I'm going to tell that Mother has a spastic colon and often feels 'sqwitty,' as the British might say, and that I had an abscessed tooth that kept draining into my throat, leaving me no choice but to hawk and spit throughout the day. But all that aside, kids, the real reason I can't formally go somewhere to dry out for you right now is, one, I have already booked a hotel over in Myrtle Beach for our anniversary, and, two, there is nothing about me to dry."

By the end of the night everyone is talking about "one more chance." Sid has easily turned the conversation to Rusty and where he plans to apply to school and to Snow Bunny and her hopes of having a "little Tommy" a year from now. They say things like that they are proud of Sid for his effort but not to be hard on himself if he can't do it on his own. He needs to realize he might have a problem. He needs to be able to say: I have a problem.

*

"So. Wonder what stirred all that up?" he asks as they watch the children finally drive away. She has yet to make eye contact with him. "I have to say I'm glad to see them leave." He turns now and waits for her to say something.

"I say *adios,* motherfuckers." She cocks her hands this way and that like the rappers do, which makes him laugh. She notices his hand shaking and reaches to hold it in her own. She waits, and then she offers to fix him a small drink to calm his nerves.

"I don't have to have it, you know," he says.

"Oh, I know that," she says. "I also know you saved the good stuff."

She mixes a weak one and goes into the living room, where he has turned off all but the small electric candle on the piano.

"Here's to the last drink," he says as she sits down beside him. He breathes a deep sigh that fills the room. He doesn't ask again if she had anything to do with what happened. He never questions her a second time; he never has. And in the middle of the night when she reaches her hand over the cool sheets, she will find him there, and when spring comes and the sticky heat disgusts her with pangs of all the failures in her life, he will be there, and when it is time to get in the car and drive to Myrtle Beach or to see the kids, perhaps even to drive all the way to Minnesota to see their grandchildren, she will get in and close the door to the passenger side without a word. She will turn and look at the house that the two of them worked so hard to maintain, and she will note as she always does the perfect green grass of the front yard and how Sid fixed it so that there is not a trace of the mess she made. It is their house. It is their life. She will fasten her seat belt and not say a word.

THOMAS McGUANE

Gallatin Canyon

FROM THE NEW YORKER

THE DAY WE PLANNED THE TRIP, I told Louise that I didn't like going to Idaho via the Gallatin Canyon. It's too narrow, and while trucks don't belong on this road, there they are, lots of them. Tourist turnoffs and wild animals on the highway complete the picture. We could have gone by way of Ennis, but Louise had learned that there were road repairs on Montana Highway 84 — twelve miles of torn-up asphalt — in addition to its being rodeo weekend, and "Do we have to go to Idaho?" she asked.

I said that I thought it was obvious. A lot rode on the success of our little jaunt, which was ostensibly to close the sale of a small car dealership I owned in the sleepy town of Rigby. But, since accepting the offer of a local buyer, I had received a far better one from elsewhere, which, my attorney said, I couldn't take unless my original buyer backed out — and he would back out only if he got sufficiently angry at me. Said my attorney: Make him mad. So I was headed to Rigby, Idaho, expressly to piss off a small-town businessman, who was trying to give me American money for a going concern on the strip east of town, and thereby make room for a rich Atlanta investor, new to our landscapes, who needed this dealership as a kind of flagship for his other intentions. The question was how to provoke the man in Rigby without arousing his suspicions, and I might have collected my thoughts a little better had I not had to battle trucks and tourists in the Gallatin Canyon.

Louise and I had spent a lot of time together in recent years, and we were both probably wondering where things would go from here. She had been married, briefly, long ago, and that fact, to-

gether with the relatively peaceful intervening years, gave a pleasant detachment to most of her relationships, including the one she
had with me. In the past, that would have suited me perfectly; but it
did not seem to suit me now, and I was so powerfully attached to
her it made me uncomfortable that she wasn't interested in discussing our mutual future, though at least she had never suggested that
we wouldn't *have* one. With her thick blond hair pulled back in a
barrette, her strong, shapely figure, and the direct fullness of her
mouth, she was often noticed by other men. After ten years in
Montana, she still had a strong Massachusetts accent. Louise was a
lawyer, specializing in the adjudication of water rights between agricultural and municipal interests. In our rapidly changing world,
she was much in demand. Though I wished we could spend more
time together, Louise had taught me not to challenge her on this.

No longer the country crossroads of recent memory, Four Corners was filled with dentists' offices, fast-food and espresso shops,
large and somehow foreboding filling stations that looked, at
night, like colonies in space; nevertheless, the intersection was true
to its name, sending you north to a transcontinental interstate, east
into town, west to the ranches of Madison County, and south, my
reluctant choice, up the Gallatin Canyon to Yellowstone and the
towns of southeast Idaho, one of which contained property with my
name on the deed.

We joined the stream of traffic heading south, the Gallatin River
alongside and usually much below the roadway, a dashing high-gra-
dient river with anglers in reflective stillness at the edges of its
pools, and bright rafts full of delighted tourists in flotation jackets
and crash helmets sweeping through its white water. Gradually, the
mountains pressed in on all this humanity, and I found myself behind a long line of cars trailing a cattle truck at well below the
speed limit. This combination of cumbersome commercial traffic
and impatient private cars was a lethal mixture that kept our canyon in the papers, as it regularly spat out corpses. In my rearview
mirror, I could see a line behind me that was just as long as the one
ahead, stretching back, thinning, and vanishing around a green
bend. There was no passing lane for several miles. A single amo-
rous elk could have turned us all into twisted, smoking metal.

"You might have been right," Louise said. "It doesn't look good."

She almost certainly had better things to do. But, looking down the line of cars, I felt my blood pressure rising. Her hands rested quietly in her lap. I couldn't possibly have rivaled such serenity.

"How do you plan to anger this guy in Rigby?" she asked.

"I'm going to try haughtiness. If I suggest that he bought the dealership cheap, he might tell me to keep the damn thing. The Atlanta guy just wants to start *somewhere*. All these people have a sort of parlay mentality and they need to get on the playing field before they can start running it up. I'm a trader. It all happens for me in the transition. The moment of liquidation is the essence of capitalism."

"What about the man in Rigby?"

"He's an end user. He wants to keep it."

I reflected on the pathos of ownership and the way it could bog you down.

"You should be in my world," Louise said. "According to the law, water has no reality except its use. In Montana, water isn't even wet. Every time some misguided soul suggests that fish need it, it ends up in the state supreme court."

Birds were fleeing the advance of automobiles. I was elsewhere, trying to imagine my buyer, red-faced, storming out of the closing. I'd offer to let bygones be bygones, I'd take him to dinner, I'd throw a steak into him, for Christ's sake. In the end, he'd be glad he wasn't stuck with the lot.

Traffic headed toward us, far down the road. We were all packed together to make sure no one tried to pass. The rules had to be enforced. Occasionally, someone drifted out for a better look, but not far enough that someone else could close his space and possibly seal his fate.

This trip had its risks. I had only recently admitted to myself that I would like to make more of my situation with Louise than currently existed. Though ours was hardly a chaste relationship, real intimacy was relatively scarce. People in relationships nowadays seemed to retain their secrets like bank deposits — they always set some aside, in case they might need them to spend on someone new. I found it unpleasant to think that Louise could be withholding anything.

But I thought I was more presentable than I had been. When Louise and I first met, I was just coming off two and a half years of peddling satellite dishes in towns where a couple of dogs doing the wild thing in the middle of the road amounted to the high point of a year, and the highest-grossing business was a methamphetamine tent camp out in the sagebrush. Now I had caught the upswing in our local economy — cars, storage, tool rental, and mortgage discounting. I had a pretty home, debt-free, out on Sourdough. I owned a few things. I could be O.K. I asked Louise what she thought of the new prosperity around us. She said, wearily, "I'm not sure it's such a good thing, living in a boomtown. It's basically a high-end carny atmosphere."

We were just passing Storm Castle and Garnet Mountain. When I glanced in the mirror, I saw a low red car with a scoop in its hood pull out to pass. I must have reacted somehow, because Louise asked me if I would like her to drive.

"No, that's fine. Things are getting a bit lively back there."

"Drive defensively."

"Not much choice, is there?"

I had been mentally rehearsing the closing in Rigby, and I wasn't getting anywhere. I had this sort of absurd picture of myself strutting into the meeting. I tried again to picture the buyer looking seriously annoyed, but I'd met him before and he seemed pretty levelheaded. I suspected I'd have to be really outlandish to get a rise out of him. He was a fourth-generation resident of Rigby, so I could always urge him to get to know his neighbors, I decided. Or, since he had come up through the service department, I could try emphasizing the need to study how the cars actually ran. I'd use hand signals to fend off objections. I felt more secure.

Some elk had wandered into the parking lot at Buck's T4 and were grazing indifferently as people pulled off the highway to admire them. I don't know if it was the great unmarred blue sky overhead or the balsamic zephyr that poured down the mountainside, but I found myself momentarily buoyed by all this idleness, people out of their cars. I am always encouraged when I see animals doing something other than running for their lives. In any case, the stream of traffic ahead of us had been much reduced by the pedestrian rubbernecking.

"My husband lived here one winter," Louise said. "He sold his pharmacy after we divorced, not that he had to, and set out to change his life. He became a mountain man, wore buckskin clothes. He tried living off the land one day a week, with the idea

that he would build up. But then he just stuck with one day a week
— he'd shoot a rabbit or something, more of a diet, really. He's a
real-estate agent now, at Big Sky. I think he's doing well. At least
he's quit killing rabbits."

"Remarried?"

"Yes."

As soon as we hit the open country around West Yellowstone,
Louise called her office. When her secretary put her on hold, Lou-
ise covered the mouthpiece and said, "He married a super gal.
Minnesota, I think. She should be good for Bob, and he's not easy.
Bob's from the south. For men, it's a full-time job being southern.
It just wears them out. It wore me out, too. I developed doubtful be-
haviors. I pulled out my eyelashes, and ate twenty-eight hundred
dollars' worth of macadamia nuts."

Her secretary came back on the line, and Louise began editing
her schedule with impressive precision, mouthing the word "sorry"
to me when the conversation dragged on. I began musing about
my capacity to live successfully with someone as competent as Louise. There was no implied hierarchy of status between us, but I wondered if, in the long run, something would have to give.

West Yellowstone seemed entirely given over to the well-being of
the snowmobile, and the billboards dedicated to it were anomalous
on a sunny day like today. By winter, schoolchildren would be peti-
tioning futilely to control the noise at night so that they could do
their schoolwork, and the town would turn a blind eye as a cloud of
smoke arose to gas residents, travelers, and park rangers alike. It
seemed incredible to me that recreation could acquire this level of
social momentum, that it could be seen as an inalienable right.

We came down Targhee Pass and into Idaho, into a wasteland of
spindly pines that had replaced the former forest, and Louise gave
voice to the thoughts she'd been having for the past few miles.
"Why don't you just let this deal close? You really have no guarantees from the man from Atlanta. And there's a good-faith issue
here, too, I think."

"A lawyerly notation."

"So be it, but it's true. Are you trying to get every last cent out of
this sale?"

"That's second. The first priority is to be done with it. It was meant to be a passive investment, and it has turned out not to be. I get twenty calls a day from the dealership, most with questions I can't answer. It's turning me into a giant bullshit machine."

"No investments are really passive."

"Mutual funds are close."

"That's why they don't pay."

"Some of them pay, or they would cease to exist."

"You make a poor libertarian, my darling. You sound like that little puke David Stockman."

"Stockman was right about everything. Reagan just didn't have the guts to take his advice."

"*Reagan.* Give me a break."

I didn't mind equal billing in a relationship, but I did dread the idea of parties speaking strictly from their entitlements across a chasm. Inevitably, sex would make chaos of much of this, but you couldn't, despite Benjamin Franklin's suggestion, "use venery" as a management tool.

Louise adjusted her seat back and folded her arms, gazing at the sunny side of the road. The light through the windshield accentuated the shape of her face, now in repose. I found her beautiful. I adored her when she was a noun and was alarmed when she was a verb, which was usually the case. I understood that this was not the best thing I could say about myself. When her hand drifted over to my leg, I hardly knew what to do with this reference to the other life we led. I knew that it was an excellent thing to be reminded of how inconsequential my worldly concerns were, but one warm hand, rested casually, and my interest traveled to the basics of the species.

Ashton, St. Anthony, Sugar City: Mormon hamlets, small farms, and the furious reordering of watersheds into industrial canals. Irrigation haze hung over the valley of the Snake, and the skies were less bright than they had been just a few miles back, in Montana. Many locals had been killed when the Teton Dam burst, and despite that they wanted to build it again: the relationship to water here was like a war, and in war lives are lost. These were the folk to whom I'd sold many a plain car; ostentation was thoroughly unacceptable hereabouts. The four-door sedan with a six-cylinder engine was the desired item, an identical one with 150,000 miles on it generally taken in trade at zero value, thanks to the manipulation of rebates against the manufacturer's suggested retail. Appearances were foremost, and the salesman who could leave a customer's smugness undisturbed flourished in this atmosphere. I had two of them, potato-fattened, bland opportunists with nine kids between them. They were the asset I was selling; the rest was little more than bricks and mortar.

We pressed on toward Rexburg, and amid the turnoffs for Wilford, Newdale, Hibbard, and Moody the only thing that had any flavor was Hog Hollow Road, which was a shortcut to France — not the one in Europe but the one just a hop, skip, and a jump south of Squirrel, Idaho. There were license-plate holders with my name on them in Squirrel, and I was oddly vain about that.

"Sure seems lonesome around here," Louise said.

"Oh, boy."

"The houses are like little forts."

"The winters are hard." But it was less that the small neat dwellings around us appeared defensive than that they seemed to be trying to avoid attracting the wrath of some inattentive god.

"It looks like government housing for Eskimos. They just sit inside waiting for a whale, or something."

This banter had the peculiar effect of making me want to cleave to Louise, and desperately, too — to build a warm new civilization, possibly in a foolish house with turrets. The road stretched before me like an arrow. There was only enough of it left before Rigby for me to say, perhaps involuntarily, "I wonder if we shouldn't just get married."

Louise quickly looked away. Her silence conferred a certain seriousness on my question.

But there was Rigby, and, in the parlance of all who have extracted funds from locals, Rigby had been good to me. Main Street was lined with ambitious and beautiful stone buildings, old for this part of the world. Their second and third floors were now affordable housing, and their street levels were occupied by businesses hanging on by their fingernails. You could still detect the hopes of the dead, their dreams, even, though it seemed to be only a matter of time before the wind carried them away, once and for all.

I drove past the car lot at 200 East Fremont without comment and — considering the amount of difficulty it had caused me in the years before I got it stabilized and began to enjoy its very modest yields — without much feeling. I remembered the day, sometime earlier, when I had tried to help park the cars in the front row and got everything so crooked that the salesmen, not concealing their contempt, had to do it all over again. The title company where we were heading was on the same street, and it was a livelier place, from the row of perky evergreens out front to the merry receptionist who greeted us, a handsome young woman, probably a farm girl only moments before, enjoying the clothes, makeup, and perquisites of the new world that her firm was helping to build.

We were shown into a spacious conference room with a long table and chairs, freshly sharpened pencils, and crisp notepads bearing the company letterhead. "Shall I stay?" Louise asked, the first thing she'd said since my earlier inadvertent remark, which I intuited had not been altogether rejected.

"Please," I said, gesturing toward a chair next to the one I meant to take. At that moment, the escrow agent entered and, standing very close to us, introduced himself as Brent Colby. Then he went to the far end of the table, where he spread his documents around in an orderly fan. Colby was about fifty, with iron-gray hair and a deeply lined face. He wore pressed jeans, a brilliant-white snap-button shirt, cowboy boots, and a belt buckle with a steer head on it. He had thick, hairy hands and a gleaming wedding band. Just as he raised his left wrist to check his watch, the door opened and Oren Johnson, the buyer, entered. He went straight to Louise and, taking her hand in both of his, introduced himself. It occurred to me that, in trying to be suave, Oren Johnson had revealed himself to be a clodhopper, but I was probably just experiencing the mild hostility that emanates from every sale of property. Oren wore a suit, though it suggested less a costume for business than one for church. He had a gold tooth and a cautious pompadour. He, too, bore an investment-grade wedding band, and I noted that there was plenty of room in his black-laced shoes for his toes. He turned and said that it was good to see me again after so long. The time had come for me to go into my act. With grotesque hauteur, I said that I didn't realize we had ever met. This was work.

Oren Johnson bustled with inchoate energy; he was the kind of small-town leader who sets an example by silently getting things done. He suggested this just by arranging his pencils and notepad and repositioning his chair with rough precision. Locking eyes with me, he stated that he was a man of his word. I didn't know what he was getting at, but took it to mean that the formalities of a closing were superfluous to the old-time handshake with which Oren Johnson customarily did business. I smiled and quizzically cocked my head as if to say that the newfangled arrangements with well-attested documents promptly conveyed to the courthouse suited me just fine, that deals made on handshakes were strictly for the pious or the picturesque. My message was clear enough that Louise shifted uncomfortably in her chair, and Brent Colby knocked his documents edgewise on the desk to align them. As far as Oren Johnson was concerned, I was beginning to feel that anyone who strayed from the basic patterns of farm life to sell cars bore watching. Like a Method actor, I already believed my part.

"You're an awfully lucky man, Oren Johnson," I said to him, leaning back in my chair. I could see Louise open-mouthed two seats away from Brent Colby, and observing myself through her eyes gave me a sudden burst of panic.

"Oh?" Oren Johnson said. "How's that?"

"How's that?" I did a precise job of replicating his inflection. "I am permitting you to purchase my car lot. You've seen the books: how often does a man get a shot at a business where all the work's been done for him?"

Brent Colby was doing an incomplete job of concealing his distaste; he was enough of a tinhorn to clear his throat theatrically. But Oren Johnson treated this as a colossal interruption and cast a firm glance his way.

"It doesn't look all that automatic to me," he said.

"Aw, hell, you're just going to coin it. Pull the lever and relax!"

"What about the illegal oil dump? I wish I had a nickel for every crankcaseful that went into that hole. Then I wouldn't worry about what's going to happen when the D.E.Q. lowers the boom."

"Maybe you ought to ride your potato harvester another year or two, if you're so risk-averse. Cars are the future. They're not for everybody."

Oren Johnson's face reddened. He pushed his pencils and notepad almost out of reach in the middle of the conference table. He contemplated these supplies a moment before raising his eyes to mine. "I suppose you could put this car lot where the sun don't shine, if that suits you."

Johnson having taken a stand, I immediately felt unsure that I even had another buyer. Had I ever acknowledged how much I longed to get rid of this business and put an end to all those embarrassing phone calls? I wanted to hand the moment off to someone else while I collected my thoughts, but as I looked around the room I found no one who was interested in rescuing me — least of all Louise, who had raised one eyebrow at the vast peculiarity of my performance. Suddenly, I was desperate to keep the deal from falling apart. I gave my head a little twist to free my neck from the constrictions of my collar. I performed this gesture too vigorously, and I had the feeling that it might seem like the first movement of some sort of dance filled with sensual flourishes and bordering on the moronic. I had lost my grip.

"Oren," I said, and the familiarity seemed inappropriate. "I was attached to this little enterprise. I wanted to be sure you valued it."

The deal closed, and I had my check. I tipped back in my chair to think of a few commemorative words for the new owner, but the two men left the room without giving me the chance to speak. I shrugged at Louise, and she, too, rose to go, pausing a moment beneath an enormous Kodachrome of a bugling elk. I was aware of her distance, and I sensed that my waffling hadn't gone over particularly well. I concluded that at no time in the future would I act out a role to accomplish anything. This decision quickly evaporated with the realization that that is practically all we do in life. Comedy failed, too. When I told Louise that I had been within an inch of opening a can of whup-ass on the buyer, I barely got a smile. There's nothing more desolating than having a phrase like that die on your lips.

It was dark when we got back to Targhee Pass. Leaving town, we passed the Beehive assisted-living facility and the Riot Zone, a "family fun park." Most of the citizens we spotted there seemed unlikely rioters. I drove past a huge neon steak, its blue T-bone flashing above a restaurant that was closed and dark. There were deer on the road, and once, as we passed through a murky section of forest, we saw the pale faces of children waiting to cross.

"What are they doing out at this hour?"

"I don't know," Louise said.

I made good time on the pine flats north of the Snowmobile Capital of the World, and I wondered what it would be like to live in a town that was the world capital of a mechanical gadget. In Rigby, we had seen a homely museum dedicated to Philo T. Farnsworth, the inventor of television, which featured displays of Farnsworth's funky assemblages of tubes and wire and, apparently, coat hangers — stuff his wife was probably always attempting to throw out, a goal Louise supported. "Too bad Mama Farnsworth didn't take all that stuff to the dump," she said.

We had the highway to ourselves, and clouds of stars seemed to rise up from the wilderness, lighting the treetops in a cool fire. Slowly, the canyon closed in around us, and we entered its flowing, dark space.

The idyll ended just past the ranger station at Black Butte, when a car pulled in behind us abruptly enough that I checked my speed to see if I was violating the limit, but I wasn't. Then the car was very close, and the driver shifted his lights to a high beam so intense that I could see our shadows on the dashboard, my knuckles on the steering wheel glaringly white. I was nearly blinded by my own mirrors, which I hastily adjusted.

I said, "What's with this guy?"

"Just let him pass."

"I don't know that he wants to."

I softened my pressure on the gas pedal. I thought that by easing my already moderate speed I would politely suggest that he might go by me. I even hugged the shoulder, but he remained glued to our bumper. There was something about this that reminded me strongly of my feeling of failure back in Rigby, but I was unable to put my finger on it. Maybe it was the hot light of liquidation, in the glare of which all motives seem laid bare. I slowed down even more without managing to persuade my tormentor to pass. "Jesus," Louise said. "Pull over." In her accent, it came out as "pull ovah."

I moved off to the side of the road slowly and predictably, but although I had stopped, the incandescent globes persisted in our rearview mirror. "This is very strange," Louise said.

"Shall I go back and speak to him?"

After considering for a moment, she said, "No."

"Why?"

"Because this is not normal."

I put the car in gear again and pulled back onto the highway. The last reasonable thought I had was that I would proceed to Bozeman as though nothing were going on, and once I was back in civilization my tormentor's behavior would be visible to all, and I could, if necessary, simply drive to the police station with him in tow.

Our blinding, syncopated journey continued another mile before we reached a sweeping eastward bend, closely guarded by the canyon walls. I knew that just beyond the bend there was a scenic turnoff, and that the approaching curve was acute enough for a small lead to put me out of sight. Whether or not this was plausible, I had no idea: I was exhilarated to be taking a firm hand in my own affairs. And a firm foot! As we entered the narrows, I pinned the accelerator, and we shot into the dark. Louise grabbed the front edges of her seat and stared at the road twisting in front of us. She emitted something like a moan, which I had heard before in a very different context. Halfway around the curve, my tormentor vanished behind us, and although my car seemed only marginally under control, the absence of blinding light was a relief as we fled into darkness.

When we emerged and the road straightened, I turned off my lights. I was going so fast I felt lightheaded, but the road was visible under the stars, and I was able to brake hard and drop down into the scenic turnoff. Seconds later, our new friend shot past, lights blazing into nowhere. He was clearly determined to catch us: his progress up the canyon was rapid and increasingly erratic. We watched in fascination until the lights suddenly jerked sideways, shining in white cones across the river, turned downward, then disappeared.

I heard Louise say, in a tone of reasonable observation, "He went in."

I had an urgent feeling that took a long time to turn into words. "Did I do that?"

She shook her head, and I pulled out onto the highway, my own headlights on once more. I drove in an odd, measured way, as if bound for an undesired destination, pulled along by something outside myself, thinking: Liquidation. We could see where he'd gone through the guardrail. We pulled over and got out. Any hope we might have had for the driver — and we shall be a long time determining if we had any — was gone the minute we looked down from the riverbank. The car was submerged, its lights still burning freakishly, illuminating a bulge of crystalline water, a boulder in the exuberance of a mountain watershed. Presently, the lights sank into blackness, and only the silver sheen of river in starlight remained.

Louise cried, "I wish I could *feel* something!" And when I reached to comfort her she shoved me away. I had no choice but to climb back up to the roadway.

After that, I could encounter Louise only by telephone. I told her that he'd had a record as long as your arm. "It's not enough!" she said. I called later to say that he was of German and Italian extraction. That proved equally unsatisfactory, and when I called to inform her that he hailed from Wisconsin she just hung up on me, this time for good.

ALICE MUNRO

Runaway

FROM THE NEW YORKER

CARLA HEARD THE CAR COMING before it topped the little rise in the road that around here they called a hill. It's her, she thought. Mrs. Jamieson — Sylvia — home from her holiday in Greece. From the barn door — but far enough inside that she could not easily be seen — she watched the road where Mrs. Jamieson would have to drive by, her place being half a mile farther along than Clark and Carla's.

If it was somebody coming to see them, the car would be slowing down by now. But still Carla hoped. *Let it not be her.*

It was. Mrs. Jamieson turned her head once, quickly — she had all she could do to maneuver her car through the ruts and puddles the rain had made in the gravel — but she didn't lift a hand off the wheel to wave, she didn't spot Carla. Carla got a glimpse of a tanned arm bare to the shoulder, hair bleached a lighter color than it had been before, more white now than silver-blond, and an expression that was both exasperated and amused at her own exasperation — just the way Mrs. Jamieson would look negotiating this road. When she turned her head there was something like a bright flash — of inquiry, of hopefulness — that made Carla shrink back.

So.

Maybe Clark didn't know yet. If he was sitting at the computer, he would have his back to the window and the road.

But he would have to know before long. Mrs. Jamieson might have to make another trip — for groceries, perhaps. He might see her then. And after dark the lights of her house would show. But this was July and it didn't get dark till late. She might be so tired that she wouldn't bother with the lights; she might go to bed early.

On the other hand, she might telephone. Anytime now.

This was the summer of rain and more rain. They heard it first thing in the morning, loud on the roof of the mobile home. The trails were deep in mud, the long grass soaking, leaves overhead sending down random showers even in those moments when there was no actual downpour from the sky. Carla wore a wide-brimmed old Australian felt hat every time she went outside, and tucked her long thick braid down her shirt.

Nobody showed up for trail rides — even though Clark and Carla had gone around posting signs at all the campsites, in the cafes, and on the tourist-office bulletin board, and anywhere else they could think of. Only a few pupils were coming for lessons, and those were regulars, not the batches of schoolchildren on vacation or the busloads from summer camps that had kept them going the summer before. And even the regulars took time off for holiday trips, or simply canceled their lessons because of the weather. If they called too late, Clark charged them anyway. A couple of them had argued, and quit for good.

There was still some income from the three horses that were boarded. Those three, and the four of their own, were out in the field now, poking disconsolately in the grass under the trees. Carla had finished mucking out in the barn. She had taken her time — she liked the rhythm of her regular chores, the high space under the barn roof, the smells. Now she went over to the exercise ring to see how dry the ground was, in case the 5:00 pupil did show up.

Most of the steady showers had not been particularly heavy, but last week there had come a sudden stirring and then a blast through the treetops and a nearly horizontal blinding rain. The storm had lasted only a quarter of an hour, but branches still lay across the road, hydro lines were down, and a large chunk of the plastic roofing over the ring had been torn loose. There was a puddle like a lake at that end of the track, and Clark had worked until after dark digging a channel to drain it away.

On the Web, right now, he was hunting for a place to buy roofing. Some salvage outlet, with prices that they could afford, or somebody trying to get rid of such material, secondhand. He would not go to Hy and Robert Buckley's Building Supply in town, which he called Highway Robbers Buggery Supply, because he owed them money and had had a fight with them.

Clark often had fights, and not just with the people he owed money to. His friendliness, compelling at first, could suddenly turn sour. There were places in town that he would not go into, because of some row. The drugstore was one such place. An old woman had pushed in front of him — that is, she had gone to get something she'd forgotten and come back and pushed in front, rather than going to the end of the line, and he had complained, and the cashier had said to him, "She has emphysema." Clark had said, "Is that so? I have piles myself," and the manager had been summoned to tell him that that remark was uncalled for. And in the coffee shop out on the highway the advertised breakfast discount had not been allowed, because it was past 11:00 in the morning, and Clark had argued and then dropped his takeout cup of coffee on the floor — just missing, so they said, a child in its stroller. He claimed that the child was half a mile away and he'd dropped the cup because no sleeve had been provided. They said that he hadn't asked for a sleeve. He said that he shouldn't have had to ask.

Et cetera.

"You flare up," Carla said.

"That's what men do."

She had not dared say anything about his row with Joy Tucker, whom he now referred to as Joy-Fucker. Joy was the librarian from town who boarded her horse with them, a quick-tempered little chestnut mare named Lizzie. Joy Tucker, when she was in a jokey mood, called her Lizzie Borden. Yesterday, she had driven out, not in a jokey mood at all, and complained about the roof's not being fixed and Lizzie looking so miserable, as if she might have caught a chill. There was nothing the matter with Lizzie, actually. Clark had even tried — for him — to be placating. But then it was Joy Tucker who flared up and said that their place was a dump, and Lizzie deserved better, and Clark said, "Suit yourself." Joy had not — or not yet — removed Lizzie, but Clark, who had formerly made the mare his pet, refused to have anything more to do with her.

The worst thing, as far as Carla was concerned, was the absence of Flora, the little white goat who kept the horses company in the barn and in the fields. There had been no sign of her for two days, and Carla was afraid that wild dogs or coyotes had got her, or even a bear.

She had dreamed of Flora last night and the night before. In the first dream, Flora had walked right up to the bed with a red apple in her mouth, but in the second dream — last night — she had run away when she saw Carla coming. Her leg seemed to be hurt, but she ran anyway. She led Carla to a barbed-wire barricade of the kind that might belong on some battlefield, and then she — Flora — slipped through it, hurt leg and all, just slithered through like a white eel and disappeared.

Up until three years ago, Carla had never really looked at mobile homes. She hadn't called them that, either. Like her parents, she would have thought the term *mobile home* pretentious. Some people lived in trailers, and that was all there was to it. One trailer was no different from another. When she moved in here, when she chose this life with Clark, she began to see things in a new way. After that, it was only the mobile homes that she really looked at, to see how people had fixed them up — the kind of curtains they had hung, the way they had painted the trim, the ambitious decks or patios or extra rooms they had built on. She could hardly wait to get to such improvements herself.

Clark had gone along with her ideas for a while. He had built new steps, and spent a lot of time looking for an old wrought-iron railing for them. He hadn't complained about the money spent on paint for the kitchen and bathroom or the material for curtains.

What he did balk at was tearing up the carpet, which was the same in every room and the thing that she had most counted on replacing. It was divided into small brown squares, each with a pattern of darker brown, rust, and tan squiggles and shapes. For a long time, she had thought that the same squiggles and shapes were arranged the same way in each square. Then, when she had had more time, a lot of time, to examine them, she decided that there were four patterns joined together to make identical larger squares. Sometimes she could pick out the arrangement easily and sometimes she had to work to see it.

She did this at times when Clark's mood had weighted down all their indoor space. The best thing then was to invent or remember some job to do in the barn. The horses would not look at her when she was unhappy, but Flora, who was never tied up, would come and rub against her, and look up with an expression that was not quite sympathy; it was more like comradely mockery in her shimmering yellow-green eyes.

Flora had been a half-grown kid when Clark brought her home from a farm where he'd gone to bargain for some horse tackle. He had heard that a goat was able to put horses at ease and he wanted to try it. At first she had been Clark's pet entirely, following him everywhere, dancing for his attention. She was as quick and graceful and provocative as a kitten, and her resemblance to a guileless girl in love had made them both laugh. But as she grew older she seemed to attach herself to Carla, and in this attachment she was suddenly much wiser, less skittish — she seemed capable, instead, of a subdued and ironic sort of humor. Carla's behavior with the horses was tender and strict and rather maternal, but the comradeship with Flora was quite different. Flora allowed her no sense of superiority.

"Still no sign of Flora?" she said as she pulled off her barn boots. Clark had posted a "lost goat" notice on the Web.

"Not so far," he said, in a preoccupied but not unfriendly voice. He suggested, not for the first time, that Flora might have just gone off to find herself a billy.

No word about Mrs. Jamieson.

Carla put the kettle on. Clark was humming to himself as he often did when he sat in front of the computer. Sometimes he talked back to it. "Bullshit," he might say, replying to some challenge. He laughed occasionally, but rarely remembered what the joke was when she asked him afterward.

Carla called, "Do you want tea?" And to her surprise he got up and came into the kitchen.

"So," he said. "So, Carla."

"What?"

"So she phoned."

"Who?"

"Her majesty. Queen Sylvia. She just got back."

"I didn't hear the car."

"I didn't ask you if you did."

"So what did she phone for?"

"She wants you to go and help her straighten up the house. That's what she said. Tomorrow."

"What did you tell her?"

"I told her sure. But you'd better phone up and confirm."

Carla said, "Why do I have to, if you told her?" She poured their mugs of tea. "I cleaned up her house before she left. I don't see what there could be to do so soon."

"Maybe some coons got in and made a mess of it while she was gone. You never know."

"I don't have to phone her right this minute. I want to drink my tea and I want to take a shower."

"The sooner the better."

Carla took her tea into the bathroom.

"We have to go to the laundromat. When the towels dry out, they still smell moldy."

"We're not changing the subject, Carla."

Even after she'd got in the shower, he stood outside the door and called to her.

"I am not going to let you off the hook, Carla."

She thought he might still be standing there when she came out, but he was back at the computer. She dressed as if she were going to town — she hoped that if they could get out of there, go to the laundromat, get a takeout at the cappuccino place, they might be able to talk in a different way, some release might be possible. She went into the living room with a brisk step and put her arms around him from behind. But as soon as she did that a wave of grief swallowed her up — it must have been the heat of the shower, loosening her tears — and she bent over him, crumbling and crying.

He took his hands off the keyboard but sat still.

"Just don't be mad at me," she said.

"I'm not mad. I hate when you're like this, that's all."

"I'm like this because you're mad."

"Don't tell me what I am. You're choking me. Go and get control of yourself. Start supper."

That was what she did. It was obvious by now that the 5:00 person wasn't coming. She got out the potatoes and started to peel them, but her tears would not stop. She wiped her face with a paper towel and tore off a fresh one to take with her and went out into the rain. She didn't go into the barn because it was too miserable in there without Flora. She walked along the lane back to the woods. The horses were in the other field. They came over to the fence to watch her, but all except Lizzie, who capered and snorted a bit, had the sense to understand that her attention was elsewhere.

It had started when they read the obituary, Mr. Jamieson's obituary, in the city paper. Until the year before, they had known the Jamiesons only as neighbors who kept to themselves. She taught botany at the college forty miles away, so she had to spend a good deal of her time on the road. He was a poet. But for a poet, and for an old man — perhaps twenty years older than Mrs. Jamieson — he was rugged and active. He improved the drainage system on his place, cleaning out the culvert and lining it with rocks. He dug and planted and fenced a vegetable garden, cut paths through the woods, looked after repairs on the house — not just the sort of repairs that almost any house owner could manage after a while but those that involved plumbing, wiring, roofing, too.

When they read the obituary, Carla and Clark learned for the first time that Leon Jamieson had been the recipient of a large prize five years before his death. A prize for poetry.

Shortly afterward, Clark said, "We could've made him pay."

Carla knew at once what he was talking about, but she took it as a joke.

"Too late now," she said. "You can't pay once you're dead."

"He can't. She could."

"She's gone to Greece."

"She's not going to stay in Greece."

"She didn't know," Carla said more soberly. "She didn't have anything to do with it."

"I didn't say she did."

"She doesn't have a clue about it."

"We could fix that."

Carla said, "No. No."

Clark went on as if she hadn't spoken.

"We could say we're going to sue. People get money for stuff like that all the time."

"How could you do that? You can't sue a dead person."

"Threaten to go to the papers. Bigtime poet. The papers would eat it up. All we have to do is threaten and she'd cave in. How much are we going to ask for?"

"You're just fantasizing," Carla said. "You're joking."

"No. Actually, I'm not."

Carla said that she didn't want to talk about it anymore, and he said O.K. But they talked about it the next day, and the next, and the next. He sometimes got notions like this, which were not practicable, which might even be illegal. He talked about them with growing excitement and then — she wasn't sure why — he dropped them. If the rain had stopped, if this had turned into a normal summer, he might have let this idea go the way of the others. But that had not happened, and during the last month he had harped on about the scheme as if it were perfectly feasible. The question was how much money to ask for. Too little and the woman might not take them seriously; she might think they were bluffing. Too much might get her back up and she might become stubborn.

Carla had stopped pretending she thought he was joking. Instead, she told him that it wouldn't work. She said that, for one thing, people expected poets to behave that way. So it wouldn't be worth paying out money to cover it up.

"How do you know?" Clark said.

He said that it would work if it was done right. Carla was to break down and tell Mrs. Jamieson the whole story. Then Clark would move in, as if it had all been a surprise to him, he had just found out. He would be outraged; he would talk about telling the world. He would let Mrs. Jamieson be the one who first mentioned money.

"You were injured. You were molested and humiliated and I was injured and humiliated because you are my wife. It's a question of respect."

Over and over again he talked to her in this way. She tried to deflect him, but he insisted.

"Promise," he said. "Promise."

All this was because of what she had told him — things she could not now retract or deny.

Sometimes he gets interested in me.

The old guy?

Sometimes he calls me into the room when she's not there.

When she has to go out shopping and the nurse isn't there, either?

A lucky inspiration of hers, one that instantly pleased him.

So what do you do then? Do you go in?

She played shy.

Sometimes.
He calls you into his room. So? Carla? So, then?
I go in to see what he wants.
So what does he want?

This was asked and told in whispers, even when there was no-body to hear, even when they were in the neverland of their bed. A bedtime story, in which the details were important and had to be added to each time, with convincing reluctance, shyness, giggles. (*Dirty, dirty.*) And it was not only he who was eager and grateful. She was, too. Eager to please and excite him, to excite herself. Grateful every time that it still worked.

And in one part of her mind it *was* true: she saw the randy old man, the bump he made in the sheet, bedridden, almost beyond speech but proficient in sign language, indicating his desire, trying to nudge and finger her into complicity, into obliging stunts and intimacies. (Her refusal a necessity, but also, perhaps, strangely, slightly disappointing to Clark.)

Now and then came an image that she had to hammer down lest it spoil everything. She would think of the real dim and sheeted body, drugged and shrinking every day in its hospital bed, glimpsed only a few times, when Mrs. Jamieson or the visiting nurse had neglected to close the door. She herself never actually coming closer to him than that.

In fact, she had dreaded going to the Jamiesons', but she needed the money, and she felt sorry for Mrs. Jamieson, who seemed so haunted and bewildered, as if she were walking in her sleep. Once or twice, Carla had burst out and done something really silly just to loosen up the atmosphere. The kind of thing she did when clumsy and terrified riders were feeling humiliated. She used to try it, too, when Clark was stuck in his moods. It didn't work with him any-more. But the story about Mr. Jamieson had worked, decisively.

At the house there was nothing for Sylvia to do except open the windows. And think — with an eagerness that dismayed without re-ally surprising her — of how soon she could see Carla.

All the paraphernalia of illness had been removed. The room that had been Sylvia and her husband's bedroom and then his death chamber had been cleaned out and tidied up to look as if nothing had ever happened in it. Carla had helped with all that, during the few frenzied days between the crematorium and the departure for Greece. Every piece of clothing Leon had ever worn and some things he hadn't, some gifts from his sisters that had never been taken out of their packages, had been piled in the back seat of the car and taken to the thrift shop. His pills, his shaving things, unopened cans of the fortified drink that had sustained him as long as anything could, cartons of the sesame-seed snaps that had at one time been his favorite snack, the plastic bottles full of the lotion that had eased his back, the sheepskins on which he had lain — all of that was dumped into plastic bags to be hauled away as garbage, and Carla didn't question a thing. She never said, "Maybe somebody could use that," or pointed out that whole cartons of cans were unopened. When Sylvia said, "I wish I hadn't taken the clothes to town. I wish I'd burned them all up in the incinerator," Carla showed no surprise.

They cleaned the oven, scrubbed out the cupboards, wiped down the walls and the windows. One day Sylvia sat in the living room going through all the condolence letters she had received. (There was no accumulation of papers and notebooks to be attended to, as you might have expected with a writer, no unfinished work or scribbled drafts. He had told her, months before, that he had pitched everything. *And no regrets.*) The sloping south wall of the house was mostly big windows. Sylvia looked up, surprised by the watery sunlight that had come out — or possibly by the shadow of Carla on top of a ladder, bare-legged, bare-armed, her resolute face crowned with a frizz of dandelion hair that was too short for her braid. She was vigorously spraying and scrubbing the glass. When she saw Sylvia looking at her, she stopped and flung out her arms as if she were splayed there, making a preposterous gargoyle-like face. They both began to laugh. Sylvia felt this laughter running through her like a sweet stream. She turned back to her letters and soon decided that all these kind, genuine, or perfunctory words, the tributes and the regrets, could go the way of the sheepskins and the crackers.

When she heard Carla taking the ladder down, heard boots on the deck, she was suddenly shy. She sat where she was with her head bowed as Carla came into the room and passed behind her, on her way to the kitchen to put the pail and the paper towels back under the sink. She hardly halted — she was as quick as a bird — but she managed to drop a kiss on Sylvia's bent head. Then she went on. She was whistling something to herself, perhaps had been whistling the whole time.

That kiss had been in Sylvia's mind ever since. It meant nothing in particular. It meant *Cheer up.* Or *Almost done.* It meant that they were good friends who had got through a lot of depressing work together. Or maybe just that the sun had come out. That Carla was thinking of getting home to her horses. Nevertheless, Sylvia saw it as a bright blossom, its petals spreading inside her with a tumultuous heat, like a menopausal flash.

Every so often there had been a special girl student in one of her classes — one whose cleverness and dedication and awkward egotism, or even genuine passion for the natural world, reminded her of her young self. Such girls hung around her worshipfully, hoped for some sort of intimacy they could not — in most cases — imagine, and soon got on her nerves.

Carla was nothing like them. If she resembled anybody in Sylvia's life, it would have to be certain girls she had known in high school — those who were bright but not too bright, easy athletes but not competitive, buoyant but not rambunctious. Naturally happy.

The day after Sylvia's return, she was speaking to Carla about Greece.

"Where I was, this little tiny village with my two old friends, well, it was the sort of place where the very occasional tourist bus would stop, as if it had got lost, and the tourists would get off and look around and they were absolutely bewildered because they weren't anywhere. There was nothing to buy."

The large-limbed, uncomfortable, dazzling girl was sitting there at last, in the room that had been filled with thoughts of her. She was faintly smiling, belatedly nodding.

"And at first I was bewildered, too. It was so hot. But it's true about the light. It's wonderful. And then I figured out what there was to do. There were just these few simple things, but they could fill the day. You walk half a mile down the road to buy some oil, and half a mile in the other direction to buy your bread or your wine, and that's the morning. Then you eat some lunch under the trees, and after lunch it's too hot to do anything but close the shutters and lie on your bed and maybe read. Later on, you notice that the shadows are longer and you get up and go for a swim. Oh," she interrupted herself. "Oh, I forgot."

She jumped up and went to get the present she had brought, which in fact she had not forgotten about at all. She had not wanted to hand it to Carla right away — she had wanted the moment to come more naturally, and while she was speaking she had thought ahead to the moment when she could mention the sea, going swimming. And then say, as she now said, "Swimming reminded me of this because it's a little replica, you know, it's a little replica of the horse they found under the sea. Cast in bronze. They dredged it up, after all this time. It's supposed to be from the second century B.C."

When Carla had come in and looked around for work to do, Sylvia had said, "Oh, just sit down a minute. I haven't had anybody to talk to since I got back. Please." Carla had sat down on the edge of a chair, legs apart, hands between her knees, looking somehow desolate. As if reaching for some distant politeness, she had said, "How was Greece?"

Now she was standing, with the tissue paper crumpled around the horse, which she had not fully unwrapped.

"It's said to represent a racehorse," Sylvia said. "Making that final spurt, the last effort in a race. The rider, too — the boy — you can see that he's urging the horse on to the limit of its strength."

She did not mention that the boy had made her think of Carla, and she could not now have said why. He was only ten or eleven years old. Maybe the strength and grace of the arm that must have held the reins, or the wrinkles in his childish forehead, the absorption and the pure effort there. It was, in some way, like Carla cleaning the windows last spring. Her strong legs in her shorts, her broad shoulders, her big dedicated swipes at the glass, and then the way she had splayed herself out as a joke, inviting or even commanding Sylvia to laugh.

"You can see that," Carla said, conscientiously now examining the little bronzy green statue. "Thank you very much."

"You are welcome. Let's have coffee, shall we? I've just made some. The coffee in Greece was strong, a little stronger than I liked, but the bread was heavenly. Sit down another moment, please do. You should stop me going on and on this way. What about here? How has life been here?"

"It's been raining most of the time."

"I can see that. I can see it has," Sylvia called from the kitchen end of the big room. Pouring the coffee, she decided that she would keep quiet about the other gift she had brought. It hadn't cost her anything (the horse had cost more than the girl could probably guess); it was only a beautiful small pinkish white stone that she had picked up on the road.

"This is for Carla," she had said to her friend Maggie, who was walking beside her. "I know it's silly. I just want her to have a tiny piece of this land."

Sylvia had already mentioned Carla to Maggie, and to Soraya, her other friend there — telling them how the girl's presence had come to mean more and more to her, how an indescribable bond had seemed to grow up between them, and had consoled her in the awful months of last spring.

"It was just to see somebody — somebody so fresh and full of health coming into the house."

Maggie and Soraya had laughed in a kindly but annoying way.

"There's always a girl," Soraya said, with an indolent stretch of her heavy brown arms, and Maggie said, "We all come to it sometime. A crush on a girl."

Sylvia was obscurely angered by that dated word — *crush*.

"Maybe it's because Leon and I never had children," she said. "It's stupid. Displaced maternal love."

But the girl was not, today, anything like the Carla that Sylvia had been remembering, not at all the calm, bright spirit, the carefree and generous creature who had kept her company in Greece.

She had been almost sullen about her gift. Almost sullen as she reached out for her mug of coffee.

"There was one thing I thought you would have liked a lot," Sylvia said energetically. "The goats. They were quite small even when they were full-grown. Some spotty and some white, and they were leaping around on the rocks just like — really like the spirits of the place." She laughed, in an artificial way; she couldn't stop herself. "I wouldn't be surprised if they'd had wreaths on their horns. How is your little goat? I forget her name."

Carla said, "Flora."

"Flora."

"She's gone."

"Gone? Did you sell her?"

"She disappeared. We don't know where."

"Oh, I'm sorry. I'm sorry. But isn't there a chance she'll turn up again?"

No answer. Sylvia looked directly at the girl — something that up to now she had not quite been able to do. She saw that her eyes were full of tears, her face blotchy — in fact, it seemed grubby — and that she was bloated with distress.

Carla didn't do anything to avoid Sylvia's look. She drew her lips tight over her teeth and shut her eyes and rocked back and forth as if in a soundless howl and then, shockingly, she did howl. She howled and wept and gulped for air, and tears ran down her cheeks and snot out of her nostrils, and she began to look around wildly for something to wipe with. Sylvia ran and got handfuls of Kleenex.

"Don't worry, here you are, here, you're all right," she said, thinking that maybe she should take the girl in her arms. But she had not the least wish to do that, and it might make things worse. The girl might feel how little Sylvia wanted to do that, how appalled she was, in fact, by this fit.

Carla said something, said the same thing again.

"Awful," she said. "Awful."

"No, it's not. We all have to cry sometimes. It's all right, don't worry."

"It's awful."

And Sylvia could not help feeling that, with every moment of this show of misery, the girl made herself more ordinary, more like one of those soggy students in her — Sylvia's — office. Some of them cried about their marks — but that was often tactical, a brief, unconvincing bit of whimpering. The less frequent, real waterworks always turned out to have something to do with a love affair, or their parents, or a pregnancy.

"It's not about your goat, is it?"

No. No.

"Then what is it?"

Carla said, "I can't stand it anymore."

What could she not stand?

It turned out to be the husband.

He was mad at her all the time. He acted as if he hated her.

There was nothing she could do right; there was nothing she could say. Living with him was driving her crazy. Sometimes she thought she already was crazy.

"Has he hurt you, Carla?"

No. He hadn't hurt her physically. But he hated her. He despised her. He could not stand it when she cried and she could not help crying because he was so mad. She did not know what to do.

"Perhaps you do know what to do," Sylvia said.

"Get away? I would if I could," Carla began to wail again. "I'd give anything to get away. I can't. I haven't any money. I haven't anywhere in this world to go."

"Well. Think. Is that altogether true?" Sylvia said in her best counseling manner. "Don't you have parents? Didn't you tell me you grew up in Kingston? Don't you have a family there?"

Her parents had moved to British Columbia. They hated Clark. When she ran away and got married, they didn't care if she lived or died.

Brothers or sisters?

One brother, nine years older. He was married and in Toronto. He didn't care, either. He didn't like Clark. His wife was a sickening snob.

"Have you ever thought of the women's shelter?"

"They don't want you there unless you've been beaten up. And everybody would find out and it would be bad for our business."

Sylvia smiled gently. "Is this a time to think about that?"

Then Carla actually laughed. "I know," she said. "I'm insane."

"Listen," Sylvia said. "Listen to me. If you had the money to go, where would you go? What would you do?"

"I would go to Toronto," Carla said, readily enough. "But I wouldn't go near my brother. I'd stay in a motel or something and I'd get a job at a riding stable."

"You think you could do that?"

"I was working at a riding stable the summer I met Clark. I'm more experienced now than I was then. A lot more."

"And all that's stopping you is lack of money?"

Carla took a deep breath. "All that's stopping me," she said.

"All right," Sylvia said. "Now, listen to what I propose. I don't think you should go to a motel. I think you should take the bus to Toronto and go to stay with a friend of mine. Her name is Ruth

Stiles. She has a big house and she lives alone and she won't mind having somebody to stay. You can stay there till you find a job. I'll help you with some money. There must be lots of riding stables around Toronto."

"There are."

"So what do you think? Do you want me to phone and find out what time the bus goes?"

Carla said yes. She was shivering. She ran her hands up and down her thighs and shook her head roughly from side to side.

"I can't believe it," she said. "I'll pay you back. I mean, thank you. I'll pay you back. I don't know what to say."

Sylvia was already at the phone, dialing the bus depot.

"Sh-h-h, I'm getting the times," she said. She listened and hung up. "I know you will. You agree about Ruth's? I'll let her know. There's one problem, though." She looked critically at Carla's shorts and T-shirt. "You can't very well go in those clothes."

"I can't go home to get anything," Carla said in a panic. "I'll be all right."

"The bus will be air-conditioned. You'll freeze. There must be something of mine you could wear. Aren't we about the same height?"

"You're ten times skinnier," Carla said.

"I didn't use to be."

In the end, they decided on a brown linen jacket, hardly worn — Sylvia had considered it to be a mistake for herself, the style too brusque — and a pair of tailored tan pants and a cream-colored silk shirt. Carla's sneakers would have to do, because her feet were two sizes larger then Sylvia's.

Carla went to take a shower — something she had not bothered with, in her state of mind that morning — and Sylvia phoned Ruth. Ruth was going to be out at a meeting that evening, but she would leave the key with her upstairs tenants and all Carla would have to do was ring their bell.

"She'll have to take a cab from the bus depot, though. I assume she's O.K. to manage that?" Ruth said.

Sylvia laughed. "She's not a lame duck, don't worry. She is just a person in a bad situation, the way it happens."

"Well, good. I mean, good she's getting out."

"Not a lame duck at all," Sylvia said, thinking of Carla trying on the tailored pants and linen jacket. How quickly the young recover from a fit of despair and how handsome the girl had looked in the fresh clothes.

The bus would stop in town at 2:20. Sylvia decided to make omelets for lunch, to set the table with the dark blue cloth, and to get down the crystal glasses and open a bottle of wine.

"I hope you can eat something," she said, when Carla came out clean and shining in her borrowed clothes. Her softly freckled skin was flushed from the shower and her hair was damp and darkened, out of its braid, the sweet frizz now flat against her head. She said that she was hungry, but when she tried to get a forkful of the omelet to her mouth her trembling hands made it impossible.

"I don't know why I'm shaking like this," she said. "I must be excited. I never knew it would be this easy."

"It's very sudden," Sylvia said judiciously. "Probably it doesn't seem quite real."

"It does, though. Everything now seems really real. It's like the time before — that's when I was in a daze."

"Maybe when you make up your mind to something, when you really make up your mind, that's how it is. Or that's how it should be. Easy."

"If you've got a friend," Carla said with a self-conscious smile and a flush spreading over her forehead. "If you've got a true friend. I mean, like you." She laid down the knife and fork and raised her wineglass with both hands. "Drinking to a true friend," she said, uncomfortably. "I probably shouldn't even take a sip, but I will."

"Me, too," Sylvia said with a pretense of gaiety, but she spoiled the moment by saying, "Are you going to phone him? Or what? He'll have to know. At least he'll have to know where you are by the time he'd be expecting you home."

"Not the phone," Carla said, alarmed. "I can't do it. Maybe if you —"

"No," Sylvia said. "No."

"No, that's stupid of me. I shouldn't have said that. It's just hard to think straight. What I maybe should do is put a note in the mailbox. But I don't want him to get it too soon. I don't want us to even drive past there when we're going into town. I want to go the back way. So if I write it — if I write it, could you, could you maybe slip it in the box when you come back?"

Sylvia agreed to this, seeing no good alternative. She brought pen and paper and poured a little more wine. Carla sat thinking, then wrote a few words.

I have gone away. I will be all write. These were the words that Sylvia read when she unfolded the paper on her way back from the bus station. She was sure that Carla knew "right" from "write." It was just that she had been talking about *writing* a note and she was in a state of exalted confusion. More confusion perhaps than Sylvia had realized. The wine had brought out a stream of talk, but it had not seemed to be accompanied by any particular grief or upset. She had talked about the horse barn where she had worked when she was eighteen and just out of high school — that was where she'd met Clark. Her parents had wanted her to go to college, and she had agreed, as long as she could choose to be a veterinarian. She had been one of those dorky girls in high school, one of those girls they made rotten jokes about, but she didn't care. All she really wanted, and had wanted all her life, was to work with animals and live in the country.

Clark was the best riding teacher they had — and good-looking, too. Scads of women were after him — they would take up riding just to get him as their teacher. She had teased him about this, and at first he seemed to like it, but then he got annoyed. She tried to make up for it by getting him talking about his dream — his plan, really — to have a riding school, a horse stable, someplace out in the country. One day, she came in to work and saw him hanging up his saddle and realized that she had fallen in love with him.

Maybe it was just sex. It was probably just sex.

When fall came and she was supposed to leave for college, she refused to go. She said she needed a year off.

Clark was very smart, but he hadn't waited even to finish high school, and he had altogether lost touch with his family. He thought families were like a poison in your blood. He had been an attendant in a mental hospital, a disk jockey on a radio station in Lethbridge, Alberta, a member of a road crew near Thunder Bay, an apprentice barber, a salesman in an army-surplus store. And those were only the jobs he had told her about.

She had nicknamed him Gypsy Rover, because of the song, an old song her mother used to sing. And she took to singing it around the house all the time, till her mother knew something was up.

> Last night she slept on a goose-feather bed
> With silken sheets for cover.
> Tonight she'll sleep on the cold cold ground —
> Beside her gypsy lo-ov-ver.

Her mother had said, "He'll break your heart, that's a sure thing." Her stepfather, who was an engineer, did not even grant Clark that much power. "A loser," he called him. "A drifter." He said this as if Clark were a bug he could just whisk off his clothes.

Carla said, "Does a drifter save up enough money to buy a farm, which, by the way, he has done?" He said, "I'm not about to argue with you." She was not his daughter, anyway, he added, as if that were the clincher.

So, naturally, Carla had had to run away with him. The way her parents behaved, they were practically guaranteeing it.

"Will you get in touch with your parents after you're settled?" Sylvia asked. "In Toronto?"

Carla raised her eyebrows, pulled in her cheeks, and made a saucy O of her mouth. She said, "Nope."

Definitely a little bit drunk.

Back home, having left the note in the mailbox, Sylvia cleaned up the dishes that were still on the table, washed and polished the omelet pan, threw the blue napkins and tablecloth in the laundry basket, and opened the windows. She did this with a confusing sense of regret and irritation. She had put out a fresh cake of apple-scented soap for the girl's shower and the smell of it lingered in the house, as it had in the air of the car.

Sometime in the last hour or so the rain had stopped. She could not stay still, so she went for a walk along the path that Leon had cleared. The gravel he had dumped in the boggy places had mostly washed away. They used to go walking every spring to hunt for wild orchids. She taught him the name of every wildflower — all of which, except for trillium, he forgot. He called her his Dorothy Wordsworth.

Last spring, she had gone out once, and picked him a bunch of dogtooth violets, but he had looked at them — as he sometimes looked at her — with mere exhaustion, disavowal.

She kept seeing Carla, Carla stepping onto the bus. Her thanks had been sincere but already almost casual, her wave jaunty. She had got used to her salvation.

At about 6:00, Sylvia put in a call to Toronto, to Ruth, knowing that Carla probably wouldn't have arrived yet. She got the answering machine.

"Ruth," Sylvia said. "Sylvia. It's about this girl I sent you. I hope she doesn't turn out to be a bother to you. I hope it'll be all right. You may find her a little full of herself. Maybe it's just youth. Let me know. O.K.? O.K. Bye-bye."

She phoned again before she went to bed but got the machine, so she said, "Sylvia again. Just checking," and hung up. It was between 9:00 and 10:00, not even really dark. Ruth would still be out, and the girl would not want to pick up the phone in a strange house. She tried to think of the name of Ruth's upstairs tenants. They surely wouldn't have gone to bed yet. But she could not remember it. And just as well. Phoning them would have been going too far.

She got into bed, but it was impossible, so she took a light quilt and went out to the living room and lay down on the sofa, where she had slept for the last three months of Leon's life. She did not think it likely that she would get to sleep there, either — there were no curtains on the huge south windows and she could tell by the sky that the moon had risen, though she could not see it.

The next thing she knew she was on a bus somewhere — in Greece? — with a lot of people she did not know, and the engine of the bus was making an alarming knocking sound. She woke to find that the knocking was at her front door.

Carla?

Carla had kept her head down until the bus was clear of town. The windows were tinted, nobody could see in, but she had to guard herself against seeing out. Lest Clark appear. Coming out of a store or waiting to cross the street, ignorant of her abandonment, thinking this an ordinary afternoon. No: thinking it the afternoon when their scheme — his scheme — had been put in motion, eager to know how far she had got with it.

Once they were out in the country, she looked up, breathed deeply, took account of the violet-tinted fields. Mrs. Jamieson's presence had surrounded her with a kind of remarkable safety and sanity, had made her escape seem the most rational thing you could imagine — in fact, the only self-respecting thing that a person in Carla's shoes could do. Carla had felt herself capable of an unaccustomed confidence, even a mature sense of humor. She had revealed her life to Mrs. Jamieson in a way that seemed bound to gain sympathy and yet to be ironic and truthful. And adapted to live up to what, as far as she could see, were Mrs. Jamieson's — Sylvia's — expectations.

The sun was shining, as it had been for some time. At lunch, it had made the wineglasses sparkle. And there was enough of a wind blowing to lift the roadside grass, the flowering weeds, out of their drenched clumps. Summer clouds, not rain clouds, were scudding across the sky. The whole countryside was changing, shaking itself loose, into the true brightness of a July day. And as they sped along she didn't see much trace of the recent past — no big puddles in the fields, showing where the seed had washed out, no miserable spindly cornstalks or lodged grain.

It occurred to her that she should tell Clark about this — that perhaps they had chosen what was, for some freakish reason, a very wet and dreary corner of the country, and there were other places where they could have been successful.

Or could be yet?

Then it came to her, of course, that she would not be telling Clark anything. Never again. She would not be concerned about what happened to him, or to the horses. If, by any chance, Flora came back she would not hear about it.

This was her second time, leaving everything behind. The first time had been just like the old Beatles song: she had put a note on the table and slipped out of the house at 5:00 in the morning to meet Clark in the church parking lot down the street. She was even humming that song as they rattled away. *She's leaving home, bye-bye.* She recalled now how the sun had come up behind them, how she had looked at Clark's hands on the wheel, at the dark hairs on his competent forearms, and breathed in the smell of the truck, a smell of oil and metal tools and horse barns. The cold air of the fall morning had blown in through the rusted seams of the sort of vehicle that nobody in her family ever rode in, that scarcely ever appeared on the streets where she lived. Clark's preoccupation with the traffic, his curt answers, his narrowed eyes, everything about him that ignored her, even his slight irritation at her giddy delight — all of that had thrilled her. As did the disorder of his past life, his avowed loneliness, the unexpectedly tender way he could have with a horse, and with her. She saw him as the sturdy architect of the life ahead of them, herself as a captive, her submission both proper and exquisite.

"You don't know what you're leaving behind," her mother wrote to her, in the one letter she received and never answered. But in those shivering moments of early-morning flight she certainly *had* known what she was leaving behind, even if she had rather a hazy idea of what she was going to. She despised their house, their backyard, their photo albums, their vacations, their Cuisinart, their powder room, their walk-in closets, their underground lawn-sprinkling system. In the brief note she left, she had used the word *authentic*.

I have always felt the need of a more authentic kind of life. I know I cannot expect you to understand this.

The bus had stopped now at a gas station in the first town on the way. It was the very station that she and Clark used to drive to, in their early days, to buy cheap gas. In those days, their world had included several towns in the surrounding countryside, and they had sometimes behaved like tourists, sampling the specialties in grimy hotel bars. Pigs' feet, sauerkraut, potato pancakes, beer. They would sing all the way home like crazy hillbillies.

But after a while all outings came to be seen as a waste of time and money. They were what people did before they understood the realities of their lives.

She was crying now — her eyes had filled up without her realizing it. She tried to think about Toronto, the first steps ahead. The taxi, the house she had never seen, the strange bed she would sleep in alone. Looking in the phone book tomorrow for the addresses of riding stables, then getting to wherever they were, asking for a job.

She could not picture it. Herself riding on the subway or a streetcar, caring for new horses, talking to new people, living among hordes of people every day who were not Clark. A life, a place, chosen for that specific reason: that it would not contain Clark.

The strange and terrible thing about that world of the future, as she now pictured it, was that she would not exist in it. She would only walk around, and open her mouth and speak, and do this and do that. She would not really be there. And what was strange about it was that she was doing all this, she was riding on this bus, in the hope of recovering herself. As Mrs. Jamieson might say — and as she herself might have said with satisfaction — *taking charge of her own life.* With nobody glowering over her, nobody's mood infecting her with misery, no implacable mysterious silence surrounding her.

But what would she care about? How would she know that she was alive?

While she was running away from him — now — Clark still kept his place in her life. But when she was finished running away, when she just went on, what would she put in his place? What else — who else — could ever be so vivid a challenge?

She managed to stop crying, but she had started to shake. She was in a bad way and would have to take hold, get a grip on herself. "Get a grip on yourself," Clark had sometimes told her, passing through a room where she was scrunched up, trying not to weep, and that indeed was what she must do now.

They had stopped in another town. This was the third town away from the one where she had got on the bus, which meant that they had passed through the second town without her even noticing. The bus must have stopped, the driver must have called out the name, and she had not heard or seen anything, in her fog of fright. Soon enough, they would reach the highway, they would be tearing along toward Toronto.

And she would be lost.

She would be lost. What would be the point of getting into a taxi and giving the new address, of getting up in the morning and brushing her teeth and going into the world?

Her feet seemed now to be at some enormous distance from her body. Her knees in the unfamiliar crisp pants were weighted with irons. She was sinking to the ground like a stricken horse.

Already the bus had loaded on the few passengers and parcels that had been waiting in this town. A woman and a baby in its stroller were waving goodbye to somebody. The building behind them, the cafe that served as a bus stop, was also in motion; a lique-fying wave passed through the bricks and windows as if they were about to dissolve. In peril, Carla pulled her huge body, her iron limbs, forward. She stumbled. She cried out, "Let me off."

The driver braked. He called back irritably, "I thought you were going to Toronto." People gave her casually curious looks. No one seemed to understand that she was in anguish.

"I have to get off here."

"There's a washroom in the back."

"No. No. I have to get off."

"I'm not waiting. You understand that? You got luggage underneath?"

"No. Yes. No."

"No luggage?"

A voice in the bus said, "Claustrophobia. That's what's the matter with her."

"You sick?" the driver said.

"No. No. I just want off."

"O.K. O.K. Fine by me."

Come and get me. Please. Come and get me.
I will.

The door was not locked. And it occurred to Sylvia that she should be locking it now, not opening it, but it was too late, she had it open.

And nobody there.

Yet she was sure, sure, that the knocking had been real.

She closed the door and this time she locked it.

There was a playful sound, a tinkling tapping sound, coming from the wall of windows. She switched the light on, but saw nothing there, and switched it off again. Some animal — maybe a squirrel? The French doors leading to the patio had not been locked, either. Not even really closed, since she had left them open an inch or so to air the house. She started to close them, and then somebody laughed, close by, close enough to be in the room with her.

"It's me," a man said. "Did I scare you?"

He was pressed against the glass of the door; he was right beside her.

"It's Clark," he said. "Clark from down the road."

She was not going to ask him in, but she was afraid to shut the door in his face. He might grab it before she could get it closed. She didn't want to turn on the light, either. She slept in a T-shirt. She should have pulled the quilt from the sofa and wrapped it around herself, but it was too late now.

"Did you want to get dressed?" he said. "What I got in here could be the very things you need."

He had a shopping bag in his hand. He thrust it at her, but did not try to move forward with it.

"What?" she said in a choppy voice.

"Look and see. It's not a bomb. There, take it."

She felt inside the bag, not looking. Something soft. And then she recognized the buttons of the jacket, the silk of the shirt, the belt on the pants.

"Just thought you'd better have them back," he said. "They're yours, aren't they?"

She tightened her jaw so that her teeth wouldn't chatter. A fearful dryness had attacked her mouth and throat.

"I understood they were yours," he said.

Her tongue moved like a wad of wool. She forced herself to say, "Where's Carla?"

"You mean my wife, Carla?"

Now she could see his face more clearly. She could see how he was enjoying himself.

"My wife, Carla, is at home in bed. Where she belongs."

He was both handsome and silly-looking. Tall, lean, well built, but with a slouch that seemed artificial. A contrived, self-conscious air of menace. A lock of dark hair falling over his forehead, a vain little mustache, eyes that appeared both hopeful and mocking, a boyish smile perpetually on the verge of a sulk.

She had always disliked the sight of him — she had mentioned her dislike to Leon, who said that the man was just unsure of himself, just a bit too friendly. The fact that he was unsure of himself would not make her any safer.

"Pretty worn out," he said. "After her little adventure. You should have seen your face — you should have seen the look on you when you recognized those clothes. What did you think? Did you think I'd murdered her?"

"I was surprised," Sylvia said.

"I bet you were. After you were such a big help to her running away."

"I helped her —" Sylvia said with considerable effort. "I helped her because she seemed to be in distress."

"Distress," he said, as if examining the word. "I guess she was. She was in very big distress when she jumped off that bus and got on the phone to me to come and get her. She was crying so hard I could hardly make out what it was she was saying."

"She wanted to come back?"

"Oh, yeah. You bet she wanted to come back. She was in real hysterics to come back. She is a girl who is very up and down in her emotions. But I guess you don't know her as well as I do."

"She seemed quite happy to be going."

"Did she really? Well, I have to take your word for it. I didn't come here to argue with you."

Sylvia said nothing.

"Actually, I came here not just to return those clothes. I came here to tell you that I don't appreciate you interfering in my life with my wife."

"She is a human being," Sylvia said, though she knew that it would be better if she could keep quiet. "Besides being your wife."

"My goodness, is that so? My wife is a human being? Really? Thank you for the information. But don't try getting smart with me. *Sylvia.*"

"I wasn't trying to get smart."

"Good. I'm glad you weren't. I don't want to get mad. I just have a couple of important things to say to you. One thing — that I don't want you sticking your nose in anywhere, anytime, in my life. Another — that I'm not going to want her coming around here anymore. Not that she is going to want to come, I'm pretty sure of that. She doesn't have too good an opinion of you at the moment. And it's time you learned how to clean your own house. Now —" he said. "Now. Has that sunk in?"

"Quite sufficiently."

"Oh, I really hope it has. I hope so."

Sylvia said, "Yes."

"And you know what else I think?"

"What?"

"I think you owe me something."

"What?"

"I think you owe me — you owe me an apology."

Sylvia said, "All right. If you think so. I'm sorry."

He shifted, perhaps just to put out his hand, and with the movement of his body she shrieked.

He laughed. He put his hand on the doorframe to make sure she didn't close it.

"What's that?"

"What's what?" he said, as if she were trying out a trick and it would not work. But then he caught sight of something reflected in the window, and he snapped around to look.

Not far from the house was a wide shallow patch of land that often filled up with night fog at this time of year. The fog was there tonight, had been there all this while. But now the fog had changed. It had thickened, taken on a separate shape, transformed itself into something spiky and radiant. First, a live dandelion ball, tumbling forward. Then it condensed itself into an unearthly sort of animal, pure white, hell-bent, something like a giant unicorn rushing at them.

"Jesus Christ," Clark said softly. He grabbed hold of Sylvia's shoulder. This touch did not alarm her at all — she accepted it with the knowledge that he did it either to protect her or to reassure himself.

Then the vision exploded. Out of the fog, and out of the magnifying light — now revealed to be that of a car traveling along this back road, probably in search of a place to park — out of this appeared a white goat. A little dancing white goat, hardly bigger than a sheepdog.

Clark let go. He said, "Where the Christ did you come from?"

"It's your goat," Sylvia said. "Isn't it your goat?"

"Flora," he said. "Flora."

The goat had stopped a yard or so away from them, had turned shy, and hung her head.

"Flora," Clark said. "Where the hell did you come from? You scared the shit out of us."

Us.

Flora came closer but still did not look up. She butted against Clark's legs.

"Goddamn stupid animal," he said shakily.

"She was lost," Sylvia said.

"Yeah. She was. Never thought we'd see her again, actually."

Flora looked up. The moonlight caught a glitter in her eyes.

"Scared the shit out of us," Clark said to her. "We thought you were a ghost."

"It was the effect of the fog," Sylvia said. She stepped out of the door now, onto the patio. Quite safe.

"Yeah."

"Then the lights of that car."

"Like an apparition," he said, recovering. And pleased that he had thought of this description.

"Yes."

"The goat from outer space. That's what you are. You are a goddamn goat from outer space," he said, patting Flora. But when Sylvia put out her hand to do the same, Flora immediately lowered her head as if preparing to butt.

"Goats are unpredictable," Clark said. "They can seem tame, but they're not really. Not after they grow up."

"Is she grown up? She looks so small."

"She's as big as she's ever going to get."

They stood looking down at the goat, as if hoping that she would provide them with more conversation. But she apparently was not going to. From this moment, they could go neither forward nor back. Sylvia believed that she might have seen a shadow of regret in his eyes that this was so.

But he acknowledged it. He said, "It's late."

"I guess it is," Sylvia said, just as if this had been an ordinary visit.

"O.K., Flora. Time for us to go home."

"I'll make other arrangements for help if I need it," she said. "I probably won't need it now, anyway." She added lightly, "I'll stay out of your hair."

"Sure," he said. "You'd better get inside. You'll get cold."

"Good night," she said. "Good night, Flora."

The phone rang then.

"Excuse me."

"Good night."

It was Ruth.

"Ah," Sylvia said. "A change in plans."

She did not sleep, thinking of the little goat, whose appearance out of the fog seemed to her more and more magical. She even wondered if, possibly, Leon could have had something to do with it. If she were a poet, she would write a poem about something like this. But in her experience the subjects that she thought a poet would write about had not appealed to Leon, who was — who had been — the real thing.

Carla had not heard Clark go out, but she woke when he came in.

He told her that he had just been checking around the barn. "A

car went along the road a while ago, and I wondered what it was doing here. I couldn't get back to sleep till I went out and checked
whether everything was O.K."

"So, was it?"

"Far as I could see. And then while I was up," he said, "I thought I
might as well pay a visit up the road. I took the clothes back."

Carla sat up in bed. "You didn't wake her up?"

"She woke up. It was O.K. We had a little talk."

"Oh."

"It was O.K."

"You didn't mention any of that stuff, did you?"

"I didn't mention it."

"It really was all made up. It really was. You have to believe me. It
was all a lie."

"O.K."

"You have to believe me."

"Then I believe you."

"I made it all up."

"O.K."

He got into bed.

"Did you get your feet wet?" she said.

"Heavy dew." He turned to her. "Come here," he said. "When I
read your note, it was just like I went hollow inside. It's true. I felt
like I didn't have anything left in me."

The bright weather had continued. On the streets, in the stores, in
the post office, people greeted one another by saying that summer
had finally arrived. The pasture grass and even the poor beaten
crops lifted up their heads. The puddles dried up, the mud turned
to dust. A light warm wind blew and everybody felt like doing
things again. The phone rang. Inquiries about trail rides, about
riding lessons. Summer camps canceled their trips to museums,
and minivans drew up, loaded with restless children. The horses
pranced along the fences, freed from their blankets.

Clark had managed to get hold of a piece of roofing at a good
price. He had spent the whole first day after Runaway Day (that was
how they referred to Carla's bus trip) fixing the roof of the exercise
ring.

For a couple of days, as they went about their chores, he and

Carla would wave at each other. If she happened to pass close to him and there was nobody else around, Carla might kiss his shoulder through the light material of his summer shirt.

"If you ever try to run away on me again I'll tan your hide," he said to her, and she said, "Who are you now — Clint Eastwood?"

Then she said, "*Would* you?"

"What?"

"Tan my hide?"

"Damn right."

Birds were everywhere. Red-winged blackbirds, robins, a pair of doves that sang at daybreak. Lots of crows, and gulls on reconnoitering missions from the lake, and big turkey buzzards that sat in the branches of a dead oak about half a mile away, at the edge of the woods. At first they just sat there, drying out their voluminous wings, lifting themselves occasionally for a trial flight, flapping around a bit, then composing themselves, to let the sun and the warm air do their work. In a day or so, they were restored, flying high, circling and dropping to earth, disappearing over the woods, coming back to rest in the familiar bare tree.

Lizzie Borden's owner — Joy Tucker — showed up again, tanned and friendly. She had got sick of the rain, and gone off on her holidays to hike in the Rocky Mountains. Now she was back. Perfect timing.

She and Clark treated each other warily at first, but they were soon joking as if nothing had happened.

"Lizzie looks to be in good shape," she said. "But where's her little friend?"

"Gone," Clark said. "Maybe she took off to the Rocky Mountains."

"Lots of wild goats out there. With fantastic horns."

"So I hear."

For three or four days they had been too busy to go down and look in the mailbox. When Carla opened it, she found the phone bill, a promise that if they subscribed to a certain magazine they could win a million dollars, and Mrs. Jamieson's letter.

My Dear Carla,

I have been thinking about the (rather dramatic) events of the last few days and I find myself talking to myself, but really to you, so often that I thought I must speak to you, even if — the best way I can do now — only in a letter. And don't worry — you do not have to answer me.

Mrs. Jamieson went on to say that she was afraid she had involved herself too closely in Carla's life and had made the mistake of thinking somehow that Carla's freedom and happiness were the same thing. All she cared for was Carla's happiness, and she saw now that she — Carla — had found that in her marriage. All she could hope was that perhaps Carla's flight and turbulent emotions had brought her true feelings to the surface, and perhaps a recognition in her husband of his true feelings as well.

She said that she would perfectly understand if Carla wished to avoid her in the future and that she would always be grateful for Carla's presence in her life during such a difficult time.

The strangest and most wonderful thing in this whole string of events seems to me the reappearance of Flora. In fact, it seems rather like a miracle. Where had she been all that time and why did she choose just that moment to reappear? I am sure your husband has described it to you. We were talking at the patio door, and I — facing out — was the first to see this white something, descending on us out of the night. Of course it was the effect of the ground fog. But truly terrifying. I think I shrieked out loud. I had never in my life felt such bewitchment, in the true sense. I suppose I should be honest and say fear. There we were, two adults, frozen, and then out of the fog comes little lost Flora.

There has to be something special about this. I know, of course, that Flora is an ordinary little animal and that she probably spent her time away getting herself pregnant. In a sense, her return has no connection at all with our human lives. Yet her appearance at that moment did have a profound effect on your husband and me. When two human beings divided by hostility are both, at the same time, mystified by the same apparition, there is a bond that springs up between them, and they find themselves united in the most unexpected way. United in their humanity — that is the only way I can describe it. We parted almost as friends. So Flora has her place as a good angel in my life and perhaps also in your husband's life and yours.

With all my good wishes,
Sylvia Jamieson

As soon as Carla had read this letter she crumpled it up. Then she burned it in the sink. The flames leaped up alarmingly and she turned on the tap, then scooped up the soft disgusting black stuff and put it down the toilet, as she should have done in the first place.

She was busy for the rest of that day, and the next, and the next. During that time, she had to take two parties out on the trails, she had to give lessons to children, individually and in groups. At night when Clark put his arms around her — he was generally in good spirits now — she did not find it hard to be cooperative. She dreamed of things that were of no importance, that made no sense.

It was as if she had a murderous needle somewhere in her lungs, and by breathing carefully she could avoid feeling it. But every once in a while she had to take a deep breath, and it was still there.

Sylvia Jamieson had taken an apartment in the college town where she taught. The house was not up for sale — or at least there wasn't a sign out in front of it. Leon Jamieson had got some kind of posthumous award — news of this was in the papers. There was no mention of any money.

As the dry golden days of fall came on — an encouraging and profitable season — Carla found that she had got used to the sharp thought that had lodged inside her. It wasn't so sharp anymore; in fact, it no longer surprised her. She was inhabited now by an almost seductive notion, a constant low-lying temptation.

She had only to raise her eyes, she had only to look in one direction, to know where she might go. An evening walk, once her chores for the day were finished. To the edge of the woods, and the bare tree where she had seen the buzzards.

Where she might find the little dirty bones in the grass. The skull, with shreds of bloodied skin still clinging to it, that she could settle in one hand. Knowledge in one hand.

Or perhaps not.

Suppose something else had happened. Suppose he had chased Flora away, or tied her in the back of the truck and driven some distance and let her loose. Taken her back to the place they'd got her from. Not to have her around, reminding them of this bad time.

The days passed and she didn't go. She held out against the temptation.

ANGELA PNEUMAN

All Saints Day

FROM VIRGINIA QUARTERLY REVIEW

WORD WAS THAT the missionary kid had a demon, though no one was supposed to know. The Boyd family was visiting East Winder only for the weekend, and already eight-year-old Prudence had heard it from her younger sister, Grace, who heard it from her new friend, Anna, whose father was going to cast it out. Prudence figured that a cast-out demon would look like a puddle of split pea soup the size of a welcome mat, and that it would move around the room like a blob, trying to absorb its way into people. Her own father, the Reverend Yancey Boyd, didn't believe in demons or in talking about demons except to say he didn't believe in them, end of discussion.

"The demon made Ryan Kitter paint himself purple all over," Grace said.

"*All* over?" Prudence asked, "even his privates?"

"That's how they found him," Grace said. She was six. "The paint dried up and he was crying because it hurt him to pee."

The girls stood in front of the mirror in the spare room at the Moberlys' house. It was the afternoon of November 1, and that night there was an All Saints Day party for kids at the First United Methodist, where the Reverend Yancey Boyd might be the new minister. Prudence was busy cutting a slit for Grace's head in a piece of old brown sheet. Everyone had to go as someone from the Bible, so she was turning Grace into John the Baptist with his head on a platter.

"There's no such thing as demons," Prudence said, only because she hadn't been the one to hear the story first. She hacked at the sheet with scissors, the blades as dull as butter knives. When she managed a hole, she threw the sheet over Grace's head.

Ryan Kitter's whole family were missionaries. They had returned from Africa ahead of schedule, due to the demon, and were camping in the church basement until they found a house. They got to cook on hot plates and take sponge baths. Prudence thought that if anyone deserved to camp in the church basement it was her own family, since her father was the one who might be the minister. He'd been ordained in three states. At the Moberlys' house, the girls were stuck in a dark, damp room that smelled like motor oil. Before the Moberlys had done it over for their daughter, who was grown, it had been a garage, and twice already Prudence had seen centipedes, one rippling into a crack between cement blocks, one behind the framed picture of Jesus over the bed.

"Ryan likes to be in a dark room," Grace said, pushing her head through the hole in the sheet. "And he doesn't talk to anyone except his mother."

"Well, maybe he doesn't have anything to say," said Prudence, regarding her with a frown. Grace still looked like herself, only in a brown sheet now, blond hair coming out of her braid, and nothing like John the Baptist.

In the picture over the bed Jesus wore a robe with billowing sleeves and a rope belt, and Prudence needed something to tie around Grace's waist. She rummaged through the cardboard box of odds and ends that Mrs. Moberly had provided. At home in North Carolina, their mother kept old towels and drapes in a trunk, and a drapery cord would have done the trick. But at home they would not be dressing like Bible characters for a party; instead they would have already gone trick-or-treating the night before. They would have worn last year's outfits switched around — Prudence as a floor lamp, Grace as a blue crayon — since their mother wasn't in any kind of shape to make new ones. Here in East Winder, Kentucky, no one was of a mind to trick-or-treat, because Halloween was pagan.

"Ryan's father thinks he has a demon and his mother isn't sure," Grace said. "They took him to doctors, but a doctor can't do anything against a demon. Anna saw a man with a demon swallow a sword in Tennessee. She saw another demon bend a man in half when her dad tried to cast it out."

Prudence made it a point not to be interested. She said, "Really?" and "Hmmm," as she unearthed a scarf and tied it around Grace's waist, so that the ends hung down, then pulled and tucked at the sheet. She put her hands on her hips and stepped back to look. "Not bad," she said. "We'll draw you a beard with eye pencil, but you've got to have a knife or a hatchet or something to make it look real. And a platter."

Mrs. Moberly stood barefoot in front of the kitchen sink, peeling apples for a pie. Her feet were puffy, and they smooched against the linoleum. It looked like she'd picked her baby toenails clean away. Prudence's mother, who was still sleeping upstairs in the Moberlys' bedroom, had always told Prudence to keep her shoes on; if anyone wanted to see her bare feet, they would ask.

"How're the costumes coming?" asked Mrs. Moberly through a mouthful of apple peel. She wore a blue-and-white-checked apron and had made covers of the same material for the toaster, coffee-maker, and some other small appliance that Prudence couldn't make out by its shape.

"Fine," Prudence said. "Could we please borrow a meat cleaver?"

"A meat cleaver?" Mrs. Moberly's hands stopped, knife poised over a peeled, cored apple. It looked naked and cold. "What Biblical character used a meat cleaver?"

"It's a secret," Prudence said, before Grace could open her mouth.

"A meat cleaver in church? I don't think so," said Mrs. Moberly. "Someone could get hurt. How about another idea? How about you go as a shepherd? Mr. Moberly has an old cane somewhere. Or Mary? Mary never used a meat cleaver."

"No one's *using* it," Prudence said.

"Meat cleavers are sharp," said Mrs. Moberly. "Meat cleavers are not toys. I don't think your mother would be happy if I allowed you to go to church with a meat cleaver. She's not feeling very well as it is." Mrs. Moberly sliced the apple into eighths in four deft strokes. "Your father tells me she likes apple pie."

"She's feeling fine," Prudence said. "She's just tired."

Mrs. Moberly looked at Prudence and smiled in the way adults sometimes smiled at Prudence, lips peeling back from patiently clenched teeth. Then Mrs. Moberly smiled at Grace, who looked at her feet. "What's that you're wearing, Grace?" Mrs. Moberly said. "Let me guess. You're Mary Magdalene, or Ruth."

Grace shook her head.

"Esther?"

"A man," Grace said.

"Moses?"

"It's a surprise," Prudence said again. "How about some tinfoil? We could save it and you could use it again to cover something."

"Tinfoil I can do," said Mrs. Moberly, and handed her the box. "Listen, girls," she said, smiling again. "What do you think of your visit so far? Think you might like to live here?"

"We won't live *here*," Prudence said. "We'll have a parsonage like at home."

"Well, yes," said Mrs. Moberly. "That's what I meant. East Winder's quite a town. I think living here would do your mother a world of good."

Prudence stared at Mrs. Moberly and raised her left eyebrow, something she'd taught herself how to do. Mrs. Moberly's eyes did not seem to be any real color. Under one eye, Prudence could see a tiny length of blue vein beneath Mrs. Moberly's skin, like a fading pen mark.

Mrs. Moberly blinked at her once and turned to Grace. "How about you, dear? Wouldn't you like to live here?"

Prudence answered for Grace as she pulled her toward the kitchen door. "We don't care," she said in her boredest voice.

I don't care was what their mother had to say about moving. Her name was Joyce, and *I don't care* was what she said about many things, usually at the end of a long, tired sigh. Then she'd talk on the phone to her sister, Char — who wasn't saved — and go to bed in the middle of the day, sometimes for days in a row, and when Prudence went in to kiss her good night she'd already be asleep and smelling like damp books. Yancey said it had to do with the baby who died before he was born in August, but when Aunt Char came to stay for a week she said no. She said this was Joyce in college all over again, or just Joyce waking up, finally, and coming apart, which he should have expected. Yancey said what's that supposed to mean, and Aunt Char said it means nothing, nothing at all, and that Joyce had made her bed. (Joyce used to testify, proudly, that her family in Greenville thought she was crazy for loving the Lord. She'd been raised a twice-a-year churchgoing Methodist, not evangelical. Yancey's preaching had been what saved her before they got married, and Prudence could tell that Aunt Char didn't like that fact one bit.)

Back in the spare room Prudence emptied out the cardboard box of odds and ends. She cut the box apart at the folds, traced the top of Grace's head in the center of one of the long sides, cut out the circle, and finally taped on sheets of tinfoil. Then she fitted the whole platter over Grace's head and bunched part of the sheet into the hole at her neck to hold it steady.

Grace squinted at herself in the mirror.

"Do your head this way," Prudence said, leaning her head to the side and fluttering her eyelids. "Try to look like you just got your head cut off."

Grace stuck out her tongue and said, "Blllhh." Her head lolled to the side. Then she shrugged her head out of the platter and began cutting out a long, curved knife shape Prudence had drawn on another piece of cardboard. "They tried sending Ryan Kitter to regular school last week," Grace said. "He went to first grade with Anna King."

"Hmmm," said Prudence. She peered into the Moberlys' closet, where she'd already found her own costume. Behind the coats and jackets and Mr. Moberly's old suits hung several leotards clipped to hangers with clothespins, and one pink tutu, the tulle gone as flat and limp as a newspaper, all from when their daughter had taken ballet. Inside a box underneath the pink tutu, Prudence had found a spangly halter top with matching tights and a long, gauzy skirt, store tags still attached.

Now Prudence took out the costume and laid it on the bed. The halter was red with long sleeves and tiny round mirrors sewn on and yellow embroidery everywhere. The neck and sleeves had silky yellow fringe, and at the bottom edge, just above where her belly-button would show, the fringe ended in tiny wooden beads that clacked softly against one another.

"In the lunchroom he stood at the trash can and ate all the bread pudding and creamed spinach that nobody wanted, and when the teacher caught him and made him stop, he cried. Then he threw up. Then he threw a fit and they took him right out of school." Grace stopped cutting, her scissors wedged deep in the cardboard, and eyed the costume. "Ooooh. Who are you again?"

"Salome," Prudence said. "The one who asked for your head on a platter."

Prudence slipped off her pants and pulled on the tights and skirt. She did a practice kick out to the side, and the gauzy material traveled up into the air with her leg, then floated down. It was see-through. In the picture Prudence had seen in a book in her father's study, Salome was a dark-skinned, smiling, barefoot girl with her hair pulled back, wearing an outfit a lot like this one. Her arms had been raised high above her head, her body in mid-sway, a gentle version of the bump-and-grind Prudence had perfected from a dance show on television, before her father found out she was watching.

No wonder the king had wanted to give Salome anything she wanted. Prudence had curly dark hair, too — almost black — and now she pulled it into a ponytail so tight it made her eyes slanty. She moved her hips in a little circle and waved her arms, first out in front of her, then to her sides, then over her head.

"Does Mrs. Moberly know you're wearing that?" Grace said.

"Mrs. Moberly is a pain."

"I want to be someone who dances."

"You can't dance if your head's cut off."

"*You're* not even supposed to dance," said Grace; and it was true, though the Reverend Yancey Boyd said it wasn't because of dancing itself, but what dancing led to.

"This is different," said Prudence. "It's pretend."

Grace crimped tinfoil onto the blade of the cardboard knife and began coloring the handle black with a Magic Marker. "Once a demon gets in, you act different," she said. "They get in when you get cut open and bleed. Anna's not allowed to have her ears pierced. In Africa, Ryan was crossing the street with their house woman and they got hit by heathens in a truck. They were holding hands and she died and he broke his arm. The bone was sticking out through his skin, and that's when it happened. Demons sneak in wherever they can, and someone has to get them out so you can go back to the way you were. Tonight Anna's dad is going to get the demon out of Ryan. It's a secret, because it's not that kind of church, but Anna's dad says it should be."

Prudence had the halter on over her shirt, and she was stuffing the bosom with Grace's dirty undershirt from the day before. "Stop talking about that," she said. "At the party they'll have to guess who we are, so I'll go first and do my dance, then I'll stop and say, 'Cut off the head of John the Baptist, voice crying in the wilderness, who eats locusts and honey, and give it to me on a silver platter.' Then you come on up and stand beside me."

"What do I say?"

"You don't say anything. We'll have the knife on the platter and ketchup for blood and you just walk like this." Prudence staggered around the bed. "You could collapse, maybe, or just follow me away. Wait and see. Everyone else will be Mary and Joseph and Noah or some other dumb thing."

"A demon could have gotten into Mom when the baby came out," Grace said.

Prudence stopped staggering. "No," she said. "She is just very tired. She just needs her rest." Prudence kept looking at Grace until Grace nodded. Then Prudence pulled up her shirt to see what the halter would look like against her stomach.

"Ryan has a demon of shock," Grace said.

Prudence sucked in her stomach until it looked hollow. Sexy. She turned her back to the mirror and looked over her shoulder for the rear view.

"Mom could have a demon of tiredness," Grace said.

Prudence kept sucking in her stomach until it hurt. "Don't say that anymore," she said, gritting her teeth. "That's the stupidest thing I've ever heard."

The Reverend Yancey Boyd had eyes so light they almost weren't blue at all, and wavy hair close to his head, and when he talked he sounded wise. Aunt Char said that Joyce married him because he looked like Paul Newman, and because he was sincere, though she said it was no excuse. Prudence was used to women going weepy around him, so it was no surprise when at dinner Mrs. Moberly started sharing the heartache of their daughter.

Belinda Moberly had grown up and gone to college, began Mr. Moberly (a good, evangelical college, put in Mrs. Moberly), and under the influence of a philosophy professor, said Mr. Moberly (who was later fired, said Mrs. Moberly), she'd first become a Unitarian, and then an atheist. And she was living in sin, out of wedlock, with a firefighter.

"We did our best," said Mrs. Moberly. "I don't know what else we could have done."

Over the table hung a low, stained-glass chandelier that Mrs. Moberly had made in a class, which cast a ring of tiny yellow crosses around the walls of the wood-paneled dining room.

"She has a good foundation," the Reverend Yancey Boyd said to Mrs. Moberly, and he patted her hand. The patting of hands was usually Joyce's department. She took care of the comforting while Yancey did the talking. It wasn't a good idea for him to touch too many women. He was that handsome. "When children have been brought up in the Lord, He marks them for life. Children" — Yancey passed a hand over Grace's blond head — "have their own kind of openness to the Lord. They may grow up and try other roads, but something inside them always knows better. I believe your daughter has a great advantage."

The Reverend Yancey Boyd sounded encouraging, but he looked sad. Before supper Prudence had found him sitting on the bed beside Joyce, trying to make her eat some crackers from the tray Mrs. Moberly had fixed. Prudence couldn't see her mother's face, but she could hear her whispering how she shouldn't have tried to come, and Prudence had seen how the curl she'd put in her hair the day before, for the trip, had flattened out against her head.

"I don't understand it," Mr. Moberly was saying about his daughter. He was a plumber with shoulders so wide that Prudence didn't see how he could crawl under any sink. He split a biscuit in half and buttered it, and when he finished he put the whole bottom of the biscuit into his mouth.

"I tell her we want her to be happy," Mrs. Moberly said, "and she tells me happiness is overrated. She says she's as happy as she can be and live with herself. I ask her, but do you know Jesus as a *personal savior*, Belinda, that's real happiness — you know, Reverend — and she tells me she would believe if she could, but she can't. I don't know what to do with her." When Mrs. Moberly paused to drink her water, her hand shook a little. "I guess we're not promised we'll always understand, are we, Reverend?"

The Reverend Yancey Boyd smiled in a way that made him look even sadder. "No," he said, "we are not."

Grace picked at her food. She had the nervous hiccups, which didn't sound like regular hiccups at all, but like breathing with little coughs. And she was chewing at the inside of her mouth, which she wasn't supposed to do. Once she'd made herself bleed. Prudence nudged Grace with her elbow, and Grace stopped.

*

By the time they reached the church parking lot that evening, it was dark and cold. The leaves smelled like fall turning into winter. Prudence had stuffed the platter down the front of Grace's long pink parka like a shield, to hide it, and she'd hidden eye pencil and lipstick and ketchup packets from Burger King in the pockets of her own coat. She'd put pants on over her tights and rolled up the gauzy skirt, too, because she thought Mrs. Moberly might recognize it before their turn.

"Where are the Kitters staying?" Prudence asked, as they walked through the parking lot toward the back entrance.

"Who?" asked Mrs. Moberly.

"The boy with the demon," said Grace, stomping up the cement steps to the door.

"What?" Mrs. Moberly said. She shifted a Tupperware container of cookies to her other hand and held open the church door. Inside she squatted down beside Grace and peered into her face. "What demon?'

"Never mind," Prudence said. "What do the Kitters sleep on? Do they have a bed or just nap mats? Do they have a sofa and chair and television or just Sunday school furniture?"

"I wouldn't know," Mrs. Moberly said. "I haven't seen it. It's their home, you know, for now, until they find a house. You can't just go charging into people's homes unannounced, even if they do live in the church."

"I wouldn't go charging in," Prudence said.

"You're going to have a great time at the party," said Mrs. Moberly, steering them down the basement steps. "Just think of all the new friends you'll make here." Mrs. Moberly spoke in a bright voice and smiled so forcefully her jaw muscles bulged.

They moved down a wide, dim hall toward the fellowship room at the far end, an open door full of light and spilling out muted voices. Three narrow halls branched off on either side of this wide hall, and at these dark openings the air came cool and quiet. Prudence lagged behind and slipped down the last hall before the fellowship room. She tried two doors, but they were locked. She peered through the long narrow windows over the doorknobs, but it was too dark to see anything.

Mrs. Moberly appeared silhouetted at the mouth of the hall. "Did we lose you?"

"No," said Prudence.

The fellowship room was full of kids and parents. A girl wearing a dingy white sheep hood with ears, her straight hair sticking stiffly out around her face, came right up to Grace and hugged her.

"Hi, Anna," Grace said. Prudence disliked hugging. She ignored Anna and checked the back of the room where tables had been set up with punch and treats, and the front of the room where kids were jumping off a foot-high wooden collapsible stage.

Mrs. Moberly hovered. "Why don't you take off your coat now," she said to Prudence. "It's warm in here, and look, Anna's in her costume."

"I'm cold," Prudence said. "We both are." She shivered, for good measure, and so did Grace.

Mrs. Moberly smiled the hard smile.

"It's very cold in here," Prudence said. "Someone should probably do something about it."

If the Reverend Yancey Boyd had been there he would have made her mind Mrs. Moberly, and then he would have marched her back to the house and made her change. He didn't want her wearing even a two-piece bathing suit that showed her belly in the summertime, much less a skimpy dance costume. But tonight he was the guest speaker at a youth lock-in across town, at the high school gym. Their mother had been the one who'd planned to come to the All Saints Day party.

"I'd be happy to carry those cookies into the kitchen for you," Prudence said, taking the Tupperware container from Mrs. Moberly.

"Well, sure," said Mrs. Moberly. "But don't go running off. You'll want to meet some girls your age."

In the kitchen across the hall, a tall, thin woman with red hair was slicing through pans of Rice Krispies treats. "Are you Al and Debbie's youngest?" she asked Prudence.

"No," said Prudence. "I'm Yancey and Joyce's oldest."

"Oh yes," said the woman, "the new pastor's daughter. I'm Mrs. Spode."

"He *might* be the new pastor," Prudence said, but she said it in a nice way.

"He will be if my husband and I have anything to say about it," said Mrs. Spode. She lifted out sticky squares with a spatula and stacked them on a plate. "This church needs someone to get it back on track. People get some strange ideas."

"What ideas?" Prudence asked.

"Oh, nothing for you to worry about," said Mrs. Spode. "Is there a costume somewhere under that pretty coat?"

"Yes," Prudence said, but just then a small Mary entered, holding a blue hand towel that was a Mary headpiece for Mrs. Spode to pin back on. Then another woman led more children into the kitchen because it was almost time to line them up for the costume show. There were two Marys, a Joseph, a Moses with swimming pool kickboards for tablets, a donkey, a sheep, a shepherd, a Noah, and a King David with a paper crown. Mostly they looked like children wearing pajamas.

Prudence found Grace and herded her into the corner. She unzipped Grace's coat and extracted the foil-covered platter. With eye pencil she sketched on a mustache and was working on the beard when she felt a poke at her shoulder.

"Well, now," said Mrs. Spode. She reached down beside them and touched the platter. "What's the story, here?"

"I'm doing her beard," Prudence said. "She's John the Baptist."

"Oh, terrific," said Mrs. Spode, clapping once. "We don't have a John the Baptist yet."

Prudence smudged the pencil marks into Grace's skin with her fingertips. Grace said, "That's my platter," trying not to move her lips.

Mrs. Spode picked up the platter and carefully turned it over in her hands. "I see," she said. "It does look like a platter. Your head goes into this hole, right here?"

Prudence took the platter from Mrs. Spode, who was frowning, and fitted it over Grace's head, securing it by tucking in the sheet. Prudence withdrew the curved cardboard knife from her coat pocket and wedged it tightly into the space between the platter and Grace's neck, at an angle so that it looked like stabbing. She was just tearing open a ketchup packet when Mrs. Spode said, "Hold on a sec."

The other children had begun to gather around Grace. "Who is she?" asked Anna King.

Grace jerked her head to the side and showed them the whites of her eyes. She staggered a few steps the way Prudence had shown her.

"Listen here," said Mrs. Spode. "This is very clever —"

"Thank you," said Prudence.

"— but maybe we could do without the blood and the platter and the knife."

"It's not real blood," Prudence said. She turned around to the children staring at them. "It's not real," she said. "It's pretend."

"Maybe I'd better see your costume, too," said Mrs. Spode.

"I'm not ready yet," Prudence said. "I have to do my hair. I have to put on my earrings."

"Now is a very good time," said Mrs. Spode.

"Not yet." Prudence raised her left eyebrow, but Mrs. Spode only raised her own eyebrows and said, "Go ahead and take off your coat, please, miss."

Prudence slowly unzipped her coat. She kept it closed until Mrs. Spode took it off her shoulders for her. When Prudence looked down she couldn't see past the halter bosom to her feet.

Mrs. Spode was silent, regarding her. She sucked her lips in against her teeth thoughtfully. Behind Mrs. Spode, the children stared.

Prudence unrolled the waistband of the gauzy skirt until the hem reached her ankles.

"You must be what's-her-name," Mrs. Spode said. She closed her eyes, then opened them.

"Salome," Prudence said. Even though her coat was off and her stomach was bare, she was growing hot. She thought about taking off her pants under the skirt, and decided against it.

"Well," said Mrs. Spode. She seemed about to say more, but instead she turned to the other children and led them out of the kitchen and into the fellowship room, where the parents had set up folding chairs. She told the biblical characters to go to the stage one at a time and let people guess, then she returned to the kitchen. She shut the door behind her, but Prudence could still make out the first clapping and laughing.

"Listen," Mrs. Spode said, squatting down. "These costumes are very creative."

"I know," Prudence said.

"The problem is," Mrs. Spode said, "is that some people might get the wrong idea."

"It's in the Bible," Prudence said. "Everyone knows how John the Baptist died."

"Not everyone will appreciate the details before them," said Mrs. Spode. "You've just got to trust me on this one." Mrs. Spode twisted her mouth at Prudence as though she was sorry she had to do what she had to do.

"It's not fair," Prudence said.

Against the wall, Grace was chewing the inside of her cheek.

Prudence remembered what she'd heard Aunt Char saying to her mother. "Don't you ever just want to cut loose?" she said to Mrs. Spode. "Don't you ever just want to live a little?"

"Oh, baby," said Mrs. Spode. "You're something else. You've got a row to hoe, I tell you." Mrs. Spode pressed her hand to her forehead. "Listen," she said. "How about I go get you a couple choir robes. They're gold and heavy, and you can be two angels."

"I don't want to be an angel," Grace said. She had a packet of ketchup between her teeth, trying to open it.

Prudence heard Mrs. Moberly before she saw her. She entered the kitchen with a quick, sharp breath that had some voice in it. "Where did you find that?" Mrs. Moberly said, staring at Prudence's chest, then at the long skirt.

"You said we could use anything," Prudence said. "You said help yourself."

"Belinda never wore that," Mrs. Moberly said, shaking her head. "We put our foot down on that one."

"We're biblical characters," Prudence said. "You said to come as a biblical character."

"I had a bad feeling about this," said Mrs. Moberly. She turned to Mrs. Spode. "I knew I should have checked to see what they came up with. Reverend Boyd's preoccupied with his wife sick."

"She's not sick," Prudence said.

Mrs. Moberly opened her mouth, then looked at Mrs. Spode, then closed it again.

"She's not," Prudence explained to Mrs. Spode. "She's very tired and needs her rest."

"She's got a little bug," Mrs. Moberly explained.

"Well, there's something going around," said Mrs. Spode.

"She's not sick," Prudence said again. "She's not sick, she's not sick." She heard herself speaking over and over, but she couldn't stop, and she couldn't seem to say anything else. She clamped her mouth tightly closed, because she thought her voice might be starting to sound like tears.

Mrs. Spode squeezed Prudence's shoulder. "Look, Mary Anne, I was telling Prudence here that they could put on choir robes — you know those pretty gold ones? — and go as angels. We could even tape on some paper wings, or make halos or something."

"I think it's a little late to construct anything fancy," Mrs. Moberly said.

Grace's ketchup packet came open and she held it between her teeth, squeezing with her lips so that the ketchup dribbled down her chin and collected in a soft gob on the platter in front of her face. From there it began a slow, red slide toward the edge.

Mrs. Spode opened the kitchen door to check on the show. The children were restless. Noah kicked the donkey, and one of the Marys had stuck the head of a baby Jesus under her robe to nurse. "Looks like I'm needed in there," she said to Mrs. Moberly. "Those gold robes are in the closet of the upstairs practice room."

When Mrs. Spode had gone, Mrs. Moberly turned to Prudence and didn't even try to smile. "You two shed these getups right now," she said, "and then you stay put and be ready when I come back, hear? I don't want to have to go back and tell your parents you didn't get to be in the show. I don't want to have to explain why."

Prudence kept her mouth tightly closed. She stared into the air just over Mrs. Moberly's head, and soon Mrs. Moberly was gone. As her footsteps faded up the back stairs off the kitchen, Prudence and Grace were sneaking past the fellowship room, headed down the hall the way they'd come in.

Prudence quickly turned off the wide main hall straight into one of the narrow dark halls of Sunday school rooms. They made two more turns until it was so dark that Prudence couldn't even see her hand in front of her. The basement went on and on. She remembered a story she heard once, about a maze so confusing that once inside you could turn down every single path you could find and never get it right. You could just keep trying out different turns until you died of hunger, or until whatever kind of animal or monster it was they'd put in the maze to go after you got to you.

The wooden beads on her halter made their small noises against one another, and Prudence wrapped her arms around her middle to still them. She was having a hard time breathing in her regular way.

"Prudence," Grace whispered. "Where are you?" Grace's platter bumped against the wall with a dull scraping.

"Here." Prudence stopped and Grace ran into her; Prudence felt ketchup, wet and sticky on her bare back.

Then Prudence could see her hand again, just barely, because down one of the hallways a light glowed through the long window above a doorknob. Prudence moved toward the light.

"I hear singing," Grace said.

"Shhhh," said Prudence, but she could hear it, too. It sounded like five or six people, and Prudence crept toward the door and peered through the bottom of the narrow window.

A small, thin boy with his arm in a cast sat in a Sunday school chair, his eyes closed. Two men and one woman had their hands on the boy's neck and head. The woman was crying and trying to sing at the same time. They were singing that song about the lovely feet of the mountains that bring good news, which had never made any real sense to Prudence. On the floor were two mattresses made up with sheets and blankets.

"Let *me* see," Grace said, but Prudence ignored her. She pressed her forehead against the glass.

"It's no big deal," she whispered after a time. "It's just people standing around a boy. They're laying hands." She knew all about laying hands — sometimes her parents touched people while praying for them so the Holy Spirit could move.

Another man and woman had placed their hands on the backs of the people touching the boy's neck. They all closed their eyes and sang the first verse of "Holy, Holy, Holy," swaying to the words. The man standing behind the boy began speaking over the singing, but it was hard to make out the words through the door. The boy had opened his eyes and was blinking quickly. The fingers of his good arm fretted at the soft, worn edge of his cast.

"Who are you?" the man said now, loud and deep, clear enough for Prudence to hear. She could feel his voice on the door.

"Help him, Lord," said another man.

"Yes, Lord," said a woman.

The first man gripped the boy's shoulder. "Who are you?" he asked again, and the boy moved his mouth, but Prudence couldn't hear.

"That's Anna's dad talking," Grace whispered, wedging her face beside Prudence's.

"No," said the man. The singing was over, and his voice was as clear as day. "No. I am not speaking to Ryan, but to the evil within."

Prudence thought the group looked too ordinary to be casting out a demon. The men were in plain old slacks and jeans, and one of the women wore sneakers with her skirt. Under the fluorescent lights their faces loomed pale and big. Even with their eyes closed they squinted, as if they were all trying very hard to remember something.

"It's no big deal," Prudence said again, but she couldn't stop watching.

Anna's dad looked up to the ceiling and started to pray. He said how Ryan was not in control of his body. He said the forces of darkness had taken advantage of this little boy's weakness, and an evil spirit had manifested itself in Ryan's behavior. He said it was a cowardly thing to use a little boy, but that was the kind of method Satan stooped to. He might look like this little boy and sound like this little boy, but indeed he was something very different, something that really wanted only to destroy Ryan. *Impostor,* Anna's dad said, and Prudence felt the word in her stomach.

Prudence pushed Grace away and covered the whole bottom of the window with her face and arms, filling up the glass so her sister couldn't see. She didn't know what was going to happen, and Grace sometimes scared easily.

One of the men began to raise his hand over his head, the movement so slow that the hand looked as if it were floating. He turned his face to the ceiling. "Ruler of all," he said when Anna's dad paused. "You triumph over evil."

Ryan began shaking all over. The woman in sneakers opened her eyes.

"The New Testament tells us we have been given the power," Anna's dad began again, and Ryan started to cry. He scrunched his face up tiny, whimpering. With his free arm he brought his hand to his shoulder and tried to pick off the fingers that clutched him.

"Please," said the woman in sneakers. "He's upset." She moved her thumb back and forth in the boy's hair.

"It's not him," Anna's dad said. From above and behind Ryan, he placed his palms on the boy's cheek. Ryan jerked his head from side to side, but the hands were firm. "What's being upset are the forces of darkness. Just hold him steady."

The woman in sneakers sniffled and shook her head. Prudence kept her eyes on Ryan Kitter.

"In the name of Jesus Christ," said Anna's dad, "I command you to exit this earthly vessel." The sound of his voice resounded off the cement-block walls even after he closed his mouth.

Prudence held her breath, watching for something to leave Ryan's body. He went so still she thought maybe he'd fainted. Anna's dad loosened his grip on the boy's face. Suddenly Ryan lurched to his feet, yanking his shoulders back and forth to shake off the hands and upending his chair, which skidded across the room on its side. The woman in sneakers cried out, "Ryan," and a man said, "Oh," in a soft, surprised way, but nobody moved. They seemed frozen, their hands still outstretched, now hovering over nothing, while the boy made for the door.

Prudence grabbed Grace and pulled her into the back hall and around a corner. The first room they came to was locked, but the door to the second one opened, and they crouched just inside, listening hard. A moment later Ryan pushed through and slammed the door shut, darting into the far corner of the room. The windows near the ceiling gave off a faint glow from the lights of the parking lot, and Prudence could just make out his dark shape against the wall. She listened to him breathing heavy through his nose, and when she heard more footsteps in the hall, she reached up and locked the door.

Then the boy was crying again, moaning softly.

Grace leaned in close to Prudence and clutched her arm as Prudence rose and made her way across the room through the dark, past tables and chairs and an upright piano. She reached out and touched the boy's head, and he scooted away. It sounded like he was saying "Oh no, oh no, oh no," over and over. Prudence had heard plenty of kids cry, but this seemed older, like the time she'd been dropped home early from school and found her mother sitting with her forehead on the kitchen table, sobbing, her arms dangling down by her chair.

"Don't be scared," Prudence said. "It's just me and my sister."

Someone jiggled the doorknob, then knocked on the narrow glass window. Prudence didn't turn around. A woman called Ryan's name, her voice muffled.

Ryan kept crying. Prudence's eyes adjusted, and she could see him huddled against the wall, hunched in on himself.

"Don't cry," Prudence said. "You shouldn't cry like that. You'll cry your eyes out." She was watching him very carefully. If there was such thing as demons, and they looked and sounded just like people, she wondered how you were supposed to know when one was gone.

"Ryan?" called the woman at the door, then her footsteps hurried away.

"Do you have a demon?" Grace asked. Her tinfoil platter glinted in the streetlight. The edge of it had bent over her shoulder on one side, and her face and neck were smeared with ketchup. The knife jutted out from her neck at a forty-five-degree angle.

Ryan looked up at her and sucked in a great, moaning sob.

Prudence knelt down beside him. "It's ketchup," she said. Then she thought that maybe they didn't have ketchup in Africa. "She's just dressed up," Prudence said. "She's John the Baptist." She told him all about John the Baptist and Salome, how the king liked Salome's dance so much that he promised her anything, and how Salome's mother, a spurned woman, had told her just what to ask for. When Prudence finished, she rose and stood in the light from the high window so the boy could see. He'd grown quieter, but when she stopped talking he started to cry again.

"Hey," Prudence said. "You just watch me. I didn't get to do my dance before. When Salome dances she gets whatever she wants, and I want you to stop crying." Prudence began humming a little tune. She started with just her hands and let the movement travel up her arms and into her shoulders, then down her whole body. The wooden beads slapped her stomach.

Ryan's mouth was open. He looked like a sad boy, sad in a part of him no one could touch. Prudence was thinking that it would be better if there *was* a demon than if there *wasn't*. That way something would be in him and then it would be gone, and he would be all right. She danced in and out of the light, and Ryan's crying grew softer. She hummed a little louder and danced some more, and soon she didn't hear him crying at all.

"It's working," Grace whispered.

There were footsteps again in the hall, and the faint jingle of keys. In a moment or two the lights would come on and Prudence knew she would be in *some kind* of trouble. They would be taken back to the Moberlys', where she would most likely be disciplined, and where her mother lay in the upstairs bedroom, her face to the wall, and there wasn't anything Prudence could do about it. But as

Prudence did a little boogie with her hips, she thought she heard Ryan giggle. Aunt Char had shown her some old-timey dances, and she did what she could remember of the twist, then she started in on the chicken, Ryan and Grace now laughing, laughing hard, gulping in air, their voices high and silly, and when the door opened and the lights came on Prudence closed her eyes and kept on dancing.

ANNIE PROULX

What Kind of Furniture
Would Jesus Pick?

FROM THE NEW YORKER

BUDGEL WOLFSCALE, a telegraph clerk from Missouri on his way
to Montana to search for the yellow metal, stopped at a Wyoming
road ranch one day in 1898 for a supper of fried venison and coffee, heard there was good range. For the next week he rode around
the country, finally staked a homestead claim on a spread east of
the Big Horns which had been cut from the holdings of a Scots
outfit that pulled out the year before.

A year-round stream, Bull Jump Creek, cut the property, fringed
by cottonwoods and willows, the shining maroon branches of water
birch. It was still open country, though barbed wire was coming in
with the nesters. He built a shotgun cabin of hauled-out lodgepole,
married one of the girls from a whorehouse in Ham's Fork, and,
naming the ranch after the harp his mother had played, thought
himself a Wyoming rancher. He wasn't that, but his sons and grandsons were.

The Harp skidded down the generations to Gilbert Wolfscale,
born on the ranch in 1945, and in middle age still living a son's life
with his mother in the old house, which had been gradually enlarged with telescoped additions until the structure resembled a
giant spyglass built of logs. He ran a cow-calf operation, usually
worked the place alone, for even inept help was hard to find. He
was a tall man with heavy bones. His coarse skin seemed made of
old leather upholstery, and, instead of lips, a small seam opened
and disclosed his cement-colored teeth. There were no horses that

could match his stamina. Despite his muscle mass he moved with fluid quickness. He surrounded himself with an atmosphere of affronted hostility, but balanced it with a wild and boisterous laugh that erupted at inappropriate times.

The old world was gone, he knew that. For some reason, a day in the 1950s when all the ranchers and their hands had worked on the road rose often in his mind and with such vividness that he could smell the mud, the mineral odor of wet rock. He had been eight years old. It was the last rainy spring before that decade's drought sucked the marrow out of the state. The county road that ran between Kingring and Sheridan passed through seven ranches over a fifty-mile stretch. Under heavy melt from the mountains, it became an impassable sump of greasy mud and standing water. The county had no money. If the ranchers wanted to get to town they would have to fix the road themselves or wait until it dried. On a drizzling morning in April his father drank his coffee standing up.

"What say, Gib? Want to come along?"

They rode together on Butch, his father's roan saddle mount. The rain had stopped, but heavy clouds moved with the bumping wind. Gilbert clutched the lard pail that held their lunch. They came to a place where men with shovels were strung out along the road. There was a section of an old corral still standing near the road and here men had leaned their tools, lunch pails, and bottles. A few had thrown their jackets on the ground. His father tethered Butch to a post.

While the men cleaned the borrow ditches and culverts, cut new drainage channels, built water bars, and hauled gravel, Gilbert hacked manfully at the mud with a broken hoe, but when Old Man Bunner told him to get out of his way or he'd chop off his legs, he went to the weathered corral to play with sticks and rocks. He built a play corral of mud and broken miner's candle stems, and placed inside it the rocks that were his horses. The wind cleared out the weather and by noon there was broken blue sky.

"Warmin up," called one of the men, stretching his back. The sun shone behind his ears, which turned the color of chokecherry jelly.

The lunch of cold pork and boiled eggs seemed the best thing

Gilbert had ever eaten. There were two squares of his mother's coarse white cake with peanut butter icing at the bottom of the pail. His father said Gilbert could have both pieces. He fell asleep on the way home, rocked by Butch's easy walk. His mother groaned with rage when she saw the mud on his clothes. The next morning his father went to work on the road without him and he cried until his mother slapped him. The work went on for a week, and when it ended a truck could get over the road. The first time they drove past the place he looked for his play corral. He could see one miner's candle stem. The rest had blown away. The rock horses were still there. Fifty years later the road was graveled and graded by the county, but he still looked when he drove past the place, the old corral now nothing but a single post. The prairie had swallowed his horse rocks.

After Gilbert Wolfscale inherited the ranch, he enlarged the two irrigated alfalfa fields, which made it possible, in bad years, to feed the cattle through the winter and, in good years, to sell hay to less fortunate outfits. These two fields kept the ledger ink black. He came up with other ideas to increase income. He thought of butchering and packing the beef himself to bypass the middlemen who took the money while the rancher did the work, but the local stores preferred to stay with the chain suppliers. So he put an ad in the paper looking for customers and found half a dozen, but they didn't eat enough beef to make the venture pay and a woman from town complained that there were bone splinters in the ground beef. He raised turkeys, thinking surefire Thanksgiving and Christmas markets, but never sold very many, even when he put strings of cranberries around their necks. His mother spent days making the cranberry necklaces, but people wanted the plastic-wrapped, prebasted Safeway turkeys with breasts like Las Vegas strippers. He and his mother ate the turkeys themselves, his mother canning most of the meat. By spring, they were sick of the smell of turkey soup.

Some of the original chock-and-log fence — built not of split rails nor slender poles but big logs — stood in the high pastures nearest the forest, but much had been replaced with five-strand barbed wire. He could almost see the ground compressing under the heavy log weight. How many men had helped his grandfather

build that fence of tree trunks? Gilbert put in his time working on
the barbed fences, which no longer had the tensile strength of
fresh wire but were patched and mended with short lengths of various gauge. In an earlier decade, struggling to finish the job on a
hot afternoon, he had cast about for a stick or something to twist
tight a diagonal cross-brace wire, but the only thing at hand was a
cow's bleached leg bone with its trochlea head, which seemed
made to jam fence wire tight. It worked so well that he collected
and used cow bones in dozens of places. These bony fences and
the coyote skulls nailed to the corner posts gave the Harp a murderous air.

He was a model of rancher stubbornness, savagely possessive of
his property. He did everything in an odd, deliberate way, Gilbert
Wolfscale's way, and never retreated once he had taken a position.
Neighbors said he was self-reliant, but there was a way they said it
that meant something else.

Seven miles north of the Harp on the Stump Hole Road lived May
and Jim Codenhead. Gilbert had gone to grade school with May —
she was then May Alwen. May's brother, Sedley Alwen, a big, good-
natured kid with stringy arms, had been Gilbert's best friend. Gilbert had courted May for a year, taken it for granted that Sedley
would be his brother-in-law, but she'd strung him along and then,
in a sudden move on Christmas Day in 1966, married Jim Codenhead. Jim then was nothing more than an illiterate Montana hand
working on the Alwen place.

May taught him to read until he could fumble through the newspaper.

"That's the shits, man," said Sedley sympathetically and took
Gilbert on a two-day drunk, as much a salute to his draft notice as
balm for Gilbert's disappointment.

The marriage wasn't unprecedented. For those who took the
long view and had patience it was the classic route for a lowly cow-
hand to own his own spread — marry the rancher's daughter. In
retaliation Gilbert went to a New Year's dance in Sheridan, found
Suzzy New, and in ten days pressured her into a fast marriage.

Suzzy New was slender and small-boned, with something French
about her child-sized wrists, a contrast to Gilbert, six feet four, bull-
necked with heavy shoulders. She was nimble-fingered and a tal-

ented embroiderer. In the flush of their first months together Gilbert bragged that she was so handy she could make a pair of chaps for a hummingbird. She was quiet, disliked arguments and shouting, the only child of elderly parents. She held herself tensely and had a way of retreating into her thoughts. She believed herself to be a very private person. She slept badly, sensitive to the slightest abnormal sound — the creak of a house timber, the rising wind, a raccoon forcing its way through the skirting of the house and under the kitchen floorboards. She had let herself be bullied into marrying Gilbert, and within days of the ruinous act she bitterly regretted it.

All her life she had heard and felt the Wyoming wind and took it for granted. There had even been a day when she was a young girl standing by the road waiting for the schoolbus when a spring wind, fresh and warm and perfumed with pine resin, had caused a bolt of wild happiness to surge through her, its liveliness promising glinting chances. But out at the ranch it was different. The house lay directly in line with a gap in the encircling hills to the northwest, and through this notch the prevailing wind poured, falling on the house with ferocity. The house shuddered as the wind punched it and slid along its sides like a released torrent from a broken dam. Week after week in winter it sank and rose, attacked and feinted. When she put her head down and went out to the truck it yanked at her clothing, shot up her sleeves, whisked her hair into a raveled fright wig. Gilbert seemed not to notice, but then, she thought, he probably regarded it as *his* wind, and no doubt took pleasure in such a powerful possession.

Sedley went to Vietnam. Gilbert, who had a growth inside his nose, was 4-F despite his strength and muscle. Sedley was captured by the Vietcong and spent several years in a bamboo cage. He came back a different person, crisscrossed with sudden rages brought on by inconsequential events such as the rattle of dishes or a truck crossing the bridge. He was thought to be unstable and in need of watchful care. He moved in with May and Jim. May could calm Sedley down when he was having one of his fits. She had always been close to him, had, from the time she was a small child with nightmares, padded down the hall to his moonless north room, climbed into his bed for warmth and protection. The infant she bore six months after she married Jim Codenhead might have been her brother's child or, for that matter, Gilbert Wolfscale's, or even Jim Codenhead's. For years, whenever Gilbert was at their house, he studied the child, Patty, trying to work out whom she resembled. He could come to no conclusion.

Vietnam nightmares tortured Sedley Alwen. Sometimes, to give May a break, Gilbert made the long drive to Cheyenne, taking Sedley to the Veterans Administration hospital, where he saw the shrink and got his prescriptions renewed. It was a two-day trip and they stayed at a motel overnight, sharing a room. After the session Sedley would be talkative. Gilbert listened attentively to his stories of torture and comrades' deaths. It was at these times that Sedley resembled the friend of his childhood, excited and eager. But he could not have whiskey. They tried it once and found out. Whiskey made him act up, smashing the motel furniture and howling at the light fixture in the ceiling.

By 1999 Gilbert was fifty-four and caught in the downward ranching spiral of too much work, not enough money, drought. It got drier and drier, grasshoppers appearing as early as April and promising a plague in August. The grass crackled like eggshells under his feet. There was no color in the landscape, the alkali dust muting sage, stones, the earth itself. When a vehicle passed along the road a fine cloud spread out and slowly settled. The air was baked of scent except for the chalky dust. He was conscious of how many things could go wrong, of how poorly he'd reckoned the ranch's problems.

To the new-moneyed suitcase ranchers who had moved in all around him — ex-California real-estate agents, fabulous doctors, and retired cola executives — the Harp looked like a skanky rundown outfit. They noticed the yard littered with stacks of rusted sheet metal held down by railroad ties, a pile of crooked fence posts inhabited by chipmunks, the long string of log additions to the old house. Some of these rich people, heated with land fever and the thought of a bargain, came to Gilbert and offered to buy his ranch. He could see in their eyes how they planned to bulldoze the house and build mansions with guest cottages.

"Them rich pricks are lower than a snake's ass in a wagon track," he said to his mother. "I told him my granddad homesteaded this place and if I ever seen his California butt on my property again I'd shoot it off. I looked him right in the eye and he got the message. He turned color so fast he farted."

His mother produced her hard little laugh.

It had always been dry country and no one born there expected more than a foot of rainfall in a good year. The drought halved that and he could see the metamorphosis of grazing land into desert. The country wanted to turn to sand dunes and rattlesnakes, wanted to scrape off its human ticks. Gilbert didn't have enough hay to feed his own stock. Everything told him that the day of the rancher was fading, but he dodged admitting it. He blamed the government, he blamed Salt Lake City. The damn Mormons, he said, had seeded the clouds for the Olympics, sucking out all the snow moisture before it reached Wyoming. The ranch-house well was eleven hundred feet deep and the water brackish. In the drought years of the 1930s and again in the 1950s his father had put in earthen dams and stock ponds, and in wet years they had held water but were now silted up and dried and stood as unsightly pits filled with weeds. In the center of one dry hole he piled an immense stack of brush, adding more every year, intending to burn it with the first good snow.

He was pestered. Some newcomer wanted a shortcut easement through the ranch to his million-dollar luxury house on the other side. A long-nosed Game and Fish biologist nagged him about fences that blocked the passage of pronghorn. Hunters wanted to shoot his deer. A busybody woman straight out of agricultural school came from the Extension Service one day and lectured him about protecting stream banks from cow-hoof erosion, about pasture rotation to prevent overgrazing.

"I heard all that shit. But I'll tell you what. I let the cows graze where they want and drink where they will. Been doin this for a while. Guess I know somethin about it." He stood in a truculent posture, legs apart, chin thrust forward. The woman shrugged and left.

His wife, Suzzy, had left him to live in Sheridan, sixty miles distant, in the spring of 1977, when the two boys, Monty and Rod, were still young. Those boys were doomed, said Gilbert, smacking his hand on the table for emphasis, to grow up without a father's guidance and example, injured because they were denied a boy's life on the ranch.

"If he wants a see the kids, why can't he just come into town?" Suzzy said to her mother on the phone after the split. Her complaining voice rose, dipped. "You know I put in years on that ranch, and nothin really worked right. Half the time there wasn't water and when there was water it was nasty. We couldn't get in or out in the winter. No telephone, no electricity, no neighbors, his mother always naggin, and the *work*! He wore me down. 'Do this, do that,' bullyin ways. Keep that old house clean? Couldn't be done. He could a sold the place fifty times over and lived decent if he got a job like a normal human bein, but would he? No. I wouldn't relive those years for nothin." Once she had made up her mind to leave, her own stubbornness emerged. But Gilbert refused to agree to a divorce and the separation and enmity dragged on.

In town she got a cash-register job at the Big Billy supermarket, and as soon as the two boys were old enough to run errands and deliver papers she made them get after-school and weekend jobs as well. She wanted to show them there were better things than cows and debt.

The Big Billy job was no good. Not only was the pay low, but she disliked having to repeat "Have a nice day" to people who deserved to be ridden bareback by the devil wearing can openers for spurs, and one day she quit to take a job as a filing clerk in the county treasurer's office. It graveled Gilbert that she handled his property-tax and vehicle-registration papers.

She wore him down on the divorce and he gave up after a fight in town in her new house. She had bought an old brick mansion with big trees in the yard and an ornamental iron fence around it. In the 1880s the house had belonged to a Chicago merchant who used it two or three times a year to oversee his ranch investments. Gilbert did not understand how she could afford this house. They had argued, then screamed. Gilbert stood with his legs apart and his arms hanging loose. Another man would have recognized this as a bad sign, but she could not stop blaming him, and he, goaded to violence, slapped her a good one, and she came at him and yanked out a clump of his hair in the front where it would show, ran to the back of the house, and called the sheriff. When the law came she accused Gilbert of assault, showing the red mark on her cheek as proof.

"What about *this?*" shouted Gilbert, pointing to his bleeding scalp, but Sheriff Brant Smich, his second cousin, ignored him. When the divorce finally came through it was settled that if he wanted the boys to help out on the ranch for a weekend he would have to drive in and fetch them and he would have to pay them for their labor. He had paid practically nothing for child support during the long separation, she said, it was the least he could do. He protested, said he had canceled checks to prove he had certainly paid adequate if not luxurious support.

"Take it to court," she said, "you think you been treated so bad."

Neither of the boys came willingly to the ranch. They appeared only in times of crisis after Gilbert telephoned Suzzy, demanding their help — spring branding, fence work. They let themselves be dragged out for a weekend then, sulky and grudging. They sassed their grandmother and whispered and snickered when they saw cows bulling. A day's work was not in them. They wanted only to ride the horses. It was clear to Gilbert that at his death they would sell the place as fast as they could. One day someone would find his stiff corpse out in the pasture, the wire cutters in his hand, or they would find him fallen in the muddy irrigation ditch, as he had found his own father. He would never be able to pass on to them how he felt about the land.

His allegiance to the place was not much of a secret, for even outsiders perceived his scalding passion for the ranch. His possessive gaze fell on the pale teeth of distant mountains, on the gullies and washes, the long draw shedding Indian scrapers and arrowheads. His feeling for the ranch was the strongest emotion that had ever moved him, a strangling love tattooed on his heart. It was his. It was as if he had drunk from some magic goblet full of the elixir of ownership. And although the margins of Bull Jump Creek had been trampled bare and muddy by generations of cows, although there were only one or two places along it still flushed with green willow, the destruction had happened so gradually that he had not noticed, for he thought of the ranch as timeless and unchanging in its beauty. It needed only young men to put it right. So his thoughts turned again and again on ways to get his sons to see and love the ranch.

In 1982, Monty was fourteen and Rod two years younger. Gilbert, waiting in the truck in front of Suzzy's house, heard Monty inside bellowing at his mother in his cracking voice, "I don't want a go. It stinks out there, there's nothin a do," and he could not dodge the fact that his sons hated the ranch. In a desperate attempt to make the place more attractive to them he had the power company run out poles and wires, a terrible expense and useless, too, as the boys came no more often. The only benefit, if benefit it was, was the small television set he bought and put in the living room, where he would lie on the sofa under one of his mother's quilts and watch men wrestling anacondas, riding motorcycles inside enormous wooden barrels. His mother liked the television, but claimed to be shocked by much of what she saw.

"It is company, I'll say that, but where they find them fool people to cut up so I don't know."

He wasn't lonely. There was his mother, he was a church deacon, a member of the Cattlemen's Association, he went to his neighbors' potluck suppers and barbecues, and about once a month drove to town and got half-drunk, bought a woman, and made it back to the ranch before the old haymaker cleared the horizon. He was not a veteran but he knew all the local veterans and often went to the V.F.W. with them to drink and listen to Vietnam stories.

He had always taken an interest in Vietnam. He wondered what it was about combat that so changed men, for all of those who had been in school with him, the ones who came back were marked by what they had seen and endured. He knew them and he didn't know them. Sedley came back angry and crazy, Russ Fleshman returned as a windbag, Pete Kitchen was reclusive and lived in a horse trailer at the back of the old Kitchen ranch. Something had gone wrong for Willis McNitt, leaving him dead-voiced and troubled. They all referred emotionally to the war, now so many years past, and Fleshman sometimes put his face in his hands and cried. And there were the ones who didn't come back: Todd Likwartz, Howard Marr, and several he hadn't known. When Gilbert thought of them a phrase came into his mind — "Now they know what Rhamses knows." His mother belonged to the generation that had memorized poems in school, and one, "Little Mattie," on the death of a thirteen-year-old girl, had fastened itself relentlessly in her recall with the tolling line "Now she knows what Rhamses knows."

She quoted from it throughout her life and still sometimes treated her son to a recitation of the entire piece with the stilted emphasis learned so long ago in a little Wyoming schoolhouse.

Gilbert Wolfscale listened to the veterans. He wanted to understand what he had missed. It had been the great experience of the time of his young manhood and he had been absent. It was as though the veterans had learned a different language, he thought, listening to Fleshman's scattershot of *didi mau,* Agent Orange, *beaucoup,* Jodies, 105s, Willy-Petes, and K-Bars. He caught at the names — Phu Bai, Khe Sanh, Quang Tri — wondering if these were the Vietnamese equivalents of Rawlins or Thermopolis. The veterans did not seem so much tragic victims as eccentric members of a select club. He felt himself an outsider. They had got the edge on him.

One year, Willis McNitt sat behind him at the August rodeo. It was the hottest summer he had ever known. The horses were blowing and their coats were white with salty sweat, the bulls stood in the chutes with their heads down and bucked feebly. There had been a freak accident at the stock pens. The rodeo grounds were old, put up in the 1930s, all wood fence and posts, and somehow a kid watering the roping calves had fallen or been knocked down and mashed his face against a splintery post. A long sliver had run into the flesh below his eyebrow and he had stumbled away from the pens, blood coursing down the back of his hand, which he had put instinctively to the wound. He had not cried out, just stumbled into sight with blood seeping between his fingers, making the crowd gasp. As the ambulance bore him away, Gilbert said to no one in particular, "They ought a tear out them damn old wood posts and get good metal."

"I seen somethin like that in Nam," said Willis behind him in his flat, heavy voice. Willis had a son at the university, studying anthropology. The kid — Coot McNitt — had a half-baked theory that rice cultivation had developed to replace a shortage of maggots in early man's diet. If you listened to him long enough he'd make you believe it. "We was in a free-fire zone and the kid next a me got shot in the eye. He said, 'I been shot in the eye,' said it five or six times, real quiet, like he couldn't quite take it in. Couldn't believe it. Then he laid down beside me and commenced a kick and thrash and ever time he kicked the blood pumped up through his eye like a school water fountain."

"God," said Gilbert. "Did he — ?"

"Died. A kid, eighteen years old, younger'n Coot. Couldn't believe he'd been shot. I was nineteen, but after that I felt like a old
man."

"You ain't old, Willis. Hell, you're my age."

"Yeah."

The word dropped like a stone.

One day, Gilbert Wolfscale's mother opened an official-looking letter from the California State Allocation Department. She read that
she had inherited a sum of money from someone in that state. All
she had to do was fill out the enclosed form, mail it back, and in six
or eight weeks she would receive the inheritance. She spent two
hours filling out the form, with its demands for address, Social Security number, date of birth, bank account numbers, and other tedious details. She sat so long at the table with this form that her left
leg went to sleep and when she got up to go to the kitchen and
make a cup of tea it buckled. She fell and broke her hip.

She recuperated very slowly. Even after the break had healed,
Gilbert had to drive her in to Sheridan for weekly therapy. He
sometimes wondered why she didn't get one of her friends to drive
her. She was always on the phone gabbing with her cronies and
most of them still drove. He heard her talking with them about
football, which she watched avidly on the television.

"I'm for them Bears. I couldn't never be for them Packers."

When he asked her why she did not arrange a trip to town with
Luce or Florence or Helen she said, "They're not family. Suppose
the doctor was to give me bad news. I'd want a be with blood kin,
not some other person."

While she was in with the therapist Gilbert walked around the
windy town streets rather than sit in a plastic chair in the stuffy waiting room. In a music store he looked at CDs, wondering at the pro-
liferation of bands with trendy, foolish names. Behind a stiff plastic
divider labeled MISCELLANEOUS he found birdcalls, tap dancing,
the whistles of steam locomotives from around the world. The last
CD was "Remembering Vietnam." The cover showed a grimy infan-
tryman staring up at a helicopter. The back copy listed "Firefight,"
"Shrapnel," "ARVN," "Jungle Patrol," "Rain," "APC Convoy." He
bought it.

In the truck driving home his mother said, "I don't have to go back there but a few more times, looks like, and thanks to heaven. Some a the strangest people settin in that waitin room. These two women got talkin about their Bible class. Sounded pretty modern, you know, tryin a link the Bible to nowadays. But this Bible class *they* went to was tryin a guess how it would be if Jesus showed up in Sheridan. That got them all excited and there they set, what would He do for work. They both said He could easy find a job workin construction. Would He have His own house and would it be like a trailer or a regular house or a apartment? Then they got at the furniture, what kind a furniture would Jesus pick for his place. And you know how you get thinkin about things you overhear? Wasn't none a my business, but there I set, crazy as they was, wonderin if He'd pick out a maple rockin chair or a sofa with that Scotchgard fabric or what."

A month before her fall his mother had bought some bright-colored kitchen sponges. One of them was purple and she had developed an affection for it, never using it on greasy pots or to wipe up nasty spills. He dribbled coffee on the counter one morning and began to mop at the spill with the distinguished sponge.

"What are you doin! Don't use that — take the pink one. You dunderhead, I'm savin that one."

"For what, Ma?"

"For the good glasses." She meant the crystal wineglasses with the gold rims that had been passed down from Granny Webb and had stood inverted in the china cupboard for as long as he could remember. He had never known them to be used. Inside the china cupboard next to the glasses was a photograph of his father's mother in a black silk twill dress, looking freeze-dried and mournful.

"Where is that stupid mailman?" his mother said, pulling back the curtain and looking for the plume of dust along the road.

It was days before he had a chance to listen to the CD. He was on his way to the bank. The soul of leaf susurration, cicadas, crickets, mortars, a calling bird with a voice like a kid hooting down a cardboard tube, snatches of talk, incoming fire, deafening helicopter fibrillation, filled the truck.

Saturday was grocery day, but his mother said, "I don't feel up to it. You just get what we need, bread and eggs. Coffee. Whatever else you see that looks good. I don't have much appetite these days anyhow. And I want a wait for the mail. I'm expectin mail."

He bought the groceries and on the way out of town passed the library. Two miles beyond it he thought of books — books on Vietnam — and he turned around. He came away with three, all they had, read them in bed that night, and fell asleep with a book on his face. He awoke frightened and shouting, thinking something was smothering him. The exhaled moisture from his mouth had formed a round dimple in the page.

It was not long after this that his mother began to give way. She would look at him and say, "Where's Gilbert? Out playin, I bet. I want him to fill up that wood box." And later she would tell him, "You'll have to fend for yourself for supper. I can't cook without no wood." He felt a pang of guilt, for there had been many times when he was a boy that he had dodged the wood box. But she kept asking if the mail had come until Gilbert, exasperated, said, "You expectin a letter from the president or what?" She shook her head and said nothing.

In 1999, Gilbert's son Monty turned thirty-two, a big dark-haired fellow, still single, who worked as a roofer in Colorado. Gilbert hadn't seen him in years. Rod, the younger one, lived in Sheridan, a block away from his mother, worked in Buffalo in a video rental store. He was married and had two children, twin girls, whom Gilbert had seen only once and had never touched nor held. The little girls had never been to the ranch. The boy's wife, Debra, worked, too, answering the telephone at Equality Cowboy Travel. Gilbert sometimes dreamed that they would have more children — boys — and that these little grandsons would love the ranch, would grow up knowing what a beautiful place the Wolfscales owned. They would love it as he did and take it on when he went.

Gilbert's mother turned eighty-one. The purple sponge, though somewhat faded, was largely unchanged, not to be used. She took to rummaging through the desk looking for pencil and paper, settled on a little notebook, spiral-bound at the top and with lined paper. She spent hours at the kitchen table bent over this notebook, thinking, occasionally scrawling something down or erasing everything, tearing out the spoiled sheet and crumpling it.

"What are you writin, Ma? Your biography? Cowgirl poetry?"

"No," she said and put her arm around the notebook so he couldn't see it, like a child protecting a test paper from a cheating neighbor.

On a very cold March day he went into town to the ranch equipment center; the used aircraft tires he'd ordered for the bush hog were in. If the weather warmed up later in the week he'd work on pulling old sagebrush out of the three-mile pasture. In town the bank thermometer read minus two and a harsh wind made it seem like the freezing pits of hell. He ordered a pizza. Clouds were moving in as he drove back, eating the cheesy slices, and as he turned in to the ranch the first fine flakes fell through the air.

The house was silent. He thought his mother might be napping and went out to the shop, where he changed the bush hog's tires. The days were growing longer and he worked until twilight. Back in the house he was disturbed by the deep silence. Usually his mother watched crime programs on television at this hour. He went to her room and knocked on the door.

"Ma! Ma, you O.K.? I'm goin a start supper now." There was no answer. He opened the door and saw his mother would not again want any supper.

It was a shock to learn that her bank account was at flat zero. He couldn't understand what she had spent the money on. He remembered her telling him when she broke her hip that she had over six thousand dollars set aside for "*you* know." And he did know. For her funeral costs. He had to scratch to come up with the money for a decent coffin.

Cleaning out her room, he came across the spiral-bound notebook. It was filled with plaintive letters to the California State Allocation Department, asking when her inheritance would come. Folded in the front of the notebook was the original letter. He telephoned the number at the bottom of the page but got a message that the number had been disconnected. Gilbert began to guess there was some sort of scam. He called Sheriff Brant Smich, asked him if he knew anything about California State Allocation.

"Hell, yes. You get a letter from them sayin about you inherited some money and askin for your bank account numbers? Don't believe none of it. Don't answer them. Bring the letter to the post office. They're after that outfit for mail fraud."

With his mother gone, civilization began to fall away from him like feathers from a molting hen. In a matter of weeks he was eating straight from the frying pan.

As is usual in the ranch world, things went from bad to worse. The drought settled deeper, like a lamprey eel sucking at the region's vitals. He had half seen the scores of trucks emblazoned with CPC — Consolidated Petroleum Company — speeding along the dusty road for the past year, and knew that they were drilling for coal-bed methane on public land adjacent to his ranch. They pumped the saline wastewater laden with mineral toxins into huge containment pits. The water was no good, he knew that, and it seemed a terrible irony that in such arid country water could be worthless. He had always voted Republican and supported energy development as the best way to make jobs in the hinterland. But when the poison wastewater seeped from the containment pits into the groundwater, into Bull Jump Creek, into his alfalfa irrigation ditches, even into the household well water, he saw it was killing the ranch.

He fought back. Like other ranchers who once again felt betrayed by state and federal government, he wrote letters and went to meetings protesting coal-bed methane drilling and the hundreds of service roads and drill rigs and heavy trucks that were tearing up the country. The meetings were strange, for ecological conservationists and crusty ranchers came together in the same room, in agreement for once. He noted with satisfaction that the schoolteacher, Dan Moorhen, a bleeding-heart liberal ecology-minded freak, admitted that ranchers were the best defense against developers chopping up the land, that ranches and ranchers kept the Old West alive. When the gas company reps or politicians came, the meetings were rancorous and loud and at the end people signed petitions with such force their pens ripped the paper, but it all meant nothing. The drilling continued, the poison water seeped, the grass and sage and alfalfa died. All he could do was hang on to the place.

He was unprepared for the telephone call from a neighbor, Fran Bangharmer. It was the morning of the Fourth of July.

"Too bad about Suzzy, all that right on the front page, too."

"What do you mean?" he said. "What was on the front page?"

"Arrested for embezzlin. Monday's paper."

"What!"

Fran's voice was subtly triumphant, tinged with schadenfreude, but Gilbert barely listened, hung up as soon as he could and drove into town to find a three-day-old paper and read for himself that his ex-wife had, for years, been siphoning tax money into a private bank account by a complex series of computer sleights of hand he could not understand.

He went to the county jail and tried to see her but was turned away.

"She don't want to see you, Gib, and she's got that right."

Half of the stores in town were closed for the holiday. Already there were clusters of people along the sidewalk, although the parade didn't start until 1:00. In despair he drove down to Buffalo to the video store where Rod worked. It was open, the windows draped with red, white, and blue ribbons. A huge poster read: RO-DEO DAYS! JULY 4 TO 10!

He found his younger son stocking the shelves with gaudy boxes. As he stood behind him he noticed the son's thinning hair and felt the hot breath of passing time.

"Rod?" he said, and the young man turned around.

"Dad." They looked at each other and the son dropped his eyes. Gilbert could smell his son's after-shave lotion. He himself had never used the stuff in his life.

"I came to . . . I want to . . . Well. Your mother?"

"Yeah. Do you want a have lunch?"

"You mean dinner?"

The son flushed at the old-fashioned word. "Yeah. 'Dinner.' Go down the KFC and eat in the car."

"I come in the truck. Come on, let's go."

"I got a tell somebody I'm goin."

That's what it was like, thought Gilbert, working for somebody else. You had to tell him what you did or were going to do and he could say no.

He drove to the fast-food strip at the north end of town, shouted into the drive-through intercom. Sitting in the truck, the windows down and the hot sun burning their arms, they gnawed at the salty, overspiced chicken as huge crumbs fell. They both sucked on straws stuck into vanilla milk shakes.

"I tried a see her," said Gilbert. "She wouldn't see me."

"She's still pretty bitter, you know. Feels like her life was wasted, or at least some years of it. She's that way. She takes a position and that's it. You can't argue her out of nothin. She's stubborn."

"I know that pretty well. How's it affectin you that your mother is a crook and a jailbird?" He glanced sideways at Rod, seeing the pale, indoor complexion, the clerk's shirt with creases ironed into the sleeves. The boy had the heavy Wolfscale jaw and beaky nose.

"Hell, I don't know. I don't think of it that way. People look at me kind a funny, but they don't say nothin. Except Deb. She is gettin a lot a snide comment down at the travel agency. It's no fun for her. It's my girls I worry about, if some kid at school this fall is goin a taunt them."

"Kids got short memories. By the time school starts they won't recall it. What do you think they'll do to her?"

"Probly go pretty light. She's got a good lawyer. You know, she made restitution of about twelve grand. That'll count for a lot. They already got a lien on the house, repossessed her car. That's what she used the most a the money for, buy the house and fix it up. That house was everthing to her. She put in a swimmin pool two years ago."

"I used a wonder how she could afford it. And I heard a couple years ago that she went out to Las Vegas?" He couldn't believe he'd found a packet of salt beneath the flabby biscuit. Did anyone ever think their chicken not salty enough?

"It was a whole bunch a them that work at the county offices. They all went. She won four thousand bucks."

For some reason this remark incensed Gilbert. Rod said it with a tone of pride that his lying, cheating, stealing, double-dealing mother had won some money gambling. He changed the subject abruptly. "What do you hear from your brother?"

"Aw, he calls up now and then. We get together with him when we take Arlene down to Denver for her treatment. You know she's had that cancer. It's in remission now and you'd never know she'd been sick a day."

Gilbert did not know his granddaughter had been sick a day. He shuddered. In the distance he could hear a school marching band. Buffalo's parade was starting, or maybe just warming up.

"Is he still workin for that roofin contractor?"

"Well, no. He's workin in a restaurant. He's workin in a Jap restaurant. But he's healthy, thank God, considerin his — lifestyle."

"What does that mean, his 'lifestyle'?" Gilbert wiped his hands of the chicken, wadded the napkin, and thrust it into the grease-stained box.

"Well, he's — you know."

"I know what?"

"Dad, it's not up to me to say nothin about Monty." Rod was folding and crushing the box. He wiped his right hand on his pants leg.

"I ain't heard or seen him for quite a few years. Not likely to. Now what the hell is this about his 'lifestyle'?"

"For Christ sake, Dad. It's nothin. Just he's sort a — more — sophisticated. He likes a different kind a stuff than most people come from Wyomin."

"I hear you talkin but I don't know what you're sayin."

But he did. As a child Monty had hung around the kitchen and his mother constantly, and to get him to help with chores had been more labor than doing the jobs himself. That is, until Myrl Otter came to work on the ranch on weekends. Myrl was a big blond Scandinavian type, muscular and good-looking. The man's wife had her work cut out for her keeping an eye on him, as girls flirted with Myrl and he reciprocated willingly. After he came to work on the ranch Monty began to tag after the fellow like a yellow jacket after pears. Gilbert noticed, but as the boy was only seven or eight it seemed just a little kid's fancy, nothing much. Kids got attached to dogs and blankets and maybe even hired men. He thought nothing of it, and after a few months Myrl Otter, in the way of so many ranch hands, stopped showing up for work and Gilbert had forgotten him until now. The marching music, carried by the light wind, seemed nearer.

"I better get goin. Don't want a get tied up in that damn parade." He got out, threw his chicken box at the trash can. Rod, too, tossed his crumpled box, but it hit the side of the can and sprayed chicken bones.

"Forget it," said Gilbert. "They get paid a pick up."

He dropped Rod back at the video store and headed north, thinking to beat the parade by taking a side street, but he was too late. He stopped for a red light that wouldn't change, and the parade came surging around a corner, passing in front of him, and he had to wait. A section of the high school band straggled past, sweaty kids, many of them obese, their white marching trousers bunched at the crotch. He remembered schoolmates in his own childhood, skinny, quick ranch kids, no one fat and sweaty, Pete Kitchen looking like he was made of kindling wood and insulation wire, Willis McNitt small enough to shit behind a sagebrush and never be noticed.

Behind the band came two teenage boys dressed as Indians, breechclouts over swim trunks, a load of beads around their necks, black wigs with braids and feathers. One carried a bongo drum, striking it irregularly with his hand. Their skin had been darkened with some streaky substance. Then two men whom he recognized as Sheridan car mechanics slouched along in buckskin suits and fur hats, carrying antique flintlocks. One had a demijohn that he lifted to his lips every thirty seconds, crying "Yee-haw!" The other had a few shiny No. 2 traps over his shoulder. Gilbert could see the hardware store price tags on them. He knew he was going to get the whole hokey Wild West treatment before he could move.

Now came two horses, both bearing kids dressed as cowboys, in heavy woolly chaps, pearl-button western shirts, limp bandannas, big hats, and boots. Both twirled guns on their fingers, aiming at friends in the crowd. They were followed by a stock outlaw and a sheriff's posse, and behind them half the town's women and small children in pioneer regalia — long calico dresses, aprons and sunbonnets, big Nikes flashing incongruously with every step. One of these women was Patty Codenhead and for a moment he was startled at how much she looked like the photograph of his father's mother in the china cupboard. It was the costume, he thought. The parade came down to a few trick riders in neon satin, and Sedley Alwen, who, crazy or not, was in every public procession showing off his roping skills, stepping in and out of his fluid loops and somehow avoiding the horse manure that marked the path. The last of all was a CPC pickup, three hard-hatted methane-gas workers sitting in back smoking cigarettes and joking with each other. Now he could go.

He could go, but he found it difficult to step on the accelerator. The light turned green, red, then green again, yet he couldn't move until drivers behind him began to sound their horns. There had been something wrong with the parade, something seriously wrong, but he couldn't think what.

Driving through the open country on the way back, he forgot the parade and thought about Monty and what form his "sophistica-tion" might take, about his embezzling wife, the other son who had not bothered to tell him that his grandchild had cancer. He couldn't tell the size of things. He was very thirsty and blamed the salty chicken.

The buildings and traffic fell away and he was on the empty road, the dusty sage flying past, the white ground. The sky was a hard cheerful blue, empty but for a few torn contrails. Plastic bags im-paled on the barbed fences flapped in the hot wind. A small herd of pronghorn in the distance had their heads down. He saw his neighbor's cattle spread out on the parched land, and it came to him that there had been no ranchers in the parade — it was all pio-neers, outlaws, Indians, and gas.

He knew what kind of furniture Jesus would pick for his place in Wyoming. He would choose a few small pines in the National For-est, go there at night, fell and limb them, debark the sappy rind with a spud, exposing the pale, worm-tunneled wood, and from the timbers he would make the simplest round-legged furniture, every-thing pegged, no nails or screws.

He wished his mother were still alive. He'd say to her, "One thing sure. He wouldn't get hisself tangled up with no ranch." It didn't come close to saying what he meant but it was all he could do.

R. T. SMITH

Docent

FROM THE MISSOURI REVIEW

GOOD AFTERNOON, ladies and gentlemen from hither and yon, and welcome to the Lee Chapel on the campus of historic Washington and Lee University. My name is Sybil Mildred Clemm Legrand Pascal, and I will be your guide and compass on this dull, dark, and soundless day, as the poet says, in the autumn of the year. You can call me Miss Sibby, and in case you are wondering about my hooped dress of ebony, my weblike hairnet and calf-leather shoes, they are authentic to the period just following the War Between the States, and I will be happy to discuss the cut and fabric of my mourning clothing with any of you fashion-conscious ladies at the end of the tour — which by the way will be concluded in the passageway between the crypt and the museum proper. If anyone should need to avail themselves of the running-water facilities, I will indicate their location before you enter the basement displays; and please, all you gentlemen, remove your caps in the chapel, and also, ladies, kindly ask your little darlings to keep a hush on their voices as they would at any shrine. No camera flashes, please, in the General Lee alcove. No smoking, of course — a habit I deplore.

Now, I am sure you know a lot already, and I may cover ground you have heard before, but please respect those who enter this tour with an open heart, and I will periodically pause to entertain questions, though I do not personally see any reason why they would arise.

The Lee Chapel, before you, was completed with intricately milled brick in 1868 on a Victorian design during the General's tenure, but it wore no green gown of ivy to begin with; I myself adore the ivy and do not care for the decision to trim it back. At this time of the afternoon it turns the light attractively spectral, wouldn't you agree? And I do not believe ivy could rip the building down. The chapel itself, which has never been officially consecrated by a legitimate denomination, should not be confused with the Robert E. Lee Episcopal Church, which you can see, with the steeple facing Washington Street, at the end of the paved walk. I am told there are two Episcopal churches in the world which are not named for saints, but that is not one of them — which is told locally as a joke, if you think such things are funny.

If you look directly above to the bell tower, you will see the black face and white numbers of the timepiece, which with its chimes duplicates the Westminster Clock in London and is dedicated to the memory of Livingston Waddell Houston, a student drowned in the North River, though I do not recall when nor deem it important. The pendulum, of course, is invisible, as in all the best devices. The numerals, you will notice, are not normal American ones with curves and circles but the *I*s and *X*s and *V*s of Latin numbers, a language which was taught here to the young men from the beginning — and still is to some few, especially those who wish to stand for the bar. Did you know that the "Lex" in "Lexington" is Latin for "law"? I have heard, however, that the young ladies who have matriculated — let's see, it's been some dozen years now since that infliction — do not enroll in dead languages. They are here, no doubt, for progress, and do not have time for such niceties. If such a perspective keeps them provided for and protected, they truly have my envy. In just ten minutes the hour will strike, and we will hear the tintinnabulation of the bells. I love that sound and will not abide random chatter once it begins.

As we proceed through the front portals, you will see on either side caracole staircases with bentwood banisters, and we will file to the left, but mind you do not cross the velvet ropes to climb the steps because insurance issues must guide our path. We are entering a National Historic Landmark that is also a museum and a tomb, and especially in these troubled modern times, we must show the greatest respect. Perhaps we could say that the very existence of this edifice — which is, as I say, a National Historic Landmark — is one of the rare benefits of that old and storied war, but watch your step: we do not want to add you to the already lamentable casualty count.

As we enter the vestibule, please do us the kindness of signing our guest register, which bears the autographs of presidents and princes, as well as luminaries from Reynolds Price to Burt Reynolds, from Maya Lin, the memorial designer, to Rosalynn Carter, Woodrow Wilson, Bing Crosby, Vincent Price, and the Dalai Lama. Fifty thousand visitors annually, I believe, many of them repeaters, from far and away, devotees of Lee, people who love the Stars and Bars or have a morbid curiosity, I suppose, about the fall of the South. If you have a morbid curiosity about the fall of the South — which is not the same as a healthy historical interest — please save your comments for your own diaries and private conversations. One of my cardinal epigrams, a compilation of which I will pen myself someday under the title "Miss Sibby Says," is this: "History is not gossip; opinion is seldom truth."

I am sure many of you all know as much about General Lee as I do, but it may be that some of the information you know is false, so I will highlight only selected facts as we file through the antechamber and into what one is tempted to call "the sanctuary" but is actually only a multipurpose auditorium, though a splendid and clean one. You could eat off the floor. When the General, who was indeed a legend but hardly a myth, agreed to come here as president, right after the sorrows and fury of the war that rent our land in half and wasted a gallant generation, he did so because, as he said, Virginia now needs all her sons — though there were fewer than forty students enrolled at the time. This chamber will seat six hundred, so we know he had a vision. He was a military man with many projects and plans — "strategies" they call them — and I was once betrothed to just such a disciplined and tactical gentleman myself, but fate has denied me that marriage, among other joys. If you have been denied a significant portion of life's joys and your own prospects, you will indeed understand.

The school, of course, was then called Washington College and had been spared from Yankee fire in the end by that revered influence and the statue of dear George atop the cupola of the main building on the colonnade (which always sounds too much like "cannonade" to suit my ear). We all wish that our dear Virginia Military Academy had been similarly spared, but alas, invaders have their own designs. Many people, such as foragers and raiders, can come into a place as easily as into a person's life and leave matters far more damaged than they found them, for they have their own designs.

And please do not hesitate to touch the pews or try them out. If you'll kindly look at the wall to your left, you will see the engraved plaque testifying that the General, whom some students wanted to call President Lee — which you must admit has a nice ring to it — sat here during services, though he often napped, accustomed as he was to catching a few winks on campaign. A man who has marched and fought as a steady diet for years will find civilian life a difficult fit, and General Lee was no exception, though it was in his ancient blood, as genealogical experts have proved that he was descended from Robert the Bruce through the Spottiswoods, though far more honorable than one Spottiswood descendant, whom I knew all too well but whom discretion prevents me from calling by his sullied name.

I daresay some of you have served your states and countries and may have posed for portraits like the two flanking the memorial gate. On the left you see the father of our country depicted on the grounds of Mount Vernon, and you will no doubt note that the Virginia militia uniform he wears so handsomely looks English, complete with gorget and musket, for he fought for the German Hanover English kings against French and Indian savagery, though he would later alter his opinion of the French. You can see he is a young man, confident and noble, even a touch haughty, with marching orders in his pocket, and the sky behind him is overcast, as with both today's sky and the current political climate, but there is a ray of light unsuppressed, and we can all hope to witness that ourselves someday. This is not to say that every officer who encamps, lays siege, then suddenly debouches is acting on official orders, for some are not to be trusted.

Before we ascend the steps and cross the stage to examine the second but primary portrait, the image of the most trustworthy man imaginable, I should inform you that this chapel has been renovated and expanded on several occasions and was almost razed in 1919 by no less fifth-column a foe than its own president of the moment, who claimed it was a firetrap with a perilous heating system and a roof that leaked like a war-worn tent — though despite today's threatening weather, you should not be alarmed. He had designs of his own and wished to replace it with a huge Georgian structure, and his name was Smith, supposedly, but the Mary Custis Chapter of the United Daughters of the Confederacy, in which I am still proud to claim emerita membership, entered the fray, along with the Colonial Dames and the DAR, until the renovation party was vanquished, the field secured, and the site declared a shrine. My own relations were in the vanguard of this action, which may bring to your mind the question of my personal role as docent, which used to mean "professor," though I am surely not one of those types. A docent is a hostess, a volunteer, like so many of our martyred sons. I like to think of my function as an older sister who opens the door to hidden history. "Decent" is only one letter removed, and decency is what I strive for daily, despite personal disappointments. My own fiancé never felt such hospitality was a function an unattached lady should perform, but since his furtive departure, I have done what I please and have risen through the ranks of a somewhat special and discreet society called the Keepers of the Magnolia, who are dedicated to preservation of the past. In France the magnolia flowers are called *les fleurs du mal,* and we Keepers have appointed ourselves sentries against the invasion of evil revisionist history and the casting of shadows over past glories. The battalions of blasphemers come into my dreams, whenever I can manage to sleep — the unholy reunderstanders and conde-scenders, and they may wear the masks of scholars but are no better than carrion rats, their tails scratching the hardwood till I wake up mouthing a silent scream.

This space is now employed by the university for a variety of pro-grams and gatherings, since as I said it is not an actual church, and the atmosphere of holiness depends entirely upon who is present. And now you and I are here and can add our reverence to the gen-eral fund. In the past few months we have hosted six weddings (all of which I have attended in my docent attire), one tipsy Irish poet, our own famous alumnus Tom Wolfe the Younger dressed in a French vanilla ice cream suit and spats while speaking of the death of art. We have heard the angry opinions of Mr. Spike Lee (no rela-tion, of course), tapped our feet to an Armenian guitar band right after a forum on cultural diversity. We have been entertained by near president Al Gore, and just yesterday the community wit-nessed the famous celebrity Dr. Maya Angelou in a headdress like a parrot and with a mighty voice, but you no doubt are eager to get back to the more historical highlights of our tour.

Yes, Theodore Pine's portrait here is the original, and the fam-ily said it was lifelike and true to their father's features, perhaps around the time of the Wilderness, though it was painted thirty years after his death on that chilling and killing October day from what some say was a stroke, and if he was in fact the victim of foul play, as I myself have sometimes suspected, *no evidence has surfaced* in all this time, but he was a strong man and a good one, younger than I am now — not old enough to succumb easily to the natural shocks that flesh is heir to. He used no spirits or nicotine and had always displayed a flirtatious vigor, though Mary Chesnutt's diaries remark that he was "so cold and quiet and grand" as a young man. No doubt he felt already the inconvenient weight of destiny, and she, as I remember, was blind to some species of charm. Yet if he was in fact the subject of knavery, *no verifiable evidence has ever surfaced*, though there was no official investigation — which should itself arouse our suspicions. We know the Northern press reviled him, and more than once public sentiment in the victorious states was roused toward trying him for treason and marching him straight to the gallows. So great a man cannot but beget enemies. I am certain you have known of plots yourself to undo the virtuous and lay waste to their peace of mind. Some men smile and smile and are villains, as the poet says. When the General breathed his last, the rain came down in torrents for days in a loud, tumultuous shouting sound, and flash floods were widespread and ruinous.

Few people are aware that the General's birthday, January 19, coincides with that of Edgar Allan Poe, who represents the dark side of our Virginia psyche. Fewer still realize that the General's extended family's loveliest estate was not Arlington, which was his wife's Custis dowry, but Ravensworth. If that connection is not enough to lend this chamber a chill, I ask you to imagine that perhaps Mr. Poe's "Annabel Lee" in fact concerns a young lady from a family the poet could only aspire to. The cosmic inequities of romance abound. A sad prospect, but we may only ponder it and move on.

Above the wrought-iron gate is the Lee family crest, with its Latin motto, *Ne incautus futuri,* which means "not without regard for the future," a valuable reminder to those who would dance light-hearted till dawn rather than consider the demands of the morrow. My favorite detail is the squirrel rampant and feeding above the argent helm, which reminds us of those animals' foraging and storage, their self-sufficient happy chatter and industry, though Lee himself in no way resembled vermin. He was five feet eleven and every inch a king.

The centerpiece, of course, here under the various regimental Stars and Bars, is this recumbent statue carved from a single block of Vermont marble by Edward Valentine — truly his name, according to sources, but deceit abounds. He was said to be from Richmond (where I came out as a debutante further back than any of you can possibly remember), and I believe it is the rival of any statuary in Italy, where I have always hoped someday to visit, though I was long ago disappointed in my best opportunity. And strong as the temptation may be, please do not touch the statue, for any mortal contact would mar the surface of the stone, which is like the magnolia blossom itself. Have you ever touched a petal and watched it rust before your eyes? Precious things are the most vulnerable, for the slightest blemish can destroy. Could that be why we are most devoted to what must perish? He looks, in this muted light, serene at last.

I would like to direct your attention to the texture Mr. Valentine's chisel has given the General's campaign blanket, the soft-leather look of his boots, the elegant beard, but please, I repeat, do not touch the statue, for the living hand with its native oils will soil this chiseled stone. Our touch could not now warm him, and see how at peace he appears, in complete repose? He is and is not at once a "touchstone," but if you bend your ear closely, you can almost hear the beating of his hidden heart.

Mrs. Lee instructed that her beloved be depicted napping before an engagement, sword at his side, gauntlets nearby. He is not to be considered dead, but only resting, and there are some who claim that he might yet rise, might return when the Commonwealth most needs him, though his actual remains are located in the crypt beneath the stairs. Doesn't that word *crypt* remind you of the writings of Mr. Poe? It means a "secret code." This chapel is, as you may have surmised, a structure with its own secrets.

Do you recall Mr. Disney's charming film *Snow White?* Since first I saw the princess in her trance I have thought of the General as someone under an enchantment, awaiting the right deliverer, but perhaps it is the trumpet of the Second Coming for which he waits. And no, I do not for a moment believe, as one rude visitor from Florida implied, that his effigy resembles a large salt lick, which animals might tongue down to nothing. The very suggestion disgusts me. He could never under any circumstances be nothing and was present even when not in attendance. Mrs. Lee was herself chair-bound and grew accustomed to his absence. She endured for three sad years of widow-weeping after his untimely passing but at last found the peace of oblivion. It is perhaps a peace we should not ourselves underestimate.

As you know, General Lee could never sleep in a bed after Appomattox, for he was haunted by the many gallant men he had led to the grave. In fact, who is to say that he ever truly left the war, as he wore his gray coat and campaign hat with a military cord until that October day when he succumbed. Considering his stern correctness and the martial bearing that he never abandoned, it would not surprise me if he did not sometimes see the students as his troopers and Lexington as beleaguered Richmond in miniature. He wore the dignity of conflict to the end. His last words were "Strike the tent."

Now, be careful as you descend the staircase. You will pass the vault itself, which is carved into the bowels of the earth like a dungeon, with its many Lees walled in, from the rogue Lighthorse Harry to his sons and grandsons, and you can see the diagram of his family tree with its fabled roots deep in the richest Virginia soil. Mrs. Lee herself is there behind the bricks, and so outspoken was her love of cats, one can only speculate as to whether some feline remains might be found there as well. Other relatives have been unearthed from the cemeteries where they were first interred and transported here in high ceremony, which is enough to make a mere mortal's skin crawl, but you will appreciate how important it was that they all come home.

Before I leave you to wander through the gallery with its pistols and portraits, documents and costumes, and his office as he left it, with maps and papers, his veteran Bible and the massive but eloquent correspondence that he sustained like a man still issuing orders, I would like — well, yes, I must remember to direct you to the restrooms yonder and the gift shop where you might purchase post cards, key chains, paperweights, bracelet charms, videos, and other keepsakes. You will no doubt desire a souvenir of this visit. As you pass his desk, I suggest you speculate on what momentous documents hide there before our very eyes, in plain sight. It was there he wrote the college honor code and there he penned his personal motto: "Misfortune nobly borne is fortune," a code I always strive to honor.

And please do not forget to express your generosity in the contribution box, for though there is no charge for admission, the chapel does not sustain and clean itself like some haunted mansion but rather requires our vigilant assistance. So long as we can generate donations, this shrine is one cause that will not be lost.

There is time, here on the threshold, for one last morsel of history from Miss Sibby — the story of Traveller, the noble steed who is finally interred outside the lower exit. What an astonishing narrative his story is. He was born in 1857 and named Jeff Davis, then purchased in 1862 by the General, who renamed his mount after Washington's favorite stallion. He carried his master through the entire war and then to Lexington, where they were close companions, often making the jaunt to the mineral waters of Rockbridge Baths. Some evenings the General could think of nothing but the mud and gunfire, the broken bodies of young men, the twisted faces of the wounded and weevils in the meal, and on those occasions he would excuse himself from table and walk out to Traveller's stable, run his burdened hands down the muzzle and brushed mane of his boon companion, then step out to the garden to relieve himself in starlight, listening for ghosts, looking heavenward and weeping. "It is all my fault," he repeated after the bloodbath of Gettysburg, for he was not one to dodge responsibility, unlike some I might name.

Traveller marched solemnly at the funeral with boots reversed in his stirrups and lived until 1871, at which time he stepped on a rusty nail and died of lockjaw. (Does that strike you also as a little bit difficult to believe?) He was himself a symbol of the South's pride and beauty, and therefore had many enemies. Death loves a shining mark, and he was buried unceremoniously in a ravine cut by Woods Creek, but his amazing journey had just begun. Raised from the grave in 1875 by the Daughters, his bones were sent away for preservation, but an inexplicable red hue had infused them, and there was no turning them white. In 1907 the skeleton was returned and mounted in the museum, where the students who had earlier plucked souvenir strands from his tail — well, not those students, obviously, but later ones of the same ilk — circulated the word that academic success was ensured by carving one's initials upon the bones, like sailors making scrimshaw. In a less harmful jest, a buck goat's bones were once smuggled into the museum, assembled beside the General's steed, and accompanied by the label "Traveller as a colt." You cannot ever guess what boys will think of next, even after they rise to manhood and begin to sow promises like seeds, or pebbles that resemble seeds but yield no issue.

Beside the door you will see Traveller's memorial stone, which is even in this cold time of the year decorated by visitors with coins and candy, apples and miniature battle flags. It is a place for wishing and the site I linger at when my day here is finished and I am waiting for evening to embrace me.

If you should care to pose any questions about the General and his highborn kinsmen, his four maiden daughters, or his influence on the liberal curriculum, I would be delighted to address them now, though I have decided it is no longer prudent for me to speculate on what the General would have thought about the admission of females to the college or what his ghost might have to tell us about his sudden decline after the war or what he thought of the works of the scandalous and ill-fated Mr. Poe, who also attended West Point, but was more bête noire than noblesse oblige.

Now I must leave you, for the security guard on duty there with the evil-looking eye has taken it upon himself to restrict my tours to the chapel proper, which is why I at once savor and regret the fact that it has never been consecrated as a church. If you do not choose to rendezvous at the monument to equestrian fidelity, I thank you for your interest and kind attention to our sepulchral treasure as well as your indulgence of an old woman's eccentric ways. I bid you, now, at this charmed threshold, a fond and wistful *adieu.*

JOHN UPDIKE

The Walk with Elizanne

FROM THE NEW YORKER

THEIR CLASS HAD GRADUATED from Olinger High School in 1952, just before the name was regionalized out of existence. Though the year 2002 inevitably figured in yearbook predictions and jokes, nobody had really believed that this much future would ever become the present. They were seventeen and eighteen; 2002 was impossibly remote. Now it was here, here in the function room of Fiorvante's, a restaurant in West Alton, half a mile from the stately county hospital where a lot of them had been born and now one of them lay critically ill.

David Kern and his second wife, Andrea, long enough his wife to be no stranger to these five-year reunions, went to visit the sick class member, Mamie Kauffman, in the hospital room where she had lain for six weeks, her bones too riddled with cancer for her to walk. She had been living alone in a house she and a long-decamped husband had bought forty years ago, and where three children had been raised on a second-grade teacher's salary. Get-well cards and artwork from generations of her pupils filled the room's sills and walls; Mamie was bubbly and hospitable, though she could not rise into even a sitting position.

"What an outpouring of love this has brought on," she told them. "I was feeling sorry for myself and, I guess you'd have to say, not enough loved, until this happened." She described getting out of bed and feeling her hip snap, feeling herself tossed into a corner like a rag doll, and reaching for the telephone, which luckily was on the floor, with her cane. She had used a cane for some time, for what she had thought was rheumatoid arthritis. At first she meant to call her daughter, Dorothy, two towns away. "I was so mad at myself, I couldn't think of Dot's phone number, though I dial it every other day, and then I told myself, 'Mamie, it's two-thirty in the morning, you don't want Dot's number, what you want is nine-one-one. What you want is an ambulance.' They came in ten minutes and couldn't have been nicer. One of the paramedics it turned out had been a second-grader of mine twenty years ago."

Andrea smiled and said, "That's lovely." In this overdecorated sickroom she looked young, vigorous, efficient, gracious; David was proud of her. She was a captive from another tribe, from a state other than Pennsylvania.

Mamie tried to tell them about her suffering. "At times I've felt a little impatient with the Lord, but then I'm ashamed of myself. He doesn't give you more than He gives you strength to bear."

In theistic Pennsylvania, David realized, people developed philosophies. Where he lived now, an unresisted atheism left people to suffer with the mute, recessive stoicism of animals. The more intelligent they were, the less they had to say in extremis.

Mamie went on, "I've been rereading Shirley MacLaine, where she says that life is like a book, and your job is to figure out what chapter you're in. If this is my last chapter, I have to read it that way, but you know I've had a lot of time to think lying here and —" In her broad, kind face, nearly as pale as her pillow, Mamie's watery blue eyes faltered, becoming quick and dry. "I don't think it is," she finished bravely. Even flat on her back, she was a teacher, knowing more than her audience and out of lifelong habit wanting to impart the lesson. "I'm not afraid of death," she told the visiting couple, smartly dressed in their reunion finery. "It's locked into my heart that — that —"

Yes, what? David thought, anxious to hear, though aware of the time ticking away. He came to this area so rarely now that he sometimes got lost on the new roads, even traveling only a mile. The reunion wouldn't wait.

"That I'll be all right," Mamie concluded. She sensed the anticlimax, the disappointment even, and made an exasperated circular motion of her hand, with its flesh-colored hospital bracelet and IV shunt. "That when it comes, I'll still be there. Here. You know what I'm saying?"

The visiting couple nodded in eager unison.

"It's the getting there," Mamie admitted, "I don't look forward to."

"No," Andrea agreed, smiling her bright healthy smile. She was dressed in a gray wool suit whose broad lapels made her look more buxom than usual.

David searched himself for something to say, but his tongue was numbed by memories of Mamie, from kindergarten on: the round-faced little girl being led to the asphalt playground by her round-faced mother; the eager student, knowing all the answers but never pushing them on others or on the teacher, never demanding attention but ready to shine when it fell on her; the cheerleader and class secretary, the pep girl. In their class plays and assembly programs, she always played the part of the impish little sister, while David, for some reason, played the father, with talcum powder in his hair. There was no need for talcum powder now; he had turned gray and then white early, like his own mother.

Mamie was saying, "So I say to myself, 'Mamie, you stop complaining, you've had a wonderful life, and three wonderful children, and it isn't over yet.' Dot offered to have me come live with them, but I wouldn't do it to her, not in the shape I'm in. Jake offered, too, out there in Arizona. He thinks the dryness would be good for me, but what would I do looking out the window at the desert, unable to open a window because of the air conditioning? The funny thing is — this will amuse you, David, you were always into irony — the rehab I'll be moving to is the same one with my mother already there. She won't be in my unit, but isn't that ironical? I lived two blocks from her most of my life, and now I'll be on the floor just under her."

The yearbook had not predicted that any of their parents would be alive in 2002. "My goodness — your mother must be ninety," David said.

"And then some. Who would have thought it, the way she smoked? And she wasn't averse to a drink now and then, either."

"She was always very nice to me. Even without you being there, I could hang out in your house, waiting for my father to get done at school. We'd play gin rummy."

"She always said, 'David will go places.'"

In memory he saw her mother at the kitchen table like a tenement solitary glimpsed from a passing train — smoke unfurling from a Chesterfield in a glass ashtray, a fanned set of cards in her hand, a glass of some tinted liquid beside her other elbow. She had pasty, deeply dimpled elbows, and she and her daughter shared curly brown hair, and full, talkative lips, curved up at the corners. For all the bubbly welcome with which the two females of the house received David's visits, there had been a melancholy nap to the furniture, a curtained gloom. It was a semidetached house with no windows on one side and those on the other giving onto a neighbor's house not six feet away. Mr. Kauffman, a small, almost rudely untalkative lathe operator, was slow to come home from work. Mamie's sunny manner, her busy happiness in high school — the long shiny halls, the organized activities, the tides of young life regulated by bells — had the relief of escape attached to it. Like David's father, who taught there, she felt at home in the broad, chaste communal setting. David's fondness for her had never made it over the edge into the mildest kind of sexual exchange.

"Speaking of going places," David said.

"Yes," Mamie said quickly, recovering her briskness, "you must be off. You two have a wonderful time. David, be sure to say something nice to Betty Lou about the decorations and favors. She *slaved* to find all those things in the class colors."

Betty Lou, though laid-back and slangy, had indeed slaved; the effect was dazzling — swags of maroon and canary yellow, floral centerpieces to match at every table, the walls thronged with enlarged photographs taken fifty and more years ago of schoolchildren in pigtails and knickers, and then of teenagers in saddle shoes and pleated skirts, corduroy shirts and leather jackets. The boys looked mildly menacing, with their greased pompadours and ducktails and flagrantly displayed cigarettes, a pack squaring their shirt pockets and an unfiltered singleton tucked behind one ear. The girls, too, with their thickly laid-on lipstick and induced blond streaks, had a touch of killer, of determination to get their share of the life to come.

Now, although that life was mostly over, the function room was full of human noise, gleeful greetings and old-fashioned kidding: "God, ugly as ever! Who's your friend, or is that a stomach?"

Betty Lou, who without Mamie here was thrown into the chief managerial role, came and seized David above the elbow and turned him away from studying the photographs on the wall to face a well-dressed, well-padded woman with button-black eyes and hair to match, cut short and tastefully frosted.

"Do you know who this is?" Betty Lou asked. Her tone was so aggressive his mind seized up. The mystery woman's features had an owlish sharpness, and the decisively shaped, jet-black eyebrows gave her a frowning look, though she was smiling hopefully, trying silently to sing her identity to David across the decades. He was reminded of walking to elementary school, when Barbara Moyer and Linda Rickenbacker would steal his hat and his rubber-lined book satchel and nimbly keep these possessions out of his reach until tears stung his eyes and he ran away in a tantrum; then the girls would chase him, to give him back what they had grabbed.

Now, again, he was being ganged up on by girls. The seconds stretched. Plump women of sixty-seven or -eight have a family resemblance. He stammered — an old problem, long outgrown — when he began to mouth the name of a girl, Loretta Haldeman, who, he realized in midstammer, this could not be, for Loretta had attended five years ago, wearing steel-rimmed spectacles with one opaque lens; an eye had given out. This woman with her stern and shiny stare was being presented as a treat, a delicacy, a rarity. He tried to remember who always annoyed the class organizers by never coming, by not coming for fifty years, and thus through the powers of deduction rather than of recognition he named her: "Elizanne!" It was a name like none other, pronounced, they had learned as children, to begin with an "ay" sound, like the mysterious "et" in Chevrolet. It bespoke an ambitious, willful mother, to brand a daughter like this, in so conservative a county.

Elizanne stepped forward to be kissed; David aimed at her cheek, though from the way she puckered she would have taken him on her mouth. "How good to have you here," he said, a bit blankly. She had not been one of the showier girls in the class, though she had aged better than most. Her dress was teal silk and understated, expensive, and suburban. Her husband, that ultimate accessory, was tall and genial, with a trace of southern accent, a man of business, retired or all but. The two of them were together embarked, David imagined, upon a well-earned sunset career of determined foreign travel, of grandchild-sitting and health-club attendance, of hardworking American leisure modeled on the hand-

some aging couples in commercials for Viagra and iron supplements. Elizanne, he sensed, had gone places; her face displayed,
along with that demure quick smile he could remember — a smile
that darted in and out — a good sense of herself, a firm social identity momentarily set aside, like a man's jacket folded into an airplane's overhead bin. Though David was happy enough to see her,
he had little to say to her, and less than that to the tan and drawling
husband, to whom they must all seem, David imagined, Pennsylvania Dutch hicks.

It was only toward the end of the evening, with their spouses
lost in the crowd, that she came up to him. There had been the
bumbling monologue by the unofficial class clown, the e-mailed
greeting from the unable-to-attend class president, the touching
message from Mamie that Betty Lou read aloud, the microphone
amplifying the catch in her throat. "We had the best of it," Mamie
had written. "No drugs, no school shootings, respect for our teachers, and faith in America." Then the Frankhauser twins, now
stooped and heavy of step, performed a soft-shoe routine last presented in senior assembly, and Betty Lou offered thanks to all the
committee members, and Butch Fogel announced how to find tomorrow's picnic, though the TV weathermen were predicting rain.
The hired entertainment, a female keyboard player with a bassist,
sang old songs freighted with nostalgic content for somebody, but
not quite for them. Their songs were overlookable oddities tucked
into the late forties and early fifties, just before Presley and doo-
wop and rock made everything before them funky — the swing
bands, the crooners, the iron-coiffed female vocalists, the novelty
numbers and moony heart-wringers, to which one did a sluggish
box step. Nobody danced. Even five years ago, one couple had
dared, and others followed. Now, nobody.

As the classmates began to shuffle toward the door and whatever
fate the next five years would bring, Elizanne came up to David,
resting a hand on his forearm and speaking with a firm, lilting urgency, almost as if she were speaking to herself. "David," she said, in
this running murmur, "there's something I've been wanting for
years to say to you. You were very important to me. You were the
first boy who ever walked me home and — and kissed me."

Her eyes, a creamy brown color nearly consumed by her widened
pupils in this dimmed function room, sought his, causing her lids

with their starry wealth of black lashes to lift. Her eyebrows were released from their frown. Her face, so close and foreshortened,
seemed arrived from a great distance. She might have had a drink
or two — Fiorvante's had its bar just outside the function room —
but she was sober, and now so was he, shocked amid the reunion's
loud adult courtesies by this remembrance of their young selves,
their true, fumbling selves.

"I remember that walk," he said. But did he?

Elizanne laughed, a bit coarsely — a modern suburban woman's
knowing laugh. "It got me started, I must tell you, on a lot of, whatever. Kissing, let's say."

He tried to ignore the experienced, sardonic woman she had become. The forgotten walk was coming back to him. The shy, lei-
surely passage, in dying light, through Olinger, and the standing
close, still talking, at the door of her parents' house, and then his
lunge into the kiss, and her equally clumsy yet fervid acceptance
of the kiss. He had loved her, for a season. When? Why had the season been so short? Had they kicked fallen leaves as they walked
through town, along the Alton Pike with its trolley tracks, into the
rectilinear streets of brick row houses, and then on to Elmdale, the
section where the streets curved, and the houses stood alone on
their lawns, the lawns weedless and the houses half-timbered and
slate-roofed and expensive, to the house where Elizanne lived?
Had it been spring, shot through with sudden green and yellow, or
summer, when bugs swarmed and girls wore shorts, or winter, when
your cheeks stung in the dark? He was stricken to have her imply,
with a knowledgeable laugh, that she had gone on to kiss others —
many others. She had added something he didn't quite catch, in
the noise of reunion farewells or in his growing deafness, about
"what you all wanted" — a sadly cheap and standard sneer, he felt,
about male sexuality, which in that place and era had been a massive, underpublicized impetus that most boys dealt with alone. But
the sneer itself dated her, and took them back.

"You were so," he breathed, groping for the word, "dewy." This
he did remember, amid so much he had forgotten — her dewiness,
a quiet, fuzzy moisture about her skin, her presence. "I'm glad," he
added, going into dry adult mode, "it was a successful initiation."

Darkly her eyes held his for a second. She realized that he
couldn't express what was there to express, and gave his forearm a

squeeze and removed her hand. "I just wanted you to know," she said. This was goodbye, for fifty more years.

Wait, he thought, but instead said, quite inanely, "Thank you, Elizanne. What a sweet thing to remember. Hey, you look great. Unlike a lot of us."

That night, twisting with the reunion's excitement next to Andrea in bed at the Alton Marriott, and for days following, he tried to recapture that walk which had ended in a kiss. Elizanne's house and neighborhood had been more expensive than his, and that had intimidated him. She was not for him. Before too long he got his first real girlfriend, from the class below theirs, who let him hold her breasts and partly undress her, as slick as a fish in the parked car. How old would they have been, he and Elizanne? Sixteen, perhaps fifteen. Had it been after a football game, or a school dance? He had not really been very social, nor, after they moved to the country, when he was fourteen, was he free to drift around Olinger as he pleased, though he continued at Olinger High, riding back and forth with his father.

She was in the marching band, he remembered. He could see her in her uniform, her black hair bundled up under her cap and her girl's body encased, somehow excitingly, in the gold-striped maroon pants and jacket. The baton twirlers in their high white boots and short flippy skirts were followed by a maroon unisex mass, and Elizanne was in that phalanx. What did she play? He thought clarinet, but this might have been a slender shadow of her coloring; unlike the other class brunettes, with their highlighted brown waves, she had truly black hair, with lashes and eyebrows to match. The skin of her face had been luminously white in contrast. A fuzz on her upper lip made two little smudges.

Remembering the dark fuzz, most noticeable in the downward view, gave him another piece of memory: dancing with her, holding her close while shuffling, her corsage and strapless taffeta bodice and the taffeta small of her back with its little ridges and his feet and armpits and shoulder blades in the rented summer tux all melting into one continuum of sweat while the streamers overhead drooped and the mirror ball flung its reflections frictionlessly across the floor and the band, its muted trombones sobbing, finished its rendition of "Stardust" or "Goodnight Irene." His and

Elizanne's cheeks felt pasted together and yet when the music stopped he didn't want to let go; he continued, pantingly, to drink her in, her foreshortened demure face with its smudged upper lip and dewy expanse of décolletage, the white edges of her strapless bra outlining her gentle bosom.

How often had they danced like that? Why hadn't more come of it? As long as he could remember, the female sex had been sending out combative, formidable scouts in his direction, mothers and grandmothers and teachers, and Barbara and Linda stealing his cap on the way to school, and fellow classroom goody-goodies like Mamie, and here the surface of femininity, that towering mystery in whose presence his life must be lived, yielded to a slight pressure. Without a word, a word that he could remember, Elizanne had submitted to his inept attentions, and indicated a demure curiosity in what he might do for her.

The walk: for weeks after the reunion his mind could not let go of the walk she reminded him they had taken. In the distorting lens of old age it loomed as one of the most momentous acts of his life. The geography of Olinger had been woven into him, into the muscles that pushed his bicycle and pulled his sled. His parents took walks on Sunday afternoons, and he had tagged behind them until his legs balked. His grandfather had worked on the borough crew that had put in some of the new streets on the north side of the main thoroughfare, the Pike. The town was older south of the Pike, where David's house sat, in a ragged neighborhood of mixed architectural styles and vacant lots, some of them planted in corn. He preferred the blocks north of the Pike, where identical brick semi-detached houses, with square-pillared porches and terraced front lawns, had been put up during the twenties. Friends like Mamie lived in these orderly cozy blocks, which had grocery stores or hobby shops or an ice cream parlor or a barbershop tucked into the front rooms of homes. He loved the houses' tightness, their uniformity, which seemed a pledge of order and shared intention missing from his own patchy neighborhood.

Beyond this section, where a harness-racing track had once tied up sixty acres, contractors in the years before the war positioned handsome limestone and clinker-brick single houses on new streets curving up the side of Shale Hill. David's walk with Elizanne must have taken him from the high school or its grounds on the Pike through the blocks of semidetached houses, which above their porches held picture windows where seasonal decorations — orange paper pumpkins and black paper bats for Halloween, Christmas tinsel, Easter baskets — announced the residents' fealty to the Christian calendar. The trees along the streets changed from horse chestnuts in the old section where he lived to dense lines of Norway maples on the solidly built-up rectilinear streets to drooping, feathery elms and blotchy-barked sycamores, locally called buttonwoods, on the streets that curved. These trees were looser, airier; there was more space and light in the section where Elizanne lived, as if you were ascending a hill, as indeed you were, but a gently sloping hill of money, of airy privilege. And yet she had let him kiss her, there by her thick-paneled front door, with its two-tone chime doorbell, and had remembered that kiss for more than fifty years, and spoke of it as her admission ticket to the wonderland of sex.

If Mamie was right and we live forever, David thought, he could imagine no better way to spend eternity than taking that walk with Elizanne over and over, until what they said, how they touched, whether or not he dared hold her hand in his, and each hair of the fine black down on her forearms all came as clear as letters deep-cut in marble. There would be time to ask her all the questions he had been too slow-witted to ask at their fiftieth. Was this her first husband, or the last of a series? Had she had affairs, in that suburb of her choosing? Had there been a lot of necking, as he had heard there was, on the band bus back from the football games? Was it the bus where she went on with her kissing, the groping that comes with kissing, the flush and hard breathing that comes with groping? Whose girlfriend had she been, in her junior and senior years? He dimly remembered her being linked with Lennie Lesher, the track star, the five-minute miler with sunken acne-scarred cheeks and tight waves of hair soaked in Vitalis. How could she have betrayed him, David, that way? Or with those faceless members of the band? Why had they, David and she, drifted apart after walking through Olinger into the region of more light? Or had it been night, after a dance or a basketball game, her white face with its strong eyebrows and quick smile a nocturnal blur?

For days he could not let her afterimage go, but in time he would, he knew. He could not write or call her, even if Mamie or Betty Lou provided him with her address and number, for there were spouses, accumulated realities, limits. At the time, obviously, there had been limits in their situation, deficiencies. He had had little to offer her but his future of going places, and that was vague and distant. The questions he was burning to ask would receive banal answers. It was an adolescent flirtation that had come to nothing.

"Well, here we are." The streetlights had just come on.

"So soon!" he exclaimed. "You have a n-nifty-looking house."

"Mother's never liked the kitchen. She says it's gloomy, all those dark-stained cabinets. She wants us to move to West Alton."

"Oh, no! Don't move, Elizanne."

"I don't want to, heaven knows. She thinks they have better schools in West Alton. A better class of student."

"My m-mother made us move to the country and I hate it."

"You can't stay in Olinger forever, David."

"Why not? Some do."

"That won't be you."

Her gaze clung to his in her seriousness; her eyebrows slightly frowned. He expected her to turn away and go into her house, but she didn't. He explained, "I ought to get back to the school, my p-poor father's p-p-probably looking for me. It must be past five." The light died earlier each day: it was October. The leaves were turning.

"Tell me honestly," she said, as if to herself, rapidly. "Did I talk too much? Just now, walking."

"No, you didn't. You didn't at all."

"That's what I do, when I let myself relax with someone. I chatter. I go on too much."

"You didn't. It was like you were singing to me."

Her face had not exactly come closer to his, but its not turning and moving away made it feel closer. Cautiously he bent his face into hers, a little sideways, and kissed her. Elizanne's lips took the fit snugly, warmly; she pressed slightly into the kiss, from underneath, looking for something in it. David felt caught up in a stream flowing counter to the current of everyday events, and began to run out of breath. He broke the contact and backed off. They stared at each other, her black eyes button-bright in the sodium streetlight, amid the restless faint shadows of the half-brown big sycamore leaves. Then he kissed her again, entering that warm still point around which the universe wheeled, with its load of stars not yet visible, the sky still blue above the streetlights. This time she backed off. A car went by, maybe containing somebody they knew, a spy or gossip. "And there was even more," she said, giggling to show that she was poking fun at herself now, "that I wanted to say."

"You will," he promised, breathlessly. His cheeks were hot, as if after gym class. He was worried, with an anxious stir of his stomach, about his father waiting for him. He felt as he had when, his one weekend at the Jersey Shore the past summer, a wave carrying his surfing body was breaking too early and about to throw him forward, down into the hard sand. "I want to hear it all," he told Elizanne. "We have t-tons of time."

MARY YUKARI WATERS

Mirror Studies

FROM ZOETROPE

THE KASHIGAWA DISTRICT, two hours from the Endos' home in Tokyo, was an isolated farming community with two claims to distinction: indigenous harrier monkeys up in the hills, and a new restaurant — Fireside Rations — that served "rice" made from locally grown yams. This restaurant had been featured in an *Asahi Shimbun* article about the trendy resurgence of wartime food, also known as nostalgia cuisine, and it had received special mention on NHK's thirty-minute *Rural Getaways* show. City dwellers, jaded by French and Madeiran cuisine, were flocking out on weekends to try it. It seemed a fitting place for Dr. Kenji Endo; his wife, Sumiko; and Dr. Ogawa to toast the start of a new primate field study.

This field study would be Kenji's last. Sumiko had insisted on it, quoting the doctor about the seriousness of his arrhythmia. "There's enough work for you at the university," she said, "where you'll have access to phones and doctors." Kenji had conceded with ill humor. Even now, at odd moments, that decision pressed hard on his chest, where he felt his heart galumphing under the skin. He was lucky, he supposed, to have this last project, a mere thirty-minute drive from this small town of Kashigawa. It would require almost no physical exertion; he had deliberately confined his mirror experiments to the provisioning area where monkeys came to feed.

Tonight, dressing for dinner at the Red Monkey Inn, Kenji stood behind his wife, who was fluffing her hair before the vanity mirror, and faced his own reflection. It pleased him that at fifty-eight he still looked good, belying the heart condition that, despite medication or perhaps because of it, had drained him over the past three months ("What happened to those pompous monologues of yours?" a close friend had joked recently). He was permanently tanned from years of working in the wilds of Borneo and Madagascar, and beneath his pressed spring suit he retained the lithe frame and hard calves of a trekker. Unlike Dr. Ogawa, whom they were meeting tonight, Kenji still had a full head of salt-and-pepper hair, which he parted in a dashing side sweep each morning. His only visible symptom of age was a tendency to walk or stand with knees slightly bent: the first sign of a curved back, according to his secretary at the university. He always caught himself, therefore, and corrected it immediately.

"I'd forgotten," his wife remarked, "how common yams are in Kashigawa. I'm surprised we didn't get one in our welcome basket." She smiled enigmatically at her reflection, turning her profile this way and that. Sumiko had grown up on the west side of this district, in a small hamlet long since swallowed up by postwar suburbs. Secure in her own sophistication, she often amused their city friends with anecdotes from her rural childhood.

"The monkeys today sure liked them, ne?" Kenji said. Ordinarily, he discussed primates for hours on end — anytime, with anyone — but lately this tendency had abated. He found himself economizing in other ways as well: if he needed a book from another room, he put off rising from his chair until it was time to use the bathroom; he sat silent in the chair while working through a complex thought process, rather than pacing the room and talking aloud as he was accustomed. He sensed how this slower pace hampered his creativity, his greatest asset, and this realization also lay heavy on his chest. For so long now, his mental agility — augmented by his affiliation with the nation's most elite university and a long and respected publishing career — had cleared his every path like a red carpet. As a young man, naturally, he had battled hard for advancement. But that was decades ago; until the advent of his arrhythmia, he could barely remember how it felt to be thwarted.

On this particular evening, however, Kenji was in fine form. He was eager to talk. His thoughts sprang up, keen and full-bodied, like stringed notes plucked by a koto master. He had felt this way for two whole days now, and he harbored a secret hope that his heart problems were receding as mysteriously as they had once ap-

peared. Luckier things had happened in his lifetime. "Did you notice," he said, "how they peeled the yams with their incisors, then
washed them in the stream?"

"Aaa, aaa," Sumiko agreed, "you showed me." She powdered her
nose, leaning in close to the mirror. "Like miniature housewives,"
she said, "with those little black dexterous hands."

There was an emotional hardiness about Sumiko that Kenji assumed came from her country stock or — more likely — from being married to him. He had always appreciated this quality in her,
like a rope to which he, the mountain climber, could entrust his
full weight. "I'm a research widow," she had mourned jokingly in
their early years, as Kenji departed for one exotic locale after another. "Wave bye-bye to Papa-san," she told their toddler, Toji, carrying him in one arm and demonstrating with the other. After Toji
entered high school, she immediately joined several women's com-
mittees; the experience had added a gloss of poise to her unruffled
core. "A charming woman!" people often said of Kenji's wife.

"Their food washing is learned behavior," Kenji told her. "It's
one of the brightest discoveries credited to Japanese researchers."

"Aaa," Sumiko murmured, blotting her lipstick with a tissue.

"Because it's proto–tool use, you see, which is a key component
of human culture."

This afternoon's tour of the site had been brief, just to confirm
all was in order. Dr. Ogawa and his assistant, who were actually here
on a project of their own, had been kind enough to set up Kenji's
freestanding mirror for him, lugging it up the dirt trail and propping it securely in the middle of the clearing. The monkeys would
have unlimited access to this mirror before official tests were performed; this would allow plenty of time for them to establish familiarity with it.

"In the first mirror study eleven years ago," Kenji explained to
Dr. Ogawa later that evening at the restaurant, "a few orangutans
actually showed signs of self-recognition. The same with chimpan-
zees. An exciting discovery! But then that study of Japanese snow
monkeys, headed by my friend Itakura — do you know Itakura?"

Dr. Ogawa, who dealt with physiology rather than cognitive behavior, did not. But he had run across articles.

"Well, anyhow, that study was a disappointment. The monkeys in-
terpreted the reflections to be either other members of the same
species or else meaningless images. So the obvious question is —"

"Is there a rift between monkey and ape," Sumiko provided, rummaging in her handbag and pulling out a handkerchief.

"Soh soh, exactly. Whether it indicates a major evolutionary discontinuity."

"Fascinating," breathed Dr. Ogawa's assistant.

"I think it's pretty early for a conclusion like *that*," said Dr. Ogawa.

Kenji halted him with a raised forefinger, nodding. Absolutely, he said. There were so many unexplored variables. Some apes, such as gorillas, showed no self-recognition whatsoever. He personally suspected a correlation between a species' level of aggression and its concept of self. "Wouldn't aggression be the natural result," he said, "of a capacity for self-awareness being developed and adapted for survival?" These Kashigawa monkeys represented a strain of macaque that was, with the exception of baboons, one of the most ferocious in the entire primate order. He hoped this characteristic would make for some interesting findings.

"On what grounds?" Dr. Ogawa asked.

"It's still a hunch at this stage," Kenji said. A good many such hunches had paid off during his career. Much of this, he knew, was sheer luck, but surely some of the credit went to a scientist's gift for inventiveness, for subconscious mental connections. He loved telling the story of Einstein, whose theory of relativity had begun with a childish fantasy of riding on a beam of light. "I have some latitude to explore as I go," he now said.

"Aggression studies must be 'in' again," Dr. Ogawa said grimly. "Psychologists, sociologists, they're all whipped up about it."

Kenji laughed. He felt invincible tonight, closer to his old self than he had been in a while; he was conscious that every good hour, indeed every good minute, was ensuring his odds of recovery. "Our nation has a hunger," he explained, forearms leaning heavily on the dinner table as if it were a podium, "given our experience with the most destructive war in modern history, to understand what seed within humans made it possible. We can look back now from the safe distance of time. Even this wartime cuisine — I think it's all part of the process."

Dr. Ogawa, a middle-aged medical man with little regard for trends of the masses and even less for culinary fads, drank his Asahi beer and looked skeptical. He was collecting DNA samples for a study of pathogens and sialic acids, a process that led him and his assistant far out into the hills with their stun guns. Dr. Ogawa vaguely reminded Kenji of alpha-male apes he had studied in the past. Not in any aggressive sense but rather in the quiet force of his linear focus, that unrelenting, almost brute push of each thought to the very end. Kenji looked forward to some interesting debates. He knew from a colleague that Dr. Ogawa was fairly well known within physiology circles.

"Soh soh, wartime cuisine," sighed Dr. Ogawa's assistant, a weary-eyed graduate student whom Dr. Ogawa perversely addressed by the babyish nickname of Kana-chan. "We're simply inundated with it," he said, with a prim moue of distaste comically identical to Dr. Ogawa's.

Kenji laughed out loud at this, slapped his thigh. His exuberance had been rising all evening. His heartbeat was returning to normal — yes! he could sense it, with that intuition for success that had seldom failed him in the past. "You're absolutely right!" he said generously. Speaking of war cuisine, he told the table, two okonomiyaki places had sprung up in his own neighborhood. Kenji, having grown up in the city during the war and the occupation that followed, remembered those crispy pancakes: meager substitutes for rationed rice, their flour content barely enough to bind together leftover scraps of cabbage or turnip stems. Nowadays, of course, such ingredients were upgraded for modern consumption.

"Rock shrimp! Calamari! Filet mignon!" Kenji crowed. "They've missed the entire point!"

His audience laughed appreciatively, the assistant most heartily of all.

"Way before your time, Kana-chan," Dr. Ogawa teased, patting the young man's shoulder. Kana-chan flushed and stopped laughing.

Their waiter approached. In the muted candlelight (Kenji took out his reading glasses), they peered down at the identical bowls set before them. Yam rice, the waiter said, was unique to this region. First, yams were mashed. Binding glutens were added, and the mixture was strained through a large-holed colander into boiling water. The resulting noodlelike strands, once cooked, were chopped into rice-sized bits. These were bleached, then finally roasted.

"All that work," murmured Sumiko, "just so they could pretend they were eating rice." The rice had a chewy, nutty texture not unlike that of brown rice, although its flavor was largely masked by salt and adzuki beans.

From nowhere, a familiar tiredness hit Kenji. The shock and disappointment of it paralyzed him; he had put so much faith in this comeback. He sat still, feeling himself descending in slow motion beneath the bright surface of the dinner conversation, as if to the bottom of a sea.

With this underwater sensation, which so often accompanied his fluctuations in blood flow, he gazed dully at his wife sitting before him. She was eating slowly, pensively, deep in a world of her own. He recalled her saying once at a dinner party that her own mother, who had died when Sumiko was in middle school, used to reminisce about eating yam rice while she was pregnant with Sumiko. He wondered if his wife was remembering this now. It was strange how these small shifts in blood flow could open him up to the sadness of things, like a receding tide exposing sea creatures crumpled on the sand. His wife's way of eating this dish struck him as profound, an acknowledgment of all the loss and longing that had created it.

"Think of all the labor they could have saved," Kana-chan was saying, "if they'd just baked their yams instead."

Tiredness poured in from all sides now, like sand into a hole, infusing Kenji with an unaccustomed sense of disadvantage. The new generation, he thought. Never gone hungry, never had a familiar world jerked out from under its feet. Before this young mind, as hard and green as an unripe peach, Kenji felt unaccountably uneasy.

"Irregular heartbeats have various causes," Kenji's doctor had told him at the beginning. "For example, minuscule heart attacks over time can build up scar tissue, which interferes with electrical impulses."

"But I have excellent arteries. My blood pressure, my cholesterol, everything's in a good range!"

"Well, then," the doctor said — briskly, as if nipping a pointless argument in the bud — "yours must be hereditary. These flaws do crop up in later years, and we can't always explain them."

It was unnerving to think how confidently he had stridden through life, utterly ignorant of what defects lurked in his genes.

Now, weeks into his study, Kenji mulled it over again, sitting at the edge of the dirt clearing and observing the macaques. Five or six of them, sated from a lunch of yams, loitered thirty meters away, grooming one another or strolling about on all fours. Directly overhead the sumac leaves rustled, intermittently letting in a blinding flash of sun. Kenji closed his eyes — it was just for a moment, the monkeys were nowhere near the mirror — and orange flooded his eyelids, the warmth pressing down on his face and body like a blanket. He felt great solace in the midst of this loudness that was nature: the back-and-forth of birds, the drilling of a woodpecker, the alternating drone and *chi-chi-chi* of insects, the grunt of a monkey.

How he would miss fieldwork: this riotous energy all about him, each cell living with all its might, yet synchronized in cycles of deceptive efficiency.

Kenji's fascination with nature had started when he was six, when his family had evacuated to the countryside to stay with relatives after the Namiki bombing. He still looked back on those months as the finest in his childhood. One day his granny had taken him to a dense pine thicket to pick shiitake mushrooms with other villagers, wicker baskets slung over their backs. They had all roared with good-natured laughter whenever someone forgot and leaned over too far, causing the contents of his basket to come tumbling out . . .

"Everything in nature is put here on purpose," his granny had told him, pushing apart mushrooms as soft as flesh, "to keep something else alive. Nature knows exactly what it's doing." And the boy, young as he was, had grasped something of this omniscient bounty. He felt secure and protected on those rainy nights when they all hunched over the brazier, mouths watering for roasted mushrooms and quail eggs.

Later, as a young man, Kenji attempted to re-create the wonder of those early days by studying the natural sciences, which promised ever widening vistas of discovery. His focus on primate sociology was a lucky accident — the influence of a particularly charismatic mentor — or so he had always believed. But in the past few months, as he looked back on his career, it had occurred to Kenji that his specialty was a logical, if somewhat extreme, extension of his nostalgia for living off the land. In primate society was the essence of oneness with nature that humans must once have had, muddied now by all the ills of modern life. At this late age, Kenji felt a rueful tenderness for his early idealism; and perhaps because of this, he had become unduly disheartened during yesterday's talk with Dr. Ogawa.

Over the past few weeks, the two men had held some interesting discussions as they drove into town in the evenings (Kana-chan had to stay behind, sorting specimens). Both Kenji and Dr. Ogawa were interested in the concept of evolutionary divergence.

"New studies tell us," Dr. Ogawa had said, as they descended past terrace after terrace of rice paddies darkening in the twilight, "that human DNA is almost identical to that of primates. Almost identical. How is this possible? What accounts, then, for the vast difference between the species?"

A few months ago, Kenji would have made an irreverent quip about not being so sure there was a vast difference, following it up with various conjectures of his own. Since the yam-rice dinner, however, his old economy had returned. This evening, weary, he merely shook his head with a *hnn* sound.

"Sialic acids," Dr. Ogawa said with quiet relish. "That's one of the clues." Characteristic of his step-by-step thought process, he started at the beginning. Sialic acids acted as a protective layer over a species' DNA structure, shielding it from invasion and alteration by outside viruses. It had been discovered, only recently, that human sialic acids have a makeup distinctly different from that of other primates'.

"Which would suggest," Dr. Ogawa said, "that each species was influenced, over time, by different viruses."

Dr. Ogawa's theory was this: Long ago, in humans, some virus tampered with the delicate balance of electrical impulses that limits the size of every mammalian brain. "So now humans are born with open sutures in the skull to accommodate further brain growth," Dr. Ogawa said, "whereas every other mammal continues to be born with a fully knit skull."

"So what you're saying," Kenji said dully, "is that our larger brains, our self-awareness, basically everything that makes us uniquely human, is in direct violation of nature's internal control system?"

"Maa maa, Endo-san, isn't that a dire interpretation! Evolution is all *about* mutation."

Kenji could sense his own brain firing, working, but in that slow, underwater way, the clean lines of scientific thought tangling in the kelp of his personal sorrows. "A mutation like this would have enormous repercussions," he said finally. "It casts a whole new light on humans running amok over the biosphere. The human brain as the supreme anomaly, a divine defect . . ." A sense of futility had washed over him, and in spite of himself he sought Dr. Ogawa's eyes for reassurance.

Dr. Ogawa's eyes, squinting suspiciously behind the lenses of his eyeglasses, seemed small and far away, as if seen from the other end of a telescope. "Defect? What, like de-evolution? What kind of unscientific talk is that?"

"Viruses, too, thrive by ravaging their own environment," Kenji said. In the deepening dusk, the dirt road glowed whitely before them.

"Interesting. I suppose one *could* find similarities." Dr. Ogawa turned his headlights on. "But why make moral judgments about life forms?"

A woodpecker, drilling directly above his head, brought Kenji back to the present. He opened his eyes. His recent problems suddenly seemed alien compared with the sunny scene before him, tasseled grasses waving and everything in perfect harmony down to the *pyoo-pyoo* of a whitetail: one giant, attuned orchestra. He had a fleeting impression that his arrhythmia was the consequence of straying so far, over the decades, from the simple faith he had once known as a boy. How much this career of his had cost him: the joys of a simple home life, the bonds he might have forged with a son now grown and distant in Wakayama.

One of the monkeys, a young male, had ambled over to the mirror and now sat hunched before it with his back to Kenji, unmoving. Typical beta behavior, he thought automatically. An alpha would have charged the mirror or bared its teeth. But in another few weeks they would all be sitting sideways before the mirror, monitoring the scene by glancing back and forth between the clearing and the reflected image.

In the freestanding mirror, Kenji could make out the monkey's close-set eyes peering unblinkingly at its own small, reddened face. Seen from the rear he looked pitifully human, tiny shoulder blades poking up through the fur, and Kenji had the same urge he used to have when his son was small, to rest his hand on that narrow back.

Primates moved him, as did children, by all they were incapable of understanding.

When Kenji came home that night (they had by now transferred from the Red Monkey Inn to a condominium overlooking the Kashigawa valley), his wife was boiling something in the kitchen. Its pungent, earthy smell hit him as soon as he opened the door.

"They're wild fuki shoots from the hills where your monkeys are," Sumiko told him. She looked excited and happy. "A woman at the market gave me the recipe." Her hair was wrapped up, peasant-style, in one of the dyed indigo kerchiefs native to the area. Her dark-skinned face, washed clean of cosmetics and glistening from the heat of the stove, put him in mind of the healthy country women of his childhood.

"Ara, you're cooking!" he said in mock surprise. "What's going on? Is this the latest in country chic?"

She gave an embarrassed little laugh, pulling off her new kerchief as she did so, and once again she was the university wife from Tokyo. "So how's your medication working?" she asked, business-like.

"So-so," Kenji said. He couldn't help an inward cringe; his condition was a fragile thing, to be cradled in the soft recesses of his mind and handled, only at the right time and with utmost delicacy, by no one but himself.

"Try not to get your hopes up," Sumiko said. "Remember what the doctor said? That a certain level of fatigue is probably unavoidable?"

"Aaa, aaa, right."

"Try to be more careful about long hours, and don't run yourself down. Remember, you have a serious condition."

"Aaa! Aaa!" He escaped to the bathroom for his predinner bath, which was ready and steaming under its heavy lid. Sumiko had purchased some old-fashioned gourd loofahs, as well as an array of local beauty products. Kenji picked up, then put down, a small jar of soy curd labeled THE BEAUTY LOTION OF OUR MOTHERS. It was unseemly, an intelligent woman like Sumiko embracing this wartime trend as if she were a member of the masses. It occurred to him, briefly, to wonder about her day-to-day life, so closely linked to his and yet riddled with mysterious gaps. He tried imagining it: a slower pace, a narrower scope, the kind of world he himself had always resisted.

Settled in his bath now, his mind restfully blank, Kenji gazed down at his body wavering beneath the shifting water. It always came as something of a jar, after a full day of observing primates, to view the naked human form: the vestigial shortness of the arms, the pink, hairless skin, vulnerable, like a fetus.

Evolution is all about mutation.

That talk with Dr. Ogawa had vaguely reminded Kenji of the ideas of another scientist, and he now remembered, with the satisfying click of a fact falling into place, who it was. Buffon — a French naturalist from the eighteenth century — had proposed that humans, biologically speaking, were born at least a year too soon. Kenji had read him many years ago, in the context of another topic, which he could not recall, and at the time he had found the man's claims entertaining but not particularly relevant to his work. Buffon claimed that man was forced to complete, within society, a psychological development that all other species accomplished within the womb. As Kenji recalled, this had to do with the human head being too large to be carried to full term. Man's problems, apparently, traced back to this prematurity of birth.

Buffon's idea had been bolstered in the 1920s by another European — Ludwig Bolk — who proved that mutations inhibiting maturation did occur naturally in animals.

Kenji closed his eyes and conjured up the perfection of the afternoon: the sound of leaves and insects and birds weaving together into one drowsy murmur, the monkeys seated on the ground, gnawing on yams with their hairy legs splayed out before them. Like Eden, according to the Western conception: the paradise from which man was banished almost immediately after his creation. Kenji recalled that Christianity, unlike the Eastern religions, held humans to be distinct from animals, born under a shadow of original sin. Well, perhaps they had tapped into something. Clues were everywhere. How odd that he had never noticed.

"Dinner's ready!" called Sumiko from the hallway.

Unfortunately, Kenji's medication brought on proarrhythmia, an exacerbation of his preexisting condition. "Saa, who knows why?" his doctor had said blandly, ignoring Kenji's glare of exasperated disgust. "Every so often, antiarrhythmic drugs have tricky side effects." An appointment had been made for a pacemaker installation.

The operation was to take place in three days. This afternoon, sprawled in a chair on the condominium terrace, Kenji mulled over the mirror test that he planned to administer the next day. It was the first and most basic of the series: anesthetizing the monkeys, painting green dye on their heads, then seeing if the recovered monkeys touched their own heads while looking in the mirror.

It worried him that, after almost two months of loose observation, he had come up with no significant brainstorms, unusual connections, or inspirations for more tailored tests. Loose observation was usually his most fertile period, when chance details coupled with spontaneous insights guided the course of his study, refining a general hunch into a testable hypothesis. But this time, although he earnestly, even desperately, watched the monkeys grooming or fingering the mirror or leaping lightly from branch to branch, nothing clicked into place. He was like a thick-witted detective at a crime scene, unable to make sense of clues right before his eyes.

Never mind, Kenji told himself. He gave a curt sigh and glanced at his watch. It was a little after 4:00. In a few hours, his new assistant from the university, whom he had recruited to handle the monkey anesthetization as well as any lifting or dragging, would be coming by to go over the checklist.

"I still don't see why you can't put off your experiment until we get back from Tokyo," Sumiko said. She was sitting beside him on the terrace, alternately squinting at an instruction manual and weaving something out of rattan.

Kenji brushed away her words with one hand, as if they were flies. She's like Ogawa, he thought with a flare of helpless fury. A horse with blinders.

They sat silent. The terrace overlooked the south end of the Kashigawa valley, and the cluttered towns lay faint and ephemeral in the dense daze. To Kenji's left loomed the hills of his final project, so close he could distinguish the colors of certain trees. Despite the patchwork of lime-colored rice paddies encroaching on their lower regions, the hills gave off an ancient air, as if they had never been shadowed by anything but clouds and an occasional red hawk.

After some time, Kenji glanced over at his wife. Her arm, weaving the rattan stalk in and out, moved as serenely as a swimmer's.

"What are you making?" he asked.

"A pouch," she replied, "for hard-boiled eggs."

"Aaa."

They fell silent once more. Below them in the valley a train whistle sliced the air, echoing the mournful, delayed quality of Kenji's mind.

"The first time I ever rode the slow train," Sumiko said, "my mother packed hard-boiled eggs in a straw pouch. We peeled them on the train, and ate them." She said this absently, unmindful of his response, as a mother might talk to herself in the company of a child. Kenji felt himself freeze as he instinctively did before creatures in the wild, peacefully eating and as yet unaware of a human presence.

"The window was open, the breeze was blowing in," Sumiko continued, "and you could smell the iron heated up by the sun. We were so hungry in those days. And the eggs tasted so *good*, with a sprinkle of salt. It was a wonderful day."

"Is that why you're making this bag?"

His wife looked up, suddenly self-conscious. She regarded him for a moment, with dark eyes as unfathomable as a primate's. "I thought it might be nice to take a train ride," she said. "Just for a couple of stops."

Kenji was jolted out of his own self-regard. His no-nonsense wife of thirty years, with her dinner-party conversations — how long had she harbored such longings? He pictured her sitting alone by the window (did train windows even open anymore?), a woman past middle age, peeling an egg. He remembered her eating yam rice at the restaurant, and he felt a pity so deep he could not tell where it ended and his arrhythmia began.

"June is nice here in Kashigawa," he said gently. Then, after a pause, "I know what you mean . . . When I was a boy, I once picked mushrooms in the forest." Nodding, his wife resumed her handicraft. They said no more.

This is married life, thought Kenji. Suddenly his underwater state seemed not so much a banishment as the entering of a new realm, with the slowly dawning kinship of divers who swim among the fish. In him welled up a strong allegiance with Sumiko, with his entire aging generation reaching back for its simple beginnings. What countless private Edens they had managed to extract from the war . . .

Sumiko got up to attend to something in the kitchen. Kenji remained sitting in the evening light, which now slanted low over the hills and cast pink shadows on the valley haze. And as effortlessly as the spreading of the light — not with the clean scientific click of old, but with a soft suffusion — his allegiance widened out over his entire flawed race, with its fierce need to create beauty for itself.

A memory floated up in his mind. Madagascar, early in his career: towering stone crags whose jagged outcroppings snapped beneath his boots with high-pitched pings, and below them, the famous sunken forests where lemurs lived. The forests had been created, millions of years ago, by earth collapsing into itself for kilometers around, destroying all life in its wake and forever changing the land's topography. Kenji was a young man, and the forest's lush beauty had astonished him.

"Isn't life a resilient force," one senior member of their party had remarked as the scientists gazed upward in wonder, faces tinted green from the virgin foliage, "turning the worst of its disasters into something like this."

JOHN EDGAR WIDEMAN

What We Cannot Speak About We Must Pass Over in Silence

FROM HARPER'S MAGAZINE

I HAVE A FRIEND with a son in prison. About once a year he visits his son. Since the prison is in Arizona and my friend lives here on the East Coast, visiting isn't easy. He's told me the planning, the expense, the long day spent flying there and longer day flying back are the least of it. The moment that's not easy, that's impossible, he said, is after three days, six hours each, of visiting are over and he passes through the sliding gate of the steel-fenced outdoor holding pen between the prison-visitation compound and visitors' parking lot and steps onto the asphalt that squirms beneath your feet, oozing hot like it just might burn through your shoe soles before you reach the rental car and fling open its doors and blast the air conditioner so the car's interior won't fry your skin, it's then, he said, taking his first steps away from the prison, first steps back into the world, when he almost comes apart, almost loses it completely out there in the desert, emptiness stretching as far as the eye can see, very far usually, ahead to a horizon ironed flat by the weight of blue sky, zigzag mountain peaks to the right and left, marking the edges of the earth, nothing moving but hot air wiggling above the highway, the scrub brush and sand, then, for an unending instant, it's very hard to be alive, he says, and he thinks he doesn't want to live a minute longer and would not make it to the car, the airport, back to this city, if he didn't pause and remind himself it's worse, far worse for the son behind him still trapped inside the prison, so for the son's sake he manages a first step away, then another and another. In these faltering moments he must prepare himself for the turnaround, the jarring transition into a world where he has no access to his son except for rare ten-minute phone calls, a blighted world he must make sense of again, beginning with the first step away and back through the boiling cauldron of parking lot, first step of the trip that will return him in a year to the desert prison.

Now he won't have it to worry about anymore. When I learned of the friend's death, I'd just finished fixing a peanut butter sandwich. Living alone means you tend to let yourself run out of things. Milk, dishwasher detergent, napkins, toothpaste — staples you must regularly replace. At least it happens to me. In this late bachelorhood with no live-in partner who shares responsibility for remembering to stock up on needful things. Peanut butter probably my only choice that evening so I'd fixed one sandwich, or two, more likely, since they'd be serving as dinner. In the mail I'd ignored till I sat down to my sorry-assed meal, a letter from a lawyer announcing the death of the friend with a son in prison, and inside the legal-sized manila envelope, a sealed white envelope the friend had addressed to me.

I was surprised on numerous counts. First, to learn the friend was gone. Second, to find he'd considered me significant enough to have me informed of his passing. Third, the personal note. Fourth, and now it's time to stop numbering, no point since you could say every event following the lawyer's letter both a surprise and no surprise, so numbering them as arbitrary as including the sluggish detail of peanut butter sandwiches, "sluggish" because I'd become intrigued by the contents of the manila envelope and stopped masticating the wad in my jaw until I recalled the friend's description of exiting prison, and the sludge became a mouthful of scalding tar.

What's surprising about death anyway, except how doggedly we insist on being surprised by what we know very well's inevitable, and of course, after a while, this insistence itself unsurprising. So I was (a) surprised and (b) not surprised by the death of a friend who wasn't much of a friend, after all, more acquaintance than intimate cut-buddy, a guy I'd met somewhere through someone and weeks later we'd recognized each other in a line at a movie or a bank and nodded and then run into each other again one morn-

ing in a busy coffee shop, and since I'm partial to the coffee there, I
did something I never do, asked if it was O.K. to share his table, and
he smiled and said sure so we became in this sense friends. I never
knew very much about him and hadn't known him very long. He
never visited my apartment nor I his. A couple years of casual
bump-ins, tables shared for coffee while we read our newspapers, a
meal, a movie or two, a playoff game in a bar once, two middle-
aged men who live alone and inhabit a small, self-sufficient corner
of a large city and take time-outs here and there from living alone
so being alone at this stage in our careers doesn't feel too depress-
ingly like loneliness. He was the kind of person you could see occasionally, enjoy his company more or less, and walk away with no
further expectations, no plan to meet again. Like the occasional
woman who consents to share my bed. If he'd moved to another
city, months might have passed before I'd notice him missing. If
we'd lost contact for good, I'm sure I wouldn't have regretted not
seeing him again. A smidgen of curiosity perhaps. Perhaps a slight
bit of vexation, like when I discover I haven't restocked paper towels or Tabasco sauce. Less, since his absence wouldn't leave a gap
I'd be obliged to fill. My usual flat response at this stage in my life
to losing things I have no power to hold on to. Most of the world
fits into this category now, so what I'm trying to say is something
about the manila envelope and its contents bothered me more
than I'm used to allowing things to bother me, though I'm not sure
why. Was it the son in prison. The friend had told me no one else
visited. The son's mother dead of cancer. Her people, like the
friend's, like mine, old, scattered, gone. Another son, whereabouts
unknown, who'd disowned his father and half brother, started a
new life somewhere else. I wondered if the lawyer who wrote me
had been instructed to inform the son in prison of his father's passing. How were such matters handled. A phone call. A registered letter. Maybe a visit from the prison chaplain. I hoped my friend had
arranged things to run smoothly, with as little distress as possible
for the son. Any alternatives I imagined seemed cruel. Cruel for
different reasons, but all equally difficult for the son. Was he even
now opening his manila envelope, a second envelope tucked inside
with its personal message. I guess I do know why I was upset — the
death of the man who'd been my acquaintance for nearly two years
moved me not a bit, but I grieved to the point of tears for a son I'd

never seen, never spoken to, who probably wasn't aware of my grief or my existence.

I could barely recall the dead friend's face. Once I twisted on the light over the mirror above the bathroom sink, thinking I might milk his features from mine. Hadn't we been vaguely similar in age and color. If I studied hard, maybe the absence in my face of some distinctive trait the friend possessed would trigger my memory, or a trait I bore would recall its absence in the friend's features and *bingo* his whole face would appear.

Seeing a stranger in the mirror, I was afraid I might be suffering from the odd neurological deficit that prevents some people from recognizing faces. Who in God's name was this person staring at me. Who'd been punished with those cracks, blemishes, the mottled complexion, eyes sunken in deep hollows, frightened eyes crying out for acknowledgment, for help, then receding, surrendering, staring blankly, bewildered and exhausted, asking me the same questions I was asking them.

How long had I been losing track of myself. Not really looking when I brushed my teeth or combed my hair, letting the image in the mirror soften and blur, become familiar and invisible as faces on money. Easier to imagine the son than deal with how the father had turned out, the splotched, puffy flesh, lines incised in forehead and cheeks, strings dragging down the corners of the mouth. I switched off the light, let the merciful hood drop over the prisoner's face.

Empathy with the son not surprising, even logical, under the circumstances, you might say. Why worry about the father. He's gone. No more tiptoeing across burning coals. Why not sympathize with a young man suddenly severed from his last living contact with the world this side of prison bars. Did he know his father wouldn't be visiting. Had he phoned. Listened to the ring-ring-ring and ring. How would the son find out. How would he bear the news.

No doubt a bit of self-pity colored my response. On the other hand I'm not a brooder. I quickly become bored when a mood's too intense or lasts too long. Luckily, I have the capacity to step back, step away, escape into a book, a movie, a vigorous walk, and if these distractions don't do the trick, then very soon I discover I'm smiling, perhaps even quietly chuckling at the ridiculous antics of

the person who's lost control, who's taking himself and his commonplace dilemmas far too seriously.

Dear Attorney Koppleman,
    I was a friend of the late Mr. Donald Whittaker. You wrote to inform
me of Mr. Whittaker's death. Thank you. I'm trying to reach Mr.
Whittaker's imprisoned son to offer my belated condolences. If you possess the son's mailing address, could you pass it on to me, please. I appreciate in advance your attention to this matter.

    In response to your inquiry of 6/24/99: This office did execute Mr.
Donald K. Whittaker's will. The relevant documents have been filed in
Probate Court and, as such, are part of the public record you may consult at your convenience.
    (P.S.) Wish I could be more helpful, but in our very limited dealings
with Mr. Whittaker he never mentioned a son in or out of prison.

I learned there are many prisons in Arizona. Large and small.
Local, state, federal. Jails for short stays, penitentiaries for lifers.
Perhaps it's the hot, dry climate. Perhaps space is cheap. Perhaps
a desert state's economy, with limited employment opportunities for its citizens, relies on prisons. Perhaps corporate-friendly
deals make prisons lucrative businesses. Whatever the reasons, the
prison industry seems to flourish in Arizona. Many people also end
up in Arizona retirement communities. Do the skills accumulated
in managing senior citizens who come to the state to die readily
translate to prison administration. Or vice versa.
    Fortunately, the state employs people to keep track of prisoners.
I'm not referring to uniformed guards charged with hands-on
monitoring of the inmates' flesh and blood. I mean computer people who know how to punch in and retrieve information. Are they
one of the resources attracting prisons to Arizona. Vast emptiness
plus a vast legion of specialists adept at processing a steady stream
of bodies across borders, orchestrating the dance of dead and living so vacancies are filled and fees collected promptly. Was it the
dead friend who told me the downtown streets of Phoenix are eerily vacant during heat-stroke daylight hours. People who do the
counting must be sequestered in air-conditioned towers or as busy
as bees underground in offices honeycombed beneath the asphalt,
their terminals regulating traffic in and out of hospices, prisons,
old folks' homes, juvenile detention centers, cemeteries, their
screens displaying Arizona's archipelago of incarceral facilities, di-

agrams of individual gulags where a single speck with its unique, identifying tag can be pinpointed at any moment of the day. Thanks to such a highly organized system, after much digging I located the son.

Why did I search. While I searched, I never asked why. Most likely because I possessed no answer. Still don't. Won't fake one now except to suggest (a) curiosity and (b) anger. Curiosity since I had no particular agenda beyond maybe sending a card or note. The curiosity that killed the cat till satisfaction brought it back. My search pure in this sense, an experiment, driven by the simple urge to know. Anger because I learned how perversely the system functions, how slim your chances of winning if you challenge it.

Anger because the system's insatiable clockwork innards had the information I sought and refused to divulge it. Refused fiercely, mindlessly, as only a mindless machine created to do a single, repetitive, mindless task can mindlessly refuse. The prison system assumes an adversarial stance the instant an inquiry attempts to sidestep the prerecorded labyrinth of logical menus that protect its irrational core. When and if you ever reach a human voice, its hostile tone insinuates you've done something stupid or morally suspect by pursuing it to its lair. As punishment for your trespass, the voice will do its best to mimic the tone and manner of the recorded messages you've been compelled to suffer in order to reach it.

Anger because I couldn't help taking the hassle personally. Hated bland bureaucratic sympathy or disdain or deafness or defensiveness or raw, aggressive antagonism, the multiplicity of attitudes and accents live and recorded transmitting exactly the same bottom-line message: yes, what you want we have, but we're not parting with it easily.

I won't bore you or myself by reciting how many times I was put on hold or switched or switched back or the line went dead after hours of Muzak or I weathered various catch-22 routines. I'll just say I didn't let it get the best of me. Swallowed my anger, and with the help of a friend persevered, till one day — accidentally I'm sure — the information I'd been trying to pry from the system's grip collapsed like an escaping hostage into my arms.

Some mornings when I awaken I look out my window and pretend to understand. I reside in a building in the bottom of somebody's pocket. Sunlight never touches its bricks. Any drawer or cabinet or closet shut tight for a day will exude a gust of moldy funk when you open it. The building's neither run-down nor cheap. Just dark, dank, and drab. Drab as the grown-ups children are brow-beaten into accepting as their masters. The building, my seventh-floor apartment, languish in the shadow of something fallen, lean-ing down, leaning over. Water, when you turn on a faucet first thing in the morning, gags on itself, spits, then gushes like a bloody jail-break from the pipes. In a certain compartment of my heart com-passion's supposed to lodge, but there's never enough space in cramped urban dwellings so I store niggling self-pity there too, try to find room for all the millions of poor souls who have less than I have, who would howl for joy if they could occupy as their own one corner of my dreary little flat. I pack them into the compartment for a visit, pack till it's full far beyond capacity and weep with them, share with them my scanty bit of good fortune, tell them I care, tell them be patient, tell them I'm on their side, tell them an old ac-quaintance of mine who happens to be a poet recently hit the lot-tery bigtime, a cool million, and wish them similar luck, wish them clear sailing and swift, painless deaths, tell them it's good to be alive, whatever, good to have been living as long as I've managed and still eating every day, fucking now and then, finding a roof over my head in the morning after finding a bed to lie in at night, grate-ful to live on even though the pocket's deep and black and a hand may dig in any moment and crush me.

I'm writing to express my condolences sympathies upon the death of your father at the death of your father your father's passing though I was barely acquainted only superficially I'm writing to you because I was a friend of your father by now prison officials must have informed you of his death his demise the bad news I assume I don't want to intrude on your grief sorrow privacy if in fact hadn't known your sorrow and the cir-cumstances of our lives known him very long only a few years permitted allowed only limited opportunities to become acquainted and the cir-cumstances of our lives I considered your father a friend I can't claim to know him your father well but our paths crossed often frequently I con-sidered him a good valuable friend fine man I was very sorry to hear learn of his death spoke often of you on many occasions his words much good love affection admiration I feel almost as if I you know you though I'm a complete stranger his moving words heart-felt about son com-pelled me to write this note if I can be helpful in any fashion manner if I can be of assistance in this matter at this difficult time place don't hesi-tate to let me know please don't

I was sorry to hear of your father's death. We were friends. Please accept my heartfelt regrets on this sad occasion.

Sir,
Some man must have fucked my mother. All I knew about him until your note said he's dead. Thanks.

It could have ended there. A case of mistaken identity. Or a lie. Or numerous lies. Or a hallucination. Or fabrication. Had I been duped. By whom. Father, son, both. Did they know each other or not. What did I know for sure about either one. What stake did I have in either man's story. If I connected the dots, would a picture emerge. One man dead, the other good as dead locked up two thousand miles away in an Arizona prison. Was any of it my business. Anybody's business.

I dress lightly, relying upon the pretty weather lady's promises.

A woman greets me and introduces herself as Suh Jung, Attorney Koppleman's paralegal assistant. She's a tiny, pleasant Asian woman with jet-black hair brutally cropped above her ears, a helmet, she'll explain later, necessary to protect herself from the cliché of submissiveness, the china-doll stereotype people immediately had applied when they saw a thick rope of hair hanging past her waist, hair that her father insisted must be uncut and worn twisted into a single braid in public, her mother combing, brushing, oiling her hair endlessly till shiny pounds of it lopped off the day the father died, and then, strangely, she'd wanted to save the hair she had hated, wanted to glue it back together strand by strand and drape it over one of those pedestaled heads you see in beauty shops so she and her mother could continue forever the grooming rituals that had been one of the few ways they could relate in a household her father relentlessly, meticulously, hammered into an exquisitely lifelike, flawless representation of his will, like those sailing ships in bottles or glass butterflies in the museum, so close to the real thing you stare and stare waiting for them to flutter away, a household the father shattered in a fit of pique or rage or boredom the day she opened the garage door after school and found him barefoot, shitty-pantsed, dangling from a rafter, beside the green family Buick.

In the lawyer's office she listened to my story about father and son, took notes carefully it seemed, though her eyes were cool, a somewhere-else distracted cool, while she performed her legal-assistant duties. Black, distant eyes framed in round, metal-rimmed old-lady spectacles belying the youthful freshness of her skin. Later when she'd talk about her dead father, I noticed the coolness of the first day, and was left to form my own impression of him since she volunteered few details, spoke instead about being a quiet, terrified girl trying to swim through shark-infested water without making waves. I guessed she had wanted to imitate the father's impenetrable gaze, practicing, practicing, till she believed she'd gotten it right, but she didn't get it right, probably because she never understood the father's coldness, never made her peace with the blankness behind his eyes where she yearned to see her image take shape, where it never did, never would. Gradually I came to pity her, her unsuccessful theft of her father's eyes, her transparent attempt to conceal her timidity behind the father's stare, timidity I despised because it reminded me of mine, my inadequacies and half measures and compromises, begging and fearing to be seen, my lack of directness, decisiveness, my deficiency of enterprise and imagination, manifested in her case by the theatrical gesture of chopping off her hair when confronted by the grand truth of her father's suicide. Timidity dooming her to cliché — staring off inscrutably into space.

Behind a desk almost comically dwarfing her (seeing it now, its acres of polished, blond wood should have alerted me to the limits, the impropriety of any intimacy we'd establish) she had listened politely, eventually dissuaded me from what I'd anticipated as the object of my visit — talking to Attorney Koppleman. She affirmed her postscript: no one in the office knew anything about a son in prison. I thanked her, accepted the card she offered that substantiated her willingness to help in any way she could.

Would you like me to call around out in Arizona. At least save you some time, get you started in the right direction.

Thanks. That's very kind of you. But I probably need to do some more thinking on this. And then I realized how stupidly wishy-washy I must have sounded. It galled me because I work hard to give just the opposite impression — appear as a man sure of himself. So perhaps that's why I flirted. Not flirting exactly, but asserting myself in the only way I could think of at the moment, by plainly, abruptly, letting her see I was interested. In her. The woman part of her. A decisive act, yet suspect from the beginning, since it sprang from no particular spark of attraction. Still, a much more decisive move than I'm usually capable of making — true or false. Hitting on her, so to speak, straight up, hard, asking for the home number she hastily scribbled on the back of her card, hurrying as if she suddenly remembered a lineup of urgent tasks awaiting our interview's termination. Her way of attending to a slightly embarrassing necessity. The way some women I've met treat sex. Jotting down the number, she was as out of character as I was, but we pulled it off.

The world is full of remarkable things. Amiri Baraka penned those words when he was still LeRoi Jones writing his way back to Newark and a new name after a lengthy sojourn among artsy, crazy white folks in the Village. One of my favorite lines from one of my favorite writers. Back in the day when I still pretended books were worth talking about, people were surprised to discover Baraka a favorite of mine, as quietly integrated and nonconfrontational a specimen as I seemed to be of America's longest, most violently reviled minority. It wasn't so much a matter of the quality of what Jones/Baraka had written as it was the chances he'd taken, chances in his art, in his life. Sacrifices of mind and body he endured so I could vicariously participate, safely holed up in my corner. Same lair where I sat out Vietnam, a college boy while my cousin and most guys from my high school were drafted, shot at, jailed, murdered, became drug addicts in wars raging here and abroad.

Remarkable things. With Suh Jung I smoked my first joint in years. At fifty-seven learned to bathe a woman and, what was harder, learned to relax in a tub while a woman bathed me. Contacting the son in prison not exactly on hold while she and I experienced low-order, remarkable things. I knew which Arizona prison held him and had received from the warden's office the information I'd requested about visiting. Completing my business with this woman, a necessary step in the process of preparing myself for whatever I decided to do next. Steaming water, her soapy hands scrubbing my shoulders, cleansed me, fortified me. I shed old skins. When the son in prison set his eyes on me, I wanted to glow. If he saw me at my best, wouldn't he understand everything.

One night I imagined the son here, his cell transformed to this room, the son imprisoned here with Suh Jung, sweet smoke settling in his lungs, mellowing him out after all the icy years. Me locked up in the black Arizona night fantasizing a woman. Would it be the same woman in both places at once or different limbs, eyes, wetnesses, scents, like those tigers whirling about Sambo, tigers no longer tigers as they chase one another faster and faster, overwhelming poor little Sambo's senses, his Sambo black brain as he tosses and turns in waking-sleep, a mixed-up colored boy, the coins his mother gave him clutched in a sweaty fist, trying once more to complete a simple errand and reach home in one piece.

The city bumps past, cut up through the bus windows. Suh Jung and I had headed for the back. Seats on the rear bench facing the driver meant fewer passengers stepping over, around, on you during the long ride uptown to the museum. Fewer people leaning over you. Sneezing. Coughing. Eavesdropping. Fewer strangers boxing you in, saying stuff you don't want to hear but you find yourself listening to anyway, the way you had watched in spite of yourself the TV set in your mother's living room she never turned off. I notice blood pooled in one of the back benches' butt-molded blue seats. A fresh, silver-dollar-sized glob. Fortunately, neither of us had splashed down in it. I check one more time the seats we're poised above, looking for blood, expecting blood, like blood's a constant danger, though I've never seen blood before on a bus bumping from uptown to downtown, downtown to uptown, in all the years of riding until this very day.

The Giacometti closes next weekend. We almost missed it.

Right on time, then. I'm away next week.

So you are going to Arizona.

I've been letting other things get in the way. Unless I set a hard date, the visit won't happen. You know. Like we kept putting off Giacometti.

You booked a flight.

Not yet.

But you're going for sure. Next week.

I think so think so think so think so think so.

I loved Giacometti's slinky dog. He was so . . . so . . . you know . . . *dog.* An alley-cat dog like the ones always upsetting garbage cans behind my father's store. Stringy and scrawny like them. Swaybacked. Always hunkered down like they're hiding or something's after them. Scruffy barbed-wire fur. Those floppy, flat dog feet like bedroom slippers.

To tell the truth, I missed her dog. I was overwhelmed by the crowd, the crowd of objects. Two floors, numerous galleries, still it was like fighting for a handhold on a subway pole. Spent most of my time reading captions. What I did see made me wonder why Giacometti didn't go insane. Maybe he did. He caught the strangeness and menace in everything. Said art always fails. Said art lied. Everybody's eyes lied. If he glanced away from a model to the image of it he was making, he said, when he looked back, the model would be different.

He understood that we go through life trying to remember what's right in front of our eyes. Experiments have demonstrated conclusively how unobservant the average person is, and, worse, how complacent, how unfazed by blindness. A man with a full beard gets paid to remove it and then goes about his usual day. The following day a researcher asks those who encountered the man, his coworkers for example, if he had a beard when they saw him the previous day. Most can't remember one way or the other, but assume he did. A few say the beard was missing. A few admit they'd never noticed a beard. A few insist vehemently they saw the invisible beard. I seem to recall the dead friend sporting a beard at one time or another during the period we were acquainted. Since I can't swear yes or no, I number myself, just as Giacometti numbered himself, among the blind.

I'd written again and the son had responded again. *Why not. My social calendar not full . . .* A smiling leopard in a cage. Step closer if you dare. A visiting form folded and tucked inside the flimsy prison envelope. Of course I couldn't help recalling the letter within a letter I'd received from the lawyer, Koppleman. The son instructed me to check the box for family and write *father* on the line following it. To cut red tape and speed up the process, I assumed, but I let the form sit a day or two, concerned some official would notice my name didn't match the son's, then realized lots of inmates wouldn't use (or know) their father's name, so I checked the family box, printed *father* in the space provided.

An official notice from the warden's office authorizing my visit took more than a month to reach me, and I began to regret lying on a form that had warned me, under penalty of law, not to perjure myself. My misgivings soured into mild paranoia. Had I compromised myself, broken a law that might send me too packing off to jail. Who reads the applications. How carefully do prison officials check alleged facts. What punishments could be levied against a person who falsifies information. The form a perfunctory measure, I had guessed, a form, properly executed and stamped, destined to gather dust in a file, retrievable just in case some official needed to cover her or his ass. Justify his or her existence. The existence of the state. Of teeming prisons in the middle of the desert.

I finally calmed down after I figured out that (a) without a DNA test no one could prove I wasn't the prisoner's father and (b) it wasn't a crime to believe I was. If what the son had written in his first letter was true, the prison would possess no record of his father. The dead friend past proclaiming his paternity. And even if he rose from the dead to argue his case, why would his claim, sans DNA confirmation, be more valid in the eyes of the law than mine. So what if he had visited. So what if he'd married the prisoner's mother. So what if he sincerely believed his belief of paternity. Mama's baby, Daddy's maybe.

Psychologists say there's a stage when a child doubts the adults raising it are its real family. How can parents prove otherwise. And why would a kid want to trade in the glamorous fairy tales he dreams up about his origins for a pair of ordinary, bumbling adults who impose stupid rules, stifling routines. Who needs their hostile world full of horrors and hate.

With Suh Jung's aid — why not use her, wasn't it always about finding uses for the people in your life, why would they be in your life if you had no use for them, and if you're using them, didn't that lend purpose to their lives, you're actually doing them a trickle-down favor, aren't you, allowing them to use you to feel themselves useful, and that's something, isn't it, better than nothing anyway, than being useless or used up — I gathered more information about the son in prison. Accumulated a file, biography, character sketch, rap sheet a.k.a. his criminal career.

Here's what the papers said: He's done lots of bad things, the worst kinds of things, and if we could kill him, we would, but we can't, so we'll never, never let him go.

Are you surprised, she'd asked.

I didn't know what to expect, I had replied. Not traveling out west to forgive him or bust him out or bring him back alive. Just visit. Just fill in for the dead father. Once. One time enough and it's finished.

You're going to wear out the words, she jokes as she glances over at me sitting beside her in her bed that occupies the same room with a pullman fridge and stove. Her jibe less joke than complaint: I'm sick and tired of your obsessive poring over a few dog-eared scraps of paper extracted from Arizona's bottomless pit of records is what she's saying with a slight curl of one side of her thin mouth, a grimace that could be construed as the beginning of a smirk she decides is not worth carrying full term.

I keep on reading. Avoid the disappointment a peek at her naked body would trigger. The eroticism between us had dulled rather too quickly it seemed. An older man's childishness partly at fault. Why else would I be impatient after a few weeks because her hips didn't round and spread, the negligible mounds beneath her nipples swell. Her boyish look not a stage, it was what I was going to get, period, even if the business between us survives longer than I have any reason to expect. No, things aren't going to get better, and I'm wasting precious time. Given my age, how many more chances could I expect.

No matter how many times you read them, she says, the words won't change. Why read the same ugly facts over and over.

(A) Because my willing, skilled accomplice gathered them for me. (B) Curiosity.

This whole visiting business way over the top, you admit it yourself, so I don't pretend I can put myself in your shoes, but still, his crimes would affect any sane person's decision to go or not.

Is he guilty. How can you be certain based on a few sheets of paper.

Too much in the record for a case of mistaken identity. Huh-uh. Plus or minus a few felonies, the man's been busy. A real bad actor.

Are you casting the first stone.

A whole building's been dumped on the poor guy. And he's thrown his share of bricks at other folks. I'd hate to bump into him in a dark alley.

Maybe you already have, my friend. Maybe you have and maybe you've enjoyed it.

You're more than a little weird about this, you know. What the hell are you talking about.

Just that people wind up in situations there's no accounting for. Situations when innocence or guilt are extremely beside the point. Situations when nothing's for sure except some of us are on one side of the bars, some on the other side, and nobody knows which side is which.

Right. But I know I haven't robbed or kidnapped or murdered anyone. Have you.

Have I. Do you really want to know. Everyone has crimes to answer for, don't they. Even you. Suppose I said my crimes are more terrible than his. A string of victims. Many, many murders. Would you believe me. Is your heart beating a little faster.

(A) No. And (B) you're not scaring me. Put those damned papers away, and turn off the light, please. I have work tomorrow.

I will, if you listen to my confession. It might sound better in the dark.

Enough already. I'm tired. I need sleep. Stop acting stupidly because you can't make up your mind about Arizona.

My mind's made up. The prison said yes. I'm on my way.

I'll be fucking glad when it's over and done.

And me back in the arms of my love. Will you be faithful while your sweet, aging serial killer's away.

She tries to snatch the papers but misses. I drop them over the side of the pullout bed. Like the bed, she is small and light. Easy to fold up and subdue even for an older fellow. When I wrap myself around her, my body's so much larger than hers, she almost vanishes. When we fuck, or now capturing her, punishing her, I see very little of her flesh. I'm aware of my size, my strength towering over her squirming, her thrashing, her gasps for breath. I am her father's stare, the steel gate dropping over the tiger pit in which she's trapped, naked, begging for food and water. Air. Light.

I arrive on Sunday. Two days late for reasons I can't explain to myself. I flew over mountains, then desert flatness that seemed to go on forever. It must have been Ohio, Illinois, Iowa, Nebraska, not actual desert but the nation's breadbasket, so they say, fruited plains, amber waves of grain, fields irrigated by giant machines day after day spreading water in the same pattern to create circles, squares, rectangles, below. Arable soil gradually giving way to sandy grit as the plane drones westward, through clouds, over another rugged seam of mountains, and then as I peer down at the undramatic nothingness beyond the far edge of wrinkled terrain, the surface of the earth flips over like a pancake. What's aboveground buried, what's below ground suddenly exposed. Upside-down mountains are hollow shells, deep, deep gouges in the stony waste, their invisible peaks underground, pointing to hell.

A bit of confusion, bureaucratic stuttering and sputtering when confronted by my tardy arrival, a private calling his sergeant, sergeant phoning officer in charge of visitation, each searching for verification, for duplication, for assurance certified in black and white that she or he is off the hook, not guilty of disrupting the checks and balances of prison routine. I present myself hat in hand, remorseful, apologetic, *please, please, give me another chance please,* forgive me for missing day one and two of the scheduled three-day visit, for checking in the morning of day three instead of day one. Am I still eligible or will I be shooed away like a starving beggar from the rich man's table.

I overhear two guards discussing a coyote whose scavenging brought it down out of the slightly elevated wilderness of rock and brush beginning a few miles or so from the prison's steel-fenced perimeter. I learn how patiently guards in the tower spied on the coyote's cautious trespass, a blip at first, up and back along the horizon, then a discernible shape — skinny legs, long pointed ears, bushy tail — a scraggly critter drawn by easy prey or coyote curiosity closer and closer to the prison until it's within rifle range and the guards take turns profiling it through their sharpshooting sniper scopes, a sad-faced, cartoon coyote they christen whatever guards would christen a creature they will kill one day, a spook, a mirage, so quick on its feet, bolder as it's allowed to approach nearer without being challenged, does it believe it can't be seen, flitting from shadow to shadow, camouflaged by hovering darkness, by mottled fur, a shadow itself, instantly freezing, sniffing the air, then trotting again back and forth along the skyline, skittish through coverless space, up and back, parry, thrust, and retreat, ears pricked to attention when the rare service vehicle enters or

leaves the prison parking lot before dawn, murky predawn the coyote's time, the darkness divulging it, a drop from a leaky pipe, a
phantom prowling nearer and nearer as if the electrified steel
fence is one boundary of its cage, an easy shot now the guards for-
bear taking, too easy, or perhaps it's more fun to observe their mascot play, watch it pounce on a mouse and pummel it in swift paws
bat-bat-bat before its jaws snap the rodent's neck, or maybe the
name they named it a kind of protection for a while till somebody
comes on duty one morning or premorning really when the first
shift after the night shift has to haul itself out of bed, out of prefab
homes lining the road to the prison entrance, shitty box houses,
a few with bright patches of something growing in boxes beside
the front steps, boxes you can't see at that black hour from your
pickup, eyes locked in the tunnel your headlights carve, a bad-
head, bad-attitude morning, thinking about quitting this stinking
job, getting the fuck out before you're caught Kilroying or cuck-
olded in the town's one swinging joint, cussed out, serving pussy
probation till further notice, cancer eating his mamma, daddy long
gone, kids sick or fighting or crazy on pot or dead or in prison so
he draws a bead and *pow,* blood seeps into the sand, the coyote buz-
zard bait by the time I eavesdrop on two guards badmouthing their
assassin colleague, laughing at him, at the coyote's surprise, the
dead animal still serving time as a conversation piece, recycled in
this desert sparseness, desert of extremes, of keepers and kept, silence and screams, cold and hot, thirst and drunkenness, no time,
too much time.

A spiffy, spit-and-polished platinum-blond guard whose nametag
I read and promptly forget, *Lieutenant,* another guard addresses
her, Lieutenant, each breast under her white blouse as large as
poor Suh Jung's head, smiles up at me from the counter where
she's installed, hands me the document she's stamped, slides me a
tray for unloading everything in my pockets, stores it when I'm finished. Now, that wasn't so bad, was it, sir. Gives me a receipt and a
green ticket with matching numbers. Points me toward a metal detector standing stark and foursquare as a guillotine whose eye I
must pass through before I'm allowed to enter the prison.

Beyond the detector one more locked door I must be buzzed
through and I'm outside again, in an open-air, tunnel-like enclosure of cyclone fencing bristling on sides and top with razor wire, a
corridor or chute or funnel or maze I must negotiate while some-

one somewhere at a machine measures and records my every step, false move, heartbeat, scream, drop of sweat, of blood when my hands tear at the razor wire.

I pass all the way through the tunnel to a last checkpoint, a small cinder-block hut squatting beside the final sliding gate guarding the visiting yard. Thirty yards away, across the yard, at an identical gated entranceway facing this one, guards are mustering inmates dressed in orange jumpsuits.

In a slot at the bottom of the hut's window you must surrender your numbered green ticket to receive a red one. Two groups of women and children ahead of me in line require a few minutes each for this procedure. Then I hold up the works. Feel on my back the helplessness and irritation of visits stalled. Five, ten minutes in the wire bullpen beside the hut, long enough to register a miraculous change in temperature. Less than an hour before, crossing the parking lot, I'd wondered if I'd dressed warmly enough. Now Arizona sun bakes my neck. I'm wishing for shade, for the sunglasses not permitted inside. My throat's parched. Will I be able to speak if spoken to. Through the hut's thick glass, bulletproof I'm guessing, I watch two officers talking. One steps away to a wall phone. The other plops down at a shelflike mini-desk, shuffles papers, punches buttons on a console. A dumb show since I couldn't hear a thing through the slab of greenish glass.

Did I stand in the cage five minutes or ten or twenty. What I recall is mounting heat, sweat spiders crawling inside my clothes, my eyes blinking, losing track of time, not caring about time, shakiness, numbness, mumbling to myself, stiffening rage, morphing combinations of all the above, yet overriding each sensation, the urge to flee, to be elsewhere, anywhere other than stalled at that gate, waiting to be snatched inside or driven away or, worse, pinned there forever. I dream of coolness, far, far away where I could bury my throbbing head, coolness miles deep below the sand, so deep you can hear the subterranean chortle of rivers on the opposite face of the planet.

At last someone exits the concrete hut from a door I hadn't noticed, addressing me, I think.

Sorry, sir. Computer says your visit's canceled. Try the warden's office after 9:00 A.M. Monday. Sorry about the mix-up. Now stand back please.

Contributors' Notes

100 Other Distinguished Stories of 2003

Editorial Addresses

Contributors' Notes

SHERMAN ALEXIE is the author of the novels *Reservation Blues* and *Indian Killer* and the short story collections *The Toughest Indian in the World, The Lone Ranger and Tonto Fistfight in Heaven,* and most recently, *Ten Little Indians.* He was named one of the "Twenty Writers for the Twenty-first Century" by *The New Yorker.*

▪ I live with my family in Seattle, which is also home to dozens of homeless Native Americans. Yes, I know that homeless folks don't have homes, but because these are aboriginal homeless folks, I think they turn the earth and air and water into houses, though they don't have the four walls and running water to prove it. Or something like that. I interact almost daily with homeless Indians, and I've always felt the need to write about them. A few years ago, I wrote "What You Pawn I Will Redeem," thought it was too sentimental on first reading, and tossed it into the U-Haul cardboard box that I use to save the crap that I want to keep for posterity but will never read again. My story about a homeless Indian became, well, sort of homeless. But last year, while putting together my short story collection *Ten Little Indians,* I reached into that U-Haul box for some reason, pulled out this story, read it again, and thought, Hey, this is pretty good. So publishing this story made me feel like an adult who'd found a beloved childhood toy in the attic. But it also makes me a little nervous. You see, my first book of short stories, *The Lone Ranger and Tonto Fistfight in Heaven,* has, in paperback, outsold all of my other books combined and remains my signature book. And now "What You Pawn I Will Redeem" has become my signature story, and because it is, in its themes and construction, very much like the stories in *Lone Ranger,* I worry that I'm just a repetitive bastard. Oh, well. Such are the worries of a worrisome author.

T. CORAGHESSAN BOYLE is the author of seventeen works of fiction, including his most recent novels, *Drop City* and *The Inner Circle;* the forthcoming collection, *Tooth and Claw;* and a college text, *Doubletakes.* His Web site, where many lively debates occur and a host of outré opinions are expressed, is tcboyle.com. All are welcome there.

▪ One of the great and little-acknowledged contributions of our friends is how often they slip us fragmented ideas for stories, just as they reveal to us their deepest fears and sexual secrets so that we can expose them to the world at large (and, it goes without saying, make money off of them). Such is the case here. An old friend told me of his college acquaintance who found himself the owner of a cat very much like the one depicted in this story. Here are the details as I received them: This man, the college acquaintance, won the cat on a roll of dice, kept it locked in the bedroom of his one-bedroom apartment, and was never able to stir much affection in the animal's felid heart; feeding times were messy. Very messy. My task was to wonder what this might mean and how it might be given shape. The result, which takes me all the way back to the Darwinian conundrum of the "Descent of Man," the title story of my first collection, is "Tooth and Claw," the title story of my next.

CATHERINE BRADY is the author of two collections of short stories, *Curled in the Bed of Love,* a cowinner of the 2002 Flannery O'Connor Award for Short Fiction, and *The End of the Class War,* a finalist for the 2000 Western States Book Award in Fiction. She teaches in the MFA in Writing Program at the University of San Francisco.

▪ I wrote this story not long after the attack on the World Trade Center, when political reality seemed like a giant maw and I felt so sharply how small and fragile the realm of the personal is — the realm where a writer resides. I was thinking about whether this small enclosure could withstand the buffeting forces of a violent, ideology-driven world. I had also been thinking about writing a story about a husband and wife who remain tied to each other even after the marriage breaks up because of another woman. I can never write until I have two stories to tell at the same time; the way one story gets disrupted by another is what drives me as a writer. The narrator of this story and Hassan, her impulsive, gregarious husband, have survived the ayatollah's revolution in Iran only to have their marriage founder years after they flee to the relatively safe soil of the United States. Their past and their present provide two incompatible frames of reference for their life together.

If the story works, each of these frames must be read in light of the other. I hope that contradictions flourish at the sentence level — in the reconfigured meanings of *urgency* and *ardor* and *allegiance* according to the prevailing currency in each country — and that the tension of the plot reveals unexpected parallels as well. Hassan's temperamental disinclination to follow rules became a political liability in Iran and is redefined by his American employer and his new lover as a symptom of alcoholism. His wife feared history would crush him, and now it has made him irrelevant twice, by forcing him into useless exile from his native country and by renaming his transgressions in his adopted country. The narrator's loyalty *might* be the residue of the terror she felt for her husband in Iran, *might* be neatly categorized as codependence, *might* constitute an entirely different kind of devotion. I tried to boot out of the story any sentences that didn't adhere to this vulnerable, uncertain, operative verb tense of fiction.

SARAH SHUN-LIEN BYNUM's first novel, *Madeleine Is Sleeping,* was published in September 2004. Her short fiction has appeared in *The Georgia Review* and *Alaska Quarterly Review* and is forthcoming in *TriQuarterly.* A graduate of Brown University and the Iowa Writers' Workshop, she has received fellowships from the MacDowell Colony and Ledig House International Writers' Colony, as well as an Iowa Arts Fellowship. She lives with her husband in Brooklyn, New York.

▪ After I graduated from college, I began teaching seventh- and eighth-grade English at a school in Park Slope, Brooklyn. After a few years, I thought I had exhausted my store of mistakes and could now finally relax into becoming a good teacher. But one of the maddening, addictive things about teaching is that it never ceases to surprise you: there are always unexpected triumphs, and also bewildering failures. I wrote this story once I was no longer a teacher, but was still trying to make sense of those miracles and calamities. "Accomplice" grew out of my efforts to understand how a well-conceived assignment managed to go awry. How could such involved, worldly, educated parents accept as real a teacher's report that was so obviously false? It was only by imagining Ms. Hempel's relationship with her father that I began to grasp what it might feel like, as a parent, to be the only one who recognizes your child's talent and greatness, and how hungrily you might welcome the news that you're not alone, after all.

I am indebted to T. R. Hummer at *The Georgia Review* for publishing the story, and especially to my former students at the Berkeley Carroll School.

CHARLES D'AMBROSIO is the author of *The Point and Other Stories.* A new collection, *The Dead Fish Museum,* is forthcoming. He lives in Portland, Oregon.

▪ Like most stories, "Screenwriter" has an archaeology of tools and graves and pottery and other crude artifacts dating back far enough so that everything I say about it now strikes me as baloney. The early characters were no better than apes, the dialogue was primitive, the plot rudimentary. Just for fun, here are four things from the dig site:

The story began with an old woman I knew who was undergoing shock treatment. Monday mornings she was wheeled downstairs for treatment. She came back an incoherent mess. The treatments turned her into a sex fiend, seventy years old and hitching up her hospital gown and dancing the cha-cha-cha in the hallways. In order to administer shock, they took away her false teeth; she'd come to dinner and stare dumbly down at her plate, her face crumpled like an empty purse. Her tongue probed her mouth constantly and without volition, like a lizard, feeling for those teeth; toothless, she lisped, each word shucked of its shell of consonants, a vowel-y mush. "I forget my name. What's my name? Winters, I don't go out," she'd say, just another voice from rat's alley.

A few years later and three thousand miles away, a friend of mine casually remarked that he'd made a million dollars the previous year but that he had nothing to show for it. This was in Hollywood, where at least some of the people, like my friend, see right through themselves, but it doesn't do them much good anyway. I admire people in whom lucidity yields insight but doesn't resolve into cynicism or pessimism, both of which are so faux-profound and boring. My friend looks a lot like Joseph Brodsky, and at one critical stage of composition I was reading nothing but Brodsky, and his great motto ("I permitted myself everything but the complaint," which so coolly trumps Ivan Karamazov's gripe, "Everything is permitted") was my prayer.

There used to be a peregrine falcon on the roof of the hospital in my story. It kept killing pigeons, and the narrator kept telling his therapist about it, but she wasn't interested. That made both the falcon and the therapist unnecessary.

Finally, the narrator was always very mean and anxious, so late in the writing I gave the ballerina my wife's blue eyes and made him tell the story again. That little trick brought out his broken capacity for sympathy.

STUART DYBEK's first two collections of stories, *Childhood and Other Neighborhoods* and *The Coast of Chicago*, were reprinted in 2003 along with a new novel-in-stories, *I Sailed with Magellan*. A new collection of poems, *Streets in Their Own Ink*, will be published in the fall of 2004.

▪ Long ago on a late afternoon, I passed an open tavern and saw two men in tank tops in the bar. One appeared to be feeling up the hairy chest of the other. I think he was kidding around.

Many years later, during a summer fiesta called El Grito, I sat on a curb eating a taco and watching the brilliant photographer Paul D'Amato, who stood at the lip of an outdoor ring, snapping pictures of the two paunchy masked wrestlers who were throwing each other about. When one of the wrestlers was flung over the ropes, almost crushing both my friend Paul and his camera, it was as if suddenly that wrestler was thrown into my story, which up to that moment did not have a wrestler in it.

"Breasts" is also based on a murder that occurred in my neighborhood when I was growing up. While writing the story I made an effort to research the actual crime. Fortunately, I wasn't able to find any official record of it.

DEBORAH EISENBERG is the author of a play, *Pastorale*, and three volumes of short fiction: *Transactions in a Foreign Currency, Under the 82nd Airborne*, and *All Around Atlantis*. She lives in New York City and teaches at the University of Virginia.

• I gave my poor character Otto just about everything you could ask for — a wonderful and continuing love, health, plenty of money, a gratifying job, and so on. He's not a casualty of the unjust workings of the world, he's a beneficiary. He's also reasonably insightful and reflective; he's intensely aware that the world *is* unjust and aware of the very serious problems that less fortunate people have — yet everything annoys him. There are people he cares about a lot, but his affection for them doesn't keep him from being irritable and thoughtless in most of his dealings with them. Lack of good fortune just isn't his problem, so what is? That is, I was thinking about the nature of the anguish that good fortune can't address, and might even, in certain ways, activate.

PAULA FOX has been writing both novels and stories for young people for over forty years. Since her first novel, *Poor George*, and her first book for children, *Maurice's Room*, she has published twenty-nine books, most recently a memoir called *Borrowed Finery*. She was born in New York City in 1923.

• Years ago, I found a small stray female dog in front of my apartment house in New York City. She wagged her tail as I looked at her and I took her in. She was both timid and willful, like Grace in the story. Its title also refers to the change in John Hillman, into a state of grace.

NELL FREUDENBERGER was born in New York City in 1975 and grew up in Los Angeles. She has taught high school students in Bangkok, New Delhi, and New York City. Her collection of stories, "Lucky Girls," won the PEN/Faulkner Malamud Award and the Sue Kaufman Prize for First Fiction. Her stories have been published in *The New Yorker, The Paris Review, Granta*, and *The O. Henry Prize Stories 2004*. She lives in New York City.

• I wrote this story after my third trip to India. I went because I wasn't sure why I kept writing stories that took place there; it seemed to me that as an American, I should be writing about people and things at home. I was especially suspicious of the idea of travel as "research" for stories. The boarding house where I stayed was picturesque — on top of a 1930s maternity hospital, behind a temple with an old-fashioned vegetable market — but the story I eventually wrote happens mostly in the kinds of apartments and rooms that could exist in any large contemporary city.

A friend in Bombay, who was tutoring high school students for the American and British college entrance exams, told me that his students generally found poetry boring, with the exception of Marvell's "To His Coy Mistress." The teenage girls responded to the poem as a seduction attempt, in spite of its archaic language. I started the story with that idea; it's funny (and somewhat reassuring) that I went all the way to India and came back with an anecdote I could just as easily have heard at home.

EDWARD P. JONES is the author of the novel *The Known World,* recipient of the 2004 National Book Critics Circle Award and the Pulitzer Prize for fiction, as well as *Lost in the City: Stories.*

▪ A minor character, Elaine, was in an earlier story, "A New Man," where she disappeared. She is again a minor character, but the new story reveals the world into which she vanished.

TRUDY LEWIS is the author of the short story collection *The Bones of Garbo,* winner of the 2002 Sandstone Prize in Short Fiction. Her stories have appeared in *The Atlantic Monthly, Chelsea, Five Points, New England Review, Third Coast,* and *Witness.* Her first novel, *Private Correspondences,* won the William Goyen Prize. She is also the recipient of a Lawrence Foundation Award from *Prairie Schooner.* Lewis is an associate professor of English and women's and gender studies at the University of Missouri, Columbia, and a member of the Anvil/lyre Studio, a multimedia arts collective founded by her husband, the poet Mike Barrett.

▪ I began writing "Limestone Diner" one spring break when my mother, Linda Lewis, was visiting me; most of my work can be traced, in one way or another, to her influence. At the time, I was studying *Persephone,* an amazing painting by Thomas Hart Benton which depicts the mythic virgin as a Missouri farm girl. I was also rereading the fiction of Alice Munro, dipping into *Open Secrets* or *The Progress of Love* almost every day over lunch. In fact, "Limestone Diner" is a tribute to Munro's "Circle of Prayer."

In Munro's story, the protagonist, Trudy, faces a life crisis when her daughter's classmate is killed in a pickup accident on a country road; my own story is an attempt to reimagine, through collage, transposition, and free interpretation, the family history of my own name. The first image of the story comes from my husband, who saw a field of smashed cupcakes at the site of a fatal accident here in central Missouri, and spoke about it long afterward. "Limestone Diner" is the first in a series of stories about the imaginary (yet historically grounded) community of Boonslick, Missouri; these stories are written in homage to my adopted state, which has brought me two sons, a dog, a livelihood, an endless array of hiking trails, and a new appreciation for the natural world. My special thanks go to Toni Hoberecht, a friend from my college days at the University of Tulsa, who gave me some insightful suggestions for revision. Thanks as well to Tina (May) Hall, whose brilliance and imagination continue to inspire me, long after she has left graduate school for an intellectual home of her own. Thanks to Carrie Wheat, former fiction editor at *Meridian,* who treated the story with great care. Finally, thanks to Lorrie Moore for selecting "Limestone Diner" to be included in the anthology; her work is a powerful touchstone.

JILL MCCORKLE is the author of five novels, among them *Tending to Virginia* and *Carolina Moon,* and three short story collections, most recently *Creatures of Habit.* She is the recipient of the John Dos Passos Prize, the New England Booksellers Award, and the North Carolina Award for Literature. She lives near Boston and teaches in the MFA Writing Program at Bennington College.

• Usually my stories begin with a line of dialogue or the idea of a particular character and then take shape along the way. With "Intervention" my idea was the ending; I imagined a person getting into a car with someone she knew should not be driving. I imagined that she was knowingly committing a kind of sacrificial suicide, if not on that particular ride, then on the next one or the next. For a year I kept toying with that idea, thinking of reasons a person would do such a thing. This is her spouse; she is devoted. But why to this extent? I began writing about the intervention about to take place within this family and before I knew it, I was in Marilyn's past and viewing the history of a marriage in which Sid's loyalty and faithfulness and forgiveness had held it all together for years. I began to see and understand how he had evolved into this man who now has a drinking problem, and I was surprised to find how I sided with him, and how Marilyn's act of getting into the car became something I admired and was in fact symbolic of her own redemption and a marriage bond that because of all it weathered is now indestructible.

THOMAS MCGUANE was born in Michigan, educated at Michigan State University, Yale, and Stanford, where he held the Wallace Stegner Fellowship in writing. He has lived in Montana since 1968.

• Writing fiction is more improvisatory than most of its practitioners care to admit; and this story's origins are a bit askew to the result, in its details. The notion was comic: a man courting a woman with modest success takes her on a trip meant to display his talents as a businessman, thinking this will finalize her commitment to him. Instead, his flaws of character are revealed and the story ends with her adamant avoidance. For the author, the surprises lay in the way the small world around these two seems to reveal the disintegration of their relationship, suggesting — I hope eerily — an unexpected connection.

ALICE MUNRO was born in Wingham, Ontario, Canada (twenty miles from where she now lives), in 1931. She married at the age of twenty, moved to British Columbia, raised three daughters, helped her husband start a bookstore, and began to write short stories while waiting to have the time (and the maturity) to write a novel. Some time ago she moved back to Ontario, and married again. She is still waiting.

▪ The story "Runaway" actually began with a landscape. The part of Ontario where I live is generally thought to lack features, and not to differ much from one county to another. I suppose you need long familiarity with it to see it as I do. At any rate, I became particularly interested in a landscape called the Dundalk Plain, ninety or so miles from where we live. This is a high, flat, sour piece of land, badly drained because of the moraines at a distance on three sides, and I must have seen it, or always imagined it, under heavy rain. That gave me the horse farm and the uneasy couple, then the woman returning from her Greek holiday, then the goat, and so on. Now that I write this down it sounds unlikely, but as far as I know it is true.

ANGELA PNEUMAN lives in San Francisco, where she works as a copywriter in the wine industry and teaches fiction writing at Stanford University. Her stories have appeared or are forthcoming in *Ploughshares, Glimmer Train, The Iowa Review, The Virginia Quarterly Review, New England Review,* and other literary magazines. She is finishing a collection of short stories and a novel.

▪ "All Saints Day" is the first story in a novel-in-stories. I grew up in a tiny Kentucky town, home to a Protestant Evangelical college and seminary as well as three Christian missionary organizations. After-church dinner discussions boiled down to fine, denominational distinctions, such as whether full-immersion baptism was more biblical than water dribbled onto the crown of the head, or whether speaking in tongues became acceptable if you could also *interpret* the language. All the stores in town closed on Sunday, and no business sold cigarettes even though we were surrounded by tobacco farms. As a child, I read the Bible every day and came to love the stories that rarely appeared in sermons — stories of violence, obsession, and the strange, silent mystery of sex. Rahab the harlot dangling spies from her window on a scarlet cord; Esther trying out for queen after months of beauty treatments; Ruth gleaning in the fields of Boaz, then perfuming herself and sneaking through the night to lie at his feet on the threshing floor. Salome, just a girl, was my favorite. My town did not go in for dancing of any kind, but I flung myself around the privacy of my room, sure that I had all the right moves.

ANNIE PROULX lives and writes in the Medicine Bow Mountains of Wyoming.

• "What Kind of Furniture Would Jesus Pick?" was written for a second collection of short stories set in Wyoming, *Bad Dirt,* reflecting various facets of life in this rural western state. It was meant to reflect some of the difficulties ranchers are experiencing in the "Cowboy State" these days.

R. T. SMITH's stories have appeared in *The Missouri Review, The Southern Review, The Virginia Quarterly Review, Prairie Schooner,* and other journals, as well as the 2002 and 2004 volumes of *New Stories from the South.* His most recent books are collections of poetry — *The Hollow Log Lounge* and *Brightwood.* Smith lives in Rockbridge County, Virginia, and edits *Shenandoah: The Washington and Lee University Review.* He is currently using a fiction writing fellowship from the Virginia Commission for the Arts to finish a manuscript collection of short stories called "Jesus Wept."

• I grew up drinking deeply and incautiously from Douglas Southall Freeman's Pulitzer Prize–winning biography of Robert E. Lee, but after many years and subsequent reading (in Foote, Emory Thomas, and most recently Roy Blount) I began to see that my idol was both more complicated and more interesting than I had imagined. Then, about a decade ago, I moved to Lexington, Virginia, and began working at Washington and Lee University, where Lee is entombed in the chapel that bears his name. I don't know how many visiting writers I have ushered through that building and up to the dignified recumbent marble likeness of Marse Robert. Eventually, though, I decided I should know a little more about the history of the place but was, at the same time, relieved that Lee Chapel provides none of those omniscient logorrhoeic docents who arrest you like Coleridge's Ancient Mariner and drain all the mystery out of a place. I have, however, encountered a few members of that tribe of museum guides, and for some reason when I was on a particularly unsettling flight back into the Deep South a couple of years ago I began to remember one somewhat charming but inexhaustible docent. To calm myself, I began imagining what that dear lady might have said about Lee Chapel, and before I knew it, I was scribbling notes and chuckling in time with the turbulence. The voice, as I imagined it, both hypnotized and irritated me, and by the time I reached home a few days later, I had a loose draft full of accidentally half-accurate details about the chapel, which meant I had some research to do. Now the ratio of facts to inaccuracies in the monologue is my intent, though not Miss Sibby's, and every time I go into the shrine, I remember to thank the stars on the general's collar that no such wraith as my invented narrator haunts the actual chapel.

JOHN UPDIKE was born in Shillington, Pennsylvania, in 1932. He attended the local public schools, Harvard College, and, for a year, the Ruskin School of Drawing and Fine Art in Oxford, England. From 1955 to 1957 he was a member of the staff of *The New Yorker*, and since 1957 he has lived in Massachusetts as a free-lance writer. This is his thirteenth appearance in *The Best American Short Stories*.

▪ I never miss a high school class reunion, and never come away without a story. Not all of them I write, but this one I did, soon after my fiftieth. It has two heroines — three, counting Betty Lou, who did the work of this particular get-together. But Mamie, being the gracious, thoughtful hostess as she lies in the hospital bed with her bones disintegrating, is the presiding spirit, the class pep girl, the embodiment of sentimental loyalty to that accident which places a group of assorted young Americans in heated daily proximity for a number of years. Her attempt to make sense of her coming death prepares the hero for the reunion nonattender, Elizanne, who brings from afar, from fifty years away, a breath of that old heat, when their lives lay all before them, and death was an unreal possibility. In villages of old, people watched one another age day by day, year by year; in modern America, where leaving home is virtually a duty, fitful illuminations show us the distances we have traversed since that initial cluster, those moist, anxious first contacts in a world that, as Prospero says to Miranda, "'tis new to thee." What a wonder it is to see a peeping out, from the crumpled face of a fellow septuagenarian, unmistakable evidence of a human identity first encountered in kindergarten! It is a miracle. All our lives, older people around us bore us with telling stories in which nothing is extraordinary except that it is *their* story; they were there. And they have not changed, not really. Yet the great stilts of time that Proust describes at the end of *Remembrance of Things Past* are undeniably there, too, under our feet. We have grown impossibly tall in a dimension we never believed in. This is a religious story, of course — at least it tries to describe the strangeness of human existence in which religion takes root.

MARY YUKARI WATERS is the recipient of a writing grant from the National Endowment for the Arts. Her fiction has appeared on NPR's *Selected Shorts* and in the following anthologies: *Best American Short Stories 2002* and *2003*, *The O. Henry Prize Stories*, *The Pushcart Book of Short Stories: The Best Short Stories from a Quarter-Century of the Pushcart Prize*, and Francis Ford Coppola's *Zoetrope: All-Story, Anthology 2*. Her debut short story collection, *The Laws of Evening*, was published in 2003. It was chosen by *Newsday* and the *San Francisco Chronicle* as one of the Best Books of 2003. *The Laws of Eve-*

ning was also a Book Sense 76 selection, a selection for Barnes & Noble's Discover Great New Writers program, and a 2004 Notable Book for the Kiriyama Prize.

• This story was written during a time when I had a brief, unreasoning fascination with monkeys. It started with a chance visit to the zoo, when I was so charmed by the monkeys' behavior that after I went home I couldn't get them out of my mind. I rented a Jane Goodall video. I checked out library books — just picture books at first, then actual scientific books. For a long time, it never occurred to me to use any of this in my fiction. As a matter of fact, I was indulging in this guilty pastime in order to avoid writing. I was under a lot of pressure to come up with a final story for my collection, which consisted of stories set in Japan and spanning a chronological period from World War II up to the present day. There was no room in such a collection for monkeys — or so I thought. It just goes to show you. What, exactly, I don't know — maybe that we should follow our hearts when something intrigues us, no matter how irrelevant it may seem. Or maybe that desperate writers will always find connections.

JOHN EDGAR WIDEMAN was born in 1941 in Washington, D.C., and attended the Pittsburgh public schools, the University of Pennsylvania, Oxford University, and the University of Iowa Writers' Workshop. He has taught at the University of Pennsylvania, the University of Wyoming, and the University of Massachusetts, and he was recently appointed the Asa Messer Professor and professor of English and Africana studies at Brown University. He has written and edited more than twenty books of fiction and essays. Wideman lives in New York City.

• I began my story about two years ago and finished it a year ago. Its title, courtesy of Ludwig Wittgenstein (which is too long and unwieldy to quote here, though not quoting it is consuming more space than quoting it), originated as a protest against the pointlessness of protest. The world is very large. Each of us is very small. Most of us at some point or another protest smallness and the powerlessness it confers. Many harbor fantasies of being larger — large, large as in hip-hop living large. Oblivious to our suffering and aspirations, the big, double-chinned world feeds on our fantasies, consumes our protests and desires, growing larger while we shrink even smaller relative to the big world's size. What to do about such an unfair, unyielding, humiliating state of affairs? Our responses land the majority of us somewhere in the middle of a continuum between Mother Teresa and a serial killer. A sense of unfairness, the frustration and rage it engenders, linger on. To alleviate discomfort, we become model prisoners. Accept the role of ant in an anthill. Or achieve the status of a relatively well tended sheep in a flock of sheep. My story protests such a pitiful fate and examines some ways it is inflicted, how it afflicts.

100 Other Distinguished Stories of 2003

SELECTED BY KATRINA KENISON

SHEPARD, KAREN
Incognito with My Brother. *Bomb*,
Fall.
SIMON, BETH
Bialy Cafe. *The Gettysburg Review*, Vol.
16, No. 4.
SONNENBERG, BRITTANI
Tierney's Gourmet. *Ploughshares*, Vol.
29, No. 4.
SPARK, DEBRA
The Revived Art of the Toy Theatre.
Agni Review, No. 58.
STEWART, TRENTON LEE
Moriah. *New England Review*, Vol. 24,
No. 2.
STUCKEY-FRENCH, ELIZABETH
Mudlavia. *The Atlantic Monthly*,
September.

UNFERTH, DEB OLIN
Mr. Simmons Takes a Prisoner.
Harper's Magazine, August.

VAPNYAR, LARA
There Are Jews in My House. *Open
City*, No. 17.
Love Lessons Mondays, 9 A.M. *The
New Yorker*, June 16 and 23.

WALLACE, DANIEL
The Town of Sarah. *Five Points*, Vol. 7,
No. 3.
WEESNER, TED, JR.
Tuscaloosa. *Ploughshares*, Vol. 29,
No. 4.
WILLIAMS, JOY
Fortune. *Tin House*, No. 16.
WOLFF, TOBIAS
The Benefit of the Doubt. *The New
Yorker*, July 14 and 21.

Editorial Addresses of American and Canadian Magazines Publishing Short Stories

African American Review
Shannon Hall 119
St. Louis University
220 North Grand Union Boulevard
St. Louis, MO 63103-2007
$38, Joe Weixlmann

Agni Review
Boston University Writing Program
Boston University
236 Bay State Road
Boston, MA 02115
$15, Sven Birkerts

Alabama Literary Review
272 Smith Hall
Troy State University
Troy, AL 36082
$10, Donald Noble

Alaska Quarterly Review
University of Alaska, Anchorage
3211 Providence Drive
Anchorage, AK 99508
$10, Ronald Spatz

Alligator Juniper
Prescott College
220 Grove Avenue
Prescott, AZ 86301
$7.50, Miles Waggener

American Letters and Commentary
850 Park Avenue, Suite 5B
New York, NY 10021
$8, Anna Rabinowitz

American Literary Review
University of North Texas
P.O. Box 311307
Denton, TX 76203-1307
$10, John Tait

Another Chicago Magazine
Left Field Press
3709 North Kenmore
Chicago, IL 60613
$8, Sharon Solwitz

Antietam Review
41 South Potomac Street
Hagerstown, MD 21740-3764
$5, Anne Knox

Antioch Review
Antioch University
150 East South College Street
Yellow Springs, OH 45387
$35, Robert S. Fogerty

Apalachee Quarterly
P.O. Box 10469
Tallahassee, FL 32032
$15, editorial group

Argosy
P.O. Box 1421
Taylor, AZ 85939
$49.95, Lou Anders, James Owen

Arkansas Review
Department of English and
Philosophy
P.O. Box 1890
Arkansas State University
State University, AR 72467
$20, William Clements

Ascent
English Department
Concordia College
901 Eighth Street
Moorhead, MN 56562
$12, W. Scott Olsen

Atlantic Monthly
77 North Washington Street
Boston, MA 02114
$14.95, C. Michael Curtis

Baffler
P.O. Box 378293
Chicago, IL 60637
$24, Thomas Frank

Bayou
Department of English
University of New Orleans
2000 Lakeshore Drive
New Orleans, LA 70148
$10, Joanna Leake

Bellevue Literary Review
Department of Medicine
New York University School of
Medicine

550 First Avenue
New York, NY 10016
$12, Danielle Ofri

Bellingham Review
MS-9053
Western Washington University
Bellingham, WA 98225
$14, Brenda Miller

Bellowing Ark
P.O. Box 55564
Shoreline, WA 98155
$15, Robert Ward

Berkshire Review
P.O. Box 23
Richmond, MA 01254-0023
$8.95, Vivan Dorsel

Black Warrior Review
P.O. Box 862936
Tuscaloosa, AL 35486-0027
$14, Dan Kaplan

Blackbird
Department of English
Virginia Commonwealth University
P.O. Box 843082
Richmond, VA 23284-3082
Gregory Donovan

Blue Mesa Review
Department of English
University of New Mexico
Albuquerque, NM 87131
Julie Shigekuni

Bomb
New Art Publications
594 Broadway, 10th floor
New York, NY 10012
$18, Betsy Sussler

Book
252 West 37th Street, 5th floor
New York, NY 10018
$19.95, Jerome V. Kramer

Boston Review
Building E 53, Room 407 MIT
Cambridge, MA 02139
$17, Joshua Cohen, Deborah Chasman

Boulevard
PMB 325
6614 Clayton Road
Richmond Heights, MO 63117
$15, Richard Burgin

Brain, Child: The Magazine for
Thinking Mothers
P.O. Box 1161
Harrisonburg, VA 22801
$18, Jennifer Niesslein, Stephanie Wilkinson

Briar Cliff Review
3303 Rebecca Street
P.O. Box 2100
Sioux City, IA 51104-2100
$10, Phil Hey

Bridges
P.O. Box 24839
Eugene, OR 97402
$15, Clare Kinberg

Callaloo
Department of English
Texas A&M University
4227 TAMU
College Station, TX 77843-4227
$37, Charles H. Rowell

Calyx
P.O. Box B
Corvallis, OR 97339
$19.50, Margarita Donnelly and collective

Capilano Review
Capilano College
2055 Purcell Way
North Vancouver
British Columbia V7J 3H5
$25, Sharon Thesen

Carolina Quarterly
Greenlaw Hall 066A

University of North Carolina
Chapel Hill, NC 27514
$12, Amy Weldon

Chariton Review
Truman State University
Kirksville, MO 63501
$9, Jim Barnes

Chattahoochee Review
Georgia Perimeter College
2101 Womack Road
Dunwoody, GA 30338-4497
$16, Lawrence Hetrick

Chelsea
P.O. Box 773
Cooper Station
New York, NY 10276
$13, Alfredo de Palchi

Chicago Quarterly Review
517 Sherman Avenue
Evanston, IL 60202
$10, S. Afzal Haider, Jane Lawrence, Elizabeth McKenzie, Brian Skinner

Chicago Review
5801 South Kenwood
University of Chicago
Chicago, IL 60637
$18, Erik Steinhoff

Cimarron Review
205 Morrill Hall
Oklahoma State University
Stillwater, OK 74078-0135
$24, E. P. Walkiewicz

Colorado Review
Department of English
Colorado State University
Fort Collins, CO 80523
$24, David Milofsky

Columbia
2960 Broadway
415 Dodge Hall
Columbia University
New York, NY 10027-6902
$15, S. K. Beringer

Commentary
165 East 56th Street
New York, NY 10022
$39, Neal Kozodoy

Confrontation
English Department
C. W. Post College of Long Island
University
Greenvale, NY 11548
$10, Martin Tucker

Conjunctions
21 East 10th Street, Suite 3E
New York, NY 10003
$18, Bradford Morrow

Connecticut Review
English Department
Southern Connecticut State University
501 Crescent Street
New Haven, CT 06515
Vivian Shipley

Crab Creek Review
P.O. Box 840
Vashon Island, WA 98070
$10, editorial group

Crab Orchard Review
Department of English
Southern Illinois University at
Carbondale
Carbondale, IL 62901
$15, Allison Joseph

Crazyhorse
Department of English
College of Charleston
66 George Street
Charleston, SC 29424
*$15, Bret Lott, Paul Allen, Carol Ann
Davis*

Crucible
Barton College
P.O. Box 5000
Wilson, NC 27893-7000
Terrence L. Grimes

CutBank
Department of English

University of Montana
Missoula, MT 59812
$12, Elizabeth Conway

Daedalus
136 Irving Street, Suite 100
Cambridge, MA 02138
$33, James Miller

Denver Quarterly
University of Denver
Denver, CO 80208
$20, Bin Ramke

Descant
P.O. Box 314
Station P
Toronto, Ontario M5S 2S8
$25, Karen Mulhallen

Descant
TCU
Box 297270
Fort Worth, TX 76129
$12, Lynn Risser, David Kuhne

Distillery
Division of Humanities and Social
Sciences
Motlow State Community College
P.O. Box 8500
Lynchburg, TN 37352-8500
$15, Dawn Copeland

Epoch
251 Goldwin Smith Hall
Cornell University
Ithaca, NY 14853-3201
$11, Michael Koch

Esquire
250 West 55th Street
New York, NY 10019
$17.94, Adrienne Miller

Eureka Literary Magazine
Eureka College
300 East College Avenue
Eureka, IL 61530-1500
$15, Loren Logsdon

Event
Douglas College
P.O. Box 2503
New Westminster
British Columbia V3L 5B2
$22, Christine Dewar

Fantasy and Science Fiction
P.O. Box 3447
Hoboken, NJ 07030
$38.97, Gordon Van Gelder

Faultline
Department of English and
Comparative Literature
University of California, Irvine
Irvine, CA 92697-2650
$16, Lorene Delany-Ullman, Lance Uyeda

Fiction
Fiction, Inc.
Department of English
The City College of New York
Convent Avenue at 138th Street
$7, Mark Mirsky

Fiction International
Department of English and
Comparative Literature
San Diego State University
San Diego, CA 92182
$12, Harold Jaffe, Larry McCaffery

Fiddlehead
UNB P.O. Box 4400
Fredericton
New Brunswick E3B 5A3
$20, Mark Anthony Jarman

Five Points
Georgia State University
Department of English
University Plaza
Atlanta, GA 30303-3083
$15, David Bottoms

Flyway
206 Ross Hall
Department of English
Iowa State University

Ames, IA 50011
$18, Sam Pritchard

Folio
Department of Literature
The American University
Washington, DC 20016
$12, rotating editorship

Frostproof Review
P.O. Box 3397
Lake Wales, FL 33859
$15, Kyle Minor

Fugue
Department of English
Brink Hall 200
University of Idaho
Moscow, ID 83844-1102
$14, Ben George, Jeff P. Jones

Furnace
Historic Bohemian House
3009 Tillman
Detroit, MI 48216
$20, Kelli B. Kavanaugh

Gargoyle
P.O. Box 6216
Arlington, VA 22206-0216
$20, Richard Peabody, Lucinda Ebersole

Georgia Review
University of Georgia
Athens, GA 30602
$24, T. R. Hummer

Gettysburg Review
Gettysburg College
Gettysburg, PA 17325-1491
$24, Peter Stitt

Gingko Tree Review
Drury University
900 North Benton Avenue
Springfield, MO 65802
$10, Randall Fuller

Glimmer Train Stories
710 SW Madison Street, Suite 504
Portland, OR 97205

*$34, Susan Burmeister-Brown,
Linda Swanson-Davies*

Gobshite Quarterly
P.O. Box 11346
Portland, OR 97205
$16, R. V. Branham

GQ
4 Times Square, 9th floor
New York, NY 10036
$19.97, Walter Kirn

Grain
Box 1154
Regina, Saskatchewan S4P 3B4
$26.95, Kent Bruyneel

Grand Street
214 Sullivan Street, Suite 6C
New York, NY 10012
$25, Jean Stein

Granta
1755 Broadway, 5th floor
New York, NY 10019-3780
$37, Ian Jack

Great River Review
Anderson Center for Interdisciplinary
Studies
P.O. Box 406
Red Wing, MN 55066
$14, Richard Broderick, Robert Hedin

Green Mountains Review
Box A58
Johnson State College
Johnson, VT 05656
$15, Tony Whedon

Greensboro Review
Department of English
134 McIver Building
P.O. Box 26170
University of North Carolina
Greensboro, NC 27412
$10, Jim Clark

Gulf Coast
Department of English

University of Houston
4800 Calhoun Road
Houston, TX 77204-3012
$22, Mark Doty

Gulf Stream
English Department
Florida International University
Biscayne Bay Campus
3000 NE 151st Street
North Miami, FL 33181
$9, John Dufresne, Cindy Chinelly

Harper's Magazine
666 Broadway
New York, NY 10012
$16, Lewis Lapham

Harpur Palate
Department of English
Binghamton University
P.O. Box 6000
Binghamton, NY 13902
$16, Letitia Moffitt, Doris Umbers

Harvard Review
Poetry Room
Harvard College Library
Cambridge, MA 02138
$16, Christina Thompson

Hawaii Review
Department of English
University of Hawaii
1733 Donaghho Road
Honolulu, HI 96822
$20, Shawna McGuire Medeiros

Hayden's Ferry Review
Box 871502
Arizona State University
Tempe, AZ 85287-1502
$10, Julie Hensley, Bill Martin

Hotel Amerika
Department of English
Ellis Hall
Ohio University
Athens, OH 45701
$18, David Lazar

Hudson Review
684 Park Avenue
New York, NY 10021
$24, Paula Deitz

Idaho Review
Department of English
Boise State University
1910 University Drive
Boise, ID 83725
$9.95, Mitch Wieland

Image
Center for Religious Humanism
3307 Third Avenue West
Seattle, WA 98119
$36, Gregory Wolfe

Indiana Review
Ballantine Hall 465
1020 East Kirkwood Avenue
Bloomington, IN 47405-7103
$14, David J. Daniels

Indy Men's Magazine
8500 Keystone Crossing, Suite 100
Indianapolis, IN 46240
Lou Harry

Inkpot
Lit Pot Press, Inc.
3909 Reche Road, Suite 132
Fallbrook, CA 92028
$30, Beverly Jackson, Carol Peters

Iowa Review
Department of English
University of Iowa
308 EPB
Iowa City, IA 52242
$18, David Hamilton

Iris
University of Virginia Women's Center
P.O. Box 800588
Charlottesville, VA 22908
$9, Abby Manzella

Italian Americana
University of Rhode Island
Providence Campus

80 Washington Street
Providence, RI 02903
$20, Carol Bonomo Albright

Jabberwock Review
Department of English
Drawer E
Mississippi State University
Mississippi State, MS 39762
$10, Sarah Asmus, Joy Murphy

James White Review
Lambda Literary Foundation
P.O. Box 73910
Washington, DC 20056-3910
Patrick Merla

Jewish Currents
22 East 17th Street
New York, NY 10003
$20, editorial board

Journal
Department of English
Ohio State University
161 West 17th Street
Columbus, OH 43210
$12, Kathy Fagan, Michelle Herman

Kalliope
Florida Community College
3939 Roosevelt Boulevard
Jacksonville, FL 32205
$12.50, Mary Sue Koeppel

Kenyon Review
Kenyon College
Gambier, OH 43022
$25, David H. Lynn

Land-Grant College Review
P.O. Box 1164
New York, NY 10159
$18, Tara Wray

Literal Latte
61 East 8th Street, Suite 240
New York, NY 10003
$11, Jenine Gordon Bockman

Literary Review
Fairleigh Dickinson University
285 Madison Avenue
Madison, NJ 07940
$18, Rene Steinke

Louisiana Literature
Box 792
Southeastern Louisiana University
Hammond, LA 70402
$12, Jack B. Bedell

Louisville Review
Spalding University
851 South Fourth Street
Louisville, KY 40203
$14, Sena Jeter Naslund

Lynx Eye
ScribbleFest Literary Group
542 Mitchell Drive
Los Osnos, CA 93402
$25, Pam McCully, Kathryn Morrison

Manoa
English Department
University of Hawaii
Honolulu, HI 96822
$22, Frank Stewart

Massachusetts Review
South College
Box 37140
University of Massachusetts
Amherst, MA 01003
$22, Mary Heath, Paul Jenkins, David Lenson

Matrix
1455 de Maisonneuve Boulevard West,
Suite LB-514-8
Montreal, Quebec H3G IM8
$18, R.E.N. Allen

McSweeney's
826 Valencia Street
San Francisco, CA 94110
$36, Dave Eggers

Meridian
Department of English

P.O. Box 400145
University of Virginia
Charlottesville, VA 22904-4145
$10, Stephen Boykewich

Michigan Quarterly Review
3032 Rackham Building
915 East Washington Street
University of Michigan
Ann Arbor, MI 48109
$25, Laurence Goldstein

Mid-American Review
Department of English
Bowling Green State University
Bowling Green, OH 48109
$12, Michael Czyzniejewski

Midnight Mind
P.O. Box 146912
Chicago, IL 60614
$12, Brett Van Emst

Minnesota Review
Department of English
University of Missouri, Columbia
107 Tate Hall
Columbia, MO 65211
$30, Jeffrey Williams

Mississippi Review
University of Southern Mississippi
Southern Station, Box 5144
Hattiesburg, MS 39406-5144
$15, Frederick Barthelme

Missouri Review
1507 Hillcrest Hall
University of Missouri
Columbia, MO 65211
$19, Speer Morgan

Ms.
Qwerty Communications
72 Madison Avenue, 12th floor
New York, NY 10016
$35, Anne Mollegen Smith

Nassau Review
English Department
Nassau Community College

One Education Drive
Garden City, NY 11530-6793
Paul A. Doyle

Natural Bridge
Department of English
University of Missouri, St. Louis
8001 Natural Bridge Road
St. Louis, MO 63121-4499
$15, Ryan Stone

Nebraska Review
Writers Workshop
WFAB 212
University of Nebraska at Omaha
Omaha, NE 68182-0324
$15, James Reed

New England Review
Middlebury College
Middlebury, VT 05753
$25, Stephen Donadio

New Letters
University of Missouri
5100 Rockhill Road
Kansas City, MO 64110
$17, Robert Stewart

New Orleans Review
P.O. Box 195
Loyola University
New Orleans, LA 70118
$12, Christopher Chambers

New Orphic Review
706 Mill Street
Nelson, British Columbia V1L 4S5
$25, Ernest Hekkanen

New Quarterly
English Language Proficiency
Programme
Saint Jerome's University
200 University Avenue West
Waterloo, Ontario N2L 3G3
$36, Kim Jernigan

New Renaissance
26 Heath Road, Suite 11

Arlington, MA 02474
$11.50, Louise T. Reynolds

New Yorker
4 Times Square
New York, NY 10036
$46, Deborah Treisman

New York Stories
English Department
La Guardia Community College
31-10 Thomson Avenue
Long Island City, NY 11101
$13.40, Daniel Caplice Lynch

Night Train
85 Orchard Street
Somerville, MA 02144
$17.95, Rod Sino, Rusty Barnes

Nimrod International Journal
Arts and Humanities Council of Tulsa
600 South College Avenue
Tulsa, OK 74104
$17.50, Francine Ringold

96 Inc.
P.O. Box 15559
Boston, MA 02215
$15, Vera Gold, Nancy Mehegan

Noon
1369 Madison Avenue
PMB 298
New York, NY 10128
$9, Diane Williams

North Carolina Literary Review
Department of English
2201 Bate Building
East Carolina University
Greenville, NC 27858-4353
Margaret Bauer

North Dakota Quarterly
University of North Dakota
P.O. Box 8237
Grand Forks, ND 58202
$25, Robert Lewis

Northwest Review
369 PLC
University of Oregon
Eugene, OR 97403
$20, John Witte

Notre Dame Review
Department of English
356 O'Shag
University of Notre Dame
Notre Dame, IN 46556-5639
$15, John Matthias, William O'Rourke

Oasis
P.O. Box 626
Largo, FL 34649-0626
$20, Neal Storrs

Oklahoma Today
15 North Robinson, Suite 100
P.O. Box 53384
Oklahoma City, OK 73102
$16.95, Louisa McCune

One Story
P.O. Box 1326
New York, NY 10156
$21, Maribeth Batcha, Hannah Tinti

Ontario Review
9 Honey Brook Drive
Princeton, NJ 08540
$16, Raymond J. Smith

Open City
225 Lafayette Street, Suite 1114
New York, NY 10012
$32, Thomas Beller, Joanna Yas

Orchid
3096 Williamsburg
Ann Arbor, MI 48108-2026
$16, Keith Hood

Other Voices
University of Illinois at Chicago
Department of English, M/C 162
601 South Morgan Street
Chicago, IL 60607-7120
$24, Gina Frangello

Oxford American
P.O. Box 1156
404 South 11th Street
Oxford, MS 38655
$24.95, Marc Smirnoff

Oyster Boy Review
P.O. Box 77842
San Francisco, CA 94107
$20, Damon Sauve

Pangolin Papers
Turtle Press
P.O. Box 241
Norland, WA 98358
$20, Pat Britt

Paris Review
541 East 72nd Street
New York, NY 10021
$34, Brigid Hughes

Parting Gifts
3413 Wilshire Drive
Greensboro, NC 27408-2923
Robert Bixby

Pearl
3030 East Second Street
Long Beach, CA 90803
*$18, Joan Jobe Smith, Marilyn Johnson,
Barbara Hauk*

Phantasmagoria
English Department
Century Community and Technical
College
3300 Century Avenue North
White Bear Lake, MN 55110
$15, Abigail Allen

Phoebe
George Mason University
MSN 2D6
4400 University Drive
Fairfax, VA 22030-4444
$12, Lisa Ampleman

Playboy
Playboy Building
919 North Michigan Avenue

Chicago, IL 60611
$29.97, *Christopher Napolitano*

Pleiades
Department of English and
Philosophy, 5069
Central Missouri State University
P.O. Box 800
Warrensburg, MO 64093
$12, *Susan Steinberg*

Ploughshares
Emerson College
120 Boylston Street
Boston, MA 02116
$22, *Don Lee*

Poem Memoir Story
Department of English
University of Alabama at Birmingham
217 Humanities Building
900 South 13th Street
Birmingham, AL 35294-1260
$7, *Linda Frost*

Porcupine
P.O. Box 259
Cedarburg, WI 53012
$15.95, *editorial group*

Post Road
P.O. Box 590663
Newton Centre, MA 02459
$16, *Catherine Parnell*

Potomac Review
Montgomery College
51 Mannakee Street
Rockville, MD 20850
$20, *Eli Flam*

Potpourri
P.O. Box 8278
Prairie Village, KS 66208
$16, *Polly W. Swafford*

Prairie Fire
423-100 Arthur Street
Winnipeg, Manitoba R3B 1H3
$25, *Andris Taskans*

Prairie Schooner
201 Andrews Hall
University of Nebraska
Lincoln, NE 68588-0334
$26, *Hilda Raz*

Primavera
Box 37-7547
Chicago, IL 60637
Editorial group

Prism International
Department of Creative Writing
University of British Columbia
Buchanan E-462
Vancouver, British Columbia V6T 1W5
$22, *Elizabeth Bachinsky*

Prose Ax
Box 22643
Honolulu, HI 96823
$6, *J. Salazar*

Puerto del Sol
Department of English
Box 3E
New Mexico State University
Las Cruces, NM 88003
$10, *Kevin McIlvoy*

Quick Fiction
JP Press
50 Evergreen Street, Unit 25
Jamaica Plain, MA 02130
Jennifer Cande, Adam Pieroni

Raritan
Rutgers University
31 Mine Street
New Brunswick, NJ 08903
$24

Red Rock Review
English Department, J2A
Community College of Southern
Nevada
3200 East Cheyenne Avenue
North Las Vegas, NV 89030
$9.50, *Richard Logsdon*

Republic of Letters
120 Cushing Avenue
Boston, MA 02125-2033
$25, Keith Botsford

River City
Department of English
University of Memphis
Memphis, TN 38152
$12, Tom Carlson

River Oak Review
River Oak Arts
P.O. Box 3127
Oak Pak, IL 60603
$12, Mary Lee MacDonald

River Styx
Big River Association
634 North Grand Boulevard, 12th
floor
St. Louis, MO 63103-1002
$20, Richard Newman

Room of One's Own
P.O. Box 46160
Station D
Vancouver, British Columbia V6J 5G5
$22, Stephanie Dayes, Zoya Harris

Salmagundi
Skidmore College
Saratoga Springs, NY 12866
$20, Robert Boyers

Salt Hill
English Department
Syracuse University
Syracuse, NY 13244
$15, Ellen Litman

Santa Monica Review
1900 Pico Boulevard
Santa Monica, CA 90405
$12, Andrew Tonkovich

Sewanee Review
University of the South
Sewanee, TN 37375-4009
$24, George Core

Shenandoah
Troubador Theater, 2nd floor
Washington and Lee University
Lexington, VA 24450-0303
$15, R. T. Smith

Slow Trains Literary Journal
Samba Mountain Press
P.O. Box 4741
Englewood, CO 80155
$14.95, Susannah Indigo

Snake Nation Review
110 West Force Street
Valdosta, GA 31601
$20, editorial group

Sonora Review
Department of English
University of Arizona
Tucson, AZ 85721
$12, Sarah Giles, Ben Gebhart

South Dakota Review
University of South Dakota
P.O. Box 111 University Exchange
Vermilion, SD 57069
$15, Brain Bedard

Southern Exposure
P.O. Box 531
Durham, NC 27702
$24, Chris Kromm

Southern Humanities Review
9088 Haley Center
Auburn University
Auburn, AL 36849
*$15, Dan R. Latimer, Virginia M.
Kouidis*

Southern Review
43 Allen Hall
Louisiana State University
Baton Rouge, LA 70803
$25, James Olney

Southwest Review
Southern Methodist University
P.O. Box 4374

Dallas, TX 75275
$24, Willard Spiegelman

Story Quarterly
431 Sheridan Road
Kenilworth, IL 60043-1220
$12, M.M.M. Hayes

Sun
107 North Roberson Street
Chapel Hill, NC 27516
$34, Sy Safransky

Sycamore Review
Department of English
1356 Heavilon Hall
Purdue University
West Lafayette, IN 47907
$12, Sean M. Conrey

Talking River Review
Division of Literature and Languages
Lewis-Clark State College
500 Eighth Avenue
Lewiston, ID 83501
$14, Nikki Allen, Eldy Schultz

Tampa Review
University of Tampa
401 West Kennedy Boulevard
Tampa, FL 33606-1490
$15, Richard Mathews

Third Coast
Department of English
Western Michigan University
Kalamazoo, MI 49008-5092
$11, Adam Schuitema, Jason Skipper

Threepenny Review
P.O. Box 9131
Berkeley, CA 94709
$16, Wendy Lesser

Timber Creek Review
8969 UNCG Station
Greensboro, NC 27413
$15, John Freiermuth

Tin House
P.O. Box 10500

Portland, OR 97296-0500
$39, Rob Spillman

Transition
69 Dunster Street
Harvard University
Cambridge, MA 02138
$28, Kwame Anthony Appiah, Henry Louis Gates, Jr., Michael Vazquez

TriQuarterly
2020 Ridge Avenue
Northwestern University
Evanston, IL 60208
$24, Susan Firestone Hahn

Two Rivers Review
P.O. Box 158
Clinton, NY 13323
Phil Memmer, Carole Burns

Virginia Quarterly Review
One West Range
P.O. Box 400223
Charlottesville, VA 22903
$18, Ted Genoways

War, Literature, and the Arts
Department of English and Fine Arts
2354 Fairchild Drive, Suite 6D45
USAF Academy, CO 80840-6242
Donald Anderson

Wascana Review
English Department
University of Regina
Regina, Saskatchewan S4S 0A2
$10, Marcel DeCoste

Washington Square
Creative Writing Program
New York University
19 University Place, 2nd floor
New York, NY 10003-4556
$6, James Pritchard

Watchword
755 54th Street
Oakland, CA 94609
Danielle Jatlow

Weber Studies
Weber State University
1214 University Circle
Ogden, UT 84408-1214
$20, Brad Roghaar

West Branch
Bucknell Hall
Bucknell University
Lewisburg, PA 17837
$10, Paula Closson Buck, Mike Carlin

Western Humanities Review
University of Utah
255 South Central Campus Drive
Room 3500
Salt Lake City, UT 84112
$16, Barry Weller

Willow Springs
Eastern Washington University
705 West 1st Avenue
Spokane, WA 99201
$11.50, Jennifer S. Davis

Windsor Review
Department of English
University of Windsor
Windsor, Ontario N9B 3P4
$29.95, Alistair MacLeod

Witness
Oakland Community College

Orchard Ridge Campus
27055 Orchard Lake Road
Farmington Hills, MI 48334
$15, Peter Stine

Words and Images
University of Southern Maine
11 Baxter Boulevard
P.O. Box 9300
Portland, ME 04104-9300
Jennifer Thomas

Yale Review
P.O. Box 208243
New Haven, CT 06520-8243
$27, J. D. McClatchy

Yankee
Yankee Publishing, Inc.
Dublin, NH 03444
$22, Judson D. Hale

Zoetrope
The Sentinel Building
916 Kearney Street
San Francisco, CA 94133
$19.95, Tamara Straus

Zyzzyva
P.O. Box 590069
San Francisco, CA 94109
$28, Howard Junker

THE BEST AMERICAN SHORT STORIES® 2004

Lorrie Moore, guest editor, Katrina Kenison, series editor. "Story for story, readers can't beat *The Best American Short Stories* series" (*Chicago Tribune*). This year's most beloved short fiction anthology is edited by the critically acclaimed author Lorrie Moore and includes stories by Annie Proulx, Sherman Alexie, Paula Fox, Thomas McGuane, and Alice Munro, among others.

0-618-19735-4 PA $14.00 / 0-618-19734-6 CL $27.50
0-618-30046-5 CASS $26.00 / 0-618-29965-3 CD $30.00

THE BEST AMERICAN ESSAYS® 2004

Louis Menand, guest editor, Robert Atwan, series editor. Since 1986, *The Best American Essays* series has gathered the best nonfiction writing of the year and established itself as the best anthology of its kind. Edited by Louis Menand, author of *The Metaphysical Club* and staff writer for *The New Yorker,* this year's volume features writing by Kathryn Chetkovich, Jonathan Franzen, Kyoko Mori, Cynthia Zarin, and others.

0-618-35709-2 PA $14.00 / 0-618-35706-8 CL $27.50

THE BEST AMERICAN MYSTERY STORIES™ 2004

Nelson DeMille, guest editor, Otto Penzler, series editor. This perennially popular anthology is a favorite of mystery buffs and general readers alike. This year's volume is edited by the best-selling suspense author Nelson DeMille and offers pieces by Stephen King, Joyce Carol Oates, Jonathon King, Jeff Abbott, Scott Wolven, and others.

0-618-32967-6 PA $14.00 / 0-618-32968-4 CL $27.50 / 0-618-49742-0 CD $30.00

THE BEST AMERICAN SPORTS WRITING™ 2004

Richard Ben Cramer, guest editor, Glenn Stout, series editor. This series has garnered wide acclaim for its stellar sports writing and topnotch editors. Now Richard Ben Cramer, the Pulitzer Prize–winning journalist and author of the best-selling *Joe DiMaggio,* continues that tradition with pieces by Ira Berkow, Susan Orlean, William Nack, Charles P. Pierce, Rick Telander, and others.

0-618-25139-1 PA $14.00 / 0-618-25134-0 CL $27.50

THE BEST AMERICAN TRAVEL WRITING 2004

Pico Iyer, guest editor, Jason Wilson, series editor. *The Best American Travel Writing 2004* is edited by Pico Iyer, the author of *Video Night in Kathmandu* and *Sun After*

THE B·E·S·T AMERICAN SERIES®

Dark. Giving new life to armchair travel this year are Roger Angell, Joan Didion, John McPhee, Adam Gopnik, and many others.

0-618-34126-9 PA $14.00 / 0-618-34125-0 CL $27.50

THE BEST AMERICAN SCIENCE AND NATURE WRITING 2004

Steven Pinker, guest editor, Tim Folger, series editor. This year's edition promises to be another "eclectic, provocative collection" (*Entertainment Weekly*). Edited by Steven Pinker, author of *The Blank Slate* and *The Language Instinct*, it features work by Gregg Easterbrook, Atul Gawande, Peggy Orenstein, Jonathan Rauch, Chet Raymo, Nicholas Wade, and others.

0-618-24698-3 PA $14.00 / 0-618-24697-5 CL $27.50

THE BEST AMERICAN RECIPES 2004–2005

Edited by Fran McCullough and Molly Stevens. "Give this book to any cook who is looking for the newest, latest recipes and the stories behind them" (*Chicago Tribune*). Offering the very best of what America is cooking, as well as the latest trends, timesaving tips, and techniques, this year's edition includes a foreword by the renowned chef Bobby Flay.

0-618-45506-x CL $26.00

THE BEST AMERICAN NONREQUIRED READING 2004

Edited by Dave Eggers, Introduction by Viggo Mortensen. Edited by the best-selling author Dave Eggers, this genre-busting volume draws the finest, most interesting, and least expected fiction, nonfiction, humor, alternative comics, and more from publications large, small, and on-line. This year's collection features writing by David Sedaris, Daniel Alarcón, David Mamet, Thom Jones, and others.

0-618-34123-4 PA $14.00 / 0-618-34122-6 CL $27.50 / 0-618-49743-9 CD $26.00

THE BEST AMERICAN SPIRITUAL WRITING 2004

Edited by Philip Zaleski, Introduction by Jack Miles. The latest addition to the acclaimed Best American series, *The Best American Spiritual Writing 2004* brings the year's finest writing about faith and spirituality to all readers. With an introduction by the best-selling author Jack Miles, this year's volume represents a wide range of perspectives and features pieces by Robert Coles, Bill McKibben, Oliver Sacks, Pico Iyer, and many others.

0-618-44303-7 PA $14.00 / 0-618-44302-9 CL $27.50

HOUGHTON MIFFLIN COMPANY www.houghtonmifflinbooks.com